"EXTRAORDINARY . . .
ONE OF UPDIKE'S FINEST NOVELS."
Los Angeles Times Book Review

"RABBIT AT REST is one of the very few modern novels in English that one can set beside the work of Dickens, Thackeray, George Eliot, Joyce and not feel the draft."
The Washington Post Book World

"Rabbit brings out the best in Updike, tests him, making him use that peerless style and that phenomenal intelligence to triumphant effect. The world comes alive as Updike takes Harry's life apart and puts it down on paper."
The Boston Globe

"His masterpiece . . . RABBIT AT REST is not just the best of the Rabbit books, of which it is the final installment, it is probably the best of all its author's novels. . . . A true and moving work, a beautiful book."
The National Review

"Brilliant . . . [The] best novel in John Updike's celebrated *Rabbit* series."
Chicago Sun-Times

Also by John Updike
Published by Fawcett Books:

THE POORHOUSE FAIR
RABBIT, RUN
PIGEON FEATHERS
THE CENTAUR
OF THE FARM
COUPLES
BECH IS BACK
RABBIT REDUX
A MONTH OF SUNDAYS
PICKED-UP PIECES
MARRY ME
TOO FAR TO GO
THE COUP
PROBLEMS
RABBIT IS RICH
THE WITCHES OF EASTWICK
ROGER'S VERSION
TRUST ME
S.
SELF-CONSCIOUSNESS

RABBIT AT REST

John Updike

FAWCETT CREST · NEW YORK

A Fawcett Crest Book
Published by Ballantine Books
Copyright © 1990 by John Updike

All rights reserved under International and Pan-American Copyright Conventions. Published in the United States by Ballantine Books, a division of Random House, Inc., New York, and simultaneously in Canada by Random House of Canada Limited, Toronto.

A portion of this novel appeared in *Playboy*.

Owing to limitations of space, acknowledgments of permission to reprint previously published material will be found on page 426.

Library of Congress Catalog Card Number: 90-52953

ISBN 0-449-21962-3

This edition published by arrangement with Alfred A. Knopf, Inc.

Manufactured in the United States of America

First International Ballantine Books Edition: April 1991
First U.S. Ballatine Books Edition: October 1991

Rabbit basks above that old remembered world, rich, at rest.

—*Rabbit Is Rich*

Food to the indolent is poison, not sustenance.

—*Life and Times of Frederick Douglass*

Chapters

I. FL

STANDING amid the tan, excited post-Christmas crowd at the Southwest Florida Regional Airport, Rabbit Angstrom has a funny sudden feeling that what he has come to meet, what's floating in unseen about to land, is not his son Nelson and daughter-in-law Pru and their two children but something more ominous and intimately his: his own death, shaped vaguely like an airplane. The sensation chills him, above and beyond the terminal air-conditioning. But, then, facing Nelson has made him feel uneasy for thirty years.

The airport is relatively new. You drive to it off Exit 21 of Interstate 75 down three miles of divided highway that for all the skinny palms in rows and groomed too-green Bermuda grass at its sides seems to lead nowhere. There are no billboards or self-advertising roadside enterprises or those low houses with cooling white-tile roofs that are built by the acre down here. You think you've made a mistake. An anxious red Camaro convertible is pushing in the rearview mirror.

"Harry, there's no need to speed. We're early if anything."

Janice, Rabbit's wife, said this to him on the way in. What rankled was the tolerant, careful tone she has lately adopted, as if he's prematurely senile. He looked over and watched her tuck back a stubborn fluttering wisp of half-gray hair from her sun-toughened little brown nut of a face. "Honey, I'm being tail-gated," he explained, and eased back into the right lane and let the speedometer needle quiver back below sixty-five. The Camaro convertible passed in a rush, a cocoa-brown black chick in a gray felt stewardess's cap at the wheel, her chin and lips pushing forward, not giving him so much as a sideways glance. This rankled, too. From the back, the way they've designed the trunk and bumper, a Camaro seems to have a mouth, two fat

1

metal lips parted as if to hiss. So maybe Harry's being spooked began then.

The terminal when it shows up at last is a long low white building like a bigger version of the sunstruck clinics—dental, chiropractic, arthritic, cardiac, legal, legal-medical—that line the boulevards of this state dedicated to the old. You park at a lot only a few steps away from the door of sliding brown glass: the whole state babies you. Inside, upstairs, where the planes are met, the spaces are long and low and lined in tasteful felt gray like that cocky stewardess's cap and filled with the kind of music you become aware of only when the elevator stops or when the dentist stops drilling. Plucked strings, no vocals, music that's used to being ignored, a kind of carpet in the air, to cover up a silence that might remind you of death. These long low tasteful spaces, as little cluttered by advertisements as the highway, remind Rabbit of something. Air-conditioning ducts, he thinks at first, and then crypts. These are futuristic spaces like those square tunnels in movies that a trick of the camera accelerates into spacewarp to show we're going from one star to the next. *2001*, will he be alive? He touches Janice at his side, the sweated white cotton of her tennis dress at the waist, to relieve his sudden sense of doom. Her waist is thicker, has less of a dip, as she grows into that barrel body of women in late middle age, their legs getting skinny, their arms getting loose like cooked chicken coming off the bone. She wears over the sweaty tennis dress an open-weave yellow cardigan hung unbuttoned over her shoulders against the chill of airport airconditioning. He is innocently proud that she looks, in her dress and tan, even to the rings of pallor that sunglasses have left around her eyes, like these other American grandmothers who can afford to be here in this land of constant sunshine and eternal youth.

"Gate A5," Janice says, as if his touch had been a technical question. "From Cleveland by way of Newark," she says, with that businesswoman efficiency she has taken on in middle age, especially since her mother died seven years ago, leaving her the lot, Springer Motors and its assets, one of only two Toyota agencies in the Brewer, Pennsylvania, area: the family all still speak of it as "the lot," since it began as a used-car lot owned and run by Fred Springer, dead Fred Springer, who is reincarnated, his widow Bessie and daughter Janice have the fantasy, in Nelson, both being wiry shrimps with something shifty about them. Which is why Harry and Janice spend half the year in

Florida—so Nelson can have free run of the lot. Harry, Chief Sales Representative for over ten years, with him and Charlie Stavros managing it all between them, wasn't even mentioned in Ma Springer's will, for all the years he lived with her in her gloomy big house on Joseph Street and listened to her guff about what a saint Fred was and her complaining about her swollen ankles. Everything went to Janice, as if he was an unmentionable incident in the Springer dynasty. The house on Joseph Street, that Nelson and his family get to live in just for covering the upkeep and taxes, must be worth three hundred thousand now that the yuppies are moving across the mountain from northeast Brewer into the town of Mt. Judge, not to mention the cottage in the Poconos where even the shacks in the woods have skyrocketed, and the lot land alone, four acres along Route 111 south of the river, might bring close to a million from one of the hi-tech companies that have come into the Brewer area this last decade, to take advantage of the empty factories, the skilled but depressed laboring force, and the old-fashionedly cheap living. Janice is rich. Rabbit would like to share with her the sudden chill he had felt, the shadow of some celestial airplane, but a shell she has grown repels him. The dress at her waist felt thick and unresponsive, a damp hide. He is alone with his premonition.

A crowd of welcomers has collected this Tuesday after Christmas in the last year of Reagan's reign. A little man with that hunched back and awkward swiftness Jews often seem to have dodges around them and shouts behind him to his wife, as if the Angstroms weren't there, "Come *on*, Grace!"

Grace, Harry thinks. A strange name for a Jewish woman. Or maybe not. Biblical names, Rachel, Esther, but not always: Barbra, Bette. He is still getting used to the Jews down here, learning from them, trying to assimilate the philosophy that gives them such a grip on the world. That humpbacked old guy in his pink checked shirt and lipstick-red slacks racing as if the plane coming in was the last train out of Warsaw. When Harry and Janice were planning the move down here their advisers on Florida, mostly Charlie Stavros and Webb Murkett, told them the Gulf side was the Christian coast as opposed to the Jewish Atlantic side but Harry hasn't noticed that really; as far as his acquaintanceship goes all Florida is as Jewish as New York and Hollywood and Tel Aviv. In their condo building in fact he and Janice are pets of a sort, being gentiles: they're considered cute. Watching that little guy, seventy if he's a day, breaking into a run, hopping zigzag through the padded pedestal chairs so he won't be beaten out at the arrival gate, Harry remorsefully feels the bulk, two hundred thirty pounds the kindest scales say, that has enwrapped him at the age of fifty-five like a set of blankets the decades have brought one by one. His doctor down here keeps telling him to cut out the beer and munchies and each night after brushing his teeth he vows to but in the sunshine of the next day he's hungry again, for anything salty and easy to chew. What did his old basketball coach, Marty Tothero, tell him toward the end of his life, about how when you get old you eat and eat and it's never the right food? Sometimes Rabbit's spirit feels as if it might faint from lugging all this body around. Little squeezy pains tease his ribs, reaching into his upper left arm. He has spells of feeling short of breath and mysteriously full in the chest, full of some pressing essence. When he was a kid and had growing pains he would be worried and the grown-ups around him laughed them off on his behalf; now he is unmistakably a grownup and must do his own laughing off.

A colorful octagonal nook of a shop selling newspapers and magazines and candy and coral souvenirs and ridiculous pastel T-shirts saying what bliss southwestern Florida is interrupts the severe gray spaces of the airport. Janice halts and says, "Could you wait here a sec till I see if they have the new *Elle*? And maybe I should go back and use the Ladies while I have the chance, the traffic going home might be terrible what with the weather continuing so beachy."

"*Now* you think of it," he says. "Well, *do* it if you're going to do it." The little Mamie Eisenhower bangs she still wears have grown skimpy with the years and curly with the humidity and saltwater and make her look childish and stubborn and cute, actually.

"We still have ten minutes at least, I don't know what that jerk was in such a hurry about."

"He was just in love with life," Harry tells her, and obediently waits. While she's in the Ladies he cannot resist going into the shop and buying something to nibble, a Planter's peanut-brittle bar for forty-five cents. Planter's Original Peanut Bar, the wrapper says. It was broken in two somewhere in transit and he thinks of saving one half to offer his two grandchildren when they're all together in the car heading home. It would make a small hit. But the first half is so good he eats the second and even dumps the sweet crumbs out of the wrapper into his palm and with his tongue licks them all up like an anteater. Then he

thinks of going back and buying another for his grandchildren
and him to share in the car—"Look what Grandpa has!" as they
turn onto Interstate 75—but doesn't trust himself not to eat it all
and makes himself stand and look out the window instead. This
airport has been designed with big windows viewing the run-
ways, so if there's a crash everybody can feast upon it with their
own eyes. The fireball, the fuselage doing a slow skidding twirl,
shedding its wings. As he tries with his tongue to clean the sticky
brittle stuff, the caramelized sugar and corn syrup, from between his teeth—all his still, thank God, and the front ones not
even crowned—Rabbit stares out at the big square of sunny afternoon. The runway tapering to a triangle, the Florida flatness
turning brown as thatch beyond the green reach of a watering
system. Winter, the shadow of it that falls down here, hasn't hit
yet. Every day the temperature has been in the eighties. After
four winters in Florida he knows how the wind off the Gulf can
cut into you on the first tee if you have an early starting time
and the sweaters can be shed only as the sun climbs toward
noon, but this December except for that one cold snap in the
middle of the month has been like early September in Pennsylvania—hot, and only the horse chestnuts turning and only a
certain weary dryness in the air and the buzz of cicadas to suggest that summer is over.

As the candy settles in his stomach a sense of doom regrows
its claws around his heart: little prongs like those that hold fast
a diamond solitaire. There has been a lot of death in the newspapers lately. Max Robinson the nation's first and only black
national anchorman and Roy Orbison who always wore black
and black sunglasses and sang "Pretty Woman" in that voice
that could go high as a woman's and then before Christmas that
Pan Am Flight 103 ripping open like a rotten melon five miles
above Scotland and dropping all these bodies and flaming
wreckage all over the golf course and the streets of this little
town like Glockamorra, what was its real name, Lockerbie.
Imagine sitting there in your seat being lulled by the hum of the
big Rolls-Royce engines and the stewardesses bringing the
clinking drinks caddy and the feeling of having caught the plane
and nothing to do now but relax and then with a roar and giant
ripping noise and scattered screams this whole cozy world dropping away and nothing under you but black space and your chest
squeezed by the terrible unbreathable cold, that cold you can
scarcely believe is there but that you sometimes actually feel
still packed into the suitcases, stored in the unpressurized hold,

when you unpack your clothes, the dirty underwear and beach
towels with the merciless chill of death from outer space still in
them. Just yesterday some jet flying from Rochester to Atlanta
tore open at thirty-one thousand feet, a fourteen-inch hole the
newspaper said, and was lucky to land in West Virginia. Everything falling apart, airplanes, bridges, eight years under Reagan
of nobody minding the store, making money out of nothing,
running up debt, trusting in God.

Harry has flown in his life to dealers' conferences here and
there and that time nine years ago with two other couples to the
Caribbean, but to Florida he and Janice always drive, so they
have the car there. Nelson will probably bitch because there's
only one, though it's a Camry station wagon that takes six comfortably, Nelson likes to do his own thing, going off on mysterious errands that take hours. Nelson. A real sore spot. Harry's
tongue begins to sting, so he stops working at a jagged bit of
corn-syrup sweetness stuck behind an eye tooth.

And also in the Fort Myers *News-Press* this morning an item
about a pregnant woman over in Fort Lauderdale shot in an
attempted robbery yesterday. Must have been black but the paper didn't say so, they don't now. She died but they saved the
baby by Caesarean section. And then there was also on the front
page this interview with a guy convicted of picking up a twelve-
year-old girl and getting her to smoke dope and raping her and
then burning her alive somehow and now complaining about the
cockroaches and rats in the cell on death row and telling the
reporter, "I've always tried to do the best I can, but I'm no
angel. And I'm no killer either." His saying this made Harry
laugh, it rang a kind of bell with him. No angel yet no killer
either. Not like this guy Bundy who murdered dozens of women
in dozens of states and has been stalling his execution for ten
years in Tallahassee down here. And Hirohito too is taking his
time. Harry can remember when Hirohito was right up there
with Hitler and Mussolini in the war propaganda.

And he has never forgot how, thirty years ago it will be this
June, his baby daughter Rebecca June drowned and when he
went back to the apartment alone there was still this tubful of
tepid gray water that had killed her. God hadn't pulled the plug.
It would have been so easy for Him, Who set the stars in place.
To have it unhappen. Or to delete from the universe whatever it
was that exploded that Pan Am 747 over Scotland. Those bodies
with hearts pumping tumbling down in the dark. How much did
they know as they fell, through air dense like tepid water, tepid

gray like this terminal where people blow through like dust in an air duct, to the airline we're all just numbers on the computer, one more or less, who cares? A blip on the screen, then no blip on the screen. Those bodies tumbling down like wet melon seeds.

A star has appeared in the daytime sky, in the blue beneath the streaks of stratocirrus, an airplane glinting, lowering, heading straight toward them. This glint, he thinks, holds his near and dear: Nelson his son, his left-handed daughter-in-law called Pru though she was christened Teresa, Judy his eight-year-old granddaughter, and Roy his four-year-old grandson, born the same fall Harry and Janice began to spend half the year in Florida. The baby actually was named after both fathers, Harold Roy, but everybody calls him Roy, something Harry could resent since Roy Lubell is a sorehead laid-off Akron steamfitter who didn't even come to the wedding and never did shit for his seven hungry kids. Pru still seems hungry and in that she reminds Harry of himself. The star grows, has become a saucer shape glinting in a number of points, a winged aluminum machine aglide and enlarging above the sulky flat scrubland and horizon thready with palms. He imagines the plane exploding as it touches down, ignited by one of its glints, in a ball of red flame shadowed in black like you see on TV all the time, and he is shocked to find within himself, imagining this, not much emotion, just a cold thrill at being a witness, a kind of bleak wonder at the fury of chemicals, and relief that he hadn't been on the plane himself but was instead safe on this side of the glass, with his faint pronged sense of doom.

Janice is at his side again. She is breathless, excited. "Harry, *hur*ry," she says. "They're *here*, ten minutes early, there must have been a tail wind from Newark. I came out of the Ladies and went down to the gate and couldn't find you, you weren't *there*. Where *were* you?"

"Nowhere. Just standing here by the window." That plane he had mentally exploded hadn't been their plane at all.

Heart thumping, his breath annoyingly short, he strides after his little wife down the wide gray carpeting. Her pleated tennis skirt flicks at the brown backs of her thighs and her multilayered white Nikes look absurdly big at the end of her skinny legs, like Minnie Mouse in her roomy shoes, but Janice's getup is no more absurd than many in this crowd of greeters: men with bankers' trim white haircuts and bankers' long grave withholding faces wearing Day-Glo yellow-green tank tops stencilled CORAL POINT or CAPTIVA ISLAND and tomato-red bicycle shorts and Bermudas patterned with like fried eggs and their permed and thick-middled women in these ridiculous one-piece exercise outfits like long flannel underwear in pink or blue, baby colors on Kewpie-doll shapes, their costumes advertising the eternal youth they have found like those skiers and tennis players and golfers now who appear on television laden with logos like walking billboards. The hunchbacked little Jewish guy in such a hurry has already met his loved one, a tall grinning woman, a Rachel or Esther with frizzed-out hair and a big pale profile, carrying over one arm her parka from Newark, her plump dumpy mother on the other side of her, Grace was her name, while the old man with angry choppy gestures is giving the women the latest version of his spiel, they listening with half an ear each to this newest little thing he feels very strongly about. Rabbit is curious to see that this grown daughter, a head taller than her parents, appears to have no mate. A tall black man, slick-looking in a three-piece gray suit, but nothing of a dude, carrying himself with a businesslike Wasp indifference to his appearance and lugging one of those floppy big bags that smart travellers use and that hog all the overhead rack space, is trailing unnaturally close behind. But he can't be a relation, he must be just trying to pass, like that black chick in the red Camaro coming in off 75. Everybody tailgating, that's the way we move along now.

Harry and Janice reach Gate A5. People get off of airplanes in clots, one self-important fusspot with three bags or some doddery old dame with a cane bunching those behind them. You wonder if we haven't gone overboard in catering to cripples. "There they are," Janice pronounces at last, adding under her breath to Harry quickly, "Nelson looks exhausted."

Not so much exhausted, Rabbit thinks, as shifty. His son is carrying his own son on his left arm, and Nelson's right eye squints, the lid seeming to quiver, as if a blow might come from that unprotected side. Roy must have fallen asleep on the flight, for his head leans against his father's neck seeking a pillow there, his eyes open with that liquid childish darkness but his plump mouth mute, gleaming with saliva, in shock. Harry goes forward as soon as the ropes allow to lift the burden from his son, but Nelson seems reluctant to let go, as if the child's own grandfather is a kidnapper; Roy, too, clings. With a shrug of exasperation Harry gives up and leans in close and kisses Roy's velvety cheek, finer than velvet, still feverish with sleep, and shakes his own son's small and clammy hand. In recent years

Nelson has grown a mustache, a tufty brown smudge not much wider than his nose. His delicate lips underneath it never seem to smile. Harry looks in vain into this fearful brown-eyed face for a trace of his blue-eyed own. Nelson has inherited Janice's tense neatness of feature, with her blur of evasion or confusion in the eyes; the puzzled look sits better on a woman than a man. Worse, Janice's high forehead and skimpy fine hair have become in Nelson a distinctly growing baldness. His receding temples have between them a transparent triangle of remaining hair soon to become an island, a patch, and at the back of his head, when he turns to kiss his mother, a swath of skin is expanding. He has chosen to wear a worn blue denim jacket down on the plane, over a crisp dressy shirt, though, pink stripes with white collar and cuffs, so he seems half cocked, like a married rock star or a weekend gangster. One earlobe bears a tiny gold earring.

"Mmmm-*wah*!" Janice says to cap her hello kiss; she has learned to make such noises down here, among the overexpressive Jewish women.

Harry carefully greets Judith and Pru. Going to be nine in less than a month, the skinny girl is a sketch of a woman, less than life-size and not filled in. A redhead like her mother. Lovely complexion, cheeks rosy under the freckles, and the details of her face—lashes, eyebrows, ears, nostril-wings, lips quick to lift up on her teeth—frighteningly perfect, as if too easy to smash. When he bends to kiss her he sees in front of her ear the sheen of childhood's invisible down. She has Pru's clear green eyes and carrot-colored hair but nothing as yet in her frail straight frame and longish calm face of the twist that life at some point gave Pru, making her beauty even when she was twenty-four slightly awkward, limping as it were, a look that has become more wry and cumbersome with the nine years of marriage to Nelson. She likes Harry and he likes her though they have never found a way around all these others to express it. "What a pair of beauties," he says now, of the mother and daughter.

Little Judy wrinkles her nose and says, "Grandpa's been eating candy again, for shame on him. I could smell it, something with peanuts in it, I can tell. He even has some little pieces stuck between his teeth. For shame."

He had to laugh at this attack, at the accuracy of it, and the Pennsylvania-Dutch way the little girl said, "for shame." Local accents are dying out, but slowly, children so precisely imitate their elders. Judy must have overheard in her house Nelson and Pru and maybe Janice talking about his weight problem and rotten diet. If they were talking, his health problems might be worse than he knows. He must look bad.

"Shit," he says, in some embarrassment. "I can't get away with anything any more. Pru, how's the world treating you?"

His daughter-in-law surprises him by, as he bends dutifully forward to kiss her cheek, kissing him flush on the mouth. Her lips have a wry regretful shy downward twist but are warm, warm and soft and big as cushions in the kiss's aftermath within him. Since he first met her in the shadows of Ma Springer's house that long-ago summer—a slender slouching shape suddenly thrust into the midst of their lives, Nelson's pregnant Roman Catholic girlfriend from Ohio, a Kent State University secretary named Teresa Lubell, to become the mother of his two grandchildren, the carrier of his genes toward eternity—Pru has broadened without growing heavy in that suety Pennsylvania way. As if invisible pry bars have slightly spread her bones and new calcium been wedged in and the flesh gently stretched to fit, she now presents more front. Her face, once narrow like Judy's, at moments looks like a flattened mask. Always tall, she has in the years of becoming a hardened wife and matron allowed her long straight hair to be cut and teased out into bushy wings a little like the hairdo of the Sphinx. Her hips and shoulders too have widened, beneath the busy pattern—brown and white and black squares and diamond-shapes arranged to look three-dimensional—of the checked suit she put on for the airplane, a lightweight suit wrinkled by the three hours of sitting and babysitting. A stuffed blue shoulder bag is slung across one shoulder and her arms and hands clutch a camel-colored topcoat, two children's jackets, several slippery children's books based on morning television shows, a Cabbage Patch doll with its bunchy beige face, and an inflated plastic dinosaur. She has big hands, with pink, cracked knuckles. Harry's mother had hands like that, from washing clothes and dishes. How did Pru get them, in this age of appliances? He stands gazing at her in a half-second's post-kiss daze. Having a wife and children soon palled for him, but he never fails to be excited by having, in the flesh, a daughter-in-law.

She says, slangily, to mask the initial awkwardness when they meet, "You're lookin' good, Harry. The sunny South agrees with you."

What did that frontal kiss mean? Its slight urgency. Some sad message there. She and Nelson never did quite fit.

"Nobody else thinks so," he says, and grabs at her shoulder

bag. "Lemme help you carry some of this stuff, I'll take the bag." He begins to pull it off.

Pru shifts the coat and toys to extend her arm to let him take it but at the same time asks him, "Should you?"

Harry asks, "Why does everybody treat me like some goddamn kind of invalid?" but he is asking the air; Pru and Janice are hugging with brisk false enthusiasm and Nelson is plodding ahead down the long gray corridor with Roy back to sleep on his shoulder. Harry is irritated to see that though Nelson has a careful haircut that looks only a few days old the barber left one of those tails, like a rat's tail, uncut and hanging down over the boy's collar, under the spreading bald spot. How old does he think he is, seventeen? Little Judy trails her father but Nelson is not waiting or looking back. The girl is just old enough to sense that in her nice proper airplane outfit she should not sacrifice all dignity and run to catch up. She wears a navy-blue winter coat over a pink summer dress; its pink hem shows below the coat, and then her bare legs, which look long, longer than when he saw her last in early November. But it is the back of her head that kills him, her shiny carrot-colored hair braided into a pigtail caught into a showy stiff white ribbon. Something of her mother's Catholic upbringing in that ribbon, decking out the Virgin or the baby Jesus or Whoever to go on parade, to go on a ride in the sky. The sleek back of Judy's head, the pigtail bouncing as she tries not to run, so docilely, so unthinkingly wears the showy ribbon her mother put there that Harry smiles. Hurrying his stride, he catches up and reaches down and says, "Hey there, good-lookin'," and takes the hand she with a child's reflex lifts to be taken. Her hand is as surprisingly moist as her mother's lips were warm. Her head with its bone-white parting is higher than his waist. She complains to her mother, Harry has heard from Janice, about being the tallest girl in her section of the fourth grade. The mean boys tease her.

"How's school going?" he asks.

"I hate it," Judy tells him. "There are all these kids think they're big shots. The girls are the absolute worst."

"Do you ever think *you're* a big shot?"

She ponders this. "Some boys are always getting after me but I tell them to fuck off."

He clucks his tongue. "That's pretty rough language for the fourth grade."

"Not really," she says. "Even the teacher says 'damn' sometimes when we get her going."

"How do you get her going?"

Judy smiles upward, her mother's quick wide-mouthed smile without the crimp. "Sometimes we all hum so she can't see our mouths move. A couple weeks ago when she tried to make us all sing Christmas carols one of these big-shot boys I told you about said it was against his parents' religion and his father was a lawyer and would sue everybody."

"He sounds like a pain in the ass," Rabbit says.

"Grandpa. Don't talk dirty."

"That's not dirty, that's just saying where it hurts. If you say somebody's a pain in the bottom it sounds dirtier. Hey. Here's the place I bought that peanut candy you smelled. Want some?"

"You better ask Mom first."

Harry turns and lets the two mothers, walking hip to hip and heads bowed in consultation, catch up. "Pru," he says, "will it rot any teeth if I buy Judy a candy bar?"

She looks up, distracted, but remembers to smile at him. "I guess it won't kill her this once, though Nelson and I try to discourage junk in their diet."

"Whatever you get her, Harry," Janice adds, "you ought to get Roy."

"But Roy's asleep and half her size."

"He'll know, though," Pru says, "if you play favorites. He's just now coming out from under her shadow."

Little Judy, casting a shadow? Did he cast a shadow over Mim? Mim certainly got far enough away from Diamond County, if that was a statement. Got into the fast lane in Las Vegas and stayed.

"Don't be forever," Janice tells Harry. "Or else give me the keys so we can get into the car. They have two more bags they made them check in Newark. Nelson's probably down there already."

"Yeah, what's his idea, rushing on ahead like that? Who's he sore at?"

"Probably me," Pru says. "I've given up trying to figure out why."

Harry digs into one pocket of his plaid golf slacks, comes up with only a few tees and a plastic ball marker with two blue Vs on it, for Valhalla Village, and then into the other to find the knobbly notched bunch of keys on the ring. Saying "Heads up," he tosses them toward Janice. Her hands jump together in a womanly panic and the keys sail past them and hit her in the stomach. Just this little effort, the search and the toss, leaves him weary, as if the arm he lifted was soggy wash. The spontaneity and fun have been taken out of buying his granddaughter a treat. She chooses not a Planter's Peanut Bar as he had envisioned but a Sky Bar, which he thinks might be truly bad for her teeth, those five different gooey fillings in the five humped segments of pure chocolate. He digs into the hip pocket of his pants, so old their plaid is sun-faded and the hem of each pocket is darkened by the sweat off his hands over the years, and pulls out his wallet and hangs for a while over the candy rack, uncertain whether or not to get himself another sugary rectangle of stuck-together nuts, wondering if this time he would be lucky enough to get one not broken in the wrapper, deciding against it because he eats too much, too much junk as Pru said, Pru and his doctor down here, old Dr. Morris, and then at the last possible split-second, with the black woman at the counter within the octagonal shop already counting out his change from a dollar for the Sky Bar, deciding to buy the peanut brittle after all. It is not so much the swallowing and ingesting he loves as the gritty-edgy feeling of the first corner in his mouth, the first right-angled fragment, slowly dissolving. To his surprise and indignation not only does he now receive no change from the dollar but owes the black woman—a severe matte undiluted color you rarely see in the U.S., dull as slate, must be a Haitian or Dominican, Florida is full of boat people—a nickel more, for the state tax. Airport prices, they nail you where there's no competition. Without competition, you get socialism and everybody freeloading and economies like they have in Cuba and Haiti. He pauses to glance at the magazines on the rack. The top row holds the skin mags, sealed in plastic, pieces of printed paper hiding details of the open-mouthed girls, open-mouthed as if perpetually astonished by their own tangible assets, *Hustler, Gallery, Club, Penthouse, Oui, Live, Fox*. He imagines himself buying one, braving the Haitian woman's disapproval—all these Caribbean types are evangelical fundamentalists, tin-roofed churches where they shout for the world to end now—and sneaking the magazine home and while Janice is asleep or cooking or out with one of her groups studying to satiety the spread shots and pink labia and boosted tits and buttocks tipped up from behind so the shaved cunt shows, with its sad little anatomy like some oyster, and sadly foreseeing that he will not be enough aroused, boredom will become his main feeling, and embarrassment at the expenditure. Four dollars twenty-five they are asking these days, promising *Sexy Sirens in the Sauna* and *Cara*

Lott Gets Hot and *Oral Sex: A Gourmet's Guide*. How disgusting we are, when you think about it—disposable meat.

"Come *on*, Grandpa—what's taking so long?"

They hurry after the others, who have vanished. Judy's shiny beribboned head makes him nervous, popping up first on one side of him and then the other, like the car keys he was a little slow to find, Janice calls him doddery when she can't even catch, the clumsy mutt. If their granddaughter gets kidnapped from his side she'll really call him doddery. "Easy does it," he tells Judy at the top of the escalator, "pick a step and stay on it. Don't get on a crack," and at the bottom, "O.K., step off, but not too soon, don't panic, it'll happen, O.K., good."

"I go on escalators all the time at the malls," she tells him, making up at him a little pinched rebuking mouth with beads of melted chocolate at the corners.

"Where the hell is everybody?" he asks her, for amid all the tan loud presences that throng the lower, higher-ceilinged floor of the Southwest Florida Regional Airport, less ductlike and cryptlike but still echoing with a muffled steely doom that worries at his stomach, there is nobody he knows, strangers as total as if he has descended into hell.

"Are we lost, Grandpa?"

"We can't be," he tells her.

In their sudden small plight he is newly aware of her preciousness, the jewel-cut of her eyes and eyelashes, the downy glaze in front of her ears and the gleam of each filament of her luxuriant hair, pulled taut into a thick pigtail adorned with an unreal stiff white ribbon. For the first time he sees she is also wearing symmetrical white barrettes, shaped like butterflies. Judy looks up toward his face and fights crying at the vagueness she sees there. "This coat is too hot," she complains.

"I'll carry it," he says. He folds its cloth weight over his arm and she is like a butterfly herself now, in her pink dress. Her green eyes have gone wide in this gray airport's bustling limbo, under reddish-brown eyebrows one of which near the flat bulge of her little freckled nose has a little cowlick fanning the hairs the wrong way; Nelson has that cowlick, and inherited it from Harry, who used to lick his middle finger and try to slick it down in the high-school boys' lavatory mirror. Amazing, that a thing so tiny could pass on. Maybe the only immortality we get, a little genetic quirk going on and on like a computerized number in your monthly bank statement. Ghostly empty shapes, people he doesn't know, push and stream past the two of them. They are an island surrounded by jokes and noisy news and embraces; people tanned that deep bluish mahogany that comes only from months and months of Florida embrace newcomers the color of wallpaper paste. Harry says, so Judy will hear her grandfather say something and not just stand there numbly, "They must be over at the baggage."

He looks up and sees above their heads the sign saying BAG- GAGE and takes her moist little hand and tugs her toward the crowd around the baggage belt, which is already moving. But neither Pru nor Janice nor Nelson nor Roy is there, as far as they can see. Face after face refuses to cohere into a known face. His eyes, always good, trouble him now in artificially lit places. The blue shoulder bag Pru let him carry for her is heavier than he would have thought; she must have packed bricks. His shoulder and eyes burn.

"I guess," he ventures, though it seems unlikely, "they're already at the car." He taps his pocket for the lump of keys, doesn't feel it, begins to panic, then remembers how he tossed them to Janice. Of course. Confidently now he approaches the brown glass exit doors, but the wrong one pops its seal and slides open when his body trips the electric eye. The wrong one as far as he is concerned; Judy was pulling him in the right direction, where a slice of hot outdoor air swiftly widens. Sun has broken through the milky stratocirrus. It bounces off the waxy leaves of the nameless tropical plants flourishing near his knees. It winks blindingly from a mass of moving cars, a brutal river of them rushing along the access strip just beyond the curb. He holds Judy's hand tighter, in case she decides to jump off the curb, we're all full of crazy impulses. They cross to a lake of shimmering cars, the lot where he parked. Where, exactly? He finds he's forgotten. He is utterly empty of the car's location.

A Camry Deluxe wagon, pearl-gray metallic, with the more potent 24-valve 2.5-liter V-6 engine. He was still so sore at being tailgated by that red Camaro and at Janice criticizing his driving that he wasn't paying any attention to where they parked. He remembers the zebra crosswalk, and the little landscaped mound of center strip where some sun-starved college kid had propped his knapsack and pillowed his head on it to soak up a few rays, and the fussy old guy who thought he was in charge gesturing at you which way the exit and the booth where you pay was, putting too much into it like that husband at the airport gabbing at his wife, Grace, as if she had no sense, meeting that frizzy-haired long-toothed smiling Jewish princess taller than either of them, but he doesn't remember which of these rows he parked the car in. He parked it in the patch of dead blank brain cells like all of our brains will be when we're dead unless the universe has cooked up some truly elaborate surprise. *The National Enquirer* which Janice sometimes brings home from the Winn Dixie keeps reporting people's near-death experiences, but for Harry they're too close to the little green men in the UFOs. Even if they're true it's not much comfort. Judy's hand has slipped out of his as he stands puzzling on the strip of Bermuda grass on the edge of the parking lot, Bermuda grows everywhere down here, watered by sprinklers, and doesn't feel like real grass to him, too matted and broad, kind of crunchy underfoot. His chest begins to hurt. A sly broad pain, a kind of band under the skin, tightly sewn there.

Judy's voice floats up to him like a thin lifeline. "What color is the car, Grandpa?"

"Oh, you know," he says, keeping his sentences short, so as not to stir up his pain. "Pale gray. Metallic finish. The same color as about half the cars in the world. Don't panic. It'll come to me where I left it."

The poor kid is losing it, in her fight not to cry. "Daddy'll drive off!" she blurts out.

"Leaving you and me? Why would he do that? He won't do that, Judy."

"He gets real mad sometimes, for no real reason."

"He probably has some reason he doesn't tell you. How about you? You ever get mad?"

"Not like Daddy. Mom says he should see a doctor."

"I guess we all should, now and then." Rabbit's sense of doom is trickling like cold water through his stomach. Doctors. His own doctor is bringing his son into the practice, so if he drops dead the kid will take right over, won't miss a Medicare form. You fill a slot for a time and then move out; that's the decent thing to do: make room. He scans the ranks of glinting metal in their slots for a strip of gray that will ring a bell, and wonders if he is misremembering the color—he has owned so many cars in his life, and sold so many more. He announces, "I think I left it over on the left. In about the third row. What happened, Judy, was there was this old guy kind of directing things, waving which way everybody should go, and the bastard distracted me. Don't you hate bossy people like that, who know everything better than you do?"

The little girl's glossy red head mutely nods at his side, too worried for words.

Rabbit rattles on, to chase their clouds away, "Whenever somebody tells me to do something my instinct's always to do the opposite. It's got me into a lot of trouble, but I've had a lot of fun. This bossy old guy was pointing one direction so I went the other and found a space." And for a second, in a kind of window between two tightenings of the band across his chest, he *sees* the space: next to a cream-colored van, a Ford Bivouac with those watery-blue Minnesota plates, parked sloppily over the white line, another cause for irritation. He had to ease in carefully so as to leave Janice room enough to open her door on the right and not rub fenders with the maroon Galaxy on the left. And now he sees from far off in the shimmering Florida heat a strip of cream risen above the other metallic rooftops. Third row, about a wedge shot in. He says in triumph, "Judy, I *see* it. Let's *go*," and takes her hand again, lest her small perfection be crushed by one of the automobiles cruising the rows looking for a spot. In some of these big white Caddys and Oldses the tiny old driver can hardly see over the hood out the windshield, just clinging to the wheel, body all shrunk and bent by osteoporosis; it hasn't got him yet, he's still six feet three as far as he knows, at least his pants don't drag on the floor, but he hears Janice talk about it, it's been on TV a fair amount, that commercial with the two women on the train, it affects women more than men, their smaller bones, she takes calcium pills along with all the other vitamin pills next to her orange juice at breakfast. God, is she healthy. She'll live forever just to spite him.

He and little Judith arrive across the hazardous hot asphalt at the pearl-gray Camry, which is his, he knows, from Janice's tennis racket and cover on the back seat, flung in there separately—the dumb mutt, what's the use of a cover if you don't put the racket in it? But nobody is here and the car is locked and Harry threw away the keys. The little girl begins to cry. Luckily he has a handkerchief in the hip pocket of his faded plaid golf pants. He lowers Pru's laden blue bag to the asphalt and puts the little winter coat he has been carrying on top of the car roof, as if to stake a claim, and kneels down and wipes the bits of melted Sky Bar from Judy's lips and then the tears from her cheeks. He too wouldn't mind having a cry, squatting here next to the car's sunstruck metallic flank, his knees complaining on top of everything else, and the small girl's hot panicked breath adding to the heat. In her distress her freckled nose has begun to run and her mouth taken on a hardness, a stiffness in the upper lip he associates with Nelson when the boy is frightened or angry.

"We can either stay here and let the others find us," Harry explains to his granddaughter, "or we can go back and look for them. Maybe we're too tired and hot to do anything but stay here. We could play a game seeing how many different states' license plates we can find."

This breaks her sniffling into a wet little laugh. "Then we'd get lost again." Her eyelids are reddened by the friction of tears and tiny flakes of light shine in her green irises like the microscopic facets that give metallic paint its tinselly quality.

"Look," he tells her. "Here's Minnesota, with its little clump of pine trees. Ten Thousand Lakes, it says. Score one for Grandpa."

Judy merely smiles this time, not granting him a laugh, she knows he's trying to get her to forgive his mistake in losing the others.

"It's not us who are lost, we know where we are," he says. "It's *them*." He stops crouching beside her, the hoity-toity little snip, and stands up, to uncreak his knees, and also to ease the crowded feeling in his chest.

He sees them. Just this side of the zebra crossing, coming this way, struggling with suitcases. He first sees Nelson, carrying Roy on his shoulders like a two-headed monster, and then Pru's head of red hair puffed out like the Sphinx, and Janice's white tennis dress. Harry, up to his chest in car roofs, waves his arm back and forth like a man on a desert island. Janice waves back, a quick toss of her hand as if he's far from what they're talking about.

But when they're all reunited Nelson is furious. His face is pale and his upper lip stiff and bristling. "Jesus Christ, Dad, where did you disappear to? We went all the way back upstairs to that stupid candy store when you didn't show up in the baggage area."

"We were there, weren't we Judy?" Harry says, marvelling at his son's growing baldness, exposed mercilessly by the Florida sunlight beating down through the thinned strands, and at his mustache, a mouse-colored stray blur like those fuzzballs that collect under furniture. He has noticed these developments before in recent years but they still have the power to astonish him, along with the crow's feet and bitter cheek lines time has etched in his child's face, sharp in the sunlight. "We didn't take more than a minute in the candy store and came right down the escalator to the baggage place," Rabbit says, pleased to be remembering so exactly, exactly visualizing the two candy bars, the extra nickel he had to fish up for the black counter woman's upturned silver-polish-colored palm, the skin magazines with the girls' open mouths, the interleaved teeth of the escalator steps he was afraid Judy might catch her foot on. "We must have slipped by each other in the crowd," he adds, trying to be helpful and innocuous. His son frightens him.

Janice unlocks the Camry. The baking heat of its interior, released like a ghost, brushes past their faces. They put the suitcases in the way-back. Pru lifts the groggy boy off Nelson's shoulders and arranges him in the shadows of the back seat; Roy's thumb is stuck in his mouth and his dark eyes open for an unseeing second. Nelson, his hands at last freed, slaps the top of the Camry and cries in his agony of irritation, "God *damn* it, Dad, we've been *frantic*, because of you! We thought you might have *lost* her!" There is a look Nelson gets when he's angry or frightened that Harry has always thought of as "white around the gills"—a tension draining color from the child's face and pulling his eyes back into his head. He gets the look from his mother, and Janice got it from hers, dark plump old Bessie, who was a hot-tempered Koerner, she liked to tell them.

"We stuck right together," Rabbit says calmly. "And don't dent my fucking car. You've damaged enough cars in your life."

"Yeah, and you've damaged enough lives in yours. Now you're kidnapping my goddamn daughter!"

"I can't believe this," Harry begins. A cold arrow of pain suddenly heads down his left arm, through the armpit. He blinks. "My own granddaughter" is all he can organize himself to say.

Janice, looking at his face, asks, "What's the matter, Harry?"

"Nothing," he tells her sharply. "Just this crazy kid. Something's bugging him and I can't believe it's me." A curious gaseous weight, enveloping his head and chest, has descended in the wake of the sudden arrow. He slumps down behind the wheel, feeling faintly disoriented but determined to drive. When you're retired, you get into your routines and other people, even so-called loved ones, become a strain. This entire other family loads itself into place behind him. Pru swings her nice wide ass in her three-dimensional checked suit into the back seat next to sleeping Roy, and Nelson climbs in on the other side, right behind Harry, so he can feel the kid's breath on the back of his neck. He turns his head as far as he can and says to Nelson, in the corner of his eye, "I resent the word 'kidnap.' "

"Resent it, then. That's what it felt like. Suddenly we looked around and you weren't there."

Like Pan Am 103 on the radar screen. "We knew where we were, didn't we, Judy?" Harry calls backward. The girl has slithered over her parents and brother into the way-back with the luggage. Harry can see the silhouette of her head with its pigtail and angular ribbon in the rearview mirror.

"I didn't know where I was but I knew you did," she answers loyally, casting forward the thin thread of her voice.

Nelson tries to apologize. "I didn't mean to get so pissed," he says, "but if you knew what a hassle it is to have *two* children, the hassle of travelling all day, and then to have your own father steal one of them—"

"I didn't *steal* her, for Chrissake," Harry says. "I bought her a *Sky* Bar." He can feel his heart racing, a kind of gallop with an extra kick in one of the legs. He starts up the Camry and puts it in drive and then brakes when the car jerks forward and puts it into reverse, trying not to make contact, as he eases out, with the side of the Minnesota Bivouac, its protruding side mirror and its racing stripe in three tones of brown.

"Harry, would you like me to drive?" Janice asks.

"No," he says. "Why would I?"

She hesitates; without looking, he can see, in the hesitation, her little pointed tongue poke out of her mouth and touch her upper lip in that way she has when she tries to think, he knows her so well. He knows her so well that making conversation with her is like having a struggle with himself. "You just had a look on your face a minute ago," she says. "You looked—"

"White around the gills," he supplies.

"Something like that."

The old guy who thinks he's directing the show directs them down the arrows painted on the asphalt toward the tollbooth. The car ahead of theirs in line, a tan Honda Accord with New Jersey plates, GARDEN STATE, has backs of the head in it that look familiar: it's that jumpy little guy who hopped through the chairs back in the waiting room, good old Grace up beside him, and in the back seat the frizzy-headed daughter and another passenger, a head even taller and the frizz even tighter—the black guy in the Waspy business suit Harry had assumed had nothing to do with them. The old guy is gabbing and gesturing and the black guy is nodding just like Harry used to do with

Fred Springer. It's bad enough even when your father-in-law is the same color. Harry is so interested he nearly coasts into the back of the Honda. "Honey, *brake*," Janice says, and out of the blur of her white tennis dress in the corner of his eye she holds out to him fifty cents for the parking-lot charge. An Oriental kid stone-deaf inside his Walkman earmuffs takes the two quarters with a hand jumping along with some beat only he can hear, and the striped bar goes up, and they are free, free to go home.

"Well," Harry says, back on the weird brief highway, "it's a helluva thing, to have your own son accuse you of *kid*napping. And as to the big deal of having two children, it can't be that much worse than having one. Either way, your freedom's gone."

Actually Nelson has, unwittingly or not, touched a sore point, for Harry and Janice did have two children. Their dead child lives on with them as a silent glue of guilt and shame, an inexpungeable sourness at the bottom of things. And Rabbit suspects himself of having an illegitimate daughter, three years younger than Nelson, by a woman called Ruth, who wouldn't admit it the last time Harry saw her.

Nelson goes on, helpless in the grip of his hardened resentments, "You go run off with Judy all palsy-walsy and haven't said boo to little Roy."

"Say boo?—I'd wake him up, saying boo, he's been asleep all the time, it's like he's drugged. And how much longer you gonna let him suck his thumb? Shouldn't he be outgrowing it by now?"

"What does it matter to you if he sucks his thumb? How is it hurting you?"

"He'll get buck teeth."

"Dad, that's an old wives' tale. Pru asked our pediatrician and he said you don't suck your thumb with your teeth."

Pru says quietly, "He did say he should outgrow it soon."

"What makes you so *down* on everything, Dad?" Nelson whines, unable it seems to find another pitch. The kid is itching and his voice can't stop scratching. "You used to be a pretty laid-back hombre; now everything you say is kind of negative."

Rabbit wants to lead the boy on, to see how bad he can make him look in front of the women. "Rigid," he smilingly agrees. "The older you get, the more you get set in your ways. Nobody at Valhalla Village sucks their thumb. There may even be a rule against it, like swimming in the pool without a bathing cap. Like swimming with an earring on. Tell me something. What's the significance of an earring when you're married with two children?''

Nelson ignores the question in silence, making his father look bad.

They are breezing along, between shoulders of Bermuda grass, the palms clicking by like telephone poles. Pru says from the back seat, to change the subject, "I can never get over how flat Florida is.''

"It gets a little rolling," Harry tells her, "away from the coasts. Ranch and orange-grove country. Rednecks and a lot of Mexicans. We could all go for a drive inland some day. See the real Florida."

"Judy and Roy are dying to see Disney World," Nelson says, trying to become reasonable.

"Too far," his father swiftly tells him. "It'd be like driving to Pittsburgh from Brewer. This is a big state. You need reservations to stay overnight and this time of year there aren't any. Absolutely impossible."

This flat statement renders them all wordless. Through the rushing noise of the air-conditioning fan and the humming of the tires Harry hears from the way-back that for a second time in this first half-hour he has made his granddaughter cry. Pru turns and murmurs to her. Harry shouts back, "There's lots else to do. We can go to that circus museum in Sarasota again."

"I *hate* the circus museum," he hears Judy's small voice say.

"We've never been to the Edison house in Fort Myers," he announces, speaking now as patriarch, to the entire carful. "The people at the condo say it's fascinating, he even invented television it turns out."

"And the beach, baby," Pru softly adds. "You know how you love the beach at the Shore." In a less maternal voice she tells Janice and Harry, "She's a lovely swimmer now."

"Driving to the Jersey Shore used to be absolutely the most boring thing we did," Nelson tells his parents, trying to get down out of his dark cloud into a family mode, willing now to reminisce and be a child again.

"Driving is boring," Rabbit pontificates, "but it's what we do. Most of American life is driving somewhere and then driving back wondering why the hell you went."

"Harry," Janice says. "You're going too fast again. Do you want to take 75, or push on to Route 41?"

* * *

Of all the roads Harry has seen in his life, Route 41, the old
Tamiami Trail, is the most steadily depressing. It is wider than
commercial-use, unlimited-access highways tend to be up north,
and somehow the competitive roadside enterprise looks worse in
constant sunlight, as if like plastic garbage bags it will never rot
away. WINN DIXIE. PUBLIX. Eckerd Drugs. K Mart. Wal-Mart.
TACO BELL. ARK PLAZA. Joy Food Store. Starvin' Marvin Discount Food Wine and Beer. Among the repeating franchises selling gasoline and groceries and liquor and drugs all mixed together
in that peculiar lawless way they have down here, low pale buildings cater especially to illness and age. Arthritic Rehabilitation
Center. Nursefinder, Inc. Cardiac Rehabilitation Center. Chiro-
practix. Legal Offices—Medicare and Malpractice Cases a Spe-
ciality. Hearing Aids and Contact Lenses. West Coast Knee
Center. Universal Prosthetics. National Cremation Society. On
the telephone wires, instead of the sparrows and starlings you see
in Pennsylvania, lone hawks and buzzards sit. Banks, stylish big
structures in smoked glass, rise higher than the wires with their
glossy self-advertisements. First Federal. Southeast. Barnett Bank
with its Superteller. C & S proclaiming All Services, servicing
the millions and billions in money people bring down here along
with their decrepit bodies, the loot of all those lifetimes flooding
the sandy low land, floating these big smoked-glass superliners.

Alongside 41, between the banks and stores and pet suppliers
and sprinkler installers, miles of low homes are roofed with fat
white cooling tile. A block or two back from the highway in the
carbon-monoxide haze tall pink condos like Spanish castles or
Chinese pagodas spread sideways like banyan trees. Banyan trees
fascinate Harry down here, the way they spread by dropping
down vines that take root, they look to him like enormous chewing gum on your shoe. Easy Drugs. NU-VIEW. Ameri-Life and
Health. Starlite Motel. JESUS CHRIST IS LORD. His carful of family
grows silent and dazed as he drives the miles, stopping now and
then at the overhead lights that signal an intersecting road, a
secondary road heading west to beaches and what mangrove
swamps are left and east to the scruffy prairie being skinned in
great square tracts for yet more development. Development!
We're being developed to death. Each turning off of Route 41
takes some people home, to their little niche in the maze, their
own parking spot and hard-bought place in the sun. The sun is
low enough over the Gulf now to tinge everything pink, the red
of the stoplights almost invisible. At the Angstroms' own turn-

off, two more miles of streets unfold, some straight and some curving, through blocks of single-family houses with half-dead little front yards ornamented by plumes of pampas grass and flowering bushes on vacation from flowering in this dry butt-end of the year. Janice and Harry at first thought they might purchase one of these pale one-story houses lurking behind their tropical bushes and orange trees, caves of coolness and dark, with their secret pools out back behind the garages with their automatic doors, but such houses reminded them unhappily of the house they had in Penn Villas that saw so much marital misery and strangeness before it burned down, half of it, so they settled for a two-bedroom condominium up high in the air, on the fourth floor, overlooking a golf course from a narrow balcony screened by the top branches of Norfolk pines. Of all the addresses where Harry has lived in his life—303 Jackson Road; Btry A, 66th FA Bn, Fort Hood, Texas; 447 Wilbur Street, Apt. #5; whatever the number on Summer Street was where he parked himself with Ruth Leonard that spring long ago; 26 Vista Crescent; 89 Joseph Street for fifteen years, courtesy of Ma Springer; 14½ Franklin Drive—this is the highest number by far: 59600 Pindo Palm Boulevard, Building B, #413. He hadn't been crazy about the thirteen, in fact he thought builders didn't put that number in things, but maybe people are less superstitious than they used to be. When he was a kid there was all sorts of worry, not altogether playful, about black cats and spilled salt and opening umbrellas in the house and kicking buckets and walking under ladders. The air was thought then to have eyes and ears and to need placating.

VALHALLA VILLAGE: a big grouted sign, the two words curved around a gold ring of actual brass, inlaid and epoxied-over to discourage vandalous thieves. You turn in at the security booth, get recognized by the guard there, park in one of two spaces with your condo number stencilled right on the asphalt, use your key on the outer door of Building B, punch out the code number to open the inner door, take the elevator, and walk to your left. The corridor is floored in peach-colored carpet and smells of air freshener, to mask the mildew that creeps into every closed space in Florida. A crew comes through three times a week vacuuming and the rug gets lathered and the walls worked once a month, and there are plastic bouquets in little things like basketball hoops next to every numbered door and a mirror across from the elevator plus a big runny-colored green and golden vase on a table shaped like a marble half-moon, but it is still not a space in which you want to linger.

With their suitcases bumping the walls of silver and peach and Janice and Pru still gamely gabbing and little Roy being made to walk on his own two feet now that he's awake for once and crying about it at every step, Harry feels they are disturbing a mortuary calm, though in fact most everybody behind these doors has contrived something to do in the afternoon, golf or tennis or a beauty-parlor appointment or a bus trip to the Everglades. You live life here as if your condo is just home base, a sort of air-conditioned anteroom to the sunny mansion of all outdoors. Stay inside, you might start to mildew. Around five-thirty, an eerie silence of many simultaneous naps descends, but at four o'clock it's too early for that.

The door to 413 has a double lock operated with two keys, one of which also opens the outer door downstairs. With the impatient mass of his entire family and its baggage pressing behind him Harry fumbles a bit, his hand jumping the way it does when he's feeling crowded in the chest, his notched key scratching at the wiggly small slot, but then it fits and turns and clicks and the door swings open and he is home. This place could belong to one of millions of part-time Floridians but in fact is his, his and Janice's. You enter in a kind of foyer, a closet door to the left and on the right see-through shelves of stained wood Janice has loaded with birds and flowers she made out of shells in a class she took that first year down here, when she was still enthusiastic about shells. Enthusiasm about shells doesn't last, nor does taking Spanish lessons so you can talk to the help. It's a phase the greenhorns, the fresh snowbirds, must go through. Baby scallops make feathers and petals, augurs do as bird beaks, slipper shells are like little boats. The shelves, which also hold a few of Ma Springer's knickknacks, including a big green glass egg with a bubble inside it, separate the foyer from the kitchen, with the dining room beyond it; straight ahead lies the living-room area, where they have the TV and the comfortable wicker chairs and a low round glass table they often eat dinner from, if a show they care about is on. To the left, a square-armed blond sofa can be folded out for a bed and a hollow door leads to the master bedroom, which has a bathroom and a storage area where Janice keeps an ironing board she never uses and an exercise bicycle she rides when she thinks she's getting overweight, to Nelson's old tapes of the Bee Gees that he outgrew long ago. The guest bedroom is entered off the living room, to the right, and has its own bathroom that backs up to the kitchen plumbing. The arrangement other years has been that Nelson and Pru take this room with a cot for the baby and Judith sleeps on the fold-out sofa, but Harry is not sure this arrangement is still proper. The little ones have grown: Roy perhaps is too big and observant to share a bedroom with his parents and the girl is getting to be enough of a lady to deserve a little privacy.

He explains his plan: "This year I thought we might put the cot in the storage room for Judy, she can use our bathroom and then shut the door, and give Roy the living-room sofa."

The small boy gazes upward at his grandfather while his thumb sneaks toward his mouth. He has a flubby sort of mouth that Rabbit associates with the Lubells; neither the Angstroms nor the Springers have bunched-up fat lips like that, like a row of plump berries run together, but Teresa's father, in the one time Harry met him, visiting Akron because he went to Cleveland for a dealer conference anyway, did, if you could see around the two days' beard and the cigarette always in the guy's fat mouth. It's as if Pru's worthless creep of a father has been disguised as a child and sent to spy on them all. The kid takes in everything and says nothing. Harry speaks down to him roughly: "Yeah, what's the matter with that?"

The thumb roots in deeper and the child's eyes, darker even than Nelson's and Janice's, shine with distrust. Judy offers to explain: "He's scared to be alone in this room all by himself, the baby."

Pru tries to help. "Sweetie, Mommy and Daddy would be right in that other room, where you used to sleep before you became so grown up."

Nelson says, "You might have discussed it first with us, Dad, before you switched everything around."

"Discuss it, when is there a chance to discuss anything with you? Every time I call the lot you're not there, or the line is busy. I used to get Jake or Rudy at least, now all I get is some fruity-voiced pal of yours you've hired."

"Yeah, Lyle tells me how you grill him about everything."

"I don't grill him, I'm just trying to act interested. I still have an interest up there, even if you do think you're running it half the year."

"*Half* the year! *All* the year, from what Mom says."

Janice intervenes: "What Mom says is her legs hurt after all that sitting in the car and she's thinking of moving the cocktail hour ahead if this is how we're all going to talk for five days. Nelson, your father was trying to be considerate about the sleeping arrangements. He and I discussed it. Judy, which would you rather, the sofa or the ironing room?''

"I didn't mind the old way," she says.

Little Roy is trying to follow the drift of this discussion and removes his thumb enough for his flubby lips to mouth something Rabbit does not understand. Whatever he's saying, it makes Roy's eyes water to think of it. "Eee*eee*" is all Harry hears, at the end of the sentence.

Pru translates: "He says she gets to watch TV."

"What a disgusting baby tattletale," says Judy, and quick as a dragonfly darting over water she skims across the carpet and with an open hand whacks her little brother on the side of his spherical head. Pru cuts his hair in a kind of inverted bowl-shape. As when a faucet gasps emptily for a second after being turned on, his outrage silences him a moment, though his mouth is open. His yell when it comes arrives at full volume; against its sonic background Judy explains to them all, with a certain condescending air, "Just Johnny Carson sometimes when everybody else was asleep, and *Saturday Night Live* once that I can remember."

Harry asks her, "So you'd rather stay in here with the lousy TV than have a little cozy room of your own?"

"It doesn't have any windows," she points out shyly, not wanting to hurt his feelings.

"Fine, *fine*," Harry says. "I don't give a fuck where anybody sleeps," and in demonstration of his indifference strides into his own bedroom, past the king-size bed they bought down here, with its padded headboard covered in quilted satin and a matching jade-green coverlet that is as hard to fold up as the ones in hotels, into the little windowless room and picks up the folding cot, with its sheets and baby-blue Orlon blanket on it, and lugs it through the doorways, banging the frames and one of the wicker armchairs in the living room, into the guest bedroom. He is embarrassed: he overestimated how fast Judy was growing, he had wanted to embower her as his princess, he doesn't know little girls, his one daughter died and his other is not his.

Janice says, "Harry, you mustn't overexert yourself, the doctor said."

"The doctor said," he mocks. "All he ever sees is people over seventy-five and he says to me just what he says to them."

But he is breathing hard, and Pru hastens after him to spare him the effort of straightening the folding leg, a U-shape of metal tubing, that has come unclicked and folded underneath, and pulls taut the sheets and blanket. Back in the living room, Harry says to Nelson, who is holding little Roy in his arms again, "*Now* are you and the brat happy?"

For answer Nelson turns to Janice and says, "Jesus, Mom, I don't know as I can stand five days of this."

But then when they all get settled—the suitcases unpacked into bureaus, Judy and Roy fed milk and cookies and changed into bathing suits and taken to the heated Valhalla Village pool by their mother and Janice, who has to sign them in—Harry and Nelson sit each with a beer at the round glass table and try to be friends. "So," Harry says, "how's the car business?"

"You know as well as I do," Nelson says. "You see the stat sheets every month." He has developed a nervous irritable habit of grimacing and hunching his shoulders, as though somebody behind him might be about to knock him on the head. He smokes a cigarette as if he's feeding himself something through a tube, constantly fiddling with the shape of the ash on the edge of a white clamshell he has borrowed from Janice's collection.

"How do you like the '89s?" Harry asks, determined not to put it off, now that he and the boy are alone. "I haven't seen the actual cars yet, just the brochures. Beautiful brochures. How many millions you think those ad agencies get for making up those brochures? I was looking at the Corolla one trying to figure out if they really *had* driven that sedan and that wagon up into the mountains or were just faking it, and I had to laugh. The cars were posed on snow but there were no tracks showing how they got there! Look at it sometime."

Nelson is not much amused. He shapes his ash into a perfect cone and then suddenly stabs it out, twisting the butt vehemently. His hands shake more than a young man's should. He sips his beer, leaving shreds of foam on his tufty mustache, and, looking level at his father, says, "You asked me what I thought of the '89s. The same thing I thought about the '88s. Dull, Dad. Boxy. They're still giving us cars that look like gas-misers when there's been a gas glut for ten years. Americans want to go back to fins and convertibles and the limo look and these Japs are still trying to sell these tidy little boxes. And not cheap, either. That's what hurts. The lousy dollar against the yen. Why should people pay seventeen grand for a GTS when in the same range you can get a Mustang or Beretta GT or Mazda MX-6?"

"A Celica doesn't cost seventeen grand," Harry says. "Mine back home listed at less than fifteen."

"Get a few options and it does."

"Don't push the options at people. You get a name in the county for loading. People come in determined to have a stripped model, you should sell 'em one without making 'em feel they're being cheapskates."

"Tell it to California," Nelson says. "Practically all they want to part with are loaded models. The automatic notchbacks, the All-Trac Turbos. You want a basic ST or GT, it takes months for the order to come through. Luxury is where the bigger profit is, all the way up the line back to Tokyo. You have to try to sell what they send us—the one machine they make that's really moving, the Camry, you can't wheedle enough out of the bastards. They treat us like dirt, Dad. They see us as soft. Soft lazy Americans, over the hill. Ten more years, they'll have bought the whole country. Some television show I was watching, they already own all of Hawaii and half of L.A. and Nevada. They're buying up thousands of acres of desert in Nevada! What're they going to do with it? Set off Japanese atom bombs?"

"Don't get down on the Japanese like that, Nelson. We've done fine riding along with the Japanese."

"Riding along, you said it. Like riding along in the back seat of a Tercel. You always talk of them with such awe, like they're supermen. They're not. Some of their design, you get away from the little safe dependable cheapie family car, is a disaster. The Land Cruiser is a dog, it doesn't begin to compete with the Cherokee, and neither does the 4-Runner, it was so underpowered they had to come with a V-6 engine that turns out to be a guzzler—fourteen miles to the gallon, I was reading in *Consumer Reports*. And that van! It's ridiculous. Where the engine is, up between the front seats, the only way to get to the front from the back is get all the way out and climb back in. In the winter in Pennsylvania, people don't like to do that. So many customers have been complaining, I drove one myself the other day just to see, and even though I'm no giant, boy, did I feel squeezed in—no foot room to speak of, and no place to put your elbow. And zilch acceleration: pull into a fast-moving highway you'll get rear-ended. The wind pushed me all over 422, the damn thing is so tall—I could hardly step up into it."

That's right, Harry is thinking, *you're no giant*. Nelson seems to him strangely precise and indignant and agitated, like a nicely made watch with one tooth off a cogwheel or a gummy spot in the lubrication. The kid keeps sniffing, and lights another cigarette, after not enjoying the one he just snuffed out. He keeps touching his nose, as if his mustache hurts. "Well," Harry says, taking a relaxed tone to try to relax his son, "vans were never the bread and butter, and Toyota knows they have a lemon. They're getting a total revamp out by '91. How do you like the new Cressida?"

"It stinks, in my humble. There's nothing new about it. Oh, it's bigger, a bit, and the engine is up from two point eight to three point oh, and twenty-four valves instead of twelve, so you get more oomph, but for a basic twenty-one K you ex*pect* a little oomph—*my God*. The dashboard is a disaster. The climate-control panel slides out like a drawer and won't budge unless the ignition's on, which is ridiculous, number one, and two, they kept from last year's model their crazy idea of two sets of audio controls so you have all these extra buttons when already there's enough for an airplane cockpit. It costs luxury, Dad, and it drives luxury you could say, but it looks cheap inside and pseudo-Audi outside. Toyota, let's face it, has about the styling imagination of a gerbil. Their cars don't ex*press* anything. Good cars, classic cars—the Thirties Packards, the little Jags with the long hood and spoked wheels, the Fifties finned jobbies, even the VW bug—ex*pressed* something, made a statement. Toyotas don't express anything but playing it safe and stealing other people's ideas. Look at their pickup. The pickup used to be hot, but now they've let Ford and GM right back into the market. Look at the MR-2. It doesn't sell for shit now."

Harry argues, "High insurance is hurting everybody's two-seaters. Toyota puts out a good solid machine. They handle well and they last, and people know that and respect it."

Nelson cuts him short. "And they're so damn dicta*tor*ial—they tell you exactly what to charge, what to put in the windows, what your salespeople should wear, how many square feet of this and that you have to have to be good enough to lick their bazoo. When I took over I was surprised at all the crap you and Charlie had been swallowing all those years. They expect you to be their *robot*."

Now Rabbit is fully offended. "Welcome to the real world, kid. You're going to be part of some organization or other in this life. Toyota's been good to us and good to your grandfather and don't you forget it. I can remember Fred Springer when he first got the Toyota franchise saying he felt like a kid at Christmas all year round." The women in the family are always saying

Nelson is a throwback to his grandfather and Harry hopes by mentioning dead Fred to bring the boy back into line. All this blaspheming Toyota makes Harry uneasy.

But Nelson goes on, "Grandpa was a *dealer*, Dad. He loved to make deals. He used to tell about it: you came up short on some and made out like a bandit on others and it was *fun*. There was some *play* in the situation, some space for creativity. Unloading the trade-ins is about the only spontaneous creative thing left in the business now, and they tell you they don't want a bunch of ugly American junk up front on the lot, you almost have to sell the used cars on the sly. At least you can cut an extra grand or so if you get a dummy; selling new is just running the cash register. I don't call that selling, just standing at the checkout counter."

"Not bad for forty-five thou plus benefits." What Nelson makes a year now. Harry and Janice quarrel about it; he says it's too much, she says he has a family to support. "When I was your age," he tells the boy, perhaps not for the first time, "I was pulling down thirteen five a year as a Linotyper and came home dirty every night. The job gave me headaches and ruined my eyes. I used to have perfect eyes."

"That was *then*, Dad, this is *now*. You were still in the industrial era. You were a blue-collar slave. People don't make money an hour at a time any more; you just get yourself in the right position and it *comes*. I know guys, lawyers, guys in real estate, no older than me and not as smart who pull in two, three hundred K on a single transaction. You must know a lot of retired money down here. It's *easy* to be rich, that's what this country is all about."

"These must be the guys doing all that selling-off of Nevada to the Japanese you're so upset about. What're you so hungry for money for anyway? You live mortgage-free in that house your mother gives you, you must be saving a bundle. Speaking of used cars—"

"Dad, I hate to break the news to you, but forty thousand just isn't a fuck of a lot if you want to live with any style."

"Jesus, how much style do you and Pru need? Your house is free, all you do is cover heat and taxes—"

"The taxes on that barn have crept up to over four grand. Mt. Judge real estate is *way* up since the new baby boom, even a semi-detached over toward that slummy end of Jackson Road where you used to live goes for six figures. Also the federal tax reform didn't do a thing for my bracket, you got to be rich to get the benefits. Lyle was showing me on a spread sheet—''

"That's something else I wanted to ask you about. Whose idea was it to replace Mildred Kroust with this guy?''

"Dad, she'd been with Springer Motors forever—''

"I know, that was the point. She could do it all in her sleep.''

"She couldn't, actually, though she *was* asleep a lot of the time. She never could handle computers, for one thing. Oh sure, she tried, but one little scramble or error message'd show up on the screen she'd blame the machine and call up the company to send a repairman over at a hundred twenty an hour when all that was wrong was she couldn't read the manual and had hit the wrong key. She was *ancient*. You should have let her go when she reached retirement age.''

The apartment door furtively clicks open. "Just me,'' Janice's voice calls. "Pru and the babies wanted to stay at the pool a little longer and I thought I'd come back and start dinner. I thought we'd just have odds and ends tonight, I'll see if there's any soup to warm up. Keep talking, boys.'' She doesn't intrude upon them; her footsteps head into the kitchen. She must imagine they are having a healing talk, father to son. In fact Harry is looking at Nelson as if the boy is a computer. There is a glitch, a secret. He talks too much, too rapidly. Nellie used to be taciturn and sullen and now he keeps spilling out words, giving more answer than there was question. Something is revving him up, something wrong. Harry says, of Mildred Kroust, "She wasn't that old, actually, was she? Sixty-eight? Sixty-nine?''

"Dad, she was in her seventies and counting. Lyle does all she ever used to do and comes in only two or three days a week.''

"He's doing something different, I can see on the stat sheets. That was the thing I wanted to ask you about, the figures on the used in the November set.''

For some reason, the kid has gone white around the gills again. He pokes his cigarette through the hole at the beer pull-tab and then crushes the can in one hand, no big trick now that they're made of paper-thin aluminum. He rises from his chair and seems to be heading toward his mother, who has been knocking things around in the kitchen.

"Janice!" Harry shouts, turning his head with difficulty, his neck stiff with fat.

She stands in the kitchen entryway in a wet black bathing suit and a purple wraparound skirt, to make herself decent for the elevator. She looks a touch foozled: she cracked open the Campari bottle before leading the others down to the pool and must have hurried back to give herself another slug. Her skimpy hair is wet and stringy. "What?" she says, responding guiltily to the urgent sound of Harry's voice.

"Where did that latest batch of sheets from the lot go? Weren't they sitting over on the desk?"

This desk is something they bought cheap down here, in a hurry to furnish their place, in the same style as the end tables flanking the blond fold-out sofa and their bedroom bureaus—white-painted wood with the legs slashed at intervals with gold paint to imitate bamboo joints. It has only three shallow drawers that stick in the humidity and some cubby holes up top where bills and invitations get lost. The desktop, of some glazed marmoreal stuff like petrified honey-vanilla ice cream, is generally covered by a drift of unanswered letters and bank statements and statements from their stockbrokers and money management fund and golf scorecards and Xeroxed announcements from the Village Activities Committee, called VAC since life down here is supposedly a perpetual vacation. Also Janice has a way of tearing out clippings from health magazines and *The National Enquirer* and the Fort Myers *News-Press* and then forgetting who she meant to send them to. She looks frightened.

"Were they?" she asks. "Maybe I threw them out. Your idea, Harry, is just pile everything on it and it'll still be there next year when you want it."

"These just came in last week. They were November's financial summaries."

Her mouth pinches in and her face seems to click shut on a decision she will stick to blindly no matter what happens, the way women will. "I don't know where they went to. What I especially hate are your old golf cards drifting around. Why do you keep them?"

"I write tips to myself on them, what I learned on that round. Don't change the subject, Janice. I want those goddamn stat sheets."

Nelson stands beside his mother at the mouth of the kitchen, the crushed can in his hand. Without the denim jacket his shirt looks even more sissified, with its delicate pink stripes and white French cuffs and round-pointed white collar. The boy and Janice are near the same height, with tense small cloudy faces. Both look furtive. "No big deal, Dad," Nelson says in a dry-mouthed voice. "You'll be getting the December summaries in a couple of weeks." When he turns toward the refrigerator, to get himself another beer, he gives Rabbit a heartbreaking view of the back of his head—the careful rat's tail, the curved sliver of earring, the growing bald spot.

And when Pru comes back from the pool with the children, all of them in rubber flipflops and hugging towels around their shoulders and their hair pasted flat against their skulls, the two small children shivering gleefully, their lips bluish, their miniature fingers white and wrinkled from the water, Harry sees Pru in a new way, as the weakest link in a conspiracy against him. That cushiony frontal kiss she gave him at the airport. That pelvis that in her high-cut but otherwise demure white bathing suit looks so gently pried wider by the passing years.

Their fifth winter down here, this is, and Harry still wakes amazed to find himself actually in Florida, beside the Gulf of Mexico. If not exactly beside it, within sight of it, at least he was until that new row of six-story condos with ornamental turrets and Spanish-tile roofs shut out the last distant wink of watery horizon. When he and Janice bought the place in 1984 you could still see from their balcony snatches of the Gulf, a dead-level edge to the world over the rooftops and broken between the raw new towers like the dots and dashes of Morse code, and in their excitement they bought a telescope and tripod at a nautical shop at the mall a mile down Pindo Palm Boulevard. In its trembling little circle of vision, that first winter, they would catch a sailboat with its striped spinnaker bellying out or a luxury yacht with tall white sides peeling back the waves silently or a fishing charter with its winglike gaffing platforms or, farthest out, a world unto itself, a rusty gray oil freighter headed motionlessly toward Mobile or New Orleans or back toward Panama or Venezuela. In the years since, their view of the water has been built shut, skyscraper hotels arising along the shore, constructions the color of oatmeal or raspberry whip or else sheer glass like vertical distillations, cold and pure, of the Gulf's blue-green.

Where these towers arise had once been nothing but sand and mangrove swamp and snaky tidal inlets slipping among the nets of roots and dimpling where an alligator or a water moccasin glided; and then a scattering of white-painted houses and unpainted shacks in feeble imitation of the South to the north, scratching out some cotton and grazing some cattle on the sandy soil, sending north shuffling herds of beef on the hoof to the starving rebel troops in the Civil War; and then houses closer together, some of brick and wrought iron and of limestone and granite barged in from Alabama quarries. Then, with the new century, to this appendage of the South came the railroads and the rich and the sick and the hopeful misfits, this being frontier in an unexpected direction. Busts followed booms; optimism kept washing in. Now, with the jets and Social Security and the national sun-worship, they can't build onto it fast enough, this city called Deleon, named after some Spanish explorer killed for all his shining black breastplate by the poisoned arrow of a Seminole in 1521 near here or a place like it, and pronounced *Deely*un by the locals, as if they are offering to deal you in. The past glimmers like a dream at the back of Harry's mind as he awakes; in his semi-retirement he has taken to reading history. It has always vaguely interested him, that sinister mulch of facts our little lives grow out of before joining the mulch themselves, the fragile brown rotting layers of previous deaths, layers that if deep enough and squeezed hard enough make coal as in Pennsylvania. On quiet evenings, while Janice sits on the sofa sipping herself into stupidity with some lamebrain TV show, he lies on the bed leaning back against its padded satiny headboard with a book, staring dizzily down into the past as if high in a jade-green treehouse.

The sound that breaks into his dreams and dispels them is the rasp of golf greens being mowed, and then the scarcely less mechanical weeping noise of the seagulls gathering on the freshly watered fairways, where the earthworms are surfacing to drink. The head of their bed is by the big glass sliding doors, left open a crack to take in the winter-morning cool, in these few months when the air-conditioner is non-essential; so the cool salt air, sweetened with the scent of fresh fairways, reminds his face of where he is, this mass-produced paradise where Janice's money has taken him. She is not in the bed, though her warmth still greets his knee as he spreadeagles into her space. In deference to his height of six three, they have at last bought a king-size bed, so for the first time in his life his feet do not hang over the bottom and force him to sleep on his belly like a dead man floating. It took him a long time to get used to it, his feet not hooking onto the mattress this way but instead being forced to bend at the ankle or else point sideways. He gets foot cramps. He tries to sleep on his side, slightly curled up; it gives his mouth space to breathe and his belly room to slop into, and it frightens his frail heart less than hanging face down over the thickness of the mattress. But his arms don't know where to go. A hand crooked under his head loses circulation at the wrist and its numbness awakes him, tingling as if with an electric shock. If he lies on his back, Janice says, he snores. She snores herself now, now that they are approaching elderly, but he tries not to blame her for it: poor mutt, she can't help what she does when asleep, snoring and sometimes farting so bad he has to bury his nose in the pillow and remind himself she's only human. Poor women: they have a lot of leaks down there, their bodies are too complicated. He hears her now in the kitchen, talking in an unreal high needling sort of voice, the way we talk to children.

Rabbit listens for the lower younger voice of the children's mother to chime in but instead hears, close to his head, a bird cheeping in the Norfolk pine whose branches can be touched from their balcony. He still can't get over Norfolk pines, the way they look like the plastic trees you buy for Christmas, the branches spaced like slats and each one of them a plume perfect as a bird's feather and the whole tree absolutely conical in shape. The bird's cheeping sounds like a piece of moist wood being rhythmically made to squeak against another. Most nature in Florida has a manufactured quality. Wall-to-wall carpet, green outdoor carpeting on the cement walks, Bermuda grass in the space between the walks, all of it imposed on top of the sand, the dirty-gray sand that sprays over your shoes when you take a divot down here.

Today is Wednesday, he has a golf date, his usual foursome, tee-off time at nine-forty: the thought gives him a reason to get out of bed and not just lie there forever, trying to remember his dream. In his dream he had been reaching out toward something his sleeping eyes didn't let him see through his lids, something round and shadowy and sad, big-bellied with the vague doom he tries to suppress during the daytime.

Up, Rabbit examines the phony-looking branches of the Norfolk pine to see if he can see the noisy bird. He expects from the self-importance of the sound a cockatoo or toucan at least, a squawky tropical something with foot-long tailfeathers hanging down, but all he sees is a small brown bird such as flicker all around in Pennsylvania. Maybe it *is* a Pennsylvania bird, a migrant down here just like him. A snowbird.

He goes into the bathroom and brushes his teeth and urinates. Funny, it used to make a throaty splash in the toilet bowl, now a kind of grudging uncertain stream comes out, he has to rise once and sometimes even twice in the night, sitting on the toilet like a woman; what with the foreskin folded over sleepily he can never be sure which direction it will come out in, bad as a woman, they can't aim either. He shaves and weighs himself. He's gained a pound. Those Planter's Peanut Bars. He moves to leave the bedroom and realizes he can't. In Florida he sleeps in his underwear; pajamas get twisted around him and around two in the morning feel so hot they wake him up, along with the pressure in his bladder. With Pru and the kids here he can't just wander into the kitchen in his underwear. He hears them out there, bumping into things. He either should put on his golf pants and a polo shirt or find his bathrobe. He decides on the bathrobe, a woolly maroon, as being more—what's that word that keeps coming up in medieval history?—seigneurial. Hostly. Grandpaternal. It makes a statement, as Nelson would say.

By the time Rabbit opens the door, the first fight of the day has begun in the kitchen. Precious little Judy is unhappy; salt tears redden the rims of her lids though she is trying, shaky-voiced, not to cry. "But half the kids in my school have been. Some of them have even been twice, and they don't even have grandparents living in Florida!" She can't reach Disney World.

Janice is explaining, "It's really a whole separate trip, sweet-heart. You should fly to Orlando if you want to go. To go from here—"

" 'd be like driving to Pittsburgh," Harry finishes for her.

"Daddy promised!" the child protests, with such passion that her four-year-old brother, holding a spoon suspended in his fist above a bowl of Total he is mushing without eating, sobs in sympathy. Two drops of milk fall from his slack lower lip.

"Dull driving, too," Harry continues. "Stoplights all down Route 27. We come that way sometime, driving down."

Pru says, "Daddy didn't mean this time, he meant some other time when we have more days."

"He said *this* time," the child insists. "He's always breaking promises."

"Daddy's very busy earning money so you can have all the things you want," Pru tells her, taking the prim tone of one woman losing patience with another. She too is wearing a bath-robe, a little quilted shorty patterned with violet morning glories and their vines. Her freckled thighs have that broad bland smoothness of car fenders. Her feet are long and bony, pink in their toe-joints and papery-white on top, in cork-soled lipstick-red clogs. Her toenail polish is chipped, and Rabbit finds that sexy too.

"Oh, *yeahhh*," the child replies, with a furious sarcastic emphasis Harry doesn't understand. Family life, life with children, is something out of his past, that he has not been sorry to leave behind; it was for him like a bush in some neglected corner of the back yard that gets overgrown, a lilac bush or privet some bindweed has invaded from underneath with leaves so similar and tendrils so tightly entwining it gives the gardener a headache in the sun to try to separate bad growth from good. Anyway he basically had but the one child, Nelson, one lousy child, though he was reading somewhere the other day that a human male produces enough sperm to populate not just the planet Earth but Mars and Venus as well, if they could support life. It's a depressing thought, too planetary, like that unreachable round object in his dream, that the whole point of his earthly existence has been to produce little Nellie Angstrom, so he in turn could produce Judy and Roy, and so on until the sun burns out.

Now Nelson is stirred up and sucked into the kitchen by the fuss. He must have heard himself being talked about, and comes in from the guest bedroom, barechested and unshaven in rumpled smoky-blue pajama bottoms that look expensive. Unease infiltrates Harry's abdomen with this observation of Nelson's expensive tastes, something he is trying to remember about numbers, something he can't reach. Janice said the boy looked exhausted and he does look thin, with faint shadows flickering between his ribs. There is a touch of aggression about the bare chest, something territorial, taken with Pru's shorty robe. The pajama game. Doris Day and, who was it, John Raitt? Despite the quality of his pajamas, Nelson looks haggard and scruffy and mean, with the unshaven whiskers and that tufty little mustache like what dead Fred Springer used to wear and his thinning hair standing up in damp spikes. Rabbit remembers how deeply Nelson used to sleep as a child, how hot and moist his skull on the pillow would feel. "What's this about promises?" the boy asks angrily, staring at a space between Judy and Pru. "I never promised to go up to Orlando this trip."

"Daddy, there's nothing to *do* in this dumb part of Florida. I *hat*ed that circus museum last year, and then on the way back the traffic was so miserable Roy threw up in the Kentucky Fried Chicken parking lot!"

"Route 41 does a job on you," Harry admits.

"There's *tons* to do," Nelson says. "Go swim in the pool. Go play shuffleboard." He runs dry almost immediately and looks in panic at his mother.

Janice says to Judy, "The Village has tennis courts where you and I can go and hit balls."

"*Roy*'ll have to come and he always *spoils* it," the little girl complains, the vision of it freshening her tears again.

"—and there's the beach—" Janice goes on.

Judy replies, just making objections now, "Our teacher says the sun gives you skin damage and the earlier you get it the more cancer you'll get later on."

"Don't be such a fucking smart-ass," Nelson says to her. "Your grandmother's trying to be nice."

His remark makes the child's tears spill, out through the curved lashes onto her cheeks like the silvery jerking tracks rain makes on windowpanes. "I *wasn't* being—" she tries to get out.

At her age, this girl should be happier than she is, Harry thinks. "Sure you were," he tells her. "And why not? It's *bor*-ing, going somewhere with family, away from your friends. We all remember what it's like, we used to drag your daddy to the Jersey Shore, and then make him go up to the Poconos and have hayfever up in those Godawful dark pines. Torture! The things we do to each other in the name of fun! O.K. Here's my plan. Anybody want to hear my plan?"

The little girl nods. The others, even Roy who's been carefully shaping his Total mush into a kind of pyramid with the back of his spoon, watch him as if he is a conjurer. It's not so hard, to get back into the swing of family life. You just have to come out of yourself a little. It's like basketball was, those first two or three minutes, when amid the jamming and yelling and body heat and crowd noise you realized that you were going to have to *do it yourself*, nobody was going to do it for you. "Today I got to play golf," he begins.

"Great," Nelson says. "That's a big help. You're not going to make Judy caddy, if that's your plan. You'll bend her spine out of shape."

"Nellie, you're getting paranoid," Harry tells him. The boy's been trying ever since that business with Jill twenty years ago to protect women against his father. His son is the only person in the world who sees him as dangerous. Harry feels the day's first twinge in the chest, a little playful burning like a child flirting with a lit match. "That wasn't my plan, no, but why not sometime? She could carry my lightweight bag, I'd take out two of the woods and one of the wedges and she and I could walk a couple holes some late afternoon when the tee times are over. I could show her the swing. But in the foursome, actually, we ride carts. I'd rather we walked, for the exercise, but the other bozos insist. Actually, they're great guys, they all have grandchildren, they'd love Judy. She could ride in my place." He can picture it, her sitting there like a slim little princess, Bernie Drechsel with his cigar in his mouth at the wheel of the electric cart.

He is losing his conjurer's audience, thinking out loud this way. Roy drops his spoon and Pru squats down to pick it up, her shorty robe flaring out over one thigh. A lacy peep of jet-black bikini underpants. A slightly shiny vaccination oval high up. Nelson groans. "Out with it, Dad. I got to go to the *bath*room." He blows his nose on a paper towel. Why is his nose always running? Harry has read somewhere, maybe *People* on the death of Rock Hudson, that that's one of the first signs of AIDS.

Harry says, "No more circus museum. Actually, they've closed it. For renovations." He had noticed a story about it in the Sarasota paper a week or so ago, headlined *Circus Redux*. He hates that word, you see it everywhere, and he doesn't know how to pronounce it. Like arbitrageur and perestroika. "My plan was this. Today, I got to play golf but tonight there's Bingo in the dining hall and I thought the kids or at least Judy would enjoy that, and we could all use a real meal for a change. Tomorrow, we could either go to this Lionel Train and Seashell Museum that Joe Gold says is just terrific, or in the other direction, south, there's the Edison house. I've always been kind of curious about it but it may be a little advanced for the kids, I don't know. Maybe the invention of the telephone and the phonograph doesn't seem too exciting to kids raised on all this computerized crap they have now."

"Dad," Nelson says in his pained voice, sniffing, "it's not even that exciting to *me*. Isn't there someplace out on Route 41 where they could go play video games? Or miniature golf. Or the beach and swimming pool, Jesus. I thought we came down here to re*lax*, and you're making some kind of educational ordeal of it. Come *on*. Lay *off*."

Rabbit is hurt. "Lay off, I was just trying to create a little structure," he says.

Pru intervenes in his defense. "Nelson, the children can't spend all day in the pool, they'll get too much ultraviolet."

Janice says, "This hot weather is bound to turn cool this time of year. It's flukey."

"It's the greenhouse effect," Nelson says, turning to go to the bathroom, showing that disgusting rat's tail at the back of his head, the glint of earring. How queer *is* the kid? "The greedy consumer society has wrecked the ozone and we'll all be fried by the year 2000," Nelson says. "Look!" He points to the Fort Myers *News-Press* someone has laid on the kitchen table. The main headline is *1988: the dry look*, and a cartoon shows a crazed-looking yellow sun wringing out some clouds for a single drop of water. Janice must have brought the paper in from the corridor, though all she cares about is the *Lifestyles* section. Who's fucking who, who's divorcing who. Normally she stays in bed and lets her husband be the one to bring the paper in from the corridor. *Lifestyles* keeps.

Pru hands back Roy's spoon to him and takes away his dreadful little bowl of Total mush, congealed like dogfood left out overnight. "Want a 'nana?" she asks in a cooing coaxing sexy voice. "A nice 'nana if Mommy peeled and sliced it?"

Janice confesses, "Teresa, I'm not sure we have any bananas. In fact I know we don't. Harry hates fruit though he should eat it and I meant to do a big shopping yesterday for you and Nelson but the tennis game I was in went to the third set and then it was time to go to the airport." She brightens; her voice goes up in volume; she tries to become another conjurer. "That's what we can do this morning while Grandpa plays his golf! We can all go to Winn Dixie and do an e*nor*mous shopping!"

"Count me out," Nelson yells from the bathroom. "I'd like to borrow the car sometime, though."

What does he want a car for, the little big shot?

Judy's tears have dried and she has snuck into the living room, where the *Today* show is doing its last recap of the news and weather. Willard Scott, beamed in from Nome, Alaska, has Jane and Bryant in stitches.

Pru is looking into the cupboards and begging Roy, "How about some Sugar Pops, honey? Grandpa and Grandma have lots of Sugar Pops. And jars of dry-roasted peanuts and cashews. Harry, do you know that nuts are loaded with cholesterol?"

"Yeah, people keep telling me that. But then I read some article said the body needs cholesterol and the whole scare's been engineered by the chicken lobby." Janice, in a pink alligator shirt and a pair of magenta slacks like the women wear down here to go shopping in, has wedged herself in at the kitchen table with the *News-Press* and a sliced-open bagel and plastic container of cream cheese. In her Florida phase she has taken to bagels. Lox, too. She has pulled out the *Lifestyles* section of the newspaper and Harry, still able to read type in any direction from his days as a Linotyper, sees sideways the headline (they use a "down" style and lots of *USA Today*-style color graphics)

Manwatchers
name the men
with the most

and in caps at the top HUGE LOSS and 'WORKING' ON ANOTHER WEDDING. He cranks his head to look at the page the right way and sees that they mean *Working Girl* star Melanie Griffith and the survivors of the Armenian tragedy and their "unique type of grief." Funny how your wife reading the newspaper makes every item in it look fascinating, and then when you look yourself it all turns dull. The Braun Aromaster percolator, with a little sludgy coffee lukewarm in its glass half, sits at the end of the counter, past where Pru is still standing trying to find something Roy might eat. To let Harry ease his belly by, she goes up on her toes and with a little soft grunt under her breath presses her thighs tight against the counter edge. All this family closeness is almost like an African hut where everybody sleeps and screws in full view of everybody else. But, then, Harry asks himself, what has Western man done with all his precious privacy anyway? To judge from the history books, nothing much except invent the gun and psychoanalysis.

Down here it's necessary to keep bread and cookies in a drawer holding a big tin box to keep out ants, even up on the fourth floor. It's awkward to pull the drawer out and then lift the lid but he does, finding a couple of empty cookie bags, one for Double-Stuf Oreos and one for Fruit Newtons, which his grandchildren left with nothing but crumbs inside, and one and a half stale sugar doughnuts that even they disdained to consume. Rabbit takes them and his mug full of sludgy coffee and squeezes back past Pru, concentrating on the sensation in his groin as her shorty robe grazes it, and with a wicked impulse gives the kitchen table a nudge with the back of his thighs to get Janice's full cup of coffee rocking so it will slosh and spill. *"Harry,"* she says, quickly lifting the newspaper. "Shit."

The sound of the shower running leaks into the kitchen. "Why the hell's Nelson so jittery?" he asks the women aloud.

Pru, who must know the answer, doesn't give it, and Janice says, mopping with a Scott Towel Pru hands her, "He's under *stress*. It's a much more competitive car world than it was ten years ago and Nelson's doing it all himself, he doesn't have Charlie to hide behind like you did.''

"He could have kept Charlie on but he didn't want to, Charlie was willing to stay part-time,'' he says, but nobody answers him except Roy, who looks at him and says, "Grampa looks ridiculous.''

"Quite a vocabulary,'' Harry compliments Pru.

"He doesn't know what he's saying, he hears these expressions on television,'' she says, brushing back hair from her forehead with a touching two-handed gesture she has.

The theme of the kitchen decor is aqua, a creamy frigid color that looked a little subtler in the paint chart Janice and he consulted four years ago, when they had the place repainted. He wondered at the time how it would wear but Janice thought it would be lighthearted and slightly daring, like their buying a condominium at all. Even the refrigerator and the Formica countertops are aqua, and looking at it all, with the creatures and flowers of seashells Janice has loaded the open shelves toward the foyer with, makes him feel panicky, shortens his breath. Being underwater is one of his nightmares. A simple off-white like the Golds next door have would have been less oppressive. He takes his mug and the doughnut-and-a-half and the rest of the *News-Press* into the living room and settles on the sofa side of the round glass table, since Judy occupies the wicker armchair that faces the television set. The pictures on the front page are of Donald Trump (*Male call: the year's hottest*), the grimacing sun wringing the clouds (*Rainfall 33% off average; year is driest since 1927*), and Fort Myers' mayor Wilbur Smith, looking like a long-haired kid younger even than Nelson, quoted saying that football star Deion Sanders' recent arrest for assault and battery on a police officer could be partially blamed upon the unruly crowd that had gathered to watch the incident. There is a story about an annual government book-length report on automobiles and consumer complaints: in a gray box highlighting *The best by the book*, under all four categories, subcompacts, compacts, intermediate, and minivans, there isn't a Toyota listed. He feels a small pained slipping in his stomach.

"Harry, you *must* eat a solid breakfast,'' Janice calls, "if you're going to play golf right through lunch. Dr. Morris told you coffee on an empty stomach is about the worst thing you can do for hypertension.''

"If there's anything makes me hypertense,'' he calls back,

"it's women telling me all the time what to eat." As he bites into the stale doughnut the sugar patters down on the paper and dusts the crimson lapels of his seigneurial bathrobe.

Janice continues to Pru, "Have you been giving any thought to Nelson's diet? He doesn't look like he's eating anything."

"He never did eat much," Pru says. "He must be where Roy gets his pickiness from."

Judy has found among all the channels of network and cable an old Lassie movie; Harry moves to the end of the sofa to get an angle on it. The collie nudges awake the lost boy asleep in the haystack and leads him home, down a dirt road toward a purple Scottish sunset. The music swells like an ache in the throat; Harry smiles sheepishly at Judy through his tears. Her eyes, that did their crying earlier, are dry. Lassie is not part of her childhood past, lost forever.

He tells her when the frog leaves his throat, "I got to go play golf, Judy. Think you can manage here today with these rude folks?"

She studies him seriously, not quite sure of the joke. "I guess so."

"They're good people," he says, not sure this is true. "How would you like to go Sunfishing some time?"

"What's Sunfishing?"

"It's sailing in a little boat. We'd go off one of the hotel beaches in Deleon. They're supposed to be just for the guests but I know the guy who runs the concession. I play golf with his father."

Her eyes don't leave his face. "Have you ever done it, Grandpa? Sunfishing?"

"Sure. A coupla times." Once, actually; but it was a vivid lesson. With Cindy Murkett in her black bikini that showed the hairs in her crotch. Her breasts slipsloppy in their little black sling. The wind tugging, the water slapping, the sun wielding its silent white hammer on their skins, the two of them alone and nearly naked.

"Sounds neat," Judy ventures, adding, "I got a prize in my camp swimming class for staying underwater the longest." She returns her gaze to the television, rapidly flicking through the channels with the hand control—channel-surfing, kids call it.

Harry tries to imagine the world seen through her clear green eyes, every little thing vivid and sharp and new, packed full of itself like a satin valentine. His own vision feels fogged no matter which glasses he puts on, for reading or far vision. He wears the latter only for movies and night driving, and refuses to get bifocals; glasses worn for more than an hour at a time hurt his ears. And the lenses are always dusty and the things he looks at all seem tired; he's seen them too many times before. A kind of drought has settled over the world, a bleaching such as overtakes old color prints, even the ones kept in a drawer.

Except, strangely, the first fairway of a golf course before his first swing. This vista is ever fresh. There, on the tee's earth platform, standing in his large white spiked Footjoys and blue sweat socks, drawing the long tapered steel wand of the Lynx Predator driver from the bag, he feels tall again, tall the way he used to on a hardwood basketball floor when after those first minutes his growing momentum and lengthening bounds and leaps reduced the court to childlike dimensions, to the size of a tennis court and then a Ping-Pong table, his legs unthinkingly eating the distances up, back and forth, and the hoop with its dainty skirtlike net dipping down to be there on the layups. So, in golf, the distances, the hundreds of yards, dissolve to a few effortless swings if you find the inner magic, the key. Always, golf for him holds out the hope of perfection, of a perfect weightlessness and consummate ease, for now and again it does happen, happens in three dimensions, shot after shot. But then he gets human and tries to force it, to make it happen, to get ten extra yards, to steer it, and it goes away, grace you could call it, the feeling of collaboration, of being bigger than he really is. When you stand up on the first tee it is there, it comes back from wherever it lives during the rest of your life, endless possibility, the possibility of a flawless round, a round without a speck of dirt in it, without a missed two-footer or a flying right elbow, without a pushed wood or pulled iron; the first fairway is in front of you, palm trees on the left and water on the right, flat as a picture. All you have to do is take a simple pure swing and puncture the picture in the middle with a ball that shrinks in a second to the size of a needle-prick, a tiny tunnel into the absolute. That would be *it*.

But on his practice swing his chest gives a twang of pain and this makes him think for some reason of Nelson. The kid jangles in his mind. As he stands up to the ball he feels crowded but is impatient and hits it outside in, trying too hard with his right hand. The ball starts out promisingly but leaks more and more to the right and disappears not far enough from the edge of the long scummy pond of water.

" 'Fraid that's alligator territory,'' Bernie says sadly. Bernie is his partner for the round.

"Mulligan?" Harry asks.

There is a pause. Ed Silberstein asks Joe Gold, "What do you think?"

Joe tells Harry, "I didn't notice that *we* took any mulligans."

Harry says, "You cripples don't hit it far enough to get into trouble. We always give mulligans on the first drive. That's been our tradition."

Ed says, "Angstrom, how're you ever going to live up to your potential if we keep babying you with mulligans?"

Joe says, "How much potential you think a guy with a gut like that still has? I think his potential has all gone to his colon."

While they are thus ribbing him Rabbit takes another ball from his pocket and tees it up and, with a stiff half-swing, sends it safely but ingloriously down the left side of the fairway. Perhaps not quite safely: it seems to hit a hard spot and keeps bouncing toward a palm tree. "Sorry, Bernie," he says. "I'll loosen up."

"Am I worried?" Bernie asks, putting his foot to the electric-cart pedal a split-second before Harry has settled into the seat beside him. "With your brawn and my brains, we'll cream these oafs."

Bernie Drechsel, Ed Silberstein, and Joe Gold are all older than Harry, and shorter, and usually make him feel good about himself. With them, he is a big Swede, they call him Angstrom, a comical pet gentile, a big pale uncircumcised hunk of the American dream. He in turn treasures their perspective; it seems more manly than his, sadder and wiser and less shaky. Their long history has put all that suffering in its pocket and strides on. Harry asks Bernie, as the cart rolls over the tamped and glistening grass toward their balls, "Whaddeya think about all this fuss about this Deion Sanders? In the paper this morning he even has the mayor of Fort Myers making excuses for him."

Bernie shifts the cigar in his mouth an inch and says, "It's cruel, you know, to take these black kids out of nowhere and give 'em all this publicity and turn them into millionaires. No wonder they go crazy."

"The paper says the crowd kept the cops from giving him room. He had flipped out at some salesclerk who said he had stolen a pair of earrings. He even took a pop at her."

"I don't know about Sanders," Bernie says, "but a lot of it's drugs. Cocaine. The stuff is everywhere."

"You wonder what people see in it," Rabbit says.

"What they see in it," Bernie says, stopping the cart and

resting his cigar on the edge of the plastic ledge for holding drinks or beer cans, "is instant happiness." He squares up to his second shot with that awful stance of his, his feet too close together, his bald head dipping down in a reverse weight-shift, and punches the ball with a four-iron: all arms and wrists. It stays straight, though, and winds up within an easy chip in front of the elevated green. "There are two routes to happiness," he continues, back at the wheel of the cart. "Work for it, day after day, like you and I did, or take a chemical shortcut. With the world the way it is, these kids take the shortcut. The long way looks too long."

"Yeah, well, it *is* long. And then when you've gone the distance, where's the happiness?"

"Behind you," the other man admits.

"What interests me about Sanders and kids like that," Rabbit says, as Bernie speeds along down the sun-baked fairway, dodging fallen brown fronds and coconuts, "is I had a little taste of it once. Athletics. Everybody cheering, loving you. Wanting a piece."

"Sure you did. It sticks out all over. Just the way you waggle the club. 'Fraid you made the palm tree, though. You're stymied, my friend." Bernie stops the cart, a little close to the ball for Harry's comfort.

"I think I can hook it around."

"Don't try it. Chip it out. You know what Tommy Armour says: take your stroke in a situation like this, and go for the green on the next one. Don't attempt a miracle."

"Well, you're already up there for a sure bogey. Let me try to bend it on." The palm tree is one of those whose trunk looks like a giant braid. It breathes on him, with its faint rustle, its dim smell like that of a friendly attic full of dried-out old school papers and love letters. There's a lot of death in Florida, if you look. The palms grow by the lower branches dying and dropping off. The hot sun hurries the life cycles along. Harry takes his stance with his hip almost touching the jagged rough trunk, hoods the five-iron, and imagines the curving arc of the miracle shot and Bernie's glad cry of congratulation.

But in fact the closeness of the tree and maybe of Bernie in the cart inhibits his swing and he pulls the ball with the hooded club, so it hits the top of the next palm along the fairway and drops straight down into the short rough. The rough, though, in Florida isn't like the rough up north; it's just spongy pale grass a half-inch longer than fairway. They tailor these courses for the elderly and lame. They baby you down here.

Bernie sighs. "Stubborn," he says as Harry gets back in. "You guys think the world will melt if you whistle." Harry knows that "guys" is polite for "goys." The thought that he might be wrong, that obstacles won't melt if he whistles, renews that dull internal ache of doom he felt in the airport. As he stands up to his third shot, an eight-iron he estimates, Bernie's disapproval weighs on his arms and causes him to hit a bit fat, enough to take the click out of the ball and leave it ten yards short.

"Sorry, Bernie. Chip up close and get your par." But Bernie fluffs the chip—all wrists again, and too quick—and they both get sixes, losing the hole to Ed Silberstein's routine bogey. Ed is a wiry retired accountant from Toledo, with dark upright hair and a slender thrusting jaw that makes him look as if he's about to smile all the time; he never seems to get the ball more than ten feet off the ground, but he keeps it moving toward the hole.

"You guys looked like Dukakis on that one," he crows. "Blowing it."

"Don't knock the Duke," Joe says. "He gave us honest government for a change. The Boston pols can't forgive him for it." Joe Gold owns a couple of liquor stores in some city in Massachusetts called Framingham. He is stocky and sandy and wears glasses so thick they make his eyes look like they're trying to escape from two little fishbowls, jumping from side to side. He and his wife, Beu, Beu for Beulah, are very quiet condo neighbors next door; you wonder what they do all the time in there, that never makes any noise.

Ed says, "He wimped out when it counted. He should have stood up and said, 'Sure, I'm a liberal, and damn proud of it.' "

"Yeah, how would that have played in the South and the Midwest?" Joe asks. "In California and Florida for that matter with all these old farts who all they want to hear is 'No more taxes'?"

"Lousy," Ed admits. "But he wasn't going to get their votes anyway. His only hope was to get the poor excited. Knock away that three-footer, Angstrom. I've already written down your six."

"I need the practice," Harry says, and strokes it, and watches it rim out on the left edge. Not his day. Will he ever have a day again? Fifty-five and fading. His own son can't stand to be in the same room with him. Ruth once called him Mr. Death.

"He was going for those Reagan Democrats," Joe continues explaining. "Except there aren't any Reagan Democrats, there're just cut-and-dried rednecks. Now that I'm down south here, I understand better what it's all about. It's all about blacks. One hundred thirty years after Abe Lincoln, the Republicans have got the anti-black vote and it's bigger than any Democratic Presidential candidate can cope with, barring a massive depression or a boo-boo the size of Watergate. Ollie North doesn't do it. Reagan being an airhead didn't do it. Face it: the bulk of this country is scared to death of the blacks. That's the one gut issue we've got."

After that episode with Skeeter twenty years ago Rabbit has had mixed feelings about blacks and whenever the subject comes up he tends to hold his tongue lest he betray himself one way or another. "Bernie, what do you think?" Harry asks while they're watching the two others hit from the second tee, a 136-yard par-three over that same scummy pond. He finds Bernie the wisest of the three, the most phlegmatic and slowest to speak. He never came back totally from some open-heart surgery he had a few years ago. He moves cumbersomely, has emphysema and a bit of a hump back and the slack look of a plump man who lost weight because his doctor told him to. His color isn't good, his lower lip in profile looks loose.

"I think," he says, "Dukakis tried to talk intelligently to the American people and we aren't ready for it. Bush talked to us like we were a bunch of morons and we ate it up. Can you imagine, the Pledge of Allegiance, read my lips—can you imagine such crap in this day and age? Ailes and those others, they made him into a beer commercial—head for the mountains." Bernie sang this last phrase, his voice quavery but touchingly true. Rabbit is impressed by this ability Jews seem to have, to sing and to dance, to give themselves to the moment. They sing at seder, he knows, because Bernie and Fern had them to a seder one April just before heading north. Passover. The angel of death passed over. Harry had never understood the word before. Let this cup pass from me. Bernie concludes, "To my mind there are two possibilities about Bush—he believed what he was saying, or he didn't. I don't know which is more terrifying. He's what we call a *pisher*."

"Dukakis always looked like he was a sore about something," Rabbit offers. This is as close as he can bring himself to admit that, alone in this foursome, he voted for Bush.

Bernie maybe guesses it. He says, "After eight years of Reagan I would have thought more people would have been sore than were. If you could ever get the poor to vote in this country, you'd have Socialism. But people want to think rich. That's the genius of the capitalist system: either you're rich, or you want to be, or you think you ought to be.''

Rabbit liked Reagan. He liked the foggy voice, the smile, the big shoulders, the way his head kept wagging during the long pauses, the way he floated above the facts, knowing there was more to government than facts, and the way he could change direction while saying he was going straight ahead, pulling out of Beirut, getting cozy with Gorby, running up the national debt. The strange thing was, except for the hopeless down-and-outers, the world became a better place under him. The Communists fell apart, except for in Nicaragua, and even there he put them on the defensive. The guy had a magic touch. He was a dream man. Harry dares say, ''Under Reagan, you know, it was like anesthesia.''

''Ever had an operation? A real operation.''

''Not really. Tonsils when I was a kid. Appendix when I was in the Army. They took it out in case I was sent to Korea. Then I was never sent.''

''I had a quadruple bypass three years ago.''

''I know, Bern. I remember your telling me. But you look great now.''

''When you come out of anesthesia, it hurts like hell. You can't believe you can live with such pain. To get at your heart, they split your whole rib cage open. They crack you open like a coconut. And they pull the best veins they can find out of your upper leg. So when you come out of it your groin's killing you as well as your chest.''

''Wow.'' Harry inappropriately laughs, since while Bernie is talking to him on the cart, Ed, with that pompous fussy setup he has, laying his hands on the club finger by finger like he's doing flower arrangement, and then peeking toward the hole five or six times before swinging, as if he's trying to shake loose cobwebs or a tick in his collar, looked up during the swing so the topped ball scuttered into the water, skipping three times before sinking, leaving three expanding, interlocking sets of rings on the water. Alligator food.

''Six hours I was on the table,'' Bernie is urging into his ear. ''I woke up and I couldn't move. I couldn't even open my eyelids. They *freeze* you, so your blood flow is down to almost nothing. I was like locked into a black coffin. No. It's like I *was* the coffin. And then out of this blackness I hear this weird voice, with a thick Indian accent, the Pakistani anesthetist.''

Joe Gold, with his partner's ball in the water, tries to hit it too quick, to get a ball in play, jerking the club back in two stages like he does and then roundhousing with that flat swing stocky guys tend to have. He pushes the shot off so he catches the pot bunker on the right.

Bernie is doing a high, spacy, Pakistani voice. " 'Ber-nie, Ber-nie,' this voice says, so honest to God I think maybe it's the voice of God, 'oper-ation a suc-cess!' "

Harry has heard the story before but laughs anyway. It's a good, scary story about the edge of death.

" 'Ber-nie, Ber-nie,' " Bernie repeats, "like it came out of the clouds to Abraham, to go cut Isaac's throat."

Harry asks, "Shall we keep the same order?" He feels he disgraced himself on the previous hole.

"You go first, Angstrom. I think it shakes you up too much to hit last. Go for it. Show these nudniks how it's done."

This is what Rabbit hoped to hear. He takes a seven-iron and tries to think of five things: keeping his head down, keeping his backswing from being too long, moving his hip while the club is still at the top, keeping his downswing smooth, and keeping the clubface square on the ball, at that point on the sphere where a clockface says 3:15. From the whistly instant way the ball vanishes from the center of his held-down vision he knows the hit is sweet; they all together watch the dark dot rise, hover that little ghostly extra bit that gives the distance, and then drop straight down on the green, a hair to the left but what looks pin high, the ball bouncing right with the slant of the bowl-shaped green. The world is beginning to melt.

"Beauty," Ed has to admit.

"How about a mulligan?" Joe asks. "We'll give you one this time."

Bernie asks, pushing himself out of the cart, "What iron was that?"

"Seven."

"Gonna hit 'em like that, my friend, you should use an eight."

"Think I'm past the hole?"

"Way past. You're on the back edge."

Some partner. There's no satisfying him. Like Marty Tothero nearly forty years ago. Get twenty-five points a game, Marty wanted thirty-five and would talk about a missed layup. The soldier in Harry, the masochistic Christian, respects men like this. It's total uncritical love, such as women provide, that makes you soft and does you in.

"For me, I think a choked-up six," Bernie says.

But in trying to take something off the shot he takes off too much and leaves it short, over the water but on the bank where it's hard to take a stance. "Tough chip from there," Harry says, unable to resist a gentle needle. He still blames Bernie for parking the cart so close on that attempted deliberate hook.

Bernie accepts the needle. "Especially after that last shitty chip of mine, huh?" he says, pushing his cut-up, deflated, humpbacked old body into the cart, Harry having slid over into the driver's seat. The guy who's on the green has earned the right to drive. Harry feels momentum building, they're going to cream these oafs. He glides over the water on an arched wooden bridge with red rubber treads laid over the planks. "From where you are," Bernie tells him as they get out, "the green slopes down. Hit your putt too hard, you'll slide miles beyond."

Ed with a ball in the water is out of it. Bernie's stance on the steep bank is so awkward he whiffs the ball once, shanks it sideways on his next swing, and picks up. But sandy Joe Gold, in his element, waggles his feet to plant himself and manages a good blast shot out of the pot bunker. With Bernie's advice preying on his mind, interfering with his own instincts, Harry strokes his long approach putt tentatively and leaves it four feet short. He marks it with a Valhalla Village marker while Joe two-putts for his bogey. Joe takes his time and gives Harry too long to study his four-footer. He sees a break, then doesn't see it. In trying to avoid lipping out on the left like he did on the last hole, he loses his par putt, very makable, an inch to the right. "Son of a son of a *bitch*," he says, frustration pressing from behind his eyes so hard he thinks he might burst into tears. "On in one, and a fucking three-putt."

"It happens," Ed says, writing down the 4 with his trained accountant's primness. "Tie hole."

"Sorry, Bern," Harry says, climbing back into the cart, on the passenger side.

"I screwed you up," his partner says. "Should have kept my yap shut about the green being downhill." He unwraps another cigar and, pushing the pedal, leans back into a long day.

Not Harry's day. The Florida sun seems not so much a single thing overhead but a set of klieg lights that pursue you everywhere with an even white illumination. Even directly under palm trees and right up against the twelve-foot pine fences that separate the Village from the rest of the world, the sun finds you, reddening the tip of Rabbit's nose and baking his forearms and the back of his non-gloved hand, which is already dotted with little white bumps of keratosis. He carries a tube of number-15 sunscreen in his golf bag and is always dabbing it on but the ultraviolet gets through anyway, cooking his squamous cells into skin cancer. The three men he plays with never use anything and just get a comfortable tan, even the bald top of Bernie's head, as smooth as an ostrich egg with only a few small specks on it as he bends over his shots with that awful reverse-shift, squeezed-feet stance of his. Harry feels Bernie's steady, mechanically repeating ineptitude—short shots, chunked chips—a burden today, since he can't quite carry him, and wonders why somebody who exudes suffering wisdom the way Bernie does never learns a thing about golf or even seems to try. To him, Harry supposes, it's just a game, a way of killing time in the sun at this stage of his life. Bernie was a boy once and then a man making money and children (a carpet business in Queens; two daughters who married nice solid guys and a son who went to Princeton and the Wharton School in Philadelphia and became a hostile-takeover specialist on Wall Street) and now he's at the other end of life's rainbow, and this is what you do: Bernie endures retirement fun in Florida the way he's endured his entire life, sucking that same acrid wet-cigar taste out of it. He doesn't see what Harry sees in the game—infinity, an opportunity for infinite improvement. Rabbit doesn't see it himself today. Around the eleventh hole—a dogleg par-five that he butchers, slicing his second shot, a four-wood, so wildly it winds up in a condo's side yard, between some plastic trash cans and a concrete slab with some rusting steel clothesline poles sunk in it (a German shepherd chained to the clothesline barks at him, lunging toward him so the taut wire sings, and Gold and Silberstein loafing in their cart cackle, and Bernie chomps deeper and looks morose), taking the out-of-bounds drop for a four while the dog keeps barking and barking, trying to hit a three-iron so hard he digs six inches behind and sprays sand all over his shoes and into the tops of his socks, pulling the next iron to the left into a bed of parched and shedding azaleas beside the twelfth tee, taking a drop for another stroke, skulling the chip clear across over the green (all three playing partners keeping a ghastly silence now, shocked, mourning for him, or is it holding in their glee?), plunking the next sand shot against the trap lip so it dribbles back, and picking up in disgust, and even hitting himself on the knee when after raking he flips the sand rake to one side—after this hole, the game and day begin to eat him into a state of depression. The grass looks greasy and unreal, every other palm tree is dying from the drought and dropping stiff brown fronds, the condos line every fairway like tall stucco outhouses, and even the sky, where your eyes can usually find relief, is dirtied by jet trails that spread and wander until they are indistinguishable from God's pure clouds.

The hours pile on, noon comes and goes, the klieg lights begin to dim but the heat is turned up higher. They finish at quarter to three, Harry and Bernie twenty dollars down—both sides of a five-dollar nassau plus the eighteen and a press on the second nine that they lost. "We'll get 'em next time," Harry promises his partner, not really believing it.

"You weren't quite yourself today, my friend," Bernie admits. "You got girlfriend trouble or something?"

Horny, Jews are: he once read a history of Hollywood about their womanizing. Harry Cohn, Groucho Marx, the Warner Brothers, they went crazy out there with the sunshine and swimming pools and all the Midwestern shiksas who'd do anything to be movie stars—participate in orgies, blow a mogul while he was talking on the telephone—yet his golf partners are all married to the same women, forty, fifty years, women with big dyed hair and thick bangles and fat brown upper arms who can't stop talking when you see them all dolled up at dinner, Bernie and Ed and Joe sitting smilingly silent beside them as if all this talking their women do is sex, which it must be—pep, life. How do they do it? Wear life like a suit made to fit exactly. "I guess I told you," Harry tells Bernie, "my son and his family are visiting."

"There's your problem, Angstrom: you felt guilty horsing around with us. You should have been entertaining your loved ones."

"Yeah, entertain 'em. They just got here yesterday and are acting bored already. They want us to live next door to Disney World."

"Take them to Jungle Gardens. Up in Sarasota, down 41 from the Ringling Museum. Fern and I go there two, three times a winter and never get bored. I could watch those flamingos sleep for hours—how do they do it? Balanced on one leg two feet long and thinner than my finger." He holds up a finger and it seems thick. "Thinner than that," he swears.

"I don't know, Bernie. When I'm around, my kid acts like he doesn't want my own grandchildren to have anything much to do with me. The little boy, he's four, is pretty much a stranger, but the girl and I could get along. She's almost nine. I was even thinking I should bring her out in a cart sometime and let her try to hit the ball. Or maybe rent a Sunfish, Ed, if your son over at the Bayview could write me up as a guest.''

The foursome is having beers and free munchies in Club Nineteen, next to the pro shop, on the bottom floor of Building A of Valhalla Village. The darkness inside—the dark panels and beams in the style of an English pub—is intensified by the subtropical brightness outside, at the round white tables under umbrellas saying *Coors*. You can hear the splashing from the pool, between Buildings A and B, and the throbbing of a generator housed on the other side of the wall, beyond the rest rooms and dart boards and video games. At night sometimes Harry imagines he can hear the generator throbbing through all the intervening apartments, carpets, air-conditioners, conversations, mattresses, and peach-colored hall wallpaper. Somehow the noise curves around and clings to the walls and comes in his big sliding window, the crack that's left open to the Gulf air.

"No problem," Ed says, as he totals their scores. "Just show up at the front desk and ask for Gregg Silvers. That's what he calls himself, don't ask me why. They'll let you walk through the lobby and downstairs to the changing rooms. I don't advise wearing bathing suits into the lobby; they try to discourage that. Do you have a day I can tell him to expect you?''

Harry gets the impression this may be a realer favor than he thought, a bigger deal than it's worth. "Friday, if ever," he says. "Does Gregg have to know for sure? Tomorrow I thought we'd head up Sarasota way.''

"Jungle Gardens," Bernie insists.

"Lionel Train Museum," Joe Gold contributes. "And right across from the Ringling Museum there's Bellm's Cars and Music of Yesterday, is I think what they call it. Over a thousand music machines, can you imagine? Antique cars from 1897, I never knew there were cars then. You're in the car business, aren't you, Angstrom? You and your boy. You'll both go ape in there.''

"I don't know," Harry begins, groping to express the curious cloud that Nelson carries with him, that dampens any outing.

"Harry, this is interesting," Ed says. "Giving you a seven, two over par for handicap purposes, on the eleventh where you picked up, and a courtesy six on the sixteenth where you put two balls in the water, you scored an even ninety even so. You weren't playing as bad as it looked. Waste a few less drives and long irons, and you'll be in the eighties every time.''

"I couldn't get my ass into it, I couldn't re*lease*,'' Harry says. "I couldn't let go.'' He has an unaskable question for these wise Jewish men: how about death? He asks them, "Hey, how about that Pan Am jet?''

There is a pause. "It has to be a bomb,'' Ed says. "When you've got splinters of steel driven right through leather luggage and wreckage strewn across fifty miles of Scotland, it has to be a bomb.''

Bernie sighs, "It's them again. The Shiiteheads.''

"Arabs,'' Joe Gold says. A patriotic glee lights his wobbling eyes. "Once we got proof, the F-111s'll be flying into Libya again. What we ought to do is keep going right into Eye-ran and stick it to the old Ayatollah.''

But their tongues are less quick than usual; Harry has made them uneasy, with what he hadn't meant to be so much a political question. With Jews, everything in the papers comes back to Israel.

"I mean,'' he says, "how the hell do you think it feels? Sitting there and having the plane explode?''

"Well, I bet it wakes you up,'' Ed says.

"They didn't feel a thing,'' Bernie says, considerately, sensing Harry's personal worry. "Zero. It was over that quick.''

Joe says to Harry, "You know what the Israelis say, don't you, Angstrom? 'If we got to have enemies, thank God they're Arabs.' ''

Harry has heard this before but tries to laugh. Bernie says, "I think Angstrom could use a new partner. I depress him.''

"It wasn't you, Bernie. I came depressed.''

Club Nineteen puts out a wonderful array of nibbles, in little china bowls monogrammed with Vahalla Village's logo, two sea-blue intertwined V's. Not just dry-roasted peanuts and almonds and hazelnuts but tiny pretzel sticks and salted pumpkin seeds and tight curls resembling Corn Chips, only finer and sharper in the mouth in that blissful instant while the tongue works one around to be crunched between the molars. The other men take only a pinch of this starchy salty salad now and then but soon the bowl is empty, Rabbit doing eighty per cent of the eating.

"That crap's loaded with sodium,'' Bernie warns him.

"Yeah, but it's good for the soul,'' Harry says, about as religious a remark as he dares put forth. "Who else is ready for another beer?" he asks. "Losers buy this round."

He is beginning to feel expansive: his dark mood is thinning like a squirt of ink in alcohol's gentle solvent. He waves for the waiter and asks him to bring along with four more beers another bowl of munchies. The waiter, a faunlike young Hispanic with an earring bigger than Nelson's and gold chains on both wrists, nods in a timid way; Harry must seem enormous to him, menacingly white and pink and sodden with sodium-retained water. The whole quartet must seem loud and potentially unruly: ugly old gringos. Another squirt of ink. Harry feels heavy again. Good times in Florida are never as good as those boozy late afternoons at his old club back in Diamond County, the Flying Eagle, before Buddy Inglefinger married that lanky crazy hippie Valerie and moved to Royersford and Thelma Harrison got too sick with lupus ever to show up and Cindy Murkett got fat and Webb divorced her so you never saw anybody any more. In Florida the people are so cautious, as if on two beers they might fall down and break a hip. The whole state is brittle.

"Your boy play golf?" Joe is asking him.

"Not really. He's never had the temperament. Or the time, he says." And, Rabbit might have added, he never really invited him.

"What does he do, for fun?" Ed asks. These men, it dawns on Harry, are being polite. By ordering another round of beers he has stretched the nineteenth-hole camaraderie beyond where it's effortless. These guys' sexy elderly wives are waiting. Gossip to catch up on. Letters from dutiful, prospering children to read. Interest to add up. Torah to study.

"Beats me," Harry says. "Hangs around with a bunch of Brewer creeps, swinging singles sort of. I never see him having much fun. He never went in for sports."

"The way you talk about him," Bernie said, "he could be the father and you the son."

Rabbit agrees enthusiastically; with a boost from the second beer he almost has a vision. "Yeah, and a delinquent son at that. That's how he sees me, an old juvenile delinquent. His wife looks miserable." Where did that come from? Was it true? *Help me, guys. Tell me how you've got on top of sex and death so they don't bother you.* He goes on, "The whole family, the two kids too, seem on edge. I don't know what's up."

"Your wife, does she know what's up?"

That mutt. Harry ignores the question. "Just last night I tried to talk to the kid in a friendly fashion and all he did was bitch about Toyotas. The company that feeds us, that saved him and his old man and his shady little crook of a grandfather from being bums, and all he does is complain about how Toyotas aren't Lamborghinis! Jesus, that beer went down fast. It felt like the Gobi Desert out there.''

"Harry, you don't want another beer.''

"You want to get home and tell your family about Bellm's. B-E-L-L-M's. I know it sounds like I can't spell. Every old car you could imagine. From before steering wheels. Before gears, even.''

"To be honest, guys, I've never been that much into cars. I drive 'em, I sell 'em, but I've never really understood the damn things. To me they're all alike. Great if they go, lousy if they don't.'' The other men are standing up.

"I want to see you out here tomorrow afternoon with your little granddaughter. Teach her the basics. Head down, slow takeaway.''

That was Bernie talking; Ed Silberstein tells him:

"Work on shortening that backswing, Harry. You don't need all that above the shoulders. The hit is right in here, right by your pecker. Best advice I ever had from a golf pro was, Imagine you're hitting it with your pecker.''

They have sensed his silent cry for help, for consolation, and are becoming more Jewish on Harry's behalf, it seems to him as he sits there.

Bernie has pushed up from the table and towers over Harry with his gray skin, his loose dewlaps full of shadows. "We have an expression,'' he says downward. "*Tsuris*. Sounds to me, my friend, like you got some *tsuris*. Not full-grown yet, not *gehoketh tsuris*, but *tsuris*.''

Pleasantly dazed with alcohol, his chest distantly stinging, the tip of his nose beginning to feel sunburn, Harry has no inclination to move, though the world around him is in motion. Two young college-kid hotshots who were pressing them from behind all afternoon have finished and are making the video games over by the rest rooms warble, zing, whistle, and bleat. Animated automatons in many colors appear and disappear on the screen. He sees his white fingers, with the big moons on their fingernails, absent-mindedly dabble at the bottom of the bowl of munchies, as if he is trying to pick up the intertwined V's. The junk food has been consumed. He cannot be absolutely sure, in memory, if the waiter ever brought a new bowl.

Joe Gold, his hair a sandy mane, his magnified eyes surging back and forth within his squarish spectacles, bends down a bit, as if rooting his feet again in a trap, and says, "Here's a Jewish joke for you. Abe meets Izzy after a long time no see. He asks, 'How many children do you have?' Izzy says, 'None.' Abe says, 'None! So what do you do for aggravation?' "

Their laughter seems speeded-up, like the action in a beer commercial; their mockery in its unnatural unison holds a premonition for Harry, that he has wasted the day, that now he must hurry, hurry to catch up, like when he used to run late to school with a watery flutter in his stomach. The three other men, returning to their solid domestic arrangements, in farewell cuff at him, even pinch the nape of his neck, as if to rouse him from a spiritual torpor. In Florida, he thinks, even friendship has a thin, provisional quality, since people might at any minute buy another condominium and move to it, or else up and die.

You leave the clubs with the pro shop, and the shoes. Rabbit walks in his moccasins, worn so loose his feet move in them without seeming to rub leather, across the parking lot and a striped piece of driveway and one of the complex's little traffic islands covered in green outdoor carpeting to the entryway of Building B. He uses his key and punches in the code on the panel in the narrow space where two closed-circuit television cameras are watching him, pulls the door—it doesn't buzz, it goes *ding ding ding* like a fire truck backing up—and takes the elevator to the fourth floor. In 413, his home away from home, Janice and Pru and the kids are playing Hearts, that is three of them are and Roy is holding a fistful of cards while his mother tells him what to do and which to discard. His face has a puffy look as though it's been an afternoon of frustrations and disappointments. They all greet Harry as if he's going to rescue them from boredom, but he feels so beat all he wants to do is lie down and let his body soak in nothingness. He asks, "Where's Nelson?"

It's not the right question, at least in front of the kids. Janice and Pru glance toward one another and then Pru volunteers, "He's out doing a few errands in the car." Down here they only have one car, the Camry, leaving Harry's Celica back in Penn Park. It works out, since most everything they need—drugs, magazines, haircuts, bathing suits, tennis balls—they can find within the Valhalla complex. The little food commissary in Building C charges airport prices, so Janice usually does a big

shopping once a week, at the Winn Dixie a half-mile down
Pindo Palm Boulevard. About once a week they visit their bank
in downtown Deleon, on a plaza two blocks back from the
beachfront where elevator music is always playing, both inside
the bank and outside; they must have speakers hidden in the
trees. Maybe twice a month they go to a movie at a cineplex in
a giant mall over on Palmetto Palm Boulevard two miles away.
But days at a stretch go by when the car just sits there in its
parking slot, attracting rust and white splotches of birdshit.

"What kind of errands does he have to do?"

"Oh Harry," Janice says. "People need things. He doesn't
like the kind of beer you buy. He likes a special kind of dental
floss, tape instead of thread. And he likes to drive around; he
gets claustrophobic."

"We all get claustrophobic," he tells her. "Most of us don't
go stealing cars about it."

"You look exhausted. Did you lose?"

"How'd you guess?"

"You always lose. He plays with these three Jewish men,"
she explains to her daughter-in-law, "and they always take twenty
dollars off of him."

"Don't be so prejudiced, you sound like your mother. And
for your information I win as often as not."

"I never hear about it when you do. They keep telling you
how good you are, and then take your money."

"You dope, one of them lost twenty dollars *with* me, he was
my partner!"

Serenely she says, just like her mother, addressing nobody in
particular, "They probably give it back to him; they're all in
cahoots."

It occurs to him that she is saying these disagreeable and
absurd things as a distraction from Nelson's rude and mysterious
absence.

Judy says, "Grandpa, come take Roy's hand and play. He
doesn't know how to even hold the cards and he's being fussy."

Roy obligingly proves her point by throwing the cards down
on the round glass table, much as this morning he threw the
spoon. "I hate games," he says, with a curious precision, like
one of those old-fashioned dolls that would say a little speech
when you pulled a string that came out of their backs.

Judy swiftly whomps him, with the hand not holding her cards.
She chops with her fist at his shoulders and neck, and when he
squalls in self-defense explains to him, "You messed up the trick

so now nobody can play. And I was going to shoot the moon!''
Pru neatly fans her hand face down on the table and with the
other arm, a downy arm of long loving bones, pulls the wailing
little boy against her chest; seeing this, Judy flares into jealousy,
goes pink-eyed the way women do before they decide to cry,
and races off toward Harry and Janice's bedroom.

Pru smiles wanly, looking exhausted herself. ''Everybody's
tired and cranky,'' she sort of sings, over the top of Roy's head
so Judy can hear it too.

Janice stands, a bit wobbly for a second. She knocks the glass
table with her shin, and next to her abandoned hand of Hearts
an orange-juice glass half full of Campari shivers, the scarlet
circlet of it, making him think of the pond when Ed's ball skipped
in. She is back into her tennis dress. Dried sweat-stains on its
side and beneath the arms are outlined like continents on a very
faint map. ''Maybe we made them do too much,'' she explains
to Harry. ''We did this enormous shopping, went to lunch at
Burger King, came back here, Pru took them for swimming and
shuffleboard for two hours, and then Judy and I went over to the
tennis courts and knocked the ball around.''

''How'd she do?'' he asks.

Janice laughs as if surprised. ''Terrific, actually. She's going
to be a jock, just like you.''

Rabbit goes into his bedroom. If nobody but Janice were here,
he would lie on this bed, push his eyes through a few pages of
the history book she gave him for Christmas, close his eyes on
the sound of the bird dryly chirping in the Norfolk pine, and
succumb to the great heaviness of being. But Judy has beat him
to his own king-size bed with its jade-green fitted coverlet. She
is curled up and hiding her face. He lies down close to the edge
and lets her press her knees against his presence. He admires
her hair, the amazing protein perfection of it, the long pale
strands that in sun deepen to a shiny orange. ''Better rest up for
Bingo tonight,'' he says.

''If Roy goes I'm not going,'' she says.

''Don't be down on Roy,'' he tells her. ''He's a good scout.''

''He's *not*. I was going to shoot the moon. I'd already took
the Queen of Spades, and I had the Ace of Hearts and the Jack
and some others and then he ruins it all and Mommy thinks
that's so cute. He gets all the attention and everything ever since
he was born, just because he's a boy!''

He admits, ''It's tough. I was in your shoes, except it was
reversed. I had a sister instead of a brother.''

"Didn't you hate her?" She removes her face from her folded arms and stares up at him with rubbed-looking green eyes.

He answers, "No. I guess, to be honest, I loved her. I loved Mim." The truth of this shocks him: he realizes how few others in his life he has loved so bluntly, without something of scorn, as his little wiry Mim. Her face seemed a narrower, harder version of his, with the same straight small nose and short upper lip, only a brunette, and a girl. Himself transposed into quite another key, and yet the melody recognizable. He remembers the sticky grip of her fingers in his when Mom and Pop would lead them on their Sunday walk, up the mountain to the Pinnacle Hotel and then back along the edge of the quarry; Mim hung on and roused protectiveness in him and perhaps used it up for everybody else, for every other female. Mim as his own blood sister had a certain unforced claim over him no woman since has been able to establish.

"Was she younger than you or older?"

"Younger. Younger even than me than Roy is than you. But she was a girl and girls are less ornery than boys. Though I guess Mim was ornery in her way. Once she got to be sixteen, she put my parents through hell."

"Grandpa, what's 'ornery'?"

"Oh, you know. Mean. Contrary. Rebellious."

"Like Daddy?"

"I don't think of your daddy as ornery, just, what's the word?—very uptight about things. People get to him more than they do to most people." Formulating even this much thickens his tongue and blurs his mind. "Judy, let's have a contest. You lie over there and I'll lie here and we'll see who can fall asleep soonest."

"Who'll be the judge?"

"Your mother," he says, letting his moccasins fall from his feet onto the floor over the edge of the bed. He closes his eyes on the posterlike Florida sunshine and in the intimate red of his brain envisions swooping on a bicycle down Jackson Road and then Potter Avenue with Mim on the handlebars of his rattly old blue Elgin, she maybe six and he twelve, if they hit a rock or pothole she'll go flying with him and the bike on top of her grinding her into the asphalt and ruining her pretty face forever, a woman's face is her fortune, but in her faith in him she sings, he can't remember the song, just the sensation of snatches of words flicked back into his ears as her long black hair whips against his eyes and mouth, making the bicycle ride more dangerous still. He led Mim into danger but always led her out. Shoo-fly pie. That was one of the songs she used to sing around the house, day after day until it drove them all crazy. *Shoo-fly pie and apple pan dowdy, makes your eyes light up, your tummy say "howdy!"* And then she would do a thing with her eyes that would make the whole rest of the family laugh.

He feels Judy ease her weight from his side and with that exaggerated, creaking stealth of small children move around the foot of the bed and out of the room. The door clicks, female voices whisper. Their whispers merge with a dream, involving an enormous scoop-shaped space, an amphitheatre, an audience somehow for whom he is performing, though there is no other person in the dream, just this sense of presence, of echoing august dreadfully serious presence. He wakes frightened, with dribble down from one corner of his mouth. He feels like a drum that has just been struck. The space he was dreaming of he now recognizes as his rib cage, as if he has become his own heart, a huffing puffing pumping man at mid-court, waiting for the whistle and the high-reaching jump-off. At some point in his sleep his chest began to ache, a stale sorrowful ache he associates with the pathetically bad way he played golf this afternoon, unable to concentrate, unable to loosen up. He wonders how long he has slept. The poster of sunshine and palm tops and distant pink red-roofed buildings pasted on the outer skin of the sliding windows has dulled in tint, gone shadowy, and the sounds of golf, its purposeful concussions alternating with intent silence and involuntary cries of triumph or disappointment, have subsided. And in the air outside, like the fluttering tinsel above a used-car lot, birds of many makes are calling to each other to wrap up the day. This hour or two before supper, when play— the last round of Horse at the basket out by the garage in the alley—used to be most intense, has become nap time as he slowly sinks toward earth with his wasting muscles and accumulating fat. He must lose some weight.

Only Judy is in the living room. She is flicking silently back and forth between channels. Faces, black in *The Jeffersons*, white in *Family Ties*, imploringly pop into visibility and then vanish amid shots of beer cans plunged into slow-motion waterfalls, George Bush lugging a gun through Texas underbrush, a Florida farmer gesturing toward his burnt fields, a Scotland Yard detective doing a little lecture with a diagram of an airplane's hold. "What's he saying?" Harry asks, but even as he asks, the image is gone, replaced by another, of a manatee being implanted with an electronic tracking device by a male pony-tailed manatee-conservation freak. An impatient rage within the child, a gluttony for images, brushes the manatee away. "Two channels back," Harry begs. "About the Pan Am plane."

"It was a bomb, silly," Judy says. "It had to be."

Children, they believe that headlines always happen to other people. "For Chrissake, cool it with the channel-changer. Lemme get a beer and I'll show you a neat card game. Where is everybody?"

"Grandma went to her women's group, Mom put Roy down for his nap."

"Your daddy—?" He thinks midway he shouldn't bring it up, but the words are out.

Judy shrugs and finishes the sentence. "Hasn't checked in yet."

It turns out she already knows how to play Rummy. In fact, she catches him with his hand full of three-of-a-kinds he was waiting to lay down when he had gin. Caught. Their laughter brings Pru out of her bedroom, in little white shorts her widened hips have stretched into horizontal wrinkles. Her face has taken wrinkles from the pillow, and seems a bit blurred and bloated by sleep, or a spell of crying. How suggestible female flesh is. Her feet are long and bare, with that chipped toenail polish. He asks his daughter-in-law, "What's up?"

She too shrugs. "I guess we'll go to dinner when Janice comes back. I'll feed Roy some applesauce to hold him."

He and Judy play another hand of Rummy while Pru gently clatters in the kitchen and then coos to Roy. Evening down here comes without much ceremony; suddenly the air beyond the balcony is gray as if with fine fog, and sea-scent drifts in through the sliding doors, and the sounds of birds and golf have gone away. This is peace. He resents it when Janice comes back, with that aggressive glow her women's group gives her. "Oh Harry, you men have been so awful! Not only were we considered chattel, but all those patriarchal religions tried to make us feel guilty about menstruating. They said we were un*clean*."

"Sorry," he says. "That was a crummy thing to do."

"That was Eve's basic sin, the lady professor told us," Janice goes on, half to Pru. "Something about apples being the color of blood, I couldn't quite follow it."

Harry interrupts, "By any chance are either of you two Eves like me, sort of starving?"

"We bought you lots of healthy snacks," Pru says. "Apricots dried without sulphur, unsalted banana chips."

"Is that what that stuff was in little plastic bags? I thought it might be like for Chinese food and I shouldn't touch it."

"Yes," Janice decides, "let's just go to dinner. We'll leave a note for Nelson. Pru, any old dress. Evenings, they won't seat shorts and men without jackets."

The Mead Hall, on the floor of Building B above Club Nineteen, is a combination restaurant and function room. On the one hand, there are menus with choices and prices, and waitresses in brief gold outfits echoing Valhalla's ring-gold theme, that figures here and there in the decor when the interior decorator remembered it, and there is even a wine steward in a summer tux and a kind of bicycle lock around his neck; on the other hand, as you go in a bulletin board is loaded with announcements and leaflets and tinted sheets about this or that set of lessons or lecture or concert or square dance or travelogue you could attend in the area, and all the time you're eating, on Wednesday and Saturday nights, Bingo goes on on the other side of the room, run from a stage and microphone somewhat out of sight behind an enormous flanged pillar that holds up the room's starry curved ceiling. The ceiling is a skylight for part of its breadth. That strange, scooping, personified space in his dream: could it have been simply this hall, conjured up because his stomach wanted food? Rabbit feels like Marty Tothero, looking at the menu, faced for the thousandth time with the same old choices among steak and veal, pork and ham, shrimps and scallops, swordfish Cajun style and fillets of sole stuffed with mussels, mushrooms, and artichoke hearts.

The pillar on two of its broad sides bears giant muddy ceramic murals about the Vikings: broadswords and horned helmets and dragon-headed ships protrude from the enamelled mass in its numerous blotchy colors, but the men wielding and wearing and sailing these protrusions are swallowed up in a crazy weave of arms and legs and lightning bolts, a kind of bloody basketwork in honor of history. "Seventy-one," the lugubrious male voice hidden behind the pillar intones. It repeats, "Seven one."

It is hard to carry on a conversation with the numbers blaring from the loudspeakers. Pru mothers Roy and coaxes a little baked potato and a single stir-fried shrimp into him. Janice talks Judy into ordering a lobster and then has to show her how to crack it, how to push out the big curved piece of white meat with a finger up through the poor boiled creature's ass, how to

suck the little tail segments, the same way you suck artichoke
leaves. Rabbit, who has ordered eye-of-round steak, can hardly
bear to watch; to him, eating lobster—its many little feathery
legs, its eyes on stalks, its antennae roasted red like the rest—is
nightmarish, a descent back into the squirmy scrabbly origins
of life. Crabs, too, and oysters and clams: all around him in
Florida he sees old people stuffing their faces with this filthy
gluey unspeakable stuff, and telling you furthermore it's good
for you, better than steak and hamburger, which is what he
usually orders, though he doesn't mind a breaded pork chop or
piece of veal, or a slice of ham with a pineapple ring or some
moon-shaped snitzes of baked apple and on the side some greasy
Dutch fries like a slipping stack of poker chips. That's how ham
comes in Pennsylvania. You can't get sausage down here, at least
not the spicy pork sausage he was raised on, or scrapple drenched
in maple syrup, or apple pie with enough cinnamon in it, or
shoo-fly pie at all. Janice went to a nutrition group a few winters
ago and came back telling him how he was clogging his arteries
with all this fat and dough. So for a while there was a rash of
salads and low-cal pasta and fish and fowl back in the condominium; but whenever he gets into the Mead Hall he can order
what he wants. With steak, you have to specify well-done or it
comes rubbery and blue-rare. Disgusting. All the things that
satisfy your appetite and seem so beautiful are disgusting when
you don't have the appetite. Disposable meat.

Judy's perfect little hands are shiny with lobster. She asks her
mother something and he can see Pru's mouth move in response
but the Godlike voice blocks their words right out with its solemn ''Twenty-seven. Two seven.''

''What're you saying, sweetie?'' he asks, embarrassed. Is his
hearing going, or do people talk a little differently, more rapidly
and softly, than they used to? On these TV shows that have
British actors, there are stretches, especially when they put on
the lower-class accents, where he can't understand a fucking
word. And movies, especially in the love scenes, when the stars
are establishing their coolness with the teen-age audience.

Pru explains, ''She's worried about Daddy not getting anything to eat,'' and makes her wry one-sided mouth. Is this grimace a communication to him, a little lament, inviting him to
conspire with her against Nelson?

Judy's shiny green eyes turn up toward her grandfather, as if
she expects him to make an unsympathetic response. Instead he
tells her, ''Don't you worry, Judy. People can get served here

until nine, and then at Club Nineteen downstairs they have sandwiches until midnight. And you saw Route 41: there's tons of eating places in Florida for your poor hungry daddy.''

The girl's lower lip trembles and she gets out, "He might not have any money.''

"Why wouldn't he have any money?''

The girl explains, "A lot of times he doesn't have any money. Bills come and even men keep coming to the house and Mommy can't pay them.'' Her eyes shift over to her mother's face as she realizes she has said too much.

Pru looks away, wiping a crumb of potato from the corner of Roy's lips. "Things have been a bit tight,'' she admits almost inaudibly.

Harry wants to pursue it. "Really? That can't be. He's making fifty grand a year, with the benefits and bonuses. My father used to support us all on less than twenty-two hundred.''

"Harry,'' Janice breaks in, in a voice that sounds like her mother's, toward the end, when the old widow got into the habit of laying down the law, "people now need more things than your father did. That was a simpler world. I remember it, I was there too. What did we use to do for fun, when you took me out for a date? Go to the movies for seventy-five cents apiece or maybe the miniature-golf course out on 422 for even less. And then a soda at the Pensupreme, and that was considered a very adequate good time.''

More than adequate, he remembers, if in the car after all that kissing and bare tit it took to warm her up Janice let him into herself, her inside warm and wet and softly grainy like a silk slipper. If she was having her period or feeling virtuous, she might hold him in her hand while he supplied the motion and the come, white as lobster meat. A shocking white, really, and tough to mop up. What he loved best in the car with Janice was when she'd sit on him, her ass in his hands and her tits in his face. And tidily take his come away with her.

Her mind on a track far distant from his, she is going on, "Nelson has to have good suits to make a good presentation of himself at the lot, and children now aren't just content with blocks and a ball, they have to have these video games—''

"Jesus—fifty thousand buys a lot of video games, he'll have enough to open an arcade soon if that's what he's spending it all on.''

"Well, you joke, but that big barn of Mother's, it's no end of expense, isn't that the case, Pru?''

Hauled back from a politely smiling daze, Pru grins and admits, "It eats up the dollars."

They are hiding something from him, Harry sees. The unseen man portentously intones, "Fifty-six. Five six," and a quavery old voice, so frantic it nearly chokes itself, croaks, "Bingo!" *Eff one eleven*, Joe Gold had said.

Harry says, "Well I don't know what the hell's going on."

No one contradicts him.

Roy is falling asleep with a sliver of shrimp shell on his slack lower lip. Harry has a sudden hankering for pecan pie. He tries to tease Judy into having dessert to keep him company. "Key-lime pie," he croons to her. "You can only get it in Florida. The chance of a lifetime."

"What makes it so special?"

He isn't quite sure. He lies. "Tiny delicate limes that only grow on the Florida Keys. Anywhere else is too coarse for them, too cold and mean."

She consents but then only picks nibbles off the crust at the back, so he, having sold it to her, has to eat it for her, on top of his pecan pie topped by a big oozing dip of butter-pecan ice cream. Nelson's absence grows bigger as their meal wears on. Janice and Pru have decaf coffee and, preoccupied, dying to talk to each other, watch Harry finish Judy's dessert. In a way, gluttony is an athletic feat, a stretching exercise. *Makes your tummy say "howdy!"* The waitress in her pleats of gold finally comes with the check and as he signs it with their condo number he feels like a god casually dispatching thunderbolts; the sum will appear on his monthly statement, next year, when the world has moved greatly on. How full he feels, stepping into the night air! A float of a man, in a parade of dependents. Harry carries Roy, who fell asleep during dessert. Janice and Pru hold Judy one by each hand and, because she has been good during the boring long meal, allow her to swing herself between them, giggling as they grunt with the strain.

Between Buildings A and B, several of the overhead sodium lights on their tall burnished wands of aluminum have been mysteriously smashed: they're out there, the criminals, watching and waiting for the security guards to nod, so the fortress of sleeping retirees can be stormed. In this gap of unillumination, the stars leap down at them out of the black warm sky. At night Florida recovers something of its old subtropical self, before men tamed its teeming flatness. Being here is exciting, like being on the deck of a ship; the air tastes of salt, of rotting palm thatch, of swamp. The stars are moister here, more plummy. The Bermuda grass has its strange spongy matted texture and each blade seems darkly metallic; the lawn snugly conceals round sprinkler heads. The skin men have imposed on bleak nature is so thin it develops holes, which armadillos wriggle through, the pathetic intricate things appearing in the middle of Pindo Palm Boulevard at dawn and being squashed flat by the first rush of morning traffic, though they curl themselves tight into protective balls. Harry, Roy's breath moist on his neck and the child's head heavy as a stone on his shoulder, looks up at the teeming sky and thinks, *There is no mercy.* The stark plummy stars press down and the depth of the galactic void for an instant makes you feel suspended upside down. The entrance to Building B looms alluringly with its cabined yellow glow. The five Angstroms each cope in their way with the sore place inside them, Nelson's gnawing absence. They fumble through the protected entrances, the elevator, the peach-and-silver hallway, avoiding each other's eyes in smiling embarrassment.

As her mother tucks her brother in, Judy settles before the television and flicks from *The Wonder Years* to *Night Court* to a French movie, starring that lunky Dépardieu who is in all of them, this time about a man who comes to a village and usurps another man's identity, including his wife. In a moment's decision the young widow, besmirched and lonely, accepts him as her husband, and this thrills Harry; there ought to be a law that we change identities and families every ten years or so. But Judy keeps flicking away from the story and Pru finally yells at the kid and tells her to get ready for bed on the sofa, they'll all clear out of the living room for her sake, though why she didn't accept Grandma and Grandpa's nice offer of a little room of her own is beyond her, Pru's, understanding. The girl breaks into tears and this is a relief for all of them, giving vent to their common unspoken sense of abandonment.

Janice tells Harry, "You go to bed, hon. You look beat. I'm too jazzed up by the coffee to sleep, Pru and I will sit in the kitchen."

"I thought the coffee was decaf." He had looked forward to having her, her little firm brown body, in bed beside him; with these other people here they don't have a second to themselves. His memories had stirred him. Fifty-two years old and she still has a solid ass. Not like Thelma, who's been losing it lately.

"That's what I ordered," Janice says, "but I never trust them really. I think a lot of the time now they just tell you it's decaf to shut you up.''

"Don't sit up too late.'' On an impulse he adds to reassure her, "The kid's all right, he's just having some kind of a toot.''

Pru glances at him in surprise, as if he's said more than he knows.

He feels goaded to elaborate: "Both me and Toyota give him a royal pain in the ass for some reason.''

Again, he is not contradicted.

Fantasies about America produced two strongly contradictory conclusions that in the end came to the same point of injecting some caution into the golden dreams, he reads in bed. It's a history book Janice gave him for Christmas, by a woman historian yet, about the Dutch role in the American Revolution, which he hadn't thought up to now had been much. *According to one school, America was too big, too divided, ever to become a single country, its communications too distended for the country ever to be united.* Just that sentence makes him feel enormous, slack, distended. The beautiful thing about history is it puts you right to sleep. He looks back up the page for something amusing he remembered reading last night. *Climate in the New World, according to a best-selling French treatise translated into Dutch in 1775, made men listless and indolent; they might become happy but never stalwart. America, affirmed this scholar, "was formed for happiness, but not for empire."* Another European scholar reported that *the native Indians "have small organs of generation" and "little sexual capacity."*

Maybe if Nelson had been bigger he'd be happier. But being big doesn't automatically make you happy. Harry was big enough, and look at him. At times the size of his reflection in a clothing-store mirror or plate-glass window startles him. Appalls him, really: taking up all that space in the world. He pushes on for a few more pages: *Expectation of lucrative commerce . . . Combat at sea . . . tangled issue . . . increased tension . . . neutral bottoms . . . French vigorously . . . Debate in the provincial states . . . Unlimited convoy would become another test of ego as a* casus belli. He rereads this last sentence twice before realizing he has no idea what it means, his brain is making those short-circuit connections as in dreams. He turns out the light. This conjures up a thin crack of light under the door like a phosphorescent transmitter, emitting sounds. He hears Janice and Pru murmuring, a clink of glass, a footstep, and then a buzzer rasping, and hasty footsteps, a woman's voice in the nervous pitch you use for talking over a loudspeaker, not trusting it, and then in a later fold of his restless, distended consciousness the door opening, Nelson's voice, deep among the women's, and most dreamlike of all, laughter, all of them laughing.

A gnashing sound, the greens being mowed by kids on those big ugly reel mowers. Excited seagulls weeping. The Norfolk pine, its branches as regularly spaced as the thin metal balusters of his balcony rail. Amazing. He is still in Florida, still alive. Morning-chilly salt air wafts from the Gulf through the two-inch crack that the sliding door was left open. Janice is asleep in bed beside him. The warmth of her body is faintly rank; night sweat has pasted dark wiggly hairs to the nape of her neck. Her hair is least gray at the nape, a secret nest of her old dark silky self. She sleeps on her stomach turned away from him, and if the night is cool pulls the covers off him onto herself, and if hot dumps them on top of him, all this supposedly in her sleep. Rabbit eases from the king-size bed, goes into their bathroom with its rose-colored one-piece Fiberglas tub and shower stall, and urinates into the toilet of a matching rose porcelain. He sits down, as it is quieter, splashing against the front of the bowl. He brushes his teeth but is too curious to shave; if he takes the time to shave Janice might get away from him and hide among the others as she has been doing. He slides back into bed, stealthily but hoping that the unavoidable rustling of sheets and the soft heaving of the mattress might wake her. When it doesn't, he nudges her shoulder. "Janice?" he whispers. "Dreamboat?"

Her voice comes muffled. "What? Leave me alone."

"What time 'dyou come to bed?"

"I didn't dare look. One."

"Where had Nelson been? What was his explanation?"

She says nothing. She wants him to think she has fallen back to sleep. He waits. Lovingly, he caresses her shoulder. His glimpse of that French movie last night had stirred him with the idea of a wife as a total stranger, of moving right in, next to her little warm brown body. A wife can be as strange as a whore, that's the beauty of male-female relations. She says, still without turning her head, "Harry, touch me once more and I'll kill you."

He thinks this over and decides upon counteraggression. "Where the hell had he been?" he asks.

She rolls over, giving up. Her breath has stale tobacco in it. She has given up smoking supposedly but whenever she's around Nelson with his Camels and Pru with her Pall Malls she takes it up again. "He didn't know exactly. Just driving around. He said he needed to get out, Florida is so claustrophobic."

The kid is right: life down here is confined to the narrow paths you make. To Winn Dixie, to the Loew's cineplex and the shops in the Palmetto Palm Mall, to the doctor's, to the pro shop and back. Between these paths there's somehow nothing, a lot of identical palm trees and cactus and thirsty lawn and empty sunshine, hotels you're not staying at and beaches you're not admitted to and inland areas where there's never any reason to go. In Pennsylvania, at least in Diamond County, everything has been paved solid by memory and in any direction you go you've already been there.

Licking her lips and making a face as if her throat aches, Janice goes on, "He drove on 41 as far as what sounds like Naples and stopped at a restaurant when he got hungry and called us but the phone didn't answer, I wondered at the time if we shouldn't have waited to go over but you said you were starving—"

"That's right. Blame me."

"I wasn't, honey. It wasn't just you. The children were antsy and worried and I thought, Life must go on, dinner will distract us; but then he says he did call just about when we were heading out the door and where he was one beer led to another and on the way back he got a little lost, you know yourself how if you miss the Pindo Palm turnoff everything looks identical, for miles."

"I can't believe it," Harry says. He feels rage coming to boil in his chest and sits up in bed to relieve the pressure. "Without so much as a fucking word to anybody he disappears for, what, eight hours? He is really becoming crazy. He's always been moody but this is crazy behavior. The kid needs help."

Janice says, "He was perfectly sober when he came back and brought a bunch of those little tiny stuffed alligators they make for souvenirs; Pru and I had to laugh. One for each of the children and even one for you, where they've made it stand and put a golf club in its little feet." She flicks the blanket back from his lap and touches his drowsy penis in his open pajama fly. "How're we doing down there? We never make love any more."

But now he is out of the mood. He slaps her hand primly and

tugs up the blanket and says, "We just *did* make love. Before Christmas."

"*Way* before Christmas," Janice says, not moving her head, and for a second he has the mad hope she will turn the blanket down again and simply, quickly, take his prick in her mouth, like Thelma used to do almost first thing when they would secretly meet in this last decade; but blowing has never been Janice's style. She has to be very drunk, and he never did like her drunk, a kind of chaos wells up within her that threatens him, that threatens to swamp the whole world. She says, "O.K. for you, buster," to register with him that she's been rejected, in case he wants her later, and pushes out of her side of the bed. Her damp nightie is stuck up above her waist and before she tugs it down he admires the taut pale buttocks above the tan backs of her thighs. Guiltily he hears her flush the toilet in the bathroom and with an angry rattle and rush of water start to run the shower. He pictures exactly how she looks stepping out of the shower, with her hair in a transparent shower cap and her bottom rosy and her pussy all whitened with dew, and regrets that they must live, he and his little dark woman, his stubborn shy mutt of a Springer, in a world of mostly missed signals. Down here they have been thrown together more than at any time of their lives and they have coped by turning their backs and growing thicker skins. He plays golf three or four times a week and she has her tennis and her groups and her errands. When she comes back from the bathroom, in a terrycloth robe, he is still in the bed, reading in his book about British interference with Dutch merchant ships and France needing to build up her decayed fleet with Baltic timber delivered by Dutch vessels, in case Janice wants to try at sex again, but now from the other end of the condo the sounds of children can be heard, and of Pru hushing them in her burdened maternal voice.

Harry says to Janice, "Let's try to concentrate on Judy and Roy today. They seem sort of woebegone, don't they?"

She doesn't answer, guardedly. She takes his remark as a slam at Nelson's parenting. Maybe it is. Nelson's the one who needs parenting; he always did and never got enough. When you don't get enough of something at the right biological moment, Rabbit has read somewhere, you keep after it until you die. He asks, "What do you and Pru talk about all the time?"

She answers, thin-lipped, "Oh, women things. You'd find them boring." Janice always gets a funny intense frowny look on her face when she's dressing herself. Even if it's just slacks and a blouse to go to Winn Dixie in, she pinches off an accusatory stare into the mirror, to face down the worst.

"Maybe so," he agrees, ending the conversation, and knowing this will make Janice want to continue it.

Sure enough, she volunteers, "She's worried about Nelson," and might go on, faltering for the next words, the tip of her tongue sneaking out and pressing on her upper lip in the effort of thought.

But Rabbit says curtly, "Who wouldn't be?" He turns his back to put on his underpants. He still wears Jockey shorts. Ruth was amused by them that night ages ago, and he always thinks of it. Today he wants to be a grandfather and tries to dress for the role. Long eggshell-colored linen pants with cuffs, instead of his dirty old plaid bell-bottom golf slacks, and instead of a polo knit a real shirt, 100-per-cent cotton, with blue pinstripes and short sleeves. He looks at himself in the mirror that Janice's image has vacated and is stunned, deep inside, by the bulk of what he sees—face swollen to a kind of moon, with his little sunburned nose and icy eyes and nibbly small mouth bunched in the center, above the jowls, boneless jowls that come up and put a pad of fat even in front of his ears, where Judy has a silky shine. Talk about Nelson—Harry's own hair, its blondness dirtied and dulled by gray, is thinning back from his temples. Tall as he is, there is no carrying the slope under his shirt as anything other than a loose gut, a paunch that in itself must weigh as much as a starving Ethiopian child. He must start to cut down. He can feel, every motion he makes, his weight tugging at his heart—that singeing sensation he gets as if a child inside him is playing with lighted matches.

On the breakfast table, today's *News-Press* has the color photograph of a tiny sickly one-year-old girl who died last night for lack of a liver transplant. Her name was Amber. Also a headline saying that according to Scotland Yard Pan Am Flight 103 was definitely bombed, just like Ed Silberstein and Judy say. Fragments of metal. Luggage compartment. Plastic explosive, can be molded into any form, probably a high-performance Czech type called Semtex: Harry can hardly bear to read about it, the thought of all those conscious bodies suddenly with nothing all around them, freezing, *Ber-nie, Ber-nie*, and Lockerbie a faint spatter of stars below, everything upside-down and void of mercy and meaning. Also the mayor of Fort Myers now thinks his police acted properly in the arrest of Deion Sanders. Also *Deadly pollution infects Lake Okeechobee*. Also *Partly cloudy, Highs in low to mid-80s.* "Today's the day," he announces, "Grandpa's going to take you to amazing places!"

Judy and Roy look doubtful but not entirely.

Janice says, "Harry, have another of these cherry Danishes before they go stale. We bought them thinking mostly of the children but they both say they hate red runny things."

"Why do you want to kill me with carbos?" he asks, but eats the Danish anyway, and cleans up the sweet sugary crumbs with his fingertips.

Pru, tall from Harry's seated angle, her hips level with his eyes, hesitantly asks, "Would you two possibly enjoy having the grandchildren to yourselves for this expedition? Nelson couldn't get to sleep last night and kept me pretty much up too. I just can't face a day in the car." She does look pale and drawn, the kid keeping her up all night with his whining and whatever else. Even her freckles look pale, and her lips, that felt so soft and warm at the airport, are resigned and tight and wryly pulled down on one side.

Janice says, "Of course, dear. You get some sleep and then maybe you and Nellie could do something healthy and fun. If you use the Valhalla pool remind him he's supposed to shower before *and* after and not to do any diving."

Judy laughs and interrupts: "Daddy does belly flops."

Roy says, "Daddy does *not* flop. You flop."

"Hey Jesus," Harry tells them, "don't start fighting yet. We aren't even in the car."

In the car by nine-thirty, provisioned with a triple-barrelled package of Double Stuf Oreos and a sixpack of Classic Coke, they begin the long day that for years to come will be known in fond family legend as The Day Grandpa Ate the Parrot Food, though it wasn't exactly for parrots, and he didn't eat much of it. They start by driving down Route 41 (PATIOLAND, Kissin' Kuzzins, Easy Drugs, LAND OF SLEEP) to Fort Myers and visiting the Thomas Alva Edison Winter Home, which nearly does them in. They park the Camry and pass underneath a giant banyan tree, a tree (a helpful sign tells them) given to Edison when it was a twig by some financial giant of the time, Harvey Firestone or Henry Ford, and that has since become the biggest banyan tree outside of India, where a single such gigantic tree may shelter an entire bazaar. Banyans spread by dangling down roots and making new trunks that become like crutches as the limbs spread out and out—these creepy trees will go for miles if nobody stops them. Harry wonders, *How do they die?*

It turns out you can't just walk around the house and grounds, you have to join a tour, for five bucks a pop. Judy and Roy both freak out when that's explained to them. They see themselves surrounded by busloads of old retired people wearing baseball caps and flip-up sunglasses and carrying those little sticks that open out into a kind of saddle to be one-legged chairs. Several wrecks in wheelchairs join their accumulating tour group as it waits to begin. Judy, looking prematurely long-legged in short pink shorts, with funny red shadows of blusher on her cheekbones, says, "I don't *care* about any dumb grounds, I want to see the machine that makes lightning," and Roy, his loose little mouth dyed by Oreo chocolate, stares with his glazed brown eyes as if he's going to melt in the heat.

Harry tells Judy, "I don't think there's any machine that makes lightning, just the very first light bulb ever invented." He tells Roy, "I'll carry you if you get too tired."

At some signal he misses, so they get caught in the back, everybody including the wheelchairs pushes out of the shed into a space of dusty gray earth and outdoor jungle stuffiness and knifelike leaf shadows. Their guide is a prissy old blue-haired girl in a billed cap reciting what she's memorized. First she points out to them *Kigelia pinnata*, the sausage tree of Africa. "The fruit resembles a sausage and that is why the name. It is not edible, but is used as a medicine by the natives of Africa and because of their superstitious nature they worship the tree for its healing power. Just across Memory Garden is the fried-egg tree. The flower looks very much like an egg, sunny side up. It was planted there just in case you like eggs with your sausage."

The group politely laughs. Some of the old folks indeed laugh more than politely, as if this is the funniest thing they've ever in their long lives heard. When do the gray cells start winking out in significant numbers? When will it start happening to him, Harry wonders. Or has it already? Their guide, heartened by the good audience response, points out more funny trees—the dynamite tree, *Hura crepitans*, whose fruit explodes when it is ripe, and the very rare *Cecropia* of South America, the sloth tree, indeed the *only* mature *Cecropia palmata* in the United States, whose leaves have the texture of chamois skin and *never* disintegrate. *Why did God bother, Harry wonders, to do all these tricks, off by Himself in the Amazon jungle?* "They are chocolate brown on one side and white on the other and because of their unusual shapes and lasting qualities are in great demand for dried floral arrangements. You can purchase these leaves in our gift shop." So He did it so people would have something to buy in gift shops.

Next we come to *Enterolobium cyclocarpum*, known as the ear tree. "The seed pods," the guide recites, "resemble the human ear." The crowd, warmed up now to laugh at almost any ridiculous thing God does, titters, and the guide allows herself a self-congratulatory smile; she knows these trees, these words, and these docile senile tourists backwards and forwards.

A little human hand tugs Harry's with a chamoislike softness of its own. He bends down to little Judy's exquisite, tarted-up, green-eyed face. He sees that Pru allowed her to put on a little lipstick, too. To sweeten this outing for her, to make it seem an occasion. Going sightseeing with Grandpa and Grandma. You'll always remember this. When they're gone to their reward. "Roy wants to know," Judy says as softly as she can, but anxiety driving her voice up, "how soon it's over."

"It's just begun," Harry says.

Janice begins to whisper with them. Her attention span is as poor as theirs. "Could we make a break for it before they make us cross the street?"

"It's a one-way tour," Harry says. "Come on, everybody. Let's stick with it."

He picks up little Roy, whose body weight has been doubled by boredom, and carries him, and they all cross the street, a street that in the very old days was a cow trail and that "Mr. Edison," as the woman keeps calling him, simpering like he's some big-dicked boyfriend of hers, took it into his head to line with royal palms. "These royal palms grow wild sixty miles off us on the fringe of the Everglades; however, it was much easier, in 1900, to bring them in from Cuba by great sailboats than to drag them by ox teams through our virtually impenetrable Florida swamplands."

On winding paths they drag themselves, dodging wheelchairs, trying not to step on the little beds of cactus and flowers that line the paths, trying to hear their guide as her voice fades in and out of its scratchy groove, trying to take an interest in the embowering green mysteries Edison brought from afar in his heavily financed search for a substitute rubber. Here are the kapok tree and the Java plum, the cannonball tree from Trinidad and the mango from India, the lipstick tree and the birdseye bush, the sweetheart orchid, which is *not* as many people think a parasite, and the lychee nut, whose fruit is much sought after by the Chinese. Harry's legs ache, and the small of his back, and that suspect area behind his left ribs, which gives him a twinge, but he cannot put Roy down because the kid is asleep: he must be one of the sleepingest four-year-olds in the world. Janice and Judy have conspiratorially separated from the group and wandered ahead to the Edison house, a house brought in four sailing schooners from Maine in 1886, the first prefabricated house in the world you could say, a house without a kitchen because Edison didn't like the smell of cooking food, a house with a wide veranda on all four sides and with the first modern pool in Florida, of blue cement reinforced not with steel but with bamboo and not a crack or leak in it to this day. Marvels! So much endeavor, ingenuity, oddity, and bravery has been compressed into history: Harry can hardly stand under the weight of it all, bending his bones, melting his mind, pressing like a turnscrew on the segments of his skull, giving him a fantastic itch under his shoulder blades, where his 100-per-cent cotton blue-pinstriped shirt has moistened and then dried. He catches up to Janice, his heart twanging, and softly begs her, "Scratch." Softly so as not to wake the child.

"Where?" She shifts her cigarette, a Pall Mall she must have borrowed from Pru, to the other hand and rakes at his back, up, down, to the right and left as he directs, until the demon feels exorcised. This jungly garden of old Edison's is a devilish place. His breathing is bothered; he makes a determined effort not to hyperventilate. The commotion wakes Roy and he drowsily announces, "I got to go pee."

"I bet you do," Harry says, and tells him, "You can't go behind any of these bushes, they're all too rare."

"The *scarlet dombeya wallichi* is known as the pink ball tree of India," the guide is telling her less unruly students with a lilt. "It has a very heavy fragrance. Mrs. Edison loved birds and always kept canaries, parakeets, and parrots. These birds live out of doors the year around and love it here."

"How does she know they love it here?" Judy asks her grandparents, a bit noisily, so that several venerable heads turn. "She's not a parrot."

"Who says she's not?" Harry whispers.

"I got to go pee," Roy repeats.

"Yeah well, your need to pee isn't the exact fucking center of the universe," Harry tells him. He is badly out of practice in this fathering business, and never was that great at it.

Janice offers, "I'll take him back along the path, there were bathrooms in the building we came in at."

Judy is alarmed to see these two escaping. "I want to come with!" she cries, so loudly the tour guide stops her recital for a moment. "Maybe I got to go pee too!"

Harry grabs her hand and holds it tight and even gives it a sadistic squeeze. "And maybe you don't," he says. "Come on, stick it out. Go with the flow, for Chrissake. You'll miss the world's oldest goddamn light bulb."

A woman in a wheelchair, not so crippled her hair isn't dyed orange and permed into more curlicues than a monkey's ass, looks over and gives them a glare. *Knowing when to quit,* Harry thinks. *Nobody knows when to quit.* Their guide has lifted her voice up a notch and is saying, "Here is the sapodilla of the American tropics. From the sap of this tree comes chicle, used in making chewing gum."

"Hear that?" Harry asks Judy, out of breath with the social tension of this endless tour and sorry about the hurtful squeeze. "The tree Chiclets come from."

"What are Chiclets?" Judy asks, looking up at him with a little new nick of a squint taken in those clear green eyes. She is sore, slightly, and wary of him now. He has nicked her innocence. Can it be she's never heard of Chiclets? Have they really gone the way of penny candy, of gumdrops and sourballs, of those little red ration tokens you had to use during the war? All as real as yesterday to Harry.

"Mr. Edison planted this chewing-gum tree for children," the guide is going on. "He loved his children and his grandchildren very much and spent long hours with them, though because of his deafness he had to do most of the talking." There is a murmur of laughter, and she preens, stretching her neck and pursing her lips, as if she hadn't expected this, though she must have, she has done this spiel so often she must have their reactions taped down to every stray chuckle. Now she leads her herd of oldsters, shuffling and bobbing solemnly in their splashy playclothes, toward a link fence and a new phase of their five-dollar pilgrimage. They are about to cross the road lined with the unnaturally straight and concrete-colored palm trunks that Edison, the amazing great American, floated in from Cuba when the century was an infant. But she can't let them cross without socking them with one more cute plant. "The shrub with the long red tassels is the chenille plant from the Bismarck Islands.

The chenille is French and means caterpillar. You can readily see the meaning for the name of the plant.''

"Yukko, *cat*erpillars," little Judy pipes up to Harry, and he recognizes this as a female attempt to rebridge the space between them, and he feels worse than ever about that hurtful squeeze. He wonders why he did it, why he tends to do mean things like that, to women mostly, as if blaming them for the world as it is, full of chenille plants and without mercy. He feels fragile, on the edge of lousy. That bad child inside his chest keeps playing with matches.

The guide announces, "We are now going across the street to the laboratory where Mr. Edison did his last experimental work."

They do at last cross over and, in Edison's breezy old laboratories, among dusty beakers and siphons and alembics and big belted black machinery, are reunited with Janice and Roy. The tour guide points out the cot where Edison used to take the ten-minute catnaps that enabled him to sit and dream in his big deaf head for hours on end, and the piece of goldenrod rubber on his desk, made from goldenrod grown right here in Fort Myers and still flexible after all these years. Finally, the guide frees them to roam, marvel, and escape. Driving north, Harry asks the three others, "So, what did you like best?"

"Going pee," Roy says.

"You're dumb," Judy tells him and, to show that she's not, answers, "I liked best the phonograph where to hear because he was deaf he rested his teeth on this wooden frame and you can see the marks his teeth made. That was interesting."

"*I* was interested," Harry says, "in all those failures he had in developing the storage battery. You wouldn't think it would be so tough. How many—nine *thou*sand experiments?"

Route 41 drones past the windows. Banks. Food and gas. Arthritis clinics. Janice seems preoccupied. "Oh," she says, trying to join in, "I guess the old movie machines. And the toaster and waffle iron. I hadn't realized he had invented those, you don't think of them as needing to be invented. You wonder how different the world would be if he hadn't lived. That one man."

Harry says, authoritatively, he and Janice in the front seat like puppet grandparents, just the heads showing, playing for their little audience of two in the back seat, "Hardly at all. It was all there in the technology, waiting to be picked up. If we hadn't done it the Swiss or somebody would have. The only modern invention that wasn't inevitable, I once read somewhere, was the zipper.''

"The zipper!" Judy shrieks, as if she has decided, since this day with her grandparents looks as though it will never end, to be amused.

"Yeah, it's really very intricate," Harry tells her, "all those little slopes and curves, the way they fit. It's on the principle of a wedge, an inclined plane, the same way the Pyramids were built." Feeling he may have wandered rather far, venturing into the terrible empty space where the Pyramids were built, he announces, "Also, Edison had backing. Look at who his friends were down there. Ford. Firestone. The giant fat cats. He got his ideas to sell them to them. All this talk about his love for mankind, I had to laugh."

"Oh yes," Janice says, "I liked the old car with daffodil-rubber tires."

"Goldenrod," Harry corrects. "Not daffodil."

"I meant goldenrod."

"I like daffodil better," Judy says from the back seat. "Grandpa, how did you like our tour lady, the awful way she talked, making that mouth like she had a sourball in it?"

"I thought she was very kind of sexy," Harry says.

"Sexy!" little Judy shrieks.

"I'm hungry," Roy says.

"Me too, Roy," says Janice. "Thank you for saying that."

They eat at a McDonald's where, for some legal reason—fear of lawsuits, the unapologetic cashier thinks when they ask her about it—the door is locked out to the playground, with its spiral slide and its enticing plastic man with a head, even bigger than Edison's, shaped like a hamburger. Roy throws a fit at the locked door and all through lunch has these big liquid googies of grief to snuffle back up into his nose. He likes to pour salt out of the shaker until he has a heap and then rub the French fries in it, one by one. The French fries and about a pound of salt are all the kid eats; Harry finishes his Big Mac for him, even though he doesn't much care for all the Technicolor glop McDonald's puts on everything—pure chemicals. Whatever happened to the old-fashioned plain hamburger? Gone wherever the Chiclet went. A little Bingo game is proceeding in a corner; you have to walk right through it on your way to the bathrooms, these old people in booths bent over their cards while a young black girl in a McDonald's brown uniform gravely reads off the numbers with a twang. "Twainty-sevvn . . . Fohty-wuhunn . . ."

Back in the hot car, Harry sneaks a look at his watch. Just noon. He can't believe it, it feels like four in the afternoon. His bones ache, deep inside his flesh. "Well now," he announces, "we have some choices." He unfolds a map he carries in the glove compartment. *Figure out where you're going before you go there:* he was told that a long time ago. "Up toward Sarasota there's the Ringling Museum but it's closed, something called Bellm's Cars of Yesterday but maybe we did enough old cars back at Edison's, and this Jungle Gardens which a guy I play golf with really swears by."

Judy groans and little Roy, taking his cue from her, begins his trembly-lower-lip routine. "Please, Grandpa," she says, sounding almost maternal, "not caterpillar trees again!"

"It's not just plants, the plants are the *least* of it, they have leopards and these crazy birds. Real leopards, Roy, that'd claw your eyes out if you let 'em, and flamingos that fall asleep standing on one leg—Bernie, this friend of mine, can't get over it, the way they can sleep standing on this one skinny leg!" He holds up a single finger to convey the wonder of it. How ugly and strange a single finger is—its knuckle-wrinkles, its whorly print, its pretty useless nail. Both the children in the back seat look flushed, the way Nelson used to when he'd be coming down with a cold—a smothery frantic look in the eyes. "Or," Rabbit says, consulting the map, "here's something called Braden Castle Ruins. How do you two sports like ruins?" He knows the answer, and cinches his point with, "Or we could all go back to the condo and take a nap." He learned this much selling cars: offer the customer something he doesn't want, to make what he half-wants look better. He peeks over at Janice, a bit miffed by her air of detachment. Why is she making this all his show? She's a grandparent too.

She rouses and says, "We can't go back so soon—they may be still resting."

"Or whatever," he says. Brawling. Fucking. There is something hot and disastrous about Nelson and Pru that scares the rest of them. Young couples give off this heat; they're still at the heart of the world's business, making babies. Old couples like him and Janice give off the musty smell of dead flower stalks, rotting in the vase.

Judy suggests, "Let's go to a *movie*."

"Yeah. Movie," Roy says, for these two words doing quite a good accidental imitation of a grown-up voice, as if they've taken on a hitchhiker in the back seat.

"Let's make a deal," Harry proposes. "We'll drive up and nip into Jungle Gardens, and if there's a guided tour or you think it'll depress you we'll nip right out again, the hell with 'em. Otherwise we'll go through and see the flamingos and then buy a Sarasota paper and see what's at the movies. Roy, you big enough to sit through a whole movie?" He starts the engine and gets into gear.

Judy says, "He cried so hard during *Dumbo* Mommy had to take him out."

"Dumbo's mommy . . ." Roy begins to explain, then starts to cry.

"Yeah," Harry says, turning onto 41 again, casting back his voice, rolling along. "That's a tough one, out there in that little prison car. The business with their trunks, remember? But it all works out. Roy, you should have stayed to the end. If you don't stay to the end the sadness sticks with you."

"He becomes a *star*," Judy tells her brother spitefully. "He shoots peanuts at all the bad clowns. You missed all that."

"That Disney," Harry says, half to Janice, half for their little audience. "He packed a punch. You had to have been raised in the Depression to take it. Even Nelson, your daddy, couldn't stand *Snow White* when it came around in rerun."

"Daddy doesn't like anything," Judy confides. "Just his dumb friends."

"What friends?" Rabbit asks her.

"Oh, I don't know their names. Slim and like that. Mommy hates them and won't go out any more."

"She won't, huh?"

"She says she's scared."

"Scared! Scared of what?"

"Harry," Janice mutters beside him. "Don't pump the children."

"Scared of Slim," Roy says, trying it out for sound.

Judy thumps him. "No, Daddy is not scared of Slim, you dumbo, he's scared of those other men."

"What other men?" Harry asks.

"*Harry,*" Janice says.

"Forget I asked," he calls back, his words lost in the squall as Roy grabs Judy's hair and won't let go. In reaching back to pull them apart Janice rips a seam of her blouse; he can hear the threads break even though at that moment he is being passed by an eighteen-wheeler whose shuddering white sides say MAYFLOWER MEANS MOVING and create an aerodynamic condition that sucks him sideways so he has to fight the Camry's wheel. A tin boat on too rough a sea. The Japanese don't build for the full range of American conditions. Like Nelson said about the van, the wind pushing him all over 422. Still, you got to sell something in life. You can't just sit there and crab. We can't all sell Lamborghinis.

Jungle Gardens works out better than anyone dared hope. A big shop full of shells and corny artifacts like that stuff of Janice's back on the condo shelves opens into a miniature outdoors. You can go one way to the Reptile Show and the Gardens of Christ and the other to the Bird Show. They all turn toward the Bird Show, and watch tattered, disgruntled-looking parrots ride bicycles and seesaws and hop through hoops. Then a curving cement path, Jungle Trail, leads them along: you shuffle obediently past mossy roots and trickling rocks and at each turn confront some fresh mild wonder—a trio of spider monkeys with long hairy arms and little worried faces, then a cageful of finches whirring up and down, roost to roost, like the tireless works of a complicated clock, then a bo-tree such as Buddha was illuminated under. Rabbit wonders how the Dalai Lama is doing, after all that exile. Do you still believe in God, if people keep telling you you *are* God?

The four Angstroms come to Mirror Lake, where mute swans float, and Flamingo Lagoon, where, as Bernie Drechsel promised, flocks of flamingos, colored that unreal orange-pink color, sleep while standing up, like big feathery lollypops, each body a ball, the idle leg and the neck and head somehow knitted in, balanced on one pencil-thin leg and wide weird leathern foot. Others, almost as marvellous, are awake and stirring, tenderly treading. "Look how they drink," Harry tells his grandchildren, lowering his voice as if in the presence of something sacred. "Upside down. Their bills are scoops that work upside down." And they stand marvelling, the four human beings, as if the space between farflung planets has been abolished, so different do these living things loom from themselves. The earth is many planets, that intersect only at moments. Even among themselves, slices of difference interpose, speaking the same language though they do, and lacking feathers, and all drinking right side up.

After the flamingos, the path takes them to a snack bar in a pavilion, and a shell-and-butterfly exhibit, and a goldfish pond, and a cage of black leopards just as Harry had promised Roy. The black-eyed child stares at the animals' noiseless pacing as if into the heart of a whirlpool that might suck him down. A small machine such as those that in Harry's youth supplied a handful of peanuts or pistachio nuts in almost every gas station and grocery store is fixed to a pavilion post near an area where peacocks restlessly drag their extravagant feathers across the dust. Here he makes his historic blunder. As his three kin move ahead he fishes in his pocket for a dime, inserts it, receives a handful of brown dry objects, and begins to eat them. They are not exactly peanuts, but perhaps some Florida delicacy, and taste so dry and stale as to be bitter; but who knows how long these machines wait for customers? When he offers some to Judy, though, she looks at them, smells them, and stares up into his face with pure wonderment. "Grandpa!" she cries. "That's to feed the birds! Grandma! He's been eating birdfood! Little brown things like rabbit turds!"

Janice and Roy gather around to see, and Harry holds open his hand to display the shaming evidence. "I didn't know," he weakly says. "There's no sign or anything." He is suffused with a curious sensation; he feels faintly numb and sick but beyond that, beyond the warm volume enclosed by his skin, the air is swept by a universal devaluation; for one flash he sees his life as a silly thing it will be a relief to discard.

Only Judy actually laughs, a laughter that turns forced, out of her fine-featured little face with its perfect teeth; Janice and Roy just look sad, and a bit puzzled.

Judy says, "Grandpa, that's the *dumb*est thing I ever saw anybody do!"

He smiles and nods at his inflated height above her; he feels short of breath and tight bands of pain pulse across his chest. In his mouth an acid taste intensifies. He turns his hand, his puffy keratotic hand, long-fingered enough to hold a basketball from above, and scatters the pellets where the peacocks can eat them. A dirty white one dragging its filmy tail through the dust eyes the turdlike food but doesn't peck. Maybe it was human food after all. Still, his day has taken a blow, and as they move along the path only Judy is gleeful; her prattle eclipses a sudden anguished crying, the noise peacocks make, behind them.

Wearying of Jungle Gardens, they move along a path that passes yet another piece of this same all-purpose lake, and a cage where a lonely ocelot dozes, and cactus gardens, and a black pool advertising a water monitor but where they see nothing, perhaps because they don't know what a water monitor is, and cages of parrots and macaws whose brilliant plumage and ornate bills seem to weigh them down. It's hell, to be a creature. You are trapped in yourself, the genetic instructions, more strictly than in a cage. At the last cage a scraggly tall emu and a rhea are snapping at the wires of the fencing with a doleful soft leathery clack of their bills. Their long-lashed great eyes stare through the diagonal wire squares. *Clip, Tap, Clip*, say their sad persistent bills, to no avail. Are they catching insects human beings cannot see? Are they delirious, like old rummies?

Harry retastes the acid pellets and the yellow-and-red glop McDonald's puts on hamburgers, with the little limp green pickle, and wishes to God he could stop eating. Janice comes to his side and touches the back of his hanging hand with the back of hers. "It was a natural mistake," she says.

"That's the kind I make," he says. "Natural ones."

"Harry, don't be so down."

"Am I?"

"You keep thinking about Nelson," she tells him. So that's what has been preoccupying her. Her, not him.

"I was thinking about emus," he confesses.

Janice says, "Let's go see if the kids want anything in the souvenir shop and then go buy a paper. I'm dying to be somewhere air-conditioned." In the souvenir shop they buy Judy a lovely glossy top shell and Roy a strikingly black-and-white murex, with rough prongs that he instantly begins to scrape along smooth surfaces—the painted rail leading back to the parking lot, and the Camry itself if Harry hadn't reached down and grabbed the little slob by his boneless little arm. Harry hates shells. Whenever he sees them he can't help thinking of the blobby hungry sluggy creatures who inhabit them, with hearts and mouths and anuses and feelers and feeble eyes, underneath the sea, a murky cold world halfway to death. He really can't stand the thought of underwater, the things haunting it, eating each other, drilling through shells, sucking each other's stringy guts out.

The interior of the car has grown broiling hot in their absence. The Florida sun has burned away those thin clouds like aging jet trails and left only a waste of pure blue above the palms and the Spanish tiles. The heat and the pressure of family life have stupefied the kids; they hardly beg for a treat when he stops at a Joy Food and Gas and buys a Sarasota *Sentinel*. The movie they all decide upon is *Working Girl* at two-forty-five at some "park" that turns out to be miles away, shimmering flat Florida miles full of big white soupy power-steered American cars being driven by old people so shrunken they can hardly see over the hood. Any time you get somewhere down here without a head-on collision is a tribute to the geriatric medicine in this part of the world, the pep pills and vitamin injections and blood thinners.

Though Judy swears Roy has been to the movies before, he doesn't seem to understand you can't just talk up as in your own living room. He keeps asking why, with a plaintive inflection: "*Why* she take off her clothes?" "*Why* she so mad at that man?" Harry likes it, in the movie, when you see that Melanie Griffith in her whorehouse underwear has a bit of honest fat to her, not like most of these Hollywood anorectics, and when she bursts in upon her boyfriend with the totally naked girl, like herself supposed to be Italian but not like her aspiring to be a Wall Street wheeler-dealer, riding the guy in the astride position, her long bare side sleek as the skin of a top shell and her dark-nippled boobs right on screen for a good five seconds. But the plot, and the farce of the hero and heroine worming their way into the upper-crust wedding, he feels he saw some forty years ago with Cary Grant or Gary Cooper and Irene Dunne or Jean Arthur. When Roy loudly asks, "*Why* don't we go now?" he is willing to go out into the lobby with him, so Janice and Judy can see the picture to the end in peace.

He and Roy split a box of popcorn and try a video game called Annihilation. Though he always thought of himself as pretty good on eye-hand coordination, Harry can't hit a single space monster as it twitches and wiggles past in computer graphics. Roy, so small he has to be held up to the control panel until his twitching, wiggling weight gives Harry a pain across his shoulders, isn't any better. "Well, Roy," he sums up, when he gets his breath back, "if it was all up to us, the world would be taken over by space monsters." The boy, more accustomed to his grandfather now, stands close, and his breath smells buttery from the popcorn, making Harry slightly queasy: this thin unconscious stream of childish breath reminds him of the overhead vent in an airplane.

When the crowd comes out of Cinema 3, Janice announces, "I think I need a job. Wouldn't you like me better, Harry, if I was a working girl?"

"Which state would you work in?"

"Pennsylvania, obviously. Florida is for vacations."

He doesn't like the idea. It has something fishy and uncomfortable about it, like that batch of November stats from Springer Motors. "What work would you do?"

"I don't know. Not work at the lot, Nelson hates us to get in his way. Sell something, maybe. My father was one and my son is one so why shouldn't I be one? A salesperson."

Rabbit doesn't know what to answer. After all these years of his grudgingly sticking with her, he can't imagine him begging her to stick with him, though this is his impulse. He changes conversational partners. "Judy. How did the movie come out?"

"Good. The man from the wedding believed her story and she got an office of her own with a window and her nasty boss broke her leg and lost the man they both liked."

"Poor Sigourney," Harry says. "She should have stuck with the gorillas." He stands way above his own little herd in the theatre lobby, where the ushers move back and forth with green garbage bags and red velvet ropes, getting ready for the five o'clock shows. "So, guys. What shall we do next? How about miniature golf? How about driving up to St. Petersburg, over this fantastic long bridge they have?"

Roy's lower lip starts to tremble, and he has such trouble getting his words out that Judy translates for him. "He says he wants to go home."

"Who doesn't?" Janice concurs. "Grandpa was just teasing. Haven't you learned that about your grandfather yet, Roy? He's a terrible tease."

Is he? He has never thought of himself that way. He sometimes says a thing to try it out, like a head fake, to open up a little space.

Judy smiles knowingly. "He pretends to be mean," she says.

"Grrr," Grandpa says.

Forty minutes of southwestern Florida rush-hour traffic bring them to the Deleon exit and Pindo Palm Boulevard and the nicely guarded entrance of Valhalla Village. Up in 413, Pru and Nelson look bathed and refreshed and act as if nothing has ever happened. They listen to the travellers' tales, foremost the incredible story of how Grandpa ate the grungy birdfood, and Pru sets about making dinner, telling Janice to take the weight off her legs, and Nelson settles on the sofa with a child on each knee in front of the local evening news, giving Harry a pang of jealousy and a sensation of injustice. The surly kid spends the whole day balling this big redhead and then is treated like a hero by these two brats Harry went and knocked himself out for.

Rabbit sits in the chair across the glass table from the sofa and delicately needles his son. "Ja catch up finally on your sleep?" he asks.

Nelson gets the dig and looks over at him with his dark swarmy eyes a little flat across the top, like a cross cat's. "I went into a place to get a bite to eat last night and stayed at the bar too long," he tells his father.

"Ya do that often?"

With a roll of his eyeballs Nelson indicates the children's heads right under his face, watching television but perhaps also listening. Little pitchers. "Naa," he allows. "Just when I'm tense it helps to take off once in a while. Pru understands. Nothing happens."

Rabbit holds up a generous hand. "None of my business, right? You're twenty-one plus. It's just you could have called. I mean, a considerate person would have called. None of us could enjoy dinner, not knowing what had happened to you. We could hardly eat."

"I *tried* to call, Dad, but I don't have your number down here memorized and the place I was in some sleazeball had stolen the phone book."

"That's your story this evening? This morning your mother told me you did call here but we were down to dinner."

"That, too, I tried once from a phone along the highway and then in this place there was no phone book."

"Where was the place? Think I'd know it?"

"No idea where," Nelson says, and smiles into the television flicker. "I get lost down here, it's like one big business strip. One nice thing about Florida, it makes Pennsylvania look unspoiled."

The local news commentator is giving the manatee update. "Manatee herds continue to populate both warm-weather feeding areas and traditional winter refuges as fair weather and eighty-degree temperatures continue. A general waterways alert is out: boaters, cut your throttle to half-speed. Throughout the weekend, encounters with manatees remain likely in widely varied habitats around Southwest Florida."

"They say that," Rabbit says, "but I never encounter one."

"That's because you're never on the water," Nelson says. "It's stupid, to be down here like you are and not own a boat."

"What do I want a boat for? I hate the water."

"You'd get to love it. You could fish all over the Gulf. You don't have enough to do, Dad."

"Who wants to fish, if you're halfway civilized? Dangling

some dead meat in front of some poor brainless thing and then pulling him up by a hook in the roof of his mouth? Cruellest thing people do is fish."

The blond newscaster, with his hair moussed down so it's stiff as a wig, tells them, "An adult manatee with calf was reported at midday on Wednesday heading inland along Cape Coral's Bimini Canal about one-half mile from the Bimini Basin. Sightings like this indicate that while a large number of the Caloosahatchee herd have moved back out into the open waters of the river and back bays, some animals may still be encountered in and near sheltered waterways. To report dead or injured manatees, call 1-800-342-1821." The number rolls across some footage of a manatee family sluggishly rolling around in the water. "And," he concludes in that sonorous way television announcers have when they see the commercial break coming, "to report a manatee sighting, call the Manatee Hotline at 332-3092."

To refresh his rapport with Judy, Rabbit calls over, "How'd you like to have a single big tooth like that mamma manatee?" But the girl doesn't seem to hear, her fair little face radiantly riveted on one of those ads with California raisins singing and dancing like black men. Like the old Mouseketeers. Where are they now? Middle-aged parents themselves. Jimmie died years ago, he remembers reading. Died young. It happens. Roy is sucking his thumb and nodding off against Nelson's chest. Nelson is still wearing the white-collared, pink-striped shirt he wore down in the plane, as if he doesn't own anything as foolish as a short-sleeved shirt.

"Tomorrow," Rabbit loudly promises he doesn't know who, "I'll get out on the water. Judy and I will rent a Sunfish. I have it all set up with Ed Silberstein's son over at the Bayview Hotel."

"I don't know," Nelson says. "How safe *are* those things?"

Rabbit is insulted. "They're like toys, for Chrissake. If they tip over, you just stand on the centerboard and up they come. Kids ten, eleven years old race them over in the Bay all the time."

"Yeah, but Judy's not even nine yet, not for another month. And, no offense, Dad, you're way into double digits. And no sailor, from what you just said."

"O.K., *you* do something with your kids tomorrow. *You* entertain 'em. I spent over eight hours at it today and dropped around eighty bucks."

Nelson tells him, "You're supposed to *want* to do things like that. You're their dear old *grand*father, remember?" He softens, slightly. "Sunfishing's a nice idea. Just make sure she wears a life jacket."

"Why don't you all come along? You, Pru, Sleeping Beauty here. It's a helluva beach. They keep it clean."

"Maybe we will, if I can. I'm expecting a call or two."

"From the lot? Can't they even manage for half a week?"

Nelson is drifting away, hiding behind the distraction of television. One of the new Toyota ads is playing, with the black-woman car salesman. At the end, she and the customer jump into the air and are frozen there. "No," Nelson is saying, so softly Rabbit can hardly hear. "It's a contact I made down here."

"A contact? What about?"

Nelson puts his finger to his lip, to signal they should not wake Roy.

Rabbit gets out his needle again. "Speaking of digits, I keep trying to remember what seemed off about that November statement. Maybe the number of used seemed down for this time of year. Usually it's up, along with the new models."

"Money's scared, with Reagan going out," Nelson answers, ever so softly. "Also, Lyle's put in a new accounting system, maybe they were deferred into the next month and will show up in the December stats. Don't worry about it, Dad. You and Mom just enjoy Florida. You've worked hard all your life. You've earned a rest."

And the boy, as if to seal in the possibility of irony, kisses little Judy on the top of her shiny-sleek, carrot-colored head. The blue light from the set penetrates the triangular patch of thinning hair between Nelson's deepening temples. A hostage he's given to fortune. Your children's losing battle with time seems even sadder than your own.

"Dinner, guys and gals," Pru calls from Janice's aqua kitchen.

Her meal is a more thought-out affair than Janice's ever are, with a spicy clear sort of minestrone soup to begin, and a salad on a separate plate, and a fresh white fish, broiled on the stove grill attachment that Janice never takes the trouble to use. Janice has become a great warmer-up of leftovers in the microwave, and a great buyer over at Winn Dixie of frozen meatloaves and stuffed peppers and seafood casseroles in their little aluminum pans that can be tossed into the trashmasher dirty. She was always a minimal housewife and now the technology has caught up with her. The vegetables Pru serves, wild rice and little tender peas and baby onions, have a delicate pointed taste that Harry feels is aimed at him, a personal message the others consume without knowing. "Delicious," he tells Pru. "What's the fish called?"

"They said snook," she says. "I said 'What?' and they said snook again and I had to laugh, it sounded so rude. But it's what they had fresh. He said it's in the pike or perch family, I forget which."

Janice explains to Harry, "Pru went into this little narrow fish store behind Eckerd's where I never thought to go. Our generation," she explains to Pru, "didn't have that much to do with fish. Except I remember Daddy used to bring home a quart of shucked Chesapeake oysters as a treat for himself sometimes."

Pru says to Harry in her personally aimed, slightly scratchy Ohio voice, "Oily deepwater fish, bluefish especially, have lots of EPA in their oil, that's a kind of acid that actually thins your blood and lowers the triglyceride level."

She would take care of me, Harry thinks. Pleasurably he complains, "What's everybody always worried about my cholesterol level for? I must look awful."

"You're a big guy," Pru says, and the assessment pierces him like a love dart, "and as we all age the proportion of fat in our bodies goes up, and the amount of LDL, that's low-density lipoprotein, the bad kind of fat, goes up and that of the high-density, good kind stays the same, so the ratio goes up, and the danger of Apo B attaching to your arteries goes up with it. And you don't exercise the way people used to, when everybody had farms, so the fats don't get burned up."

"Teresa, you know so *much,*" Janice says, not quite liking being upstaged and using Pru's baptismal name as a tiny check, to keep her in place.

The other woman lowers her eyes and drops her voice. "You remember, I took that course at the Brewer Penn State extension. I was thinking, when Roy gets into school full-time, I should have something to do, and thought maybe nutrition, or dietetics . . ."

"*I* want to get a job, too," Janice says, annoying Harry with her intrusion into Pru's demure lecture about his very own, he felt, fatty insides. "The movie we saw this afternoon, all these women working in New York skyscrapers, made me so *jea*lous." Janice didn't use to dramatize herself. Ever since her mother died and they bought this condo, she has been building up an irritating confidence, an assumption that the world is her stage and her performance is going pretty well. Around Valhalla

Village, she is one of the younger women and on several house committees. Just not being senile is considered great down here. When they went to the Drechsels' seder, she turned out to be the youngest and had to ask the four questions.

Harry jealously asks Pru, "Does Nelson get the benefit of all this nutrition?"

Pru says, "He doesn't need it, really—he hardly ever eats, and he has all this nervous energy. He could *use* more lipids. But the children—they say now that after two in most American children the cholesterol level is too high. When they did autopsies on young men killed in the Korean War, three-quarters of them had too much fat in their coronary arteries."

Harry's chest is beginning to bind, to ache. His insides are like the sea to him, dark and wet and full of things he doesn't want to think about.

Nelson has done nothing to contribute to this conversation but sniff occasionally. The kid's nose seems to run all the time, and the line of bare skin above his mustache looks chafed. Now he pushes back from his half-eaten snook and announces complacently, "The way I figure, if one thing doesn't kill you, another will." Though he rests his palms on the edge of the table, his hands are trembling, the nerves snapping.

"It's not *what* we worry about, it's *when*," his father tells him.

Janice looks alarmed, her eyes shuttling from one to the other. "Let's all be cheerful," she says.

For dessert, Pru serves them frozen yogurt—much better for you than ice cream, with no cholesterol at all. When the meal is done, Harry hangs around the kitchen counter long enough to dig into the cookie drawer and stuff himself with three quick vanilla Cameos and a broken pretzel. Down here they don't have the variety of pretzels you get in Brewer but Sunshine sells a box of thick ones that are not too tasteless. He has an impulse to help Janice with the dishes and suppresses it; it's just throwing plates into the dishwasher and what else did she contribute to the meal? His feet hurt from all that walking they did today; he has a couple of toes that over the years have twisted enough in his shoes to dig their nails into each other if he doesn't keep them cut close. Pru and Roy and Nelson retreat into their room and he sits a while and watches while Judy, the remote control in hand, bounces back and forth between *The Cosby Show*, some ice capades, and a scare documentary about foreigners buying up American businesses, and then between *Cheers* and a drama about saving a fourteen-year-old girl from becoming a prostitute like her mother. So many emergencies, Harry thinks, so much canned laughter, so many actors' tears, all this effort to be happy, to be brave, to be loved, all this wasted effort. Television's tireless energy gnaws at him. He sighs and laboriously rises. His body sags around his heart like a tent around a pole. He tells Judy, "Better pack it in, sweetie. Another big day tomorrow: we're going to go to the beach and sailing." But his voice comes out listless, and perhaps that is the saddest loss time brings, the lessening of excitement about anything. These four guests are a strain; he looks forward to their departure Saturday, the last day of 1988.

Judy continues to stare at the screen and ply her channel changer. "Just the first part of *L.A. Law*," she promises, but flicks instead to an ABC news special about "American Kids— Their Diet of Danger." In their bedroom Janice is reading *Elle*, looking at the pictures, of superslim models looking stoned.

"Janice," he says. "I have something to ask you."

"What? Don't get me stirred up, I'm reading to make myself sleepy."

"Today," he says. "In that crowd going through the Edison place. Did I look as though I fit in?"

It takes her a while to shift her focus; then she sees what he wants. "Of course not, Harry. You looked much younger than the other men. You looked like one of their sons, visiting."

He decides this is as much reassurance as he dare ask for. "At least," he agrees with her, "I wasn't in a wheelchair." He reads a few pages of history, about the fight between the *Bonhomme Richard* and the *Serapis*, and how when amid the bloody explosions his chief gunner cried out "Quarter! quarter! for God's sake!" John Paul Jones *hurled a pistol at the man, felling him. But the cry had been heard by Pearson, the* Serapis' *commander, who called, "Do you ask for quarter?" Through the clash of battle, gunshot and crackle of fire the famous reply came faintly back to him: "I have not yet begun to fight!"* The victorious American ship was so damaged it sank the next day, and Jones took the captured *Serapis*, shorn of its mast, into Holland, *exacerbating the British resentment that already existed.* All this fury and bravery seems more wasted effort. Rabbit feels as if the human race is a vast colorful jostling bristling parade in which he is limping and falling behind. He settles the book on the night table and switches off the lamp. The bar of light beneath the door transmits distant shots and shouts from some TV show, any TV show. He falls asleep with unusual speed, with scarcely a turn into his pillow. His arms, which usually get in the way, fold themselves up like pieces of blanket. His dreams include one in which he has come to a door, a door with a round top to it, and pushes at it. The glass door at McDonald's except that one you could see the hamburger head through. In his dream he knows there is a presence on the other side, a presence he dreads, hungry and still, but pushes nevertheless, and the dread increases with the pressure, so much that he awakes, his bladder aching to go to the bathroom. He can't get through the night any more. His prostate, his bladder, losing stretch like goldenrod rubber. His mistake was drinking a Schlitz while channel-surfing with Judy. Falling asleep again is not so easy, with Janice's deep breathing now and then dipping into a rasping snore just as he begins to relax and his brain to generate nonsense. The luminous bar beneath the door is gone but a kind of generalized lavender light, the light that owls and other animals of the night see to kill by, picks out the planes and big objects of the bedroom. A square bureau holds the glassy rectangle of Nelson's high-school graduation photo; a fat pale chair holds on one arm Harry's discarded linen trousers, the folds of cloth suggesting a hollow-eyed skull stretched like chewing gum. Air admitted from the balcony under the folds of the drawn curtain grazes his face. A way of going to sleep is to lie on your back and try to remember the dream you were having. Unease seizes him like a great scaly-footed parrot claw and puts him down again on his face. The next thing he knows he is hearing the mowing machines on the golf course, and the stirred-up seagulls weeping.

The lobby of the Omni Bayview, entered from under a wide maroon marquee through sliding glass doors tinted opaque like limousine windows, knocks you out, virtually blinds you with its towering space and light, its great prismatic chandelier and splashing fountain and high rear wall of plate glass flooded with the view of Deleon Bay: beach in the foreground and sea like a scintillating blue-green curtain hung from a horizon line strung between two pegs of land, rich men's islands. "Wow," Judy breathes at Harry's side. Pru and Roy, coming behind them, say nothing; but the shuffle of their sandals slows and hushes. They feel like four trespassers. The woman at the black-marble front desk is an exotic color, her skin mixed of Negro and Indian or Oriental tints and stretched tight over her cheekbones and nose-bone; her eyelids have been painted a metallic green and her earlobes covered by ribbed shells of gold.

Harry is so awed he makes a mistake in uttering the magic name of admission, saying "Silberstein."

The woman blinks her amazing metallic lids, then graciously tells him, "You must mean Mr. Silvers. He is this morning's beach supervisor." With merciful disdain she directs them across the lobby, her ringed hand gesturing like a Balinese dancer's, without letting go of a slim gold pen. He leads his little party into the vast air-conditioned space, across a floor of black marble inset with strips of brass that radiate out like rays of the sun from an aluminum fountain suggesting a pipe organ, beneath a remote ceiling of hanging rectangles of gilded metal like those glittering strips farmers hang to scare away birds. A flight of downward stairs is marked TO POOL AND BEACH in solemn letters such as you see on post-office façades. After taking a wrong turn in the milky-green terrazzo corridors on the ground floor and confronting a door marked STAFF ONLY, Harry and his group find Ed Silberstein's son Gregg in a glassed-in, straw-matted area on the way to the hotel swimming pool—pools, since Harry sees there are three, fitted together like the blobs in an intelligence test, one for waders, one for divers, and a long one marked in lanes. Gregg is a curly-haired man brown as an Arab from being off and on the beach all day. In little black elastic European-style trunks and a hooded sweatshirt bearing the five-sided Omni logo, he stands less tall than his father, and his inherited sharp-chinned accountant's jaw has been softened by a mother's blood and a job of holiday facilitation. He smiles, showing teeth as white as Ed's but rounder: Ed's were so square they looked false, but Harry has never seen them slip. When Gregg speaks, his voice seems too young for his age; his curls hold arcs of gray and his smile rouses creases in the sunbeaten face. He shouldn't still be horsing around on the beach.

"My father said you'd be coming. This is Mrs. Angstrom?" He means Pru, who has come instead of Janice, who after all that tramping around yesterday wanted to stay home and catch up on her errands and go to her aerobics class and bridge group and spend a little time with Nelson before he goes home. Harry is stunned that Ed's son could make this blunder but then thinks he must deal all the time with men in advanced middle age who have younger wives. And anyway Pru is no longer that young. Tall and fair-skinned like he is, she might well be his.

"Thanks for the compliment, Gregg," Harry says, pretty

smoothly, considering, "but this is my daughter-in-law, Teresa." Teresa, Pru—she is like him even in having two names, an inner and an outer. "And these are my two grandchildren, Judy and Roy."

Gregg tells Judy, "So you're the one who wants to be a sailor girl."

Her eyes when she lifts them to Gregg's face flood here by the pools with a skyey light that washes out their green and makes her pupils small as pencil leads. "Sort of."

Moving and speaking in a relaxed thorough way that suggests his whole day could happily be devoted to them, Ed's son leads them back into the terrazzo corridors and arranges for locker keys for them with a boy at a desk—a young black with his hair shaved into one of those muffin-tops they do now, an ugly style, with bald sides—and then leads them to the locker-room doors, and tells them how to exit directly onto the beach, where he will meet them and manage the Sunfish rentals. "How much do I owe you for all this?" Harry asks, half-expecting it will be free, arranged for by Ed in compensation for the twenty Harry dropped to him at Wednesday's golf.

But Gregg sheds a bit of his amiability and says, "The boats are exclusively for the use of hotel guests and get included in their charges, but I think about a hundred twenty for the four of you would cover it, with the lockers and beach access and two Sunfish for an hour each."

Pru speaks up. "We don't want two. I'd be terrified."

He looks her up and down and says with a new thrust in his voice, a little friendly lean in from a guy who deals with a lot of women in this job, "No need to be terrified, Teresa. They can't sink, and lifesavers are compulsory. Worst case and you feel you have no control, just let go of the sail and we'll come out for you in the launch."

"Thanks but no thanks," Pru says, a bit perkily Harry thinks, but, then, she and this guy are about the same age. Baby boomers. Rock and roll, dope, *Leave It to Beaver*, physical fitness. And wait till they discover they both come from Ohio.

Gregg Silvers turns to him and says, "Ninety should about do it, then."

The sum seems an invitation to tip him ten, but Harry wonders if this wouldn't be insulting, since he is here as a family friend, and waits for Gregg to fetch the bill from the muffin-topped boy at the desk. When Rabbit and Roy are alone in the locker room, he tells the child, "Jesus, Roy, that just about cleaned out poor old Grandpa's wallet!"

Roy looks up at him with frightened inky eyes. "Will they put us in jail?" he asks, his voice high and precise, like wind chimes.

Harry laughs. "Where'd you get that idea?"

"Daddy hates jail."

"Well who doesn't!" Harry says, wondering if the child is quite right in the head. Roy doesn't understand you should loosen the string of bathing trunks to pull them on, and while he fumbles and struggles his little penis sticks straight out, no longer than it is thick, cute as a button mushroom. He is circumcised. Rabbit wonders what his own life would have been like if he had been circumcised. The issue comes up now and then in the newspapers. Some say the foreskin is like an eyelid; without it the constantly exposed glans becomes less sensitive, it gets thick-skinned and dull rubbing against cloth all the time. A letter he once read in a skin magazine was from a guy who got circumcised in midlife and found his sexual pleasure and responsiveness went so far down his circumcised life was hardly worth living. If Harry had been less responsive he might have been a more dependable person, not so crazy to have his eye down there opened. Getting a hard-on you can feel the foreskin sweetly tug back, like freezing cream lifting the paper cap on the old-time milk bottles. From the numb look of his prick Roy will be a solid citizen. His grandfather reaches down a hand to lead him out to the beach.

Harry and Janice after their first year or two in Florida, when in their excitement at being here they bought a telescope for the balcony and three or four times a week would drive the two miles to the Deleon public beach for a walk and picnic supper if not a swim, gradually stopped visiting the Gulf. So it hits him now as something fresh, unforeseen, this immensity of water, of air, of a surface of flux battered into a million oscillating dents. The raw glory of it all overpowers for a moment the nagging aches and worries in his chest and releases him into self-forgetfulness. Such light-struck and level grandeur is like nothing he knew in the Pennsylvania landscape, hemmed in by woods and hills and housetops, a land dingy with centuries of use, where even the wild patches, the quarries and second-growth woodland and abandoned factories and mineshafts, had been processed by men and discarded. Here, all feels virgin, though in fact there is a history too, of Indians and conquistadores and barefoot mailmen who served the mosquito-plagued coastal settlements. On the right and left of the horizon are islands where the millionaires used to come by private railroad car for the tarpon fishing in April. Spanish and French pirates once hid among these islands. Gold is still buried in their sands. They are flat and seem very distant from where Harry and Roy stand on the beach wall. It is all so bright, so open, the world feels created anew, in synthetic elements. Sailboats, windsurfing rigs, those motorcycles that buzz along on top of the water, plastic paddleboats, and inflated rafts dot the near water with colors gaudy as a supermarket's. A distance down the beach, in front of another hotel, someone is flying a kite—a linked pair of box kites that dip and dive and climb again in unison, trailing glittering orange ribbons. For a mile in either direction, a twinkling party of tan flesh and cloth patches is assembling itself, grainlike live bodies laid on top of the beach of sand.

Pru and Judy come out of the hotel to join them and they descend concrete steps. The hour has passed ten o'clock, and at their backs the tall hotel, shaped like an S fifteen stories high, fringed at each story with balconies like fine-toothed red combs, still has its face in shadow, though its shadow has shrunk back to the innermost of its pools. The sand is freshly raked underfoot; yesterday's footprints and plastic glasses and emptied lotion bottles have been taken away and the wooden beach chaises stacked. Today's sunbathers are arranging themselves and their equipment, their towels and mystery novels (Ruth used to read those, and what she got out of them was another mystery) and various color-coded numbers of sunscreen. Couples are greasing each other. Old smoothies already the color of leather are rubbing oil into their bald heads, the hair of their chests pure white. The smell of lotion rises to intertwine with the odor of salt air, of dead crab, of seaweed. As he leads his group across the sand Harry feels heads lift and eyes behind sunglasses slide; he feels proud and strange to be seen with this much younger woman and two small children. His second family. Or his third or fourth. Life moves through us family after family.

At the water's slapping, hissing, frothing edge sandpipers scurry and halt, stab the foam for some morsel, and scurry on. Their feet and heads are so quick they appear mechanical. Roy cannot catch them, though they seem like toys. When Harry takes off his unlaced Nikes, the sand bites his bare feet with an unexpected chill—the tide of night still cold beneath the sunny top layer of grains. The tops of his feet show wormy blue veins, and his shins are all chalky and crackled, as if he is standing up to his knees in old age. A tremor of fright comes alive in his legs. The sea, the sun are so big: cosmic wheels he could be ground between. He is playing with fire.

Gregg is waiting for them at a hut of corrugated Fiberglas on the beach, back from the water near some palms with their roots exposed. He has taken from the hut a rudder, a centerboard, and two life jackets of black foam rubber. Rabbit doesn't like the color, the texture; he wants old fashioned Day-Glo kapok from Thomas Edison's kapok trees. Gregg asks him, "You've done this before?"

"Sure."

But something in Harry's tone leads Gregg to be instructive: "Push the tiller away from the sail. Watch the tips of the waves for the direction of the wind. When the wind gets behind you, hold the mainsheet loose."

"O.K., sure," Harry says, having not quite listened, thinking instead, resentfully, of Ed Silberstein's bogey on the first hole yesterday and how its being enough for a win got the whole round off to a lousy start.

Gregg turns to Pru and asks, "Your little girl can swim?"

"Oh, sure," she says, picking up Harry's lazy word. "She was the champion in her swimming class at summer camp."

"*Mom,*" the girl pleads. "I came in *second*."

Gregg looks down at Judy, the sun at his back so bright the shadow on his face has a blue light of its own. "Second's pretty close to champ." Still needing to talk to Pru, Gregg says, "I wouldn't advise your little boy to go. There's an offshore breeze today, you can't feel it in the lee of the hotel here, but it takes you out there pretty fast. There's no cockpit, it's easy to slip off."

She gives Gregg Silvers her crooked wry grin and shifts her weight, as if the closeness of this man her own age makes her awkwardly aware of her near-nakedness. She is wearing a tie-dyed brown dashiki over her one-piece white suit with those high sides that expose leg up to the hipbone. The cut means you have to shave the sides off your pussy. What women go through. There's even a kind of wax job you can have done to make it permanent. But suppose bathing-suit fashions change again? Rabbit preferred that pre-Reagan look of the two-piece bikini with the lower half like a little skimpy diaper slung under the belly, like Cindy Murkett used to slosh around in. Still, this new style nicely lengthens Pru's already long legs and keeps her thickening middle in. "He's going to stay with me right on the beach," she tells Gregg Silvers, and by way of emphasis bows down, so her red hair flings forward, and pulls off her dashiki, revealing string straps and white wide shoulders mottled with pale freckles.

"How long do I have it for?" Harry, feeling ignored, asks Ed's son. Those tight little European-style bathing trunks definitely show the bump of a prick.

"One hour, sir." The "sir" just popped in absent-mindedly and the boy tries to revert to friendly casualness. "No sweat if you don't bring it in on the dot. There's not much action today, a lot of people don't like taking them out in this much wind. Take number nineteen, on the end there."

As Harry moves off, he hears Gregg ask Pru, "Where're you folks from up north?"

"Pennsylvania. Actually, I'm from Akron, Ohio."

"Hey! You'll never guess where I was raised—Toledo!"

The boats are up on the dry sand in a line, along with some other big water toys—those water bikes, and squarish paddleboats. Harry pulls at the nylon painter attached to the bow and the hull is heavier than he thought; by the time he's dragged it forty feet through the sand his breathing feels shallow and that annoying binding pain has begun to flicker on the left side of his ribs. He gives the boat one more heave and sits down in the sand, near where Pru is settling herself on a beach chaise Gregg has dragged down from the stack for her. Another beachgoer has momentarily called him away. "You like those?" Rabbit pants. "Don't you like feeling the sand under your—you know, like sort of a nest?"

She says, "It gets into the bathing suit, Harry. It gets in *ev*erywhere."

This needless emphasis, when he had got the picture, excites him, here in the bewildering brightness. He dimly remembers an old joke in high school about women making pearls. Cunts like Chesapeake oysters. That sly old Fred. He tells Judy, "Give me a second to get my breath, couldja honey? Go for a quick swim in the water so it won't be a shock when we're out on it. I'll be with you in one minute."

He should try to talk to Pru about Nelson. Something rotten there. Roy is already gouging at the sugary sand with a plastic shovel Janice thought to buy him at Winn Dixie. Frowningly the dark-eyed child dumps the sand into a bucket shaped like an upside-down Garfield. Pru says, since Harry seems unable to begin, "You're awfully nice to have arranged all this. I was astonished, how much he charged."

"Well," he says, feeling slowly better as his bare legs absorb heat from the top layer of sand, "you're only a grandfather once. Or twice, in my case. You and Nelson plan any more?" This feels forward, but not in a class with the sand getting in everywhere.

"Oh no, my God," she too swiftly answers, in a trough of silence as one long low wave follows another in and breaks in a frothy cresting of glitter and a mechanical scurrying of sandpipers. "We're not ready for any more."

"You're not, huh?" he says, not sure where to take this.

She helps him, her voice in his ear as he gazes out into the Gulf. He doesn't dare turn his head to look at her bare feet, their pink toe-joints and cracked nail polish, and her long legs lifted on the chaise, exposing contrasting white pieces of spandex crotch and soft flesh underside. These new bathing suits don't do much to hold a woman's ass in. She confesses to Harry, "I don't think we're doing justice to the two we've got, with Nelson how he is."

"Yeah, how is he? He seems jumpy, and only half here."

"That's *right*," she says, too enthusiastically agreeing. That's all she says. Another wave collapses and shooshes up the sand. She has pulled back. She is waiting for him to make an inspired guess.

"He hates Toyotas," he offers.

"Oh, he'd complain if they were Jaguars," Pru says. "Nothing would satisfy him, the way he is now."

The way he is. The secret seems to be in that phrase. Was the poor kid with his white-around-the-gills look dying of something, of leukemia like that girl in *Love Story*? Of AIDS he caught somehow—how, Harry can't bear to think—hanging around that faggy Slim crowd Lyle the new accountant is part of. But it all seems distant, like those islands where pirates hid gold and rich men caught tarpon, mere thickenings of the horizon from this angle three feet above sea level. He can't focus on it, with the sun on his head. He maybe should have brought a hat, to protect his Swedish complexion. His suspicion has always been he looks foolish in a hat, his head too big already. Roy has filled the bucket and pretty carefully, considering he's only four, dumps it upside down and lifts it off. He expects to have a sand Garfield but the shape is too tricky and crumbles on one side. A bad principle, fancy shapes. Stick with simple castles and let the kids use their imaginations. Harry volunteers, speaking into the air, not quite daring to turn his head and face Pru's crotch, and those nameless bits exposed by the way her legs are up, "He was never what you'd call a terrifically happy child. I guess me and Jan are to blame for that."

"He's willing to blame you," Pru admits in her flat Ohio voice. "But I don't think you should reinforce him by blaming yourself." Her language here, as when she spoke about cholesterol the other night, seems to him disagreeably specific, like a pet's fur that is coarse and more prickly than you expect when you touch it. "I'd refuse," she says firmly, "to let a child of *mine* send me on a guilt trip."

"I don't know," Harry demurs. "We put him through some pretty wild scenes back there in the late Sixties."

"That's what the late Sixties were for everybody, wild scenes," Pru says, and goes back into that coarse semi-medical talk. "By continuing to accept the blame he's willing to assign you, you and Janice continue to infantilize him. After thirty, shouldn't we all be responsible for our own lives?"

"Beats me," he says, "I never know who was responsible for mine," and he pushes himself up from the trough his body has warmed in the sand, but not before flicking his eyes back to that strip of stretched spandex flanked by soft pieces of Pru that have never had enough sun to freckle. Little Judy has come back from swimming, her red hair soaked tight to her skull and her navy-blue bathing suit adhering to the pinhead bumps of her nipples.

"You promised a *minute*," she reminds him, water running down her face and beaded in her eyelashes like tears.

"So I did," he agrees. "Let's go Sunfishing!" He stands, and the Florida breeze catches in every corner of his skin, as if he is the kite down the beach. He feels tall under the high blue sky; the elements poured out all around him—water and sand and air and sun's fire, substances lavished in giant amounts yet still far from filling the limitless space—reawaken in him an old animal recklessness. His skin, his heart can never have enough. "Put your life jacket on," he tells his granddaughter.

"It makes me feel fat," she argues. "I don't need it, I can swim for miles, honest. At camp, way across the lake and back. When you're tired, you just turn on your back and float. It's easier in saltwater, even."

"Put it on, honey," he repeats serenely, pleased that blood of his has learned ease in an element that has always frightened him. He puts his own jacket on, and feels armored, and female, and as the kid says fat. His legs and arms have never gained much weight, only his abdomen and his face, strangely; shaving each morning, he seems to have acres of lather to remove, and catching himself sideways in a reflecting surface in glassy downtown Deleon he is astonished by this tall pale guy stuffed with kapok. "You keep an eye on us," he tells Pru, who has risen to solemnize this launching. Near-naked as she is, she helps pull the hull to the water's agitated slipslopping edge. She quiets the flapping sail, which wants to swing the boom, while he sorts out the lines, more complicated than he remembers from the time he went Sunfishing in the Caribbean years ago with Cindy Murkett and her bikini, and clips in the rudder. He lifts Judy up and on. Little Roy, when he sees his sister about to go somewhere without him, screams and stalks into a wave that knocks him down. Pru picks him up and holds him on her hip. The air is so bright everything seems to be in cutout, with that violet halo you see in movies where the scenery is faked. Harry wades in up to his waist to walk the boat out, then heaves himself aboard, barking his shin on a cleat, and grabs at the line attached to the aluminum boom. What did Cindy call it, that piece of nylon rope? The sheet. Sweet Cindy, what a gumdrop she once was. He steadies the rudder and pulls the sail taut. The boat is dipping and patting the waves one by one as the offshore breeze, in the dreamlike silence that comes within the wind, moves the boat away from the solidity of land, of beach, of Pru in her pristine suit holding screaming Roy on her hip.

Judy is stationed on this side of the mast, poised to push the centerboard down its slot; Harry sits awkwardly on the wet Fiberglas with his legs bent and one hand behind him on the tiller and the other clutching the sheet. His mind begins to assemble a picture of directional arrows, the shining wind pressing on the sail's straining striped height. Certain tense slants begin in his hands and fan out to the horizon and zenith. *Like a scissors,* Cindy had said, and a sensation of funnelled invisible power grows upon him. "Centerboard down," he commands, a captain at last, at the mere age of fifty-five. His scraped shin stings and his buttocks in his thin wet bathing suit resent the pressure of bald Fiberglas. His weight is so much greater than Judy's the hollow hull tips upward in front. The waves are choppier, the tugs on the sail ruder, and the water a dirtier green than in his enhanced memory of that Caribbean adventure at the beginning of this decade.

Still, his companion is happy, her bright face beaded with spray. Her thin little arms stick goosebumped out of her dull-black rubber vest, and her whole body shivers with the immersion in motion, the newness, the elemental difference. Rabbit looks back toward land: Pru, the sun behind her, is a forked silhouette against the blaze of the beach. Her figure in another minute will be impossible to distinguish from all the others tangled along the sand, the overprinted alphabet of silhouettes. Even the hotel has shrunk in the growing distance, a tall slab among many, hotels and condos for as far as he can see in either direction along this stretch of the Florida coast. The power he finds in his hands to change perspectives weighs on his chest and stomach. Seeing the little triangular sails out here when he and Janice drove the shore route or visited their bank in downtown Deleon had not prepared him for the immensity of his perspectives, any more than the sight of men on a roof or scaffold conveys the knee-grabbing terror of treading a plank at that height. "Now, Judy," he says, trying to keep any stiffness of fear from his voice, yet speaking loudly lest the dazzling amplitudes of space suck all sense from his words, "we can't keep going forever in this direction or we'll wind up in Mexico. What I'm going to do is called coming about. I say—I know it seems silly—'Coming about, hard alee,' and you duck your head and don't slide off when the boat changes direction. Ready? Coming about, hard alee."

He is not quite decisive enough in pushing the tiller away from him, and for too many seconds, with Judy crouched in a little acrobatic ball though the boom has already passed over her head, they head lamely into the wind, in a stillness wherein the slapping of water sounds idle and he feels they are being carried backward. But then an inertia not quite squandered by his timidity swings the bow past the line of the wind and the sail stops impatiently rippling and bellies with a sulky ripple in the direction of the horizon and goes tight, and Judy stops looking worried and laughs as she feels the boat tug forward again, over the choppy, opaque waves. He pulls in sail and they move at right angles to the wind, parallel to the color-flecked shore. In their moment of arrested motion the vastness all around had transfixed them as if with arrows from every empty shining corner of air and sea, but by moving they escape and turn space to their use; the Gulf, the boat, the wind, the sun burning the exposed tips of their ears and drying the spray from the erect pale body hairs on their goosebumped arms all make together a little enclosed climate, a burrow of precise circumstance that Harry gradually adjusts to. He begins to know where the wind is coming from without squinting up at the faded telltale at the top of the mast, and to feel instinctively the planes of force his hands control, just as on a fast break after a steal or rebound of the basketball in the old days he would picture without thinking the passing pattern, this teammate to that, and the ball skidding off the backboard into the hoop on the layup. Growing more confident, he comes about again and heads toward a distant green island tipped with a pink house, a mansion probably but a squat hut from this distance, and pulls in the sail, and does not flinch when the boat heels on this new tack.

Like a good grandfather, he explains his actions to Judy as they go along, the theory and the practice, and both of them become infected by confidence, by the ease with which this toy supporting them can be made to trace an angled path back and forth, teasing the wind and the water by stealing a fraction of their glinting great magnitudes.

Judy announces, "I want to steer."

"You don't *steer* it, sweetie, like you steer a bicycle. You can't just point it where you want to go. You have to keep the wind in mind, what direction it's coming from. But yeah, O.K., scrootch your like backside back toward me and take hold of the tiller. Keep the boat pointed at that little island with the pink house out there. That's right. That's good. Now you're slipping off a little. Pull it a bit toward you to make it come left. That's called port. Left is port, starboard is right. Now I'm letting out the sail a little, and when I say 'Ready about,' you push the tiller toward me as hard as you can and hold it. Don't panic, it takes a second to react. Ready? Ready, Judy? O.K. Ready about, hard alee."

He helps her through the last part of the arc, her little arm doesn't quite reach. The sail slackens and flaps. The boom swings nervously back and forth. The aluminum mast squeaks in its Fiberglas socket. A far gray freighter sits on the horizon like a nickel on a high tabletop. A bent-winged tern hangs motionless against the wind and cocks its head to eye them as if to ask what they are doing so far out of their element. And then the sail fills; Harry tugs it in; his hand on top of Judy's little one sets the angle of the tiller for this tack. Their two weights toward the stern lift the bow and make the Sunfish slightly wallow. The patter of waves on the hull has settled into his ears as a kind of deafness. She tacks a few more times and, seeing that's all there is to it, grows bored. Her girlish yawn is a flower of flawless teeth (the chemicals they put in toothpaste now, these kids will never know the agony he did in dental chairs) and plush arched tongue. Some man some day will use that tongue.

"You kind of lose track of time out here," Harry tells her. "But from the way the sun is it must be near noon. We should head back in. That's going to take some time, since the wind's coming out against us. We don't want your mother to get worried."

"That man said he'd send a launch out."

Harry laughs, to release the tension of the tenderness he feels toward this perfect child, all coppery and bright and as yet unmarred. "That was just for an emergency. The only emergency we have is our noses are getting sunburned. We can sail in, it's called beating against the wind. You work as close to the wind as you can. Here, I'll pull in the sail and you try to keep us pointed toward that hotel. Not the hotel at the very far right. The one next to it, the one like a pyramid."

The merged bodies on the beach have lost their flecks of color, the twinkle of their bathing suits, and seem a long gray string vibrating along the Bay for miles. The water out here is an uglier color, a pale green on top of a sunken bile green, than it seems from the shore.

"Grandpa, are you cold?"

"Getting there," he admits, "now that you ask. It's chilly, this far out."

"I'll say."

"Isn't your life jacket keeping you warm?"

"It's slimy and awful. I want to take it off."

"Don't."

Time slips by, the waves idly slap, the curious tern keeps watch, but the shore doesn't seem to be drawing closer, and the spot where Roy and Pru wait seems far behind them. "Let's come about," he says, and this time, what with the child's growing boredom and his own desire to get in and conclude this adventure, he tries to trim the wind too closely. A puff comes from an unexpected direction, from the low pirate islands instead of directly offshore, and instead of the Sunfish settling at a fixed heel in a straight line at a narrow angle to the direction they have been moving in, it heels and won't stop heeling, it loses its grip on the water, on the blue air. The mast passes a certain point up under the sun and as unstoppably as if pushed by a giant malevolent hand topples sideways into the Gulf. Rabbit feels his big body together with Judy's little lithe one pitch downward feet-first into the abyss of water, his fist still gripping the line in a panic and his shin scraped again, by an edge of Fiberglas. A murderous dense cold element encloses his head in an unbreathable dark green that clamps his mouth and eyes and then pales and releases him to air, to sun, and to the eerie silence of halted motion.

His brain catches up to what has happened. He remembers how Cindy that time stood on the centerboard and the Sunfish came upright again, its mast hurling arcs of droplets against the sky. So there is no great problem. But something feels odd, heartsuckingly wrong. Judy. Where is she? "Judy?" he calls, his voice not his out here between horizons, nothing solid under him and waves slapping his face with a teasing malice and the hull of the Sunfish resting towering on its edge casting a narrow shade and the striped sail spread flat on the water like a many-colored scum. *"Judy!"* Now his voice belongs entirely to the hollow air, to the heights of terror; he shouts so loud he swallows water, his immersed body offering no platform for him to shout from; a bitter molten lead pours instead of breath into his throat and his heart's pumping merges with the tugs and swellings of the sea. He coughs and coughs and his eyes take on tears. She is not here. There are only the dirty-green waves, kicking water, jade where the sun shines through, layered over bile. And clouds thin and slanting in the west, forecasting a change in the weather. And the hollow mute hull of the Sunfish hulking beside him. His bladder begs him to pee and perhaps he does.

The other side. She must be there. He and the boat and sail exist in a few square yards yet enormous distances feel ranged against him. He must dive under the hull, quickly. Every second is sinking everything. The life jacket buoys him but impedes. Currents in the water push against him. He has never been a natural swimmer. Air, light, water, silence all clash inside his head in a thunderous demonstration of mercilessness. Even in this instant of perfectly dense illumination there is space for his lifelong animal distaste for putting his head underwater, and for the thought that another second of doing nothing might miraculously bring it all right; the child's smiling face will surface with saltwater sparkling in her eyelashes. But the noon sun says now or never and something holy in him screams that all can be retrieved and he opens his mouth and sucks down panicked breath through a sieve of pain in his chest and tries to burrow through a resistant opacity where he cannot see or breathe. His head is pressed upward against something hard while his hands sluggishly grope for a snagged body and find not even a protuberance where a body could snag. He tries to surface. Fiberglas presses on his back like sharkskin and then the tiller's hinged wood, dangling down dripping, scrapes his face.

"Judy!" This third time he calls her name he is burbling; gobbets of water make rainbow circles in his vision as he faces straight up into the sun; in these seconds the boat is slowly twirling and its relation to the sun, the shadow it casts on the water, is changing.

Under the sail. She must be under the sail. It seems vast in the water, a long nylon pall with its diagonal seams, its stitched numbers and sunfish silhouette. He must. His bowels burn with all the acid guilt that has accumulated since creation; he again forces himself under into a kind of dirty-green clay where his bubbles are jewels. Against the slither of cloth on his back he tries to tunnel forward. In this tunnel he encounters a snake, a flexible limp limb that his touch panics so it tries to strangle him and drag him down deeper. It claws his ear; his head rises into the sail and a strained white light breaks upon his eyes and there is a secret damp nylon odor but no air to breathe. His body convulsively tries to free itself from this grave; he flounders with his eyes shut; the sail's edge eventually nuzzles past his drowning face and he has dragged along Judy into the light.

Her coppery wet hair gleams an inch from his eyes; her face makes a blurred clotted impression upon him but she is writhingly alive. She keeps trying to climb on top of him and locking her arms around his head. Her body feels hot under its slippery glaze. Dark water persistently rebounds into his eyes and mouth, as if a bursting spider keeps getting between him and the sun. With his long white arm he reaches and grasps the aluminum mast; though it sinks to a steeper angle with the addition of weight, the sail and the hollow hull refuse to let it sink utterly. Harry gasps and in two jerks pulls them higher up, where the mast is out of the water. Joy that Judy lives crowds his heart, a gladness that tightens and rhythmically hurts, like a hand squeezing a ball for exercise. The space inside him has compressed, so that as he hangs there he must force down thin wedges of breath into a painful congestion. Judy keeps hanging around his neck and coughing, coughing up water and fright. The rough motion of her little body wrenches twinges out of his tender, stunned chest, where something living flutters and aches.

It is as if amidst all this seawater his chest is a beaker of the same element holding an agitated squid.

Perhaps a minute has passed since their spill. After another minute, she has breath enough to attempt a smile. Her eyewhites are red from within, from the tears of her coughing. Her long little face sparkles all over, as if sprinkled with tinsel, and then a slow twirl of the Sunfish places their heads in the narrow clammy band of shadow the hull casts. To his eyes she looks in her breathless frightened pallor less like Pru than Nelson, fine-boned and white around the gills, and with shadows under her eyes as if after a night of sleeplessness.

Though his pains continue underwater he can speak. "Hey," he says. "Wow. What happened, exactly?"

"I don't know, Grandpa," Judy says politely. Getting these words out sends her into another spasm of coughing. "I came up and there was this thing over me and when I tried to swim nothing happened, I couldn't get out from under."

He realizes that her fright has its limits; she thinks that even out here nothing more drastic than discomfort can befall her. She has a child's sense of immortality and he is its guardian.

"Well, it worked out," he pants. "No harm done." Besides the pain, that will not let go and is reaching up the arm that clings to the mast, there is a bottom to his breathing, and from lower down a color of nausea, of seasickness it may be, and enclosing that a feebleness, a deep need to rest. "The wind changed on us," he explains to Judy. "These things tip over too damn easy."

Now the grand strangeness of where they are, hundreds of yards from shore and hundreds of feet above sea bottom, begins to grab her. Her eyes with their perfectly spaced lashes widen and her carefully fitted thin lips begin to loosen and blur. Her voice has a quaver. "How do we get it back up?"

"Easy," he tells her. "I'll show you a trick." Did he remember how? Cindy had done it so quickly, diving right under the boat, in those glassy Caribbean waters. A line, she had to have pulled on a line. "Stay close to me but don't hang on me any more, honey. Your life vest will hold you up."

"It didn't before."

"Sure it did. You were just under the sail."

Their voices sound diminished out here in the Gulf, flying off into space without lingering in the air the way words spoken in rooms do. Treading water takes all of his breath. He mustn't black out. He must hold the sunlit day from dropping its shutter on its head. He thinks if he ever gets out of this he will lie down on a firm dry stretch of grass—he can picture it, the green blades, the thatchy gaps of rubbed earth like at the old Mt. Judge playground—and never move. Gently he lets go of the mast and with careful paddling motions, trying not to jar whatever is disturbed in his chest, takes the two nylon lines floating loose and, with an effort that by recoil action pushes his face under, tosses them over to the other side. The waves are rough enough that Judy clings to his shoulder though he asked her not to. He explains to her, "O.K. Now we're going to doggie-paddle around the boat."

"Maybe that man who liked Mom will come out in his launch."

"Maybe. But wouldn't that be embarrassing, being rescued with Roy watching?"

Judy is too worried to laugh or respond. They make their way past the tiller, the ugly wooden thing that scraped his face. The tern has left the sky but floating bits of brown seaweed, like paper mops or wigs for clowns, offer proofs of other life. The slime-stained white hull lying sideways in the water seems a corpse he can never revive. "Back off a little," he tells the clinging child. "I'm not sure how this will go."

As long as he is in the water, at least he doesn't weigh much; but when, taking hold of the line threaded through the top of the aluminum mast, he struggles to place his weight on the centerboard, at first with his arms and then with his feet, he feels crushed by his own limp load of slack muscle and fat and guts. The pain in his chest gathers to such a red internal blaze that he squeezes his eyes shut to blot it out, and blindly then he feels with a suck of release the sail lift free of the water and the centerboard under him plunge toward vertical. The boat knocks him backward as it comes upright, and the loose wet sail swings its boom back and forth in a whipping tangle of line. He has no breath left and has an urge to give himself to the water, that hates him yet wants him.

But the child with him cheers. "Yaay! You did it! Grandpa, you O.K.?"

"I'm great. Can you get on first, honey? I'll hold the boat steady."

After several failed leaps out of the water Judy plops her belly on the curving deck, her blue-black bottom gleaming in two arcs, and scrambles to a crouching position by the mast.

"Now," he announces, "here comes the whale," and, lifting

his mind clear of the striated, pulsing squeezing within his rib cage, rises up enough out of the water to seize the tipping hull with his abdomen. He grabs a cleat. The fake grain of the Fiberglas presses its fine net against his cheekbone. The hungry water still sucks at his legs and feet but he kicks it away and shakily arranges himself in his position at the tiller again. He tells Judy, "We're getting there, young lady."

"You O.K., Grandpa? You're talking kind of funny."

"Can't breathe too well. For some reason. I might throw up. Let me rest a minute. And think. We don't want to. Tip this fucker over again." The pain now is down both arms and up into his jaw. Once Rabbit told someone, a prying clergyman, *somewhere behind all this there's something that wants me to find it*. Whatever it is, *it* has found *him*, and is working him over.

"Do you hurt?"

"Sure. My ear where you pulled it. My leg where I scraped it." He wants to make her smile but her starry-eyed study of him is unremittingly solemn. How strange, Rabbit thinks, his thoughts weirdly illumined by his agony, children are, shaped like us, torso and legs and ears and all, yet on a scale all their own—subcompact people made for a better but also a smaller planet. Judy looks at him uncertain of how seriously to take him, like yesterday when he ate the false peanuts.

"Stay just where you are," he tells her. "Don't rock the boat. As they say."

The tiller feels oddly large in his hands, the nylon rope unreally rough and thick. He must manage these. Untended, the boat has drifted dead into the wind. What was Cindy's phrase for that? *In irons*. He is in irons. He waggles the tiller, hard one way and gently the other, to get an angle on the wind, and timidly pulls in sail, fearing the giant hand will push them over again. Surprisingly, there are other Sunfish out in the bay, and two boys on jet skis, brutally jumping the waves, at such a distance that their yells and the slaps of impact arrive in his ears delayed. The sun has moved past noon, onto the faces of the tall hotels. The windows glint now, their comblike balconies stand out, the crowd on the beach twinkles, another kite flyer has joined the first. The sheet of water between here and shore is dented over and over by downward blows of light that throw sparks. Rabbit feels chilled in his drying skin. He feels full of a gray unrest that wants to ooze poison out through his pores. He stretches his legs straight in front of him and leans back on an elbow in an awkward approximation of lying down. Sinking into sleep would be a good idea if he weren't where he was, with this child to deliver back to her parents unharmed.

He speaks rapidly, between twinges, and clearly, not wanting to repeat. "Judy. What we're going to do is as quietly as we can take two big tacks and get to shore. It may not be exactly where your mother is but we want to get to land. I feel very tired and strange and if I fall asleep you wake me up."

"Wake you up?"

"Don't look so worried. This is a fun adventure. In fact, I have a fun job for you."

"What's that?" Her voice has sharpened; she senses now this isn't like the parrot food.

"Sing to me." When he pulls the sail tighter, it's as if he's tightening something within himself; pain shoots up the soft inner side of that arm to his elbow.

"Sing? I don't know any songs, Grandpa."

"Everybody knows some songs. How about 'Row, Row, Row Your Boat' to start off with?"

He closes his eyes intermittently, in obedience to the animal instinct to crawl into a cave with your pain, and her little voice above the slipslop of the waves and resistant creaking of the mast picks its wavery way through the words of the round, which he used to sing in the second grade back in the days of corduroy knickers and Margaret Schoelkopf's pigtails and high-buttoned shoes. His mind joins in, but can't spare the effort to activate his voice box, *Gently down the stream, Merrily, merrily, merrily* . . . "Life is but a dream," Judy ends.

"Nice," he says. "How about 'Mary Had a Little Lamb'? Do they still teach you that at school? What the hell *do* they teach you at school these days?" Being laid so low has loosened his language, his primal need to curse and his latent political indignation. He goes on, thinking it will make him seem less alarming to his grandchild, and humorously alive, "I know we're sucking hind titty in science education, the papers keep telling us that. Thank God for the Orientals. Without these Chinese and Vietnam refugees we'd be a nation of total idiots."

Judy does know "Mary Had a Little Lamb," and "Three Blind Mice," and the verses of "Farmer in the Dell" up to the wife takes a cow, but then they both lose track. "Let's do 'Three Blind Mice' again," he orders her. "*See* how they *run*. The *mice* ran after the farmer's *wife*. . . . "

She does not take up the verse and his voice dies away. Their tack is taking them far out toward the north, toward Sarasota and Tampa and the rich men's islands where the pirates once were, but the people on the beach do look a little less like gray string, the colors of their bathing suits twinkle a bit closer, and he can make out the darting tormented flight of a volleyball. A pressure in the center of his chest has intensified and to his nausea has been added an urgent desire to take a crap. In trying to picture his real life, the life of simple comforts and modest challenges that he abandoned when his foot left the sand, he now envisions foremost the rose-colored porcelain toilet bowl in the condo, with matching padded seat, and the little stack of *Consumer Reports* and *Times* that waited on the bottom shelf of the white-painted bamboo table Janice kept her cosmetics on top of, next to the rose-tinted bathroom basin. It seems to have been a seat in paradise.

"Grandpa, I can't think of any more songs." The child's green eyes, greener than Pru's, have a watery touch of panic.

"Don't stop," he grunts, trying to keep everything in. "You're making the boat go."

"No I'm not." She manages a blurred smile. "The wind makes it go."

"In the wrong fucking direction," he says.

"Is it wrong?" she asks with the quickness of fear.

"No, I'm just kidding." It was like that sadistic squeeze he gave her hand yesterday. Must stop that stuff. When you get children growing under you, you try to rise to the occasion. "We're fine," he tells her. "Let's come about. Ready? Duck your head, honey." No more sailor talk. He yanks the tiller, the boat swings, sail sags, sun shines down through the gap of silence, hammering the water into sparks. The bow drifts across a certain imaginary line, the sail hesitantly and then decisively fills, and they tug off in another direction, south, toward the remotest glass hotel and Naples and the other set of rich men's islands. The small effort and anxiety of the maneuver wring such pain from his chest that tears have sprung into his own eyes. Yet he feels good, down deep. There is a satisfaction in his skyey enemy's having at last found him. The sense of doom hovering over him these past days has condensed into reality, as clouds condense into needed rain. There is a lightness, a lightening, that comes along with misery: vast portions of the world are shorn off, suddenly ignorable. You become simply a piece of physical luggage to be delivered into the hands of others. Stretched out on the Fiberglas deck he is pinned flat to the floor of the world. The sensation of pressure, of unbearable fullness, within him now has developed a rhythm, an eccentric thrust as if a flywheel has come unconnected from its piston. Pain you can lift your head above, for a little; he minds more the breathing, the sensation that his access to the air has been narrowed to a slot that a fleck of mucus would clog, and worse even than the breathing, which if you can forget it seems to ease, is the involvement of his guts, the greasy gray churning and the desire to vomit and shit and yet not to, and the clammy sweating, which chills him in the wind and the sun's quick drying.

"Splish, splash, I was takin' a bath," Judy's faint voice sings, little feathers of music that fly away, "along about Saturday night. . . . " She has moved from nursery rhymes to television commercials, the first few lines of them until she forgets. "The good times, great taste, of McDonald's . . ." "I wish I were an Oscar Mayer wiener. That is what I'd truly like to be. 'Cause if I were an Oscar Mayer wiener, everyone would be in love with me." And the one the toilet paper sings, and the "Stand by Me" imitation by those California raisins, and the "Mack the Knife" by Ray Charles as the man in the moon, and the reassurance that if you want it, we've got it, "Toy-o-ta. . . . " It is like switching channels back and forth, her little voice lifting and blowing back into his face, his eyes closed while his mind pays furtive visits in the dark to the grinding, galloping, lopsided maladjustment in his chest, and then open again, to check their bearings and the tension in the sail, to test the illusion of blue sky and his fixed belief that her voice is powering the Sunfish toward the shore. "Coke is it," Judy sings, "the most refreshing taste around, Coke is it, the one that never lets you down, Coke is it, the biggest taste you ever found!"

He has to tack twice more, and by then his granddaughter has discovered within herself the treasure of songs from videos she has watched many times, of children's classics Rabbit saw when they were new, the first time in those old movie theatres with Arabian decors and plush curtains that pulled back and giant mirrors in the lobby, songs of departure, "We're off to see the Wizard, the wonderful Wizard of Oz" and "Hi-ho, hi-ho, it's off to work we go," and sad songs of something in the sky to distract us from the Depression, "Somewhere over the Rainbow," and "When You Wish upon a Star," little Jiminy Cricket out there with his top hat and furled umbrella on that moon-bathed windowsill. *That Disney, he really packed a punch.*

"Nice, Judy," Rabbit grunts. "Terrific. You were really getting into it."

"It was fun, like you said. Look, there's Mommy!"

Harry lets the sheet and tiller go. The Sunfish bobs in the breaking waves of shallow water, and Judy pulls up the centerboard and jumps off into water up to her shiny hips and pulls the boat like a barge through the last yards before the bow scrapes sand. "We tipped over and Grandpa got sick!" she shouts.

Not just Pru and Roy but Gregg Silvers have come to meet them, about a good six-iron shot up the beach from where they set out. Gregg's too-tan face gives a twitch, seeing the way Harry keeps stretched out beside the useless tiller, and seeing something Harry can't, perhaps the color of his face. How bad is he? He looks at his palms; they are mottled with yellow and blue. Gregg takes the painter from Judy and asks Harry, "Want to stay where you are?"

Harry waits until a push of pain passes and says, "I'm getting off this fucking tub if it kills me."

But the action of standing and easing off the tipping Sunfish and wading a few feet does bad things to his slipped insides. He feels himself wade even through air, on the packed sand, against pronounced resistance. He lies down on the sand at Pru's feet, her long bare feet with chipped scarlet nails and their pink toejoints like his mother's knuckles from doing the dishes too many times. He lies face up, looking up at her white spandex crotch. Little Roy, thinking Harry's posture playful, toddles over and stands above his grandfather's head, shedding grains of sand down into Rabbit's ears, his clenched mouth, his open eyes; his eyes squeeze shut.

The sky is a blank redness out of which Pru's factual Ohio voice falls with a concerned intonation. "We saw you go over but Gregg says it happens all the time. Then it seemed to take so long he was just about to come out in the launch."

The redness pulses with a pain spaced like ribs, stripes of pain with intervals of merciful nothingness between them. Very high up, slowly, an airplane goes over, dragging its noise behind it. "Judy got under the sail," he hears his own voice say. "Scared me." He lies there like a jellyfish washed up, bulging, tremblingly full of a desire for its lost element. Another complicated warmish thing, with fingers, is touching his wrist, feeling his pulse. First-aid training must be part of Gregg's job. To assist him in his diagnosis Harry volunteers, "Sorry to be such a crump. I had this terrific desire to lie down."

"You keep lying there, Mr. Angstrom," Gregg says, sounding suddenly loud and crisp and a touch too authoritative, like his father adding up the golf scores. "We're going to get you to the hospital."

In his red blind world this news is such a relief he opens his eyes. He sees Judy standing huge and sun-haloed above him, fragments of rainbows confused with her tangled drying hair. Rabbit tries to smile comfortingly and tells her, "It must have been that birdfood I ate."

Nelson was still sleeping at eleven, but Janice was in no hurry for the confrontation. She sat out on the balcony for a while after Harry and Pru and the children went, coming back twice for things they forgot and forgetting two flippers and a bottle of sun lotion anyway, and she discovered there is a place, one step to the left of where the Norfolk pine gets in the way, from which you can see a patch, a little squarish sparkling patch between an ornamental condo turret and a Spanish-tile roof, of blue-green water, of Gulf. But of course there was no hope of seeing their sail; from this distance it would take a yacht like the one they raced off San Diego this September, the Americans outwitting with a catamaran the New Zealanders in their giant beautiful hopeless boat. Looking from their balcony always a little saddens her, reviving something buried within her, the view they had from their windows in the apartment on Wilbur Street, of all the town, Mt. Judge's slanting streets busy and innocent below. Then as now, Harry had gone off, and she was alone with Nelson.

When Nelson finally comes out in his expensive smoky-blue pajamas he is surprised and annoyed to find her here, though he does try not to show it. "I thought you'd be with the others. They sure as hell made a racket getting out of here."

"No," she tells her son, "I get enough sun and wanted to spend a little time with you before you rush back."

"That's nice," he says, and goes back into his room, and comes out a minute later wearing his bathrobe, for modesty she supposes, with his own mother. You think of all the times you changed their diapers and gave them a bath and then one day you're shut out. It's a summer-weight robe, purply paisley, that reminds her of what rich people used to wear in movies when she was a girl. Robes, smoking jackets, top hats and white ties, flowing white gowns if you were Ginger Rogers, up to your chin in ostrich feathers or was it white fox? Young people now don't have that to live up to, to strive toward, the rock stars just wear dirty blue jeans and even the baseball players, she has noticed looking over Harry's shoulder at the television, don't bother to shave, like the Arab terrorists. When she was a girl nobody had money but people had dreams.

She offers to make Nelson what was once his favorite breakfast, French toast. Those years on Vista Crescent before they all got into such trouble she would make a thing of its being Sunday morning with the French toast, before Nelson went off to Sunday school. He had really been such a trusting child, so easy to please, with his little cowlick in his eyebrow and his brown eyes shuttling so anxiously between her and Harry.

He says, "No thanks, Mom. Just let me get some coffee and don't hassle me with food. The thought of fried bread full of syrup makes me want to barf."

"Your appetite does seem poor lately."

"Whaddeyou want, me to get hog fat like Dad? He should lose fifty pounds, it's going to kill him."

"He's too fond of snacky things, that's where he gets the weight. The salt attracts water."

There are tarry dregs left in the Aromaster, enough to fill half a cup. Janice remembers buying that percolator at the K Mart on Route 41 when she and Harry were new down here; she had been drawn to the Krups ten-cup Brewmaster but Harry was still sold on *Consumer Reports* and said they said the Braun twelve-cup Aromaster was better. Nelson makes that face he used to make as a child with cod-liver oil and pours the eleventh-and-a-half cup down the sink. He sniffs prolongedly and picks up the *News-Press* from the counter under the see-through window. He reads aloud, "City reduces charge against football star. Lake Okeechobee's cure may be hard to swallow," but it is clear to both of them that they must talk really.

Janice says, "You sit in the living room and read the paper a minute while I make a fresh pot of coffee. Would you like the last of those Danish we bought? If you don't your father will eat it."

"No, Mom, like I said. I don't want to eat any crap."

As the water in the percolator comes to a boil, he laughs to himself in the living room. "Get this," he calls, and reads aloud, " 'The highly commended head of Cape Coral's police narcotics team will be fired because of an investigation that showed he mishandled nearly one thousand dollars' worth of cocaine he borrowed from the Sanibel Police Department. The borrowed cocaine is missing, police say, and has been replaced with a handful of baking soda in a department storage box.' '' Nelson adds, as if she is too dumb to get the point, ''Everybody's snorting and stealing down here, even the head of the narc squad.''

''How about you?'' Janice asks.

He thinks she means coffee and says ''Sure'' and holds out his cup without taking his eyes from the newspaper. ''Says here southwestern Florida was the hottest place in the country yesterday.''

Janice brings the percolator and sets it on the glass table, on a section of the newspaper she folds over to make an insulating pad. She has a superstitious fear of cracking the glass with heat, though Harry laughs at her and says you couldn't crack it with a blowtorch. Men laugh about things like this and electricity but don't always know. Bad things do happen, and then men try to pretend they didn't, or it was some other man's fault. She settles firmly on the fold-out sofa next to the wicker armchair Nelson is in, and spreads her thighs to broaden her lap the way she often saw her mother do when she was determined to be firm, and tells him, ''No, I meant about you and cocaine. What *is* the story, baby?''

When he looks over at her she is reminded of that frightened sly way he looked that whole summer when he was twelve, or was it thirteen—1969, he must have been only twelve until September. Among the things she can never forgive herself for was the way he would come over on his bicycle to Eisenhower Avenue and stand outside Charlie's place hoping to get a glimpse of her, his mother run off with another man. He asks, ''Who says there's a story?''

''Your wife says, Nelson. She says you're hooked and you're blowing a lot of money you don't have.''

''That crazy lying bitch. You know how she'll say anything to make a dramatic effect. When did she fill you full of this crap?''

''Don't be so rude in your language. A body can see at a glance things aren't right. Teresa let a little out the night before last when you didn't come home till after midnight, and then yesterday we had more chances to talk, while your father was walking ahead with the children.''

''Yeah, what's he trying to do, anyway, this great-big-lovable-grandpa routine he's pulling on my kids? He was never that way with *me*.''

''Don't keep changing the subject. Maybe he's trying to make up with them for some of his mistakes with you. Anyway your father's not who concerns me these days. He had a hard time when we were younger giving up his dreams and his freedom but he seems to be at peace now. Which is what I can't say about you. You're jumpy and rude and your mind isn't on anything that's in this room or has to do with your family. You're thinking of something else every minute and I can only think from what I read and see on television that it's drugs. Pru says it's cocaine, and probably crack now, she believes you've stayed clear of heroin, though evidently the two go together in something called speedballing.''

"You need to inject that, Ma, and I'll never go near a needle. That you can count on. Jesus, you can get AIDS that way.''

"Yes, well, AIDS. We all have that to worry us now.'' She closes her eyes and wordlessly thinks of all the misery sex has caused the world, with precious little pleasure in compensation. Nelson may have his weaknesses but her sense of him is that he has never been crazy about sex like his father—that his generation got enough of it early enough for the magic to wear off. Her poor Harry, until he began to slow down, he hopped into bed every night expecting wonders. And maybe she, too, at a time in her life, was as foolish. That time she felt she brought Charlie back from the edge of the grave with it. With sheer love. For a woman it's power, the only power they let you have until recently.

Nelson takes advantage of her silence to marshal an attack. "What if I *do* do a little toot on the weekends? It's no worse than all that sipping you do. Ever since I can remember you've had a little glass next to you in the kitchen or wherever. You know, Mom, alcohol kills, eventually. There are these scientific studies that show coke is much less harmful to the body than booze.''

"Well,'' she says, tugging her short khaki skirt down over her thighs, "it may be less harmful but it seems to be a lot more expensive.''

"That's because idiotic laws make it illegal.''

"Yes, that's right—whatever bad you can say about alcohol at least it's legal. When your granddaddy Springer was young it wasn't and he never developed the taste for it, or he might not have made such a good thing out of his life for us all to enjoy.'' She sees his lips parting to interrupt and lifts her voice to continue, "And you're a lot like him in a lot of respects, Nelson. You have his nervous energy, you always have to be figuring at something, all the time, and I hate to see that energy of yours wasted on a self-destructive thing like this.'' She sees him trying to break in and concludes, ''Now, you must tell me about cocaine, Nelson. You must help an old lady understand. What makes it worth it? Pru says your unpaid bills are piling way up, so it must be worth quite a lot.''

Nelson in exasperation slaps his body back into the chair, so that the wicker creaks; she hears something snap. ''*Mom*. I don't want to talk about my private life. I'm thirty-two years old, for Chrissake.''

''Even at eighty-two you'll still be my son,'' she tells him.

He tells her, ''You're trying to act and talk like your mother but you and I both know you're not that sharp, you're not that tough.'' But saying this makes him feel so guilty he looks away, toward the bright breezy Florida day beyond the balcony, with its squeaky birdsong and muffled sounds of golf, the day climbing toward noon and temperatures in the mid-eighties, the warmest spot in the entire nation. His mother keeps her eyes on his face. In the wash of light his skin looks transparent, worn thin by unhealth, by unnatural consumption. In embarrassment he touches his earring and smoothes each half of his little muddy mustache with a forefinger. ''It relaxes me,'' he tells her at last.

Janice waits for more, and prompts, ''You don't seem that relaxed.'' She adds, ''You were a tense child, Nelson. You took everything very seriously.''

He says rapidly, ''How else're you supposed to take it? Like a big joke, like Dad does, as if the fucking world is nothing but a love letter to yours truly?''

''Let's try to keep talking about you, not your father. As you say, I'm a simple woman. Not sharp, not tough. I'm very ignorant about a lot of things. The simplest things about this, like how much it takes and how much it costs. I don't even know how you take it—up the nose or smoke it or what you put it in to smoke it or any of that. All I know about cocaine is what's on *Miami Vice* and the talk shows and they don't explain very much. It's just not something I ever thought would make a difference in my life.''

His embarrassment increases, she sees, as when he was six and sick and she would quiz him about his bowel movements. Or once when he was fourteen and she mentioned the stains on his bedsheets. But he wants to talk, she also sees, about these details, to show off the knowledge his manhood has obtained. He sighs in surrender and closes his eyes and says, ''It's hard to describe. You know that expression about drunks, 'feeling no pain'? After a hit, I feel no pain. I guess that means I feel pain the rest of the time. Everything goes from black and white to color. Everything is more intense, and more hopeful. You see the world the way it was meant to be.'' This last confidence is so intimate the boy bats his eyelids, his lashes long as a girl's, and blushes.

Janice feels slightly queasy, brought this close to the something neutral and undecided in her son's sexual nature—something scared out of him—and brings her legs up on the sofa under her, the short skirt hiking up above the knees. Her legs are still firm and trim at fifty-two, her best feature as a girl and woman, her hair having always been skimpy and her breasts small and her face nondescript. She especially loves her legs here in Florida, where they turn brown and compare favorably with those of the other women, who have let themselves get out of shape or never had a shape to start with. These Jewish women tend to have piano legs, and low hips. Letting her son enjoy her ignorance, Janice asks, ''How many of these snorts do you need at a time, to feel the bright colors?''

He laughs, superior. ''They're called lines, Mom, if you snort them. You chop up this powder with a razor blade on a mirror usually and make them into lines about an eighth of an inch wide and an inch or two long. You inhale them into your nose with a straw or a glass tooter you can buy at these places down in Brewer near the bridge. Some of the guys use a rolled-up dollar bill; if say it's a hundred-dollar bill, that's considered cool.'' He smiles, remembering these crisp, glittering procedures, among friends in their condos and apartments in the high northern section of Brewer, backing up to Mt. Judge.

His mother asks, ''Does Pru do this with you?''

His face clouds. ''She used to, but then stopped when she was pregnant with Roy, and then didn't take it up again. She's become quite rigid. She says it destroys people.''

''Is she right?''

''Some people. But not really. Those people would have gone under to something. Like I say, it's better for you physically than alcohol. You can do a line at work quick in the john and nobody can tell the difference, except you feel like Superman. Sell like Superman, too. When you feel irresistible, you're hard to re-sist.'' He laughs again, showing small grayish teeth like hers. His face is small like hers, as if not wanting to put too much up front where the world can damage it. Whereas Harry in his middle age has swelled, his face a moon above it all. People down here, these smart Jews, like to kid him and take advantage like the three in that foursome.

She touches her upper lip with her tongue, not certain where to take this interview now. She knows she will not be able to pry Nelson this open soon again. He is flying back tomorrow afternoon, to make a New Year's party. She asks, "Do you do crack, too?"

He becomes more guarded. He lights a Camel and throws his head back to drink the last of the coffee. A nerve in his temple is twitching, under the gray transparent skin. "Crack's just coke that's been freebased for you—little pebbles, they call them rock. You smoke them in a kind of pipe, usually." He gestures; smoke loops around his face. "It's a nice quick lift, quicker than snorting. But then you crash quicker. You need more. You get in a run."

"You do this, then. Smoke crack."

"I've been known to. What's the diff? It's handy, it's all over the street these last couple years, it's dirt cheap, what with the competition between the gangs. Fifteen, even ten dollars a rock. They call it candy. Mom, it's no big *deal*. People your age are superstitious about drugs but it's just a way of relaxing, of getting your kicks. People since they lived in caves have had to have their kicks. Opium, beer, smack, pot—it's all been around for ages. Coke's the cleanest of them all, and the people who use it are successful by and large. It *keeps* them successful, actually. It keeps them sharp."

Her hand has come to rest on her own bare foot there on the sofa cushion. She gives her toes a squeeze, and spreads them to feel air between. "Well you see how stupid I am," she says. "I thought it was all through the slums and behind most of the crime we read about."

"The papers exaggerate. They exaggerate everything, just to sell papers. The government exaggerates, to keep our minds off what morons they are."

She bleakly nods. Daddy used to hate it, when people blamed the government. She unfolds first one leg, resting her heel on the round glass table, and then brings the other parallel, so the bare calves touch; she arches her brown, tendony insteps as if to invite admiration. Her legs still look young, and her face never did. She knifes her legs down and sets her feet on the rug, all business again. "Let me heat up the coffee. And wouldn't you like to split that stale Danish with me? Just to keep it out of your father's stomach?''

"You can have it all," he tells her. "Pru doesn't let me eat junk like that." Janice finds this rude. She's his mother, not Pru. As she stands in the kitchen waiting for the coffee to heat, Nelson calls in to her comfortably, finding another subject, "Here's an off-duty assistant fire chief hit a motorcycle with his blinkers and siren on—probably stoned. And they think it might rain on New Year's."

"We need it," Janice says, returning with the Aromaster and the Danish cut in half on a plate. "I like the weather warm, but this December has been unreal."

"Did you notice in the kitchen what time it was?"

"Getting toward noon, why?"

"I was thinking what a pain in the ass it is to have only one car down here. If nobody minds, when they get back, I could run some errands."

"What sort of errands would they be?"

"You know. Stuff at the drugstore. I could do with some Sominex. Roy has a rash from leaving his wet bathing suit on after swimming in all that chlorine; isn't there some ointment I could get him?''

"You wouldn't be going back to the people you were with in the fish restaurant the night before last? People who can sell you some lines, or rocks, or whatever you call them?''

"Come on, Mom, don't play detective. You can't grill me, I'm an adult. I'm sorry I told you half of what I did."

"You didn't tell me what really interests me, which is how much this habit is costing you."

"Not much, honest. Do you know, computers and cocaine are about the only items in the economy that are coming down in price? In the old days it cost a fortune, nobody but pop musicians could afford it, and now you can get a whole gram for a lousy seventy-five dollars. Of course, you don't know how much it's been cut, but you learn to get a dealer you can trust."

"Did you have any this morning? Before you came out of your bedroom to face me?''

"Hey, give me a break. I'm trying to be honest, but this is ridiculous."

"I think you did," she says, stubbornly.

He disappoints her by not denying even this. Children, why are they afraid of us? "Maybe a sniff of what was left over in the envelope, to get me started. I don't like this idea of Dad taking Judy off on a little sailboat—he can't sail for shit, and seems sort of dopey anyway these days. He seems depressed, have you noticed?''

"I can't notice everything at once. What I do notice about you, Nelson, is that you're not at all yourself. You're in what my mother used to call a state. This dealer you trust so much, do you owe him any money? How much?''

"Mom, is that any business of yours?''

He is enjoying this, she sadly perceives; he is glad to have it wormed out of him, and to place his shameful burden on her. He shows relief in just the way his voice is loosening, the way his shoulders sag in his fancy paisley bathrobe. She tells him, "Your money comes from the lot and the lot's not yours yet; it's mine, mine and your father's.''

"Yeah, in a pig's eye it's his.''

"How much money, Nelson?''

"There's a credit line I've developed, yeah.''

"Why can't you pay your bills? You get forty-five thousand a year, plus the house.''

"I know to your way of thinking that's a lot of jack, but you're thinking in pre-inflation dollars.''

"You say this coke is seventy-five a gram or ten dollars a rock. How many grams or rocks can you use a day? Tell me, honey, because I want to help you.''

"You do? What kind of help?''

"I can't say unless I know what kind of trouble you're in.''

He hesitates, then states, "I owe maybe twelve grand.''

"Oh, my.'' Janice feels an abyss at her feet; she had envisioned this conversation as confession and repentance and, at the end, her generous saving offer of a thousand or two. The ease with which he named a much bigger figure indicates a whole new scale of things. "How could you do it, Nelson?'' she asks lamely, limply, all of Bessie Springer's righteous stiffness scared out of her.

Nelson's pale little face, sensing her shock, begins to panic, to get pink. "What's such a big deal? Twelve grand is less than a stripped Camry costs. What do you think your liquor bill runs to a year?''

"Nothing like that. Your father has never been a drinker, though back in the Murkett days he used to try.''

"Those Murkett days—you know what was in them for him, doncha? Getting into Cindy Murkett's pants, that's all he cared about.''

Janice stares and almost laughs. How young he is, how long ago that was, and how different from what Nelson thinks. She feels a hollowness spreading inside her. She wishes she had something to sip, a little orange-juice glass of blood-red Campari, not weakened by soda the way the women down here like to have spritzers, for luncheon or out by the pool. Her half of the cherry-filled Danish feels heavy on her stomach and now in her nervousness she can't stop picking the sugar icing off Nelson's half. His refusal to eat—his acting so superior to the mild poisons she and Harry like—is the most annoying thing about him. She tells him, stiffly, "Whatever our bill is, we pay it. We have the money and can afford it." She holds out a hand toward him and twiddles two fingers. "Could I bum one cigarette?"

"You don't smoke," he tells her.

"I don't, except when I'm around you and your wife." He shrugs and takes his pack of Camels from the table and tosses it toward her. Their complicity is complete now. The lightness of it all—the cigarette itself, the dry tingling in her nostrils as she exhales—restores matters to a scale that she can manage. She asks, "What do these men do, these dealers, when you don't pay?" She could bite her lips—she has gone over into his territory, where he is an innocent victim.

"Oh," he says, enjoying posing as casually brave, shaping the ash of his cigarette on the edge of a lovely Macoma tellin he uses as an ashtray, "it's mostly talk. They say they'll break your legs. Threaten to kidnap your kids. Maybe that's what makes me so nervous about Judy and Roy. If they threaten you often enough, they have to do something eventually. But, then, they don't like to lose a good customer."

Janice says, "Nelson. If I gave you the twelve thousand, would you swear off drugs for good?" She strives to make eye contact.

She expects at least an eager vow from him to cinch her gift, but the boy has the audacity, the shamelessness, to sit there and say, without giving her a glance, "I could try, but I can't honestly promise. I've tried before, to please Pru. I love coke, Mom. And it loves me. I can't explain it. It's right for me. It makes me feel *right*, in a way nothing else does."

She finds herself crying, without sobs, just the dry-straw ache in the throat and the wetness on her cheeks, as if a husband were calmly confessing his love for another woman. When she gets her voice together enough to speak she says, clearly enough, "Well then I'd be foolish to contribute to your ruining yourself."

He turns his head and looks her full in the face. "I'll give it up, sure. I was just thinking out loud."

"But, baby, *can* you?"

"Cinchy. I often go days without a hit. There's no withdrawal, is one of the beautiful things—no heaves, no DTs, nothing. It's just a question of making up your mind."

"But is your mind made up? I don't get the feeling it is."

"Sure it is. Like you say, I can't afford it. You and Dad own the lot, and I'm your wage slave."

"That's a way of putting it. Another way might be that we've bent over backwards to give you a responsible job, heading things up, without our interference. Your father's very bored down here. Even I'm a little bored."

Nelson takes an abrupt new tack. "Pru's no help, you know," he says.

"She isn't?"

"She thinks I'm a wimp. She always did. I was the way out of Akron and now she's out. I get none of the things a man's supposed to get from a wife."

"What are those?" Janice is truly interested; she has never heard a man spell them out.

He makes a cross evasive face. "You know—don't play naïve. Reassurance. Affection. Make the guy think he's great even if he isn't."

"I may be naïve, Nelson, but aren't there things we can only do for ourselves? Women have their own egos to keep up, they have their own problems." She hasn't been attending a weekly women's discussion group down here for nothing. She feels indignant enough, independent enough, to get up and march into the kitchen and open the cabinet doors and pull down the Campari bottle and an orange-juice glass. The aqua-enamelled clock on the stove says 12:25. The phone right beside her on the wall rings, startling her so that the bottle jumps in her hand and some of the Campari spills, watery red on the Formica counter, like thinned blood.

"Yes . . . yes . . . oh my God . . ." Nelson, sitting in the wicker chair planning his next move and wondering if twelve thou was too little to ask for, it sure as hell is less than he owes, hears his mother's voice make each response with a tightened breathlessness, and sees by her face when she hangs up and hurries toward him that indeed the scale of things has changed; a new order has dawned. His mother's Florida tan has fled, leaving her face a greenish gray. "Nelson," she says, speaking as efficiently as a newscaster, "that was Pru. Your father's had a heart attack. They've taken him to the hospital. They're coming right back so I can have the car. No point in your coming, he isn't allowed any visitors except me, and then for only five minutes every hour. He's in intensive care."

The Deleon Community General Hospital is a modern set of low white buildings added onto a bisque-colored core, dating from the Thirties, with a Spanish-tile roof and curved grillework at the windows. The complex fills two blocks on the southern side of Tamarind Avenue, which runs parallel to Pindo Palm Boulevard about a mile to the north. Janice spent most of yesterday here, so she knows the way into the parking garage, and which arrows painted on the floor to follow out of the parking garage, across a glass-enclosed second-story pedestrian bridge, which takes them above the parking-garage ticket booths and a breadth of busy asphalt and a hexagonal-tiled patio with arcs of oleander hedge and of convalescents in glinting steel wheelchairs, and down a half-flight of stairs into a lobby where streetpeople, multiracial but the whites among them dyed on hands and face a deep outdoorsy brown, doze beside the neatly tied bundles and plastic garbage bags containing all their possessions. The lobby smells of oleander, urine, and air freshener.

Janice, wearing a soft salmon-colored running suit with powder-blue sleeves and pants stripes, leads, and Nelson, Roy, Pru, and Judy, all in their airplane clothes, follow, hurrying to keep up. In just one day Janice has acquired a widow's briskness, the speed afoot of a woman with no man to set the pace for her. Also some remnant of old love—of old animal magnetism revived in this thronged institutional setting not so different from the high-school corridors where she first became aware of Rabbit Angstrom, he a famous senior, tall and blond, and she a lowly ninth-grader, dark and plain—pulls her toward her man, now that his animal fragility has resharpened her awareness of his body. His, and her own. Since his collapse she is proudly, continuously conscious of her body's elastic health, its defiant uprightness, the stubborn miracle of its functioning.

The children are frightened. Roy and Judy don't know what they will see in this visit. Perhaps their grandfather has been monstrously transformed, as by a wicked witch in a fairy story, into a toad or a steaming puddle. Or perhaps a monster is what he has been all along, underneath the friendly kindly pose and high coaxing voice he put on for them like the wolf in grandmother's clothes who wanted to eat Little Red Riding Hood. The sugary antiseptic smells, the multiplicity of elevators and closed doors and directional signs and people in white smocks and white stockings and shoes and plastic badges, the hollow purposeful sound their own crowd of feet makes on the linoleum floors, scrubbed and waxed so shiny they hold moving ripples like water, widens the ominous feeling in their childish stomachs, their suspicion of a maze there is no escaping from, of a polished expensive trap whose doors and valves only open one way. The world that grownups construct for themselves seems such an extravagant creation that malice might well be its motive. Within a hospital you feel there is no other world. The palm trees and jet trails and drooping wires and blue sky you can see through the windows seem part of the panes, part of the trap.

The vaulted lobby holds two murals—at one end, happy people of many colors work in orange groves above which the sun seems one more round orange and, at the other, bearded Spaniards in armor woodenly exchange obscure gifts with nearly naked Indians, one of whom crouches with a bow and arrow behind a spiky jungle bush. This Indian scowls with evil intent. The explorer will be killed.

A skinny strict woman at the main desk consults a computer printout and gives them a floor number and directions to the correct elevator. This family of five crowds onto it among a man who holds a bouquet and keeps clearing his throat, a Hispanic boy carrying a clinking tray of vials, and a big-jawed bushy-haired middle-aged woman pushing an ancient version of herself, only the hair not so thick or so brightly dyed, in a wheelchair. She drags her mother out to let other people off and on and then forces the wheelchair's way back in. Judy rolls her clear green eyes heavenward in protest of how obnoxious and clumsy grownups are.

Their floor is the fourth, the topmost. Janice is struck by how much less elaborate the nurses' station is here than in the intensive cardiac-care unit. There, the uniformed women sat barricaded behind a bank of heart monitors each giving in a twitching orange line the imperfect beats from the rows of individual rooms, on three sides, with glass front walls, some doors open so you could see a dazed patient sitting up under his spaghetti of tubes, some of them closed but the curtains not drawn so you could see the two dark nostrils and triangular dying mouth of an unconscious head, and yet others with the curtains ominously

drawn, to hide some desperate medical procedure in progress.
She has borne two babies and escorted both of her parents into
the grave so she is not a total stranger to hospitals. Here, on
Floor Four, there is just a single high counter, and a few desks,
and a waiting area with a hard walnut settee and a coffee table
holding magazines titled *Modern Health* and *Woman's Day* and
The Watchtower and *The Monthly Redeemer*. A big black
woman, with waxy tight-woven corn rows looped beneath her
white cap, stops the anxious herd of Angstroms with a smile.
"Only two visitors in the room at a time, please. Mr. Angstrom
came out of the ICCU this morning he's still not ready for too
much fun."

Something in her wide gleaming face and elaborately braided
hair transfixes little Roy; suddenly he begins under the stress of
accumulating strangeness to cry. His inky eyes widen and then
squeeze shut; his rubbery lips are pulled down as if by a terrible
taste. His first cry turns a number of heads in the corridor, where
attendants and doctors are busy with the routines of early afternoon.

Pru takes him from Nelson's arms and presses his face into
her neck. She tells her husband, "Why don't *you* take Judy in?"

Nelson's face, too, undergoes a displeased, alarmed stretching. "*I* don't want to be the first. Suppose he's delirious or
something. Mom, you ought to go in first."

"For heaven's sake," she says, as if Harry's burdens of exasperation with their only living child has passed to her. "I
talked to him two hours ago over the phone and he was perfectly
*nor*mal." But she takes the little girl by the hand and they go
down the shiny rippled corridor looking for the room number,
326. The number rings a faint bell with Janice. Where before?
In what life?

Pru sits on the hard settee—uncushioned perhaps to discourage loiterers—and tries to murmur and joggle Roy into calm
again. In five minutes, with a sob like a hiccup, he falls asleep,
heavy and hot against her, rumpling and making feel even more
oppressive the checked suit which she put on for disembarking
in the Northeastern winter. The air-conditioning in here feels
turned off; the local temperature has again climbed into the
eighties, ten degrees warmer than normal this time of year. They
have brought this morning's *News-Press* as a present to Harry
and while they are waiting on the bench Nelson begins to read
it. *Reagan, Bush get subpoenas*, Pru reads over his shoulder.
Regional killings decrease in 1988. Team owner to pay for Am-

ber's funeral. Unlike the Brewer *Standard* this one always has color on the page and today features a green map of Great Britain with Lockerbie pinpointed and insets of a suitcase and an exploding airplane. *Report describes sophisticated bomb.* "Nelson," Pru says softly, so as not to wake Roy or have the nurses hear what she wants to say. "There's been something bothering me."

"Yeah? Join the crowd."

"I don't mean you and me, for a change. Do you possibly think—? I can't make myself say it."

"Say what?"

"Shh. Not so loud."

"Goddamn it, I'm trying to read the paper. They think they know now exactly what kind of bomb blew up that Pan Am flight."

"It occurred to me immediately but I kept trying to put it out of my mind and then you fell asleep last night before we could talk."

"I was beat. That's the first good night's sleep I've had in weeks."

"You know why, don't you? Yesterday was the first day in weeks you've gone without cocaine."

"That had nothing to do with it. My body and blow get along fine. I crashed because my father suddenly near-died and it's damn depressing. I mean, if he goes, who's next in line? I'm too young not to have a father."

"You crashed because that chemical was out of your system for a change. You're under terrible neurological tension all the time and it's that drug that's doing it."

"It's my fucking whole neurological life doing it and has been doing it ever since you and I got hitched up; it's having a holier-than-thou wife with the sex drive of a frozen yogurt now that she's got all the babies she wants."

Pru's mouth when she gets angry tenses up so the upper lip stiffens in vertical wrinkles almost like a mustache. You see that she does have a faint gauzy mustache; she is getting whiskery. Her face when she's sore becomes a kind of shield pressing at him, the crepey skin under her eyes as dead white as the parting in her hair, her whisper furious and practiced in its well-worn groove. He had heard this before: "Why should I risk my life sleeping with you, you addict, you think I want to get AIDS from your dirty needles when you're speedballing or from some cheap coke whore you screw when you're gone until two in the morning?''

Roy whimpers against her neck, and two younger nurses behind the counter in the desk area ostentatiously rustle papers as if to avoid overhearing.

"You shitty dumb bitch," Nelson says in a soft voice, lightly smiling as if what he's saying is pleasant, "I don't do needles and I don't fuck coke whores. I don't know what a coke whore is and you don't either."

"Call them what you want, just don't give me their diseases."

His voice stays low, almost caressing. "Where did you get so goddamn high and mighty, that's what I'd love to know. What makes you so fucking pure, you weren't too pure to get yourself knocked up when it suited you. And then to send Melanie back home to Brewer with me to keep putting out ass so I wouldn't run away somehow. That was really the cold-blooded thing, pimping for your own girlfriend."

Nelson finds a certain chronic comfort in his wife's fair-skinned, time-widened face, with its mustache of rage crinkles and its anger-creased triangular brow, pressing upon him, limiting his vision. It shuts out all the threatening things at the rim. She says, faltering as if she knows she is being put through a hoop, "We've been through this a million times, Nelson Angstrom, and I had no idea you'd hop into bed with Melanie, I was foolish enough to think you were in love with *me* and trying to work things out with your *parents*." This cycle of complaint is stale and hateful yet something familiar he can snuggle into. At night, when both are asleep, it is she who loops her arm, downy and long, around his sweating chest and he who curls closer to the fetal position, pressing his backside into her furry lap.

"I was," he says, plainly teasing now, "I did work them out. So what were you starting to say?"

"About what?"

"What you were going to tell me but couldn't because I fell asleep because according to you I wasn't as wired as usual." He leans his head against the bench's headrest and sighs in this new blood-clean weariness of his. Coming down makes you realize how high up you usually are. "God," he says, "it'll be good to get back to the real world. You're sort of right about yesterday, I was stuck, with Mom grabbing the car as soon as you got back. All you can deal for around Valhalla Village is Geritol."

Her voice in marital sympathy softens. "I like you like this," she confides. "Just yourself. No additives." He looks, with his tidy taut profile sealed upon his tired thoughts, his thinning temples balanced by his jutting little mustache, almost handsome. The scattered gray hairs in his rat's-tail haircut touch her, as if they are her fault.

Wearily in Pru's forgiving tone of voice he hears that she is not yet ready to let this marriage go. He has plenty of margin still. "I'm always the same," he disagrees. "I can take or leave the stuff. Yesterday, maybe you're right, out of respect for the old guy, or something. I just decided to do without. What nobody seems to understand is, it's not addictive."

"Wonderful," Pru says, the softness in her voice ebbing. "My husband the exception that proves the rule."

"Don't we have any other topic?"

"This story," she decides to begin, "of Judy's being trapped under the sail. Aren't the sails awfully small? You know what a good swimmer she is. Do you possibly think—?"

"Think what?"

"That she was just pretending, hiding from your father as a sort of game, and then it got out of hand?"

"So it just about killed him? What a thought. Poor Dad." Nelson's profile smiles; his mustache lifts closer to the underside of his small straight irritated nose. "I don't think so," he says. "She wouldn't be that cool. Think of how far out there it must have seemed to her, surrounded by sharks in her mind. She wouldn't be playing games."

"We don't know really how it was out there, or how many seconds it all took. Children's minds don't work exactly like ours, and your father's way with her is to be teasing, the way he talks to her. It's something she could have done not to be mean but a child's idea, you know, of teasing back."

His smile now shows his small inturned teeth, which always look a little gray no matter how hard he brushes them, and flosses, and uses those handles with rubber tips once he gets into his pajamas. "I knew it was a bad idea, him taking her out there when he doesn't know shit about boats," he says. "You say he acted proud of saving her life?"

"On the beach, before the paramedics came—it seemed to take forever but they said it was only seven minutes—he seemed happy, relieved somehow even with the terrible pain and struggling for breath. He kept trying to make jokes and get us to laugh. He told me I should put new polish on my toenails."

Nelson's eyes open and he stares, not at the opposite wall

where a dead benefactor's oil portrait preens, but unseeing into the past. "I had that baby sister, you know," he says, "who drowned."

"I know. How could any of us ever forget it?"

He stares some more, and says, "Maybe he was happy to have saved this one."

And indeed to Harry, as he lies on his back drugged and tied down by tubes and wires in what seems a horizonless field of white, the sight of little Judy alive and perfect in each red hair and freckle, her long eyelashes spaced as if by a Linotype machine with one-point spaces, is a pure joy. She had tangled with the curse and survived. She is getting out of Florida alive.

His collapse twenty-six hours ago did have its blissful aspect: his sense, beginning as he lay helpless and jellyfishlike under a sky of red, of being in the hands of others, of being the blind, pained, focal point of a world of concern and expertise, at some depth was a coming back home, after a life of ill-advised journeying. Sinking, he perceived the world around him as gaseous and rising, the grave and affectionate faces of paramedics and doctors and nurses released by his emergency like a cloud of holiday balloons. His many burdens have been lifted away in this light-drenched hospital, this businesslike emporium where miracles are common if not cheap. They have relieved him of his catheter, and his only problem is a recurrent need to urinate—all this fluid they keep dripping into him—sideways into a bed pan, without pulling loose the IV tube and the wires to the heart monitor and the oxygen tubes in his nostrils.

Another small problem is fog: a football game he has been looking forward to seeing, the NFC playoff game between the Eagles and the Bears at Soldier Field in Chicago, is on the television set that comes out on a tan enamelled metal arm not two feet from his face, but the game, which began at twelve-thirty, as it goes on has become dimmer and dimmer, swallowed by an unprecedented fog blowing in off Lake Michigan. Television coverage has been reduced to the sideline cameras; people up in the stands and the announcers in their booth can see even less than Rabbit lying doped-up here in bed. "Heck of a catch by somebody," said one color commentator, Terry Bradshaw as a matter of fact, Bradshaw who in the Super Bowl at the beginning of the decade was bailed out by a circus catch by that lucky stiff Stallworth. The crowd, up high in the fog, rumbles and groans in poor sync with the television action, trying to read the game off the electronic scoreboard. The announcers—a black guy with froggy pop eyes, maybe that same guy who married Bill Cosby's television wife, and a white guy with a lumpy face—seem indignant that God could do this, mess with CBS and blot out a TV show the sponsors are paying a million dollars a minute for and millions are watching. They keep wondering aloud why the officials don't call off the game. Harry finds the fog merciful, since before it rolled in the Eagles looked poor, two perfectly thrown TD passes by Cunningham called back because of bonehead penalty plays by Anthony Toney, and then this rookie Jackson dropping a pass when he was a mile open in the end zone. The game flickering in the fog, the padded men hulking out of nothingness and then fading back again, has a peculiar beauty bearing upon Rabbit's new position at the still center of a new world, personally. The announcers keep saying they've never seen anything like it.

He has trouble at first realizing he must perform for his visitors, that it's not enough to lie here and accept the apparition of them like another channel of television. During the commercial, the one for Miller that shows the big black guy lifting the pool table so all the balls roll into the pocket supposedly, he lowers his eyes to Judy's eager face, bright and precise as watchworks free of dust and rust, and says to her, "We learned, didn't we, Judy? We learned how to come about."

"It's like a scissors," the girl says, showing with her hands. "You push toward the sail."

"Right," he says. Or is it away from? His thinking is foggy. His voice, nasal and husky, doesn't sound like his; his throat feels raw from something they did to him when he was brought into the hospital, something with oxygen, he was half out of it and then all the way out thanks to something they slipped into him in the confusion.

"Harry, what do the doctors say about you?" Janice asks. "What's going to happen?" She sits in a chair near his bed, a new kind of vinyl-cushioned wheelchair, like a revved-up version of Fred Springer's pet Barcalounger. She has that anxious skinned look to her forehead and her mouth is a dumb slot open a dark half-inch. She looks in that two-tone running suit and those bulky Adidas like a senior-league bowling champion, her face hard from too much sun, with two little knobs like welts developing over her cheekbones. The delicate skin beneath her eyebrows is getting puckery. With age we grow more ins and outs.

He tells her, "One doc told me I have an athlete's heart. Too big. Too big on the outside, that is, and too small on the inside. The muscle is too thick. Apparently the heart isn't a nice valentine like you'd think, it's a muscle. It pumps with a kind of twisting motion, like this.'' He shows his little audience with a twitching fist: beat, pause, beat, pause. Judy's face is transfixed by the screen of the heart monitor, which he can't see; but he supposes the effort of his small demonstration is showing up in his running cardiogram. Janice watches it too, their four eyes shiningly reflecting the electronic jiggle and their two mouths both open to make identical slots of darkness. He has never before seen any sign of heredity between them. He goes on, ''They want to put some dye into my heart, by putting a long tube into some artery down at the top of my leg, so they can see exactly what's going on, but offhand they think at least one of the coronary arteries is plugged. Too many pork chops on top of all that hustle on the court when I was a kid. No problem, though. They can bypass anything, they do it every day now, as simple as plumbing with plastic pipe. They tell me it's amazing, what they've learned to do in the last ten years.''

''You're going to have open-heart surgery?'' Janice asks in alarm.

The fist that impersonated a heart feels cloudy and heavy; he lowers it carefully to his side on the sheet, and momentarily closes his eyes, to spare himself the sight of his worried wife. ''Nothing for now. Maybe eventually. It's an option. Another option is, this catheter has a balloon in it somehow that they inflate when it's inside the plugged-up artery. It cracks the plaque. That's what they call it, plaque. I thought a plaque was what you got for winning the championship.'' Rabbit has to keep suppressing the impulse to laugh, at his inability to share with Janice the drug-induced peace inside his rib cage, the sense of being at last at the still center. Painkiller, blood-thinner, tranquillizer, vasodilator, and diuretic all drip into his system from above, painting the hospital world with rosy tints of benevolence and amusement. He loves the constant action, the visits to extract blood and measure blood pressure and check instruments and drips, and the parade of firm-bodied odorless young females in starchy cotton and colors of skin from every continent who tend to his helpless flesh with a sexy mix of reverence and brutal condescension, with that *trained* look on their pretty faces like actresses or geisha girls. His little white-walled room seems in his entrancement to be a stage set, crowded with unpredictable exits and entrances. Semi-private, it even has a curtain, which conceals his roommate, who was burbling and vomiting and groaning this morning but has fallen since into a silence that might be death. But for Harry, the play goes on, and on cue another actor enters. "Here's a doc now," he announces to Janice. "You ask him whatever you want. I'll watch the game and Judy'll watch my heart monitor. Tell me if it stops, Judy."

"Grandpa, don't joke," the dear child scolds.

The cardiologist is a big red-skinned immigrant Australian named Dr. Olman. He has a pink hooked nose, brilliant white teeth, and bleached lank hair. Years of the good life in Florida have overlaid his clipped native accent with a Southern drawl. He takes Janice's little narrow brown hand into his meaty red one and they become, in Rabbit's eyes, his cardiac parents—worried little nut-brown mother and outwardly calm and factual father. "He's been a pretty sick lad," Dr. Olman tells her, "and we've got to teach him how to take better care of himself."

"What's wrong with his heart, exactly?" Janice asks.

"The usual thing, ma'am. It's tired and stiff and full of crud. It's a typical American heart, for his age and economic status et cetera."

That strangely intense and slightly embarrassing Gallo-wine commercial, about the guy who has a blind date with a girl who turns out to be the very liquor saleswoman who advised him what bottle to take the date as a present, comes on.

"As best we can tell without cardiac catheterization," Dr. Olman is saying, "the principal narrowing is the standard one, the left anterior descending, the workhorse of the system. Luckily, he appears to have fairly well-developed collaterals, which have kept him going. You see, ma'am, whenever the heart's been starving for oxygen, it tries to develop alternative routes to get blood to the muscle. Also, from the murmur we think we hear there may be a fair bit of stenosis around the aortic valve. Not a pretty picture, but by no means the worst we've ever seen."

Janice looks at her husband almost with pride. "Oh, Harry! You would mention the little aches and breathing problems, and I never took you seriously. You didn't complain hard enough."

"It was perfect," the girl in the commercial sighingly says, at the end of their date, starry-eyed and in soft focus; you can see they will fuck, if not this date the next, and marry and live happily ever after, all by the grace of Gallo.

Dr. Olman has sized Janice up as educable and moves into a heavier sell. "Now, if his luck holds and the lesion isn't located at a bifurcation and there's not too much calcification a lot of doctors would advise you to begin modestly, with an angioplasty, and wait and see. To my own way of thinking, though, you have to offset the relative lack of trauma and expense—we can't forget expense, now can we, what with Medicare's pulling in its horns and this new chappie's promising no new taxes?— we have to offset those psychological pluses against the minus kicker, the likelihood of recurrent stenosis and having to do it all over again, the odds of which, to be honest about it, are on the shady side of fifty per cent. For my money, not to keep beating about the bush, the artery bypass is the sucker that does the job. What do you say in the States, never send a boy when you can send a man? Now, ma'am, how much do you want to know about the heart?''

"Everything,'' Janice says, starry-eyed over this man willing to explain things to her, her tongue peeking through as she prepares to concentrate.

"Way to go,'' Dr. Olman gamely says, and makes a big fist with one hand and with the fingers of the other begins to show her how the coronary arteries lie on the heart's surface, their branches burrowing into the hardworking muscle. Harry has seen this demonstration earlier in the day and signals Judy to come closer to his bed. She is wearing the pink party dress she came down on the airplane in, and the stiff white ribbon around her braided pigtail. Yesterday's experience at sea has given her a sunburn on her nostril wings and beneath her clear green eyes, where her freckles are thinnest. She keeps staring at his heart monitor.

"What do you see?'' he asks her huskily.

"It's like a little twitchy worm, that just goes and goes.''

"That's life,'' he tells her. "That's your granddad.''

Judy yields to an impulse: leaning against the bed, she tries to embrace the old man, disarraying and tugging at the tubes and wires attached to his upper body. "Oh Grandpa,'' she confesses, "it's all my fault!''

Her breath feels hot on his neck. He hugs her, as best he can, with the arm not pierced by the IV. "Don't be silly. What's your fault?''

"Yesterday. I scared you out there.''

"You didn't scare me, sweetie. The Gulf of Mexico scared me. You weren't scared?''

Tearily she shakes her head No.

This seems another wonder to him. "Why not?'' he asks.

Her smooth little face gets that tiptoe look which in a mature woman signals that she is about to lie. She says, a bit mincingly, "You were out there with me, Grandpa. And there were lots of other boats around."

He renews his trammelled hug and her slender little body is unresisting, something has gone out of it; he feels a roughness in his throat, perhaps from yesterday's gulps of saltwater. His eyes film over with the hot relief of tears. On television, men with wide shoulders and narrow hips move like gods on Olympus among the clouds. You can't even see who is white and who is black. Blinded though they are, the announcers keep yelling in those straining excited voices they have. A commercial shows a Subaru bumpily climbing a mountain of dead car chassis.

"Want to change the channel?" he asks Judy, and moves her hand from his bandaged wrist, where it is hurting him, to the hand control for the television set on its beige metal arm. He lies back feeling the white walls stretch all around him just like the ocean yesterday, his bed a raft. Judy flickers the TV through a wrestling match, a parade, a scare commercial with Karl Malden barking that with American Express Travellers Checks you can't be robbed, a man and a woman in black skating in a sparkle of ice, a tongue-in-cheek horror movie about being a teenage werewolf in London, and another movie called, they learn from the station break, *The Fists of Bruce Lee*. The kung-fu violence is arresting enough to hold Judy's attention for a few minutes. Fragments of what Dr. Olman is confidentially yet, in that preppy Australian way, quite audibly telling Janice weave into the action—murderous kicks turned into slow motion by the director, graceful blurs of Oriental color. ". . . preliminary test . . . pulmonary congestion common after a myocardial infarction . . . backup of blood, leakage into the lung tissue . . . hydralazine . . . inflammation of the pericardium . . . Dilantin . . . skin rashes, diarrhea, loss of hair . . . hate to go to a pacemaker for a man this age . . ."

Bruce Lee kicks out, once, twice, thrice, and three handsomely costumed thugs slowly fly toward the corners of the room, furniture shattering like fortune cookies, and suddenly Judy has switched channels again, coming upon a commercial Harry loves, for some skin moisturizer whose name he can never remember, but he could never forget the look on the model's face, the way she smiles over her naked shoulder as she slinks behind the bathroom door, and then when she comes out the satisfied wicked purr in her expression, her wet hair turbanned in a bulky soft towel, her breasts showing cleavage but the nipples just off the screen, if only the screen were a little wider, if he could only slow the action down like in a kung-fu movie, for a thirtieth of a second there might have been a nipple, and the way she relaxes into a blue velvet sofa as if ever so profoundly satisfied, lovely eyes closed with their greasy lids, her eyebrows slightly thick like Cindy Murkett's, and then the part coming up where she is dressed to go out for the evening, all moisturized still beneath her gold lamé. . . . "No, wait, honey": he senses that Judy is about to change channels and reaches out to stop her but fails, it's back to the werewolf, the boy's face is growing fur as he crouches in a telephone booth, and then the ice skaters, the woman sliding backward at you with her little skirt flipped up; and then the back of Harry's wrist stings from the tug he gave the IV, and a flirtatious ghost of yesterday's pain plays across his chest. The Demerol must be wearing off. They gave him a little brown bottle of nitroglycerin on his bedside table next to the telephone and a glass of stale water and he shakes one out shakily and puts it beneath his tongue as they have taught him. It burns under his tongue and then, the funny thing, a minute or two later, his asshole tingles.

"How much junk food does he eat?" Dr. Olman is asking.

"Oh," Janice says, with enthusiasm, "he's a real addict." His wife is, it occurs to Harry, a channel that can't be switched. The same slightly too-high forehead, the same dumb stubborn slot of a mouth, day after day, same time, same station. She looks up into the doctor's big red blond face as if at an instructively beautiful sunset. The two of them make a duo, dividing him up. One takes the inside, the other the outside.

Now a cherry-red Subaru is spinning along one of those steep spiky Western landscapes that the makers of automobile commercials love. A shimmery model, skinny as a rail, dimpled and square-jawed like a taller Audrey Hepburn from the *Breakfast at Tiffany's* days, steps out of the car, smiling slyly and wearing a racing driver's egg-helmet with her gown made up it seems of ropes of shimmering light. Maybe Nelson is right, Toyota is a dull company. Its commercials show people jumping into the air because they're saving a nickel. The channel jumps back to the Fiesta Bowl Parade. Youth, flowers, a giant Garfield the cat jiggling majestically along. Harry's internal climate of drugs and their afterwash seems to be undergoing a distant storm, like sunspots or those faint far hurricanes on Jupiter. Along with history, Harry has a superstitious interest in astronomy. Our Father, Who art in Heaven . . .

". . . tons of fat through his system," Dr. Olman is saying, "*rivers* of it, some of it *has* to stick. Marbled meats, pork sausage, liverwurst, baloney, hot dogs, peanut butter, salted nuts . . ."

"He loves all that stuff, he's a terrible nibbler," Janice chimes in, anxious to please, courting, betraying her husband. "He loves nuts."

"Worst thing for him, absolutely the worst," Dr. Olman responds, his voice speeding up, losing its drawl, "*full* of fat, not to mention sodium, and cashews, macadamia nuts, they're the worst, macadamia nuts, but it's all bad, bad." In his intensity he has begun to crouch above her, as if over a slippery putt. "Anything made with hydrogenated vegetable shortenings, coconut oil, palm oil, butter, lard, egg yolk, whole milk, ice cream, cream cheese, cottage cheese, any organ meats, all these frozen TV dinners, commercial baked goods, almost anything you buy in a package, in a waxpaper bag, any of it, ma'am, is poison, bloody poison. I'll give you a list you can take home."

"You can, but my daughter-in-law is studying nutrition. She has a lot of lists already." On cue, Pru appears, hesitantly filling the doorway with her womanly-wide frame in its nappy travelling suit of three-dimensional checks. Unawares, Janice goes on buttering up Dr. Olman. "She's been saying everything you've been saying for years to Harry, but he just won't listen. He thinks he's above it all, he thinks he's still a teenager."

The doctor snorts. "Even the teenagers with their supercharged metabolism aren't burning up the fats and sugars this country's food industry is pumping into them. We're having adolescent heart attacks all over"—his voice softens to Southerliness again—"God's green creation."

Pru steps forward, in her three dimensions. "Janice, I'm sorry," she says, still shy of using her mother-in-law's name, "I know he shouldn't have so many visitors at once but Nelson is getting frantic, he's afraid we're going to miss the plane."

Janice stands, so briskly the wheelchair recoils under her. She staggers but keeps her feet. "I'll leave. You say hello and bring Judy when you come. Harry, I'll drop by on my way back when I've put them on the plane. But there's an origami demonstration tonight at the Village I don't want to miss." She exits, and Judy switches off the television in the middle of an especially amusing slapstick commercial for Midas mufflers, and exits with her.

Dr. Olman shakes Pru's hand fiercely and tells her, baring his shark-white teeth, "Ma'am, teach this stubborn bastard to *eat*."

He turns and punches Harry with a loosened fist on the shoulder. "For half a century, my friend," he says, "you've been pouring sludge through your gut." Then he, too, is gone.

He and Pru, suddenly alone together, feel shy. "That guy," Harry says, "keeps attacking America. If he doesn't like the food here, why doesn't he go back where he came from and eat kangaroos?"

His tall daughter-in-law fiddles with her long red hands, twisting at her wedding ring, yet moves forward, to the foot of the bed. "Harry," she says. "Listen. We're *stricken* at what's happened to you."

"You and who else?" he asks, determined to be debonair—Bogie at the airport in Casablanca, Flynn at Little Big Horn, George Sanders in the collapsing temple to Dagon, Victor Mature having pushed apart the pillars.

"Nelson, obviously. I don't think he slept a wink last night, you were so much on his mind. He can't say it, but he loves you."

Harry laughs, gently, since there is this valentine inside him that might rip. "The kid and I have something going between us. Not sure love is what you'd call it." Since she hesitates in replying, looking at him with those staring mud-flecked greenish eyes that Judy's clearer paler eyes were distilled from, he goes on, "I love him all right, but maybe it's a him that's long gone. A little tiny kid, looking right up to you while you're letting him down—you never forget it."

"It's still there, under it all," Pru assures him, without saying what "it all" is. Her Sphinx-do hair is slightly wild, Harry sees in the brilliant hospital light—colorless stray filaments stand out all around her head. He feels there is a lot she wants to say but doesn't dare. He remembers how she appeared hovering above him as he lay breathless on the beach, anxious and womanly, her face in shadow, unlookable at, and right beside it like a thunderhead the face of Ed Silberstein's son, his salt-stiffened black curls, his butternut skin, his prick making its bump in his tight black trunks, beside the five-sided Omni logo—a smoothie, on the make, on the rise. Hi-ho, Silvers.

"Tell me about you, Pru," Rabbit says, the words gliding out of his hoarse throat as if his being in bed and chemically relaxed has moved them to a new level of intimacy. "How's it going for *you*, with the kid? With Nelson."

People do respond, surprisingly, to the direct approach, as if we're all just waiting in our burrows to be ferreted out. She says without hesitation, "He's a wonderful father to the children. That I can say sincerely. Protective and concerned and involved. When he can focus."

"Why can't he always focus?"

Now she hesitates, unthinkingly revolving the ring on her finger.

As if all of Florida is made up of interchangeable parts, a Norfolk pine stands outside his hospital window and holds an invisible bird that makes the sound of wet wood squeaking. He heard it this morning and he hears it now. His chest seems to echo with a twinge. Just to be on the safe side he takes another nitroglycerin.

Pru blurts out, "The lot worries him, I think. Sales have been off these last years with the weaker dollar and all, and what he says are boring models, and I think he's afraid Toyota might lift the dealership."

"It would take a bomb to make them do that. We've done O.K. by Toyota over the years. When Fred Springer got that franchise Japanese products were still considered a joke."

"That was a long time ago, though. Things don't stand still," Pru says. "Nelson has trouble being patient, and to tell the truth I think it scares him to have none of the old-timers around any more, Charlie and then Manny and now Mildred, even though he fixed her, and you down here half the year, and Jake gone over to Volvo-Olds over near that new mall in Oriole, and Rudy opening his own Toyota-Mazda over on 422. He feels alone, and all he has for company are these flaky types from north Brewer."

At the thought of "these flaky types" more of her hairs, glowing like electric filaments here in Florida's fluorescent light, stand out from her head in agitation. She is trying to tell him something, something is slipping, but how can a man tied up helpless in bed track it down? Rabbit has his heart to nurse. This is life and death. His drugs must be wearing off. The deadly awfulness of his situation is beginning to rise in his throat, burning like an acid regurgitation. His asshole tingles, right on schedule. He has something evil and weak inside him that might betray him at any minute into that icy blackness Bernie talked about.

Pru shrugs her wide shoulders in delayed answer to his question about how it was going. "What's a life supposed to be? They don't give you another for comparison. I love the big house, and Pennsylvania. In Akron we only ever had apartments, and the rent was always behind, and it seemed like the toilet bowl always leaked.''

Rabbit tries to lift himself onto her level, out of his private apprehension of darkness, its regurgitated taste. ''You're right,'' he says. ''We ought to be grateful. But it's hard, being grateful. It seems like from the start you're put here in a kind of fix, hungry and scared, and the only way out is no good either. Hey, listen. Listen to me. You're still young. You're great-looking. Smile. Smile for me, Teresa.''

Pru smiles and comes around the end of the bed and bends down to give him a kiss, not on the mouth this time like in the airport, but on the cheek, avoiding the tubes feeding oxygen into his nose. Her close presence feels huge, checked, clothy, a cloud come over him like the shadow of that hull on its side out there on the Gulf, where it was cold and hot both at once. He feels sick; the facts of his case keep wanting to rise in his throat, burning, on the verge of making him gag. ''You're a sweet man, Harry.''

''Yeah, sure. See you in the spring up there.''

''It seems terrible, us leaving like this, but there's this party in Brewer Nelson's determined to go to tonight and changing plane reservations is impossible anyway, everything's jammed this time of year, even into Newark.''

''What can you do?'' he asks her. ''I'll be fine. This is probably a blessing in disguise. Put some sense into my old head. Get me to lose some weight. Go for walks, eat less crap. The doc says I gotta become a new man.''

''And I'll paint my toenails.'' Pru, standing tall again, says in a level low voice he has not exactly heard before, aimed flat at him as a man, ''Don't change *too* much, Harry.'' She adds, ''I'll send Nelson in.''

''If the kid's wild to go, tell him to just go. I'll catch him later, up there.''

Her mouth pinches down at one corner, her face goes slightly stiff with the impropriety of his suggestion. ''He *has* to see his father,'' she says.

Pru exits; the white clean world around Harry widens. When everybody leaves, he will give himself the luxury of ringing for the nurse and asking for more Demerol. And see how the Eagles are doing in the fog. And close his eyes for a blessed minute.

Nelson comes in carrying little Roy in his arms, though visitors under six years old aren't supposed to be allowed. The kid wears the child like defensive armor: as long as he's carrying a kid of his own, how much can you say against him? Roy stares at Harry indignantly, as if his grandfather being in bed connected with a lot of machinery is a threatening trick. When Harry tries to beam him a smile and a wink, Roy with a snap of his head hides his face in his father's neck. Nelson too seems shocked; his eyes keep going up to the monitor, with its orange twitch of onrunning life, and then gingerly back to his father's face. Cumbersomely keeping his grip on the leaden, staring child, Nelson steps toward the bed and sets a folded copy of the *News-Press* on the chrome-edged table already holding the water glass and the telephone and the little brown bottle of nitroglycerin. "Here's the paper when you feel like reading. There's a lot in it about the Pan Am crash you're so interested in. They think they know now exactly what kind of bomb it was—there's a kind with a barometric device that activates a timer when a certain altitude is reached."

Up, up; the air thins, the barometer registers, the timer begins to tick as the plane snugly bores through darkness and the pilot chats on the radio while the cockpit lights burn and wink around him and the passengers nod over their drinks in their slots of pastel plastic. The image, like a seed at last breaking its shell in moist soil, awakens in Harry the realization that even now as he lies here in this antiseptic white fog tangled in tubes and ties of blood and marriage he is just like the people he felt so sorry for, falling from the burst-open airplane: he too is falling, helplessly falling, toward death. The fate awaiting him behind this veil of medical attention is as absolute as that which greeted those bodies fallen smack upon the boggy Scottish earth like garbage bags full of water. *Smack, splat,* bodies bursting across the golf courses and heathery lanes of Lockerbie drenched in night. What met them was no more than what awaits him. Reality broke upon those passengers as they sat carving their airline chicken with the unwrapped silver or dozing with tubes piping Barry Manilow into their ears and that same icy black reality has broken upon him; death is not a domesticated pet of life but a beast that swallowed baby Amber and baby Becky and all those Syracuse students and returning soldiers and will swallow him, it is truly there under him, vast as a planet at night, gigantic and totally his. His death. The burning intensifies in his sore throat and he feels all but suffocated by terror.

"Thanks," he hoarsely tells his son. "I'll read it when you go. Those damn Arabs. I'm nervous about your missing *your* plane."

"Don't be. We got tons of time still. Even Mom can't get lost on the way, can she?"

"Drive east from here to 75 and then south to Exit 21. The road feels like it's going nowhere but after three miles the airport shows up." Harry remembers his own drive along that weird highway, the lack of billboards, the palm trees skinny as paint drips, the cocoa-colored chick in the red Camaro and stewardess cap who tailgated him and then didn't give him a sideways glance, her tipped-up nose and pushed-out lips, and it seems unreal, coated in a fake sunshine like enamel, like that yellow sunlight they make on TV shows from studio lights. He didn't have a worry in the world back then. He was in paradise and didn't know it. He feels his body sweating from fear, he smells his own sweat, clammy like something at the bottom of a well, and sees Nelson standing there bathed in the artificial light of the world that hasn't broken through into death yet, neat and taut in the putty-colored suit he is wearing instead of the denim jacket he wore on the flight down, but with his shirt collar still open, so he looks like an all-night gambler who took off his tie in a poker game, down here nearly a week and hardly ever saw the sun. The little smudge of his mustache annoys Harry and the kid keeps calling attention to it, sniffing and touching the underside of his nose as if he smells his father's clammy fear.

He says, "Also, Dad, I noticed the Deion Sanders case is being pushed back into the sports pages and somewhere in Section B there's an article about fighting flab that'll give you a laugh."

"Yeah, flab. I'm flabby on the inside even."

This is the cue for his son to look sincere and ask, "How're you doing anyway?" The kid's face goes a little white around the gills, as if he fears his father will really tell him. His haircut is annoying, too—short on top and too long in the back, that pathetic rat-tail. And the tiny earring.

"Pretty good, considering."

"Great. This big beefy doctor with the funny accent came out and talked to us and said that the first one is the one a lot of people don't survive and in your case now, for a while at least, it's just a matter of changing your lifestyle a little."

"That guy has a thing about potato chips and hot dogs. If God didn't want us to eat salt and fat, why did He make them taste so good?"

Nelson's eyes get dark and swarmy, the way they do whenever his father mentions God. The conversation keeps sticking, it doesn't flow, Harry keeps thinking how he is falling, the kid is like a weight on his chest. *Come on*, he says to himself, *try. You only live once.*

"Pru told me you were up all night with worry."

"Yeah, well, she exaggerates, but sort of. I don't know why I can't sleep down here. It all feels phony to me, and there's all this stuff back in Brewer I should be tending to."

"Like at the lot? Between holidays is a slow week usually. Everybody's feeling broke after Christmas."

"Well, yeah, and other stuff. I keep feeling hassled."

"That's life, Nelson. Hassle."

"I suppose."

Harry says, "I been thinking about our conversation, about Toyotas being so dull. Give 'em credit, they're trying to sex the line up. They're coming out with this Lexus luxury sedan next fall. V-8 engine even."

"Yeah, but they won't let us regular dealerships handle it. They're establishing a whole new retail network. Let 'em, it's going to flop anyway. The Japanese aren't Italians. Luxury isn't their bag."

"I forgot about that separate Lexus network. I tell ya, Nelson, I'm not quite with it. I'm in a fog."

"Join the crowd," Nelson says.

"And oh yeah—the stat sheets. I've been thinking about that. Are you having trouble moving the used? Don't get greedy. Ten-per-cent markup is all you should expect, it's worth shaving the profit just to keep the inventory flowing."

"O.K., Dad. If you say so. I'll check it out."

The conversation sticks again. Roy squirms in his father's grip. Harry is falling, the light is just a skin of the dark, thinner than an airplane's skin, thinner than an aluminum beer can. Grab something, anything. "She's turned out to be quite a fine woman, Pru," he volunteers to his son.

The boy looks surprised. "Yeah, she's not bad." And he volunteers, "I should try to be nicer to her."

"How?"

"Oh—you know. Clean up my act. Try to be more mature."

"You always seemed pretty mature to me. Maybe too, early on. Maybe I didn't set such a good example of maturity."

"All the more reason, then. For me, I mean."

Does Harry imagine it, or is there a stirring, a tiny dry coughing, behind the curtain next to him, in the bed he cannot see?

His phantom roommate lives. He says, "I'm really getting anxious about you making your plane."

"Sorry about that, by the way. I feel crummy leaving. Pru and I were talking last night, if we ought to stay a few more days, but, I don't know, you make plans, you get socked in."

"Don't I know it. What could you do, staying? Your old man's fine. He's in great hands. I just have to learn to live with a not so great heart. A bum ticker. Charlie's done it for twenty years, I can do it." But then Rabbit adds, threatening to pass into the maudlin, the clingy, the elegiac, "But, then, he's a wiry little Greek and I'm a big fat Swede."

Nelson has become quite tense. He radiates a nervous desire to be elsewhere. "O.K., Dad. You're right, we'd better get moving. Give Grandpa a kiss," he tells Roy.

He leans the boy in, like shovelling off a wriggling football, to kiss his grandfather's cheek. But Roy, instead of delivering a kiss, grabs the double-barrelled baby-blue oxygen tube feeding into Harry's nose and yanks it out.

"Jesus!" Nelson says, showing emotion at last. "You all right? Did that hurt?" He whacks his son on the bottom, and sets him down on the floor.

It did hurt slightly, the sudden smarting violence of it, but Harry has to laugh. "No problem," he says. "It just sits in there, like upside-down glasses. Oxygen, I don't really need it, it's just one more perk."

Roy has gone rubber-legged with rage and collapses on the shiny floor beside the bed. He writhes and makes a scrawking breathless noise and Nelson bends down and hits him again.

"Don't hit the kid," Harry tells him, not emphatically. "He just wanted to do me a favor." As best he can with his free hand, he resettles the two pale-blue tubes one over each ear as they come from the oxygen box hung on the wall behind him and resettles the clip, with its gentle enriching whisper, on his septum. "He maybe thought it was like blowing my nose for me."

"You little shit, you could have killed your own grandfather," Nelson explains down at the writhing child, who has to be hauled, kicking, out from under the bed.

"Now who's exaggerating," Harry says, "I'm tougher to kill than that," and begins to believe it. Roy, white in the gills just like his father, finds his voice and lets loose a yell and tries to throw himself out of Nelson's grasp. The rubber heels of nurses are hurrying toward them down the hall. The unseen roommate suddenly groans behind his white curtain, with a burbly, deep-pulmonary-trouble kind of groan. Roy is kicking like a landed fish and must be catching Nelson in the stomach; Harry has to chuckle, to think of the child doing that. On one grab: deft. Maybe in his four-year-old mind he thought the tubes were snakes eating at his grandfather's face; maybe he just thought they were too ugly to look at.

Full though his arms are, Nelson manages to lean in past the tangle of life-supporting connections and give Harry's cheek the quick kiss he meant Roy to bestow. A warm touch of mustache. A sea-urchin's sting. The watery monster stirring behind the bed curtain releases another burbling, wracking groan from the deeps. Alarmed nurses enter the room; their cheeks are flushed. The head nurse looms, with her waxy woven tresses, like oodles of black noodles or packets of small firecrackers.

"Oh yeah," Harry thinks to add as Nelson hurries his yelling, writhing burden away, down the hall, toward Pennsylvania. "Happy 1989!"

II. PA

SUN and moon, rise and fall: the well-worn wheels of nature that in Florida impinge where beach meets sea are in Pennsylvania muffled, softened, sedimented over, clothed in the profoundly accustomed. In the Penn Park quarter-acre that Janice and Harry acquired a decade ago, there is, over toward the neighboring house built of clinker bricks, a weeping cherry tree, and he likes to be back when it blossoms, around April tenth. By then, too, baseball has come north—Schmidt this year hitting two home runs in the first two games, squelching all talk that he was through—and lawns are sending up tufts of garlic. The magnolias and quince are in bloom, and the forsythia is out, its glad cool yellow calling from every yard like a sudden declaration of the secret sap that runs through everybody's lives. A red haze of budding fills the maples along the curbs and runs through the woods that still exist, here and there, ever more thinly, on the edge of developments old and new.

His first days back, Rabbit likes to drive around, freshening his memory and hurting himself with the pieces of his old self that cling to almost every corner of the Brewer area. The streets where he was a kid are still there, though the trolley cars no longer run. The iron bridges, the railroad yards rust inside the noose of bypasses that now encircles the city. The license plates still have an orange keystone in the middle, but now say *You've Got a Friend in Pennsylvania*, which he always found sappy, and sappier still those imitation plates that can be bolted on the front bumper and say *You've Got a Friend in* JESUS. The covers of telephone directories boast *The UnCommonwealth of Pennsylvania*. Behind the wheel of his car, he gravitates to Mt. Judge, the town where he was born and raised, on the opposite side of Brewer from Penn Park. In this cumbersome sandstone church with its mismatching new wing, the Mt. Judge Evangelical Lutheran, he was baptized and confirmed, in a shirt that chafed his neck like it had been starched in lye, and here, further along Central, in front of a candy store now a photocopying shop, he first felt himself in love, with Margaret Schoelkopf in her pigtails and hightop shoes. His heart had felt numb and swollen above the sidewalk squares like one of those zeppelins you used to see in the sky, the squares of cement like city blocks far beneath his floating childish heart. Every other house in this homely borough holds the ghost of someone he once knew who now is gone. Empty to him as seashells in a collector's cabinet, these plain domiciles with their brick-pillared porches and dim front parlors don't change much; even the slummier row houses such as he and Janice lived in on Wilbur Avenue when they were first married are just the same in shape, climbing the hill like a staircase, though those dismal old asphalt sidings the tints of bruise and dung have given way to more festive substances imitating rough-hewn stone or wooden clapboards, thicker on some façades than others, so there is a little step up and down at the edges as your eye moves along the row. Harry always forgets, what is so hard to picture in flat Florida, the speckled busyness, the antic jammed architecture, the distant blue hilliness forcing in the foreground the gabled houses to climb and cling on the high sides of streets, the spiky retaining walls and sharp slopes crowned by a barberry hedge or tulip bed, slopes planted more and more no longer in lawn but ground cover like ivy or juniper that you don't have to mow once a week with those old-fashioned reel mowers. Some people would rig their mowers with a rope on the handle so they could let it slither clattering down and then pull it back up. Rabbit smiles in his car, remembering those wooden-handled old mowers and that long-dead Methodist neighbor of theirs on Jackson Road Mom used to feud with about mowing the two-foot strip of grass between the cement walks that ran along the foundation walls of their houses. The old Methodist couple had bought the house from the Zims when they moved to Cleveland. Carolyn Zim had been so pretty—like Shirley Temple only without the dimple, more of a Deanna Durbin sultriness, on this little girl's body—that Mr. and Mrs. fought all the time, Mom said, Mrs. being jealous. He used to wait by his window for a glimpse in the soft evening of Carolyn undressing for bed, across the little air space. His room: he can almost remember the wallpaper, its extra-yellowed look above the radiator, the varnished shelf where his teddy bears sat, the bushel basket his Tinker Toy spokes and hubs and his rubber soldiers and lead airplanes lived in. There was a taste, oilclothy, or like hot windowsill paint, or the vanilla and nutmeg when Mom baked a cake, to that room he can almost taste again, but not quite, it moves into the shadows, it slips behind the silver-painted radiator with its spines imprinted with scrolling designs in blurred low relief.

Brewer, too, that torpid hive, speaks to him of himself, of his past grown awesomely deep, so that things he remembers personally, V-E day or the Sunday Truman declared war on North Korea, are history now, which most of the people in the world know about only from books. Brewer was his boyhood city, the only city he knew. It still excites him to be among its plain flowerpot-colored blocks, its brick factories and row housing and great grim churches all mixed together, everything heavy and solid and built with an outmoded decorative zeal. The all but abandoned downtown, wide Weiser Street which he can remember lit up and as crowded as a fairgrounds in Christmas season, has become a patchwork of rubble and parking lots and a few new glass-skinned buildings, stabs at renewal mostly occupied by banks and government agencies, the stores refusing to come back in from the malls on Brewer's outskirts. The old Baghdad, once one of a half-dozen first-run movie theatres along Weiser, now stands between two vacant lots, its Arab-style tiles all stripped away and its marquee, that last advertised triple-X double features, peeling and rusting and holding the letters ELP and on the line below that SAV ME—scrambled remnant of an appeal for historic restoration. The movie palaces of his boyhood, packed with sweet odors and dark velvet, murmurs and giggles and held hands, were history. HELP SAVE ME. There had been a kind of Moorish fountain in the lobby, colored lights playing on the agitated water. The music store, Chords 'n' Records, that Ollie Fosnacht used to run twenty years ago a few doors up from the Baghdad, and that then became Fidelity Audio, is still a store, called now The Light Fantastic, selling running shoes, two whole windows of them. Must be a market for them among the minorities. Mug and run.

In Rabbit's limited experience, the more improvements they've loaded onto running shoes, the more supporting pads and power wedges and scientifically designed six-ply soles and so on, the stiffer and less comfortable they've become: as bad as shoes. And those running tights the young women wear now, so they look like spacewomen, raspberry red and electric green so tight they show every muscle right into the crack between the buttocks, what is the point of them? Display. Young animals need to display. Ollie Fosnacht's estranged wife Peggy died about eight years ago, of breast cancer that had metastasized. Rabbit reflects that she was the first woman he has slept with who has died, has actually bitten the bullet. Then realizes this is not true. There was Jill. He used to fuck Jill that crazy summer, though he could tell she didn't much like it. Too young to like it. And maybe that whore in Texas who with a curious drawling courtesy made him an unvirgin is dead now too. They don't have long lives, with the hours, the booze, the beatings. And the drugs that most of them are into, and AIDS. But, then, who does live forever? We all take a beating. Must be the way they figure, it's sooner or later. They're just like us only more so. These guys in prison now who bite the guards to give them AIDS with their saliva. We're turning into mad dogs—the human race is one big swamp of viruses.

Back from the hollow center of Brewer, in the tight brick rows built a century ago when the great mills now abandoned or turned into factory outlet stores still smoked and vibrated, spinning textiles and casting steel, life goes on as lively as ever, though in a darker shade. He likes cruising these streets. In April at least they brim with innocent energy. Four leggy young blacks cluster about a bicycle being repaired. A Hispanic girl in the late-afternoon slant of sun steps out of her narrow slice of a house in high silk heels and a lilac-colored party dress and a diagonal purple sash and at her waist a great cloth rose: she is a flower, the moment says, and a swarm of boys has gathered, jostling, bumbling, all dressed in steel-gray windbreakers and green Army pants, a gang uniform of sorts, Harry supposes. In Brewer people still use the streets, they sit out on their steps and little porches in an expectant way you never see in Deleon. And the Pennsylvania row houses take a simple square approach to shelter, not so different from those cities of aligned cereal boxes the teacher had you set up with cut-out doors and crayoned-on windows in first grade; it makes Harry happy after his winter in Florida with its condominiums interwoven with golf courses, its tile-roofed towers of time-shared apartments, its villages that aren't villages, its thousand real-estate angles and prettifications of the flimsy.

In the slate-gray two-door Celica he and Janice lock into their garage when they take the Camry wagon south in the fall, he feels safe gliding along and attracts not too many stares, though

in the tough section near the tracks, on the rounded corner step
of a boarded-up tavern, a little rounded dark girl in a sweatshirt
sits in the lap of a boy already barechested though the spring air
is still chilly, and alternately kisses him with a languid and determined open mouth and gazes insolently at the cars streaming
by. The half-naked boy is too stoned to stare, perhaps, but she
gives Harry a look through the Celica's side window that would
wipe him away if it could. Fuck her. Fuck him, her eyes say.
She seemed to sense what he was doing, rolling by, trying to
steal a little life for himself out of the south Brewer scene, all
these lives that are young and rising like sap where his is old
and sinking.

There has been a lot of living in these tired streets. The old
row houses have been repainted, residinged, updated with aluminum awnings and ironwork railings themselves grown old.
They are slots still being filled, with street numbers the builders
set in stained-glass fanlights above the doors. The blocks were
built solid, there would never be any renumbering. Once he
lived in one of these, number 326, with Ruth, and used to shop
for quick necessities at that corner store there, now called ROSA'S
GROCERIES (*Tienda de Comestibles*), and stare out the window
at the rose window of a limestone church now become the PAL
Community Center/Centro Comunidad. The city is quicker than
he remembers it, faster on the shuffle, as the blocks flicker by,
and buildings that he felt when a boy were widely spaced now
appear adjacent. The coughdrop factory, the skyscraper courthouse, the Y where he tried to take swimming lessons and caught
pneumonia instead, coming out into the winter streets with wet
hair, are all around corners from one another, and close to the
post office with its strange long empty lobby, busy and lighted
only at one end where a grate or two is up, and to the Ben
Franklin, a proud gilded downtown hotel now a Ramada Motor
Inn. There his class, Mt. Judge '51, had its senior prom, he in
a summer tux and Mary Ann in a lavender satin strapless gown
whose crinoline petticoats gave them so much trouble in the car
afterward they had to laugh, her round white thighs lost in all
those rustling folds and hems, Easter eggs in a papery nest, her
underpants damp from all the dancing, a spongy cotton pillow,
stuffed with her moss, a powerful moist musk scent, Mary Ann
the first woman whose smell he made his own, all of her his
own, every crevice, every mood, before he went off to do his
two years in the Army and she without a word of warning married somebody else. Maybe she sensed something about him.

A loser. Though at eighteen he looked like a winner. Whenever he went out with Mary Ann, knowing she was his to harvest in the warm car, he felt like a winner, offhand, calm, his life set at an irresistible forward slant.

Two blocks toward the mountain from the Ben Franklin, under Eisenhower Avenue where it lifts up in a wooden-railed hump to pass over, the laborers of old hand-dug a great trench to bring the railroad tracks into the city, tracks disused now, and the cut, walled in limestone, a pit for tossing beer cans and soda bottles down into, whole garbage bags even, mattresses; Brewer was always a tough town, a railroad town, these blocks along the tracks full of tough men, bleary hoboes who'd offer to blow you for a quarter, sooty hotels where card games went on for days, bars whose front windows were cracked from the vibration of the trains going past, the mile-long trains of coal cars pulling right across Weiser, stopping all traffic, like the time he and Ruth waited for one to pass, the neon lights of a long-gone Chinese restaurant flickering in her many-colored hair.

These red-painted bricks, these imitation gray stones, have seen heartbreaking things but don't know it. A block or two toward the mountain from Ruth's old street—Summer Street it was, though they had lived there in spring, summer spelled their end—Rabbit is suddenly driving in a white tunnel, trees on both sides of the street in white blossoms, the trees young and oval in shape and blending one into the other like clouds, the sky's high blue above tingeing the topmost blossoms as it does the daytime moon. And up top where there is most light the leaves are beginning to unfold, shiny and small and heart-shaped, as he knows because he is moved enough to pull the Celica to the curb and park and get out and pull off a single leaf to study, as if it will be a clue to all this glory. Along the sidewalk in this radiant long grove shadowy people push baby carriages and stand conversing by their steps as if oblivious of the beauty suspended above them, enclosing them, already shedding a confetti of petals: they are in Heaven. He wants to ask one of them the name of these trees, and how they came to be planted here in these hard brick blocks of Brewer, luxuriant as the ficus trees that line the avenues of Naples down in Florida, but feels shy in their gaze toward him, himself a shadow in this filtered tunnel light of blossoms, a visitor, an intruder from the past, and figures they would not know anyway, or if they did know would think him too strange for asking.

But Janice knows. When he describes this experience to her,

she says, "Those are these Bradford pear trees the city is planting everywhere the old elms and buttonwoods are dying off. It blossoms but doesn't bear any fruit, and is very hardy in city conditions. It doesn't mind carbon dioxide or any of that."

"Why have I never seen them before?"

"You have, Harry, I'm sure. They've been putting them in for ten years now at least. There've been articles in the paper. One of the girls over at the club's husband is on the Improvement Commission."

"I never saw anything like it. It broke me all up."

She is busy re-establishing them in the Penn Park house, cleaning away the winter's cobwebs and polishing the Koerner silver her mother left her, and she moves away from him impatiently. "You've seen, it's just you see differently now."

Since his heart attack, she means. Since nearly dying. He faintly feels with Janice now like one of the dead they used to say came back and watched over the survivors, living with them invisibly like the mice in the walls. She often doesn't seem to hear him, or take him quite seriously. She goes off across Brewer to visit Nelson and Pru and their children in Mt. Judge, or to remake acquaintance with her female buddies over at the Flying Eagle Country Club, where the clay tennis courts are being rolled and readied and the golf course is already green and receiving play. And she is looking for a job. He thought she had been kidding after seeing *Working Girl*, but no, the women her age almost all do something now—one of her tennis buddies is a physical therapist with muscles in her arms and shoulders like you wouldn't believe, and another, Doris Eberhardt, who used to be Doris Kaufmann, has become a diamond expert and takes the bus over to New York practically every week and carries hundreds of thousands of dollars' worth of gems back and forth, and a third woman she knows works in the booming new field of de-asbestosizing homes and buildings like factories and schools. It seems there's no end of old asbestos to ferret out. Janice thinks she might go into real estate. A friend of a friend works mostly on weekends and makes over fifty thousand a year in commissions.

Harry asks her, "Why not go over and help Nelson run the lot? Something's going flooey over there."

"That's no fun, hiring myself. And you know how sensitive Nelson is at the idea of us interfering."

"Yeah—why is that?"

Janice has all the answers, now that she is back with her

female crowd of know-it-alls over at the Flying Eagle. "Because he's grown up in the shadow of a dominating father."

"I'm *not* dominating. I'm a pushover, if you ask me."

"You are to him. Psychologically dominating. You're certainly a lot taller. And were a wonderful athlete."

"Were is right. A wonderful athlete whose doctors say he has to ride a golf cart and not do anything more violent than brisk walking."

"And you don't *do* it, Harry. I haven't seen you walk further than to the car and back."

"I've been doing some gardening."

"If you can call it that."

He likes to get out into their yard toward the end of the day and break off last year's dead flower stalks and bone-white old poke plants and burn them in a fire kindled on the day's newspaper, the Brewer *Standard*. The lawn needed a mowing badly when they arrived and the bulb beds should have been uncovered in March. The snowdrops and crocuses came and went while they were in Florida; the hyacinths are at their peak and the tulips up but still with pointy green heads. Rabbit feels peace at the moment of the day when the light dims and the weeping cherry glows in the dusk, its florets like small pink bachelor buttons and the whole droop-branched womanly forgiving shape of it gathering to itself a neon pallor as the shadows lengthen and dampen; the earth's revolution advances a bit more and the scraps of sunlight linger longer under the April sky with its jet trails and icy horsetails, just a few golden rags caught in the shaggy forsythia over toward the neighboring mansion built of thin yellow bricks, and the struggling hemlock, and the tallest of the rhododendrons by the palisade fence you see from the kitchen window. Janice put up a bird feeder in the hemlock a few falls ago, even though Doris Kaufmann or some other busybody told her it was cruel to birds to put up a feeder when you weren't there in the winter, a plastic sphere tilted like Saturn, and he fills it with sunflower seed when he thinks of it. Putting up bird feeders was the sort of thing her mother used to do but would never have occurred to Janice when they were younger and old Bessie was still alive. Our genes keep unfolding as long as we live. Harry tastes in his teeth a sourness that offended him on his father's breath. Poor Pop. His face yellowed like a dried apricot at the end. Bessie had the feeders all on wires and poles in her Joseph Street back yard to frustrate the squirrels. The copper beech by their old bedroom, with the nuts that would

pop on their own all night, attracted the squirrels, she would
say, making her lap and setting her hands on her knees as if God
had cooked up squirrels just to bedevil her. Harry had liked
Bessie, though she screwed him in her will. Never forgave him
for that time in '59. Died of diabetes and its circulatory com-
plications the day after Princess Di gave birth to little Prince
William, the last living thing Bessie was interested in, would
there be a future king of England?—that and the Hinckley trial,
she thought they should hang the boy on the steps of the Capitol,
right there in the sunshine, letting him off as insane was a scandal. The old lady was terrified of having her legs amputated at
the end the way her own mother had. Harry can even remember
Bessie's mother's name. Hannah. Hannah Koerner. Hard to believe he will ever be as dead as Hannah Koerner.

Before the April evening falls, the birds, big and little, that
the feeder attracts flutter and hop to take a drink or splash their
feathers in the blue-bottomed cement pond some earlier owner
of this little place, this snug limestone cottage tucked in among
the bigger Penn Park homes, created. The cement pool is
cracked but still holds water. Like himself, Rabbit thinks, turning toward his house with its lit windows that seem as far away
and yet as strangely close as his parents' house used to when he
was a kid playing 21 or Horse with Mim and the other children
of the neighborhood out at the backboard on the garage in the
alley behind their long narrow yard on Jackson Road. Then as
now, waking from twilit daydreams, he discovered himself
nearer a shining presence than he thought, near enough for it to
cast a golden shadow ahead of his steps across the yard; then it
was his future, now it is his past.

During those spring months with Ruth on Summer Street, he
used to wonder what it would be like to run to the end of the
street, straight as far as the eye could see. In the thirty years
since, he has often driven this way, to Brewer's northwestern
edge and beyond, where the highway with its motels (*Economy
Lodge, Coronet, Safe Haven*) melts into farmland and signs
pointing the way to Harrisburg and Pittsburgh begin to appear.
One by one the farms and their stone buildings, the bank barns
put together with pegs and beams and the farmhouses built square
to the compass with walls two feet thick, are going under to real-
estate developments. Two miles beyond the pike to Maiden
Springs, where the Murketts used to live before they got divorced, there is a fairly new development called Arrowdale after

the old Arrowhead Farm that was sold off by the nieces and nephews of the old spinster who lived there so many years and had wanted to leave it to some television evangelist as a kind of salvation park, a holy-roller retreat, but whose lawyers kept talking her out of it. Rabbit as these recent years have gone by has watched the bulldozed land lose its raw look and the trees and bushes grow up so it almost seems houses have always been here. The streets curve, as they did in the Murketts' development, but the houses are more ordinary—ranch houses and split levels with sides of aluminum clapboards and fronts of brick varied by flagstone porchlets and unfunctional patches of masonry facing. Cement walks traverse small front yards with azaleas not quite in bloom beneath the picture windows. Bark mulch abounds, and matching porch furniture, and a tyrannical neatness absent in the older more blue-collar towns like Mt. Judge and West Brewer.

Ronnie and Thelma Harrison moved to one of these modest new houses when their three boys grew up and went off. Alex, the oldest, is an electronics engineer somewhere south of San Francisco; the middle boy, Georgie, who had had reading problems in school, is trying to be a dancer and musician in New York City; and their youngest, Ron Junior, has stayed in the county, as a part-time construction worker, though he put in two years of college at Lehigh. Thelma doesn't complain about her sons or her house, though to Harry they seem disappointing, disappointingly ordinary, for a woman of Thelma's intelligence and, in his experience of her, passion.

Thelma's disease, systemic lupus erythematosus, has cost a fortune over the years, even with the benefits from Ronnie's insurance company's health plan. And it has meant that she has not been able to go back to teaching elementary school when her boys were gone, as she had hoped. Her health has been too erratic; it has kept her at home, where Harry could usually find her. This noon when he called from a pay phone in Brewer he expected her to answer and she did. He asked if he might drive over and she said he might. She didn't sound happy to hear from him, but not distressed either: resigned, merely. He leaves the Celica out front at the curving curb, though usually over the years she opened the garage for him and closed the door electronically from within the kitchen, to hide the evidence. But now that he is as sick as if not sicker than she, he doesn't know how much they still have to conceal. The neighborhood is empty during the midday, until the buses bring the children home from school. A single whining engine is at work somewhere out of sight in Arrowdale, and the air holds a pervasive vibration and hum of traffic out of sight, on the Maiden Springs Pike. Also out of sight, some birds are chirping, raucous in their nesting frenzy, though the development is skimpy on trees. A robin hops on the bit of lawn beside Thelma's cement walk, and thrashes into the air as Harry approaches. He doesn't remember robins as seeming such big fierce birds; this one looked the size of a crow. He climbs two flagstone steps and crosses a little porch; Thelma opens the front door before he can ring the bell.

She seems smaller, and her hair grayer. Her prim, rather plain face always had a sallow tinge, and this jaundice has deepened, he can observe through the makeup she uses to soften her butterfly rash, a reddening the disease has placed like a soreness across her nose and beneath her eyes. Nevertheless, her deeply known presence stirs him. They lightly kiss, when she has closed the door, a long light-blocking green shade pulled down over its central pane of bevelled glass. Her lips are cool, and faintly greasy. She stays a time within his embrace, as if expecting something more to happen, her body relaxed against his in unspeakable confession.

"You're thin," she says, drawing at last away.

"A little less fat," he tells her. "I've a long way to go before I satisfy the doctors and Janice." It seems only natural to mention Janice, though he had to make his tongue do it. Thelma knows the score, and did from the start. The whole affair was her idea, though he grew used to it over the years, and built it in. Her walk as she moves away from him into the living room seems stiff, a bit of a waddle; arthritis is part of the lupus.

"Janice," she repeats. "How *is* Wonder Woman?" Once he confided that he called Janice that and Thelma has never forgotten. Women don't forget, especially what you wish they would.

"Oh, no different. She keeps busy in Florida with all these different groups, she's kind of the baby of our condo, and a shiksa besides. You'd hardly know her, she's so on the ball. Her tennis is terrific, the people who play tell me." He is getting too enthusiastic, he realizes. "But we were happy to leave. It got *cold*. March was miserable. At least up here you expect it and have the clothes."

"You never told us about your heart attack." That "us" is a little payback for his mentioning Janice right off. You trail your spouses after you like shadows, right into bed; they becloud the sheets.

"It didn't seem worth bragging about."

"We heard about it from little Ron, who knows a boy who knows Nelson. The kiddie network. Imagine how I felt, learning about it that way. My lover nearly dies and never tells me."

"How would we, I, whoever, tell you? It's not the kind of thing they have cards for in the drugstore."

In recent years he and Janice have seen less and less of the Harrisons. Rabbit and Ron were Mt. Judge boys together and played on the high-school basketball varsities that, coached by Marty Tothero, were league champions for two out of their three years in senior high. But he has never liked Ronnie: loud-mouthed, pushy, physically crude, always playing with himself in the locker room, flicking towels, giving redbellies, terrorizing the JVs. Women don't mind this kind of prick as much as Harry does. Part of Thelma's fascination for him has been that she could stand the guy, put up with his sexual tricks and crudity and remain outwardly such a prim, plain schoolteacher-type. Not really plain: with her clothes off her body is somehow better than her clothes have led you to expect. The first time they ever slept together, her breasts seemed like a girl's in *Playboy*—nipples like perfect little doorbells.

"What can I offer you?" Thelma asks. "Coffee. A beer?"

"Both are no-nos for the new me. Do you have anything like a Diet Coke or Pepsi?" He remembers Judy's little quavering voice singing *Coke is it* on that long zigzag ride into shore.

"Sure. We don't drink much any more ourselves, now that we've resigned from the Flying Eagle."

"You ever coming back?"

"I don't think so. We heard the fees went up again, as you maybe didn't notice, you're so rich, plus the assessment for repairs to the two greens close to the road that are always being vandalized. Even three years ago Ronnie figured it was costing him over eighty dollars a round, it wasn't worth it. There's a whole new younger crowd out at the Eagle now that dominates everything. They've changed the tone. It's gotten too yuppie."

"Too bad. I miss playing with old Ronnie."

"Why? You can't stand him, Harry."

"I liked beating him."

Thelma nods, as if acknowledging her own contribution to Harry's beating Ronnie. But she can't help it, she loves this man, his soft pale bemusement and cool hard heart, his uncircumcised prick, his offhand style, and in her slow dying has not denied herself the pleasure of expressing this love, as much as Harry has been able to bear it. She has kept her strongest feelings contained, and the affair has enriched her transactions with God, giving her something to feel sinful about, to discuss with Him. It seems to explain her lupus, if she's an adulteress. It makes it easier on Him, if she deserves to be punished.

She goes into the kitchen for the soft drinks. Rabbit roams quietly in the living room; in preparation for his visit she has pulled not only the narrow shade on the front door but the wide one on the picture window. He pities the room, its darkness as if even weak windowlight would penetrate her skin and accelerate the destruction of her cells, its hushed funereal fussiness. Wild though she can be, with a streak of defiance as though daring to be damned, Thelma maintains a conventional local decor. Stuffed flowered chairs with broad wooden arms, plush chocolate-brown sofa with needlepointed scatter pillows and yellowing lace antimacassars, varnished little knickknack stands and taborets, a footstool on which an old watermill is depicted, symmetrical lamps whose porcelain bases show English hunting dogs in gilded ovals, an oppressively patterned muddy neo-Colonial wallpaper, and on every flat surface, fringed runners and semi-precious glass and porcelain elves and parrots and framed photographs of babies and graduating sons and small plates and kettles of hammered copper and pewter, objects to dust around but never to rearrange. This front room, but for the television set hulking in its walnut cabinet with its powdery gray-green face wearing a toupee of doilies and doodads, could have come out of Harry's adolescence, when he was gingerly paying calls on girls whose mothers came forward from the kitchen, drying their hands on their aprons, to greet him in motionless stuffed rooms such as this. The houses he has kept with Janice have had in comparison a dishevelled, gappy quality that has nevertheless given him room to breathe. This room is so finished, he feels in it he should be dead. It smells of all the insurance policies Ron sold to buy its furnishings.

"So tell me about it," Thelma says, returning with a round painted tray holding along with the two tall glasses of sparkling dark soft drink two matching small bowls of nuts. She sets the tray down on a glass-topped coffee table like an empty long picture frame.

He tells her, "For one thing, I'm not supposed to have stuff like that—salted nuts. Macadamia nuts yet! The worst thing for me, and they cost a fortune. Thel, you're wicked.''

He has embarrassed her; her jaundiced skin tries to blush. Her basically thin face today looks swollen, perhaps from the cortisone she takes. ''Ronnie buys them. They just happened to be around. Don't eat them if you can't, Harry. I didn't know. I don't know how to act with you, it's been so long.''

''A couple won't kill me,'' he reassures her, and to be polite takes a few macadamia nuts into his fingers. Nuggets, they are like small lightweight nuggets with a fur of salt. He especially loves the way, when he holds one in his mouth a few seconds and then gently works it between his crowned molars, it breaks into two halves, the surface of the fissure smooth to the tongue as glass, as baby skin. ''And cashews, too,'' he says. ''The second-worst thing for me. Dry-roasted yet.''

''I seem to remember you like dry-roasted.''

''There's a lot I bet you seem to remember,'' he says, taking a tasteless sip of his Diet Coke. First they take the cocaine out, then the caffeine, and now the sugar. He settles back with a small handful of cashews; dry-roasted, they have a little acid sting to them, the tang of poison that he likes. He has taken the rocking chair, painted black with stencilled red designs and a red-and-yellow flat pillow tied in place, to sit in, and she the plush brown sofa, not sinking into it but perching on the edge, her knees together and touching the raised edge of the coffee table. They have made love on that sofa, which was not long enough to stretch out on but long enough if both parties kept their knees bent. In a way he preferred it to one of the beds, since she seemed to feel guiltier and less free with herself in a real bed, a bed her family used, and her unease would spread to him. Moving the table, he could kneel beside the sofa and have the perfect angle for kissing her cunt. On and on, deeper into her darkness where things began to shudder and respond, it got to be an end in itself. He loved it when she would clamp his face between her damp thighs like a nut in a nutcracker and come. He wondered if a man ever got his neck broken that way.

A shadow has crossed Thelma's face, a flinching as if he has consigned her to merely remembering, to the sealed and unrepeatable past like the photographs on the silent television set. But he had meant it more comfortably, settling in his rocker opposite the one person who for these last ten years has given him nothing but what he needed. Sex. Soul food.

''You too,'' she says, her eyes lowered to the items on the

tray, which she hasn't touched, "have things to remember, I hope."

"I just was. Remembering. You seem sad," he says, accusing, for his presence should make her glad, in spite of all.

"You don't seem quite you yet. You seem—more careful."

"Jesus, you'd be too. I'll have some more macadamia nuts, if that'll please you." He eats them one by one and between bouts of chewing and feeling their furry nuggets part so smoothly in his mouth tells her about his heart attack—the boat, the Gulf, little Judy, the lying on the beach feeling like a jellyfish, the hospital, the doctors, their advice, his attempts to follow it. "They're dying to cut into me and do a bypass. But there's this less radical option they can do first and I'm supposed to see a guy up here at St. Joseph's about having it done this spring. It's called an angioplasty. There's a balloon on the end of a catheter a yard long at least they thread up into your heart from a cut they make just under your groin, the artery there. I had it done kind of in Florida but instead of a balloon it was a bunch of dyes they put in to see what my poor old ticker actually looked like. It's a funny experience: it doesn't exactly hurt but you feel very funny, demoralized like, while it's being done and terrible for days afterward. When they put the dye in, your chest goes hot like you're in an oven. Deep, it feels too deep. Like having a baby but then no baby, just a lot of computerized bad news about your coronary arteries. Still, it beats open-heart, where they saw through your sternum for starters"—he touches the center of his chest and thinks of Thelma's breasts, their nipples so perfect to suck, waiting behind her blouse, waiting for him to make his move—"and then run all your blood through a machine for hours. I mean, that machine is *you*, for the time being. It stops, you die. A guy I play golf with down there had a quadruple and a valve replacement and a pacemaker while they were at it and he says he's never been the same, it was like a truck ran over him and then backed up. His swing, too, is terrible; he's never got it back. But enough, huh? What about you? How's *your* health?"

"How do I look?" She sips the Coke but leaves all the nuts in their twin bowls for him. The pattern imitates sampler stitch, squarish flowers in blue and pink.

"Good to me," he lies. "A little pale and puffy but we all do at the end of winter."

"I'm losing it, Harry," Thelma tells him, looking up until he meets her eyes. Eyes muddier than Pru's but also what they call hazel, eyes that have seen him all over, that know him as well as a woman's can. A wife fumbles around with you in the dark; a mistress you meet in broad daylight, right on the sofa. She used to tease him about his prick wearing a bonnet, with the foreskin still on. "My kidneys are worse and the steroid dose can't go any higher. I'm so anemic I can hardly drag around the house to do the work and have to take naps every afternoon— you're right in the middle of my nap time, as a matter of fact." He makes an instinctive motion, tightening his hands on the chair arms to pull himself up, and her voice lifts toward anger. "No. Don't go. Don't you dare. For God's sake. I don't see you at all for nearly six months and then you're up here a week before you bother to call."

"Thelma, *she's* around, I can't just wander off. I was getting reacclimated. I have to take it more easy on myself now."

"You've never loved me, Harry. You just loved the fact that I loved you. I'm not complaining. It's what I deserve. You make your own punishments in life, I honest to God believe that. You get exactly what you deserve. God sees to it. Look at my hands. I used to have pretty hands. At least I thought they were pretty. Now half the fingers—*look* at them! Deformed. I couldn't even get my wedding ring off if I tried now."

He looks, leaning forward so the rocker tips under him, to examine her extended hands. The knuckles are swollen and shiny, and some of the segments with the fingernails go off at a slight angle, but he wouldn't have noticed without her calling his attention to it. "You don't want to get your wedding ring off," he tells her. "As I remember, you and Ronnie are stuck together with glue. You even eat the glue sometimes, I seem to remember your telling me."

Her hands have made Thelma angry and he is fighting back, as if she blames her hands on him. She says, "You always minded that, that I was a wife to Ronnie, along with serving you whenever it suited. But who were you to mind that, stuck fast to Janice and her money? I never tried to take you away from her, though it would have been easy at times."

"Would it?" He rocks back. "I don't know, something about that little mutt still gets to me. She won't give up. She never really figured out how the world is put together but she's still working at it. Now she's got the idea she wants to be a working girl. She's signed up at the Penn State annex over on Pine Street for those courses you have to take to get a real-estate broker's license. At Mt. Judge High I don't think she ever got over a C, even in home ec. Come to think of it, I bet she flunked home ec, the only girl in the history of the school.''

Thelma grudgingly smiles; her sallow face lights up in her shadowy living room. ''Good for her,'' she says. ''If I had my health, I'd be getting out myself. This being a homemaker—they sold us a bill of goods, back there in home ec.''

''How *is* Ronnie, by the way?''

''The same,'' she says, with a note of that languid, plaintive music the women of the county inject into their saga of their stoic days. ''Not hustling so hard for the new customers now, coasting along on the old. He's out from under the children's educations, so his only financial burden is me and the doctor bills. Not that he wouldn't be willing to pay for little Ron to finish up at Lehigh if he wanted; it's been a disappointment, his becoming a kind of hippie the way he has. The funny thing was he was the cleverest of the three at school. Things just came too easy to him, I guess.''

Harry has heard this before. Thelma's voice is dutiful and deliberately calm, issuing small family talk when both know that what she wants to discuss is her old issue, that flared up a minute ago, of whether he loves her or not, or why at least he doesn't need her as much as she does him. But their relationship at the very start was established with her in pursuit of him, and all the years since, of hidden meetings, of wise decisions to end it and thrilling abject collapses back into sex, have not disrupted the fundamental pattern of her giving and his taking, of her fearing their end more than he, and clinging, and disliking herself for clinging, and wanting to punish him for her dislike, and him shrugging and continuing to bask in the sun of her love, that rises every day whether he is there or not. He can't believe it, quite, and has to keep testing her.

''These kids,'' he says, taking a bluff tone as if they are making small talk in public instead of enjoying this stolen intimacy behind drawn shades in Arrowdale, ''they break your heart. You ought to see Nelson when he's down there in Florida and has to live with me a little. The poor kid was jumping out of his skin.''

Thelma makes an annoyed motion with her hands. ''Harry, you're not actually the center of the universe, it just feels that way to you. Do you really think Nelson was jumpy because of you?''

''Why else?''

She knows something. She hesitates, but cannot resist, perhaps, a bit of revenge for his taking her always for granted, for his being in Pennsylvania a week before calling. "You must know about Nelson. My boys say he's a cocaine addict. They've all used it, that generation, but Nelson they tell me is really hooked. As they say, the drug runs him, instead of him just using the drug."

Harry has rocked back as far as the rocker will take him without his shoes leaving the rug and remains in that position so long that Thelma becomes anxious, knowing that this man isn't sound inside and can have a heart attack. At last he rocks forward again and, gazing at her thoughtfully, says, "That explains a lot." He fishes in the side pocket of his tweedy gray sports coat for a small brown bottle and deftly spills a single tiny pill into his hand and puts it in his mouth, under his tongue. There is a certain habituated daintiness in the gesture. "Coke takes money, doesn't it?" he asks Thelma. "I mean, you can go through hundreds. Thousands."

She regrets her telling him, now that the satisfaction is past of shocking him, of waking him up to her existence once again. She is still at heart too much a schoolteacher; she enjoys administering a lesson. "I can't believe Janice doesn't know and hasn't discussed it with you, or that Nelson's wife hasn't come to you both."

"Pru's pretty close-mouthed," he says. "I don't see them that much. Even when we're all in the county, it's on opposite sides of Brewer. Janice is over there at her mother's old place a fair amount, but not me. She owns it, I don't."

"Harry, don't look so stunned. It's all just rumor, and really is his business, his and his family's. We all do things our parents wouldn't approve of, and they know it, and don't want to know, if you follow me. Oh, Harry, *damn* it! Now I've made you sad, when I'm dying to make you happy. Why don't you like me to make you happy? Why have you always fought it?"

"I haven't. I haven't fought it, Thel. We've had great times. It's just, we've never been exactly set up for a lot of happiness, and now—"

"Now, dear?"

"Now I know how you've been feeling all these years."

She wants for him to explain, but he can't, he is suddenly afflicted by tact. She prompts, "Mortal?"

"Yeah. Close to it. I mean, things wearing thin so you sort of look right through them."

"Including me."

"Not you. Cut it out, making me jump through this same fucking hoop all the time. Why do you think I'm here?"

"To make love. To screw me. Go ahead. I mean come ahead. Why do you think I answered the door?" She has leaned forward across the table, her knees white where they press against the edge, and her face has taken on that melting crazy look women get at the decision to go with it, to fuck in spite of all, which frightens him now because it suggests a willing slide down into death.

"Wait. Thel. Let's think about this." On cue, the nitroglycerin has worked its way through and he gets that tingle. He sits back, suppressing it. "I'm supposed to avoid excitement."

She asks, amused somehow by the need to negotiate, "Have you made love with Janice?"

"Once or twice maybe. I kind of forget. You know, it's like brushing your teeth at night, you forget if you did or didn't."

She takes this in, and decides to tease him. "I made up Alex's old bed for us."

"You didn't use to like to use real beds."

"I've become very liberated," she says, smiling, extracting what pleasure she can out of his evasions.

He is tempted, picturing Thelma in bed naked, her tallowy willing body, her breasts that have nursed three boy babies and two men at least but look virginal and rosy like a baby's thumbtips, not bumply and chewed and dark like Janice's, her buttocks glassy in texture and not finely gritty like Janice's, her pubic hair reddish and skimpy enough to see the slit through unlike Janice's opaque thick bush, and her shameless and matter-of-fact mouth, Thelma's, her frank humorous hunger, amused at being caught in the trap of lust over and over, not holding it against him all these years of off and on, in and out. But then he thinks of Ronnie—who knows where that obnoxious prick's prick has been, Rabbit can't believe he's as faithful as Thelma thinks he is, not from the way he used to carry on in the locker room, not from the way he was screwing Ruth before Harry was, and cashing in Cindy that time in the Caribbean—and of AIDS. That virus too small to imagine travelling through our fluids, even a drop or two of saliva or cunt slime, and unlocking our antibodies with its little picks, so that our insides lose their balance and we topple into pneumonia, into starvation. Love and death, they can't be pried apart any more. But he can't tell Thelma that. It would be spitting in her wide-open face.

On her own she sees he isn't up to it. She asks, "Another

Coke?'' He has drunk it all, he sees, and consumed without thinking both the little bowls of fatty, sodium-soaked nuts.

"No. I ought to run. But let me sit here a little longer. Being with you is such a relief.''

"Why? It seems I make claims, like all the others.''

A little lightning of pain flickers across his chest, narrowing his scope of breath. Claims lie heavy around him, squeezing. Now a sexually unsatisfied mistress, another burden. But he lies, "No you don't. You've been all gravy, Thel. I know it's cost you, but you've been terrific.''

"Harry, *please*. Don't sound so maudlin. You're still young. What? Fifty-five? Not even above the speed limit.''

"Fifty-six two months ago. That's not old for some guys— not for a stocky little plug-ugly like Ronnie, he'll go forever. But if you're the height I am and been overweight as long, the heart gets tired of lugging it all around.'' He has developed, he realizes, an image of his heart as an unwilling captive inside his chest, a galley slave or one of those blinded horses that turn a mill wheel. He feels that Thelma is looking at him in a new way—clinically, with a detached appraising look far distant from the melting crazy look. He has forfeited something by not fucking her: he has lost full rank, and she is moving him out, without even knowing it. Fair enough. With her lupus, he moved her out a long while ago. If Thelma had been healthy, why wouldn't he have left Janice for her in this last decade? Instead he used all the holes she had and then hustled back into whatever model Toyota he was driving that year and back to Janice in her stubborn, stupid health. What *was* there about Janice? It must be religious, their tie, it made so little other sense.

Two ailing old friends, he and Thelma sit for half an hour, talking symptoms and children, catching up on the fate of common acquaintances—Peggy Fosnacht dead, Ollie down in New Orleans she heard, Cindy Murkett fat and unhappy working in a boutique in the new mall out near Oriole, Webb married for the fourth time to a woman in her twenties and moved from that fancy modern house in Brewer Heights with all his home carpentry to an old stone farmhouse in the south of the county, near Galilee, that he has totally renovated.

"That Webb. Anything he wants to do, he does. He really knows how to live.''

"Not really. I was never as impressed with him as you and Janice were. I always thought he was a smart-ass know-it-all.''

"You think Janice was impressed?''

Thelma is slightly flustered, and avoids his eye. "Well, there was that one night at least. She didn't complain the next morning." They are remembering a vacation night in the Caribbean when the three couples swapped, Janice getting Webb, Ronnie getting Cindy, and he, to his disappointment, Thelma. She told him that night that she had loved him for years.

"Neither did I," he says gallantly, though what he chiefly remembers is how tired he was the next morning, and how weird golf seemed, with impossible jungle and deep coral caves just off the fairway.

She nods in sarcastic acknowledgment of the compliment, and says, returning to an earlier point in their conversation, "About being mortal—I suppose it affects different people different ways, but for me there's never been a thinning out. Being alive, no matter how sick I feel, is an absolute right to the end. You're absolutely alive and when you're not you'll be absolutely something else. Do you and Janice ever go to church?"

Not too surprised, since Thelma has always been religious in her way, it goes with her conventional decor and secretive sexiness, he answers, "Rarely, actually. The churches down there have this folksy Southern thing. And most of our friends happen to be Jewish."

"Ronnie and I go every Sunday now. One of these new denominations that goes back to fundamentals. You know—we're lost, and we're saved."

"Oh yeah?" These marginal sects depress Harry. At least the moldy old denominations have some history to them.

"I believe it, sometimes," she says. "It helps the panic, when you think of all the things you'll never do that you always thought vaguely you might. Like go to Portugal, or get a master's degree."

"Well, you did some things. You did Ronnie, and me, me up brown I'd say, and you did raise three sons. You might get to Portugal yet. They say it's cheap, relatively. The only country over there I've ever wanted to go to is Tibet. I can't believe I won't make it. Or never be a test pilot, like I wanted to when I was ten. As you say, I still think I'm the center of the universe."

"I didn't mean that unkindly. It's charming, Harry."

"Except maybe to Nelson."

"Even to him. He wouldn't want you any different."

"Here's a question for you, Thel. You're smart. What ever happened to the Dalai Lama?"

In her clinical appraising mood, nothing should surprise her, but Thelma laughs. "He's still around, isn't he? In fact, hasn't he been in the news a little, now that the Tibetans are rioting again? Why, Harry? Have you become a devotee of his? Is that why you don't go to church?"

He stands, not liking being teased about this. "I've always kind of identified with him. He's about my age, I like to keep track of the guy. I have a gut feeling this'll be his year." As he stands there, the rocking chair on the rebound taps his calves and his medications make him feel lightheaded. "Thanks for the nuts," he says. "There's a lot we could still say."

She stands too, stiffly fighting the plushy grip of the sofa, and with her arthritic waddle steps around the table, and places her body next to his, her face at his lapel. She looks up at him with that presumptuous solemnity of women you have fucked. She urges him, "Believe in God, darling. It helps."

He squirms, inside. "I don't *not* believe."

"That's not quite enough, I fear. Harry, darling." She likes the sound of "darling." "Before you go, let me see him at least."

"See who?"

"Him, Harry. You. With his bonnet."

Thelma kneels, there in her frilled and stagnant dim living room, and unzips his fly. He feels the clinical cool touch of her fingers and sees the gray hairs on the top of her head, radiating from her parting; his heart races in expectation of her warm mouth as in the old days.

But she just says, "Just lovely," and tucks it back, half hard, into his Jockey shorts, and rezips his fly and struggles to her feet. She is a bit breathless, as if from a task of housework. He embraces her and this time it is he who clings.

"The reason I never left Janice and never can," he confesses, suddenly near tears, maudlin as she said, "is, without her, I'm shit. I'm unemployable. I'm too old. All I can be from here on in is her husband."

He expects sympathy, but perhaps his mention of Janice is one too many. Thelma goes dead, somehow, in his arms. "I don't know," she says.

"About what?"

"About your coming here again."

"Oh let me," he begs, perversely feeling at last in tune with this encounter and excited by her. "Without you, I don't have a life."

"Maybe Nature is trying to tell us something. We're too old to keep being foolish."

"Never, Thelma. Not you and me."

"You don't seem to want me."

"I want you, I just don't want Ronnie's little bugs."

She pushes at his chest to free herself. "There's nothing wrong with Ronnie. He's as safe and clean as I am."

"Yeah, well, that goes without saying, the way you two carry on. That's what I'm afraid of. I tell you, Thelma, you don't know him. He's a madman. You can't see it, because you're his loyal wife."

"Harry, I think we've reached a point where the more we say, the worse it'll get. Sex isn't what it used to be, you're right about that. We must all be more careful. *You* be careful. Keep brushing your teeth, and I'll brush mine."

It isn't until he is out on Thelma's curved walk, the door with its pulled curtain and bevelled glass shut behind him, that he catches her allusion to toothbrushing. Another slam at him and Janice. You can't say anything honest to women, they have minds like the FBI. The robin is still there, on the little lawn. Maybe it's sick, all these animals around us have their diseases too, their histories of plague. It gives Rabbit a beady eye and hops a bit away in Thelma's waxy April grass but disdains to take wing. Robin, hop. The bold yellow of dandelions has come this week to join that of daffodils and forsythia. Telltale. Flowers attracting bees as we attract each other. Our signals. Smells. Believe in God. If only he were back in her house he'd fuck her despite the danger. Instead he finds safety inside his gray Celica; as he glides away the stillness of Arrowdale is broken by the return of the lumbering yellow school buses, and their release, at every corner of the curved streets, of shrilly yelling children.

THE TOYOTA TOUCH, a big blue banner says in the display windows of Springer Motors over on Route 111. *36 Months / 36,000 Miles • Limited Warranty on All New Models*, a lesser poster proclaims, and another *All-New* CRESSIDAS • *Powerful New 3.0-Liter Engine • 190 Horsepower • 4-Speed Electronically Controlled Overdrive Transmission • New Safety Shift Lock*. Nelson isn't in, to Harry's considerable relief. The day is a desultory Tuesday and the two salesmen on the floor are both young men he doesn't know, and who don't know him. Changes have been made since last November. Nelson has had the office area repainted in brighter colors, pinks and greens like a Chinese teahouse, and has taken down the old blown-up photos of Harry in his glory days as a basketball star, with the headlines calling him "Rabbit."

"Mr. Angstrom left for lunch around one o'clock and said he might not be back this afternoon," a pudgy salesman tells him. Jake and Rudy used to have their desks out in the open along the wall, in the direction of the disco club that failed and when the Seventies went out became an appliance-rental center. One of Nelson's bright ideas was to take these desks away and line the opposite wall with cubicles, like booths in a restaurant. Maybe it creates more salesman-customer intimacy at the ticklish moment of signing the forms but the arrangement seems remote from general business operations and exposed to the noise of the service garage. In this direction, and behind toward the river and Brewer, lies the scruffy unpaved area of the lot Harry has always thought of in fantasy as Paraguay, which in reality just got rid of its old dictator with the German name, Harry read in the papers recently.

"Yeah, well," he tells this fat stranger, "I'm a Mr. Angstrom too. Who is here, who knows anything?" He doesn't mean to sound rude but Thelma's revelation has upset him; he can feel his heart racing and his stomach struggling to digest the two bowls of nuts.

Another young salesman, a thinner one, comes toward them, out of a booth at the Paraguay end, and he sees it's not a man; her hair being pulled back tight from her ears and her wearing a tan trench coat to go out onto the lot to a customer fooled him. It's a female. A female car salesman. Like in that Toyota commercial, only white. He tries to control his face, so his chauvinism doesn't show.

"I'm Elvira Ollenbach, Mr. Angstrom," she says, and gives him a narrow hard hand that, after Thelma's pasty cold touch a half-hour ago, feels hot. "I'd know you were Nelson's dad even without the pictures he keeps on his wall. You look just like him, especially around the mouth."

Is this chick kidding him? She is a thin taut young woman, overexercised the way so many of them are now, with deep bony eyesockets and a deep no-curves voice and thin lips painted a pale luminous pink like reflecting tape and a neck so slender it makes her jaws look wide, coming to points under the lobes of her exposed white ears, which stick out. She wears gold earrings shaped like snail shells. He says to her, "I guess you've come onto the job since I was last here."

"Just since January," she says. "But before that I was three years with Datsun out on Route 819."

"How do you like it, selling cars?"

"I like it very much," Elvira Ollenbach says, and no more. She doesn't smile much, and her eyes are a little insistent.

He puts himself on the line, telling her, "You don't think of it usually as a woman's game."

She shows a little life. "I know, isn't that strange, when it's really such a natural? The women who come in don't feel so intimidated, and the men aren't so afraid to show their ignorance as they would be with another man. I love it. My dad loved cars and I guess I take after him."

"It all makes sense," he admits. "I don't know why it's been so long in coming. Women sales reps, I mean. How's business been?"

"It's been a good spring, so far. People love the Camry, and of course the Corolla plugs right along, but we've had surprisingly good luck with the luxury models, compared to what we hear from other dealers. Brewer's economy is looking up, after all these years. The dead industries have been shaken out, and the new ones, the little specialty and high-tech plants, have been coming in, and of course the factory outlets have had a fabulous reception. They're the key to the whole revival."

"Super. How about the used end of it? That been slow?"

Her deeply set eyes—shadowy, like Nelson's, but not sullen and hurt—glance up in some puzzlement. "Why no, not at all. One of the reasons Nelson had for hiring a new rep was he wanted to devote more of his own attention to the used cars, and not wholesale so many of them out. There was a man who used to do it, with a Greek name—"

"Stavros. Charlie Stavros."

"Exactly. And ever since he retired Nelson feels the used cars have been on automatic pilot. Nelson's philosophy is that unless you cater to the lower-income young or minority buyer with a buy they can manage you've lost a potential customer for a new upscale model five or ten years down the road."

"Sounds right." She seems awfully full of Nelson, this girl. Girl, she may be thirty or more for all he can tell, everybody under forty looks like a kid to him.

The pudgy salesman, the one who's a man—a nice familiar Italian type, Brewer is still producing a few, with husky voices, hairy wrists, and with old-fashioned haircuts close above the ears—feels obliged to put his two cents in. "Nelson's really been making the used cars jump. Ads in the *Standard*, prices in shaving cream on the windshield knocked lower every two or three days, discounts for cash. Some people swing by every day to see what's up for grabs.'' He has an anxious way of standing too close and hurrying his words; his cheeks could use a shave and his breath a Cert or two. Garlic, they use it on everything.

"Discounts for cash, huh?" Harry says. "Where *is* Nelson, anyway?"

"He told us he needed to unwind," Elvira says. "He wanted to get away from the calls."

"Calls?"

"Some man keeps calling him," Elvira says. Her voice drops. "He sounds kind of foreign." Harry is getting the impression she isn't as smart as she seemed at first impression. Her insistent eyes catch a hint of this thought, for she self-protectively adds, "I probably shouldn't be saying a thing, but seeing as you're his father . . ."

"Sounds like a dissatisfied customer," Rabbit says, to help her out of it.

"Toyota doesn't get many of those," the other salesman crowds in. "Year after year, they put out the lowest-maintenance machines on the road, with a repair-free longevity that's absolutely unbelievable."

"Don't sell me, I'm sold," Harry tells him.

"I get enthusiastic. My name's Benny Leone, by the way, Mr. Angstrom. Benny for Benedict. A pleasure to see you over here. The way Nelson tells us, you've washed your hands of the car business and glad of it."

"I'm semi-retired." Do they know, he wonders, that Janice legally owns it all? He supposes they pretty much have the picture. Most people do, in life. People know more than they let on.

Benny says, "You get all kinds of kooky calls in this business. Nelson shouldn't let it bug him."

"Nelson takes everything too seriously," Elvira adds. "I tell him, Don't let things get to you, but he can't help it. He's one of those guys so uptight he squeaks."

"He was always a very caring boy," Harry tells them. "Who else is here, besides you two? Talk about automatic pilot—"

"There's Jeremy," Lenny says, "who comes in generally Wednesdays through Saturdays."

"And Lyle's here," Elvira says, and glances sideways to

where a couple in bleached jeans are wandering in the glinting
sea of Toyotas.

"I thought Lyle was sick," Harry says.

"He says he's in remission," Benny says, his face getting a
careful look, as maybe Harry's did when he was trying not to
appear a chauvinist in Elvira's eyes. She for her part has suddenly moved, in her spring trench coat, toward the bright outdoors, where the pair of potential buyers browse.

"Glad to hear it," Harry says, feeling less constrained and
ceremonious talking to Benny alone. "I didn't think there was
any remission from his disease."

"Not in the long run." The man's voice has gone huskier, a
touch gangsterish, as if the woman's presence had constrained
him too.

Harry jerks his head curtly toward the outdoors. "How's she
doing really?"

Benny moves an inch even closer and confides, "She gets 'em
to a certain point, then gets rigid and lets the deal slip away.
Like she's afraid the rest of us will say she's too soft."

Harry nods. "Like women are always the stingiest tippers.
Money spooks 'em. Still," he says, loyal to the changing times
and his son's innovations, "I think it's a good idea. Like lady
ministers. They have a people touch."

"Yeah," the jowly small man cautiously allows. "Gives the
place a little zing. A little something different."

"Where is Lyle, did you say?" He wonders how much these
two are concealing from him, protecting Nelson. He was aware
of eye signals between them as they talked. A maze of secrets,
this agency he built up in his own image since 1975, when old
man Springer suddenly popped, one summer day, like an over-
heated thermometer. A lot of hidden stress in the auto business.
Chancy, yet you're stuck with all that inventory.

"He was in Nelson's office ten minutes ago."

"Doesn't he use Mildred's?" Harry explains, "Mildred
Kroust was the bookkeeper for years here, when you were just
a kid." In terms of Springer Motors he has become a historian.
He can remember when that appliance-rental place up the road
had a big sign saying D I S C O remade from a Mr. Peanut in
spats and top hat brandishing his stick in neon.

But Benny seems to know all he wants to. He says, "That's
a kind of conference room now. There's a couch in there if
anybody needs all of a sudden to take a nap. Lyle used to, but
now he works mostly at home, what with his illness."

"How long has he had it?"

Benny gets that careful look again, and says, "At least a year. That HIV virus can be inside you for five or ten before you know it." His voice goes huskier, he comes closer still. "A couple of the mechanics quit when Nelson brought him in as accountant in his condition, but you got to hand it to Nelson, he told them go ahead, quit, if they wanted to be superstitious. He spelled out how you can't get it from casual contact and told them take it or leave it."

"How'd Manny go for that?"

"Manny? Oh yeah, Mr. Manning in Service. As I understand it, that was the reason he left finally. He'd been shopping, I hear, at other agencies, but at his age it's hard to make a jump."

"You said it," Harry says. "Hey, looks like another customer out there, you better help Elvira out."

"Let 'em look, is my motto. If they're serious, they'll come in. Elvira tries too hard."

Rabbit walks across the display floor, past the performance board and the Parts window and the crash-barred door that leads into the garage, to the green doorway, set in old random-grooved Masonite now painted a dusty rose, of what used to be his office. Elvira was right; the photographic blowups of his basketball headlines and halftone newspaper cuts haven't been tossed out but are up on Nelson's walls, where the kid has to look at them every day. Also on the walls are the Kiwanis and Rotary plaques and a citation from the Greater Brewer Chamber of Commerce and a President's Touch Award that Toyota gave the agency a few years ago and a *Playboy* calendar, the girl for this month dressed up as a bare-assed Easter bunny, which Harry isn't so sure strikes quite the right note but at least says the whole agency hasn't gone queer.

Lyle stands up at Nelson's desk before Harry is in the room. He is very thin. He wears a thick red sweater under his gray suit. He extends a skeletal bluish hand and an unexpectedly broad smile, his teeth enormous in his shrunken face. "Hello, Mr. Angstrom. I bet you don't remember me."

But he does look dimly familiar, like somebody you played basketball against forty years ago. His skull is very narrow, the crew-cut hair so evenly blond it looks dyed; the accountant's half-glasses on his nose are of thin gold wire. He is so pale, light seems to be coming through his skin. Squinting, Harry takes the offered hand in a brief shake and tries not to think of those little HIVs, intricate as tiny spaceships, slithering off onto his palm and up his wrist and arm into the sweat pores of his armpit and burrowing into his bloodstream there. He wipes his palm on the side of his jacket and hopes it looks like he's patting his pocket.

Lyle tells him, "I used to work in Fiscal Alternatives on Weiser Street when you and your wife would come and trade gold and silver."

Harry laughs, remembering. "We damn near broke our backs, lugging one load of silver dollars up the street to the fucking bank."

"You were smart," Lyle says. "You got out in time. I was impressed."

This last remark seems a touch impertinent, but Harry says amiably, "Dumb luck. That place still functioning?"

"In a *very* restricted way," Lyle says, overemphasizing, for Harry's money, the "very." It seems if you're a fag you have to exaggerate everything, to bring it all up to normal pitch. "The whole metals boom was a fad, really. They're *very* depressed now."

"It was a nifty little place. That beauty who used to do the actual buying and selling. I could never figure out how she could run the computer with those long fingernails."

"Oh, Marcia. She committed suicide."

Rabbit is stunned. She had seemed so angelic in her way. "She did? Why?"

"Oh, the usual. Personal problems," Lyle says, flicking them away with the back of his transparent hand. In Rabbit's eyes globules of blurred light move around Lyle's margins, like E.T. in the movie. "Nothing to do with the metals slump. She was just the front, the money behind it came out of Philadelphia."

As Lyle talks airily, Harry can hear his intakes of breath, a slight panting that goes with the bluish shadows at the temples, the sense of him having come from space and about to go back to space. *This guy's even worse off than I am,* Rabbit thinks, and likes him for it. He sees no signs of the Kaposi's spots, though, just a general radiant aura of a body resisting life, refusing sustenance, refusing to go along with its own system. There is a sweetish-rotten smell, like when you open the door of the unused refrigerator in a vacation place, or maybe Rabbit imagines it. Lyle suddenly, limply, sits down, as if standing has been too much effort.

Harry takes the chair across the desk, where the customers usually sit, begging for easier terms. "Lyle," Harry begins.

"I'd like to inspect the books. Bank statements, receipts, payments, loans, inventory, the works."

"Why on earth why?" Lyle's eyes, as the rest of his face wastes away, stand out, more in the round than healthy people's eyes. He sits erect, one fleshless forearm for support laid in its gray sleeve parallel to the edge of Nelson's desk. Either to conserve his energy or protect the truth, he has set himself to give minimal answers.

"Oh, human curiosity. Frankly, there's something fishy about the statements I've been getting in Florida." Harry hesitates, but can't see that being specific would do any harm at this point. He still has the hope that everything can be explained away, that he can go back to not thinking about the lot. "There aren't enough used-car sales, proportionally."

"There aren't?"

"You could argue it's a variable, and with the good economy under Reagan people can afford to buy new; but in my years here there's always been a certain proportion, things average out over the course of a couple months, and that hasn't been happening in the statements since November. In fact, it's been getting weirder."

"Weirder."

"Funnier. Phonier. Whatever. When can I see the books? I'm no accountant, I want Mildred Kroust to go over them with me."

Lyle makes an effort and shifts his arm off the desk and rests with both hands out of sight, on his lap. Harry is reminded by the way he moves of the ghostly slowness of the languid dead floppy bodies at Buchenwald being moved around in the postwar newsreels. Naked, loose-jointed, their laps in plain view, talk about obscene, here was something so obscene they had to show it to us so we'd believe it. Lyle tells Harry, "I keep a lot of the data at home, in my computer."

"We have a computer system here. Top of the line, an IBM. I remember our installing it."

"Mine's compatible. A little Apple that does everything."

"I bet it does. You know, frankly, just because you're sick and have to stay home a lot's no reason the Springer Motors accounts should be scattered all over Diamond County. I want them here. I want them here tomorrow."

This is the first acknowledgment either has made that Lyle is sick, that Lyle is dying. The boy stiffens, and his lips puff out a little. He smiles, that skeleton-generous grin. "I can only show the books to authorized persons," he says.

"I'm authorized. Who could be more authorized than me? I used to run the place. That's my picture all over the walls."

Lyle's eyelids, with lashes darker than his hair, lower over those bulging eyes. He blinks several times, and tries to be delicate, to keep the courtesies between them. "My understanding from Nelson is that his mother owns the company."

"Yeah, but I'm her husband. Half of what's hers is mine."

"In some circumstances, perhaps, and perhaps in some states. But not, I think, in Pennsylvania. If you *wish* to consult a lawyer—" His breathing is becoming difficult; it is almost a mercy for Harry to interrupt.

"I don't need to consult any lawyer. All I need is to have my wife call you and tell you to show me the books. Me and Mildred. I want her in on this."

"Miss Kroust, I believe, resides now in a nursing home. The Dengler Home in Penn Park."

"Good. That's five minutes from my house. I'll pick her up and come back here tomorrow. Let's set a time."

Lyle's lids lower again, and he awkwardly replaces his arm on the desktop. "When and *if* I receive your wife's authorization, and Nelson's go-ahead—"

"You're not going to get that. Nelson's the problem here, not the solution."

"I say, even *if*, I would need some days to pull all the figures together."

"Why is that? The books should be up-to-date. What's going on here with you guys?"

Surprisingly, Lyle says nothing. Perhaps the struggle for breath is too much. It is all so wearying. Harry's heart is racing and his chest twingeing but he resists the impulse to pop another Nitrostat, he doesn't want to become an addict. He slumps down lower in the customer's chair, as if negotiations for now have gone as far as they can go. He tries another topic. "Tell me about it, Lyle. How does it feel?"

"What feel?"

"Being so close to, you know, the barn. The reason I ask, I had a touch of heart trouble down in Florida and still can't get used to it, how close I came. I mean, most of the time it seems unreal, I'm *me*, and all around me everything is piddling along as normal, and then suddenly at night, when I wake up needing to take a leak, or in the middle of a TV show that's sillier than hell, it hits me, and wow. The bottom falls right out. I want to crawl back into my parents but they're dead already.''

Lyle's puffy lips tremble, or seem to, as he puzzles out this new turn the conversation has taken. "You come to terms with it," he says. "Everybody dies.''

"But some sooner than others, huh?''

A spasm of indignation animates Lyle. "They're developing new drugs. All the time. The French. The Chinese. Trichosanthin. TIBO derivatives. Eventually the FDA will have to let them in, even if they are a bunch of Reaganite fascist homophobes who wouldn't mind seeing us all dead. It's a question of hanging on. I have hope.''

"Well, great. More power to you. But medicine can only do so much. That's what I'm learning, the hard way. You know, Lyle, it's not as though I'd never thought about death, or never had people near to me die, but I never, you could say, had the actual taste of it in my mouth. I mean, it's not kidding. It wants it all.'' He wants that pill. He wonders if Nelson keeps a roll of Life Savers in the desk the way he himself used to. Just something to put in your mouth when you get nervous. Harry finds that every time he thinks of his death it makes him want to eat—that's why he hasn't lost more weight.

This other man's attempt to open him up has made Lyle more erect behind the desk, more hostile. He stares at Harry with those eroded-around eyes, beneath eyebrows the same metallic blond as his hair. "One good thing about it,'' he offers, "is you become harder to frighten. By minor things. By threats like yours, for example.''

"I'm not making any threats, Lyle, I'm just trying to find out what the fuck is going on. I'm beginning to think this company is being ripped off. If I'm wrong and it's all on the up and up, you've nothing to be frightened of.'' Poor guy, he's biting the bullet, and less than half Harry's age. At his age, what was Harry doing? Setting type the old-fashioned way, and dreaming about ass. Ass, one way or another, does us in: membrane's too thin, those little HIVs sneak right through. Black box of nothingness, is what it felt like with Thelma. Funny appetite, for a steady diet. Being queer isn't all roses.

Lyle moves his arms around again with that brittle caution. His body has become a collection of dead sticks. "Don't make allegations, Mr. Angstrom, you wouldn't want to defend in court.''

"Well, is it an allegation or a fact that you refuse to let me and an impartial accountant examine your books?"

"Mildred's not impartial. She's furious at me for replacing her. She's furious because I and my computer can do in a few hours what took her all week."

"Mildred's an honest old soul."

"Mildred's senile."

"Mildred's not the point here. The point is you're defying me to protect my son."

"I'm not defying you, Mr. Angstrom—"

"You can call me Harry."

"I'm not defying you, sir. I'm just telling you I can't accept orders from you. I have to get them from Nelson or Mrs. Angstrom."

"You'll get 'em. Sir." A smiling provocative hovering in Lyle's expression goads him to ask, "Do you doubt it?"

"I'll be waiting to hear," Lyle says.

"Listen. You may know about a lot of things I don't but you don't know shit about marriage. My wife will do what I tell her to. Ask her to. In a business like this we're absolutely one."

"We'll see," Lyle says. "My parents were married, as a matter of fact. I was raised in a marriage. I know a *lot* about marriage."

"Didn't do you much good."

"It showed me something to avoid," Lyle says, and smiles as broadly, as guilelessly, as when Harry came in and the old days at Fiscal Alternatives for a moment returned, the stacks of gold and silver, and flawless cool Marcia with her long red nails. Poor beauty, did herself in. She and Monroe. Rabbit admits to himself the peculiar charm queers have, a boyish lightness, a rising above all that female muck, where life breeds.

"How's Slim?" Harry asks, rising from the chair. "Nelson used to talk a lot about Slim."

"Slim," Lyle says, too weak or rude to stand, "died. Before Christmas."

"Sorry to hear it," Harry lies. He holds out his hand over the desk to be shaken and the other man hesitates to take it, as if fearing contamination. Feverish loose-jointed bones: Harry gives them a squeeze and says, "Tell Nelson if you ever see him I like the new decor. Kind of a boutique look. Cute. Goes with the new sales rep. You hang loose, Lyle. Hope China comes through for you. We'll be in touch."

On the radio on the way home, he hears that Mike Schmidt,

who exactly two years ago, on April 18, 1987, slugged his five hundredth home run, against the Pittsburgh Pirates in Three Rivers Stadium, is closing in on Richie Ashburn's total of 2,217 hits to become the hittingest Phillie ever. Rabbit remembers Ashburn. One of the Whiz Kids who beat the Dodgers for the pennant the fall Rabbit became a high-school senior. Curt Simmons, Del Ennis, Dick Sisler playing first because Eddie Waitkus got shot by some woman. Beat the Dodgers the last game of the season, then lost to the Yankees four straight. In 1950 he was seventeen and had led the county B league with 817 points his junior season. Remembering these statistics helps settle his agitated mood, stirred up by seeing Thelma and Lyle, a mood of stirred-up unsatisfied desire at whose fringes licks the depressing idea that nothing matters very much, we'll all soon be dead.

Janice's idea of a low-sodium diet for him is to get these frozen dinners in plastic pouches called Low-Cal. Most of this precooked chicken and beef is full of chemicals so it doesn't go bad on the shelf. To work it all through his system he usually has a second beer. Janice is distracted these days, full of excitement about taking real-estate courses at the Penn State extension. "I'm not sure I totally understand it, though the woman at the office over on Pine Street—hasn't *that* neighborhood gone downhill, since you and your father used to work at Verity!— she was very patient with my questions. The classes meet three hours a week for ten weeks, and there are two required and four electives to get this certificate, but I don't think you need the certificate to take the licensing exam, which for a salesperson— that's what I'd be—is given monthly and for a broker, which maybe I'd try to be later, only quarterly. But the gist of it is I could begin with two this April and then take two more from July to September and if all goes well get my license in September and start selling, strictly on a commission basis at first, for this firm that Doris Eberhardt's new brother-in-law is one of the partners in. She says she's told him about me and he's interested. It's in your favor evidently to be middle-aged, the clients assume you're experienced."

"Honey, why do you need to do this? You have the lot."

"I don't have the lot. Nelson has the lot."

"Does he? I dropped over there today and he wasn't there, just these kids he's hired. One fag, one wop, and a skirt."

"Harry. Now who's sounding prejudiced?"

He doesn't push ahead with his story, he wants to save it for when they both can focus. After dinner Janice likes to watch *Jeopardy!* even though she never knows any of the answers, and then the Phillies are playing the Mets on Channel 11. The little stone house with its fractional number on Franklin Drive draws darkling about them, just them, in the evening as the gradual Northern dusk (in Florida the sun just suddenly shuts down, and the moon takes over) seeps into the still-bare trees, quelling the birdsong, and a lemon tinge of sky in the west beyond the craggy chimneys of the big clinker-brick house deepens to an incendiary orange and then the crimson of last embers. Another few weeks, the trees will leaf in, and there won't be any sunset to see from the lozenge-pane windows of his den, when he turns his eyes aside from watching the television screen.

In the third inning, with two men on, Schmidt hits a home run, his fourth of the young season and the five hundred forty-sixth of his career. It puts the Phils ahead five to zero, and Rabbit starts switching channels, finding no basketball playoffs, only *Matlock* and *The Wonder Years*. Much as Janice irritates him when she's with him, when she isn't in the room with him, or when he can't hear her knocking around in the kitchen or upstairs above his head, he grows uneasy. He switches off the set and goes looking for her, full of his troubling news as once he was full of gold, Krugerrands.

She is already in one of her nighties, upstairs, and those infuriating Florida sandals that go *flop-flop* as she walks around when he is still trying to sleep in the morning. Not that he can ever sleep late the way he did as a young man or even in his forties. He wakes around six with a little start and ever since his heart attack there is a gnawing in his stomach whose cause he can't locate until he realizes it is the terror of being trapped inside his perishing body, like being in a prison cell with a madman who might decide to kill him at any moment. She is paddling back and forth, *flop-flop*, carrying small stacks of folded cloth, laundry she has brought up the back stairs; one square stack he recognizes as folded handkerchiefs, another, less trim, as his Jockey shorts with their slowly slackening elastic waists, a third as her own underthings, which still excite him, not so much when they are on her as when empty and laundry-clean. He doesn't know how to begin. He throws his big body across the bed diagonally and lets the nubbles of its bedspread rub his face. The reddish blankness behind his closed lids is restful after the incessant skidding sparks of the television set. "Harry, is anything the matter?" Janice's voice sounds alarmed. His fragility gives him a new hold over her.

He rolls over and can't help smiling at the lumpy figure she cuts in her nightie. She looks not so different from how Judy looks in hers and not very much larger. Her scant bangs don't quite hide her high forehead, its Florida tan dulling, and her tired eyes look focused elsewhere. He begins, "There's something going wrong over at the lot. When I was over there today I asked to see the books and this fag with AIDS Nelson has put in as bookkeeper instead of Mildred told me he couldn't show them to me unless you authorized it. You're the boss, according to him."

The tip of her little tongue creeps out and presses on her upper lip. "That was silly," she says.

"I thought so, but I kept my cool. Poor guy, he's just covering up for Nelson."

"Covering up for Nelson why?"

"Well"—Harry sighs heavily, and arranges himself on the bed like an odalisque, with a hippy twist to his body—"you really want to hear this?"

"Of course." But she keeps moving around with her little stacks.

"I have a new theory. I think Nelson takes cocaine, and that's why he's so shifty and jumpy, and kind of paranoid."

Janice moves carefully to the bureau, *flop* and then *flop*, carrying what Harry recognizes as her salmon-colored running suit with the blue sleeves and stripes, which she never wears on the street around here, where the middle-aged are more careful about looking ridiculous. "Who told you this?" she asks.

He squirms on the bed, pulling up his legs and pushing off his shoes so as not to dirty the bedspread of white dotted Swiss. "Nobody *told* me," he says. "I just put two and two together. Cocaine's everywhere and these yuppie baby boomers Nelson's age are just the ones who use it. It takes money. Lots of money, to maintain a real habit. Doesn't Pru keep complaining about all these bills they can't pay?"

Janice comes close to the bed and stands; he sees through her cotton nightie shadows of her nipples and her pubic hair. From his angle she looks strangely enormous, and in his diagonal position he undergoes one of those surges of lightheadedness as when he stands up too fast; it is not clear who is upright and who is not. Her body has kept the hard neatness it had when they were kids working at Kroll's but underneath her chin there are ugly folds that ramify into her neck. She was determined not to get fat like her mother but age catches you anyway. Janice says carefully, "Most young couples have bills they can't pay."

He sits up, to shake the lightness in his head, and because her body is there puts his arms around her hips. On second thought he reaches under her nightie and cups his hands around her solid, slightly gritty buttocks. He says, looking up past her breasts to her face, "The worst of it is, honey, I think he's been bleeding the company. I think he's been stealing and Lyle has been helping him, that's why they let Mildred go."

Her buttocks under his hands tense; he feels them squeeze together and become more spherical, with the tension of a basketball a few pounds under regulation pressure. A watery glimmer of arousal winks below his waist. Her blurred eyes look down upon him with somber concentration, the skin of her face sagging downward from the bone. He nuzzles one breast and closes his eyes again, smelling the faintly sweaty cotton, hiding from her intent downward eyes. Her voice asks, "What evidence do you have?"

This irritates him. She is dumb. "That's what I was saying. I asked to look at the accounts and bank statements today and they wouldn't let me, unless you authorized it. All you have to do is call up this Lyle."

He hears in her chest a curious stillness, and feels in her body a tension of restraint. Her nightie is transparent but she is opaque. "If you did see these figures," she asks, "would you know enough to understand them?"

He flicks her nipple with his tongue through the cotton. The glimmer below has grown to a steady glow, a swelling warmth. "Maybe not altogether," he says. "But even the monthly statements we got in Florida didn't look quite right to me. I'd take Mildred with me, and if she's too far gone—he said she's senile and over at Dengler's—I think we should hire somebody, a professional accountant in Brewer. You could call our lawyer for who he'd recommend. This may be something we have to bring the cops in on eventually." A nice April shower has started up outdoors, kindled by the slow sunset.

Her body has stiffened and jerked back an inch. "Harry! Your own son!"

"Well," he says, irritated again, "his own mother. Stealing from his own mother."

"We don't know anything for sure," Janice tells him. "It's only your theory."

"What else could Lyle have been hiding today? Now they'll have the wind up so we should start moving or they'll shred everything like Ollie North."

Now Janice is getting agitated, backing out of his arms and rubbing the back of one hand with the other, standing in the center of the carpet. He sees that the sex isn't going to happen, the first time in weeks he's really had the urge. Damn that Nelson. She says, "I think I should talk to Nelson first."

"*You* should? Why not *we*?"

"According to Lyle, I'm the only one who counts."

This hurts. "You're too soft on Nelson. He can do anything he wants with you."

"Oh, Harry, it used to be so awful, that time I ran off with Charlie! Nelson was only twelve, he'd come over on his bicycle all the way into Eisenhower Avenue and he'd stand there for an hour across the street, looking up at our windows, and a couple of times I saw him and I *hid*, I hid behind the curtain and let him just stand there until he got exhausted and rode away." Staring over Harry's head, seeing her little boy across the street, so patient and puzzled and hopeful, her dark eyes fill with tears.

"Well, hell," Rabbit says, "nobody *asked* him to go over there spying on you. *I* was taking care of him."

"With that poor crazy girl and perfectly hideous black man you were. It's just dumb luck the house didn't burn down with Nelson in it too."

"I would have got him out. If I'd been there I would have got them all out."

"You don't *know*," she says, "you don't know what you would have done. And you don't know now what the real story is, it's all just your suspicions, somebody's been poisoning your mind against Nelson. I bet it was Thelma."

"Thelma? We never see her anymore, we ought to have the Harrisons over sometime."

"*Pfaa!*" She spits this refusal, he has to admire her fury, the animal way it fluffs out her hair. "Over my dead body."

"Just a thought." This is not a good topic. He reverts: "I don't know what the real story is, but you do, huh? What has Nelson told you?"

She pinches her mouth shut so she seems to have no lips at all, like Ma Springer used to look. "Nothing really," she lies.

"Nothing *really*. Well O.K. then. You know more than I do. Good luck. It's you he's ripping off. It's your father's company he and his queer buddies are taking down the tube."

"Nelson wouldn't steal from the company."

"Honey, you don't understand the power of drugs. Read the papers. Read *People*, Richard Pryor tells all. Just the other day they pulled Yogi Berra's kid in. People who are into coke will kill their grandmother for a fix. It used to be heroin was the bottom of the barrel but crack makes heroin look mild."

"Nelson doesn't do crack. Much."

"Oh. Who says?"

She almost tells him, but gets frightened. "Nobody. I just know my own son. And from what Pru lets drop."

"Pru talks, does she? What does she say?"

"She's miserable. And the children too. Little Roy acts very odd, you must have noticed. Judy has nightmares. If it weren't for the children, Pru confessed to me, she would have left Nelson long ago."

Harry feels evaded. "Let's keep to the subject. Pru's got her problems, you've got yours. You better get your man-child out of Springer Motors fast."

"I'll talk to him, Harry. I don't want you to say a word."

"Why the fuck not? What's the fucking harm if I do?"

"You'll come on too strong. You'll drive him deeper into himself. He—he takes you too seriously."

"But not you?"

"He's sure of me. He knows I love him."

"And I don't?" His eyes water at the thought. The shower outside has already lifted, leaving a trickle in the gutters.

"You do, Harry, but there's something else too. You're another man. Men have this territorial thing. You think of the lot as yours. He thinks of it as his."

"It'll be his some day, if he's not in jail. I was looking at him down in Florida and there suddenly came into my mind the word *criminal*. Something about the shape of his head. I hate the way he's going bald. He'll look like Ronnie Harrison."

"Will you promise to let me talk to him and you do nothing?"

"You'll just let him weasel out." But in fact he has no desire to confront Nelson himself.

She knows this. She says, "No I won't, I promise." She stops rubbing the back of one hand with the fingers of the other and moves back toward him, *flop-flop*, as he sits on the bed. She rests her fingers above his ears and by the short hairs there pulls him softly toward her. "I do like the way you want to defend me," she says.

He yields to her insistent tug and rests his face on her chest again. Her nightie has a damp spot on it where he diddled her nipple with his tongue. Her nipples are chewed-looking, less perfect, realer than Thelma's. Being little, Janice's tits have kept their tilt pretty much, that perky upward thrust through those Forties angora sweaters in the high-school halls. Through the cotton her body gives off a smell, a stirred-up smoky smell. "What's in it for me?" he asks, his mouth against the wet cloth.

"Oh, a present," she says.

"When do I get it?"

"Pretty soon."

"With the mouth?"

"We'll see." She pushes his face back from her smoky warm body and with her fingers poking under his jaws makes him look up at her. "But if you say another single word about Nelson, I'll stop, and you won't get any present."

His face feels hot and his heart is racing but in a steady sweet way, contained in his rib cage the way his hard-on is contained in his pants, sweetly packed with blood; he is pleased that the Vasotec may make him lightheaded but leaves him enough blood pressure for one of these unscheduled, once in a while. "O.K., not a word," Rabbit promises, becoming efficient. "I'll quick go to the bathroom and brush my teeth and stuff and you turn off the lights. And somebody ought to take the phone off the hook. Downstairs, so we don't hear the squawking."

Strange phone calls have been coming through. Grainy voices with that rich timbre peculiar to black males ask if Nelson Angstrom is there. Harry or Janice responds that Nelson does not live here, that this is the home of his parents. "Well I ain't had no luck at the number he give me for a home number and at the place he works this here secretary always say the man is out."

"Would you like to leave a message?"

A pause. "You just tell him Julius called." Or Luther.

"Julius?"

"That's right."

"And what's it about, Julius? You want to say?"

"He'll know what it's about. You just tell him Julius called." Or Perry. Or Dave.

Or the caller would hang up without leaving a name. Or would have a thin, faintly foreign, precise way of speaking, and once wanted to speak not to Nelson but with Harry. "I am regretful to bother you, sir, but this son you have leaves me no recourse but to inform you in person."

"To inform me of what?"

"To inform you that your son has incurred serious debts and gentlemen to which I am associated, against any advice which I attempt to give them, talk of doing physical harm."

"Physical harm to Nelson?"

"Or even to certain of his near and dear. This is sorry to say and I do apologize, but these are not perhaps such gentlemen. I myself am merely the bearer of bad tidings. Do not put the blame with me." The voice seemed to be drawing closer to the telephone mouthpiece, closer to Harry's ear, growing plaintively earnest, attempting to strike a conspiracy, to become Harry's friend and ally. The familiar room, the den with its frost-faced TV and two silvery-pink wing chairs and bookshelves holding a smattering mostly of history books and on the upper shelves some china knickknacks—fairies under toadstools, cherubic bald monks, baby robins in a nest of porcelain straws—that used to be in Ma Springer's breakfront, all this respectable furnishing changes quality, becomes murky and fluid and useless, at the insertion of this menacing plaintive voice into his ear, a voice with a heart of sorts, with an understandable human mission, an unpleasant duty to do, calling out of an extensive slippery underground: just so, the balmy blue air above the Gulf of Mexico changed for him, as if a filter had been slipped over his eyes, when the Sunfish tipped over.

Harry asks, treading water, "How did Nelson incur these debts?"

The voice likes getting his own words back. "He incurred them, sir, in pursuit of his satisfactions, and that is within his privileges, but he or someone on his behalf must pay. My associates have been assured that you are a very excellent father."

"Not so hot, actually. Whajou say your name was?"

"I did not say, señor. I did not give myself a name. It is the name of Angstrom that is of concern. My associates are eager to settle with anyone of that excellent name." This man, it occurred to Harry, loves the English language, as an instrument full of promise, of unexplored resources.

"My son," Harry tells him, "is an adult and his finances have nothing to do with me."

"That is your word? Your very final word?"

"It is. Listen, I live half the year in Florida and come back and—"

But the caller has hung up, leaving Harry with the sensation that the walls of his solid little limestone house are as thin as diet crackers, that the wall-to-wall carpet under his feet is soaked with water, that a pipe has burst and there is no plumber to call.

He turns to his old friend and associate Charlie Stavros, retired from being Springer Motors' Senior Sales Representative and moved from his old place on Eisenhower Avenue to a new condominium development on the far east side of the city, where the railroad had sold off an old freight yard, twenty acres of it, it's amazing what the railroads owned in their heyday. Harry isn't sure he can find the place and suggests they have lunch at Johnny Frye's downtown; Johnny Frye's Chophouse was the original name for this restaurant on Weiser Square, which became the Café Barcelona in the Seventies and then the Crêpe House later in the decade and now has changed hands again and calls itself Salad Binge, explaining in signs outside *Your Local Lo-Cal Eatery* and *Creative Soups and Organic Fresh-Food Health Dishes*, to attract the health-minded yuppies who work in the glass-skinned office building that has risen across from Kroll's, which still stands empty, its huge display windows whitewashed from the inside and its bare windowless side toward the mountain exposed in rough-mortared brick above the rubbly parking lot that extends up to the old Baghdad. ELP. SAV ME.

The downtown is mostly parking space now but the strange thing is that the space is all full. Though there is little to shop at downtown any more, except for some discount drugstores and a McCrory's five-and-dime that still peddles parakeet food and plastic barrettes to old people who haven't changed clothes since 1942, the number of trim youngish professionals in lightweight suits and tight linen skirts has ballooned; they work in the banks and insurance companies and state and federal agencies and there is no end of them somehow. On a sunny day they fill the woodsy park the city planners—not local, a fancy architectural firm that came in and won the competition with their design and then flew back to Atlanta—have made out of Weiser Square, where the squeaking, sparking trolley cars used to line up for passengers. They bask, these young paper-pushers, beside the abstract cement fountains, reading *The Wall Street Journal* with their coats off and neatly folded on the anodized, vandal-proof benches beside them. The women of this race especially fascinate Harry; they wear running shoes instead of high heels but their legs are encased in sheer pantyhose and their faces adorned by big round glasses that give them a comical sexy look, as if their boobs are being echoed above in hard hornrims and coated plastic. They look like Goldie Hawns conditioned by Jane Fonda. The style these days gives them all wide mannish shoulders, and their hips have been pared and hardened by exercise bicycles and those ass-hugging pants that mold around every muscle like electric-colored paint. These women seem visitors from a slimmed-down future where sex is just another exercise and we all live in sealed cubicles and communicate through computers.

You would have thought Charlie would be dead by now. But these Mediterranean types don't even seem to get gray and paunchy. They hit a plateau around fifty that doesn't change until they drop off of it suddenly somewhere in their eighties. They used their bodies up neatly, like mopping up a dinner plate with bread. Charlie had rheumatic fever as a kid but, though carrying a heart murmur inside him and subject to angina, he hasn't ever had an episode as severe as Harry's down in the Gulf. "How the fuck do you do it, Charlie?" Rabbit asks him.

"You learn to avoid aggravation," Charlie tells him. "If anything looks to be aggravating, walk away from it. Things over at the lot had got to be aggravating, so I walked away. Christ, am I glad to be away from Toyotas! First thing I did was buy myself an old-fashioned American boat, an Olds Toronado. Soft shocks, single-finger steering, guzzles gas, I'm crazy about it. Five-liter V-8, tomato red with a white padded half-roof."

"Sounds great. You park it close by?"

"I tried and couldn't. Circled up around Spring Street twice and finally gave up and left it in a lot up past the old Baghdad and took a bus the three blocks down. So it costs a few pennies. Avoid aggravation, champ."

"I still don't understand it. Downtown Brewer's supposed to be dead and there's nowhere to park. Where are all the cars coming from?"

"They breed," Charlie explains. "They get pregnant as teenagers and go on welfare. They don't give a damn."

One of the things Harry has always enjoyed about Charlie is the man's feel for the big picture; the two of them used to stand by the display window over at the lot on dull mornings and rehash the day's news. Rabbit has never gotten over the idea that the news is going to mean something to him. As they seat themselves at one of the tile-topped tables that remain from the days when this was the Café Barcelona, he says, "How about Schmidt last night?" Against the Pirates in Three Rivers Stadium, the

Phillies' veteran third baseman had doubled twice and surpassed Richie Ashburn's team record for total hits.

"This is still spring," Charlie tells him. "Wait till the pitchers' arms warm up. Schmidt'll wilt. He's old, not compared to you and me but in the game he's in he's old, and there's no hiding from the young pitchers over the long season."

Harry finds it salutary, to have his admiration for Schmidt checked. You can't live through these athletes, they don't know you exist. For them, only the other players exist. They go to the ballpark and there's thirty thousand there and a big bumbly roar when their names are announced and that's all of you they need. "Does it seem to you," he asks Charlie, "there's a lot of disasters lately? That Pan Am plane blowing up, and then those soccer fans in England the other day getting crushed, and now this gun exploding on the battleship for no apparent reason."

"Apparent's the key word," Charlie says. "Everything has some little tiny reason, even when we can't see it. A little spark somewhere, a little crack in the metal. Also, champ, look at the odds. How many people in the world now, five billion? With the world jammed up like it is the wonder is more of us aren't trampled every day or blown up or whatever. There's a crush on, and it's not going to get better."

Rabbit's heart dips, thinking that from Nelson's point of view he himself is a big part of the crowding. That time he screamed outside the burning house at 26 Vista Crescent, *I'll kill you.* He didn't mean it. A spark, a crack in metal. A tiny flaw. When you die you do the world a favor.

Charlie is frowning down into the menu, which is enormous, printed in photocopy in green ink on rough flecked acid-free paper. The things they can do with Xerox now. Who still uses a place like Verity Press? First letterpress went, then photo-offset. Charlie no longer wears thick squarish hornrims that set a dark bar across his eyebrows but gold aviator frames that hold his thick lavender-tinted lenses to his nose like fingers pinching a wine-glass. Charlie used to be thickset but age has whittled him so his Greek bones show—the high pinched arch to his nose, the slanting hollow temples below his dark hairline. His sideburns are gray but he is shaving them shorter. Studying the menu, he chuckles. "Beefsteak Salad," he reads. "Pork Kebob Salad. What kind of salads are those?"

When the waitress comes, Charlie kids her about it. "What's with all this high-cal high-fat meat?" he asks. "You giving us a beefsteak with a little lettuce on the side?"

"The meat is shoelaced and worked in," the waitress says. She is tall and almost pretty, with her hair bleached and trained up in a fluffy Mohawk, and a row of little earrings all around the edge of one ear, and dark dusty-rosy spots rouged behind her eyes. Her tongue has some trouble in her mouth and it's cute, the earnest, deliberate way her lips move. "They found there was a call for these, you know, heartier ingredients."

So underneath everything, Rabbit thinks, it's still Johnny Frye's Chophouse. "Tell me about the Macadamia and Bacon Salad," he says.

"It's one of people's favorites," she says. "The bacon is crisp and in, like, flakes. Most of the fat has been pressed out of it. Also there's alfalfa sprouts, and some radishes and cucumber sliced real thin, and a couple kinds of lettuce, I forget the different names, and I don't know what all else, maybe some chuba—that's dried sardines."

"Sounds good," Rabbit says, before it doesn't and he has to choose again.

Charlie points out, "Nuts and bacon aren't exactly what the doctor ordered."

"You heard her, the fat's been squeezed out. Anyway a little bit can't kill you. It's more a matter of internal balance. Come on, Charlie. Loosen up."

"What's in the Seaweed Special?" Charlie asks the waitress, because both men like to hear her talk.

"Oh, hijiki of course, and wakame, and dulse and agar in with a lot of chickpeas and lentils, and leafy greens, it's wonderful if you're going macrobiotic seriously and don't mind that slightly bitter taste, you know, that seaweed tends to have."

"You've done talked me out of it, Jennifer," Charlie says, reading her name stitched onto the bodice of the lime-green jumper they wear for a uniform at Salad Binge. "I'll take the Spinach and Crab."

"For salad dressing, we have Russian, Roquefort, Italian, Creamy Italian, Poppyseed, Thousand Island, Oil and Vinegar, and Japanese."

"What's in the Japanese?" Harry asks, not just to see her lips curl and pucker around the little difficulty in her mouth, but because the Japanese interest him professionally. How do they and the Germans do it, when America's going down the tubes?

"Oh, I could ask in the kitchen if you really care, but umeboshi, I think, and tamari, of course—we don't use that commercial soy sauce—and sesame oil, and rice vinegar." Her eyes harden as she senses that these men are flirtatiously wasting her time. Feeling apologetic, they both order Creamy Italian and settle to each other.

It has been a long time, their rapport has grown rusty. Charlie does seem older, drier, when you look. The thin gold aviator frames take out of his face a lot of that masculine certainty that must have appealed to Janice twenty years ago. "Cute kid," Charlie says, arranging the silver around his plate more neatly, square to the edges of the paper placemat.

"What ever happened to Melanie?" Rabbit asks him. Ten years ago, they sat in this same restaurant and Melanie, a friend of Nelson's and Pru's living at the time at Ma Springer's house, had been their waitress. Then she became Charlie's girlfriend, old as he was, relatively. At least they went to Florida together. One of the things maybe that had made Florida seem attractive. But no bimbo there had offered herself to Harry. The only flickers he got were from women his own age, who looked ancient.

"She became a doctor," Charlie says. "A gastroenterologist, to be exact, in Portland, Oregon. That's where her father wound up, you'll recall."

"Just barely. He was a kind of late-blooming hippie, wasn't he?"

"He settled down with the third wife and has been a big support to Melanie. It was her mother, actually, who was flipping out, back in Mill Valley. Alcohol. Guys. Drugs."

The last word hurts Harry's stomach. "How come you know all this?"

Charlie shrugs minimally, but cannot quite suppress his little smile of pride. "We keep in touch. I was there for her when she needed a push. I told her, 'Go for it.' She still had a bit of that poor-little-me-I'm-only-a-girl thing. I gave her the boost she needed. I told her to go out there where her dad was living with his squaw and kick ass."

"Me you tell avoid aggravation, her you told to go for it."

"Different cases. Different ages. You her age, I'd tell you, 'Go for it.' I'll still tell you. As long as you avoid aggravation."

"Charlie, I have a problem."

"That's news?"

"A couple of 'em, actually. For one, I ought to do something about my heart. I just can't keep drifting along waiting for my next MI."

"You're losing me, champ."

"You know. Myocardial infarction. Heart attack. I was lucky

to get away with the one I did have. The docs tell me I ought to have an open-heart, a multiple bypass.''

"Go for it."

"Sure. Easy for you to say. People die having those things. I notice you never had one.''

"But I did. In '87. December, you were in Florida. They replaced two valves. Aortic and mitral. When you have rheumatic fever as a kid, it's the valves that go. They don't close right. That's what gives you the heart murmur, blood running the wrong way.''

Rabbit can hardly bear these images, all these details inside him, valves and slippages and crusts on the pipe. "What'd they replace them with?''

"Pig heart valves. The choice is that or a mechanical valve, a trap with a ball. With the mechanical, you click all the time. I didn't want to click if I could help it. They say it keeps you awake.''

"Pig valves." Rabbit tries to hide his revulsion. "Was it terrible? They split your chest open and ran your blood through a machine?''

"Piece of cake. You're knocked out cold. What's wrong with running your blood through a machine? What else you think you are, champ?''

A God-made one-of-a-kind with an immortal soul breathed in. A vehicle of grace. A battlefield of good and evil. An apprentice angel. All those things they tried to teach you in Sunday school, or really didn't try very hard to teach you, just let them drift in out of the pamphlets, back there in that church basement buried deeper in his mind than an air-raid shelter.

"You're just a soft machine," Charlie maintains, and lifts his squarish hands, with their white cuffs and rectangular gold links, to let Jennifer set his salad before him. He saw her coming with eyes in the back of his head. She circles the table gingerly—these men are doing something to her, she doesn't know what—and puts a bacon-flecked green mound bigger than a big breast in front of Harry. It looks rich, and more than he should eat. The tall awkward girl with her strange white rooster-comb trembling in the air still hovers, the roundnesses in her green uniform pressing on Harry's awareness as he sits at the square tiled table trying to frame his dilemmas.

"Is there anything more I can get you gentlemen?" Jennifer asks, her lips gently struggling to articulate. It's not a lisp she has, quite; it's like her tongue is too big. "Something to drink?''

Charlie asks her for a Perrier with lime. She says that San Pellegrino is what they have. He says it's all the same to him. Fancy water is fancy water.

Rabbit after an internal struggle asks what kinds of beer they have. Jennifer sighs, feeling they are putting her on, and recites, "Schlitz, Miller, Miller Lite, Bud, Bud Light, Michelob, Löwenbräu, Corona, Coors, Coors Light, and Ballantine ale on draft." All these names have an added magic from being tumbled a bit in her mouth. Not looking Charlie in the eye, Harry opts for a Mick. Jennifer nods unsmiling and goes away. If she doesn't want to excite men, she shouldn't wear all those earrings and go so heavy on the makeup.

"Piece of cake, you were saying," he says to Charlie.

"They freeze you. You don't know a thing."

"Guy I know down in Florida, not much older than we are, had an open-heart and he says it was hell, the recuperation took forever, and furthermore he doesn't look so great even so. He swings a golf club like a cripple."

Charlie does one of his tidy small shrugs. "You got to have the basics to work with. Maybe the guy was too far gone. But you, you're in good shape. Could lose a few pounds, but you're young—what, fifty-five?"

"Wish I was. Fifty-six last February."

"That's young. Would you believe, I hit the big six-oh last October?"

"The way I'm going I'll be happy to hit sixty. I look at all these old crocks down in Florida, shrivelled-up mummies toddling right into their nineties in their shorts and orthopedic sneakers, perky as bejesus, and I want to ask 'em, 'What makes you so great? How did you do it?' "

"A day at a time," Charlie suggests. "One day at a time, and don't look down." Harry can tell he's getting bored with issuing reassurances, but Charlie's all he's got, now that he's unloaded Thelma.

"There's this other thing they can do now. An angioplasty. They cut open an artery in your groin—"

"Hey. I'm eating."

"—and poke it up all the way to your heart, would you believe. Then they pop out this balloon in the narrow place of the coronary artery and blow the damn thing up. Not with air, with saltwater somehow. It cracks the plaque. It stretches the artery back to the way it was."

"With a lot of luck it does," Charlie says. "And a year later you're back in the same boat, plugged up with macadamia nuts and beer yet.''

Beer has come on the end of Jennifer's lean arm, in a frosted glass mug, golden and foam-topped and sizzling with its own excited bubbles. "If I can't have a single beer now and then, I'd just as soon be dead," Harry lies. He sips, and with a bent forefinger wipes the foam from under his nose. That gesture of Nelson's. He wonders when she fucks how protective Jennifer has to be of that wobbly Mohawk. Some punk girls, he's read, put safety pins through their nipples.

"Coronary bypass is what you want," Charlie is telling him. "These balloons, they can only do one artery at a time. Bypass grafts, they can do four, five, six once they get in there. Whadde-*you* care if they pull open your rib cage? You won't be there. You'll be way out of it, dreaming away. Actually, you don't dream. It's too deep for that. It's a big nothing, like being dead.''

"I don't want it," Harry hears himself say sharply. He softens this to, "Not yet anyway." Charlie's word *pull* has upset him, made it too real, the physical exertion, pulling open these resistant bone gates so his spirit will fly out and men in pale-green masks will fish in this soupy red puddle with their hooks and clamps and bright knives. Once on television watching by mistake over Janice's shoulder one of these PBS programs on childbirth—they wouldn't put such raunchy stuff on the networks—he saw them start to cut open a woman's belly for a Caesarean. The knife in the rubber-gloved hand made a straight line and on either side yellow fat curled up and away like two strips of foam rubber. This woman's abdomen, with a baby inside, was lined in a *material*, just like foam rubber. "Down in Florida," he says, "I had a catheterization"—the word makes trouble in his mouth, as if he's become the waitress—"and it wasn't so bad, more boring than anything else. You're wide awake, and then they put like this big bowl over your chest to see what's going on inside. Where the dye is being pumped through, it's *hot*, so hot you can hardly stand it." He feels he's disappointing Charlie, being so cowardly about bypasses, and to deepen his contact with the frowning, chewing other man confides, "The worst thing of it, Charlie, is I feel half dead already. This waitress is the first girl I've wanted to fuck for months.''

"Boobs," Charlie says. "Great boobs. On a skinny body. That's sexy. Like Bo Derek after her implant."

"Her hair is what gets me. Tall as she is, she adds six inches with that hairdo.''

"Tall isn't bad. The tall ones don't get the play the cute little short ones do, and do more for you. Also, being skinny has its advantages, there's not all that fat to come between you and the clitoris."

This may be more male bonding than Rabbit needs. He says, "But all those earrings, don't they look painful? And is it true some punk girls—"

Charlie interrupts impatiently, "Pain is where it's at for punks. Mutilation, self-hatred, slam dancing. For these kids today, ugly is beautiful. That's their way of saying what a lousy world we're giving them. No more rain forests. Toxic waste. You know the drill."

"When I came back this spring, I did a certain amount of driving around the city, all the sections. Some of these Hispanics were practically screwing on the street."

"Drugs," Charlie says. "They don't know what they're doing half the time."

"Did you see in the *Standard*, some spic truck driver from West Miami was caught over near Maiden Springs with they estimate seventy-five million dollars' worth of cocaine, five hundred kilos packed in orange crates marked 'Fragile'?"

"They can't stop dope," Charlie says, aligning his knife and fork on the edge of his empty plate, "as long as people are willing to pay for it."

"The guy was a Cuban refugee evidently, one of those we let in."

"These countries go Communist, they let us have all their crooks and crackpots." Charlie's tone is level and authoritative, but Harry feels he's losing him. It's not quite like the old days, when they had all day to kill, over in the showroom. Charlie has finished his Spinach and Crab and Rabbit has barely made a dent in his own heaping salad, he's so anxious to get advice. He gets a slippery forkful into his mouth and finds among the oily lettuce and alfalfa sprouts a whole macadamia nut, and delicately splits it with his teeth, so his tongue feels the texture of the fissure, miraculously smooth, like a young woman's body, like a marble tabletop.

When he swallows, he gets out, "That's the other thing preying on my mind. I think Nelson is into cocaine."

Charlie nods and says, "So I hear." He picks up the fork he's just aligned and reaches over with it toward Harry's big breast of bacon-garnished greenery. "Let me help you out with all that, champ."

"You've heard he's into cocaine?"

"Mm. Yeah. He's like his granddad, jumpy. He needs crutches. I never found the kid easy to deal with."

"Me *neither*," Harry says eagerly, and it comes tumbling out. "I went over there last week to have it out with him about cocaine, I'd just got wind of it, and he was off somewhere, he usually is, but this accountant he's hired, a guy dying of AIDS would you believe, was there and when I asked to look at the books just about gave me the up-yours sign and said I had to get Janice's say-so. And she, the dumb mutt, doesn't want to give it. I think she's scared of what she'll find out. Her own kid robbing her blind. The used sales are down, the monthly stat sheets have been looking fishy to me for months."

"You'd know. Doesn't sound good," Charlie agrees, reaching again with his fork. A macadamia nut—each one nowadays costs about a quarter—escapes in Harry's direction and only his quick reflexes prevent it from falling into his lap and staining with salad oil the russet slacks he took out of the cleaner's bag and put on for the first time today, the first spring day that's felt really warm. The sudden motion gives him a burning pang behind his rib cage. That evil child is still playing with matches in there.

He tries to ignore the pain and goes on, "And now we get these phone calls at funny hours, guys with funny voices asking for Nelson or even telling *me* they want money."

"They play rough," Charlie says. "Dope is big business." He reaches once more.

"Hey, leave me *some*thing. How do you stay so skinny? So what shall I do?"

"Maybe Janice should talk to Nelson."

"That's just what I told her."

"Well then."

"But the bitch won't. At least she hasn't so far that I know of."

"This is good," Charlie says, "this health stuff, but it's all like Chinese food, it doesn't fill you up."

"So what did you say your verdict was?"

"Sometimes, between a husband and wife, all the history gets in the way. Want me to sound old Jan-Jan out, see where she's coming from?"

Harry hesitates hardly at all before saying, "Charlie, if you could, that would be super."

"Would you gentlemen like some dessert?"

Jennifer has materialized. Turning his head in surprise at the sound of her sweetly impeded voice, Harry sees, inches from his eyes, that Charlie as usual is right: great boobs, gawky and self-hating as the rest of her is. Her parents must have put a lot of protein, a lot of Cheerios and vitamin-enriched bread, into those boobs. In his fragile freighted mood they seem two more burdens on his brain. The stretched chest of her green jumper lifts as she takes in breath to say, "Today our special is a cheese-cake made from low-fat goat's milk topped with delicious creamed gooseberries."

Rabbit, his eyebrows still raised by the waitress's breasts, looks over at Charlie. "Whaddeyou think?"

Charlie shrugs unhelpfully. "It's your funeral."

The phone is ringing, ringing, like thrilling cold water poured into the mossy warm crevices of his dream. He was dreaming of snuggling into something, of having found an aperture that just fit. The phone is on Janice's side; he gropes for it across her stubbornly sleeping body and, with a throat dry from mouth-breathing, croaks, "Hello?" The bedside clock seems to have only one hand until he figures out it's ten minutes after two. He expects one of those men's voices and tells himself they should take the phone off the hook downstairs whenever they go to bed. His heart's pounding seems to fill the dark room to its corners, suffocatingly.

A tremulous young woman's voice says, "Harry? It's Pru. Forgive me for waking you up, but I—" Shame, fear trip her voice into silence. She feels exposed.

"Yeah, go on," he urges softly.

"I'm desperate. Nelson has gone crazy, he's already hit me and I'm afraid he'll start in on the children!"

"Really?" he says stupidly. "Nelson wouldn't do that." But people do it, it's in the papers, all the time.

"Who on earth is it?" Janice asks irritably, yanked from her own dreams. "Tell them you have no money. Just hang up."

Pru is sobbing, on the end of the line, ". . . can't *stand* it any more . . . it's been such hell . . . for *years*."

"Yeah, yeah," Harry says, still feeling stupid. "Here's Janice," he says, and passes the hot potato into her fumbling hand, out from under the covers. His sudden window into Pru, the hot bright unhappy heart of her, felt illicit. He switches on his bedside light, as if that will help clear this all up. The white jacket of the history book he is still trying to get through, with its clipper ship in an oval of cloud and sea, leaps up shiny under the pleated lampshade. Since he began reading the book last Christmas afternoon, the author herself has died, putting a kind of blight on the book. Yet he feels it would be bad luck never to finish it.

"Yes," Janice is saying into the phone, at wide intervals. "Yes. Did he really? Yes." She says, "We'll be right over. Stay away from him. What about going into Judy's room with her and locking yourselves in? Mother had a bolt put on the door, it must be still there."

Still Pru's voice crackles on, like an acid eating into the night's silence, the peace that had been in the room ten minutes before. Bits of his interrupted dream come back to him. A visit to some anticipated place, on a vehicle like a trolley car, yes, it had been an old-time trolley car, the tight weave of cane seats, he had forgotten how they looked, the way they smelled warmed by the sun, and the porcelain loops to hang from, the porcelain buttons to press, the dusty wire grates at the windows, the air and light coming in, on old-fashioned straw hats, the women with paper flowers in theirs, all heading somewhere gay, an amusement park, a fair, who was with him? There had been a companion, a date, on the seat beside him, but he can't come up with her face. The tunnel of love. The trolley car turned into something carrying them, him, into a cozy tunnel of love. It fit.

"Could the neighbors help?"

More crackling, more sobbing. Rabbit gives Janice the "cut" signal you see on TV—a finger across the throat—and gets out of bed. The aroma of his old body lifts toward him as he rests his bare feet on the carpet, a stale meaty cheesy scent. Their bedroom in the limestone house has pale-beige Antron broadloom; a houseful of unpatterned wall-to-wall seemed snug and modern to him when they ordered it all, but in their ten years of living here certain spots—inside the front door, the hall outside the door down to the cellar, the bedroom on either side of the bed—have collected dirt from shoes and sweat from feet and turned a gray no rug shampoo could remove, a grimy big fingerprint your life has left. Patterned carpets like people had when he was a boy—angular flowers and vines and mazes he would follow with his eyes until he felt lost in a jungle—swallowed the dirt somehow, and then the housewives up and down Jackson Road would beat it out of them this time of year, on their back-yard clotheslines, making little swirling clouds in the cool April air, disappearing into the dust of the world. He collects clean underwear and socks from the bureau and then is a bit stumped, what to wear to an assault. Harry's brain is skidding along like a surfer on the pumping of his heart.

"Hi honey," Janice is saying in another tone, high-pitched and grandmotherly. "Don't be scared. We all love you. Your daddy loves you, yes he does, very much. Grandpa and I are coming right over. You must let us get dressed now so we can do that. It'll take just twenty minutes, honey. We'll hurry, yes. You be good till then and do whatever your mother says." She hangs up and stares at Harry from beneath her skimpy rumpled bangs. "My God," she says. "He punched Pru in the face and smashed up everything in the bathroom when he couldn't find some cocaine he thought he hid in there that he wanted."

"He wants, he wants," Harry says.

"He told her we're all stealing from him."

"Ha," Harry says, meaning it's the reverse.

Janice says, "How can you laugh when it's your own son?"

Who is this woman, this little nut-hard woman, to chasten him? Yet he feels chastened. He doesn't answer but instead says in a measured, mature manner, "Well, it's probably good this is coming to a head, if we all survive it. It gets it out in the open at least."

She puts on what she never wears in the daylight up north, her salmon running suit with the powder-blue sleeves and stripe. He opts for a pair of pressed chinos fresh from the drawer and the khaki shirt he puts on to do light yard chores, and his oldest jacket, a green wide-wale corduroy with leather buttons: kind of a casual Saturday-afternoon look. Retirement has made them both more clothes-conscious than before; in Florida, the retirees play dress-up every day, as if they've become their own paper dolls.

They take the slate-gray Celica, the more Batmobilelike and steely car, on this desperate mission in the dead of the night. Along the stilled curving streets of Penn Park, the oaks are just budding but the maples are filling in, no longer red in tint but dense with translucent tender new leaves. The houses have an upstairs night light on here and there, or a back-porch light to keep cats and raccoons away from the garbage, but only the streetlamps compete with the moon. The trimmed large bushes of the groomed yards, the yews and arborvitae and rhododendrons, look alert by night, like jungle creatures come to the waterhole to drink and caught in a camera's flash. It seems strange to think that while we sleep these bushes are awake, exhaling oxygen, growing; they do not sleep. Stars do not sleep, but above the housetops and tree crowns shine in a cold arching dusty sprinkle. Why do we sleep? What do we rejoin? His dream, the way it fit him all around. At certain angles the lit asphalt feels in the corners of his eyes like snow. Penn Park becomes West Brewer and a car or two is still awake and moving on blanched deserted Penn Boulevard, an extension of Weiser with a supermarket parking lot on one side and on the other a low brick row of shops from the Thirties, little narrow stores selling buttons and bridal gowns and pastry and Zipf Chocolates and Sony TVs and hobby kits to make model airplanes with—they still manufacture and sell those in this era when all the kids are supposedly couch potatoes and all the planes are these wallowing wide-body jets with black noses like panda bears, not sleek killing machines like Zeros, Messerschmitts, Spitfires, Mustangs. Funny to think that with all that world-war effort manufacturers still had the O.K. to make those little models, keeping up morale in the kiddie set. All the shops are asleep. A flower shop shows a violet growing light, and a pet store a dimly lit aquarium. The cars parked along the curbs display a range of unearthly colors, no longer red and blue and cream but cindery lunar shades, like nothing you can see or even imagine by daylight.

Harry pops a nitroglycerin pill and tells Janice accusingly, "The doctors say I should avoid aggravation."

"It wasn't me who woke us up at two in the morning, it was your daughter-in-law."

"Yeah, because your precious son was beating up on her."

"According to *her*," Janice states. "We haven't heard Nelson's side of it."

The underside of his tongue burns. "What makes you think he has a side? What're you saying, you think she's lying? Why would she lie? Why would she call us up at two in the morning to lie?"

"She has her agenda, as people say. He was a good bet for her when she got herself pregnant but now that he's in a little trouble he's not such a good bet and if she's going to get herself another man she better move fast because her looks won't last forever."

He laughs, in applause. "You've got it all figured out." Discreetly, distantly, his asshole tingles, from the pill. "She *is* good-looking, isn't she? Still."

"To some men she would seem so. The kind that don't mind

big tough women. What I never liked about her, though, was she makes Nelson look short.''

"He *is* short,'' Harry says. "Beats me why. My parents were both tall. My whole family's always been tall.''

Janice considers in silence her responsibility for Nelson's shortness.

There are any number of ways to get to Mt. Judge through Brewer but tonight, the streets all but deserted and the stoplights blinking yellow, he opts for the most direct, going straight over the Running Horse Bridge, that once he and Jill walked over in moonlight though not so late at night as this, straight up Weiser past the corner building that used to house JIMBO's *Friendly* LOUNGE until trouble with the police finally closed it and that now has been painted pastel condo colors and remodelled into a set of offices for yuppie lawyers and financial advisers, past Schoenbaum Funeral Directors with its stately building of white brick on the left and the shoeshine parlor that sells New York papers and hot roasted peanuts, the best peanuts in town, still selling them all those years since he was a kid not much older than Judy now. His idea then of the big time was to take the trolley around the mountain and come into downtown Brewer on a Saturday morning and buy a dime bag of peanuts still warm from the roaster and walk all around cracking them and letting the shells fall where they would, at his feet on the sidewalks of Weiser Square. Once an old bum grumbled at him for littering; even the bums had a civic conscience then. Now the old downtown is ghostly, hollow in lunar colors and closed to traffic at Fifth Street, where the little forest planted by the city planners from Atlanta to make a pedestrian mall looms with ghostly branches under the intense blue lights installed to discourage muggings and sex and drug transactions beneath these trees which grow taller every year and make the downtown gloomier. Rabbit turns left on Fifth, past the post office and the Ramada Inn that used to be the Ben Franklin with its grand ballroom, which always makes him think of Mary Ann and her crinolines and the fragrance between her legs, and over to Eisenhower Avenue, above number 1204 where Janice hid out with Charlie that time, and takes an obtuse-angled turn right, heading up through the Hispanic section, which used to be German working-class, across Winter, Spring, and Summer streets with the blinding lights and occasional moving shadows, spics out looking for some kind of a deal, the nights still a little cool to bring out all the street trash, to Locust Boulevard and the front of Brewer

High School, a Latin-inscribed Depression monument, ambitious for the common good like something Communists would put up, the whole country close to Communism in the Thirties, people not so selfish then, put up the year Harry was born, 1933, and going to outlast him it looks like. Of pale-yellow brick and granite quoins, it clings to the greening mountainside like a locust husk.

"What do you think she meant," he asks Janice, " 'gone crazy'? How crazy can you go from cocaine?"

"Doris Kaufmann, I mean Eberhardt, has a brother-in-law whose stepson by his wife's first marriage had to go to a detox center out near the middle of the state. He got to be paranoid and thought Hitler was still alive and had agents everywhere to get just him. He was Jewish."

"Did he beat up his wife and children?"

"He didn't have a wife, I think. We don't know for sure Nelson's threatened the children."

"Pru said he did."

"Pru was very upset. It's the money I think upsets her, more than anything."

"It doesn't upset you?"

"Not as much as it seems to you and Pru. Money isn't something I worry about, Harry. Daddy always said, 'If I don't have two nickels to rub together, I'll rub two pennies.' He had faith he could always make enough, and he did, and I guess I inherited his philosophy."

"Is that the reason you keep letting Nelson get away with murder?"

Janice sighs and sounds more than ever like her mother, Bessie Koerner Springer, who lived her whole life overweight, without a lick of exercise except housework, sitting in her big house with its shades down to protect the curtains and upholstery from sunlight and sighing about the pains in her legs. "Harry, what can I do, seriously? It's not as if he's still a child, he's thirty-two."

"You could fire him from the lot, for starters."

"Yes, and shall I fire him as my son, too—tell him I'm sorry, but he hasn't worked out? He's my father's grandson, don't forget. Daddy built that lot up out of nothing and he would have wanted Nelson to run it, run it even if he runs it into the ground."

"Really?" Such a ruinous vision startles him. Having money makes people reckless. Bet a million. Junk bonds. "Couldn't you fire him provisionally, until he shapes up?"

Janice's tone has the bite of impatience, of fatigue. "All this is so easy for you to say—you're just sore since Lyle told you I was the real boss, you're trying to make me suffer for it. *You* do it, you do whatever you think should be done at the lot and tell them I said you should. I'm tired of it. I'm tired of you and Nelson fighting your old wars through me."

Streetlights flicker more swiftly on his hands as the Celica moves more rapidly through the city park, above the tennis courts and the World War II tank painted a thick green to forestall rust, repainted so often they've lost the exact military green Harry remembers. What did they call it? Olive drab. He feels under the barrage of streetlights bombarded, and Brewer seems empty of life like those bombed-out German cities after the war. "They wouldn't believe me," he tells her spitefully, "they'd still come to you. And I'm like you," he tells her more gently, "scared of what I'll stir up."

After the park there is a stoplight that says red, and a locally famous old turreted house roofed in round fishscale slate shingles, and then a shopping mall where the cineplex sign advertises SEE YOU DREAM TEAM SAY ANYTHING OUT OF CONTROL. Then they're on 422 and a territory bred into their bones, streets they crossed and recrossed in all seasons as children, Central, Jackson, Joseph, the hydrants and mailboxes of the borough of Mt. Judge like buttons fastening down their lives, their real lives, everything drained of color at this nadir of the night, the streets under the burning blue sodium looking rounded like bread-loaves and crusted with snow, the brick-pillared porches treacherous emplacements up behind their little flat laps of lawn and tulip bed. Number 89 Joseph, the Springers' big stucco house where when Rabbit was courting Janice he used to hate to come because it made his own family's semi-detached house on Jackson Road look poor, has all its lights ablaze, like a ship going down amid the silent darkened treetops and roof peaks of the town. The huge spreading copper-beech tree on the left side where Harry and Janice's bedroom used to be, a tree so dense the sun never shone in and its beech nuts popping kept Harry awake all fall, is gone, leaving that side bare, its windows exposed and on fire. Nelson had it cut down. *Dad, it was eating up the whole house. You couldn't keep paint on the woodwork on that side, it was so damp. The lawn wouldn't even grow.* Harry couldn't argue, and couldn't say that the sound of the rain in that great beech had been the most religious experience of his life. That, and hitting a pure golf shot.

They park outside, under the maples that are shedding chartreuse fuzz and sticky stuff this time of year. He always hates that about parking here. He'll get the car washed Monday.

Pru has been watching for their arrival. She pulls the door open as their feet hit the porch, as if there's an electric eye. Like Thelma the other week. Judy is with her, in some fuzzy Oshkosh b'Gosh pajamas that are too small for her. The child's feet look surprisingly long and white and bony, with the inches of exposed ankle.

"Where's Roy?" Harry asks instantly.

"Nelson's putting him in bed," Pru says, with a wry downward tug of one side of her mouth, a kind of apology.

"To bed?" Harry says. "You trust him with the kid?"

She says, "Oh yes. He's calmed down since I called. I think he shocked himself, hitting me so hard. It did him good." In the illumination of the front hall they can see the pink welt along one cheekbone, the lopsided puffiness of her upper lip, the redness around her eyes as if rubbed and rubbed with a scouring pad. She is wearing that quilted shorty morning-glory bathrobe but not as in Florida over bare legs; under it she has on a long blue nightgown. But you can see the outline of her legs through the thin cloth, like fish moving through murky water. Fake-fur-lined bedroom slippers clothe her feet, so he can't check out her toenail polish.

"Hey, is this some kind of false alarm?" Harry asks.

"When you see Nelson I don't think you'll think so," Pru tells him, and turns to the other woman. "Janice, I've had it. I want out. I've kept the lid on as long as I can and now I've *had* it!" And the eyes that have scoured the lids with tears begin to water again, and she embraces the older woman before Janice has quite straightened out from bending down to kiss and hug Judy hello.

Harry's guts give a tug: he can feel Pru's attempt to make a sweeping connection; he can feel his wife's resistance. Pru was raised a Catholic, showy, given to big gestures, and Janice a tight little Protestant.

Judy takes Harry's fingertips. When he stoops to peck her on the cheek, her hair gets in his eye. The little girl giggles and says in his ear, "Daddy thinks ants are crawling all over him."

"He's always feeling itchy," Pru says, sensing that her attempt to sweep Janice into her escape plan has failed, she must do some more selling of the situation. "That's the coke. They call it formication. His neurotransmitters are fucked up. Ask me anything, I know it all. I've been going to Narc-Anon in Brewer for a year now.''

"Huh," Rabbit says, not quite liking her tough tone. "And what else do they tell you?''

She looks straight at him, her green eyes glaring with tears and shock, and manages that smile of hers, downtwisted at the corner. Her upper lip being puffy gives it a sad strangeness tonight. "They tell you it's not your problem, the addicts can only do it themselves. But that still leaves it your problem.''

"What happened here tonight, exactly?" he asks. He has to keep speaking up. He feels Janice pulling back, distancing herself irritatingly, like that time they took the kids to Jungle Gardens in the Camry.

Judy doesn't find her grandparents as much fun as usual and leaves Harry's side to go lean against her mother, pressing her carrot-colored head back against Pru's belly. Pru protectively encircles the child's throat with a downy freckled forearm. Now two pairs of greenish eyes stare, as if Harry and Janice are not the rescue squad but hostile invaders.

Pru's voice sounds tough and weary. "The usual sort of garbage. He came home after one and I asked him where he'd been and he told me none of my business and I guess I didn't take it as docilely as usual because he said if I was going to be that way he needed a hit to calm his nerves, and when the coke wasn't in the bathroom where he thought he hid it in an aspirin bottle he smashed things up and when I didn't like that he came out after me and started slugging me all over the place.''

Judy says, "It woke me up. Mommy came into my room to get away and Daddy's face was all funny, like he wasn't really seeing anything.''

Harry asks, "Did he have a knife or anything?''

Pru's eyebrows knit crossly at the suggestion. "Nelson would never go for a knife. He can't stand blood and never helps in the kitchen. He wouldn't know which end of a knife to use.''

Judy says, "He said he was real sorry afterwards.''

Pru has been smoothing Judy's long red hair back from her face and now, just the middle fingers touching her forehead and cheeks, tucks back her own. She has outgrown the Sphinx look; it hangs limp to her shoulders. "He calmed down after I called you. He said, 'You called them? I can't believe it. You called my parents?' It was like he was too stunned to be angry. He kept saying this is the end and how sorry he was for everything. He makes no sense.'' She grimaces and lightly pushes Judy away from her body and tightens the robe around her middle, with a shiver. For a second they all seem to have forgotten their lines. In crises there is something in our instincts which whittles, which tries to reduce the unignorable event back to the ignorable normal. "I could use a cup of coffee," Pru says.

Janice asks, "Shouldn't we go upstairs to Nelson first?"

Judy likes this idea and leads the way upstairs. Following her milky bare feet up the stair treads, Harry feels guilty that his granddaughter has to wear outgrown pajamas while all those Florida acquaintances of theirs have different-colored slacks for every day of the week and twenty sports coats hanging in cleaner's bags. The house, which he remembers from way back in the days of the Springers, when they were younger than he is now, seems rather pathetically furnished, now that he looks, in remnants from the old days, including the battered old brown Barcalounger that used to be Fred Springer's throne, along with nondescript newer stuff from Schaechner's or one of the shabby furniture places that have sprung up along the highways leading out of the city, mingled among the car lots and fast-food joints. The stairs still have the threadbare Turkish runner the Springers had tacked down forty years ago. The house has descended to Nelson and Pru in stages and they never really have taken it on as their own. You try to do something nice for kids, offer them a shortcut in life, a little padding, and it turns out to be the wrong thing, undermining them. This was no house for a young couple.

All the lights being turned on gives the house a panicky over-heated air. They ascend the stairs in the order Judy, Harry, Janice, and Pru, who maybe regrets having called them by now and would rather be nursing her face and planning her next move in solitude. Nelson greets them in the hallway, carrying Roy in his arms. "Oh," he says, seeing his father, "the big cheese is here."

"Don't mouth off at me," Harry tells him. "I'd rather be home in bed."

"It wasn't my idea to call you."

"It was your idea though to go beating up your wife, and scaring the hell out of your kids, and otherwise acting like a shit." Harry fishes in the side pocket of his chinos to make sure the little vial of heart pills is there. Nelson is trying to play it cool, still wearing the black slacks and white shirt he was out on the town in, and having the kid on his arm, but his thinning hair is bristling out from his head and his eyes in the harsh hallway light are frantic, full of reflected sparks like that time outside the burning house at 26 Vista Crescent. Even in the bright light his pupils look dilated and shiny-black and there is a tremor to him, a shiver now and then as if this night nearly in May is icy cold. He looks even thinner than in Florida, with that same unpleasant sore-looking nose above the little half-ass blur of a mustache. And that earring yet.

"Who are you to go around deciding who's acting like a shit?" he asks Harry, adding, "Hi, Mom. Welcome home."

"Nelson, this just won't do."

"Let me take Roy," Pru says in a cool neutral voice, and she pushes past the elder Angstroms and without looking her husband in the face plucks the sleepy child from him. Involuntarily she grunts with the weight. The hall light, with its glass shade faceted like a candy dish, crowns her head with sheen as she passes under it, into Roy's room, which was Nelson's boyhood room in the old days, when Rabbit would lie awake hearing Melanie creep along the hall to this room from her own, the little room at the front of the house with the dress dummy. Now she's some gastroenterologist. In the harsh overhead light, Nelson's face, white around the gills, shows an electric misery and a hostile cockiness, and Janice's a dark confused something, a retreat into the shadows of her mind; her capacity for confusion has always frightened Harry. He realizes he is still in charge. Little Judy looks up at him brightly, titillated by being awake and a witness to these adult transactions. "We can't just stand here in the hall," he says. "How about the big bedroom?"

Harry and Janice's old bedroom has become Nelson and Pru's. A different bedspread—their old Pennsylvania Dutch quilt of little triangular patches has given way to a puff patterned with yellow roses, Pru does like flowered fabrics—but the same creaky bed, with the varnished knobbed headboard that never hit your back quite right when you tried to read. Different magazines on the bedside tables—*Racing Cars* and *Rolling Stone* instead of *Time* and *Consumer Reports*—but the same cherry table on Harry's old side, with its sticky drawer. Among the propped-up photographs on the bureau is one of him and Janice, misty-eyed and lightly tinted, taken on their twenty-fifth wedding anniversary in February of 1981. They look embalmed, Rabbit thinks, suspended in that tinted bubble of time. The ceiling light in this room, glass like the hall light, is also burning. He asks, "Mind if I switch that off? All these lights on, I'm getting a headache."

Nelson says sourly, "You're the big cheese. Help yourself."

Judy explains, "Mommy said to turn them all on while Daddy was chasing her. She said if it got worse I should throw a chair through a front window and yell for help and the police would hear."

With the light switched off, Rabbit can see out into the dark gulf of air where the copper beech used to be. The neighbor's house is closer than he ever thought, in his fifteen years of living here. Their upstairs lights are on. He can see segments of wall and furniture but no people. Maybe they were thinking of calling the police. Maybe they already have. He switches on the lamp on the cherry table, so the neighbors can look in and see everything under control.

"She overreacted," Nelson explains, fitfully gesturing. "I was trying to make a point and Pru wouldn't hold still. She never listens to me any more."

"Maybe you don't say enough she wants to hear," Harry tells his son. The kid in his white shirt and dark trousers looks like a magician's assistant, and keeps tapping himself on the chest and back of the neck and rubbing his arms through the white cloth as if he's about to do a trick. The boy is embarrassed and scared but keeps losing focus, Rabbit feels; there are other presences for him in the room besides the bed and furniture and his parents and daughter, a mob of ghosts which only he can see. A smell comes off him, liquor and something chemical. He is sweating; his gills are wet.

"O.K., O.K.," Nelson says. "I treated myself to a bender tonight, I admit it. It's been a helluva week over there. California wants to have this nationwide Toyotathon to go with a TV-commercial blitz and they expect to see a twenty-per-cent increase of new sales to go with the discounts they're offering. They let me know they haven't been liking our figures lately."

"Them and who else?" Harry says. "Did your buddy Lyle tell ya I was over there the other day?"

"Snooping around last week, yeah, he sure did. He hasn't come to work since. Thanks a bunch. You put Elvira into a snit, too, with all your sexist flirtatious stuff."

"I wasn't sexist, I wasn't flirtatious. I was just surprised to see a woman selling cars and asked her how it was going. The cunt, I was just as pleasant as I could be."

"She didn't think so."

"Well screw her, then. From my look at her she can take care of herself. What's your big huff for—you boffing her?"

"Dad, when are you going to get your mind off boffing? You're what, fifty-seven?—"

"Fifty-six."

"—and you're so damn adolescent. There's more things in the world than who's boffing who."

"Tell me about it. Tell me about how the me generation has a bender. You can't keep snorting this stuff every half-hour to keep high, your nose'd burn out. Yours looks sort of shot already. What do you do with crack? How do you take it in? It's just little crystals, isn't it? Do you need all that fancy burning stuff and tubes they show on TV? Where do you do it, then? You can't just haul all that paraphernalia into the Laid-Back or whatever they call it now."

"Harry, please," Janice says.

Judy contributes, bright-eyed at three in the morning. "Daddy has lots of funny little pipes."

"Shut up honey, would you mind?" Nelson says. "Go find Mommy and she'll put you to bed."

Harry turns on Janice. "Let me *ask* him. Why should we all go around on tiptoe forever pretending the kid's not a hophead? Face it, Nellie, you're a mess. You're a mess and you're a menace. You need help."

Self-pity focuses the boy's features for a second. "People keep telling me I need help but *they're* no help is what I notice. A wife who doesn't give me shit, a father who's no kind of father at all and never was, a mother . . ." He trails off, not daring offend his one ally.

"A mother," Harry finishes for him, "who's letting you rob her blind."

This gets to him a little, burns through the jittery buzz in his eyes. "I'm not robbing anybody," he says, numbly, as though a voice in his head told him to say it. "Everything's been worked out. Hey, I feel sick. I think I have to throw up."

Harry raises his hand in lofty blessing. "Go to it. You know where the bathroom is."

The bathroom door is to the right of the dresser with the color snapshots of the kids at various stages of growing and the tinted one of Harry and Janice looking embalmed, mistily staring at the same point in space. Looking in, Harry sees all sorts of litter on the floor. Prell, Crest, pills. Luckily most things come in plastic containers these days so there isn't much breakage. The door closes.

Janice tells him, "Harry, you're coming on too strong."

"Well, hell, nobody else is coming on at all. You expect it to go away by itself. It won't. The kid is hooked."

"Let's just not talk about the money," she begs.

"Why not? Just what is so fucking sacred about money, that everybody's scared to talk about it?"

The tip of her tongue peeks from between her worried lips. "With money you get into legal things."

Judy is still with them and has been listening: her clear young eyes with their bluish whites, her reddish-blond eyebrows with their little cowlick, her little face pale as a clock's face and as precise pluck at Harry's anger, undermine his necessary indignation. Retching noises from behind the bathroom door now frighten her. Harry explains, "It'll make your daddy feel better. He's getting rid of poison." But the thought of Nelson being sick upsets him too, and those bands of constriction around his chest, the playful malevolent singeing deep within, reassert their threat. He fishes in his pants pocket for the precious brown vial. Thank God he remembered to bring it. He unscrews the top and shakes out a small white Nitrostat and places it, as debonairly as he used to light a cigarette, beneath his tongue.

Judy smiles upward. "Those pills fix that bad heart I gave you."

"You didn't give me my bad heart, honey, I wish you'd get that out of your mind." He is bothered by Janice's remark about money and legal things and the implication that they are getting in over their heads. ANGSTROM, SON INCARCERATED. *Joint Scam Sinks Family Concern.* The lights in the neighbor's upstairs windows have gone off and that relieves some pressure. He could feel Ma Springer turning in her grave at the possibility that her old house has become a bother to the neighborhood. Nelson comes out of the bathroom looking shaken, wide-eyed. The poor kid has seen some terrible things in his day: Jill's body carried from the burned-out house in a rubber bag, his mother hugging the little dead body of his baby sister. You can't really blame him for anything. He has washed his face and combed his hair so his pallor has this gleam. He lets a shudder run from his head down into his body, like a dog shaking itself dry after running in a ditch.

For all his merciful thoughts Harry goes back on the attack. "Yeah," he says, even as the kid is closing the bathroom door, "and another new development over there I wasn't crazy about is this fat Italian you've hired. What are you letting the Mafia into the lot for?"

"Dad, you are incredibly prejudiced."

"I don't have prejudices, just facts. The Mafia is a fact. It's being scared out of the drug trade, too violent, and is getting into more and more legitimate businesses. It was all on *60 Minutes*."

"Mom, get him off me."

Janice gets up her courage and says, "Nelson, your father's right. You need some help."

"I'm fine," he whines. "I need some *sleep*, is what I need. You have any idea what time it is?—it's after three. Judy, you should go back to bed."

"I'm too wired," the child says, smiling, showing her perfect oval teeth.

Harry asks her, "Where'd you learn that word?"

"I'm too jazzed," she says. "Kids at school say that."

Harry asks Nelson, "And who're these guys keep calling our house at all hours asking for money?"

"They think I owe them money," Nelson answers. "Maybe I do. It's temporary, Dad. It'll all work out. Come, Judy. I'll put you to bed."

"Not so fast," Harry says. "How much do you owe, and how're you going to pay 'em?"

"Like I said, I'll work it out. They shouldn't be calling your number, but they're crude guys. They don't understand term financing. Go back to Florida if you don't like your phone ringing. Change your number, that's what I did."

"Nelson, when will it end?" Janice asks, tears making her voice crack, just from looking at him. In his white shirt with his electric movements Nelson has the frailty and doomed alertness of a cornered animal. "You must get off this stuff."

"I am, Mom. I am off. Starting tonight."

"Ha," Harry says.

Nelson insists to her, "I can handle it. I'm no addict. I'm a recreational user."

"Yeah," Harry says, "like Hitler was a recreational killer." It must be the mustache made him think of Hitler. If the kid would just shave it off, and chuck the earring, he maybe could feel some compassion, and they could make a fresh start.

But, then, Harry thinks, how many fresh starts for him are left? This room, where he spent fifteen years sleeping beside Janice, listening to her snore, smelling her nice little womanly sweat, her unconscious releases of gas, making some great love sometimes, that time with the Krugerrands, and other times

disgustedly watching her stumble in tipsy from a night downstairs sipping sherry or Campari, this room with the copper
beech outside the window leafing in and changing the light and
then losing its leaves and giving the light back and the beech
nuts popping like little firecrackers and Ma Springer's television
mumbling on and making the bedside lamp vibrate when a certain pitch was reached on the program-ending surge of music,
Ma sound asleep and never hearing it, this room soaked in his
life, fifteen long years of it, how many more times will he see
it? He hadn't expected to see it tonight. Now all at once, as
happens at his age, fatigue like an inner overflowing makes him
feel soggy, dirty, distracted. Little sparks are going off and on
in the corners of his eyes. Avoid aggravation. He'd better sit
down. Janice has sat down on the bed, their old bed, and Nelson
has pulled up the padded stool patterned with yellow roses Pru
must use to perch on in her underwear when she sits putting on
makeup at her dresser mirror before going out with him to the
Laid-Back or some yuppie buddies' party in northeast Brewer.
How sorry is he supposed to feel for his son when the kid has a
big tall hippy dish like that to boff?

Nelson has changed his tune. He leans toward his mother, his
fingers intertwined to still their shaking, his lips tensed to bite
back his nausea, his dark eyes full of an overflowing confusion
like her own. He is pleadingly, disjointedly, explaining himself:
". . . the only time I feel *hu*man, like other people I guess feel
all the time. But when I went after Pru that way tonight it was
like a monster or something had taken over my body and I was
standing outside watching and felt no connection with myself.
Like it was all on television. You're right, I got to ease off. I
mean, it's getting so I can't start the day without . . . a hit . . .
and all day all I think about . . . That's not human either."

"You poor baby," she says. "I know. I know just what you're
saying. It's lack of self-esteem. I had it for years. Remember,
Harry, how I used to drink when we were young?"

Trying to pull him into it, make him a parent too. He won't
have it, yet. He won't buy in. "When we were young? How
about when we were middle-aged, like now even? Hey look,
what's this supposed to be, a therapy session? This kid just
clobbered his wife and is conning the pants off us and you're
*let*ting him!"

Judy, lying diagonally on the bed behind her grandmother,
and studying them all with upside-down eyes, joins in, observ-

ing, "When Grandpa gets mad his upper lip goes all stiff just like Mommy's does."

Nelson comes out of his fog of self-pity enough to say to her, "Honey, I'm not sure you should be hearing all this."

"Let me put her back to bed," Janice offers, not moving though.

Harry doesn't want to be left alone with Nelson. He says, "No, I'll do it. You two keep talking. Hash it out. I've had my say to this jailbait."

Judy laughs shrilly, her head still upside down on the bed, her reversed eyelids monstrous. "That's a funny word," her mouth says, the teeth all wrong, big on bottom and little on top. " 'Jailbait.' You mean 'jailbird.' "

"No, Judy," Harry tells her, taking her hand and trying to pull her upright. "First you're jailbait, then you're a jailbird. When you're in jail, you're a jailbird."

"Where the holy fuck is her mother?" Nelson asks the air in front of his face. "That damn Pru, she's always telling me what a jerk I am, then she's out to lunch half the time herself. Notice how broad in the beam she's getting? That's alcohol. The kids come home from school and find her sound asleep." He says this to Janice, placating her, badmouthing his wife to his mother, then suddenly turns to Harry.

"Dad," he says. "Want to split a beer?"

"You must be crazy."

"It'll help bring us down," the boy wheedles. "It'll help us to sleep."

"I'm fighting sleep; Jesus. It's not *me* who's wired or whatever you call it. Come on, Judy. Don't give Grandpa a hard time. He hurts all over." The child's hand seems damp and sticky in his, and she makes a game of his pulling her off the bed, resisting to the point that he feels a squeeze in his chest. And when he gets her upright beside the bed, she goes limp and tries to collapse onto the rug. He holds on and resists the impulse to slap her. To Janice he says sharply, "Ten more minutes. You and the kid talk. Don't let him con you. Set up some kind of plan. We got to get some order going in this crazy family."

As he pulls the bedroom door halfway shut, he hears Nelson say, "Mom, how about you? Wouldn't half a beer be good? We have Mick, and Miller's."

Judy's room, wherein Ma Springer used to doze and pretend to watch television, and from whose front windows you can see patches of Joseph Street, deserted like tundra, blanched by the streetlights, through the sticky Norway maples, is crowded with stuffed toys, teddy bears and giraffes and Garfields; but Harry feels they are all old toys, that nobody has brought this child a present for some time. Her childhood is wearing out before she is done with it. She crawls without hesitation or any more stalling into her bed, under a tattered red puff covered with Peanuts characters. He asks her if she doesn't need to go pee-pee first. She shakes her head and stares up at him from the pillow as if amused by how little he knows about her insides. Slant slices of streetlight enter around the window shades and he asks her if she would like him to draw the curtains. Judy says No, she doesn't like it totally dark. He asks her if the cars going by bother her and she says No, only the big trucks that shake the house sometimes and there's a law that says they shouldn't come this way but the police are too lazy to enforce it. "Or too busy," he points out, always one to defend the authorities. Strange that he should have this instinct, since in his life he hasn't been especially dutiful. Jailbait himself on a couple of occasions. But the authorities these days seem so helpless, so unarmed. He asks Judy if she wants to say a prayer. She says No thanks. She is clutching some stuffed animal that looks shapeless to him, without arms or legs. Monstrous. He asks her about it and she shows him that it is a stuffed toy dolphin, with gray back and white belly. He pats its polyester fur and tucks it back under the covers with her. Her chin rests on the white profile of Snoopy wearing his aviator glasses. Linus clutches his blanket; Pigpen has little stars of dirt around his head; Charlie Brown is on his pitcher's mound, and then is knocked head over heels by a rocketing ball. Sitting on the edge of the bed, wondering if Judy expects a bedtime story, Harry sighs so abjectly, so wearily, that both are surprised, and nervously laugh. She suddenly asks him if everything will be all right.

"How do you mean, honey?"

"With Mommy and Daddy."

"Sure. They love you and Roy, and they love each other."

"They say they don't. They fight."

"A lot of married people fight."

"My friends' parents don't."

"I bet they do, but you don't see it. They're being good because you're in the house."

"When people fight a lot, they get divorced."

"Yes, that happens. But only after a *lot* of fighting. Has your daddy ever hit your mommy before, like tonight?"

"Sometimes she hits him. She says he's wasting all our money."

Harry has no ready answer to that. "It'll work out," he says, just as Nelson has. "Things work out, usually. It doesn't always seem that way, but they usually do."

"Like you that time you fell on the sand and couldn't get up."

"Wasn't that a funny way to act? Yes, and see, here I am, as good as new. It worked out."

Her face broadens in the dark; she is smiling. Her hair is spread in dark rays across the glowing pillow. "You were so funny in the water. I teased you."

"You teased me how?"

"By hiding under the sail."

He casts his weary mind back and tells her, "You weren't teasing, honey. You were all blue and gaspy when I got you out. I saved your life. Then you saved mine."

She says nothing. The dark pits of her eyes absorb his version, his adult memory. He leans down and kisses her warm dry forehead. "Don't you worry about anything, Judy. Grandma and I will take good care of your daddy and all of you."

"I know," she says after a pause, letting go. We are each of us like our little blue planet, hung in black space, upheld by nothing but our mutual reassurances, our loving lies.

Emerging opposite to the closed door of the old sewing room, where Melanie used to sleep, Rabbit sneaks down the hall past the half-closed door to the master bedroom—he can hear Janice and Nelson talking, their voices braided into one—and to the room beyond, a back room with a view of the back yard and the little fenced garden he used to tend. This was Nelson's room in the distant days when he went to high school and wore long hair and a headband like an Indian and tried to learn the guitar that had been Jill's and spent a small fortune on his collection of rock LPs, records all obsolete now, everything is tapes, and tapes are becoming obsolete, everything will be CDs. This room is now little Roy's. Its door is ajar; with three fingertips on its cool white wood Harry pushes it open. Light enters it not as sharp slices from the proximate streetlights above Joseph Street but more mistily, from the lights of the town diffused and scattered, a yellow star-swallowing glow arising foglike from the silhouettes of maples and gables and telephone poles. By this dim light he sees Pru's long body pathetically asleep across Roy's little bed. One foot has kicked off its fake-furry slipper and sticks out bare from its nightie, so filmy it clings to the shape of her bent full-thighed leg, her short quilted robe ruched up to her waist, rumpled in folds whose valleys seem bottomless in the faint light. One long white hand of hers rests extended on the rumpled covers, the other is curled in a loose fist and fitted into the hollow between her lips and chin; the bruise on her cheekbone shows like a leech attached there and her hair, its carrotcolor black in the dark, is disarrayed. Her breath moves in and out with a shallow exhausted rasp. He inhales through his nose, to smell her. Perfume traces float in her injured aura.

As he bends over for this inspection, Rabbit is startled by the twin hard gleam of open eyes: Roy is awake. Cuddled on his bed by his mother, sung a song that has put the singer to sleep, the strange staring child reaches up through the darkness to seize the loose skin of his grandfather's looming face and to twist it, his small sharp fingernails digging in so that Harry has to fight crying out. He pulls this fierce little crab of a hand away from his cheek, disembeds it finger by finger, and with a vengeful pinch settles it back onto Roy's chest. In his animal hurt he has hissed aloud; seeing Pru stir as if to awake, her hand making an agitated motion toward her tangled hair, Harry backs rapidly from the room.

Janice and Nelson are in the bright hall looking for him. With their thinning hair and muddled scowling expressions they seem siblings. He tells them in a whisper, "Pru fell asleep on Roy's bed."

Nelson says, "That poor bitch. She'd be O.K. if she'd just get off my case."

Janice tells Harry, "Nelson says he feels much more like himself now and we should go home to bed."

Their voices seem loud, after the foglit silence of Roy's room, and he pointedly keeps his own low. "What have you two settled? I don't want this to happen again."

In Nelson's old room, Roy has begun to cry. He should cry; it's Harry's cheek that hurts.

"It won't, Harry," Janice says. "Nelson has promised to see a counsellor."

He looks at his son to see what this means. The boy visibly suppresses a smile of collusion, over the necessity of placating women. Harry tells Janice, "I *said*, Don't let him con ya."

Her forehead, which her bangs do not cover, creases in impatience. "Harry, it's time to go." She is, as Lyle informed him, the boss.

On the drive back, he vents his indignation. "What did he

say? What about the money?'' Route 422 shudders with tall trucks, transcontinental eighteen-wheelers. They make better time in the dead of the night.

Janice says, ''He's running the lot and it would be too unmanning to take it from him. I can't run it and you're going into the hospital for that angio-thing. Plasty.''

''Not till the week after next,'' he says. ''We could always put it off.''

''I know that's what you'd like but we just can't go on pretending you're fine. It's been nearly four months since New Year's and in Florida they said you should recover enough in three. Dr. Breit told me you're not losing weight and avoiding sodium the way you were told and you could have a recurrence of what happened on the Sunfish any time.''

Dr. Breit is his cardiologist at the St. Joseph's Hospital in Brewer—a fresh-faced freckled kid with big glasses in flesh-colored plastic rims. Janice's telling him all this in her mother's matter-of-fact, determined voice carves a dreadful hollowness within him. The sloping park as they cruise through on Cityview Drive seems fragile and papery, the illuminated trees unreal. There is nothing beneath these rocks, these steep lawns and proud row houses, but atoms and nothingness, waiting for him to take his tight-fitting place among them. *Dear God, reach down. Pull my bad heart out of me.* Thelma said it helped. Janice's mind, far from prayer, is moving on, her voice decided and a bit defiant. ''As for the money, Nelson did allow as there has to be some financial restructuring.''

''Restructuring! That's what everybody up the creek talks about. South American countries, those Texas S and Ls. Did he really say 'restructuring'?''

''Well, it's not a word *I* would have thought to use. Though I expect when I start with my courses it'll be one of the things they teach.''

''Your courses, Jesus,'' he says. That tank, painted the wrong green, how much longer before nobody remembered why it was there—the ration stamps, the air-raid drills, the screaming eight-column headlines every morning, God versus Satan a simple matter of the miles gained each day on the road to Aachen? ''What did he say about himself and Pru?''

''He doesn't think she's found another man yet,'' Janice says. ''So we don't think she'll really leave.''

''Well, that's nice and hard-boiled of you both. But what about *her*, her own welfare? You saw her battered face tonight. How much more should she take? Face it, the kid is utterly gonzo. Do you see the way he was twitching all the time? And throwing up then? Did you hear him offer me a beer? A beer, for Chrissake, when we should have been the cops really. He's damn lucky the neighbors didn't call 'em.''

"He was just trying to be hospitable. It's a great trial to him, Harry, that you're so unsympathetic.''

"Unsympathetic! What's to be sympathetic with? He cheats, he snivels, he snorts or whatever, he's a lush besides, over at the lot he hires these gangsters and guys with AIDS—''

"Really, you should hear yourself. I wish I had a tape recorder.''

"So do I. So what's he going to do about dope?'' Even at this hour, going on four, a few men in sneakers and jeans are awake in the park, conferring behind trees, waiting on benches. "Did he promise to give it up?''

"He promised to see a counsellor,'' Janice says. "He admits he might have a problem. I think that's a good night's work. Pru has all sorts of names and agencies from these Narc-Anon meetings she's been going to.''

"Names, agencies, we can't expect society to run our lives for us, to baby us from cradle to grave. That's what the Communists try to do. There comes a point when you got to take responsibility.'' He fingers his pants pocket to make sure the little hard cylindrical bottle is there. He won't take a pill now, but save it for when they get home. With a small glass of milk in the kitchen. And a Nutter-Butter cookie to dip into the milk. Shaped like a big peanut, a Nutter-Butter is delicious dipped into milk, first up to the peanut waist, and then the rest for a second bite.

Janice says, "I wish my parents were still alive to hear you talk about responsibility. My mother thought you were the most irresponsible person she ever met.''

This hurts, slightly. He had liked Ma Springer toward the end, and thought she liked him. Hot nights out on the screened porch, pinochle games up in the Poconos. They both found Janice a bit slow.

Out of the park, he heads the slate-gray Celica down Weiser, through the heart of Brewer. The Sunflower Beer Clock says 3:50, above the great deserted city heart. Something cleansing about being awake at this forsaken hour. It's a new world. A living, crouching shadow—a cat, or can it be a raccoon?—stares with eyes like circular reflectors in his headlights, sitting on the cement stairs of a dry fountain there on the edge of the little woods the city planners have created. At the intersection of Weiser and Sixth, he has to turn right. In the old days you could drive straight to the bridge. The wild kids in high school liked to drive down the trolley tracks, between the islands where passengers would board.

As his silence lengthens, Janice says placatingly, "Weren't those children dear? Harry, you don't want them to live in one of those sad one-parent households."

Rabbit has always been squeamish about things being put into him—dental drills, tongue depressors, little long knives to clean out earwax, suppositories, the doctor's finger when once a year he sizes up your prostate gland. So the idea of a catheter being inserted at the top of his right leg, and being pushed along steered with a little flexible tip like some eyeless worm you find wriggling out of an apple where you just bit, is deeply repugnant to him, though not as much so as being frozen half to death and sawed open and your blood run through some complicated machine while they sew a slippery warm piece of your leg vein to the surface of your trembling poor cowering heart.

In the hospital in Deleon they gave him some articles to try to read and even showed him a little video: the heart sits in a protective sac, the pericardium, which has to be cut open, *snipped* the video said cheerfully like it was giving a sewing lesson. It showed it happening: cold narrow scalpels attack the shapeless bloody blob as it lies there in your chest like a live thing in a hot puddle, a cauldron of tangled juicy stew, convulsing, shuddering with a periodic sob, trying to dodge the knives, undressed of the sanitary pod God or whoever never meant human hands to touch. Then when the blood has been detoured to the gleaming pumping machine just like those in those horrible old Frankenstein movies with Boris Karloff the heart stops beating. You see it happen: your heart lies there dead in its soupy puddle. You, the natural you, are technically dead. A machine is living for you while the surgeons' hands in their condomlike latex gloves fiddle and slice and knit away. Harry has trouble believing how his life is tied to all this mechanics—that the *me* that talks inside him all the time scuttles like a waterstriding bug above this pond of body fluids and their slippery conduits. How could the flame of him ever have ignited out of such wet straw?

The angioplasty seemed far less deep a violation than the coronary bypass. It was scheduled for a Friday. Youngish-old

Dr. Breit, with his painfully fair skin, the pale freckles merged
into a mottle, and his plastic-rimmed glasses too big for his
button nose, explained the operation—the procedure, he preferred to call it—in the lulling voice of a nightclub singer who
has done the same lyrics so often her mind is free to wander as
she sings. The cardiologist's real preference was the bypass,
Harry could tell. The angioplasty to Breit was just a sop, kid
snuff, until the knives could descend. "The rate of restenosis is
thirty per cent in three months' time," he warned Harry, there
in his office with the framed color photos of a little freckled
woman who resembled him as one hamster resembles another
and of little children arranged in front of their parents like a
small stepladder, all with curly pale hair and squints and those
tiny pink noses, "and twenty per cent of PTCA patients wind
up having a CABG eventually anyway. Sorry—that's percuta-
neous transluminal coronary angioplasty versus coronary artery
bypass graft."

"I guessed," Harry said. "Still, let's do the balloon first, and
save the knives for later."

"Fair enough," said Dr. Breit, semi-singingly, his tone
clipped and grim and even-tempered and resigned. Like a golfer:
you lose this match but you'll play again next week. "You think
the way ninety per cent of all heart patients do. They love the
idea of the PTCA, and no heart specialist can talk them out of
it. It's irrational, but so's the human species. Tell you what,
Harold." No one had told him Harry was never called Harold,
though that was his legal name. Rabbit let it go; it made him
feel a child again. His mother used to call him Hassy. "We'll
give you a treat. You can watch the whole procedure on TV.
You'll be under local anesthetic, it'll help you pass the time."

"Do I have to?"

Dr. Breit seemed momentarily bothered. For so fair a man,
he sweated a great deal, his upper lip always dewy. "We screen
off the monitor usually, for the patients we think are too excitable
or frail. There's always a slight chance of a coronary occlusion
and that wouldn't be too good, to be watching it happen. But
you, you're not frail. You're no nervous nelly. I've sized you up
as a pretty tough-minded guy, Harold, with a fair amount of
intellectual curiosity. Was I wrong?"

It was like a ten-dollar press, when you're already thirty dollars down. You can't refuse. "No," he told the young doctor.
"That's me all right."

Dr. Breit actually does not perform the procedure: it needs a specialist, a burly menacing man with thick brown forearms, Dr. Raymond. But Breit is there, his face peeping like a moon—big specs glinting, upper lip dewy with nervous perspiration—over the mountainous lime-green shoulders of Dr. Raymond and the surgical caps of the nurses. The operation takes two attending nurses; this is no little "procedure"; Harry's been sandbagged. And it takes two rooms of the hospital, the room where it happens and a monitoring room with several TV screens that translate him into jerking bright lines, vital signs: the Rabbit Angstrom Show, with a fluctuating audience as the circulating nurse and Dr. Breit and some others never named to him, lime-green extras, come and watch a while and leave again. There is even, he has been casually told, a surgical team standing by just in case he needs immediate bypass surgery.

Another double-cross: they shave him, down beside his privates, without warning, where the catheter will go in. They give him a pill to make him light in the head and then when he's helpless on the operating table under all these lights they scrape away at the right half of his groin area and pubic bush; he's never had much body hair and wonders if at his age it will ever grow back. The needle that follows feels bigger and meaner than the Novocain needle the dentist uses; its "pinch"—Dr. Raymond murmurs, "Now you'll feel a pinch"—doesn't let go as quickly. But then there's no pain, just an agony of mounting urinary pressure as the dyes build up in his system, injected repeatedly with a hot surge like his chest is being cooked in a microwave. Jesus. He closes his eyes a few times to pray but it feels like a wrong occasion, there is too much crowding in, of the actual material world. No old wispy Biblical God would dare interfere. The one religious consolation he clings to through his three-and-a-half-hour ordeal is a belief that Dr. Raymond, with his desert tan and long melancholy nose and bearish pack of fat across his shoulders, is Jewish: Harry has this gentile prejudice that Jews do everything a little better than other people, something about all those generations crouched over the Torah and watch-repair tables, they aren't as distracted as other persuasions, they don't expect to have as much fun. They stay off booze and dope and have a weakness only (if that history of Hollywood he once read can be trusted) for broads.

The doctors and their satellites murmurously crouch over Harry's sheeted, strategically exposed body, under a sharp light, in a room whose tiles are the color of Russian salad dressing, on the fourth floor of St. Joseph's Hospital, where decades ago his two children were born—Nelson, who lived, and Rebecca, who died. In those years nuns ran the place, with their black and white and cupcake frills around their pasty faces, but now nuns have blended into everybody else or else faded away. Vocations drying up, nobody wants to be selfless any more, everybody wants their fun. No more nuns, no more rabbis. No more good people, waiting to have their fun in the afterlife. The thing about the afterlife, it kept this life within bounds somehow, like the Russians. Now there's just Japan, and technology, and the profit motive, and getting all you can while you can.

Turning his head to the left, Rabbit can see, over the shoulders that crowd around his body like green cotton tummocks, the shadow of his heart on an X-ray monitor screen, a twitching pale-gray ghost dimly webbed by its chambered structure and darkened in snaky streaks and bulbous oblongs by injections of the opacifying dye. The thin wire tip of the catheter, inquisitive in obedience to Dr. Raymond's finger on the trigger, noses forward and then slowly eels, in little cautious jerking stabs, diagonally down into a milky speckled passageway, a river or tentacle within him, organic and tentative in shape where the catheter is black and positive, hard-edged as a gun. Harry watches to see if his heart will gag and try to disgorge the intruder. Like a finger down his throat, he thinks, feeling a wave of nausea and yet a test pilot's detachment from this picture on the screen, blanched and hard to read like a section of aerial map, and these conferring voices around him. "We're home," Dr. Breit murmurs, as if not to awaken something. "That's your LAD, your left anterior descending. The widow-maker, they call it. By far the most common site of lesions. See how stenotic those walls are? How thickened with plaque? Those little agglutinated specks—that's plaque. I'd say your luminal narrowing is close to eighty-five per cent."

"Rice Krispies," Harry tries to say, but his mouth is too dry, his voice cracks. All he wanted was to acknowledge that yes, he sees it all, he sees his tangled shadowy self laid out like a diagram, he sees the offending plaque, like X-rayed Rice Krispies. He nods a little, feeling even more gingerly than when getting a haircut or having his prostate explored. Too vigorous a nod, and his heart might start to gag. He wonders, is this what having a baby is like, having Dr. Raymond inside you? How do women stand it, for nine months? Not to mention being screwed in the first place? Can they really like it? Or queers being buggered? It's something you never see really discussed, even on Oprah.

"Now comes the tricky part," Dr. Breit breathes, like a golf commentator into the mike as a crucial putt is addressed. Harry feels and then sees on the monitor his heart beat faster, twist as if to escape, twist in that convulsive spiral motion Dr. Olman in Florida demonstrated with his fist; the shadowy fist is angry, again and again, seventy times a minute; the anger is his life, his soul, mind over matter, electricity over muscle. The mechanically precise dark ghost of the catheter is the worm of death within him. Godless technology is fucking the pulsing wet tubes we inherited from the squid, the boneless sea-cunts. He feels again that feathery touch of nausea. Can he possibly throw up? It would jar and jam the works, disrupt the concentrating green tummocks he is buried beneath. He mustn't. He must be still.

He sees, on the monitor, behind the inquisitive tip, a segment of the worm thicken and swell, pressing the pallid Rice Krispies together against the outlines of the filmy crimped river descending down his heart, and stay inflated, pressing, filling, so that (it has been explained to him) if the LAD has not developed any collateral arteries the blood flow will cease and another heart attack begin, right on camera.

"Thirty seconds," Dr. Breit breathes, and Dr. Raymond deflates the balloon. "Looking good, Ray." Harry feels no pain beyond the knifelike sweet pressure in his bladder and a soreness in the far back of his throat as if from swallowing all that saltwater out on the Gulf. "Once more, Harold, and we'll call it a day."

"How're ya doing?" Dr. Raymond asks him, in one of those marbles-in-the-mouth voices muscular men sometimes have, Pennsylvanians especially.

"Still here," Harry says, in a brave voice that sounds high in his ears, as if out of a woman's throat.

The tense insufflation repeats, and so do the images on the TV screen, silent like the bumping of molecules under the microscope on a nature program, or like computer graphics in an insurance commercial, where fragments flickeringly form the logo. It seems as remote from his body as the records of his sins that angels are keeping. Were his heart to stop, it would be mere shadowplay. He sees, when the catheter's bulge subsides a second time, that the Rice Krispies have been pushed to the sides of his LAD. He pictures blood flowing more freely into his heart, rich in combustible oxygen; his head in gratitude and ecstasy grows faint.

"Looking good," Dr. Breit says, sounding nervous.

"Whaddya mean?" Dr. Raymond responds—"looking *great*," like those voices on television that argue about the virtues of Miller Lite.

The nurse who that evening comes into his room (a private room, $160 more a day, but it's worth it to him; in Florida the guy in the bed next to him finally died, gurgling and moaning all day and then shitting all over himself as a last pronouncement) and takes Harry's temperature and blood pressure and brings his allotment of pills in a little paper cup has a round kind face. She is a bit overweight but it's packed on firm. She looks familiar. She has pale-blue eyes in sockets that make a dent above the cheekbones in the three-quarters view, and her upper lip has that kind of puffy look he likes, like Michelle Pfeiffer. Her hair shows under her nurse's cap as browny-red, many-colored, with visible strands of gray, though she is young enough to be his daughter.

She lifts the strange plastic rocket-shaped thermometer that gives its reading in red segmented numbers from his mouth and enwraps his left arm with the Velcro-fastened blood-pressure cuff. As she inflates it she asks, "How's the Toyota business?"

"Not bad. The weak dollar doesn't help. My son runs the place now, basically. How'd you know I sold Toyotas?"

"My boyfriend then and I bought a car from you about ten years ago." She lifts those bleached blue eyes mockingly. "Don't you remember?"

"It's *you*! Yes. Of course. Of course I remember. An orange Corolla." She is his daughter; or at least he imagines she is, though Ruth out of spite would never admit it to him. As the girl stands close to his bed, he reads her badge: ANNABELLE BYER, R.N. She still has her maiden name.

Annabelle frowns, and deflates the blood-pressure cuff, as tight around his arm as a policeman's grip. "Let's try that again in a minute. It shot up while we were talking."

He asks her, "How'd the Corolla work out? How'd the boyfriend work out, for that matter? What the hell was his name? Big red-eared country kid."

"Don't talk, please, until I've got my reading. I'll be quiet. Try to think of something soothing."

He thinks of Ruth's farm, the Byer place, the slope down

through the orchard from the line of scrub trees he used to spy behind—the little square stone house, the yellow shells of the abandoned school buses, the dark collie that tried to herd him down there, as though he knew Harry belonged there with the others. Fritzie, that was that dog's name. Sharp teeth, black gums. *Oo boy, scary.* Calm down. Think of the big sky of Texas, above the hot low barracks at Fort Hood, himself in fresh khaki, with a pass for the evening. Freedom, a soft breeze, a green sunset on the low horizon. Think of playing basketball against Oriole High, that little country gym, the backboards flush against the walls, before all the high schools merged into big colorless regionals and shopping malls began eating up the farmland. Think of sledding with Mim in her furry hood, in Mt. Judge behind the hat factory, on a winter's day so short the streetlights come on an hour before suppertime calls you home.

"That's better," the nurse says. "One forty over ninety-five. Not great, but not bad. In answer to your questions: the car lasted longer than the boyfriend. I traded in the car after eight years; it had a hundred twenty thousand miles on the speedometer. Jamie moved out about a year after we moved into town. He went back to Galilee. Brewer was too tough for him."

"And you? Is it too tough for you?"

"No, I like it. I like the action."

Action like her mother used to get? *You were a real hooer?* Dusk and May's fully arrived leafiness soften his private room; it is a quiet time on the hospital floor, after dinner and the post-work surge of visitors. Harry dares ask, "You married now? Or live with a guy?"

She smiles, her natural kindness contending a moment with surprise at his curiosity, his presumption, and then smoothing her face into calm again. The dusk seems to be gathering it closer, the pale round glimmer of her face. But her voice discloses a city dryness, a guardedness that might rise up. "No, as a matter of fact I live with my mother. She sold the farm we inherited from my father and moved in with me after Jamie moved out."

"I think I know that farm. I've passed it on the road." Harry's violated, tired heart feels weighted by so much information, by the thought of that other world, with all its bushes and seasons and green days and brown, where this child's life had passed without him. "Does Ruth—" he begins, and ends, "What does she do? Your mother."

The girl gives him a look but then answers readily, as if the question passed some test. "She works for one of these investment companies from out of state, money markets and mutual funds and all that, that have branch offices in the new glass building downtown, across from where Kroll's used to be."

"A stenographer," Rabbit remembers. "She could type and take dictation."

The girl actually laughs, in surprise at his groping command of the truth. She is beginning to be pert, to drop her nurse's manner. She has backed off a step from his bed, and her full thighs press against the crisp front of her white uniform so that even standing up she has a lap. Why is Ruth turning this girl into a spinster? She tells him, "She was hired for that but being so much older than the other women they've let her have some more responsibility. She's a kind of junior exec now. Did you know my mother, ever?"

"I'm not sure," he lies.

"You must have, in the days when she was single. She told me she knew quite a few guys before meeting up with my father." She smiles, giving him permission to have known her mother.

"I guess she did," Harry says, sad at the thought. Always he has wanted to be every woman's only man, as he was his mother's only son. "I met her once or twice."

"You should see her," Annabelle goes on pertly. "She's lost a lot of weight and dresses real snappy. I kid her, she has more boyfriends than I do."

Rabbit closes his eyes and tries to picture it, at their age. *Come on. Work.* Dressing snappy. Once a city girl, always a city girl. Her hair, that first time he saw her, rimmed with red neon like wilt.

The girl he thinks is his daughter goes on, "I'll tell her you're in here, Mr. Angstrom." Though he is trying now to withdraw, into his evening stupor, an awakening affinity between them has stirred her to a certain forwardness. "Maybe she'll remember more than you do."

Outside the sealed hospital windows, in the slowly thickening dusk, sap is rising, and the air even in here feels languid with pollen. Involuntarily Harry's eyes close again. "No," he says, "that's O.K. Don't tell her anything. I doubt if she'd remember anything." He is suddenly tired, too tired for Ruth. Even if this girl is his daughter, it's an old story, going on and on, like a radio nobody's listening to.

* * *

They keep him in the hospital for five nights. Janice visits him Saturday. She is very busy on the outside; the classes she has to take to be a real-estate salesman have begun to meet, "The Laws of Real Property and Conveyancing" for three hours one night, and the other, "Procedures of Mortgages and Financing," on another. Also, she has been spending a lot of daytime hours with Pru and the grandchildren, and Charlie Stavros called her up and took her out to lunch.

Rabbit protests, "The bastard, he did? I'm not even dead yet."

"Of course not, darling, and nobody expects you to be. He said it was your idea, from when *you* had lunch together. Charlie's concerned about us, is all. He thinks I shouldn't just be letting things slide but should get an outside accountant and our lawyer and look at the books over at the lot, just like you wanted."

"You believe it when Charlie tells you, but not when I do."

"Honey, you're my husband, and husbands get wives all confused. Charlie's just an old friend, and he has an outsider's impartiality. Also, he loved my father, and feels protective toward the firm."

Harry has to chuckle, though he doesn't like to laugh now or do anything that might joggle his heart, that delicate web of jumping shadow he saw on the radiograph monitor during his operation. Sometimes, when shows like *Cosby* or *Perfect Strangers* or *Golden Girls* begin to tickle him too much, he switches off the set, rather than stress his heart with a laugh. These shows are all idiotic but not as totally stupid as this new one everybody raves about, *Roseanne*, starring some fat woman whose only talent as far as he can see is talking fast without moving her mouth. "Janice," he says seriously, "I think the only person who ever loved your father was you. And maybe your mother, at the beginning. Though it's hard to picture."

"Don't be rude to the dead," she tells him, unruffled. She looks plumped up, somehow; without that steady diet of tennis and swimming Valhalla Village provides she is maybe gaining weight. They are still members up at the Flying Eagle, but haven't made it out that way as much as in past springs. They had enjoyed good friendly times up there without realizing they would end. And, with his heart, Harry doesn't quite know how much to get into golf again. Even with a cart, you can be out there on the seventh hole and keel over and by the time they bring you in, through the other foursomes, there's been no oxygen to the brain for ten minutes. Five minutes is all it takes, and you're a vegetable.

"Well, are you going to do it? Call in another accountant."

"I've done it already!" she announces, the proud secret she's been waiting for the conversation to elicit. "Charlie had called up Mildred on his own already and we went over there to this very nice nursing home right near us, she's *per*fectly sensible and competent, just a little unsteady on her legs, and we went over to the lot and this Lyle who was so mean to you wasn't there but I was able to reach him over the phone at his home number. I said we wanted to look over the accounts since October and he said the accounts were mostly in these computer disks he keeps at his house and he was too sick to see us today, so I said maybe he was too sick to be our accountant then."

"You said that?"

"Yes I did. The first thing they teach you in this class on conveyancing is never to pussy-foot around, you do somebody and a potential sale more harm by not being clear than by speaking right out, even if they might not like hearing it at first. I told him he was fired and he said you can't fire somebody with AIDS, it's discrimination, and I said he should bring in his books and disks tomorrow or a policeman would be out to get them."

"You said all that?" Her eyes are bright and her hair bushes out from her little nut of a face, getting tan again, with a touch of double chin now that she's putting on weight. Harry admires her as you admire children you have raised, whose very success pulls them away, into the world's workings, into distance and estrangement.

"Maybe not as smoothly as I'm saying it to you, but I got it all out. Ask Charlie, he was right there. I don't like what these queers have done to Nelson. They've corrupted him."

"Gay," Harry says wearily. "We call them gay now." He is still trying to keep up with America, as it changes styles and costumes and vocabulary, as it dances ahead ever young, ever younger. "And what did Lyle say then?"

"He said we shall see. He asked whether I'd consulted with Nelson about all this. I said no but I wasn't sure Nelson was fit to consult with these days. I said in my opinion he and his friends were milking Nelson for all he was worth and had turned him into a human wreck and a dope addict and Charlie wrote on a pad of paper for me to see, 'Cool it.' Elvira and Benny were out in the showroom all ears even though the office door was closed. *Oh*, but that fairy got me mad," Janice explains, "he sounded so above-it-all and bored on the phone, as if dealing with women like me was just more than his poor sensitive body and spirit could bear.''

Rabbit is beginning to know how Lyle felt. "He probably was tired,'' he says in his defense. "That disease he has does an awful job on you. Your lungs fill up.''

"Well, he should have kept his penis out of other men's bottoms then,'' Janice says, lowering her voice though, so the nurses and orderlies in the hall don't hear.

Bottoms. Thelma. That casket of nothingness. Probing the void. "And I don't know,'' Rabbit wearily pursues, "in a situation like Nelson's, who corrupts who. Maybe *I* corrupted the poor kid, twenty years ago.''

"Oh Harry, don't be so hard on yourself. It's depressing to see you like this. You've changed so. What have they done to you, these doctors?''

He's glad she asked. He tells her, "They stuck a long thin thing into me and I could see it on television in my heart. Right on the screen, my own poor heart, while it was pumping to keep me alive. They shouldn't be allowed to go into your heart like that. They should just let people die.''

"Darling, what a stupid way to talk. It's modern science, you should be grateful. You're going to be fine. Mim called all worried and I told her how minor it was and gave her your number here.''

"Mim." Just the syllable makes him smile. His sister. The one other survivor of that house on Jackson Road, where Mom and Pop set up their friction, their heat, their comedy, their parade of days. At nineteen Mim took her bony good looks and went west, to Las Vegas. One of her gangster pals with a sentimental streak set her up with a beauty parlor when her looks began to go, and now she owns a laundromat as well as the hairdresser's. Vegas must be a great town for laundromats. Nobody lives there, everybody is just passing through, leaving a little bit of dirt like on the pale Antron carpets back at 14½ Franklin Drive. Harry and Janice visited Mim once, seven or eight years ago. These caves of glowing slot machines, no clocks anywhere, just a perpetual two o'clock in the morning, and you step outside and to your surprise the sun is blazing, and the sidewalks so hot a dog couldn't walk on them. What with Sinatra and Wayne Newton, he expected a lot of glitz, but in fact the gambling addicts were no classier than the types you see pulling at the one-armed bandits down in Atlantic City. Only there was a Western flavor, their voices and faces lined with little tiny cracks. Mim's face and voice had those tiny cracks too, though she had had a face-lift, to tighten up what she called her "wattles." Life is a hill that gets steeper the more you climb.

"Harry." Janice has been telling him something. "What did I just say?"

"I have no idea." Irritably he adds, "Why bother to talk to me when you've got Charlie back advising you to say the least?"

She flares a little; her lips pinch in and her face comes forward. "Advising me is all he's doing and he's doing that because you asked him to. Because he loves you."

She wouldn't have spoken this way before going to Florida and those women's groups, of "love" as something that spills everywhere, like gasoline. She is trying to stir him, he dimly recognizes, back into life, into the fray. He tries to play along. "Me?"

"Yes, you, Harry Angstrom."

"Why would he, for Chrissake?"

"I have no idea," Janice says. "I've never understood what men see in each other." She tries a joke. "Maybe he's gone *gay* in his old age."

"He's never married," Harry admits. "You think he'd be interested in coming back to work for Springer Motors?"

She is gathering up her things—a black leather pocketbook packed like a bomb, the old-fashioned round kind people used to throw and not the flattened Semtex that terrorists smuggle into suitcases in airplanes, and her real-estate textbook and photocopied sample documents stapled together, for her class tonight, and a new spring coat she's got herself, a kind of jonquil-yellow gabardine with a broad belt and wide shoulders. She looks girlish, fluffy-haired, putting it on. "I asked him," she says, "and he says absolutely not. He says he's into these partnerships with his cousins, rental properties in the north end of the city and over toward the old fairgrounds, and a rug-cleaning business his nephew started up with another boy and they needed backers, and Charlie says that's enough for him, he couldn't stand to go back into a salaried job and all that withholding tax and the aggravation of being expected somewhere like at the lot every day. He likes his freedom."

"We all do," sighs Rabbit. "Hey, Janice. I was thinking just the other day we ought to get the wall-to-wall carpets in our house cleaned. No fault of yours, but they're filthy, honey."

* * *

Dr. Breit comes in Sunday morning and tells him, "Harold, you're looking A-1. Ray does beautiful work. They say around the OR, 'He could tickle a tapeworm under the chin with that catheter.' " Breit looks up through his furry eyelashes for the expected laugh, doesn't get it, and perches on the edge of the bed for extra intimacy. "I've been reviewing our own films plus the stuff the jerks down at Deleon Community finally got around to sending us. Your lumen in the LAD has gone up from fifteen per cent of normal to sixty. But I can't say I'm crazy about your RCA, the right coronary artery; it shows I'd put it at about eighty-per-cent blockage, which is fine and dandy as long as the well-developed collateral is supplying the right ventricle from the circumflex. But a lesion is developing at the bifurcation of the circumflex and the LAD, and a lesion at a bifurcation is tougher to treat with angioplasty. Same thing—I assume you're interested in this—if the lesion is too long, or in a hyperkinetic AV groove, or in a situation where in the middle of the procedure you might get stranded without enough collateral circulation. In those kinds of cases, it can get hairy."

His legs are a little short for sitting on the bed comfortably; he bounces his ham a little closer to Harry's legs, and Harry feels the blood inside his supine body sway. Breit smiles and his voice grows confidential, like when he was murmuring over Dr. Raymond's shoulders. "The fact is, Harold, PTCA is a pretty Mickey Mouse treatment, and what I want you to seriously consider as you lie here these few days, even though as I say this procedure appears to have produced good results for the time being, is, now that you've tested the waters, going ahead with a CABG. Not right away. We're talking four, six months down the road before we go in again. We'd bypass both the RCA and the CFX, and the LAD depending on the restenosis, and you'll be a new man, with damn close to a brand-new heart. While we're in there we might want to look at that leaky aortic valve and think about a pacemaker. Frankly, we may have had a little postoperative MI; your electrocardiogram shows some new Q waves and there's been an elevation of the CPK isoenzyme, with positive MB bands."

"You mean," Harry says, not totally snowed, "I've been having a heart attack just lying here?"

Dr. Breit shrugs daintily. All his gestures have a daintiness that goes with his milky-pink skin. His voice is a bit squeaky, piped through his blistered-looking lips. He says, "PTCA is an invasive procedure, nobody said it wasn't. A little trauma is to be expected. Your heart shows myocardial scarring from way back. All a heart attack is is some heart muscle dying. A little can die without your noticing. It happens to all of us, just as everybody over a certain age has some emphysema. It's called the aging process and there's no escaping it. Not in this life.''

Harry wonders about the next life, but decides not to ask. He doubts that Breit knows more than *The National Enquirer*. ''You're telling me I've come into this hospital for I don't know how many thousands of dollars for a Mickey Mouse operation?''

''Rome wasn't built in a day, Harold, and your heart isn't going to be rebuilt in a week. Angioplasty does some good, at least for a while, in about eighty per cent of the cases. But bypass is up around ninety-nine per cent initial success. Look. It's the difference between scrubbing out your toilet bowl with a long brush and actually replacing the pipes. There are places you can't reach with a brush, and deposits that have become chemically bonded. A man your age, in generally good health, shouldn't be thinking twice about it. You owe it not only to yourself but to your wife and son. And those cunning little grandchildren I've heard about.''

The faster Breit talks, the more constricted Harry's chest feels. He gets out, ''Let me see if I understand it. They rip veins out of your legs and sew them to your heart like jug handles?''

A frown clouds the young doctor's face. He is overrunning the allotted time for his visit, Rabbit supposes. With visible patience he licks his sore-looking lips and explains, ''They take a superficial vein from your leg and in some cases the mammary chest artery, because arteries hold up better under arterial pressure than veins. But you don't have to worry about any of that. You're not the surgeon, it's our bailiwick. This operation is done tens of thousands of times in the United States every year— believe me, Harold, it's a piece of cake.''

''You'd do it here?''

Breit's eyes behind his flesh-colored glasses are strange furry slits, with puffy pink lids. ''The facilities don't exist yet in this physical plant,'' he admits. ''You'd have to go to Philadelphia, I doubt we could slot you into Lancaster, they're booked solid for months.''

''Then it can't be such a *very* little deal, if you need all these facilities.'' Since childhood, Rabbit has had a prejudice against Philadelphia. Dirtiest city in the world: they live on poisoned water. And Lancaster is worse—Amish farmers, overwork their animals to death, inbred so much half are humpbacks and dwarfs. He saw them in the movie *Witness* being very quaint, Kelly McGillis sponging her bare tits with a sponge and everybody chipping in to build that barn, but it didn't fool him. "Maybe Florida would be the place," he offers Dr. Breit. Florida always seems unreal to him when he's up here and having the operation there might be the same as not having it at all.

Dr. Breit's sore-looking mouth gets stern; his upper lip has sweat on it. Why is he selling this so hard? Does he have a monthly quota, like state cops with speeding tickets? "I haven't been that impressed by our dealings with Deleon," he says. "But you think about it, Harold. If I were in your shoes, it's what I'd have done—without any hesitation. You're just toying with your life otherwise."

Yeah, Rabbit thinks when the doctor is gone from the room, *but you're not in my shoes. And what's life for but to toy with?*

Mim phones. He takes a moment to recognize her voice, it is so dry and twangy, so whisky-and-cigarette-cracked. "What are they doing to you now?" she asks. She has always taken the attitude that he is a lamb among wolves in Diamond County, he should have gotten out like she did.

"They've got me in the hospital," he tells her. He could almost cry, like a boy. "They stuck a balloon up through my leg into my heart and pumped it full of saltwater to open up an artery that was plugged up with old grease I've been eating. Then afterwards they put a sandbag on the incision down at my thigh and told me not to move my leg for six hours or I'd bleed to death. That's how hospitals are; they tell you what they're going to do is about as simple as having a haircut and then midway through they tell you you might bleed to death. And then this morning the doctor comes around and tells me it was a Mickey Mouse operation and hardly worth bothering with. He wants me to go for broke and have a multiple bypass. Mim, they split you right open like a coconut and rip veins out of your legs."

"Yeah, I know," she says. "You gonna do it?"

Rabbit says, "I suppose they'll talk me into it eventually. I mean, they've got you by the balls. You're scared, and what else is there?"

"Guys I know out here have had open-heart and swear by it. I can't see it made that much difference, they still spend all day sitting on their fat asses getting manicures and talking on the phone, but then they weren't such dynamite before either. When you get to our age, Harry, it's work to stay alive."

"Come on, Mim. You're only fifty."

"For a woman out here, that's ancient. That's cow pasture. That's hang-it-up time, if you're a woman. You don't get the stares any more, it's like you've gone invisible."

"Boy, you did use to get the stares," he says proudly. He remembers her when she was nineteen—dyed-in blond streak, big red cinch-in belt, sexy soft sweaters, skinny arms ending in a clash of bangle bracelets, buck teeth she couldn't help revealing when she smiled, lips smeared with lipstick like she had eaten a jam sandwich, a leggy colt of a girl dying to break out of Brewer, to kick or fuck her way through the fence. She made it, too. Rabbit never could have made it out there. He was too soft. Even Florida bakes the spirit out of him. He needed to stay where they remembered him when. "So when are you coming east?" he asks Mim.

"Well, how bad are you, Harry?"

"Not that bad. I just complain a lot. All I have to do is stay away from animal fats and salt and don't get aggravated."

"Who would aggravate you?"

"The usual," he says. "Nellie's been having some problems. Hey, you'll never guess who's back on the scene squiring Janice around while I'm laid up. Your old boyfriend, Charlie Stavros."

"Chas was not what I'd ever call a boyfriend. I took him on that time to get him off your wife's back. Around here you're not a boyfriend until you at least set the girl up in a condo."

He is striving to keep her interested. People who've made it like she has, they get bored easily. "How the hell *is* Vegas?" he asks. "Is it hot there yet? How about you coming east to get away from the heat for a couple of weeks? We'll put you up in the guest room above the den and you'll get to know your great-niece and -nephew. Judy's a real little lady now. She's gonna be a looker—not like you, but a looker."

"Harry, the last time I came to Pennsylvania I nearly died from the humidity. I don't know how you people do it, day after day; it was like being wrapped in warm washcloths. It's that heavy climate I bet is doing you in."

"Yeah," he weakly agrees. The phone receiver feels soggy in his hand. His own capacity to be interested isn't what it should be. He's free to wander the halls now, and you see amazing things: less than an hour ago, an amazing visitor, a young Brewer girl, she couldn't have been more than fifteen, all in black, black jacket, tight black pants, pointed black boots, and her hair dyed yellowy white and cut short and mussed every which way so her skull reminded him of a wet Easter chick, plus a little flowery cruciform tattoo pricked right beside her eye. But his heart couldn't quite rise to it, he felt he'd seen even this before, girls doing wicked things to themselves believing their youth would shine through and all would heal.

"Maybe I'll come in the fall if you can last it out," Mim tells him.

"Oh I can last," he says. "You aren't going to get rid of big brother so easy." But the connection feels strained, and he can sense Mim groping, in the little pauses, for what to say next. "Hey, Mim," he says. "Do you remember if Pop complained of chest pains?"

"He had emphysema, Harry. Because he wouldn't stop smoking. You stopped. You were smart. Me, I'm down to a pack a day. But I don't think I ever really inhaled."

"I seem to remember him complaining of feeling full in the chest. He'd sneak his hand inside his shirt and rub his chest."

"Maybe he itched. Harry, Pop died because he couldn't breathe. Mom died because of her Parkinson's. I suppose their hearts failed in the end but so does everybody's, because that's what life is, a strain on the heart."

His little sister has become so dogmatic, everything cut and dried. She's mad at something, too. Just like little Roy. "Hey," he says, not wanting to let go however, "and another thing I was wondering about. Remember how you used to always sing, 'Shoo-fly pie and apple pan dowdy?' "

"Yeah. Kind of."

"What's the line that comes after 'Makes your eyes light up, your tummy say "howdy" '?"

In the silence he can hear chatter in the background, beauty-parlor chatter, and a hair dryer whirring. "I have no fucking idea," she says finally. "Are you sure I used to sing this song?"

"Well, I was, but never mind. How's *your* life?" he asks. "Any new irons in the fire? When're we going to marry you off?"

"Harry, come off it. The only reason anybody out here'd marry an old bag like me would be as some kind of cover. Or a tax dodge, if the accountant could figure one."

"Speaking of accountants," he begins, and he might have told her all about Nelson and Lyle and Janice, and the voices on the phone, but she doesn't want to hear him; she says hurriedly, in a lowered voice, "Harry, a real special customer has just come in, even *you've* heard of her, and I got to hang up. You take care of yourself, now. You sound on the mend. Any time they get to be too much for you, you can come on out here for some sun and fun."

What sort of fun, he would have liked to ask—in the old days she was always offering to get a girl for him if he came out alone, though he never did—and he would have liked to have heard more of why she thinks he is on the mend. But Mim has hung up. She has a life to get on with. His arm hurts in its crook from holding the phone. Ever since they invaded his arteries with dyes and balloons, he has aches and pains in remote and random joints, as if his blood is no longer purely his own. Once you break the cap on a ginger-ale bottle, there is never again as much fizz.

The nurse with the round pale face—a country kind of face— comes in Monday evening and says to him, "My mother is having to drop something off for me tonight. Should I ask her to come up and see you for a second?"

"Did she say she'd be willing?" *When I think of you thinking she's your daughter it's like rubbing her all over with shit,* Ruth had said the last time they talked.

The young woman in her folded cap smiles. "I mentioned the other night, casual-like, that you were here, and I think she would be. She didn't say anything rude or anything." There is on her face a trace of a blush, a simper, a secret. If something does not soon happen to her, it will become a silly empty face. Innocence will dull down into stupidity.

This has not been the best day for Harry. The sounds of traffic and work resuming on the street outside reminded him of how out of it he still is. Janice didn't visit, and now her evening class has begun. All day gray clouds packed the sky, in long rolls of nimbus, and trailed black wisps above the brick chimneys, but no rain has actually fallen. The view from his window consists of several intricately notched bands of ornamental brickwork capping the third stories of narrow buildings that hold at street level a coffee shop, a dry cleaner's, an office-supplies store. The corner building is painted gray, the middle one blue, and the third, with the most ornate window framing, beige. It has slowly dawned upon the people of Brewer that you can paint over brick with any color you choose, not just brick red. People live behind the upper windows across the street, but though Harry faithfully stares he has not yet been rewarded with the sight of a woman undressing, or even of anyone coming to the window to look out. Further depressing him, he has not been able to have a bowel movement since entering St. Joseph's three days ago. The first day, he blamed the awkwardness of the bedpan and his solicitude for the nurses who would have to carry what he produced away, and the second day, the change of diet from what he usually eats—the food the hospital dieticians conjure up looks pretty good but tastes like wet cardboard and chews like chaff, so bland as to shut down his salivary glands—but on the third day, when he can wander the halls and use the bathroom behind a closed door in his room, he blames himself, his decrepitude, his drying up, the running down of his inner processes. Running out of even gas.

It is strange that this girl (hardly that, she would be only three years younger than Nelson) should offer to bring him her mother, for last night he dreamed about Ruth. As the world around him goes gray, his dreams have taken on intense color. Ruth—Ruth as she had been, the spring they lived and slept together, both of them twenty-six, she fleshy, cocky, pretty in a coarse heavy careless way—was wearing a sea-blue dress, with small white polka dots, and he was pressing his body against it, with her body inside it, and telling her how lovely a color it was on her, while the hair on her head glistened red, brown, and gold, close to his eyes. Ruth had turned her head not, he felt, in aversion from him but in natural embarrassment at the situation, for she seemed to be living with him and Janice, all together, and Janice was somewhere near them—upstairs, though the furniture around them was sunstruck floral-patterned wicker, as from their Florida condo, which has no upstairs. His embrace of Ruth felt semi-permitted, like an embrace of a legal relation, and his praise of her vivid dress was meant to urge her into his own sense of well-being, of their love being at last all right. He hid his face beside her throat, in the curtain of her many-colored hair, and knew he could fuck her forever, on and on, bottomlessly spilling himself into her solid beauty. When he awoke it was with the kind of absolute hard-on he almost never has while awake, what with the anti-hypertensive medicine and his generally gray mood. He saw while the dream still freshly clung to him in sky-blue shreds that the white polka dots were the confettilike bits of blossom that littered the sidewalk a month ago on that street of Bradford pear trees up near Summer, where he had once lived with Ruth, and that the splashy sunlight was what used to pour in on Ma Springer's iron table of ferns and African violets, in the little sunroom across the foyer from the gloomy living room. For though the furniture of the dream was Florida, the house they were all sharing had certainly been the old Springer manse.

Harry asks the round-faced nurse, "How much do you know about me and your mother?"

The blush deepens a shade. "Oh, nothing. She never lets on about the time before she settled down with my father." It now sounds rather conventional, Ruth's time as a single woman; but at the time she was beyond the pale, a lost soul scandalous to the narrow world of Mt. Judge. "I figure you were a special friend."

"Maybe not that special," Harry tells her.

He feels bad, because there is nothing much she can say to that, his lie, just stand there polite with her puffy upper lip, a nurse being patient with a patient. He is leaving her out on a limb. He loves her; love flows through him like a blind outpouring, an anesthesia. He tells his possible daughter, "Look, it's a cute idea, but if she came up it would be because you asked her to rather than she wanted to on her own, and, frankly, Annabelle"—he has never called her by her name before—"I'd just as soon she didn't see me like this. You say she's lost weight and looks snappy. I'm fat and a medical mess. Maybe she'd be too much for me."

The girl's face returns to being pale and prim. Boundaries have been restored, just as he's getting to feel paternal. "Very well," Annabelle says. "I'll tell her you've been released, if she asks."

"Might she ask? Wait. Don't get prissy. Tell me, why did you want to get us together?"

"You seem so interested in her. Your face comes to life when I mention her."

"It does? Maybe it's looking at you that does it." He dares go on, "I've been wondering, though, if you should still be living with her. Maybe you ought to get out from under her wing."

"I did, for a while. I didn't like it. Living alone is tough. Men can get nasty."

"Can we really? I'm sorry to hear it."

Her face softens into a dear smile, that curls her upper lip at the edges and buckles the plump part in the middle. "Anyway, she says just what you say. But I like it, for now. It's not like she's my mother any more, she's a roommate. Believe me, bad things can happen to women who live alone in this city. Brewer isn't New York but it isn't Penn Park, either.''

Of course. She can read his address right off the chart at the foot of the bed. To her he is one of those Penn Park snobs he himself has always resented. ''Brewer's a rugged town,'' he agrees, sinking back into his pillow. ''Always was. Coal and steel. Bars and cathouses all along the railroad tracks right through the middle of the city, when I was young.'' He glances away, at the ornamental brickwork, the hurrying dry dark clouds. He tells his nurse, ''You know best how to live your own life. Tell your mother, if she asks, that maybe we'll meet some other time.'' Under the pear trees, in paradise.

Lying there these days, Harry thinks fondly of those dead bricklayers who bothered to vary their rows at the top of the three buildings across the street with such festive patterns of recess and protrusion, diagonal and upright, casting shadows in different ways at different times of the day, these men of another century up on their scaffold, talking Pennsylvania Dutch among themselves, or were Indians doing all the masonry even then? Lying here thinking of all the bricks that have been piled up and knocked down and piled up again on the snug square streets that lift toward Mt. Judge, he tries to view his life as a brick of sorts, set in place with a slap in 1933 and hardening ever since, just one life in rows and walls and blocks of lives. There is a satisfaction in such an overview, a faint far-off communal thrill, but hard to sustain over against his original and continuing impression that Brewer and all the world beyond are just frills on himself, like the lace around a plump satin valentine, himself the heart of the universe, like the Dalai Lama, who in the news lately—Tibet is still restless, after nearly forty years of Chinese rule—was reported to have offered to resign. But the offer was greeted with horror by his followers, for whom the Dalai Lama can no more resign godhood than Harry can resign selfhood.

He watches a fair amount of television. It's right there, in front of his face; its wires come out of the wall behind him, just like oxygen. He finds that facts, not fantasies, are what he wants: the old movies on cable AMC seem stiff and barky in their harshly lit black and white, and the old TV shows on NIK impossibly tinny with their laugh tracks and spray-set Fifties hairdos, and even the incessant sports (rugby from Ireland, curling from Canada) a waste of his time, stories told people with time to kill, where he has time left only for truth, the truth of DSC or Channel 12, MacNeil-Lehrer so gravely bouncing the news between New York and Washington and reptiles on *Smithsonian World* flickering their forked tongues in the desert blaze or the giant turtles of Galápagos on *World of Survival* battling for their lives or the Russians battling the Nazis in the jumpy film clips of World War II as narrated by Sir Laurence Olivier ("Twenty million dead," he intones at the end, as the frame freezes and goes into computer-blur and the marrow-chilling theme music comes up, thrilling Harry to think he was there, on the opposite side of the Northern Hemisphere, jumping on tin cans and balling up tin foil for his anti-Hitler bit, a ten-year-old participant in actual history) and *War and Peace in the Nuclear Age* and *Nature's Way* and *Portraits of Power* and *Wonders of the World* and *Wildlife Chronicles* and *Living Body* and *Planet Earth* and struggle and death and cheetahs gnawing wildebeests and tarantulas fencing with scorpions and tiny opossums scrambling for the right nipple under the nature photographer's harsh lights and weaverbirds making the most intricate damn nests just to attract one little choosy female and the incredible cleverness and variety and energy and waste of it all, a kind of crash course he is giving himself in the ways of the world. There is just no end to it, no end of information.

The nightly news has a lot of China on it—Gorbachev visiting, students protesting in Tiananmen Square, but not protesting Gorbachev, in fact they like him, all the world likes him, despite that funny mark on his head shaped like Japan. What the Chinese students seem to want is freedom, they want to be like Americans, but they look like Americans already, in blue jeans and T-shirts. Meanwhile in America itself the news is that not only President George Bush but Mrs. Bush the First Lady take showers with their dog Millie, and if that's all the Chinese want we should be able to give it to them, or something close, though it makes Harry miss Reagan a bit, at least he was dignified, and had that dream distance; the powerful thing about him as President was that you never knew how much he knew, nothing or everything, he was like God that way, you had to do a lot of it yourself. With this new one you know he knows something, but it seems a small something. Rabbit doesn't want to have to picture the President and middle-aged wife taking showers naked with their dog. Reagan and Nancy had their dignity, their computer-blur, even when their bowel polyps and breasts were being snipped off in view of billions.

Janice comes in at six on Tuesday while he is eating his last bland supper—he is being released tomorrow. She is wearing her new coat and a gray skirt and a low-cut magenta blouse almost as vivid as the polka-dot dress Ruth wore in his dream. His wife looks energized, businesslike, her salt-and-pepper hair trimmed and given body by a hairdresser who has eliminated the bangs, gelled them back into a softly bristling mass, parted low on one side. Janice reminds him of those heightened and rapid-talking women on television who give the news. She in fact is brimming with news. Her eyes seem to be wearing contact lenses of an unnatural glitter until he realizes those are tears, prepared for him during the station break.

"Oh Harry," she begins, "it's worse than we thought! Thousands and thousands!"

"Thousands of what?"

"Of dollars Nelson stole! Charlie and I and this accountant his nephew knows—Mildred says she was too old for doing an audit and anyway is too busy in the nursing home—went over there today, Charlie said I *had* to be there, he and the accountant weren't enough, and I asked to see the books, Nelson *was* there for once, and he looked at me in this heartbreaking hopeless way I'll never forget as long as I live and said, Sure, Mom, what did I want to know? He told us everything. At first, when he needed money so desperately for the, you know, the cocaine, he would just write himself a check marked 'Expenses' or 'Operating Cash,' but Mildred, she was still around then, questioned him about it and he got scared. Anyway, these little amounts, a hundred or even two at a time, weren't really enough to keep him going, so he got the idea of offering people a discount on the used cars if they paid in cash or with a check written directly out to him."

"I *told* you there weren't enough used sales on the statements," Harry says, in a triumph that feels rather flat. Ever since they poked that catheter in, there's been something drained about his emotional responses. "How many cars did he pull this stunt with?"

"Well, he doesn't really remember, but Charlie says we can reconstruct it from the records, the NV-1s and so on, it will just take time. Of course, Nelson didn't approach every customer with this sort of shady deal, he had to pick and choose, the ones that looked poor enough not to look a gift horse in the face. He was clever about it, Nelson is much more clever than you ever gave him credit for."

"I never said the kid wasn't clever."

"Oh, but Harry"—the shell of tears is refreshed, the brown eyes spill, shiny trails glitter beside her blunt little knob of a nose, a nose with no more character than a drawer pull. She tugs a paper facial tissue from the box the hospital puts on his night table—as she leans forward he glimpses the tops of her tidy breasts through the loose neck of the magenta peasant-style blouse he has never seen before, something she has bought for the real-estate course and these meetings with Charlie and her general stepping-out into the world, without him. He feels a flash of unpleasant heat, as in catheterization. His own wife's tits, surprising him like that. Janice dabbles at her face, her muddled mutt's face, and leans even farther forward, so he feels her breath on his face, smells some faint mint of a Life Saver. To hide the tobacco on her breath. Her tears shine under his eyes; her shaky voice is low so only he can hear. "—he didn't even stop with that. He was doing crack by this time and the amount of money he needed was incredible. He and Lyle worked out this scheme, here it gets very technical—"

"Wait," he tells her. The culinary aide has come in to remove his tray. She is a plump Hispanic woman with long red fingernails and a distinct mustache.

"You no eat enough," she scolds, with her shy smile of pearl-size teeth.

"Enough," he says. "For now. Very good. Bueno."

She has a notebook on which she writes the percentages of the food he has consumed. A third of the overcooked watery string beans, half the pale oval of tasteless veal, scarcely a leaf of the coarse green salad drowned in an orange grease, a bite of the tapioca pudding, whose wobbly texture in his mouth made him shudder. "For breakfast," she reads from her clipboard, "pieces pineapple, cream of wheat, whole-wheat toast, coffee decaf."

"I can hardly wait," he tells her.

"Eat more now," she suggests.

He holds firm. "No thanks, too cold now. My wife's here."

She reads from the chart. "Says here last day tomorrow."

"How about that?" Harry asks her. "The big wide world. I'll miss you. And all your healthy eats."

As she removes his plastic tray, her long red fingernails scrape on its underside with a noise that puts his teeth on edge. He is reminded of that platinum-haired bimbo who used to tickle the computer keys at Fiscal Alternatives. Her fingernails were too long too. Dead, Lyle said. If there *is* an afterlife where the dead all gather, would he get a chance to deepen their acquaintance? But without money around, what would they talk about?

When the woman goes, Janice resumes. The tip of her tongue protrudes a second or two between her lips as she tries to think. "I'm not sure I understand it entirely, but you know how we keep a rolling inventory—so many trucks and vans and cars a month from Mid-Atlantic Toyota in Maryland."

"Between twenty and twenty-five a month is how it's been running," Harry tells her, to let her know he may be flat on his back but knew his business. "We haven't been able to move three hundred new units a year except that one year, '86, after Nelson first took over. The strong yen's been killing us, and Honda and Nissan taking a bigger bite. Ford Ranger put a real dent in our one-ton pickup last year."

"Harry, try to focus. The way it was explained to me is that there's this Toyota Motors Credit Corporation in California that finances our inventory direct with Mid-Atlantic and gets paid when we sell a car and adds to our credit account when we order one for the lot. What Nelson was doing, each month he'd report one or two sales fewer than there actually were and so Toyota would roll over the indebtedness on these cars while he and Lyle put the proceeds in a separate account they'd opened up in the company name, you know how banks now are always offering you all these different accounts, savings and checking with savings and capital accounts with limited checks and so on. So every month we'd owe this TMCC for one or two more cars than were actually on the lot and our debt to them kept getting bigger and our actual inventory was getting smaller; in two or three years if nothing had happened we would have had no new cars in stock at all and owed Mid-Atlantic Toyota a fortune!"

"How much do we actually owe 'em?" His mind can't quite assign weight to these facts, these phantom Toyotas, yet. He is still thinking hospital thoughts—the pineapple he's been promised for breakfast, and whether or not he has taken his digitalis for the evening.

"Nobody knows, Harry. Nelson doesn't exactly remember and Lyle says a lot of the disks he was keeping the accounts on have been accidentally erased."

"Accidentally on purpose, as they used to say," he says. "What a shit. What a pair of shits."

"I know, it's *horrible*," Janice says, "and Lyle is horrible on the phone. He says he's dying and doesn't care *what* we do to him! He sounded kind of crazy in the head; isn't that one of the things that happens?'' The weight of the facts hits her and bears her suddenly down into hysteria; the tears flow accompanied by sobs and she tries to rest her wet face on his blanketed chest, but she is too short, perched on the chair beside his high bed, and instead presses her eyes and mouth against the hard mattress edge, burbling her disbelief that he would do this to her.

"He" means Nelson; Harry is off the hook for once. In her grief her whole head is hot, even the top of her skull, like a pot come to boil. He comfortingly rubs it, through her little new hairdo, and tries not to smile. *Serve them both right,* he thinks. Springers. Her dark hair with its gray strands is so fine it sticks to his fingers like cobwebs. For a good five minutes he massages her warm unhappy head with his fingertips while staring at the blank television screen and thinking that he is missing the six o'clock news, followed by national news at six-thirty. Somehow he can't believe that what Janice is trying to tell him ranks with the national news, for reality. She may be his wife but she's no Connie Chung, let alone Diane Sawyer with her wide-apart blue eyes and melting mouth and stunned look like some beautiful blonde ox. "So what's going to happen?" he asks Janice at last.

She lifts her tear-smeared face and, surprisingly, has some answers. Charlie must have been coaching her. "Well, once we found out how much we owe TMCC we'll have to settle up. We've been paying interest on the inventory so they shouldn't care too much, it's like a mortgage, only Nelson has sold the house without telling them."

"If he faked any signatures, that's forgery," Harry says, and a black dye of despair is beginning to enter his heart, as he sees what a lost cause his son is. *Human garbage,* like his own father once said of him. He asks, "What's going to happen with the kid?"

Janice blinks her wet lashes. What she has to say seems to her so momentous she withholds it a moment. Her voice has the juicy precision Ma Springer would speak with when she had made up her mind. "He's agreed to enter a rehab place. Immediately."

"Good, I guess. What made him agree?"

"I said it was either that or I'd fire him from the lot. And prosecute."

"Wow. You said that?"

"I did, Harry. I made myself."

"To your own son?"

"I had to. He's been sinking, and he knows it. He was grateful, really. We had it out right there on the lot, out where the weeds are, while Charlie and the accountant stayed inside. Then we made some phone calls, from your old office."

"Where *is* this rehab place?"

"In North Philadelphia. It's the one his counsellor recommends, if he can get Nelson in. They're all overcrowded, you know. Society can't keep up. There are some day-treatment programs in Brewer but his counsellor says the important thing is to get away from the entire environment the drugs are part of."

"So he really did go to a counsellor, after that blowup with Pru."

"Yes, to everybody's surprise. And even more surprisingly, Nelson seems to like him. Respect him. It's a black man."

Harry feels a jealous, resentful pang. His boy is being taken over. His fatherhood hasn't been good enough. They're calling in the professionals. "For how long is the rehab?"

"The complete program is ninety days. The first month is detox and intensive therapy, and then he lives in a halfway house for sixty days and gets some kind of a job, a community-service sort of thing probably, just something to get him back out into the normal world."

"He'll be gone all summer. Who'll run the lot?"

Janice puts her hand over his, a gesture that feels to him learned, coached. "You will, Harry."

"Honey, I can't. I'm a sick son of a bitch."

"Charlie says your attitude is terrible. You're giving in to your heart. He says the best thing is a positive spirit and lots of activity."

"Yeah, why doesn't he come back and run the lot if he's so fucking active?"

"He has all these other fish to fry these days."

"Yeah, and you seem to be one of them. I'm hearing you sizzle."

She giggles, along with the ugly tears drying on her face. "Don't be so silly. He's just an old friend, who's been wonderful in this crisis."

"While I've been useless, right?"

"You've been in the *hos*pital, dear. You've been being brave in *your* way. Anyway as we all know there are things you can't do for me, only I can do them for myself."

He is disposed to argue this, it sounds pious in a new-fashioned way he distrusts, but if he's ever going to get back into the game he must let up and avoid aggravation. He asks, "How did Nelson take your getting tough?"

"Like I said, he liked it. He's just been begging for the rest of us to take over, he knew he was way out of control. Pru is thrilled to think he's going to get help. Judy is thrilled."

"Is Roy thrilled?"

"He's too little to understand, but as you say yourself the atmosphere around that house has been poisonous."

"Did I say poisonous?"

She doesn't bother to answer. She has straightened up and is wiping her face with a licked facial tissue.

"Will I have to see the kid before he goes?"

"No, baby. He's going tomorrow morning, before we bring you home."

"Good. I just don't know as I could face him. When you think of what he's done, he's flushed the whole bunch of us, not just you and me but his kids, *every*body, right down the toilet. He's sold us all out to a stupid drug."

"Well, my goodness, Harry—I've known you to act selfishly in your life."

"Yeah, but not for a little white powder."

"They can't help it. It becomes their life. Anyway, evidently they were buying drugs for Lyle, too. I mean drugs for his illness—medicines for AIDS you can't buy yet in this country and are terribly expensive, they have to be smuggled."

"It's a sad story," Rabbit says, after a pause. Inky depression circulates in his veins. He's been in the hospital too long. He's forgotten what life is like. He asks Janice, "Where are you going now, in that snappy blouse?"

She rolls her eyes upward at him, from the mirror of her purse as she fixes her face, and then her face goes wooden and stubborn, bluffing it through. "Charlie said he'd take me out to dinner. He's worried I'm going to crash, psychologically, after all this trauma. I need to process."

"Process?"

"Talk things through."

"You can talk them through with me. I'm just lying here with nothing to do, I've already missed the sports section of the news."

She makes that *mmmm* mouth women make after putting on lipstick, rolling her lips together in a complacent serious way, and tells him, "You're not impartial. You have your own agenda with Nelson, and with me for that matter."

"What's so impartial about Charlie, he wants to get into your pants again. If he hasn't already."

She pops the lipstick back into her bomb-shaped pocketbook and touches up her new hairdo with her fingers, glancing from several angles at herself in the mirror, and snaps the lid shut. She says, "That's sweet of you, Harry, to pretend to think I'm still interesting to anybody in that way, but in fact I'm not, except maybe once in a while to my own husband, I hope."

He says, embarrassed, for he knows he's been letting her down in that department lately, "Sure, but you know, for a man, it's all a matter of blood pressure, and—"

"We'll talk about it when you're home. I told Charlie I'd meet him at seven—"

"Where? The salad bar that used to be Johnny Frye's? It's only two blocks from here. You can walk."

"No, actually. There's a new Vietnamese place out near Maiden Springs he wanted to try. It's a bit of a drive and, you know me, I'll probably get lost. And then on top of everything I have fifty pages of a book on British realty law, full of all these funny old obsolete words, I have to read before tomorrow night."

"You won't be home tomorrow night? My first night home?" He is making a complaint of it, scoring points, but he wishes she'd go and leave him alone with the television screen.

"We'll see," Janice says, rising. "I have an idea." Then she asks, "Aren't you proud of me?" She bends forward to press her hot busy face against his. "Managing everything the way I am?"

"Yeah," he lies. He preferred her incompetent. She leaves with her jonquil-yellow new coat over her arm and he thinks she is gaining weight behind, she has that broad-beamed look women of the county wear when they come into their own.

Harry watches what is left of Tom Brokaw and is settling into a seven o'clock show on life in Antarctica when, of all people, the Harrisons come visiting. Not just Thelma—she's brought Ron along, or Ron has brought her, since she is thinner and sallower than he has ever seen her, and moves as if every step might break a bone. She smiles regretfully; her eyes apologize for the shape she's in, for Ronnie's being with her, for her being unable to stay away. "We were here in the hospital seeing my doctor," she explains, "and Ron Junior had heard you were in."

"For what they call a little procedure," he says, and gestures toward the chair Janice has pulled up to the bed and that's probably still warm from her broad beam. "Ron, there's that big padded chair over in the corner if you want to pull it over; it's on wheels."

"I'll stand," he says. "We can only stay a minute."

He is sullen, but Rabbit didn't ask the Harrisons to come visit and doesn't see why he should be bullied. "Suit yourself." He asks Thelma, "How are *you*?"

Thelma sighs elaborately. "You know doctors. They never admit they don't have an answer. I'm on home dialysis twice a week, Ronnie's a saint to put up with me. He took a course on how to cope with the machine."

"Ronnie always was a saint," Harry tells her, everybody in the room knowing that Ronnie Harrison was just about his least favorite person in the world, though he had known him from kindergarten. A dirty-mouthed plug-ugly even at the age of five, and now bald as a prick's tip, with wisps above his big droopy ears. Ronnie in high school and afterward had a certain chunkiness, but the approach of old age has pulled the chunkiness like taffy, leaving hollows in his face and lumps and a painful stringiness around the throat. Harry says, as if she doesn't already know, "Janice is taking courses too, to learn how to sell real estate. I guess so she has a trade in case I pop off."

Thelma's eyelids flutter, a bony hand wearing a wedding ring gestures the possibility away. The sicker she gets, the more dried-out and schoolteacherish she looks. That was one of the jokes of her being his mistress, her looking so prim and being so wild in bed, but maybe the real her was the schoolteacher and the other was put on for him, like an insect imitating a flower. "Harry, you're not going to pop off," she tells him urgently, afraid for him. That strange way women have, of really caring about somebody beyond themselves. "They do wonderful things with hearts now, they stitch and mend them just like rag dolls." She manages a thin smile. "Want to see what I have?"

He thinks he knows what she has, all of it, but she unbuttons her sleeve and with that matter-of-fact baring which was her style Thelma shows him the underside of her bared arm. Two purple bruised patches on her slender wrist are connected by a translucent U of some plastic tubing taped flat against the jaundiced skin. "That's called my shunt," she says, pronouncing the last word carefully. "It connects an artery and vein and when I have the dialysis we take it off and connect me to the machine.''

"Pretty," seems all he can say. He tells them about his angioplasty, but is already tired of describing it, and trying to convey the creepy business of seeing the dark shadow of the catheter like a snaky forefinger inch ever more intimately into his heart's paler, trembling shades. "My coronary artery could have occluded and I would have gone into CA. Cardiac arrest.''

"But you didn't, you jerk," Ronnie says, standing erect and abandoning his shadow on the wall. "The Old Master," he says, a sardonic phrase he used to kid Harry with in their basketball-playing days. Funny, all of his life Harrison has been shadowing Harry with a fleshly mockery, a reminder of everything sweaty and effortful Rabbit hoped squeamishly to glide over and avoid. "Nobody lays a finger on the Old Master. He makes it all look easy." Ronnie used to resent how Marty Tothero would put him, Ronnie, into the game when the bruisers on the other side were roughing Harry up, to give rough stuff back. An enforcer, they call it now.

"It was never as easy as I made it look," Rabbit tells him. He turns to Thelma, wanting to be tender, since she had braved her husband's anger by bringing him here. She had never balked at humiliating Ronnie to give Harry her gift of love, and indeed, sick as the two lovers are, her nearness does give him that socketed feeling you have with certain women, that graceful feeling you can do no wrong. "How about you, Thel? Your docs think they're licking it?''

"Oh, they never say die, but a body gets tired. You can fight only so long. The pains I can live with, and the weakness all the time, but the kidneys going is really demoralizing. It takes away your pleasure in life if you can't take such things for granted. Harry, you know that part of the Bible they used to read to us in assembly, before the Bible got outlawed, about a time for everything? A time to gather up stones, a time to cast them away? I'm beginning to think there's a time to give up.''

"Thel, don't say that," Ronnie says, with an urgency of his own. He loves this woman too, also calls her Thel. It occurs to Harry that two men for a woman and vice versa is about right, just as we need two kinds of days, workdays and holidays, and day and night. Ronnie sounds angry, that she would talk of giving up, but this May evening is slowly melting him into the shadowy wall, so it is beginning to seem that Harry and Thelma are alone together, as in so many stolen afternoons, their hearts beating, the school buses braking outside on the curved street, and as in that room in the Caribbean, their first time together, when they stayed awake until dawn, and then fell asleep as one as the tropical blue air between the louvers paled and the palm trees ceased their nighttime stirring. Ronnie's disembodied voice says angrily, "You have three boys who want to see you grow old."

Thelma smiles slyly at Harry, her face colorless and waxy in the May day fading above the fancy brickwork cornices and chimneys visible through the windows. "Why would they want to see that, Ron?" she asks mischievously, not taking her gaze from Harry's face. "They're grown men. I've done all I can do for them."

Poor Ron has no answer. Maybe he's choked up. Rabbit takes pity and says to him, "How's the insurance business going, Ron?"

"It's levelled out," his voice says gruffly. "Not bad, not good. The S and L mess hurt some companies but not ours. At least people've stopped borrowing against their policies at five per cent and investing at ten the way they were. That was killing our figures."

"One of the nice things about getting to be old geezers like us," Harry says, "is people like you stop trying to sell me insurance." Footsteps and tingling pans sound from the hall, where the lights seem bright suddenly. Night has come.

"Not necessarily," Ron is saying. "I could get you a pretty good deal on some twenty-payment straight life, if you and Janice are interested. I know a doctor who doesn't look too close. You've survived one coronary, that's in your favor. Let me work up some figures."

Harry ignores him. To Thelma he says, "Your boys are in good shape?"

"We think so. Good enough. Alex has had an offer from a high-tech place in Virginia, outside Washington. Georgie thinks he has a spot with a musical-comedy troupe in the Catskills this summer."

"Here's something Janice just told me. She's got Nelson to sign up for a drug rehab."

"That's nice," Thelma says, so softly and sincerely here in the gloom that her voice seems to exist not in the air but already in his blood, inserted intravenously. All the afternoons when their bodies intertwined and exchanged fluids are not gone but safe inside him, his cells remembering.

"You're nice to say so," he says, and dares to grasp her cool hand, the one without the shunt, and move it up from her lap so the back of his own hand brushes a breast.

Ronnie's voice comes forward from the wall. "We gotta go, Thel."

"Ron, thanks for bringing her by."

"Anything for the Old Master. We were in the building."

"Master of nothing at this point."

Ronnie grunts. "Who's to say?" He's not all bad.

Thelma has stiffly stood and, bending by his bed, asks, right out in front of Ronnie, "Darling, can you manage a little kiss?"

He may imagine it, but Thelma's pale cool departing face, swiftly pressed against his, their lips meeting a bit askew, gives off a faint far tang of urine. When he is alone in his room again he remembers how sometimes when he kissed Thelma goodbye at her house her mouth would be flavored by the sour-milk taste of his prick, the cheesy smegma secreted beneath his foreskin. She would be still all soft and blurred by their lovemaking and unaware, and he would try to conceal his revulsion, a revulsion at his own smell on her lips. It was like, another sad thing to remember, the time when Nixon, with Watergate leaking out all around him, during one of the oil crunches went on television to tell us so earnestly to turn our thermostats down, for not only would it save oil but scientific studies showed that colder houses were healthier for us. That big scowling scared face on television, the lips wet and fumbling. Their President, crook or not, going down in disgrace but trying to say what needed to be said; Harry as a loyal American did go and turn his thermostat down.

Janice wakes up early out of nervousness; it is going to be a long and complicated day for her, of seeing Nelson off at nine and picking Harry up at noon and taking a quiz in British property law at seven, in the Brewer extension of Penn State in a renovated disused elementary school on South Pine Street, a section she isn't too easy about parking the car in at night. In Penn Park in mid-May the day begins with a kiss of coolness as in Florida; the little limestone house is cozier now that the surrounding trees are fully leafed. She has enjoyed, enough to add to her feelings of guilt, these days of Harry's being in the hospital and her being free to come and go without explanation, and to get into bed as early or late as she pleases, and to watch what television shows she wants to. Wednesday nights, for instance, she likes *Unsolved Mysteries*, but Harry is always sitting beside her in the study or in bed telling her how ridiculous these so-called mysteries are and how they always derive, if you think about it, from the testimony of people who are either mentally unbalanced or have something to gain financially. The older Harry gets the more cynical he is; he used to be religious in a funny way. They couldn't put the show on television if there weren't some truth to it and that Robert Stack seems ever so sensible. Last night, what with being out with Charlie at that Vietnamese place along the Maiden Springs Pike (it was nice, but she never figured out what she was supposed to do with those bubbly brittle rice things like warped pancakes that were so tasteless you must be supposed to dip them in something), she missed all but the last ten minutes of *thirtysomething* which she likes to watch Tuesdays because it's so different from how she was when she was thirty-something, all those demands on her, mother wife daughter, and then being Charlie's mistress for a while and feeling so inadequate and guilty and having no female friends really except Peggy Fosnacht who went and slept with Harry anyway and now is dead, terrible to think, all rotten and parchment like a mummy in her casket, too hideous for the mind to grasp but it happens anyway, even to people your own age. With Harry gone, she can eat Campbell's chicken noodle soup cold out of the can if she wants, with a few Ritz crackers crushed in, and not have to worry about giving him a good balanced low-fat low-sodium meal that he complains to her is tasteless. Maybe being a widow won't be so very bad is the thought she keeps trying not to think.

Last night it rained hard for an hour, she was kept awake by its drumming on the air-conditioner, and they say showers this evening again, though the sun is making a kind of tawny fog slanting across the yard through the neighbor's tall trees to where Harry has his little vegetable garden in imitation of the one his parents had in the back yard on Jackson Road, all he grows is lettuce and carrots and kohlrabi, he does love to nibble. She sees with her coffee that Bryant and Willard are getting along better on the *Today* show after that unfortunate thing with Bryant's private memo being exposed in all the papers, really nothing's private any more, the scandalmongers never rest, always hoping for another Watergate, her father's death was brought on by Watergate she has always felt. The news is mostly about China and Gorbachev, you can never trust Communists not to gang up on you, and Panama where that evil pockmarked Noriega just won't leave, and how Pennsylvania voters yesterday turned down the tax reform that Governor Casey wanted; people thought it would mean a tax increase and if there's anything you can count on Americans to be these last ten years it's selfish.

She tries to pick an outfit suitable for seeing your son off to a drug clinic and then babysitting for Roy all morning while Pru drives Nelson into North Philadelphia, which she's very nervous about, who wouldn't be, they do terrible things now, deliberately rear-end you and then drive off with your car when you get out, there is no such thing any more as a good Philadelphia neighborhood, and for a striking-looking younger woman like Pru is it's worse. Pru hopes to be back by noon so Janice can go pick Harry up at the hospital, by twelve-thirty at the latest the nurse on duty warned, they don't like to give them lunch that last day and the girls coming round to make the beds don't like having somebody in one of them dirtying the sheets and then leaving. It makes her stomach nervous to think of Harry and his heart, men are so fragile it turns out, though that nice Dr. Breit with all his freckles seemed delighted with what the balloon did, but Harry's image of himself has changed, he speaks of himself almost as if he's somebody he knew a long time ago, and he seems more of a baby than he ever did, letting her make all the decisions. She doesn't see how she can leave him alone in their house his first night out of the hospital, but she can't miss the quiz either, it really makes more sense with all this coming and going and the children upset about their father's going off to the rehab to shift her base of operations to Mother's house and to wear the smart light wool outfit she bought two years ago at the Wanamaker's out at the mall on the old fairgrounds (didn't they use to get excited in school, getting the day off and all the rides, the one where four of you were in a kind of cylinder and the boy opposite would be above you and then below and the sky every which way and your skirt doing heaven knows what, the smells of sawdust and cotton candy, and the freaks and animals and prizes for tossing little hoops at pegs that were bigger than they looked), a navy-blue-and-white outfit with a kicky blue pleated skirt and off-white satin jersey and blue buttonless jacket with wide shoulders that always come back from the cleaner's with the padding askew or bent or torn loose, it's a terrible fashion as far as dry cleaning goes. The first time she posed for Harry in that suit he said it made her look like a little policeman—the shoulders and the piping on the pockets, she supposed, gave it the look of a uniform but it would do all day, she thinks, from having not to break down in saying goodbye to Nelson to taking this quiz with all the strange old terms in it, curtilage and messuage and socage and fee simple and fee tail and feoffee and copyhold and customary freehold and mortmain and devises and *lex loci rei sitae*. The little old elementary-school desks have been uprooted and taken away in favor of one-armed chairs of combination aluminum tubing and orange plastic, but the old blackboards are still there, gray with chalk dust rubbed in over the years, and the high windows you have to have a pole to raise and lower, and those high floating lights like flattened moons, like big hollow flowers upside down on their thin stems. Janice loves being back in class again, trying to follow the teacher and learn new things but also aware of the other students, their breathing and their feet scraping and the silent effort of their minds. The class is women three out of four and most younger than she but not all, to her relief she is not the oldest person in the class and not the dumbest either. The years with their heartbreak and working off and on over at the lot have taught her some things; she wishes her parents were alive to see her, sitting with these twenty-five others studying to get their licenses, the city sounds and Hispanic music and customized Hispanic cars violently revving on Pine Street beyond the tall windows, sitting there with her notebooks and pencils and yellow highlighter (they didn't have those when she went to high school); but of course if they were alive she wouldn't be doing this, she wouldn't have the mental space. They were wonderful parents but had never trusted her to manage by herself, and her marrying Harry confirmed them in their distrust. She made bad decisions.

The teacher, Mr. Lister, is a doleful tall rumpled man with jowls that make him look like a dog. He gave her a B on the last quiz and likes her, she can tell. The other students, even the younger ones, like her too, and lend her cigarettes in the bathroom break at eight-thirty and invite her to come out with them for a beer afterward at ten. She hasn't accepted yet but she might some night when things are more normal with Harry, just to show she's not stuck-up. At least she hasn't let herself go to fat like some of the women her age in the class—shocking, really, to see flesh piled up like that, and not doing anything to reduce, just carrying these hundreds of pounds back and forth and scarcely able to squeeze them into the desks. You wonder how long people can live like that. One of the few natural blessings God handed Janice was a tidy figure and that she has tried to keep, for Harry's sake as well as her own. He does seem prouder of her, the older they get. He looks at her sometimes as if she's just dropped down out of the moon.

Even with hurrying this morning, she gets caught in the slow traffic through the thick of Brewer rush hour. All these cars, where are they going? By the side of the highway as it heads around the side of the mountain you can see erosion from last night's heavy rain—big twisted ditches of red clay washed away, weeds and all. At Joseph Street she parks and goes up the walk scared of what chaos she'll find, but Nelson is dressed in one of those putty-colored suits he has and Pru in brown slacks and a khaki-colored mannish shirt under a red cardigan sweater with the arms loosely knotted around her shoulders, an outfit to drive in. Both she and Nelson look pale and drawn; you can almost see the agitated psychic energy around their heads, like one of those manifestations Harry scoffs at on *Unsolved Mysteries*.

In the kitchen, showing Janice the special peanut-butter-and-honey sandwich she has made just the way Roy likes it (otherwise he throws everything on the floor, even the TastyKake for dessert), Pru perhaps thinks the older woman notices something wrong in her manner and explains in a hurried low voice, "Nelson had some coke hidden around the house and thought we should use it up before he goes. It was too much even for him, so I did a few lines. I honestly don't know what he sees in it—it burned and I sneezed and then couldn't fall asleep but otherwise felt nothing. *Nothing.* I said to him, 'If this is all it is I don't see any problem in giving it up.' I'd have a harder time giving up Hershey bars."

But just the fact that she is talking so much, confessing so freely, stroking the lank red hair back from her forehead with a caressing gesture of both hands, with trembling fingertips, indicates to Janice that there has been a chemical event. Her son is poisonous. Everything he touches. With all her maternal effort she's brought destruction into the world.

Nelson has stayed in the front room, sitting on the Barcalounger with Roy in his arms, murmuring to the boy and gently blowing to tickle his ear. He looks up at his mother with offense written all over his face. He says to her, "You know why I'm doing this, don't you?"

"To save your own life," Janice tells him, lifting the child out of his lap. Roy is growing heavier by the day and she puts him down on his own legs. "Time you start making him walk," she explains to Nelson.

"Just like you're making me go to this stupid useless place,"

Nelson says. "I want that perfectly clear. I'm going because you're making me and not because I admit I have any problem."

A weight of weariness floods her, as if she is at the end and not the beginning of her day. "From what it seems you've done with the money, we all have a problem."

The boy scarcely flinches, but does for an instant lower his eyelids, with their beautiful lashes, a little long for a boy's. She has always found those lashes heartbreaking. "It's just debt," he says. "If Lyle weren't so sick now he'd have explained it to you better. We were just borrowing against future income. It would have all worked out."

Janice thinks of the quiz she must face tonight and of poor Harry with that metal worm they put into his heart and she tells her son, "Darling, you've been stealing, and not just pennies from the change jar. You're an addict. You've been out of your head. You've not been yourself for I don't know how long and that's all any of us want, for you to be yourself again."

His lips, thin like her own, tighten so as to disappear under his mustache, that seems to be growing out, getting droopier. "I'm a recreational user just like you're a social drinker. We need it. We losers need a lift."

"I'm not a loser, Nelson, and I hope you're not." She feels a tightening growing in her but she tries to keep her voice low and level like Charlie would. "We had this same conversation in Florida and you made promises then you didn't keep. Your problem is too much for me, it's too much for your wife, it's too much for your father—much too much for him."

"Dad doesn't give a damn."

"He does. Don't interrupt. And your problem is too much for you. You need to go to this place where they've developed a method, where they're experienced. Your counsellor wants you to go."

"Ike says it's all a con. He says everything's a con."

"That's just his black way of talking. He got you in, he wants you to go."

"Suppose I can't stand it?" She and Harry never sent him off to summer camp, for fear he couldn't stand it.

"You must stand it, or—"

"Yeah, or what, Mom?"

"Or else."

He tries to mock her: "Oh sure. What are you and Charlie and old Harry going to do to me, put me in jail?" It is a real question; in nervousness he loudly sniffs, and then rubs his pink nostrils.

She tries to give him a real answer, saying in the level soft voice, "We wouldn't be the ones doing it. The Toyota Company and the police would be doing it, if they were called in."

He sniffs again, in disbelief. "Why would you call them in? I'll put the money back. I was always going to put it back. You care more about the dumb lot than you care about me."

His tone is trying for a bantering lightness, but her own mood has hardened; outrage has seized her, and self-righteousness. "You stole from me, never mind that. But you stole from your grandfather. You stole from what he had built."

Nelson's guarded eyes widen; his pallor seems a prisoner's in the murky parlor light. "Grandpop always wanted me to run the lot. And what about my kids? What about Judy and Roy if you carry through on all these threats?" Roy has whimpered and collapsed to the floor, and is leaning against her ankles, hoping to distract her, hating the sounds of this conversation.

"You should have been thinking of them before now," Janice says stonily. "You've been stealing from them, too." She takes a weary pride in her stoniness; her head is numb but clear, with the product of her own womb pleading and wriggling beneath her. This numbness she feels must be the *power* her women's group in Florida talks about, the power men have always had.

Nelson tries outrage of his own. "Ah, fuck, Mom. Don't give me all this, all this 'How could you do this to your mother and father?' What about what you did to me, all that mess around when Becky died so I never had a sister, and then that time you ran away with your oily Greek and crazy Dad brought Jill and then Skeeter into the house and they tried to make me take dope when I was just a little kid?"

Janice realizes that with all her stoniness and inner hardness she has been crying, her throat feels raw and tears have been flowing stupidly down her face. She wipes at them with the back of her hand and asks shakily, "How much dope did they make you do?"

He squirms, retreats a bit. "I don't know," he says. "They let me take a puff of pot now and then. But they were doing worse stuff and didn't try to hide it from me."

She works with a balled-up Kleenex at drying her face and eyes, thinking what a messy start she is having to this day, in a costume that was supposed to see her through the roles of mother, grandmother, ministering wife, eager student, and prospective working girl. "Your childhood I guess wasn't ideal," she admits, stabbing under her eyes, feeling distracted, ready for her next role, "but then whose is? You shouldn't sit in judgment of your parents. We did the best we could while being people too."

He protests, "Being people too!"

She tells him: "You know, Nelson, when you're little you think your parents are God but now you're old enough to face the fact that they're not. Your father isn't well and I'm trying to make something of what little life I have left and we just can't focus on you and your misbehavior as much as you think we should. You're of an age now to take responsibility for your own life. It's plain to everybody who knows you that your only chance is to stick with this program in Philadelphia. We're all going to try to hold the fort here for three months but when you come back in August you'll be on your own. You won't get any favors at least from me."

He sneers. "I thought mothers were supposed to love their kids no matter what." As if to challenge her physically he pushes up out of his grandfather's Barcalounger and stands close, a few inches taller than she.

She feels the rawness in her throat and the heat in her eyes beginning again. "If I didn't love you," she says, "I'd let you go on destroying yourself." Her store of words is exhausted; she launches herself toward the white sneering face and embraces the boy, who grudgingly, after a resistant wriggle, responds and hugs her back, patting her shoulder blade with what Harry's mother used to call "those little Springer hands." Now, *there*, Janice thinks, was a hateful mother, who never said No to her son in all her life.

Nelson is saying in her ear that he'll be fine, everything will be fine, he just got a little overextended.

Pru comes downstairs carrying two big suitcases. "I don't know how often they wear suits," she says, "but I thought they must have a lot of physical therapy so I packed all the shorts and athletic socks I could find. And blue jeans, for when they make you scrub the floors."

"Bye bye Daddy," Roy is saying down among their legs. Since Pru has her hands full, Janice hoists him up, heavy and leggy though he is getting to be, for his father's farewell kiss. The child hangs on to Nelson's ear in parting and she wonders where Roy got this idea of inflicting pain to show affection.

When his parents have gone off in the burgundy-red Celica

Supra that Nelson drives, Roy leads his grandmother into the back yard where Harry's old vegetable garden with the little chicken-wire fence he could step over has been replaced with a swing-and-slide set bought five years ago for Judy and pretty well gone to rust and disuse. Already, though the summer is young, tall weeds flourish around the metal feet of it. Janice thinks she recognizes the ferny tops of carrots and kohlrabi among the plantain and dandelions, the dandelions' yellow flowers now seedy white pompons that fly apart at the swat of the broken hockey stick whose taped-up handle little Roy swings like a samurai sword. The Springers moved to this house when Janice was eight and from the back yard the big house looks naked to her without the copper beech. The sky is full of puffy scudding clouds with those purply-dark centers that can bring rain. The weatherman this morning had called for more, though not as violent as last night's showers. She takes Roy for a little walk over the sidewalk squares of Joseph Street, some of them replaced but here and there a crack she remembers still unmended and two slabs still tilted up by a sycamore root in a way that made a treacherous little hill for a girl on roller skates. She tells Roy some of this, and the names of families that used to live in the houses of the neighborhood, but he gets cranky and tired within the block; children now don't seem to have the physical energy, the eagerness to explore, that she remembers, girls as well as boys, her knees always skinned and dirty, her mother always complaining about the state of her clothes. Roy's interest during their walk flickers up only when they come to a string of little soft anthills like coffee grounds between two sidewalk cracks. He kicks them open and then stamps the scurrying armies suddenly pouring out to defend the queen. Such slaughter wearies him, the ants keep coming, and she finally has to pick the lummox up and carry him back to the house, his sneakers drumming sluggishly against her belly and pleated skirt.

One of the cable channels has cartoons all morning. Gangs of outlined superheroes, who move one body part at a time and talk with just their lower lips, do battle in space with cackling villains from other galaxies. Roy falls asleep watching, one of Pru's oat-bran low-sugar cookies broken in two wet crumbling halves in his hands. This house where Janice lived so long—the potted violets, the knickknacks, the cracked brown Barcalounger Daddy loved to relax on, to wait with closed eyes for one of his headaches to subside, the dining-room table Mother used to complain was being ruined by the lazy cleaning women who like to spray on Pledge every time and ruin the finish with gummy wax build-up—deepens her guilt in regard to Nelson. His pale frightened face seems still to glow in the dark living room: she pulls up the shade, surprising the sleepy wasps crawling on the sill like arthritic old men. Across the street, at what used to be the Schmehlings' house, a pink dogwood has grown higher than the porch roof; its shape in bloom drifts sideways like those old photos of atomic bomb–test clouds in the days when we were still scared of the Russians. To think that she could be so cruel to Nelson just because of money. The memory of her hardness with him just makes her shake, chilling the something soft still left in the center of her bones, giving her a little physical convulsion of self-disgust such as after you vomit.

Yet no one will share these feelings with her. Not Harry, not Pru. Pru comes back not at noon but after one o'clock. She says traffic was worse than anyone would imagine, miles of the Turnpike reduced to one lane, North Philadelphia enormous, block after block of row houses. And then the rehab place took its own sweet time about signing Nelson in; when she complained, they let her know that they turned down three for every one they admitted. Pru seems a semi-stranger, taller in stature and fiercer in expression than Janice remembered as a mother-in-law. The link between them has been removed.

"How did he seem?" Janice asks her.

"Angry but sane. Full of practical instructions about the lot he wanted me to pass on to his father. He made me write them all down. It's as if he doesn't realize he's not running the show any more."

"I feel so terrible about it all I couldn't eat any lunch. Roy fell asleep in the TV chair and I didn't know if I should wake him or not."

Pru pokes back her hair wearily. "Nelson kept the kids up too late last night, running around kissing them, wanting them to play card games. He gets manicky on the stuff, so he can't let anybody alone. Roy has his play group at one, I better quick take him."

"I'm sorry, I knew he had the play group but didn't know where it was or if Wednesday was one of the days."

"I should have told you, but who would have thought driving to Philadelphia and back would be such a big deal? In Ohio you just zip up to Cleveland without any trouble." She doesn't directly blame Janice for missing Roy's play group, but a sternness in the triangular brow expresses irritation nevertheless.

Janice still seeks absolution from this younger woman, asking, "Do *you* think I should feel so terrible?"

Pru, whose eyes have been shuttling from detail to detail of what is, after all, as far as use and occupancy go, her house, now for a moment focuses on Janice a look of full cold clarity. "Of course not," she says. "This is the only chance Nelson has. And you're the only one who could make him do it. Thank God you did. You're doing exactly the right thing."

Yet the words are so harshly stated Janice finds herself unreassured. She licks the center of her upper lip, which feels dry. There is a little crack in the center of it that never quite heals. "But I feel so—what's the word?—mercenary. As if I care more about the company than my son."

Pru shrugs. "It's the way things are structured. You have the clout. Me, Harry, the kids—Nelson just laughs at us. To him we're negligible. He's sick, Janice. He's not your son, he's a monster con artist who used to be your son."

And this seems so harsh that Janice starts to cry; but her daughter-in-law, instead of offering to lend comfort, turns and sets about, with her air of irritated efficiency, waking up Roy and putting him in clean corduroy pants for play school.

"I'm late too. We'll be back," Janice says, feeling dismissed. She and Pru have previously agreed that, rather than risk leaving Harry alone in the Penn Park house while she does her three hours at the Penn State extension, she will bring him back here for his first night out of the hospital. As she drives into Brewer she looks forward to seeing him on his feet again, and to sharing with him her guilt over Nelson.

But he disappoints her just as Pru did. His five nights in St. Joseph's have left him self-obsessed and lackadaisical. He seems brittle and puffy, suddenly; his hair, still a dull blond color, has been combed by him in the same comb-ridged pompadour he used to wear coming out of the locker room in high school. His hair has very little gray, but his temples are higher and the skin there, in the hollow at the corner of the eyebrows, has a crinkly dryness. He is like a balloon the air just slowly goes out of: over days it wrinkles and sinks to the floor. His russet slacks and blue cotton sports coat look loose on him; the hospital diet has squeezed pounds of water out of his system. Drained of spirit as well, he seems halting and blinky the way her father became in his last five years, closing his eyes in the Barcalounger, waiting for the headache to pass. It feels wrong: in their marriage in the past Harry's vitality always towered over hers—his impulsive

needs, his sense of being generally cherished, his casual ability
to hurt her, his unspoken threat to leave at any moment. It feels
wrong that she is picking him up in her car, when he is dressed
and wet-combed like the boy that comes for you on a date. He
was sitting meekly in the chair by his bed, with his old gym
bag, holding medicine and dirty underwear, between his feet in
their big suede Hush Puppies. She took his arm and with cautious steps he moved to the elevator, as the nurses called goodbye. One plump younger one seemed especially sad to see him
go, and the Hispanic culinary aide said to Janice with flashing
eyes, "Make him eat right!"

She expects Harry to be more grateful; but a man even slightly
sick assumes that women will uphold him, and in this direction,
men to women, the flow of gratitude is never great. In the car,
his first words are insulting: "You have on your policeman's
uniform."

"I need to feel presentable for my exam tonight. I'm afraid I
won't be able to concentrate. I can't stop thinking about Nelson."

He has slumped down in the passenger seat, his knees pressed
against the dashboard, his head laid back against the headrest in
a conceited way. "What's to think?" he asks. "Did he wriggle
out of going? I *thought* he'd run."

"He didn't run at all, that was one of the things that made it
so sad. He went off just the way he used to go to school. Harry,
I wonder if we're doing the right thing."

Harry's eyes are closed, as if against the battering of sights to
see through the car windows—Brewer, its painted brick buildings, its heavy sandstone churches, its mighty courthouse, its
new little green-glass skyscraper, and the overgrown park where
Weiser Square had once been and which is now the home of
drug addicts and the homeless who live in cardboard boxes and
keep their clothes in stolen shopping carts. "What else can we
do?" he asks indolently. "What does Pru think?"

"Oh, she's for it. It gets him off her hands. I'm sure he's been
a handful lately. You can see in her mind she's single already,
all independent and brisk and a little rude to me, I thought."

"Don't get touchy. What does Charlie think? How was your
Vietnamese dinner last night?"

"I'm not sure I understand Vietnamese food, but it was nice.
Short but sweet. I even got home in time to catch the end of
thirtysomething. It was the season finale—Gary tried to protect
Susannah from a magazine exposé being written by Hope, who

found out that Susannah was stealing from the social-service center." All this in case he thinks she slept with Charlie, to show there wasn't time. Poor Harry, he doesn't believe you can grow beyond that.

He groans, still keeping his eyes shut. "Sounds awful. Sounds like life."

"Charlie's real proud of me," she says, "for standing up to Nelson. We had a grim little talk this morning, Nelson and me, where he said I loved the company more than him. I wonder if he isn't right, if we haven't become very materialistic since you first knew me. He seemed so little, Harry, so hurt and defiant, just the way he was the time I went off to live with Charlie. Abandoning a twelve-year-old like that, I'm the one should have been put in jail, what *was* I thinking of? It's true what he says, who am I to lecture him, to send him off to this dreary place? I was just about the age he is now when I did it, too. So *young*, really." She is crying again; she wonders if you can become addicted to tears like everything else. All the darkness and fumbling and unthinkable shames of her life feel regurgitated in this unstoppable salty outpour. She can hardly see to drive, and laughs at her own snuffling.

Harry's head rolls loosely on the headrest, as if he is basking in an invisible sun. The clouds are crowding out even light-gray sky, their dark hearts merging into an overcast. "You were trying something out," Harry tells her. "You were trying to live while you were still alive."

"But I had no *right*, you had no right either, to do the things we did!"

"For Chrissake, don't bawl. It was the times," he says. "The Sixties. The whole country was flipping out back then. We weren't so bad. We got back together."

"Yes, and sometimes I wonder if that wasn't just more self-indulgence. We haven't made each other happy, Harry."

She wants to face this with him but he smiles as if in his sleep. "You've made me happy," he says. "I'm sorry to hear it didn't work both ways."

"Don't," she says. "Don't just score points. I'm trying to be serious. You know I've always loved you, or wanted to, if you'd let me. Ever since high school, at least ever since Kroll's. That's one of the things Charlie was telling me last night, how crazy about you I've always been." Her face heats; his failure to respond embarrasses her; she hurries on, turning left on Eisenhower. A gap in the clouds makes the hood of the Camry glare;

then it is dipped deeper into cloud shadow. "It really was a pretty restaurant," she says, "the way they've fixed it up and everything, these little Vietnamese women so petite they made me feel like a horse. But they spoke perfect English, with Pennsylvania accents—second generation, can it be? Has it been that long since the war? We should go there sometime."

"I wouldn't dream of intruding. It's your and Charlie's place." He opens his eyes and sits up. "Hey. Where're we going? This is the way to Mt. Judge."

She says, "Harry, now don't get mad. You know I have to go to class and take the quiz tonight, and I'd feel too funny leaving you alone for three hours just out of the hospital, so Pru and I worked it out that you and I would sleep in Mother's old bed, which they moved across the hall into the old sewing room when Mother's room became Judy's room. This way you'll have babysitters while I'm off."

"Why can't I go to my own fucking house? I was looking forward to it. I lived in that damn barn of your mother's for fifteen years and that was enough."

"Just for one night, honey. Please—otherwise I'll be sick with worry and flunk my quiz. There are all those Latin and funny old English words you're expected to know."

"My heart's fine. Better than ever. It's like a sink trap after all the hair and old toothpaste has been cleaned out. I saw the bastards do it. Nothing will happen if you leave me alone, I promise."

"That nice Dr. Breit told me before they did it there was a chance of a coronary occlusion."

"That was while they were doing it, with the catheter in. The catheter's out now. It's been out nearly a week. Come on, honey. Take me home."

"Just one night, Harry, please. It's a kindness to everybody. Pru and I thought it would distract the children from their father's not being there. They can think they're helping take care of you."

He sinks back into his seat, giving up. "What about my pajamas? What about my toothbrush?"

"They're there. I brought them over this morning. I tell you, this day. I've really had to plan. Now, after we've got you settled, I *must* study, absolutely."

"I don't want to be in the same house with Roy," he says, sulking humorously, resigned to what after all is a tiny adventure, a night back in Mt. Judge. "He'll hurt me. Down in Florida he yanked the oxygen tube right out of my nose."

Janice remembers Roy stamping on all those ants but nevertheless says, "I spent the whole morning with him and he couldn't have been sweeter."

Pru and Roy are not there. Janice leads Rabbit upstairs and suggests he lie down. Ma's old bed has been freshly made up; his off-white pajamas are folded nicely on his pillow. He sees in the murky far corner next to an old wooden-cased Singer sewing machine the dressmaker's dummy, dust-colored, eternally headless and erect. Ma's big bed crowds the room so there are just a few inches of space on one side next to the window and on the other beside the wall with its wainscoting. The sewing room has a wainscoting of varnished beaded boards, set upright and trimmed at chest-level with a strip of molding. The door of a shallow closet in the corner is made of the same boards. When he opens it, the door bumps annoyingly on the bedpost of Ma's old bed, a bedpost turned with a flattened knob at the top like a hard, brown-painted mushroom, and the paint on it has crackled into small rectangles, like a puddle that has dried. He opens the door to hang up his blue coat, among cobwebby crammed old irons and toasters, coverlets folded and preserved in yellowing cellophane moth bags, and a rack of Fred Springer's dead neckties. He folds back his shirtsleeves and begins to feel like himself; the idea of spending a day back in Mt. Judge is beginning to amuse him. "Maybe I'll take a little walk."

"Should you?" Janice asks.

"Absolutely. It's the best thing for you, that's what everybody at the hospital says. They had me walking the halls."

"I thought you might want to lie down."

"Later, maybe. You go study. Go on, this quiz of yours is making me nervous."

He leaves her at the dining-room table with her book and her photocopies and heads up Joseph Street to Potter Avenue, where the ice-plant water used to run down in the gutter. The gutter has been long dry but the cement was permanently tinged green. Rabbit walks away from the center of the borough with its dry cleaners and Turkey Hill Minit Market and Pizza Hut and Sunoco and discount stereo and new video store that used to be a shoe store and aerobics class above what had been a bakery when he was a boy. The smell of warm dough and icing out of its doors would make him drool. He walks uphill to where Potter Avenue meets Wilbur Street; here a green mailbox used to lean on a concrete post and now the bigger boxy kind with the rounded top stands instead, painted blue. A fire hydrant painted red, white, and blue for the Bicentennial in the Seventies has been given a fresh and garish coat of the orange you see on life jackets and joggers' vests and hunters' outfits, as if a fog creeping into our way of life is making everything harder to see. He walks up Wilbur, feeling the steep slope tug at his heart. The street in its lower blocks holds pretentious large houses like the Springers', stucco and brick and slate, fortresslike, with gables and acres of roof, some of them now split up into condos reached by wooden outside stairs that look tacky. Beyond the alley where long ago there used to be a telephone pole with a backboard bolted to it, Rabbit's chest has that full feeling, his ribs like bands of pressure, and he pops a Nitrostat under his tongue and waits, while cool cloud shadows slide rapidly across the forested edge of the mountain above him, for the relief and the tingle. He had hoped he would need to take fewer pills but maybe it takes time for the operation to sink in.

He continues hiking, alone on the sloping sidewalk, up into the block where he and Janice lived when they were first married. Built all at once in the Thirties, a row of frame semi-detached climbs the hill like a staircase. Like the fire hydrant, they have become brighter, painted in fanciful storybook colors, pale purple and lime green, even turquoise and scarlet, colors that no respectable Pennsylvania householder would have applied when Harry was young. Life was not only bigger but more solemn then. Colors were bruise and dung, in gritty sidings that rubbed off on your fingers and were tar underneath.

His own house, the seventh in the row, number 447, had tired wooden steps that have been replaced with concrete inset with irregular multicolored pieces of broken tile and covered with a central runner of green outdoor carpeting; the house door into the vestibule has been painted a high-gloss ochre on its panels and maroon on its stiles, so a bold double cross is figured forth, ornamented by a brass knocker in the shape of a fox's head. Camaros and BMWs are parked out front; glass curtains and splashy abstract prints dress the windows. This row, a kind of slum when Harry and Janice and two-year-old Nelson lived here, and their infant daughter died, has been spruced up: festive yuppie money has taken it over. These apartments are fashionable, high above the town as they are. Back then, thirty years ago, from the third floor, the view across the tar rooftops to the peaked houses and parked cars lower down just seemed an enlargement of their discontent, their defeat, a sense of defeat the years have brought back to him, after what seemed for a while to be triumphs. There had been, being here makes him remember, those cheap sliding screens at the windows, and a rusty furnace odor in the vestibule, and a plastic clown some kid had left in the dirt under the front-porch steps, now concrete carpeted green like those traffic islands down at the condo.

This row used to end Wilbur Street; development had stopped at a gravel turnaround, and an abandoned gravel quarry made the transition to the mountain's shaggy back side. Now a double row, not quite new, of shingled condominiums, with strangely exaggerated chimneys and gables like houses in a child's storybook, occupies still higher ground. The windows and doors and trim boards of these condos are tinted in pale and playful colors. The plantings and little lawns are still tenuous; last night's downpour washed from the deforested acres of the mountain reddish mud that has drifted, hardening, all along the fresh curbs and overflowed onto the street's blue-black asphalt. *We're using it all up.* Harry thinks. The world.

He turns and walks downhill. On Potter Avenue he continues past Joseph and goes into a Turkey Hill Minit Market and to suppress his melancholy buys a ninety-nine-cent bag of Corn Chips. NET WT. 6¼ OZ. 177 grams. *Manufactured by Keystone Food Prod., Inc., Easton, Pa. 18042 U.S.A. Ingredients: Corn, vegetable oil (contains one or more of the following oils: peanut, cottonseed, corn, partially hydrogenated soybean), salt.* Doesn't sound so bad. KEEP ON KRUNCHIN', the crinkly pumpkin-colored bag advises him. He loves the salty ghost of Indian corn and the way each thick flake, an inch or so square, solider than a potato chip and flatter than a Frito and less burny to the tongue than a triangular red-peppered Dorito, sits edgy in his mouth and then shatters and dissolves between his teeth. There are certain things you love putting into your mouth—Nibs, Good & Plentys, dryroasted peanuts, lima beans cooked not too soft—and the rest is more or less disagreeable mush, or meat that gives the teeth too tough a fight and if you think about it almost makes you gag. Ever since childhood, Rabbit has had mixed feelings about eating, especially the creatures that not too long ago were living just like you. Sometimes he imagines he can taste the terror of the ax in the slice of turkey or chicken and the happy snorting and wallowing in pork and the stupid monotony of a cow's life in beef, and in lamb a hint of urine like that whiff from Thelma's face in the hospital. Her dialysis now and their night in that tropical hut, bodily fluids, but there were limits to what bodies can do, and limits of involvement what with Janice and Ron and the kids and fussy living rooms all over Diamond County, and some limitation within him really, a failure or refusal to love any substance but his own. And she too, she did tend afterwards to be curiously severe with him, as though he had become disgusting now that she had eaten, his sour-milk smell tainting her satisfied mouth. His meat having been eaten by her and now she being eaten by all that microscopic chewing from within. Lupus means wolf, she had told him, one of the autoimmune diseases in which the body attacks itself, antibodies attack your own tissue, self-hatred of a sort. Thinking of Thelma, Harry feels helpless and in his helplessness hard-hearted. The Corn Chips as he walks along the pavement begin to accumulate in his gut into a knotted muchness, a little ball of acid, and yet he cannot resist putting just one more into his mouth, to feel its warped salty edges, its virgin crunchiness, on his tongue, between his teeth, among these salivating membranes. By the time he gets back to 89 Joseph behind its wall of sticky leafed-out Norway maples he has consumed the full bag, even the fragments of salt and corn small enough for an ant to carry back to his brown queen bloated in her maze beneath the sidewalk; he has wrapped himself around all 6¼ ounces of sheer poison, pure sludge in his arteries, an oily aftertaste in his throat and between his teeth. He hates himself, with a certain relish.

Janice is working at the dining-room table, making lists for herself to memorize. When she looks up, her eyes have a rubbed frowning look and her mouth is open a dark slot. He hates to see it, hates to see her struggling so hard not to be dumb. His long walk has left him so tired he goes upstairs and takes off his slacks to keep the crease and lies down on Ma Springer's bed, on top of the covers but under the Amish quilt, a patchwork quilt that releases to his nostrils a memory of how Ma smelled toward the end, musty far odor of fleshly corners gone unwashed. He finds himself suddenly scared to be out of the hospital whiteness, the antisepsis, the halls of softly clattering concern focused upon him . . . sick him.

He must have fallen asleep, for when he opens his eyes the day has a different tone through the room's single window: a cooler, shadowed menace. The rain coming closer. The clouds and treetops merging. From the sounds downstairs, Pru and both children are home, and footsteps move about in the hall outside much as years ago he would hear Melanie and Nelson sneak back and forth at night. It is not night, it is late afternoon. The children, home from school, have been instructed to be quiet because Grandpa is sleeping; but they are unable to resist the spurts of squalling and of glee that come over them. Life is noise. Rabbit's stomach hurts, he forgets why.

After they hear him make a trip down the hall to the bathroom, they come and visit him, the poor little semi-orphans. Their four eyes, two green, two brown, feast on him from the bed's edge. Judy's face seems longer and graver than it was in Florida. She will have an Angstrom leanness, a hunted look. Her dress is lilac-colored, with white smocking. Does he imagine a touch of extra redness to her lips? Does Pru allow that? Certainly the child's hair has been given an artificial wave, a carrot-colored crimp. She asks, "Grandpa, did it hurt in the hospital?"

"Not much, Judy. It hurt my feelings, mostly, to be there at all."

"Did they fix that thing inside you?"

"Oh, yes. Don't you worry about that. My doctors says I'm better than ever."

"How come you're in bed, then?"

"Because Grandma was studying for her quiz and I didn't want to bother her."

"She says you're going to sleep over."

"Looks that way, doesn't it? A pajama party. Before you were born, Judy, Grandma and I lived here for years and years, with your great-grandmother Springer. You remember her?"

The child's eyes stare, their green intensified by the maple trees at the window. "A little bit. She had fat legs and wore thick orange stockings."

"That's right." But can Ma be no more than that in this child's memory? Do we dwindle so fast to next to nothing?

"I used to hate her stockings," Judy goes on, as if sensing his need for more and trying to meet it.

"Those were Sup-Hose," Harry explains.

"And she wore funny little round glasses she never took off. She'd let me play with the case. It snapped."

Roy, bored to hear all this about a woman he never met, begins to talk. His round face strains upward as if he's trying to swallow something rough, and his arched eyebrows pull his dark shiny eyes painfully open. "Daddy—Daddy won't—" or perhaps he said "went"; he seems unable to wrestle his thoughts into shape and begins again with the strained word "Daddy."

Impatiently Judy gives him a push; he falls against a bedpost, there in the narrow space between the mattress edge and the beaded wainscoting. "Shut up if you can't talk," she tells him. "Daddy's in a rehab place getting better."

The child has hit his head; he stares at his grandfather as if waiting to be told what to do. "Ouch," Harry says for him, and, sitting up against Ma Springer's old brown headboard, opens his arms to the child. Roy dives against his chest and lets himself bawl, about his hurt head. His hair, when Harry rubs it, is stickily fine, like Janice's yesterday, when she cried. Something about being helpless in bed, people hit you up for sympathy. They've got you where they want you.

Judy talks right through Roy's aggrieved noise. "Grandpa, want to watch one of my videos with me? I have *Dumbo* and *The Sound of Music* and *Dirty Dancing*."

"I'd love to see *Dirty Dancing* sometime, I've seen the other two, but shouldn't you be doing your homework before dinner?"

The child smiles. "That's what Daddy always says. He never wants to watch a video with me." She looks at Roy being cradled and pulls at her brother's arm. "Come on, stupid. Don't lean on Grandpa's chest, you'll hurt him."

They go away. A ghostly moment as Judy stood by the bed reminded him of Jill, another of the many dead people he knows. The numbers are growing. Life is like a game they used to play on the elementary-school playground, Fox-in-the-Morning. You all lined up on one side of the asphalt area marked out for games. One person was "it," and that one would call out "Fox in the morning," and you would all run to the other side, and "it" would grab one victim from the running throng and drag him or her into the circle painted on the asphalt, and then there would be two "its", and these would capture a few more on the next massed gallop from safety to safety, and these four would become eight, and soon a whole mob would be roving the center; the proportions were reversed. The last person left uncaught became "it" for the next game.

Sparse specks of rain have appeared on the panes. His eyelids feel heavy again; a fog within is rising up to swallow his brain. When you are sleepy an inner world smaller than a seed in sunlight expands and becomes irresistible, breaking the shell of consciousness. It is so strange; there must be some other way of being alive than all this eating and sleeping, this burning and freezing, this sun and moon. Day and night blend into each other but still are nothing the same.

The call to dinner comes from far away, through many thicknesses of lath and plaster and hollow air, and from its sharp tone is being repeated. He can't believe he's been asleep; no time has passed, just a thought or two took a strange elastic shape as it went around a corner. His mouth feels furry. The specks of rain on the window are still few, few enough to be counted. He recalls remembering today the window screens they had in the Wilbur Street apartment, the kind you used to buy in hardware stores before combination storms made them obsolete. They never precisely fit, leaving splinters of light through which the mosquitoes and midges could crawl, but that wasn't the something tragic about them. Tragedy lay in a certain filtered summer breath they admitted, the glint of sun along segments of the mesh, an overlooked fervor in their details—the bent screening, the sliding adjustable frame stamped with the manufacturer's name, the motionless molding of the window itself, like the bricks that all through Brewer loyally hold their pattern though the masons that laid them long ago are dead. Something tragic in matter itself, that keeps watch no matter how great our misery. He went back to the apartment that day after Becky died and nothing was changed. The water in the tub, the chops in the skillet. The call to dinner repeats again, closer, in Janice's sharp voice, at the foot of the stairs: "*Har*ry. *Din*ner."

"*Com*ing, for Chrissake," he says.

Janice called but the meal was cooked by Pru; it is light, delicious, healthful. Pieces of some white fish garnished with parsley and chives and flavored with pepper and lemon, asparagus served steaming in a rectangular microwave dish, and in a big wooden bowl a salad including celery and carrot slices and dates and green grapes. The salad bowl and microwave equipment are new since Ma Springer died.

Everybody eats but nobody has much to say except Janice, who chatters on bravely about her quiz, her class, the people in it, some of them women like herself developing midlife careers and others young people that seem much the way we were in the Fifties, running scared, economically, and playing everything safe. She mentions her teacher, Mr. Lister, and Judy laughs out loud at the name, repeating it, the rhyme of it. "Don't laugh, Judy, he has such a sad face," Janice says.

Judy tells some involved story about what a boy at school did today: he accidentally spilled paint for a poster they were making all over the floor and when the teacher bawled him out took the spilled jar and shook it at her so some got on her dress.

Meanwhile there is this one black boy in the class, his family has just moved to Mt. Judge from Baltimore, and he was painting his face all over with these designs that have a secret meaning, he said. Her talk is a little like her excited channel-flipping and it occurs to Harry that she is making it up or confusing her own classroom with classroom shows she has seen on television.

Pru asks Harry how he is feeling. He says fine; his breathing does feel freer since the operation—"the procedure the doctors like to call it"—and his memory for that matter better. He wonders how soft in the head he was getting before without realizing it. Really, he says, apologizing to her for her trouble, thanking her for the good healthy meal that he has managed to get down on top of the fermenting lump of Corn Chips, he could perfectly well have been left alone in his own house tonight.

Janice says she knows it is probably foolish but she could never forgive herself if he took a bad turn while she was in class and how could she concentrate on liens and curtilage and *lex loci* thinking he was back in the house drowning?

The other adults at the table hold their breaths at this slip; Harry gently says, when the silence gets unbearable, "You don't mean drowning," and Janice asks, "Did I say drowning?," knowing now in her ear's recall that she did. Harry sees that she only seems to have forgotten Rebecca, that in her own mind she is always and will always be the woman who drowned her own baby. Thirty years ago. It was this time of year, late spring, they are approaching the anniversary, in June. Janice rises, flustered, blushing, shamed.

"Who wants coffee besides me?" she asks, all eyes upon her, like an actress who must come up with some line.

"And there's some butter-pecan ice cream for dessert if anybody wants," Pru says, her flat Ohio voice having fallen over the years into the local locutions, that considerate Pennsylvania way of speaking as if to make things clear in a stupefying haze. She has taken off the cardigan and folded back the cuffs of her mannish khaki shirt so that half her downy freckled forearms show, there at the kitchen table, under the faceted-glass light fixture overhead.

"My favorite flavor," Harry says, pitying his wife, wanting to help her out of the brightly lit center of the stage; even little Roy with his inky eyes is staring at Janice, sensing something strange, a curse nobody mentions.

"Harry, that's the worst possible thing for you," Janice says, grateful for this opportunity he has given her for a quarrel, a scene. "Ice cream and nuts both."

Pru says, "I got some frozen yogurt with Harry in mind. Peach and banana I think are the flavors."

"It's not the same," Harry says, clowning to keep the attention of both women. "I want butter pecan. *With* something. How about some good old-fashioned apple strudel, with all that sort of wallpaper paste inside? Or some sticky buns? Or shoofly pie? *Yum*: huh, Roy?"

"Oh, Harry, you're going to kill yourself!" Janice cries, excessively, her grief centered elsewhere.

"There's something called ice milk," Pru is saying, and he feels that her heart too is elsewhere, that throughout the meal she has been maneuvering around the covered-up hole of Nelson's absence, which no one has mentioned, not even the wide-eyed children.

"Shoo-fly pie," Roy says, in an oddly deep and mannish voice, and when they explain to him that there isn't really any, that it was just a joke of Grandpa's, he feels he has made a mistake, and in his weariness at learning all day to be more independent he begins to whimper.

"Makes your eyes light up," Rabbit sings to him, "and your tummy say 'howdy.' "

Pru takes Roy upstairs while Janice serves Judy butter-pecan ice cream and stacks the dishes into the dishwasher. Harry kept his spoon and digs into Judy's dish while Janice's back is turned. He loves that second when the tongue flattens the ice cream against the roof of the mouth and the fragments of pecan emerge like stars at evening. "Oh Grandpa, you shouldn't," Judy says, looking at him with genuine fright, though her lips want to smile.

He touches his own lips with a finger and promises, "Just one spoonful," while going for another.

The child calls for help: "Grandma!"

"He's just teasing," Janice says, but asks him, "Would you like your own dish?"

This gets him up from the table. "I shouldn't have ice cream, that's the worst thing for me," he tells her, and scolds, seeing the jumble of plates she has stacked in Pru's (Ma's old) dishwasher, "My God, you have no system—look at all the space you're wasting!"

"You stack it, then," she says, a modern woman, and while he does, fitting the dishes closer together, in harrowlike rows, she gathers together her papers and book and purse from the dining-room table. "Damn," she says, and comes to the kitchen to tell Harry, "All my planning this morning what to wear and I forget to bring a raincoat." The rain has settled in outside; sheathing the house in a loud murmur.

"Maybe Pru could lend you one."

"It would fall off me," she says. But she goes upstairs to where Pru is putting Roy to bed and after a conversation Harry can't hear comes down in a cherry-red waterproof plastic coat, with wide lapels and a belt too long and gleaming zigzags under the light. "Do I look ridiculous?"

"Not exactly," he tells her. It excites him, this transposition: you follow the zigzagging creases up expecting to see red-haired Pru staring back and instead it's Janice's middle-aged face, framed in a splashy bandanna not hers either.

"Also, *damn*, I'm so mad at myself, I left my lucky pen on the upstairs table back home. And there's no time to drive back for it, in all this rain."

"Maybe you're taking all this too seriously," he says. "What're you trying to prove to the teacher?"

"I'm trying to prove something to my*self*," she says. "Tell Pru I've left and that I'll be back at ten-thirty, maybe eleven if we decide to go out for beers afterward. You go to bed and rest. You look tired, honey." She gives him in parting a pointed little lingering kiss, grateful for something. Glad to go. All these other male advisers she suddenly has—Charlie, Mr. Lister, the new accountant—seem an invasion as devious as that televised catheter nudging forward into his shadowy webbed heart.

The murmur around the house sounds louder after Janice's footsteps on the porch and the sound of the Camry starting up. She has a panicky way of racing the engine before she puts a car in gear, and usually jumps off like a drag-racer. Janice is wrapped in Pru's red raincoat, and he is the man of Pru's house.

On the set in the living room, he and Judy watch the end of ABC news on Channel 6 (that Peter Jennings: here he is telling Americans all about America and he still says "aboot" for "about," he's so Canadian) and then, with Judy punching the remote control, they skip back and forth between *Jeopardy!* and *Simon and Simon* and the seven o'clock syndicated reruns of *Cosby* and *Cheers*. Pru drifts downstairs, having put Roy down, and into the kitchen to tidy up totally after Janice's half-ass job and then through the dining room checking that all the windows are shut against the rain and into the sun room where she picks a few dead leaves off the plants on Ma Springer's old iron table there. Finally she comes into the living room and sits on the old sofa beside him, while Judy in the Barcalounger channel-surfs. On the *Cosby Show* rerun, the Huxtables are having one of those child-rearing crises bound to dissolve like a lump of sugar in their warm good humor, their mutual lovingness: Vanessa and her friends get all excited about entering a local dance contest, with lip synching, and get instruction from an old black night-club pianist and when the time comes to demonstrate for their parents in their living room they bump and grind with a sexuality so startling and premature that Mrs. Huxtable, Claire, in real life the terrific Phylicia Rashad, married to the frog-eyed black sports commentator, restores decency, stopping the record and sending the girls back upstairs, yet with that smile of hers, that wide white slightly lippy black woman's smile, implying that indecency is all right, in its place, its wise time, as in one of those mutually ogling Huxtable snuggles that end many a *Cosby Show*. Beside him on the sofa Pru is staring at the screen with a jewel, a tear glittering in a corner of the eye toward him. From the Barcalounger Judy snaps the channel to a shot of tropical sky and a huge turtle turning its head slowly while a Godlike voiceover intones, *". . . determined to defend its breeding grounds."*

"Goddamn it, Judy, put it back to the Cosbys right *now*," Harry says, furious less for himself than for Pru, to whom the show seemed to be a vision of lost possibilities.

Judy, startled just like the girls on the show, does put it back, but by now it's a commercial, and she cries, as the insult sinks in, "I want Daddy back! Everybody else is mean to me!"

She starts to cry, Pru rises to comfort her, Rabbit retreats in disgrace. He circles the house, listening to the rain, marvelling that he once lived here, remembering the dead and the dead versions of the living who lived here with him, finding a half-full jar of dry-roasted cashews on a high kitchen shelf and, on the kitchen television set, a cable rerun of last night's play-off game between the Knicks and the Bulls. He hates the way Michael Jordan's pink tongue rolls around in his mouth as he goes up for a dunk. He has seen Jordan interviewed, he's an intelligent guy, why does he swing his tongue around like an imbecile? The few white players there are on the floor look pathetically naked, their pasty sweat, their fuzzy armpit hair; it seems incredible to Harry that he himself was ever out there in the game, though in those days the shorts were a little longer and the tank-top armholes not quite so big. He has finished off the jar of cashews without noticing and suddenly the basketball—Jordan changing direction in midair not once but twice and sinking an awkward fall-back jumper with Ewing's giant hand square in his face—pains him with its rubbery activity, an extreme of bodily motion his nerves but not his muscles can remember. He needs a Nitrostat from the little bottle in the coat jacket in that shallow closet upstairs. The hauntedness of the downstairs is getting to him. He turns off the kitchen light and holds his breath passing Ma Springer's old breakfront in the darkened dining room, where the wallpaper crawls with the streetlight projections of rain running down the windows.

In the upstairs hall, he hears from Ma's old room, now Judy's, the murmur of a television set, and dares tap the door and push in. The little girl has been put into a sleeveless nightie and, holding her stuffed dolphin, sits propped up on two pillows while her mother sits on the bed beside her. The TV set flickering at the foot of the bed picks out pale patches—the whites of Judy's eyes, her bare shoulders, the dolphin's belly, Pru's long forearms laid across the child's flat chest. He clears his throat and says, "Hey, Judy—sorry if I got a bit mean down there."

With a hushing impatient hand motion she indicates that her grandfather is forgiven and ought to come in and watch with them. In the blue unsteady light, he picks out a child's straight chair and brings it close to the bed and lowers himself to it; he virtually squats. Raindrops glint on the panes in the light from Joseph Street. He looks at Pru's profile for the glint of a tear but her face is composed, her nose sharp, her lips clamped together. They are watching *Unsolved Mysteries*: pale, overweight American faces float into the camera's range, earnestly telling of UFOs seen over sugar-beet fields, above shopping malls, in Navajo reservations, while the plaid furniture and striped wallpaper of their rooms, exposed to the glaring lights the cameras require, have the detailed hard weirdness of diatoms seen under a microscope. Harry is struck by how well, really, these small-town sheriffs and trailer-camp housewives, and even the drifters and dropouts who just happened to be tripping out on a deserted picnic grounds when the giant minds commanding the UFOs decided to land and sample the terrestrial fauna, speak—a nation of performers, of smoothly talking heads, has sprung up under the lights, everybody rehearsed for their thirty seconds of nationwide attention. During the commercials, Judy skips to other channels, to Jacques Cousteau in a diving suit, to Porky Pig in his big-buttoned blue vest (odd, those old cartoon animals all going around with bare bottoms), to a stringy-haired rock singer mouthing his mike in a lathered-up agony like a female porn star approaching a blow job, to a courtroom scene where the judge's shifty eyes in a second show that he is in on a deal, a hummingbird beating its surprisingly flexible wings in slow motion, Angela Lansbury looking shocked, Greer Garson looking gently out of focus in black and white, and back to *Unsolved Mysteries*, now about an infant who disappeared from a New York hospital, making Robert Stack, in his mystical raincoat, extra quizzical. Having been rude before, Rabbit holds his tongue. He feels fragile. The flickering images bear down upon him, relentless as heartbeats. With the mystery of the vanished baby still unsolved, he rises and kisses Judy goodnight, his face gliding past the bigger one next to hers. "Love you, Grandpa," the child mechanically says, forgiving or forgetful.

"Lights are off downstairs," he mutters to Pru.

"I need to go down anyway," she says, softly, both of them fearful of breaking the spell that exists between the child and the television set.

Her face, as his face glided past it on the way to kiss another, exuded an aura, shampooey-powdery, just as the trees outside the house are yielding to the rain a leafy fresh tree-smell. This green wet fragrance is present in his room too, the old sewing room, where the headless dress dummy stands. He changes into the clean pajamas Janice uncharacteristically had the foresight to bring. A blooming cottony weariness has overtaken him, enveloping him like the rain. In the narrow room its sound is more distinct than elsewhere, and complicated, a conversation involving the porch roof, the house gutter, the echoing downspout, the yielding leaves of the maples, the swish of a passing car. Closest to him, periodic spurts of dripping between the storm window and the wooden sash suggest some leakage into the walls and an eventual trouble of rot. Not his problem. Fewer and fewer things are. The window is open a little for air and stray droplets prick the skin of his hands as he stands a moment looking out. Mt. Judge doesn't change much, at least here in the older section, but has dropped away beneath his life as if beneath a rising airplane. His life flowed along this shining asphalt, past these tilted lawns and brick-pillared porches, and left no trace. The town never knew him, the way he had imagined as a child it did, every pebble and milkbox and tulip bed eyelessly watching him pass; with friendliness but at the moment this thought is not frightening. A blurred lit window across the street displays an empty easy chair, a set of brass-headed fireplace tools, a brick mantel supporting a pair of oblivious candlesticks.

Rabbit hurries in bare feet down the hall to the bathroom and back and into bed, before it is nine o'clock. At the hospital by now the last visitors would be long gone, the flurry of bathroom-going and pill-taking that followed their departure subsided, the lights and nurses' voices in the hall turned down. There is no reading lamp in his room, just a paper-shaded overhead he resists switching on. He noticed a stack of old *Consumer's Digests* in the closet but figures the products they evaluated will all be off the market by now. The history book Janice gave him, that he can't get through although he is more than halfway, is back in the Penn Park den. Nor is the streetlight enough to read by. It projects rhomboidal ghosts of the windowpanes, alive with a spasmodic motion as raindrops tremblingly gather and then break downward in sudden streaks. Like the origins of life in one of those educational television shows he watches: molecules collecting and collecting at random and then twitched into life by lightning. Behind his head, past the old brown headboard with its jigsaw scrolls and mushroom-topped posts, his dead mother-in-law's sewing machine waits for her little swollen foot to press its treadle into life, and her short plump fingers to poke a wetted thread through its rusted needle. About as likely that to happen as life just rising up out of molecules. A smothered concussion, distant thunder, sounds in the direction of Brewer, and the treetops stir. Harry's head is up on two pillows so the full feeling in his chest is eased. His heart is giving him no pain, just floats wounded on the sea of ebbing time. Time passes, he doesn't know how much, before the door handle turns and clicks and a slant rod of hall light stabs into the amniotic isolation of the little borrowed room.

Pru's head, with coppery highlights on the top of her hair, pokes in. "You awake?" she asks in almost a whisper. Her voice seems roughened and her face is a milky heart-shaped shadow.

"Yep," Rabbit says. "Just lying here listening to the rain. You get Judy settled?"

"*Finally*," the young woman says, and with the exasperated emphasis enters the room wholly, standing erect. She is wearing that shorty bathrobe of hers, her legs cased in a white shadow descending to her ankles. "She's very upset about Nelson, naturally."

"Naturally. Sorry I blew up at her," he says. "The last thing the poor kid needs." He pushes up on his elbows, feeling himself somehow host, his heart thundering at the strangeness, though after his days in the hospital he should be used to people seeing him in bed.

"I don't know," Pru says. "Maybe it was just what she needed. A little structure. She thinks she has a right to all the TV sets in the world. Mind if I smoke?"

"Not at all."

"I mean, I see the window's a little bit open, but if it—"

"It doesn't," he says. "I like it. Other people's smoke. Almost as good as your own. After thirty years, I still miss it. How come you haven't given it up, with all this health kick?"

"I had," Pru says. Her face in the blue-green flare of her Bic lighter—a little tube as of lipstick—looks flinty, determined, a face stripped to essentials, with a long shadow leaping across her cheek from her nose. The flame goes out. She loudly exhales. Her voice continues in the renewed shadows. "Except for maybe one or two at night to keep myself from eating. But now, this thing with Nelson—why not? What does anything matter?" Her hovering face shows one profile, then the other. "There's no place to sit in here. This is an awful room."

He smells not only her cigarette smoke but her femininity, the faint department-store sweetness that clings to women, in the lotions they use, the shampoo. "It's cozy," he says, and moves his legs so she can sit on the bed.

"I bet you were asleep," Pru says. "I'll only stay for this cigarette. I just need a little adult company." She inhales like a man, deep, so the smoke comes out thin in a double jet from her mouth and nostrils, and keeps coming for several breaths. "I hope putting the kids down with Nelson gone isn't such a nightmare every night. They need so much reassurance."

"I thought he wasn't here a lot of nights."

"This time of night he usually was. The action over at the Laid-Back doesn't begin until around ten. He'd come home from work, eat, be with the kids, and then get restless. I honestly think most nights he didn't plan to go out for a couple hits again, it just came over him and he couldn't help himself." She takes another drag. He hears her intake, like a sigh with several levels, and remembers how it was, to smoke. It was creating out of air an extension of yourself. "With the kids, he was helpful. However much of a shit he was to everybody else, he wasn't a bad father. Isn't. I shouldn't talk about him as if he's dead."

He asks her, "What time is it, anyway?"

"Quarter after nine or so."

Janice would get back at ten-thirty at the earliest. There was plenty of time to see this through. He relaxes back into his pillows. Good he had that nap this afternoon. "Is that how you see it?" he asks. "He was a shit to you?"

"Absolutely. Terrible. Out all night doing God knows what, then this snivelling and begging for forgiveness afterwards. I hated that worse than the chasing; my father was a boozer and a chaser, but then he wouldn't whine to Mom about it, he'd at least let her do the whining. This immature dependence of Nelson's was totally outside my experience."

Her cigarette tip glows. A distant concussion of thunder steps closer. Pru's presence here feels hot in Harry's mind, she is awkwardly big and all sharp angles in the sac of his consciousness. Her talk seems angular and tough, the gritty Akron toughness overlaid with a dismissive vocabulary learned from professional copers. He doesn't like hearing his son called immature. "You knew him for some time out at Kent," he points out, almost hostilely. "You knew what you were taking on."

"Harry, I *did*n't," she says, and the cigarette tip loops through an agitated arc. "I thought he'd grow, I never dreamed how enmeshed he was, with you two. He's still trying to work out what you two did to him, as if you were the only parents in the world who didn't keep wiping their kid's ass until he was thirty. I tell him: Get real, Nelson. Lousy parents are par for the course. My God. Nothing's ideal. Then he gets sore and tells me what a cold fish I am. He means sex. A thing that goes fast with coke is shame; these women that are hooked will do *any*thing. I say to him, You're not going to give me AIDS from one of your coke whores. So he goes out again. It's a vicious circle. It's been going on for years."

"How many years, would you say?"

When she shrugs her shoulders, Ma's old bed shakes. "More than you'd think. That crowd around Slim was always doing pot and uppers—gays don't give a damn, they have all this money only for themselves. Maybe two years ago Nelson became a big enough user on his own to need to steal. At first he just stole from us, money that should have gone into the house and stuff, and then he started stealing from you—the company. I hope you send him to jail, I really do." She has been cupping her hand beneath the cigarette, to catch the ash, and now she looks around for an ashtray and sees none and finally flips the butt toward the window, where it sparks against the screen and sizzles out on the wet sill. Her voice is hoarsening and finding a certain swing, a welling up. "I have no use for him any more. I'm scared to fuck him, I'm scared to be legally associated with him. I've wasted my life. You don't know what it's like. You're a man, you're free, you can do what you want in life, until you're sixty at least you're a buyer. A woman's a seller. She has to be. And she better not haggle too long. I'm thirty-four. I've had my shot, Harry. I wasted it on Nelson. I had my little hand of cards and played them and now I'm folded, I'm through. My husband hates me and I hate him and we don't even have any money to split up! I'm scared—*so* scared. And my kids are scared, too. I'm trash and they're trash and they know it."

"Hey, hey," he has to say. "Come on. Nobody's trash." But even as he says it he knows this is an old-fashioned idea he would have trouble defending. We're all trash, really. Without God to lift us up and make us into angels we're all trash.

Her sobbing is shaking the bed so badly that in his delicate post-op state he feels queasy. To quiet her big body he reaches out and pulls her toward him. As if expecting his touch, she huddles tightly, though a blanket and a sheet are between them, and continues sobbing in a bitter, lower register, her breath hot on his chest, where a pajama button has come undone. His chest. They want to carve it up. "At least you're healthy," he tells her. "Me, all they need to do is nail down the coffin lid. I can't run, I can't fuck, I can't eat anything I like, I know damn well they're going to talk me into a bypass. *You're* scared? You're still young. You've got lots of cards still. Think of how scared I feel."

In his arms Pru says in a voice gone calm again, "People have bypass operations all the time now."

"Yeah, easy for you to say. Like me telling you people are married to shits all the time. Or you telling me people have their kids turn out to be dope-addict embezzlers all the time."

A small laugh. A flash of light outside and, after some seconds, thunder. Both listen. She asks, "Does Janice say you can't fuck?"

"We don't talk about it. We just don't do it much lately. There's been too much else going on."

"What did your doctor say?"

"I forget. My cardiologist's about Nelson's age, we were all too shy to go into it."

Pru sniffs and says, "I hate my life." She seems to him to be unnaturally still, like a rabbit in oncoming headlights.

He lets the hand of the arm around her broad back move up across the bumps of the quilted robe and enter the silken cave at the nape of her neck, to toy with the warm hair there. "I know the feeling," he says, content to toy, aware through the length of his body of a cottony sleepiness waiting to claim him.

She tells him, "You were one of the things I liked about Nelson. Maybe I thought Nelson would grow into somebody like you."

"Maybe he did. You don't get to see what a bastard I can be."

"I can imagine," she says. "But people provoke you."

He goes on, "I see a lot of myself in the kid." The nape of her neck tingles under his fingers, the soft hairs rising to his electricity. "I'm glad you're letting your hair grow long," he says.

"It gets too long." Her hand has come to rest on his bare chest, where the button is unbuttoned. He pictures her hands with their pink-knuckled vulnerable raw look. She is left-handed, he remembers. The oddity of this excites him further. Not waiting too long to think about it, he with his free hand lifts hers from his chest and places it lower, where an erection has surprisingly sprouted from his half-shaved groin. His gesture has the pre-sexual quality of one child sharing with another an interesting discovery—a stone that moves, or a remarkably thick-bodied butterfly. Her eyes widen in the dim face inches from his on the pillow. Tiny points of light are caught in her lashes. He lets his face drift, on the tide of blood risen within him, across those inches to set their mouths together, carefully testing for the angle, while her fingers caress him in a rhythm slower than that of his thudding heart. As the space narrows to nothing he is watchful of his heart, his accomplice in sin. Their kiss tastes to him of the fish she so nicely prepared, its lemon and chives, and of asparagus.

Rain whips at the screen. The leak onto the windowsill accelerates its tapping. A brilliant close flash shocks the air everywhere and less than a second later a heart-stopping crack and splintering of thunder crushes the house from above. As if in overflow of this natural heedlessness, Pru says *"Shit,"* jumps from the bed, slams shut the window, pulls down the shade, tears open her bathrobe and sheds it, and, reaching down, pulls

her nightie up over her head. Her tall pale wide-hipped naked-
ness in the dimmed room is lovely much as those pear trees in
blossom along that block in Brewer last month were lovely, all
his it had seemed, a piece of paradise blundered upon, incredible.

III. MI

B Y MID-JUNE the weeds have taken over: burdock and chicory stand three feet tall along the stony dry shoulders of Route 111, and the struggling little yew hedge meant to dress up the base of the Springer Motors display window has crabgrass and purslane spreading through the rotting bark mulch, which hasn't been renewed for a couple of years. It's one of the things Harry keeps making a mental note to do: call the landscaping service and renew the mulch and replace the dead yews, about a third of them, they look like hell, like missing teeth. Across the four-lane highway, its traffic thicker and faster than ever though the state still holds to the fifty-five-mile-an-hour speed limit, the takeout restaurant called the Chuck Wagon has been replaced by a Pizza Hut, one of the six or so around Brewer now. What do people see in it? All those gummy wedges of dough and cheese, that when you try to eat them pull long strings out in front of your face. But, on Saturdays when in the weekend mood Benny runs over and brings back an order for whoever wants it, Harry allows himself a pepperoni with peppers and onions but no anchovies, please. Like little snails stuck in the mud.

Today is not Saturday, it is Monday, the day after Father's Day. Nobody sent Harry a card. He and Janice have visited Nelson twice, for family therapy at this gloomy big rehab center in North Philly, full of bannisters and bulletin boards and a damp mimeograph smell that reminds him of the basement Sunday school he went to, and both times it was like a quarrel around the kitchen table only with a referee, a lean pale colored woman with fancy spectacles and one of these sweet church-going smiles Harry associates with the better type of Philadelphia black. They go over the old stuff—the baby's death, the mess in the Sixties with Janice moving out and Jill and Skeeter moving in, the crazy way Nelson got himself married to this Kent State secretary an inch taller and a year older than he, a Catholic furthermore, and the kind of crazy way the young couple moved into the old Springer house and the older couple moved out and in fact lives half the year in Florida, all so the kid can run wild with the car agency; Harry explains how from his point of view Nelson's been spoiled rotten by his mother because of her guilt complex and that's why the kid feels entitled to live in never-never land with all these fags and druggies and let his wife and children go around in rags. When he talks, the mocha-colored therapist's smile gets even more pious and patient and then she turns to one of the others, Nelson or Janice or Pru, and asks them how they feel about what they've just heard, as if what he's saying isn't a description of facts but a set of noises to be rolled into some general mishmash. All this "talking through" and "processing" therapists like to do cheapens the world's facts; it reduces decisions that were the best people could do at the time to dream moves, to reflexes that have been "processed" in a million previous cases like so much shredded wheat. He feels anticipated and discounted in advance, whatever he says, and increasingly aggravated, and winds up telling Janice and Pru to go next time without him.

Benny comes over to where Harry stands at the window looking out and asks, "Whajja do for Father's Day?"

Harry is pleased to have an answer. "Nelson's wife brought our grandchildren over in the afternoon and I did a cookout for everybody on the outdoor grill." It sounds ideally American but had its shaky underside. Their grill, for one thing, is a metal sphere that *Consumer Reports* said years ago was a classic but that Harry never has quite the patience for, you must wait until the briquettes are gray and ashy, but he's afraid of waiting too long, so there was a lot of staring at the raw hamburger patties not cooking, with Janice annoying him by offering to cook them in the kitchen, since the children were being eaten alive by mosquitoes. For another, the grandchildren brought him cute grandfather's cards, all right, both by this new artist Gary Larson that everybody else thinks is so funny, but this uniformity—they were even signed by the same red pen, Judy's with quite a girlish flourish to the "y" and Roy's a bunch of aimless but intense pre-literate stabs—suggested a lack of planning, a quick stop at the drugstore on the way over from the Flying Eagle. Pru and

the kids arrived with their hair wet from the pool. She brought
a bowl of salad she had made at home.

"Sounds terrific," Benny says, in his husky small voice.

"Yeah," Harry agrees, explaining, as if his image of Pru with
her wet long hair holding this big wooden bowl of lettuce and
sliced radishes on her hip was visible to them both, "we've
arranged a temporary membership for Nelson's wife over at the
country club, and they'd been swimming over there most of the
day."

"Nice," Benny says. "She seems a nice gal, Teresa. Never
came over here to the lot much, but I hate to see a family like
that having a hard time."

"They're managing," Harry says, and changes the subject.
"D'jou watch any of the Open?" Somebody really should go
out and pick up all the wrappers that blow over from the Pizza
Hut and get caught in the struggling little yew hedge. But he
doesn't like to bend over, and doesn't quite feel he can order
Benny to do it.

"Naa, I can't get turned on by games," the pudgy young sales
representative says, more aggressively than the question re-
quires. "Even baseball, a game or two, I'm bored. You know,
what's in it for me? So what?, if you follow me."

There used to be a stately old maple tree across Route 111 that
the Pizza Hut cut down to expand its red-roofed facility. The
roof is shaped like a hat, with two slants. He ought to be grateful, Harry thinks, to have a lively business along this struggling
little strip. "Well," he tells Benny, not wanting to argue, "with
the Phils in last place you aren't missing much. The worst record
in baseball, and now they've traded away two of their old all-
stars. Bedrosian and Samuel. There's no such thing as loyalty
any more."

Benny continues to explain himself, unnecessarily. "Me, I'd
rather do something my*self* on a nice Sunday, not sit there like
a couch potato, you know what I mean? Get outdoors with my
little girl at the neighbor's pool, or go take the family for a walk
up the mountain, if it's not too hot, you know."

These people who keep saying "you know": as if if they don't
keep nailing your attention to their words it'll drift off. "That's
the way I used to be," Harry tells him, relaxing as the disturbing
image of Pru holding the great bowl on her hip recedes, and
feeling philosophical and pleasurably melancholic the way he
usually does gazing out this big window. Above his head the big
blue paper banner spelling AMAЯATOYOT with the sun shining

through it is beginning to come unstuck from the glass. "Always doing some sport as a kid, and up until recently out on the golf course, flogging the stupid ball."

"You could still do that," Benny says, with that Italian huskiness, faintly breathless. "In fact, I bet your doc advises it. That's what mine advises, exercise. You know, for my weight."

"I probably should do something," Harry agrees, "to keep the circulation going. But, I don't know, golf suddenly seemed stupid. I realized I'd never get any better at it, at this point. And the guys I had my old foursome with have pretty well moved away. It's all these blond beefy yuppie types up at the club, and they all ride carts. They're in such a fucking hurry to get back to making money they ride around in carts, wearing the grass off the course. I used to like to walk and carry. You'd strengthen your legs. That's where the power of a golf swing is, believe it or not. In the legs. I was mostly arms. I knew the right thing to do, I could see it in the other guys and the pros on TV, but I couldn't make myself do it."

The length and inward quality of this speech make Benny uneasy. "You ought to be getting some exercise," he says. "Especially with your history."

Rabbit doesn't know if he means his recent medical history, or his ancient history of high-school athletics. The framed blow-ups of his old basketball photos have come out of Nelson's office and back onto the walls, rose-colored though they are, above the performance board. That was something he did carry through on, unlike the rotting bark mulch. ANGSTROM HITS FOR 42. "When Schmidt quit, that got to me," he tells Benny, even though the guy keeps saying he is no sports nut. Maybe he enjoys bullying him with it, boring him. He wonders how much Benny was in on Nelson's shenanigans, but didn't have the heart or energy to fire him when he came back to run the lot. Get through the day, and the cars sell themselves. Especially the Camry and Corolla. Who could ask for anything more?

"All he had to do," he explains to Benny, "to earn another half million was stay on the roster until August fifteenth. And he began the season like a ball of fire, two home runs the first two games, coming off that rotator-cuff surgery. But, like Schmidt himself said, it got to the point where he'd tell his body to do something and it wouldn't do it. He knew what he had to do and couldn't do it, and he faced the fact and you got to give him credit. In this day and age, he put honor over money."

"Eight errors," Elvira Ollenbach calls in her deep voice from over in her booth, on the wall toward Paraguay, where she has been filling out the bill of sale and NV-1 for an ivory Corolla LE she sold yesterday to one of these broads that come in and ask to deal with her. They have jobs, money, even the young ones that used to be home making babies. If you look, more and more, you see women driving the buses, the delivery trucks. It's getting as bad as Russia; next thing we'll have women coalminers. Maybe we already do. The only difference between the two old superpowers is they sell their trees to Japan in different directions. "An error each in the last two games against the Giants," Elvira inexorably recites. "And hitting .203, just two hits his last forty-one at bats." Her head is full, between her pretty little jug ears, with figures. Her father was a sports addict, she has explained, and to communicate with him she followed all this stuff and now can't break the habit.

"Yeah," Rabbit says, he feels weakly, taking some steps toward her desk. "But still, it took a lot of style. Just a week ago, did you see, there was this interview in some Philadelphia paper where he said how great he felt and he was only in a slump like any overeager kid? Then he was man enough to change his mind. When all he had to do was hang around to collect a million and a half total. I like the way he went out," Rabbit says, "quick, and on his own nickel."

Elvira, not looking up from her paperwork, her pendulous gold earrings bobbing as she writes, says, "They would have cut him by August, the way he was going. He spared himself the humiliation."

"Exactly," Harry says, still weakly, torn between a desire to strike an alliance with this female and an itch to conquer her, to put her in her place. Not that she and Benny have been difficult to deal with. Docile, rather, as if anxious that they not be swept out of the lot along with Lyle and Nelson. It was easiest for Harry to accept them as innocents and not rock the agency worse than it was being rocked. Both of them have connections in Brewer and move Toyotas, and if the conversations during idle time—"down" time, young people called it now—weren't as satisfying, as clarifying, as those he used to have with Charlie Stavros, perhaps the times were less easy to clarify. Reagan left everybody in a daze, and now the Communists were acting confused too. "How about those elections in Poland?" he says. "Voting the Party out—who ever would have thought we'd live to see the day? And Gorby telling all the world the contractors who put up those sand castles in Armenia were crooks? And in

China, what's amazing isn't the crackdown but that the kids were allowed to run the show for a month and nobody knew what to do about it! It's like nobody's in charge of the other side any more. I miss it," he says. "The cold war. It gave you a reason to get up in the morning."

He says these things to be provocative, to get a rise out of Benny or Elvira, but his words drift away like the speech of old people on the porches when he was a boy. Not for the first time since returning to the lot does he feel he is not really there, but is a ghost being humored. His words are just noises. In Nelson's old office, and the office next to it where Mildred used to be, the accountant Janice has hired on Charlie's advice is going through the books, a task so extensive he has brought a full-time assistant. These two youngish men, who dress in gray suits of which they hang up the jackets when arriving, putting them on again when they depart, feel like the real management of the firm.

"Elvira," he says, always enjoying pronouncing her name, "did you see this morning in the paper where four men were charged with a felony for chaining themselves to a car in front of an abortion clinic? And with contributing to the delinquency of a minor since they had a seventeen-year-old boy along?" He knows where she stands: pro-choice. All these independent bimbos are. He takes a kind of pro-life tilt to gall her but his heart isn't really in it and she knows it. She leaves her desk and comes striding toward him, thrillingly thin, holding the completed NV-1s, her wide-jawed little head balanced with its pulled-back shiny-brown hair on her slender neck, her dangling big earrings shaped like Brazil nuts. He retreats a step and the three of them stand together at the window, Harry between them and a head taller.

"Wouldn't you *know*," she says, "it would be all men. Why do they *care* so much? Why are they so passionate about what some women they don't even know do with their bodies?"

"They think it's murder," Harry says. "They think the fetus is a little separate person from the morning after on."

His way of putting it feeds into her snort of disgust. "*Tccha*, they don't know what they think," she says. "If men could get knocked up this wouldn't even be a debate. Would it, Benny?"

She is bringing him in to dilute whatever Harry is trying to do to her with this provocative topic. Benny says carefully, huskily, "My church says abortion is a sin."

"And you believe them, until you want to do it, right? Tell

us about you and Maria—you use birth control? Seventy per cent of young married Catholics do, you know that?''

A strange aspect of his encounter with Pru, Harry remembers, had been the condom she had produced, out of the pocket of her shorty bathrobe. Either she always kept one there or had foreseen fucking him before coming into the room. He wasn't used to them, not since the Army, but went along with it without a protest, it was her show. The thing had been a squeeze, he had been afraid he couldn't keep up his own pressure against it, and his pubic hair, where he had some left after the angioplasty, the way they shaved him, got caught at the base in the unrolling, a little practical fussing there, she helped in the dim light, it maybe had made him slower to come, not a bad thing, as she came twice, under him once and then astraddle, rain whipping at the window behind the drawn shade, her hips so big and broad in his hands he didn't feel fat himself, her tits atwitter as she jiggled in pursuit of the second orgasm, he near to fainting with worry over joggling his defective heart. A certain matter-of-fact shamelessness about Pru reduced a bit the poetry of his first sight of her naked and pale like that street of blossoming trees. She did it all but was blunt about it and faintly wooden, as if the dressmaker's dummy in the dark behind him had grown limbs and a head with swinging carrot-colored hair. To keep his prick up he kept telling himself, *This is the first time I've ever fucked a left-handed woman.*

Benny is blushing. He's not used to talking this way with a woman. ''Maybe so,'' he admits. ''If it's not a mortal sin, you don't have to confess it unless you want to.''

''That saves the priest a lot of embarrassment,'' Elvira tells him. ''Suppose no matter what you two use Maria kept getting knocked up, what would you do? You don't want that precious little girl of yours to feel crowded, you can give her the best the way things are. What's more important, quality of life for the family you already have, or a little knot of protein the size of a termite?''

Benny has a kind of squeaking girlish voice that excitement can bring out. ''Lay *off*, Ellie. Don't make me think about it. You're offending my religion. I wouldn't mind a couple more kids, what the hell. I'm young.''

Harry tries to help him out. ''Who's to say what's the quality of life?'' he asks Elvira. ''Maybe the extra kid is the one that's going to invent the phonograph.''

"Not out of the ghetto he isn't. He's the kid that mugs you for crack money sixteen years later."

"You don't have to get racist about it," Harry says, having been mugged in a sense by a white kid, his own son.

"It's the opposite of racist, it's realistic," Elvira tells him. "It's the poor black teenage mother whose right to abortion these crazy fundamentalist jerks are trying to take away."

"Yeah," he responds, "it's the poor black teenage mother who wants to have the baby, because she never had a doll to play with and she loves the idea of sticking the taxpayer with another welfare bill. Up yours, Whitey—that's what the birth statistics are saying."

"Now who's sounding racist?"

"Realistic, you mean."

Relaxed in the aftermath of love, and grateful to be still alive, he had asked Pru how queer she thought Nelson was, with all this palling around with Lyle and Slim. Her breath, in the watery light from the window, was made visible by fine jets of inhaled cigarette smoke as she thoughtfully answered, only a little taken aback by the question, "No, Nelson likes girls. He's a mamma's boy but he takes after you that way. They just look bigger to him than to you." Coming into the room less than an hour later, Janice had sniffed the cigarette smoke but he had pretended to be too sleepy to discuss it. Pru took the second butt away with the condom but the first one, drowned over on the windowsill, was next morning so saturated and flattened it could have been there for ages, a historical relic of Nelson and Melanie. Rabbit sighs and says, "You're right, Elvira. People should have a choice. Even if they make bad ones." From the room he was in with Pru his mind moves to the one he had shared with Ruth, one flight up on Summer Street, and the last time he saw it: she told him she was pregnant and called him Mr. Death and he begged her to have the baby. *Have it, have it you say: how? Will you marry me?* She mocked him, but pleaded too, and in the end, yes, to be realistic, probably did have the abortion. *If you can't work it out, I'm dead to you; I'm dead to you and this baby of yours is dead too.* The nurse with the round face and sweet disposition in St. Joseph's had nothing to do with him, just like Ruth told him the last time he saw her, in her farmhouse ten years ago. He had had one daughter and she died; God didn't trust him with another. He says aloud, "Schmidt did what Rose is too dumb to: quit, when you've had it. Take your medicine, don't prolong the agony with all these lawyers."

Benny and Elvira look at him, alarmed by how his mind has wandered. But he enjoys his sensation, of internal roaming. When he first came to the lot as Chief Sales Rep, after Fred Springer had died, he was afraid he couldn't fill the space. But now as an older man, with his head so full of memories, he fills it without even trying.

Through the plate glass he sees a couple in their thirties, maybe early forties, everybody looks young to him now, out on the lot among the cars, stooping to peek into the interiors and at the factory sticker on the windows. The woman is plump and white and in a halter top showing her lardy arms, and the man darker, much darker—Hispanics come in all these shades—and skinny, in a grape-colored tank top cut off at the midriff. Their ducking heads move cautiously, as if afraid of an Indian ambush out in the prairie of glittering car roofs, a pioneer couple in their way, at least in this part of the world where the races don't much mix.

Benny asks Elvira, "You want 'em, or do I?"

She says, "You do. If the woman needs a little extra, bring her in and I'll chat her up. But don't aim it all at her, just because she's white. They're both going to be miffed if you snub the man."

"Whaddeya think I am, a bigot?" Benny says mock-comically, but his demeanor is sad and determined as he walks out of the air-conditioning into the June humidity and heat.

"You shouldn't ride him about his religion," Harry tells Elvira.

"I don't. I just think that damn Pope he's got ought to be put in jail for what he does to women."

Peggy Fosnacht, Rabbit remembers, before she had a breast cut off and then upped and died, had been wild with anger toward the Pope. Anger is what gives you cancer, he has read somewhere. If you've been around long enough, he reflects, you've heard it all, the news and the commentary both, churned like the garbage in a Disposall that doesn't drain, the media every night trying to whip you up into a frenzy so you'll run out and buy all the depressing stuff they advertise, laxatives and denture adhesive cream, Fixodent and Sominex and Tylenol and hemorrhoid medicine and mouthwash against morning mouth. Why does the evening news assume the people who watch it are in such decrepit plugged-up shape? It's enough to make you switch the channel. The commercials revolt him, all that friendly jawing among these folksy crackerbarrel types about rectal itching and burning, and the one of the young/old beautiful woman in soft focus stretching so luxuriously in her white bathrobe because she's just taken a shit and all those people in the Ex-Lax ad saying "Good morning" one after the other so you can't help picturing the world filling up with our smiling American excrement, we'll have to pay poor third-world countries to dump it pretty soon, like toxic waste. "Why pick on the Pope?" Harry asks. "Bush is just as bad, anti-choice."

"Yes, but he'll change when the women start voting Republicans out. There's no way to vote the Pope out."

"Do you ever get the feeling," he asks her, "now that Bush is in, that we're kind of on the sidelines, that we're sort of like a big Canada, and what we do doesn't much matter to anybody else? Maybe that's the way it ought to be. It's a kind of relief, I guess, not to be the big cheese."

Elvira has decided to be amused. She fiddles with one of her Brazil-nut earrings and looks up at him slantwise. "You matter to everybody, Harry, if that's what you're hinting at."

This is the most daughterly thing she has ever said to him. He feels himself blush. "I wasn't thinking of me, I was thinking of the country. You know who I blame? The old Ayatollah, for calling us the Great Satan. It's like he put the evil eye on us and we shrank. Seriously. He really stuck it to us, somehow."

"Don't live in a dream world, Harry. We still need you down here."

She goes out to the lot, where a quartet of female teenagers have showed up, all in jackets of stone-washed denim. Who knows, even teenagers these days have money enough for a Toyota. Maybe it's an all-girl rock band, shopping for a van to tour in. Harry wanders in to the office where the visiting accountants are nesting, day after day, in piles of paper. The one in charge has a rubbery tired face with dark rings under his eyes, and the assistant seems to be a kind of moron, a simpleton at speaking anyway, with not enough back to his head. As if to make up for any deficiency he always wears a clean white shirt with a tight necktie, pinned to his chest with a tieclip.

"Ah," the one in charge says, "just the guy we need. Does the name Angus Barfield mean anything to you?" The rings under his eyes are so deep and deeply bruised they go all the way around his sockets; he looks like a raccoon. Though his face shows a lot of wear, his hair is black as shoe polish, and lies as flat on his head as if painted in place. These accountants have to be tidy, all those numbers they write down, thousands and millions, and never a five that could be confused with a three or a seven with a one. As he cocks a ringed eye at Harry waiting for an answer, his rubbery mouth slides around in a restless wise-guy motion.

"No," Harry says, "and yet, wait. There's a faint bell. Barfield."

"A good guy for you to know," the accountant says, with a sly grimace and twist of his lips. "From December to April, he was buying a Toyota a month." He checks a paper under his shirtsleeved forearm. He has very long black hairs on his wrists. "A Corolla four-door, a Tercel five-speed hatchback, a Camry wagon, a deluxe two-passenger 4-Runner, and in April he really went fancy and took on a Supra Turbo with a sport roof, to the tune of twenty-five seven. Totals up to just under seventy-five K. All in the same name and the same address on Willow Street."

"Where's Willow?"

"That's one of the side streets up above Locust, you know. The area's gotten kind of trendy."

"Locust," Harry repeats, struggling to recall. He has heard the odd name "Angus" before, from Nelson's lips. Going off to a party in north Brewer.

"Single white male. Excellent credit ratings. Not much of a haggler, paid list price every time. The only trouble with him as customer," the accountant says, "is according to city records he's been dead for six months. Died before Christmas." He purses his lips into a little bunch under one nostril and lifts his eyebrows so high his nostrils dilate in sympathy.

"I got it," Harry says, with a jarring pounce of his heart. "That's Slim. Angus Barfield was the real name of a guy everybody called Slim. He was a, a gay I guess, about my son's age. Had a good job in downtown Brewer—administered one of those HUD job-training programs for high-school dropouts. He was a trained psychologist, I think Nelson once told me."

The moronic assistant, who has been listening with the staring effort of a head that can only hold one thing at a time, giggles: the humor of insanity spills over onto psychologists. The other twists up the lower part of his face in a new way, as if demonstrating knots. "Bank loan officers love government employees," he says. "They're sure and steady, see?"

Since the man seems to expect it, Harry nods, and the accountant dramatically slaps the tidy chaos of papers spread out on the desk. "December to April, Brewer Trust extended five car loans to this Angus Barfield, made over to Springer Motors.''

"How could they, to the same guy? Common sense—''

"Since computers, my friend, common sense has gone out the window. It's joined your aunt Matilda's ostrich-feather hat. The auto-loan department of a bank is just tiddledywinks; the computer checked his credit and liked it and the loan was approved. The checks were cashed but never showed up in the company credits. We think your pal Lyle opened a dummy somewhere.'' The man stabs a stack of bank statements with a finger; it has black hairs between the knuckles and bends back so far Rabbit winces and looks away. This rubbery guy is one of those born teachers Rabbit has instinctively avoided all his life. "Let me put it like this. A computer is like a Frenchman. It seems real smart until you know the language. Once you know the language, you realize it's dumb as hell. Quick, sure. But quick ain't the same as smart.''

"But," Harry gropes to say, "but for Lyle and Nelson, Lyle especially, to use poor Slim's name in a scam like this when he had just died, when he was just about buried—would they have actually been so hardhearted?''

The accountant slumps a little under the weight of such naïveté. "These were hungry boys. The dead have no feelings, that I've heard about. The guy's credit hadn't been pulled from the computer, and between these loans from Brewer Trust and the diddled inventory with Mid-Atlantic Toyota, some two hundred grand was skimmed from this operation, that we can verify so far. That's a lot of Toll House cookies.''

The assistant giggles again. Rabbit, hearing the sum, goes cold with the premonition that this debt will swallow him. Here amid all these papers arrayed on the desk where he himself used to work, keeping a roll of Life Savers in the lefthand middle drawer, a fatal hole is being hatched. He taps his jacket pocket for the reassuring lump of the Nitrostat bottle. He'll take one as soon as he gets away. The night he and Pru fucked, both of them weary and half crazy with their fates, the old bed creaking beneath them had seemed another kind of nest, an interwoven residue of family fortunes, Ma Springer's musty old-lady scent released from the mattress by this sudden bouncing where for years she had slept alone, an essence of old mothballed blankets stored in attic cedar chests among plush bound family albums and broken cane-seated rockers and veiled hats in round hatboxes, an essence arising not only from the abused bed but from the old sewing apparatus stored here and Fred's forgotten neckties in the closet and the dust balls beneath the venerable fourposter. All those family traces descended to this, this coupling by thunder and lightning. It was now as if it had never been. He and Pru are severely polite with each other, and Janice, ever more the working girl, has ceased to create many occasions when the households mingle. The Father's Day cookout was an exception, and the children were tired and cranky and bitten by the time the grilled hamburgers were finally ready to be consumed.

Harry laughs, as idiotically as the assistant accountant. "Poor Slim," he says, trying to harmonize with the head accountant's slanginess. "Some pal Lyle turned out to be, buying him all those wheels he didn't need."

On July Fourth, for Judy's sake, he marches in a Mt. Judge parade. Her Girl Scout troop is in it and the troop leader's husband, Clarence Eifert, is on the organizing committee. They needed a man tall enough to be Uncle Sam and Judy told Mrs. Eifert that her grandfather was wonderfully tall. Actually, six three isn't tall by today's standards, you'd be a dwarf in the NBA at that height, but several members of the committee, a generation older than Mr. Eifert, remembered Rabbit Angstrom from his high-school glory days and became enthusiastic, even though Harry lives now in Penn Park on the other side of Brewer. He was a Mt. Judge boy and something of a hero once and though he has become more corpulent than our national symbol should be has the right fair skin and pale blue eyes and a good soldierly bearing. He served during Korea. He did his bit.

The bell-bottom trousers with their broad red stripes have to be left unbuttoned at the stomach, but since they are held up by tricolor suspenders, and a pale-blue vest patterned in stars comes down over the belt area, it doesn't much matter. Harry and Janice fuss a good deal at the costume in the week before the Fourth. They actually go buy a formal shirt with French cuffs and a wing collar to go with the floppy red cravat, and decide that somehow his suede Hush Puppies go better with the red-striped trousers, look more like boots, than the formal black shoes he keeps for weddings and funerals. The swallowtail coat, a wool darker blue than the vest, with three unbuttonable brass buttons on both sides, fits well enough, but the fuzzy flared top hat with its hatband of big silver stars perches on his high head unsteadily, a touch tight with the white nylon wig, so it feels like it might totter and fall off. He never did like hats.

Janice bites the tip of her tongue thoughtfully. "Do you need the wig? Your hair's so pale anyway."

"But it's cut too short for Uncle Sam. I would have let it grow out if I'd known."

"Well," she says, "why wouldn't Uncle Sam have a modern haircut? He's not dead, is he?"

He tests the hat without the wig and says, "It does feel better, actually."

"And frankly, Harry, the wig on you is somehow alarming. It makes you look like a very big red-faced woman."

"Look, I'm doing this for our granddaughter, there's no need to get insulting."

"It's not insulting, it's interesting. I never saw your feminine side before. I bet you would have made a nicer woman than either your mother or Mim. They should have been men, both of them."

Mom was mean to Janice from the moment he first brought her home from Kroll's, and Mim once stole Charlie Stavros from her, or so Janice interpreted it. "I'm getting hot and itchy in this outfit," Harry says. "Let's try the goatee."

The goatee in place, Janice says, "Oh, *yes*. It slims your face right down. I wonder why you never grew a beard." There is this subtle past tense that keeps creeping into her remarks about him. "Mr. Lister is growing a beard now, and it makes him look a lot less doleful. He has these sagging jowls."

"I don't want to hear about that creep." He adds, "When I talk, the stickum doesn't feel like enough."

"It must be, it's gone through a lot of other parades."

"That's its problem, you dope. Is there any way to renew the stickum?"

"Just don't move your chin too much. I could call up Doris Eberhardt; when she was married to Kaufmann they were big into amateur theatricals."

"Don't get that pushy bitch on my case. Maybe somebody at the parade will have some spare stickum."

But the mustering of the parade is a confused and scattered business, held on the grounds of the old Mt. Judge High School, now the junior high school and slated to be torn down because of the asbestos in it everywhere and the insurance rates on the wooden floors. When Harry went there, they all just breathed the asbestos and took their chances on the floors catching fire.

There are marching bands and antique cars and 4-H floats and veterans in their old uniforms all milling around on the asphalt of the parking lot and the brown grass of the baseball outfield, with the only organizing principle provided by men and women in green T-shirts stencilled MT. JUDGE INDEPENDENCE DAY COMMITTEE and those plastic truck-driver caps with a bill in front and a panel of mesh at the back. Looking to be told where to go, Rabbit wanders in this area where long ago he had roamed with wet-combed duck-tailed hair and a corduroy shirt tight across his back, the sleeves folded back and, out of basketball season, a cigarette pack squaring the shirt pocket. He expects to come across his old girlfriend, Mary Ann, as she had been then, in saddle shoes and white socks and a short pleated cheerleader's skirt, her calves straight and smooth and round-muscled between the skirt and the socks, and her face, with the dimple in one cheek and the touch of acne on her forehead, springing into joy at the sight of him. Instead, strange people with puzzled Eighties faces keep asking directions, because he is dressed as Uncle Sam and should know. He has to keep telling them he doesn't know anything.

The old high school, built in the Twenties of orange brick, had a tall windowless wall at the back, across from a board-and-tarpaper equipment shed long since torn down, and this black and gravelly area has profound associations for him, a power in its mute bricks and secluding space, for it was here after school and until twilight called you home that the more questing and footloose of the town's children tended to gather, girls as well as boys, hanging out, shooting baskets at the hoop attached to the blank brickwork (flat on the wall like those in the gym in Oriole), necking against the torn-tarpaper boards of the equipment shed, talking (the girls held by the boys' braced arms as in a row of soft cages), teasing, passing secrets, feeling their way, avoiding going home, so that the gritty leftover space here behind the school was charged with a solemn electricity, the questing energy of adolescents. Now in this area, repaved and cleaned up, the shed and backboards gone, Rabbit comes upon Judy's Girl Scout troop, some of them in uniform and some posed in costume on a flatbed truck, a float illustrating Liberty, the tallest and prettiest girl in a white bedsheet and spiked crown holding a big bronze book and gilded torch, and others grouped around her cardboard pedestal with their faces painted red and brown and black and yellow to represent the races of mankind, the faces painted because there aren't any Indian or Negro or

Asian little girls in Mt. Judge, at least any that have joined the Girl Scouts.

Judy is one of those in badged and braided khaki uniform around the truck, and she is so amazed to see her grandfather in his towering costume that she takes his hand, as if to tie him to the earth, to reality. He has difficulty bending his head to see her, for fear that his top hat might fall off. As if addressing the distant backstop of the baseball diamond, he asks her, "How does the goatee look? The little beard, Judy."

"Fine, Grandpa. You scared me at first. I didn't know who you were."

"It feels to me like it might fall off any second."

"It doesn't look that way. I love the big stripy pants. Doesn't the vest squeeze your tummy?"

"That's the least of my problems. Judy, listen. Think you could do me a favor? It just occurred to me, they make a Scotch tape now that's sticky on both sides. If I gave you a couple dollars think you could run over to the little store across Central and get me some?" Always, under names and managements that shift with the years, there has been a store across from the school to sell its students bubble gum and candy and cap-guns and caps and tablets and cigarettes and skin magazines and whatever else young people thought they had to have. With difficulty, keeping his head stiffly upright, he digs through the layers of his costume to his wallet in a pouchy side pocket of the striped pants and, holding it up to his face, digs out two one-dollar bills. Just in case, he adds another. Things these days always cost more than he expects.

"Suppose it's not open because of the holiday!"

"It'll be open. It was always open."

"Suppose the parade starts; I got to be on the truck!"

"No it won't, the parade can't start without me. Come on, Judy. Think of all I've done for you. Think of how I saved you on the boat that time. Who got me into this damn parade in the first place? *You* did!"

He doesn't dare look down, lest his hat come off, but he can hear from her voice she is near tears. Her hair makes a reddish blur in the bottom of his vision. "O.K., I'll try, but . . ."

"Remember," he says, and as his chin stiffens in admonishment he feels his goatee loosen, "sticky on *both* sides. Scotch makes it. Run, honey!" His heart is racing; he gropes through his clothes to make sure he remembered to bring the little bottle of nitroglycerin. He finds its life-giving nugget deep in the

pouchy pocket. When he brings his fingers to his face, to tamp
down the goatee, he sees they are trembling. If his goatee doesn't
stick, he won't be Uncle Sam, and the entire parade will floun-
der; it will jam up here on the school grounds forever. He walks
around with little steps, ignoring everybody, trying to quiet his
heart. This is aggravating.

When Judy at last comes back, panting, she tells him, "They
were *dumb*. They mostly sell only food now. Junky things like
Cheez Doodles. The only Scotch tape they have is sticky on one
side only. I got some anyway. Was that O.K.?"

Drum rolls sound on the parking lot, scattered at first, a few
kids impatiently clowning around, and then in unison, gathering
mass, an implacable momentum. The motors of antique cars
and trucks bearing floats are starting up, filling the holiday air
with blue exhaust. "O.K.," Harry says, unable to look down
at his granddaughter lest his hat fall off, pocketing the tape and
the change from three dollars, pressed upon him from below.
Estranged from his costumed body, he feels on stilts, his feet
impossibly small.

"I'm sorry, Grandpa. I did the best I could." Judy's little
light voice, out of sight beneath him, wobbles and crackles with
tears, like water sloshing in sun.

"You did great," he lies.

A frantic stocky woman in a green committee T-shirt and
truck-driver hat comes and hustles him away, to the head of the
parade, past floats and drum-and-bugle corps, Model A Fords
and civic leaders in neckties and a white limousine. A Mt. Judge
patrol car with its blue light twirling and its siren silent will be
the spearhead, then Harry at a distance. As if he doesn't know
the route: as a child he used to participate in parades, in the
crowd of town kids riding bicycles with red, white, and blue
crepe paper threaded through the spokes. Down Central to Market a block short of 422, through the heart of the little slanting
diagonal downtown, then left and uphill along Potter Avenue,
through blocks of brick semi-detached houses up on their terraced lawns behind the retaining walls, then downhill past Kegerise Alley as they used to call it, Kegerise Street it is now, with
its small former hosiery factories and machine shops renamed
Lynnex and Data Development and Business Logistical Sys-
tems, up to Jackson, the high end, a block from his old house,
and on down to Joseph and past the big Baptist church, and
sharp right on Myrtle past the post office and the gaunt old
Oddfellows' Hall to end at the reviewing stand set up in front

of the Borough Hall, in the little park that was full in the Sixties of kids smoking pot and playing guitars but now on a normal day holds just a few old retired persons and homeless drifters with million-dollar tans. The green-chested woman, along with a marshal with a big cardboard badge, a squinty stooped jeweller called Himmelreich—Rabbit was in school a few grades behind his father, whom everybody called a pansy—makes sure he delays enough to let a distance build between him and the lead car, so Uncle Sam doesn't look too associated with the police. Immediately next in the parade is the white limousine carrying the Mt. Judge burgess and what borough councilmen weren't off in the Poconos or at the Jersey Shore. From further behind come the sounds of the drum-and-bugle corps and some bagpipers hired from Chester County and the scratchy pop tunes playing on the floats to help illustrate Liberty and the Spirit of 1776 and ONE WORLD/UN MUNDO and Head, Heart, Hands, and Health, and at the tail end a local rock singer doing ecstatic imitations of Presley and Orbison and Lennon while a megawatt electric fan loudly blows on all the amplifying equipment stacked on his flatbed truck. But up front, at the head of the parade, it is oddly silent, hushed, and what a precarious weird feeling it is for Harry at last to put his suede-booted feet on the yellow double line of the town's main street and start walking. He feels giddy, ridiculous, enormous. Behind him there is the white limousine purring along in low gear, so he cannot stop walking, and far ahead, so far ahead it twinkles out of sight around corners and bends in the route, the police car; but immediately ahead there is nothing but the eerie emptiness of normally busy Central Street under a dazed July sky blue above the telephone wires. He is the traffic, his solitary upright body. The stilled street has its lunar details, its pockmarks, its scars, its ancient metal lids. The tremor in his heart and hands becomes an exalted sacrificial feeling as he takes those few steps into the asphalt void, rimmed at this end of the route with only a few spectators, a few bare bodies in shorts and sneakers and tinted shirts along the curb.

They call to him. They wave ironically, calling "Yaaaay" at the idea of Uncle Sam, this walking flag, this incorrigible taxer and frisky international mischief-maker. He has nothing to do but wave back, carefully nodding so as not to spill his hat or shake loose his goatee. The crowd as it thickens calls out more and more his name, "Harry," or "Rabbit"—"Hey, Rabbit! Hey, hotshot!" They remember him. He hasn't heard his old nickname so often in many years; nobody in Florida uses it, and his grandchildren would be puzzled to hear it. But suddenly from these curbstones there it is again, alive, affectionate. This crowd seems a strung-out recycled version of the crowd that used to jam the old auditorium-gym Tuesday and Friday nights, basketball nights, in the dead of the winter, making their own summer heat with their bodies, so that out on the floor sweat kept burning your eyes and trickling down from under your hair, behind your ears, diagonally sliding down your neck. Now the sweat builds under his wool swallowtail coat, on his back and his belly, which indeed is squeezed as Judy said, and under his hat even without the wig, thank God Janice got him out of that, she isn't always a dumb mutt.

His sweat, as with increasing ease and eagerness he waves at the crowd that clusters at the corners and in the shade of the Norway maples and on the sandstone retaining walls and terraced lawns up into the cool shadow of the porches, loosens his goatee, undermines the adhesive. He feels one side of it softly separate from his chin and without breaking stride—Uncle Sam has a bent-kneed, cranky stride not quite Harry's loping own— he digs out the Scotch tape from the pouchy pocket and tears off an inch, with the tab of red plaid paper. It wants to stick to his fingers; after several increasingly angry flicks it flutters away onto the street. Then he pulls off another piece, which he presses onto his own face and the detaching edge of synthetic white beard; the tape holds, though it must make a rectangular gleam on his face. The spectators who see him improvise this repair cheer. He takes to doffing his tall heavy hat, with a cautious bow to either side, and this stirs more applause and friendly calling.

The crowd he sees from behind his wave, his smile, his adhesive gleam amazes him. The people of Mt. Judge are dressed for summer, with a bareness that since Harry's childhood has crept up from children into the old. White-haired women sit in their aluminum lawn chairs down by the curb dressed like fat babies in checks and frills, their shapeless veined legs cheerfully protruding. Middle-aged men have squeezed their keglike thighs into bicycle shorts meant for boys. Young mothers have come from their back-yard aboveground swimming pools in bikinis and high-sided twists of spandex that leave half their buttocks and breasts exposed. On their cocked hips they hold heat-flushed babies in nothing but diapers and rubber pants. There seem so many young—babies, tots, a bubbling up of generation on generation since the town brought him forth. Then it was full of the old: as he walked to school of a morning, severe and scolding women would come out of their houses shaking brooms and wearing thick dark stockings and housedresses with buttons all down the front. Now a cheerful innocent froth of flesh lines Jackson Road. Bare knees are bunched like grapes, and barrels of naked brown shoulders hulk in the dappled curbside shade. There are American flags on gilded sticks, and balloons, balloons in all colors, even metallic balloons shaped like hearts and pillows, held in hands and tied to bushes, to the handles of strollers containing yet more babies. A spirit of indulgence, a conspiring to be amused, surrounds and upholds his parade as he leads it down the stunning emptiness at the center of the familiar slanting streets.

Harry puts some Scotch tape on the other side of his goatee and out of the same pocket fishes his pill vial and pops a Nitrostat. The uphill section of the route tested him, and now turning downhill jars his heels and knees. When he draws too close to the cop car up ahead, carbon monoxide washes into his lungs. Mingled music from behind pushes him on: the gaps of "American Patrol" are filled with strains of "Yesterday." He concentrates on the painted yellow line, besmirched here and there by skid marks, dotted for stretches where passing is permitted by mostly double like the inflexible old trolley tracks, long buried or torn up for scrap. Cameras click at him. Voices call his several names. They know him, but he sees no face he knows, not one, not even Pru's wry red-haired heart-shape or Roy's black-eyed stare or Janice's brown little stubborn nut of a face. They said they would be at the corner of Joseph and Myrtle, but here near the Borough Hall the crowd is thickest, the summer-cooked bodies four and five deep, and his loved ones have been swallowed up.

The whole town he knew has been swallowed up, by the decades, but another has taken its place, younger, more naked, less fearful, better. And it still loves him, as it did when he would score forty-two points for them in a single home game. He is a legend, a walking cloud. Inside him a droplet of explosive has opened his veins like flower petals uncurling in the sun. His eyes are burning with sweat or something allergic, his head aches under the pressure cooker of the tall top hat. The greenhouse effect, he thinks. The hole in the ozone. When the ice in Antarctica goes, we'll all be drowned. Scanning the human melt for the glint of a familiar face, Harry sees instead a beer can being brazenly passed back and forth, the flash of a myopic

child's earnest spectacles, a silver hoop earring in the lobe of a
Hispanic-looking girl. Along the march he noticed a few black
faces in the crowd, as cheerful and upholding as the rest, and
some Orientals—an adopted Vietnamese orphan, a chunky Filipino wife. From far back in the still-unwinding parade the bagpipers keen a Highland killing song and the rock impersonator
whimpers ". . . imagine all the *people*" and, closer to the front,
on a scratchy tape through crackling speakers, Kate Smith belts
out, dead as she is, dragged into the grave by sheer gangrenous
weight, "God Bless America"—". . . to the *oceans, white with
foam.*" Harry's eyes burn and the impression giddily—as if he
has been lifted up to survey all human history—grows upon him,
making his heart thump worse and worse, that all in all this is
the happiest fucking country the world has ever seen.

It was the sort of foolish revelation he might have once shared
with Thelma, in the soft-speaking shamelessness that follows
making love. Thelma was suddenly dead. Dead of kidney failure, thrombocytopenia, and endocarditis, toward the end of July,
as the cool dawn of another hot blue-gray day broke on the
ornamental roof-level brickwork opposite St. Joseph's Hospital
in Brewer. Poor Thelma, her body had just been plain worn out
by her long struggle. Ronnie tried to keep her at home to the
end, but that last week she was too much to handle. Halluci-
nations, raving, sarcastic anger. Quite a lot of anger, at Ron of
all people, who had been so devoted a husband, after being such
a scapegrace in his young unmarried days. She was only fifty-
five—a year younger than Harry, two years older than Janice.
She died the same week the DC-10 bringing people from Denver
to Philadelphia by way of Chicago crashed in Sioux City, Iowa,
trying to land at two hundred miles an hour, running on no
controls but the thrust of the two remaining engines, cartwheel-
ing on the runway, breaking up in a giant fireball, and yet well
over a hundred surviving, some of them dangling upside down
from the seat belts in a section of fuselage, some of them walking away and getting lost in the cornfields next to the runway. It
seemed to Rabbit the first piece of news that summer that wasn't
a twentieth anniversary of something—of Woodstock, the Manson murders, Chappaquidick, the moon landing. The TV news
has been full of resurrected footage.

The funeral service is in a sort of no-brand-name church about
a mile beyond Arrowdale. Looking for it, Harry and Janice got
lost and wound up at the mall in Maiden Springs, where a six-

theatre cineplex advertised on its crammed display board HONEY
I SHRUNK BATMAN GHOSTBUST II KARATE KID III DEAD POETS
GREAT BALLS. The lazy girl in the booth didn't know where the
church might be, nor did the pimply usher inside, in the big
empty scarlet lobby smelling of buttered popcorn and melting
M&Ms. Harry was angry with himself: all those times he
sneaked out to Arrowdale to visit Thelma, now he can't find her
goddamn church. When finally, hot, embarrassed, and furious
at each other's incompetence, the Angstroms arrive, the church
is just a plain raw building, a warehouse with windows and a
stump of an anodized aluminum steeple, set in a treeless acre
of red soil sown skimpily with grass and crisscrossed by car
ruts. Inside, the walls are cinder-block, and the light through
the tall clear windows bald and merciless. Folding chairs do
instead of pews, and childish felt banners hang from the metal
beams overhead, showing crosses, trumpets, crowns of thorns
mixed in with Biblical verse numbers—Mark 15:32, Rev. 1:10,
John 19:2. The minister wears a brown suit and necktie and
shirt with an ordinary collar, and looks rather mussed, and
breathless, like the plump young manager of an appliance store
who sometimes has to help out in handling the heavy cartons.
His voice is amplified by a tiny stalk of a microphone almost
invisible at the oak lectern. He talks of Thelma as a model
housewife, mother, churchgoer, sufferer. The description describes no one, it is like a dress with no one in it. The minister
senses this, for he goes on to mention her ''special'' sense of
humor, her particular way of regarding things which enabled her
to bear herself so courageously throughout her long struggle
with her physical affliction. During a pastoral visit to Thelma in
her last tragic week in the hospital, the minister had ventured to
speculate with her on the eternal mystery of why the Lord visits
afflictions upon some and not upon others, and cures some and
lets many remain uncured. Even in the divine Gospel, let us
remind ourselves, this is so, for what of the many lepers and
souls possessed who did *not* happen to be placed in Jesus' path,
or were *not* aggressive enough to press themselves forward in
the vast crowds that flocked to Him on the Plain and on the
Mount, at Capernaum and at Galilee? And what was Thelma's
reply? She said, there in that hospital bed of pain and suffering,
that she guessed she deserved it as much as the next. This woman
was truly humble, truly uncomplaining. On an earlier, less
stressful occasion, the minister recalls with a quickening of his
voice that indicates an anecdote is coming, he was visiting her

in her immaculate home, and she had explained her physical affliction to him as a minor misunderstanding, as a matter of some tiny wires in her system being crossed. Then she had suggested, with that gentle humorous expression that all of us here who loved her remember—and yet in all grievous seriousness as well—that perhaps God was responsible only for what we ourselves could experience and see, and not responsible for anything at the microscopic level.

He looks up, uncertain of the effect this reminiscence has made, and the little congregation of mourners, perhaps hearing Thelma's voice in the odd remark and thus enabled to conjure up the something schoolteacherish and sardonic and strict in her living manner, or perhaps sensing the minister's need to be rescued from the spectre of unjustifiable suffering, politely titters. With relief, the brown-suited man, like a talk-show host wrapping up, rolls on to the rote assurances, the psalm about green pastures, the verses from Ecclesiastes about a time for everything, the hymn that says now the day is over.

Harry sits there beside snuffly Janice in her policeman's outfit thinking of the wanton naked Thelma he knew, how little she had to do with the woman the minister described; but maybe the minister's Thelma was as real as Harry's. Women are actresses, tuning their part to each little audience. Her part with him was to adore him, to place her body at his service as if disposing of it. Her body was ill and sallow and held death within it like a silky black box. There was a faint insult, a kind of dismissal, in her attitude of helpless captivity to the awkward need to love. He could not love her as she did him, there was a satisfying self-punishment in his relative distraction, an irony she relished. Yet however often he left her she never wanted him to leave. The glazed ghost of her leans up against him when he stands for the blessing, stands close to his chest with sour-milk breath silently begging him not to go. Janice snuffles again but Harry keeps his own grief for Thelma tight against his heart, knowing Janice doesn't want to see it.

Outside, in the embarrassing sunlight, Webb Murkett, his face smilingly creased more deeply than ever, a cigarette still dangling from his long upper lip like a camel's, goes from group to group introducing his new wife, a shy girl in her twenties, younger than Nelson, younger than Annabelle, a fluffy small blonde dressed in dark ruffles and shaped like a seal, like a teen-aged swimming champ, with no pronounced indentations. Webb does like them zaftig. Harry feels sorry for her, dragged up to this religious warehouse to bury the wife of an old golf partner of her husband's. Cindy, Webb's last wife, whom Harry adored not so many years ago, is also here, alone, looking dumpy and irritated and unsteady on black heels skimpy as sandals, as she takes a pose on the thickly grassed ruts of red earth that do for a church parking lot. While Janice sticks with Webb and his bride, Harry gallantly goes over to Cindy standing there like a lump, squinting in the hot hazed sun.

"Hi," he says, wondering how she could let herself go so badly. She has taken on the standard Diamond County female build—bosom like a shelf and ass like you're carrying your own bench around with you. Her dear little precise-featured face, in the old days enigmatic in its boyish pertness, with its snub nose and wide-apart eyes, is framed by fat and underlined by chins; she has no neck, like those Russian dolls that nest one inside the other. Her hair that used to be cut short has been teased and permed into that big-headed look young women favor now. It adds to her bulk.

"Harry. How are you?" Her voice has a funereal caution and she extends a soft hand, wide as a bear's paw, for him to shake; he takes it in his but also under cover of the sad occasion bends down and plants a kiss on her damp and ample cheek. Her look of irritated lumpiness slightly eases. "Isn't it awful about Thel?" she asks.

"Yeah," he agrees. "But it was coming a long time. She saw it coming." He figures it's all right to suggest he knew the dead woman's mind; Cindy was there in the Caribbean the night they swapped. He had wanted Cindy and wound up with Thelma. Now both are beyond desiring.

"You know, don't you?" Cindy says. "I mean, you sense when the time is near if you're sick like that. You sense everything." Rabbit remembers a little cross in the hollow of her throat you could see when she wore a bathing suit, and how, like a lot of people of her generation, she was soft on spookiness in general—astrology, premonitions—though not as bad as Buddy Inglefinger's girlfriend Valerie, a real old-style hippie, six feet tall and dripping beads.

"Maybe women more than men," he says to Cindy tactfully. He lurches a bit deeper into frankness. "I've had some physical problems lately and they give me the feeling I've walked through my entire life in a daze."

This is too deep for her, too confessional. There was always in his relations with Cindy a wall, just behind her bright butterscotch-brown eyes, a barrier where the signals stopped. *Silly Cindy*, Thelma called her. Yet Rabbit had seen Polaroids, sneaking into the Murketts' bedroom one drunken night, proving that Cindy functioned. She fucked, she blew. Now indeed she did look silly, and unhappy.

"Somebody told me," he tells her, "you're with a boutique over in that new mall near Oriole."

"I'm thinking of quitting, actually. Whatever I earn is taken off Webb's alimony so why should I bother? You can see how welfare mothers get that way."

"Well," he says, "a job gets you out in the world. Meet people." *Meet a guy, get married again,* is his unspoken thought. But who would want to hitch up with such a slab of beef? She'd sink any Sunfish you'd try to sail with her now.

"I'm thinking of maybe becoming a physical therapist. Another girl at the boutique is learning to do holistic massage."

"Sounds nice," Harry says. "Which holes?"

This is crude enough that she dares begin, "You and Thelma—" But she stops and looks at the ground.

"Yeah?" That old barrier keeps him from encouraging her. She is not the audience for which he wants to play the part of Thelma's bereft lover.

"You'll miss her, I know," Cindy says weakly.

He feigns innocence. "Frankly, Janice and I haven't been seeing that much of the Harrisons lately—Ronnie's resigned from the club, too much money he says, and I've hardly had a chance this summer to get over there myself. It's not the same, the old gang is gone. A lot of young twerps. They hit the ball a mile and win all the weekend sweeps. My daughter-in-law uses the pool, with the kids."

"I hear you're back at the lot."

"Yeah," he says, in case she knows anyway, "Nelson screwed up. I'm just holding the fort."

He wonders if he is saying too much, but she is looking past him. "I must go, Harry. I can't stand another second of watching Webb cavort with that simpering ridiculous baby doll of his. He's over sixty!"

The lucky stiff. He made it to sixty. In the little silence her indignant sharp remark imposes on the air, an airplane goes over, dragging its high dull roar behind it. With a smile not fully friendly he tells her, "You've all kept him young," recalling those Polaroids. A woman you've endured such a gnawing of desire for, you can't help bearing a little grudge against, when the ache is gone.

A number of people are making their escapes and Harry thinks he should go over and say a word to Ronnie. His old nemesis is standing in a loose group with his three sons and their women. Alex, the computer whiz, has a close haircut and a nerdy near-sighted look. Georgie has a would-be actor's long pampered hair and the coat and tie he put on for his mother's funeral look like a costume. Ron Junior has the pleasantest face—Thelma's smile—and the muscle and tan of an outdoor worker. Shaking their hands, Harry startles them by knowing their names. When you're sexually involved with a woman, some of the magic spills down into her children, that she also spread her legs for.

"How's Nelson doing?" Ron Junior asks him, from the look on his face not trying to be nasty. It must have been this boy, around Brewer as he is, who told Thelma about Nelson's habit.

Harry answers him man to man. "Good, Ron. He went through the detox treatment for a month and now he's living with about twenty other, what do they say, substance abusers, at what they call a 'concept house,' a halfway house in North Philly. He's got a volunteer job working with inner-city kids at a playground."

"That's great, Mr. Angstrom. Nelson's a great guy, basically."

"I don't go visit him any more, I couldn't stand this family therapy they try to give you, but his mother and Pru swear he loves it, working with these tough black kids."

Georgie, the prettiest boy and Thelma's favorite, has been overhearing and volunteers, "The only trouble with Nelson, he's too sensitive. He lets things get to him. In show business you learn to let it slide off your back. You know, fuck 'em. Otherwise you'd kill yourself." He pats the back of his hairdo.

Alex, the oldest, adds in his nerdy prim way, "Well I tell you, the drugs out in California were getting to *me*, that's why I was happy when this job in Fairfax came through. I mean, *every*body does it. All weekend they do it, on the beaches, on the thruways; *every*body's stoned. How can you raise a family? Or save any money?"

Her boys are men now, with flecks of gray hair and little wise wrinkles around their mouths, with wives and small children, Thelma's grandchildren, looking to their fathers for shelter in the weedy tangle of the world. Her boys look more mature in

Harry's eyes than Ronnie, in whom he must always see the ob-noxious brat from Wenrich Alley, and the loud-mouthed locker-room showoff of high-school days. People he once loved slide from him but Ronnie is always there, like the smelly underside of his own body, like the Jockey underpants that get dirty every day.

Ronnie is playing the grieving widower to a T; he looks like he's been through a washer, his eyelashes poking white from his tear-reddened lids, his kinky brass-colored hair reduced to gray wisps above his droopy ears. Rabbit tries to overcome his old aversion, their old rivalry, by giving the other man's hand an expressive squeeze and saying, "Really sorry."

But the old hostile devil lights up in Harrison's face, once meaty and now drawn and hollowed-out and stringy. With a glance at his sons and a small over-there jab of his head, he takes Harry's arm in a grip purposely too hard and leads him out of earshot, a few steps away on the rutted dried mud. He says to him, in the hurried confidential voice of men together in an athletic huddle, "You think I don't know you were banging Thel for years?"

"I—I've never much thought about what you know or don't know, Ronnie."

"You son of a bitch. That night we swapped down in the islands was just the beginning, wasn't it? You kept seeing her up here."

"Ron, I thought you said you knew. You should have asked Thelma if you were curious."

"I didn't want to hassle her. She was fighting to live and I loved her. Toward the end, we talked about it."

"So you *did* hassle her?"

"She wanted to clear the slate. You son of a bitch. The Old Master. You're the coldest most selfish bastard I ever met."

"Why? What makes me so bad? Maybe she wanted me. Maybe the favors were mutual." Over Ronnie's shoulder, Harry sees mourners waiting to say goodbye, hesitant, conscious of the heat of this hurried conversation. Harrison has become pink in the face and perhaps Rabbit has too. He says, "Ronnie, people are watching. This isn't the time."

"There won't be another time. I don't ever want to see you again as long as I live. You disgust me."

"Yeah, and you disgust me. You always have, Ron. You got a prick where your head ought to be. Who can blame her, if

Thelma gave herself a little vacation from eating your shit now and then?''

Ronnie's face is quite pink and his eyes are watering; he has never let go of Harry's forearm, as if this hold is his last warm contact with his dead wife. His voice lowers into a new intensity; Harry has to bend his head to hear. ''I don't give a fuck you banged her, what kills me is you did it without giving a shit. She was crazy for you and you just lapped it up. You narcissistic cocksucker. She wasted herself on you. She went against everything she wanted to believe in and you didn't even appreciate it, you didn't love her and she knew it, she told me herself. She told me in the hospital asking my forgiveness.'' Ronnie takes breath to go on, but tears block his throat.

Rabbit's own throat aches, thinking of Thelma and Ronnie at the last, her betraying her lover when her body had no more love left in it. ''Ronnie,'' he whispers. ''I *did* appreciate her. I did. She was a fantastic lay.''

''You cocksucker'' is all Ronnie can get out, repetitively, and then they both turn to face the mourners waiting to pay their respects and climb into their cars and salvage what is left of this hot hazy Saturday, with lawns to mow and gardens to weed all across Diamond County. Janice and Webb are among those staring. They must guess what the conversation has been about; in fact, most of those here must guess, even the three sons. Though he had always been discreet on his visits to Arrowdale, hiding his Toyota in her garage and never getting caught in bed with her by a sick child returning early from school or a repairman letting himself in an unlocked door, these things have a way of getting out into the air. Like a tire, it needs only a pinhole of a leak. People sense it. Word has got around, or it will now. Well, fuck 'em, like Georgie said. Fuck 'em all, including Webb's child bride, who from the shape of her might be pregnant. That Webb, what a character.

A nice thing happens. Ronnie and Harry, Harrison and Angstrom, with a precision as if practiced, execute a crisscross. They smile, despite their pink eyelids and raw throats, at the little watching crowd and neatly cross paths as they move toward their kin, Harry toward Janice in her navy-blue suit with white trim and wide shoulders, and Ronnie back to his sons and the center of his sad occasion. Once teammates, always teammates. Rabbit, remembering how Ronnie once screwed Ruth a whole weekend in Atlantic City and then bragged to him about it, can't feel sorry for him at all.

* * *
I Love What You Do for Me, Toyota. That is the new paper
banner the company has sent down to hang in the big display
window. At times, standing at the window, when a cloud dense
with moisture darkens the atmosphere or an occluding truck
pulls up past the yew hedge for some business at the service
doors, Harry catches a sudden reflection of himself and is startled by how big he is, by how much space he is taking up on the
planet. Stepping out on the empty roadway as Uncle Sam last
month he had felt so eerily tall, as if his head were a giant
balloon floating above the marching music. Though his inner
sense of himself is of an innocuous passive spirit, a steady small
voice, that doesn't want to do any harm, get trapped anywhere,
or ever die, there is this other self seen from outside, a six-foot-
three ex-athlete weighing two-thirty at the least, an apparition
wearing a sleek gray summer suit shining all over as if waxed
and a big head whose fluffy shadowy hair was trimmed at Shear
Joy Hair Styling (unisex, fifteen bucks minimum) to rest exactly
on the ears, a fearsome bulk with eyes that see and hands that
grab and teeth that bite, a body eating enough at one meal to
feed three Ethiopians for a day, a shameless consumer of gasoline, electricity, newspapers, hydrocarbons, carbohydrates. A
boss, in a shiny suit. His recent heart troubles have become,
like his painfully and expensively crowned back teeth, part of
his respectability's full-blown equipage.

Harry needs a good self-image today, for the lot is going to
be visited at eleven by a representative of the Toyota Corporation, a Mr. Natsume Shimada, hitherto manifested only as a
careful signature, each letter individually formed, on creamy
stiff stationery from the American Toyota Motor Sales head-
quarters in Torrance, California. Word of the financial irregu-
larities anatomized by the two accountants Janice hired under
Charlie's direction has filtered upward, higher and higher, as
letters from Mid-Atlantic Toyota in Glen Burnie, Maryland, were
succeeded by mail from the Toyota Motor Credit Corporation's
offices in Baltimore and then by courteous but implacable communications from Torrance itself, signed with what seems an
old-fashioned stub-tipped fountain pen by Mr. Shimada, in
sky-blue ink.

"Nervous?" Elvira asks, sidling up beside him in a slim seer-
sucker suit. For the hot weather she had her hair cut short behind, exposing sexy dark down at the back of her neck. Did
Nelson used to boff her? If Pru wasn't putting out, he had to

boff somebody. Unless coke whores were enough, or the kid was secretly gay. Insofar as he can bear to contemplate his son's sex life, Elvira seems a little too classy, too neuter to go along with it. But maybe Harry is underestimating the amount of energy in the world: he tends to do that, now that his own is sagging.

"Not too," he answers. "How do I look?"

"Very imposing. I like the new suit."

"It's kind of a gray metallic. They developed the fabric while doing the moon shots."

Benny is doing a dance of door-opening and hood-popping out on the lot with a couple so young they keep looking at each other for confirmation, both talking at once and then falling silent simultaneously, paralyzed by their wish not to be tricked out of a single dollar. August sales are on and Toyota is offering thousand-dollar rebates. In the old days you sold only at their list price, no haggling, take it or leave it, a quality product. Their old purity has been corrupted by American methods. Toyota has stooped to the scramble. "You know," he tells Elvira, "in all the years the lot has been selling these cars I don't recall it ever being visited by an actual Japanese. I thought they all stayed over there in Toyota City enjoying the tea ceremony."

"And the geisha girls," Elvira says slyly. "Like Mr. Uno."

Harry smiles at the topical allusion. This girl—woman—keeps up. "Yeah, he wasn't Numero Uno very long, was he?"

Her earrings today are like temple bells, little curved lids of dull silver wired together in trembling oblongs the size of butterfly cocoons. They shiver with a touch of indignation when she tells him, "It's really Nelson and Lyle should be facing Mr. Shimada."

He shrugs. "What can you do? The lawyer got Lyle on the phone finally and the guy just laughed at him. Said he was taking oxygen just to get out of bed and go to the toilet and could die any time. Furthermore he said the disease had spread to his brain and he had no idea what the lawyer was talking about. And he'd had to sell his computer and didn't keep any of the disks. In other words he told the lawyer to—to go jump in the lake." Suppressing "fuck himself" like that was maybe a way of courting Elvira, he doesn't know. Late in the game as it is, you keep trying. He likes her being so thin—she makes Pru and even Janice look thick—and there is something cool and quiet about her he finds comforting, like a television screen when you can't hear the words, just see the flicker. "I had to laugh," he says, of Lyle's last communications. "Dying has its advantages."

She asks at his side, "Won't Nelson be home in a week or so?"

"That's the schedule," Harry says. "Summer flies by, doesn't it? You notice it in the evening now. It's still warm but gets dark earlier and earlier. It's a thing you forget from year to year, that late-summer darkness. The cicadas. That smell of baked-out lawns. Except this summer's been so damn rainy—in my little garden, God, the weeds won't stop growing, and the lettuce and broccoli are so leggy they're falling over. And the pea vines have spread like Virginia creeper, up over the fence and into the neighbor's yard."

"At least it hasn't been so terribly hot like it was the summer before," Elvira says, "when everybody kept talking about the greenhouse effect. Maybe there is no greenhouse effect."

"Oh, there is," Rabbit tells her, with a conviction he didn't know he had. Across Route 111, above the red hat-shaped roof of the Pizza Hut, a flock of starlings, already migrating south, speckle on telephone wires like a bar of musical notation. "I won't live to see it," he says, "but you will, and my grandchildren. New York, Philly, their docks will be underwater, once Antarctica starts melting. All of the Jersey Shore." Ronnie Harrison and Ruth: what a shit, that guy.

"How is he doing, have you heard much? Nelson."

"He's dropped us a couple of cards of the Liberty Bell. He sounded cheerful. In a way, the kid's been always looking for more structure than we could ever give him, and I guess a rehab program is big on structure. He talks to Pru on the phone, but they don't encourage too much outside contact at this point."

"What does Pru think about everything?" Does Harry imagine it, an edge of heightened interest here, as if the sound on the TV set clicked back in?

"Hard to know what Pru thinks," he says. "I have the impression she was about ready to pack it in, the marriage, before he sent himself off. She and Janice and the kids have been up at the Poconos."

"That makes it lonely for you," Elvira Ollenbach says.

Could this be a feeler? Is he supposed to have her come on over? Have a couple daiquiris in the den, stroke the dark nape of her neck, see if her pussy matches up, up in that slanty spare bedroom where all the old *Playboy*s were stashed in the closet when they moved in—the thought of that wiry young female body seeking to slake its appetites on his affects him like the thought of an avalanche. It would make a wreck of his routine. "At my age I don't mind it," he says. "I can watch the TV shows I want. *National Geographic, Disney, World of Nature.* When Janice is there she makes us watch all these family situation shows with everybody clowning around in the living room. This *Roseanne*, I asked her what the hell she sees in it, she told me, 'I like her. She's fat and messy and mean, like most of the women in America.' I watch less and less. I try to have just one beer and go to bed early."

The young woman silently offers to move away, back to her cubicle in the direction of Paraguay. But he likes her near him, and abruptly asks, "You know who I'm sick of hearing about?"

"Who?"

"Pete Rose. 'Djou read in the *Standard* the other day how he's been in hot water before, in 1980 when he and a lot of the other Phils were caught taking amphetamines and the club traded away Randy Leach, the only player who admitted to it, and the rest of 'em just brazened it through?"

"I glanced at it. It was a Brewer doctor supplying the prescriptions."

"That's right, our own little burg. So that's why he thinks he can bluff it through now. Nobody else has to pay for what they do, everybody else gets away with everything. Ollie North, drug dealers, what with the jails being full and everybody such a bleeding heart anyway. Break the law, burn the flag, who the fuck cares?"

"Don't get yourself upset, Harry," she says, in her maternal, retreating mode. "The world is full of cheaters."

"Yeah, we should know."

She makes no response at all, having turned her back. Maybe she had been balling Nelson after all.

"I always thought he was an ugly ballplayer, anyway," he feels compelled to say, concerning Rose. "If you have to do it all with hustle and grit, you shouldn't be out there."

Out there, in the dog-days outdoors whose muggy alternation of light and shadow flickeringly gives him back his own ominous reflection, Harry notices that the refurbished yew hedge—he had a lawn service replace the dead bushes and renew the bark mulch—has collected a number of waxpaper pizza wrappers and Styrofoam coffee cups that have blown in from Route 111. He can't have their Japanese visitor see a mess like that. He goes outside, and the hot polluted air, bouncing off the asphalt, takes his breath away. The left side of his ribs gives a squeeze. He puts a Nitrostat to melt beneath his tongue before he begins to stoop. The more wastepaper he gathers, the more it seems there is—candy wrappers, cigarette-pack cellophane, advertising fliers and whole pages of newspaper wrinkled by rain and browned by the sun, big soft-drink cups with the plastic lid still on and the straw still in and the dirty water from melted ice still sloshing around. There is no end of crud in the world. He should have brought out a garbage bag, he has both hands full and can feel his face getting red as he tries to hold yet one more piece of crumpled sticky cardboard in his fanned fingers. A limousine cracklingly pulls into the lot while Harry is still picking up the trash, and he has to run inside to cram it all into the wastebasket in his office. Puffing, his heart thudding, his metallic-gray suit coat pulling at the buttons, he rushes back across the showroom to greet Mr. Shimada at the entrance, shaking his hand with a hand unwashed of street grit, dried sugar, and still-sticky pizza topping.

Mr. Shimada is an impeccable compact man of about five six, carrying an amazingly thin oxblood-red briefcase and wearing a smoke-blue suit with an almost invisible pinstripe, tailored to display a dapper breadth of his gold-linked French cuffs and high white collar, on a shirt with a pale-blue body. He looks dense, like a beanbag filled to the corners with buckshot, and in good physical trim, though stocky, with a burnish of California tan on his not unfriendly face. "Is very nice meeting you," he says. "Area most nice." He speaks English easily, but with enough of an accent to cost Harry a second's response time answering him.

"Well, not around here exactly," he answers, instantly thinking that this is tactless, for why would Toyota want to locate its franchise in an ugly area? "I mean, the farm country is what we're famous for, barns with hex signs and all that." He wonders if he should explain "hex sign" and decides it's not worth it. "Would you like to look around the facility? At the setup?" In case "facility" didn't register. Talking to foreigners really makes you think about the language.

Mr. Shimada slowly, stiffly turns his head and shoulders together, one way and then the other, to take in the showroom. "I see," he smiles. "Also in Torrance I study many photos and froor pran. Oh! Rovely rady!"

Elvira has left her desk and sashays toward their visitor, sucking in her cheeks to make herself look more glamorous. "Miss

Olshima, I mean Mr. Shimada"—Harry had been practicing the name, telling himself it was like Ramada with shit at the beginning, only to botch it in the crunch—"this is Miss Ollenbach, one of our best sales reps. Representatives."

Mr. Shimada first gives her an instinctive little hands-at-the-sides bow. When they shake hands, it's like both of them are trying to knock each other out with their smiles, they hold them so long. "Is good idea, to have both sexes serring," he says to Harry. "More and more the common thing."

"I don't know why it took us all so long to think of it," Harry admits.

"Good idea take time," the other man says, curbing his smile a little, letting an admonitory sternness tug downward his rather full yet flat lips. Harry remembers from his boyhood in World War II how very cruel the Japanese were to their prisoners on Bataan. The first thing you heard about them, after Pearl Harbor, was that they were ridiculously small, manning tiny submarines and planes called Zeros, and then, as those early Pacific defeats rolled in, that they were fanatic in the service of their Emperor, robot-monkeys that had to be torched out of their caves with flame-throwers. What a long way we've come since then. Harry feels one of his surges of benevolence, of approval of a world that isn't asking for it. Mr. Shimada seems to be asking Elvira if she prays.

"Play tennis, you mean?" she asks back. "Yes, as a matter of fact. Whenever I can. How did you know?"

His flat face breaks into twinkling creases and, quick as a monkey, he taps her wrist, where a band of relative pallor shows on her sunbrowned skin. "Sweatband," he says, proudly.

"That's clever," Elvira says. "You must play, too, in California. Everybody does."

"All free time. Revel five, hoping revel four."

"That's fabulous," she comes back, but a sideways upward glance at Harry asks how much longer she has to be a geisha girl.

"Good fetch, no backhand," Mr. Shimada tells her, demonstrating.

"Turn your *back* to the net, and take the racket back *low*," Elvira tells him, also demonstrating. "Hit the ball out *front*, don't let it *play you*."

"Talk just as pro," Mr. Shimada tells her, beaming.

No doubt about it, Elvira is impressive. You can see how rangy and quick she would be on the court. Harry is beginning to relax. When the phantom tennis lesson is over, he takes their guest on a quick tour through the office space and through the shelved tunnel of the parts department, where Roddy, the Assistant Parts Manager, a viciously pretty youth with long lank hair he keeps flicking back from his face, his face and hands filmed with gray grease, gives them a dirty white-eyed look. Harry doesn't introduce them, for fear of besmirching Mr. Shimada with a touch of grease. He leads him to the brass-barred door of the rackety, cavernous garage, where Manny, the Service Manager Harry had inherited from Fred Springer fifteen years ago, has been replaced by Arnold, a plump young man with an advanced degree from voke school, where he was taught to wear washable coveralls that give him the figure of a Kewpie doll, or a snowman. Mr. Shimada hesitates at the verge of the echoing garage—men's curses cut through the hammering of metal on metal—and takes a step backward, asking, "Emproyee moraru good?"

This must be "morale." Harry thinks of the mechanics, their insatiable gripes and constant coffee breaks and demands for ever more costly fringe benefits, and their frequent hungover absences on Monday and suspiciously early departures on Friday, and says, "Very good. They clear twenty-two dollars an hour, with bonuses and benefits. The first job I ever took, when I was fifteen, I got thirty-five cents an hour."

Mr. Shimada is not interested. "Brack emproyees, are any? I see none."

"Yeah, well. We'd like to hire more, but it's hard to find qualified ones. We had a man a couple years ago, had good hands and got along with everybody, but we had to let him go finally because he kept showing up late or not showing up at all. When we called him on it, he said he was on Afro-American time." Harry is ashamed to tell him what the man's nickname had been—Blackie. At least we don't still sell Black Sambo dolls with nigger lips like they do in Tokyo, he saw on *60 Minutes* this summer.

"Toyota strive to be fair-practices emproyer," says Mr. Shimada. "Wants to be good citizen of your pruraristic society. In prant in Georgetown, Kentucky, many bracks work. Not just assembry line, executive positions."

"We'll work on it," Rabbit promises him. "This is a kind of conservative area, but it's coming along."

"Very pretty area."

"Right."

Back in the showroom, Harry feels obliged to explain, "My son picked these colors for the walls and woodwork. My son Nelson. I would have gone for something a little less, uh, choice, but he's been the effective manager here, while I've been spending half the year in Florida. My wife loves the sun down there. She plays tennis, by the way. Loves the game."

Mr. Shimada beams. His lips seem flattened as if by pressing up against glass, and his eyeglasses, their squarish gold rims, seem set exceptionally tight against his eyes. "We know Nelson Angstrom," he says. He has trouble with the many consonants of the last name, making it "Ank-a-stom." "A most famous man at Toyota company."

A constriction in Harry's chest and a watery looseness below his belt tell him that they have arrived, after many courtesies, at the point of the visit. "Want to come into my office and sit?"

"With preasure."

"Anything one of the girls could get you? Coffee? Tea? Not like your tea, of course. Just a bag of Lipton's—"

"Is fine without." Rather unceremoniously, he enters Harry's office and sits on the vinyl customer's chair, with padded chrome arms, facing the desk. He sets his wonderfully thin briefcase on his lap and lightly folds his hands upon it, showing two dazzling breadths of white cuff. He waits for Harry to seat himself behind the desk and then begins what seems to be a prepared speech. "Arways," he says, "we in Japan admire America. As boy during Occupation, rooked way up to big GI soldiers, their happy easy-go ways. Enemy soldiers, but not bad men. Powerful men. Our Emperor's advisers have red him down unfortunate ways, so General MacArthur, he seemed to us as Emperor had been, distant and first-rate. We worked hard to do what he suggest—rebuild burned cities, learn democratic ways. Japanese very humble at first in regard to America. You know Toyota story. At first, very modest, then bigger, we produce a better product for the rittle man's money, yes? You ask for it, we got it, yes?"

"Good slogan," Harry tells him. "I like it better than some of the recent ones've been coming down."

But Mr. Shimada does not expect to be even slightly interrupted. His burnished, manicured hands firmly flatten on the thin oxblood briefcase and he inclines his upper body forward to make his voice clear. "Nevertheress, these years of postwar, Japanese, man and woman, have great respect for United States. Rike big brother. But in recent times big brother act rike rittle brother, always cry and comprain. Want many favors in trade, saying Japanese unfair competition. Why unfair? Make something, cheaper even with duty and transportation costs, people rike, people buy. American way in old times. But in new times America make nothing, just do mergers, do acquisitions, rower taxes, raise national debt. Nothing comes out, all goes in—foreign goods, foreign capital. America take everything, give nothing. Rike big brack hole.''

Mr. Shimada is proud of this up-to-date analogy and of his unanswerable command of English. He smiles to himself and opens, with a double snap as startling as a gunshot, his briefcase. From it he takes a single sheet of stiff creamy paper, sparsely decorated with typed figures. ''According to figures here, between November '88 and May '89 Springer Motors fail to report sale of nine Toyota vehicles totarring one hundred thirty-seven thousand four hundred at factory price. This sum accumurating interest come to as of this date one hundred forty-five thousand eight hundred.'' With one of his reflexive, half-suppressed bows, he hands the paper across the desk.

Harry covers it with his big hand and says, ''Yeah, well, but it's accountants *we* hired reported all this to you. It's not as if Springer Motors as a company is trying to cheat anybody. It's a screwy—an unusual—situation that developed and that's being corrected. My son had a drug problem and hired a bad egg as chief accountant and together they ripped us all off. The Brewer Trust, too, in another scam—they had a dead mutual friend buying cars, would you believe it? But listen: my wife and I—technically she's the owner here—we have every intention of paying Mid-Atlantic Toyota back every penny we owe. And I'd like to see, sometime, how you're computing that interest.''

Mr. Shimada leans back a bit and makes his briefest speech. ''How soon?''

Harry takes a plunge. ''End of August.'' Three weeks away. They might have to take out a bank loan, and Brewer Trust is already on their case. Well, let Janice's accountants work it out if they're so smart.

Mr. Shimada blinks, behind those lenses embedded in his flat face, and seems to nod in concord. ''End of August. Interest computed at twelve per cent monthly compounded as in standard TMCC loan.'' He snaps shut his briefcase and balances it on its edge beside his chair. He gazes obliquely at the framed photographs on Harry's desk: Janice, when she still had bangs, in a spangly long dress three or four years ago, about to go off to the Valhalla Village New Year's Eve party, a flashlit color print Fern Drechsel took with a Nikkomat Bernie had just given her for a Hanukkah present and that came out surprisingly well, Janice's face in anticipation of the party looking younger than her years, a bit overexposed and out of focus and starry-eyed; Nelson's high-school graduation picture, in a blazer and necktie but his hair down to his shoulders, long as a girl's; and, left over from Nelson's tenure at this desk, a framed black-and-white posed school photo of Harry in his basketball uniform, holding the ball above his shining right shoulder as if to get off a shot, his hair crewcut, his eyes sleepy, his tank top stencilled MJ.

Mr. Shimada's less upright posture in the chair indicates a new, less formal level of discourse. "Young people now most interesting," he decides to say. "Not scared of starving as through most human history. Not scared of atom bomb as until recently. But scared of something—not happy. In Japan, too. Brue jeans, rock music not make happiness enough. In former times, in Japan, very simple things make men happy. Moonright on fish pond at certain moment. Cricket singing in bamboo grove. Very small things bring very great feering. Japan a rittle ireand country, must make do with very near nothing. Not rike endless China, not rike U.S. No oiru wells, no great spaces. We have only our people, their disciprine. Riving now five years in Carifornia, it disappoints me, the rack of disciprine in people of America. Many good qualities, of course. Good tennis, good hearts. Roads of fun. I have many most dear American friends. Always they aporogize to me for Japanese internment camps in Frankrin Roosevelt days. Always I say to them, surprised, 'Was war!' In war, people need disciprine. Not just in war. Peace a kind of war also. We fight now not Americans and British but Nissan, Honda, Ford. Toyota agency must be a prace of disciprine, a prace of order.''

Harry feels he must interrupt, he doesn't like the trend of this monologue. "We think this agency is. Sales have been up eight per cent this summer, bucking the national trend. I'm always saying to people, 'Toyota's been good to us, and we've been good to Toyota.' "

"No more, sorry," Mr. Shimada says simply, and resumes: "In United States, is fascinating for me, struggle between order and freedom. Everybody mention freedom, all papers terevision anchor people everybody. Much rove and talk of freedom. Skateboarders want freedom to use beach boardwalks and knock down poor old people. Brack men with radios want freedom to self-express with super-jumbo noise. Men want freedom to have guns and shoot others on freeways in random sport. In Carifornia, dog shit much surprise me. Everywhere, dog shit, dogs must have important freedom to shit everywhere. Dog freedom more important than crean grass and cement pavement. In U.S., Toyota company hope to make ireands of order in ocean of freedom. Hope to strike proper barance between needs of outer world and needs of inner being, between what in Japan we call *giri* and *ninjō*.'' He leans forward and, with a flash of wide white cuff, taps the page of figures on Harry's desk. "Too much disorder. Too much dog shit. Pay by end of August, no prosecution for criminal activities. But no more Toyota franchise at Singer Motors.''

"Springer," Harry says automatically. "Listen," he pleads. "No one feels worse about my son's falling apart than I do.''

Now it is Mr. Shimada who interrupts; his own speech, with whatever beautiful shadows in Japanese it was forming in his mind, has whipped him up. "Not just son," he says. "Who is father and mother of such son? Where are they? In Frorida, enjoying sunshine and tennis, while young boy prays games with autos. Nelson Ank-a-stom too much a boy still to be managing Toyota agency. He roses face for Toyota company.'' This statement tugs his flat lips far down, in a pop-eyed scowl.

Hopelessly Harry argues, "You want the sales staff young, to attract the young customers. Nelson'll be thirty-three in a month.'' He thinks it would be a waste of breath, and maybe offensive, to explain to Mr. Shimada that at that same age Jesus Christ was old enough to be crucified and redeem mankind. He makes a final plea: "You'll lose all the good will. For thirty years the people of Brewer have known where to come to buy Toyotas. Out here right on Route One One One.''

"No more," Mr. Shimada states. "Too much dog shit, Mr. Ank-strom.'' His third try and he almost has it. You got to hand it to them. "Toyota does not enjoy bad games prayed with its autos.'' He picks up his slim briefcase and stands. "You keep invoice. Many more papers to arrive. Most preasant if regretful visit, and good talk on topics of general interest. Perhaps you would be kind to discuss with rimo driver best way to find Route Four Two Two. Mr. Krauss has agency there.''

"You're going to see Rudy? He used to work here. I taught him all he knows.''

Mr. Shimada has stiffened, in that faintly striped smoky-blue suit. "Good teacher not always good parent.''

"If he's going to be the only Toyota in town, he ought to get rid of Mazda. That Wankel engine never really worked out. Too much like a squirrel cage."

Harry feels lightheaded, now that the ax has fallen. Anticipation is the worst; letting go has its pleasant side. "Good luck with Lexus, by the way," he says. "People don't think luxury when they think Toyota, but things can change."

"Things change," says Mr. Shimada. "Is world's sad secret." Out in the showroom, he asks, "Rovely rady?" Elvira with her clicking brisk walk traverses the showroom floor, her earrings doing a dance along the points of her jaw. Their visitor asks, "Could prease have business card, in case of future reference?" She digs one out of her suit pocket, and Mr. Shimada accepts it, studies it seriously, bows with his hands at his sides, and then, to strike a jocular American note, imitates a tennis backhand.

"You've got it," she tells him. "Take it back *low*."

He bows again and, turning to Harry, beams so broadly his eyeglass frames are lifted by the creasing of his face. "Good ruck with many probrems. Perhaps before too rate should buy Rexus at dealer price." This is, it would seem, a little Japanese joke.

Harry gives the manicured hand a gritty squeeze. "Don't think I can afford even a Corolla now," he says and, in a reflex of good will really, manages a little bow of his own. He accompanies his visitor outdoors to the limousine, whose black driver is leaning against the fender eating a slice of pizza, and a cloud pulls back from the sun; a colorless merciless dog-day brilliance makes Harry wince; all joking falls away and he abruptly feels fragile and ill with loss. He cannot imagine the lot without the tall blue TOYOTA sign, the glinting still lake of well-made cars in slightly bitter Oriental colors. Poor Janice, she'll be knocked for a loop. She'll feel she's let her father down.

But she doesn't react too strongly; she is more interested these days in her real-estate courses. Janice has completed one pair of ten-week courses and is into another. She has long phone conversations with her classmates about the next exam or the fascinating personality of their teacher, Mr. Lister with his exciting new beard. "I'm sure Nelson has some plan," she says. "And if he doesn't, we'll all sit down and negotiate one."

"Negotiate! Two hundred thousand disappearing dollars! And you don't have Toyotas to sell any more."

"Were they really so great, Harry? Nelson hated them. Why can't we get an American franchise—isn't Detroit making a big comeback?"

"Not so big they can afford Nelson Angstrom."

She pretends he's joking, saying, "Aren't you awful?" Then she looks at his face, is startled and saddened by what she sees there, and crosses their kitchen to reach up and touch his face. "Harry," she says. "You *are* taking it hard. Don't. Daddy used to say, 'For every up there's a down, and for every down there's an up.' Nelson will be home in a week and we can't do a thing really until then." Outside the kitchen window screen, where moths keep bumping, the early-August evening has that blended tint peculiar to the season, of light being withdrawn while summer's warmth lingers. As the days grow shorter, a dryness of dead grass and chirring insects has crept in even through this summer of heavy rains, of more thunderstorms and flash floods in Diamond County than Harry can ever remember. Out in their yard, he notices now a few dead leaves shed by the weeping cherry, and the flower stalks of the violet hosta dying back. In his mood of isolation and lassitude he is drawing closer to the earth, the familiar mother with his infancy still in her skirts, in the shadows beneath the bushes.

"Shit," he says, a word charged for him with magic since the night three months ago when Pru used it to announce her despairing decision to sleep with him, once. "What kind of plans can Nelson have? He'll be lucky to stay out of jail."

"You can't go to jail for stealing from your own family. He had a medical problem, he was sick the same way you were sick only it was addiction instead of angina. You're both getting better."

He hears in the things she says, more and more, other voices, opinions and a wisdom gathered away from him. "Who have you been talking to?" he says. "You sound like that know-it-all Doris Kaufmann."

"Eberhardt. I haven't talked to Doris for weeks and weeks. But some of the women taking the real-estate program, we go out afterwards to this little place on Pine Street that's not too rough, at least until later, and one of them, Francie Alvarez, says you got to think of any addiction as a medical condition just like they caught the flu, or otherwise you'd go crazy, blaming the addicts around you as if they can help it."

"So what makes you think Nelson's cure will take? Just because it cost us six grand, that doesn't mean a thing to the kid.

He just went in to let things blow over. You told me yourself he told you once he loves coke more than anything in the world. More than you, more than me, more than his own kids.''

"Well, sometimes in life you have to give up things you love."

Charlie. Is that who she's thinking of, to make her voice sound so sincere, so sadly wise and wisely firm? Her eyes for this moment in dying August light have a darkness that invites him in, to share a wisdom her woman's life has taught her. Her fingers touch his cheek again, a touch like a fly that when you're trying to fall asleep keeps settling on your face, the ticklish thin skin here and there. It's annoying; he tries to shake her off with a snap of his head. She pulls her hand back but still stares so solemnly. "It's you I worry about, more than Nelson. Is the angina coming back? The breathlessness?"

"A twinge now and then," he admits. "Nothing a pill doesn't fix. It's just something I'm going to have to live with."

"I wonder if you shouldn't have had the bypass."

"The balloon was bad enough. Sometimes I feel like they left it inside me."

"Harry, at least you should do more exercise. You go from the lot to the TV in the den to bed. You never play golf any more."

"Well, it's no fun with the old gang gone. The kids out there at the Flying Eagle don't want an old man in their foursome. In Florida I'll pick it up again."

"That's something else we ought to talk about. What's the point of my getting the salesperson's license if we go right down to Florida for six months? I can never build up any local presence."

"Local presence, you've got lots of it. You're Fred Springer's daughter and Harry Angstrom's wife. And now you're a famous coke addict's mother."

"I mean professionally. It's a phrase Mr. Lister uses. It means the people know you're always there, not off in Florida like some person who doesn't take her job seriously."

"So," he says. "Florida was good enough to stash me in when I was manager at Springer Motors, to get me out of Nelson's way, but now you think you're a working girl we can just forget it, Florida."

"Well," Janice allows, "I *was* thinking, one possibility, to help with the company's debts, might be to sell the condo."

"*Sell* it? Over my dead body," he says, not so much meaning it as enjoying the sound of his voice, indignant like one of those perpetually outraged fathers on a TV sitcom, or like silver-haired Steve Martin in the movie *Parenthood*, which they saw the other night because one of Janice's real-estate buddies thought it was so funny. "My blood's got too thin to go through a Northern winter."

In response Janice looks as if she is about to cry, her dark-brown eyes warm and glassy-looking just like little Roy's before he lets loose with one of his howls. "Harry, don't confuse me," she begs. "I can't even take the license exam until October, I can't believe you'd immediately make me go down to Florida where the license is no good just so you can play golf with some people older and worse than you. Who beat you anyway, and take twenty dollars every time."

"Well what am *I* supposed to do around here while you run around showing off? The lot's finished, *kaput*, or whatever the Japanese word is, *finito*, and even if it's not, if the kid's halfway straightened out you'll want him back there and he can't stand me around, we have different styles, we get on each other's nerves."

"Maybe you won't now. Maybe Nelson will just have to put up with you and you with him."

Harry humbly tells her, "I'd be willing." Father and son, together against the world, rebuilding the lot up from scratch: the vision excites him, for the moment. Shooting the bull with Benny and Elvira while Nelson skitters around out there in the lake of rooftops, selling used cars like hotcakes. Springer Motors back to what it used to be before Fred got the Toyota franchise. So they owe a few hundred thousand—the government owes trillions and nobody cares.

She sees hope in his face and touches his cheek a third time. At night now, Harry, having to arise at least once and sometimes, if there's been more than one beer with television, twice, has learned to touch his way across the bedroom in the pitch dark, touching the glass top of the bedside table and then with an outreached arm after a few blind steps the slick varnished edge of the high bureau and from there to the knob of the bathroom door. Each touch, it occurs to him every night, leaves a little deposit of sweat and oil from the skin of his fingertips; eventually it will darken the varnished bureau edge as the hems of his golf-pants pockets have been rendered grimy by his reaching in and out for tees and ball markers, round after round, over the years; and that accumulated deposit of his groping touch, he sometimes thinks when the safety of the bathroom and its luminescent light switch has been attained, will still be there, a shadow on the varnish, a microscopic cloud of his body oils, when he is gone.

"Don't push me, honey," Janice says, in a rare tone of direct appeal that makes his hard old heart accelerate with revived husbandly feeling. "This horrible thing with Nelson really has been a stress, though I may not always show it. I'm his mother, I'm humiliated, I don't know what's going to happen, exactly. Everything's in flux."

His chest feels full; his left ribs cage a twinge. His vision of working side by side with Nelson has fled, a pipe dream. He tries to make Janice, so frighteningly, unusually somber and frontal, smile with a tired joke. "I'm too old for flux," he tells her.

Nelson is scheduled to return from rehab the same day that the second U.S. Congressman in two weeks, a white Republican this time, is killed in a plane crash. One in Ethiopia, one in Louisiana; one a former Black Panther, and this one a former sheriff. You don't think of being a politician as being such a hazardous profession; but it makes you fly. Pru drives to get her husband at the halfway house in North Philadelphia while Janice babysits. Soon after they arrive, Janice comes home to Penn Park. "I thought they should be alone with each other, the four of them," she explains to Harry.

"How did he seem?"

She thoughtfully touches her upper lip with the tip of her tongue. "He seemed . . . serious. Very focused and calm. Not at all jittery like he was. I don't know how much Pru told him about Toyota withdrawing the franchise and the hundred forty-five thousand you promised we'd pay so soon. I didn't want to fling it at him right off the bat."

"What *did* you say, then?"

"I said he looked wonderful—he looks a little heavy, actually—and told him you and I were very proud of him for sticking it out."

"Huh. Did he ask about me? My health?"

"Not exactly, Harry—but he knows we'd have said something if anything more was wrong with you. He seemed mostly interested in the children. It was really very touching—he took them both off with him into the room where Mother used to have all the plants, what we called the sun parlor, and apologized for having been a bad father to them and explained about the drugs and how he had been to a place where they taught him how to never take drugs again.''

"Did he apologize to you for having been a bad son? To Pru for being a crappy husband?''

"I have no idea what he and Pru said to each other—they had hours in the car together, the traffic around Philadelphia is getting worse and worse, what with all the work on the Expressway. All the roads and bridges are falling apart at once.''

"He didn't ask about me at all?''

"He did, of course he did, honey. You and I are supposed to go over there for dinner tomorrow night.''

"Oh. So I can admire the drugless wonder. Great.''

"You mustn't talk like that. He needs all of our support. Returning to your milieu is the hardest part of recovery.''

"Milieu, huh? So that's what we are.''

"That's what they call it. He's going to have to stay away from that druggy young people's crowd that meets at the Laid-Back. So his immediate family must work very hard to fill in the gap.''

"Oh my God, don't sound so fucking goody-goody,'' he says. Resentment churns within him. He resents Nelson's getting all this attention for being a prodigal son. He resents Janice's learning new words and pushing outward into new fields, away from him. He resents the fact that the world is so full of debt and nobody has to *pay*—not Mexico or Brazil, not the sleazy S and L banks, not Nelson. Rabbit never had much use for old-fashioned ethics but their dissolution eats at his bones.

The night and the next day pass, in bed and at the lot. He tells Benny and Elvira that Nelson is back and he looked fat to his mother but didn't announce any plans. Elvira has received a call from Rudy Krauss asking if she wanted to come over to Route 422 and sell for him. A Mr. Shimada spoke very highly of her. Also she hears that Jake is leaving the Volvo-Olds in Oriole and heading up a Lexus agency toward Pottstown. For now though she would rather hang loose here and see what Nelson has in mind. Benny's been asking around at other agencies and isn't too worried. "What happens happens, you know what I mean? As long as I got my health and my family—those are my priorities.'' Harry has asked them not to tell anyone in Service yet about Mr. Shimada's surprise attack. He feels increasingly detached; as he walks the plastic-tiled display floor, his head seems to float above it as dizzily high as his top-hatted head above the pitted, striped asphalt that day of the parade. He drives home, catches the beginning of Brokaw on 10 (he may have a kind of harelip, but at least he doesn't say "aboot") before Janice insists he get back in the Celica with her and drive across Brewer to Mt. Judge for the zillionth time in his life.

Nelson has shaved his mustache and taken off his earring. His face has a playground tan and he does look plump. His upper lip, exposed again, seems long and puffy and bulging outward, like Ma Springer's used to. That's who it turns out he resembles; she had a tight stuffed-skin sausage look that Harry can see now developing in Nelson. The boy moves with a certain old-lady stiffness, as if the rehab has squeezed the drugs and the jitters out of him but also his natural nervous quickness. For the first time, he seems to his father middle-aged, and his thinning hair and patches of exposed scalp part of him and not just a condition that will heal. He reminds Harry of a minister, a slightly sleek and portly representative of some no-name sect like that lame-brain who buried Thelma. A certain acquired formality extends to his clothes: though the evening is seasonably humid and warm, he wears a striped necktie with a white shirt, making Harry feel falsely youthful in his soft-collared polo shirt with the Flying Eagle emblem.

Nelson met his parents at the door and after embracing his mother attempted to do the same with his father, awkwardly wrapping both arms around the much taller man and pulling him down to rub scratchy cheeks. Harry was taken by surprise and not pleased: the embrace felt showy and queer and forced, the kind of thing these TV evangelists tell you to do to one another, before they run off screen and get their secretaries to lay them. He and Nelson have hardly touched since the boy's age hit double digits. Some kind of reconciliation or amends was no doubt intended but to Harry it felt like a rite his son has learned elsewhere and that has nothing to do with being an Angstrom.

Pru in her turn seems bewildered by suddenly having a minister for a husband; when Harry bends down expecting the soft warm push of her lips on his, he gets instead her dry cheek, averted with a fearful quickness. He is hurt but can't believe he has done anything wrong. Since their episode that wild and windy night, the silence from her side has indicated a wish to pretend it never happened, and with his silence he has indicated that he is willing. He hasn't the strength any more, the excess vitality, for an affair—its danger, its demand performances, the secrecy added like a filigree to your normal life, your gnawing preoccupation with it and with the constant threat of its being

discovered and ended. He can't bear to think of Nelson's knowing, whereas Ronnie's knowing he didn't much mind. He even
enjoyed it, like a sharp elbow given under the basket. Thelma
and he had been two of a kind, each able to gauge the risks and
benefits, able to construct together a stolen space in which they
could feel free for an hour, free of everything but each other.
Within your own generation—the same songs, the same wars,
the same attitudes toward those wars, the same rules and radio
shows in the air—you can gauge the possibilities and impossi-
bilities. With a person of another generation, you are treading
water, playing with fire. So he doesn't like to feel even this small
alteration in Pru's temperature, this coolness like a rebuke.

The children eat with them, Judy and Harry on one side of
the Springers' mahogany dining-room table, set as if for a holiday, Janice and Roy on the other, Pru and Nelson at the heads.
Nelson offers grace; he makes them all hold hands and shut their
eyes and after they're ready to scream with embarrassment pronounces the words, "Peace. Health. Sanity. Love."

"Amen," says Pru, sounding scared.

Judy can't stop staring up at Harry, to see what he makes of
it. "Nice," he tells his son. "That something you learned at the
detox place?"

"Not detox, Dad, rehab."

"Whatever it was, it was full of religion?"

"You got to admit you're powerless and dependent on a higher
power, that's the first principle of AA and NA."

"As I remember it, you didn't use to go much for any higher-
power stuff."

"I didn't, and still don't, in the form that orthodox religion
presents it in. All you have to believe in is a power greater than
ourselves—God as we understand Him."

Everything sounds so definite and pat, Harry has to fight the
temptation to argue. "No, great," he says. "Anything that gets
you through the night, as Sinatra says." Mim had quoted that
to him once. In this Springer house tonight Harry feels a huge
and regretful distance from Mim and Mom and Pop and all that
sunken God-fearing Jackson Road Thirties-Forties world.

"You used to believe a lot of that stuff," Nelson tells him.

"I did. I do," Rabbit says, irritating the kid, he knows, with
his amiability. But he has to add, "Hallelujah. When they stuck
that catheter into my heart, I saw the light."

Nelson announces, "They tell you at the center that there'll be people who mock you for going straight, but they don't say one of them will be your own father."

"I'm not mocking anything. Jesus. Have all the peace and love and sanity you want. I'm all for it. We're all all for it. Right, Roy?"

The little boy stares angrily at being suddenly singled out. His loose wet lower lip begins to tremble; he turns his face toward his mother's side. Pru tells Harry, in a soft directed voice in which he does sense a certain mist of acknowledgment, of rain splashing at a screened window, "Roy's been very upset, readjusting to Nelson's coming back."

"I know how he feels," Harry says. "We'd all gotten used to his not being around."

Nelson looks toward Janice in protest and appeal and she says, "Nelson, tell us about the counselling work you did," in the fake tone of one who has already heard about it.

As Nelson speaks, he sits with a curious tranquillized still-ness; Harry is used to the kid, from little on up, being full of nervous elusive twitches, that yet had something friendly and hopeful about them. "Mostly," he says, "you just listen, and let them work it out through their own verbalization. You don't have to say much, just show you're willing to wait, and listen. The most hardened street kids eventually open up. Once in a while you have to remind them you've been there yourself, so their war stories don't impress you. A lot have been dealers, and when they start bragging how much money they made all you have to do is ask, 'Where is it now?' They don't have it," Nelson tells the listening table, his own staring children. "They blew it."

"Speaking of blowing it—" Harry begins.

Nelson overrides him with his steady-voiced sermon. "You try to get them to see themselves that they are addicts, that they weren't outsmarting anybody. The realization has to come from them, from within, it's not something they can accept imposed on them by you. Your job is to listen; it's your silence, mostly, that leads them past their own internal traps. You start talking, they start resisting. It takes patience, and faith. Faith that the process will work. And it does. It invariably does. It's thrilling to see it happen, again and again. People want to be helped. They know things are wrong."

Harry still wants to speak but Janice intercedes by telling him, loudly for their audience at the table, "One of Nelson's ideas about the lot is to make it a treatment center. Brewer doesn't have anything like the facilities it needs to cope with the problem. The drug problem.''

"That's the absolutely dumbest idea I've ever heard," Harry says promptly. "Where's the money in it? You're dealing with people who have *no* money, they've blown it all for drugs."

Nelson is goaded into sounding a bit more like his old self. He whines, "There's *grant* money, Dad. Federal money. State. Even do-nothing Bush admits we got to do *some*thing."

"You've got twenty employees you've fucked up over there at the lot, and most of 'em have families. What happens to the mechanics in Service? What about your sales reps—poor little Elvira?''

"They can get other jobs. It's not the end of the world. People don't stick with jobs the way your scared generation did."

"Yeah, scared—with your generation on the loose we got reason to be scared. How would you ever turn that cement-block shed over there into a hospital?''

"It wouldn't be a hospital—"

"You're already one hundred fifty thousand in the hole to Toyota Inc. and two weeks to pay it off in. Not to mention the seventy-five grand you owe Brewer Trust.''

"Those purchases in Slim's name, the cars never left the lot, so there's really no—"

"Not to mention the used you sold for cash you put in your own pocket.''

"Harry," Janice says, gesturing toward their audience of listening children. "This isn't the place.''

"There *is* no place where I can get a handle on what this lousy kid has done! Over two hundred thousand fucking shekels—where's it going to come from?'' Sparks of pain flicker beneath the muscles of his chest, he feels a dizziness in which the faces at the table float as in a sickening soup. Bad sensations have been worsening lately; it's been over three months since that angioplasty opened his LAD. Dr. Breit warned that restenosis often sets in after three months.

Janice is saying, "But he's learned so much, Harry. He's so much wiser. It's as if we sent him to graduate school with the money.''

"School, all this school! What's so great about school all of a sudden? School's just another rip-off. All it teaches you is how to rip off dopes that haven't been to school yet!''

"I don't want to get back to school," Judy pipes up. "Everybody there is stuck-up."

"I don't mean *your* school, honey." Rabbit can hardly breathe; his chest feels full of bits of Styrofoam that won't dissolve. He must get himself unaggravated.

From the head of the table Nelson radiates calm and solidity. "Dad, I was an addict. I admit it," he says. "I was doing crack, and a run of that gets to be expensive. You're afraid to crash, and need a fresh hit every twenty minutes. If you go all night, you can run through thousands. But that money I stole didn't all go to my habit. Lyle needed big money for some experimental stuff the FDA jerks are sitting on and has to be smuggled in from Europe and Mexico."

"Lyle," Harry says with satisfaction. "How is the old computer whiz?"

"He seems to be holding his own for the time being."

"He'll outlive me," Harry says, as a joke, but the real possibility of it stabs him like an icicle. "So Springer Motors," he goes on, trying to get a handle on it, "went up in coke and pills for a queer." How queer, he wonders, staring at his middle-aged, fattened-up, rehabilitated son, is the kid? Pru's answer to that had never quite satisfied him. If Nelson wasn't queer, how come she let Harry ball her? A lot of pent-up hunger there, her coming twice like that.

Nelson tells him, in that aggravating tranquillized nothing-can-touch-me tone, "You get too excited, Dad, about what really isn't, in this day and age, an awful lot of money. You have this Depression thing about the dollar. There's nothing holy about the dollar, it's just a unit of measurement."

"Oh. Thanks for explaining that. What a relief."

"As to Toyota, it's no big loss. The company's been stale for years, in my opinion. Look at their TV ads for the Lexus compared with Nissan's for the Infiniti: there's no comparison. Infiniti's are fan*tas*tic, there's no car in them, just birds and trees, they're selling a *con*cept. Toyota's selling another load of tin. Don't be so fixated about Toyota. Springer Motors is still there," Nelson states. "The company still has assets. Mom and I are working it out, how to deploy them."

"Good luck," Harry says, rolling up his napkin and reinserting it in its ring, a child's ring of some clear substance filled with tiny needles of varied color. "In our thirty-three years of marriage your mother hasn't been able to deploy the ingredients of a decent meal on the table, but maybe she'll learn. Maybe Mr. Lister'll teach her how to deploy. Pru, that was a lovely meal. Excuse the conversation. You really have a way with fish.

Loved those little spicy like peas on top." As he shakes out a
Nitrostat from the small bottle he carries everywhere, he sees
his hands trembling in a new way—not just a tremor, but jumping, as if with thoughts all their own, that they aren't sharing
with him.

"Capers," Pru says softly.

"Harry, Nelson is coming back to the lot tomorrow," Janice
says.

"Great. That's another relief."

"I wanted to say, Dad, thanks for filling in. The summer stat
sheets look pretty good, considering."

"Con*sid*ering? We pulled off a miracle over there. That Elvira
is dynamite. As I guess you know. This Jap that gave us the ax
wants to hire her for Rudy over on 422. The inventory is being
shifted to his lot." He turns to Janice and says, "I can't believe
you're putting this loser back in charge."

Janice says, in the calm tone everybody at the table is acquir-
ing, as if to humor a madman, "He's not a loser. He's your son
and he's a new person. We can't deny him a chance."

In a voice more wifely than Janice's, Pru adds, "He really
has changed, Harry."

"A day at a time," Nelson recites, "with the help of a higher
power. Once you accept that help, Dad, it's amazing how nothing gets you down. All these years, I think I've been seriously
depressed; everything seemed too much. Now I just put it all in
God's hands, roll over, and go to sleep. You have to keep up the
program, of course. There're local meetings, and I drive down
to Philly once a week to see my therapist and check on some of
my old kids. I love counselling." He turns to his mother and
smiles. "I love it, and it loves me."

Harry asks him, "These druggy kids you deal with, they all
black?"

"Not all. After a while you don't even see that any more.
White or black, they have the same basic problem. Low self-
esteem."

Such knowingness, such induced calm and steadiness and
virtue: it makes Rabbit feel claustrophobic. He turns to his
granddaughter, looking for an opening, a glint, a ray of undoc-
tored light. He asks her, "What do you make of all this, Judy?"

The child's face wears a glaze of perfection—perfect straight
teeth, perfectly spaced lashes, narrow gleams in her green eyes
and along the strands of her hair. Nature is trying to come up
with another winner. "I like having Daddy back," she says,

"and not so crazy. He's more responsible." Again, he feels that words are being recited, learned at a rehearsal he wasn't invited to attend. But how can he wish anything for this child but the father she needs?

Out on the curb, he asks Janice to drive the Celica, though it means adjusting the seat and the mirrors. Heading back around the mountain, he asks her, "You really don't want me back at the lot?" He looks down at his hands. Their jumping has subsided but is still fascinating.

"I think for now, Harry. Let's give Nelson the space. He's trying so hard."

"He's full of AA bullshit."

"It's not bullshit if you need it to live a normal life."

"He doesn't look like himself."

"He will as you get used to him."

"He reminds me of your mother. She was always laying down the law."

"Everybody knows he looks just like you. Only not as tall, and he has my eyes."

The park, its shadowy walks, its decrepit tennis courts, its memorial tank that will never fire another shot. You can't see these things so clearly when you're driving. They go by like museum exhibits whose labels have all peeled off. He tries to climb out of his trapped and angry mood. "Sorry if I sounded ugly at dinner, in front of the grandchildren."

"We were prepared for much worse," she says serenely.

"I didn't mean to bring up the money or any of that stuff at all. But somebody has to. You're in real trouble."

"I know," Janice says, letting the streetlights of upper Weiser wash over her—her stubborn blunt-nosed profile, her little hands tight on the steering wheel, the diamond-and-sapphire ring she inherited from her mother. "But you have to have faith. You've taught me that."

"I have?" He is pleasantly surprised, to think that in thirty-three years he has taught her anything. "Faith in what?"

"In us. In life," she says. "Another reason I think you should stay away from the lot now, you've been looking tired. Have you been losing weight?"

"A couple pounds. Isn't that good? Isn't that what the hell I'm supposed to be doing?"

"It depends on how you do it," Janice says, so annoyingly full of new information, new presumption. She reaches over and gives his inner upper thigh, right where they inserted the catheter and he could have bled to death, a squeeze. "We'll be fine," she lies.

Now August, muggy and oppressive in its middle weeks, is bringing summer to a sparkling distillation, a final clarity. The fairways at the Flying Eagle, usually burnt-out and as hard as the cart-paths this time of year, with all the rain they've had are still green, but for the rough of reddish-brown buckgrass, and an occasional spindly maple sapling beginning to show yellow. It's the young trees that turn first—more tender, more attuned. More fearful.

Ronnie Harrison still swings like a blacksmith: short backswing, ugly truncated follow-through, sometimes a grunt in the middle. No longer needed at the lot, needing a partner if he was going to take up golf again, Rabbit remembered Thelma's saying how they had had to resign from the club because of her medical bills. Over the phone, Ronnie had seemed surprised—Harry had surprised himself, dialling the familiar digits trained into his fingers by the dead affair—but had accepted, surprisingly. They were making peace, perhaps, over Thelma's body. Or reviving a friendship—not a friendship, an involvement—that had existed since they were little boys in knickers and hightop sneakers scampering through the pebbly alleys of Mt. Judge. When Harry thinks back through all those years, to Ronnie's pugnacious thick-lipped dull-eyed face as it loomed on the elementary-school playground, to Ronnie crowingly playing with his big pale cucumber of a prick (circumcised, and sort of flat on its upper side) in the locker room, and then to Ronnie on the rise and on the make in his bachelor years around Brewer, one of the guys it turned out who had gone with Ruth before Rabbit did, Ronnie in those years full of smart-ass talk and dirty stories, a slimy operator, and then to Ronnie married to Thelma and working for Schuylkill Mutual, a kind of a sad sack really, plugging along doggedly, delivering his pitch, talking about "your loved ones" and when you're "out of the picture," slowly becoming the wanly smiling bald man in the photo on Thelma's dresser whom Harry could feel looking up his ass, so once to Thelma's amusement he got out of bed and put the photo flat on the bureau top, so afterwards she always turned it away before he arrived of an afternoon, and then to Ronnie as a widower, with the face of a bleached prune, pulled-looking wrinkles down from his eyes, an old guy's thin skin showing pink at the cheekbones, Harry feels that Ronnie has always been with him, a presence he couldn't avoid, an aspect of himself he didn't want to face but now does. That clublike cock, those slimy jokes, the blue eyes looking up his ass, what the hell, we're all just human, bodies and brains at one end and the rest just plumbing.

Their first round, playing as a twosome, they have a good enough time that they schedule another, and then a third. Ronnie has his old clients but he's no longer out there generating new business among the young husbands, he can take an afternoon off with a little notice. Their games are rusty and erratic, and the match usually comes down to the last hole or two. Will Harry's fine big free swing deliver the ball into the fairway or into the woods? Will Ronnie look up and skull an easy chip across the green into the sand trap, or will he keep his head down, his hands ahead, and get the ball close, to save a par? The two men don't talk much, lest the bad blood between them surface; the sight of the other messing up is so hilariously welcome as to suggest affection. They never mention Thelma.

On the seventeenth, a long par-four with a creek about one hundred ninety yards out, Ronnie plays up short with a four-iron. "That's a chickenshit way to play it," Harry tells him, and goes with a driver. Concentrating on keeping his flying right elbow close to his body, he catches the ball sweet, clearing the creek by thirty yards. Ronnie, compensating, tries too hard on his next shot: needing to take a three-wood, he roundhouses a big banana ball into the pine woods on the Mt. Pemaquid side of the fairway. Thus relieved of pressure, Rabbit thinks *Easy does it* on his six-iron and clicks off a beauty that falls into the heart of the green as if straight down a drainpipe. His par leaves him one up, so he can't lose, and only has to tie to win. Expansively he says to Ronnie as they ride the cart to the eighteenth tee, "How about that Voyager Two? To my mind that's more of an achievement than putting a man on the moon. In the *Standard* yesterday I was reading where some scientist says it's like sinking a putt from New York to Los Angeles."

Ronnie grunts, sunk in a losing golfer's self-loathing.

"Clouds on Neptune," Rabbit says, "and volcanos on Triton. What do you think it means?"

One of his Jewish partners down in Florida might have come up with some angle on the facts, but up here in Dutch country Ronnie gives him a dull suspicious look. "Why would it mean anything? Your honor."

Rabbit feels rubbed the wrong way. You try to be nice to this guy and he snubs you. He is an ugly prick and always was. You offer him the outer solar system to think about and he brushes it aside. He crushes it in his coarse brain. Harry feels a fine excessiveness in that spindly machine's feeble but true transmissions across billions of miles, a grace of sorts that chimes with the excessive beauty of this crystalline late-summer day. He needs to praise. Ronnie must know some such need, or he and Thelma wouldn't have attended that warehouse of a no-name church. "Those three rings nobody ever saw before," Harry insists, "just like drawn with a pencil," echoing Bernie Drechsel's awe at the thinness of flamingo legs.

But Ronnie has moved off, over by the ball washer, pretending not to hear, and takes a series of vicious practice swings, anxious to begin the hole and avenge his previous poor showing. Disappointed, distracted by thoughts of brave Voyager, Rabbit lets his right elbow float at the top of the backswing and cuts weakly across the ball, slicing it, on a curve as uncanny as if plotted by computer, into the bunker in the buckgrass to the right of the fairway. The eighteenth is a par-five that flirts with the creek coming back but should be an easy par; in his golfing prime he more than once birdied it. Yet he has to come out of the bunker sideways with a wedge and then hits his three-iron, not his best club but he needs the distance, fat, trying too hard just like Ronnie on the last hole, and winds up in the creek, his yellow Pinnacle finally found under a patch of watercress. The drop consumes another stroke and he's so anxious to nail his nine-iron right to the pin he pulls it, so he lies five on the deep fringe to the left of the green. Ronnie has been poking along, hitting ugly low shots with his blacksmith swing but staying out of trouble, on in four, so Rabbit's only hope is to chip in. It's a grassy lie and he fluffs it, like the worst kind of moronic golfing coward he forgets to hit down and through, and the ball moves maybe two feet, onto the froghair short of the green in six, and Ronnie has a sure two putts for a six and a crappy, crappy win. If there's one thing Harry hates, it's losing to a bogey. He picks up his Pinnacle and with a sweeping heave throws the ball into the pine woods. Something in his chest didn't like the big motion but it is bliss of sorts to see the tormenting orb disappear in a distant swish and thud. The match ends tied.

"So, no blood," Ronnie says, having rolled his twelve-footer to within a gimme.

"Good match," Harry grunts, deciding against shaking hands. The shame of his collapse clings to him. Who says the universe isn't soaked in disgrace?

As they transfer balls and tees and sweaty gloves to the pocket of their bags, Ronnie, now that it's his turn to feel expansive, volunteers, "Didja see last night on Peter Jennings, the last thing, they showed the photographs of the rings and the moon moving away and then a composite they had made of the various shots of Neptune projected onto a ball and twirled, so the whole planet was there, like a toy? Incredible," Ronnie admits, "what they can do with computer graphics."

The image faintly sickens Harry, of Voyager taking those last shots of Neptune and then sailing off into the void, forever. How can you believe how much void there is?

The golf bags in the rack here by the pro shop throw long shafts of shadow. These days are drawing in. Harry is thirsty, and looks forward to a beer on the club patio, at one of the outdoor tables, under a big green-and-white umbrella, beside the swimming pool with its cannonballing kids and budding bimbos, while the red sun sinks behind the high horizon of Mt. Pemaquid. Before they head up for the beers, the two men look directly at each other, by mistake. On an unfortunate impulse, Rabbit asks, "Do you miss her?"

Ronnie gives him an angled squint. His eyelids look sore under his white eyelashes. "Do you?"

Ambushed, Rabbit can barely pretend he does. He used Thelma, and then she was used up. "Sure," he says.

Ronnie clears his ropy throat and checks that the zipper on his bag is up and then shoulders the bag to take to his car. "Sure you do," he says. "Try to sound sincere. You never gave a fuck. No. Excuse me. A fuck is exactly what you gave."

Harry hangs between impossible alternatives—to tell him how much he enjoyed going to bed with Thelma (Ronnie's smiling photo watching) or to claim that he didn't. He answers merely, "Thelma was a lovely woman."

"For me," Ronnie tells him, dropping his pugnacious manner and putting on his long widower's face, "it's like the bottom of the world has dropped out. Without Thel, I'm just going through the motions." His voice gets all froggy, disgustingly. When Harry invites him up on the patio for the beers, he says, "No, I better be getting back. Ron Junior and his newest significant other are having me over for dinner." When Harry tries to set a date for the next game, he says, "Thanks, old bunny, but you're the member here. You're the one with the rich wife. You know the Flying Eagle rules—you can't keep having the same guest. Anyway, Labor Day's coming. I better start getting back on the ball, or Schuylkill'll think I'm the one who died.''

He drives his slate-gray Celica home to Penn Park. Janice's Camry is not in the driveway and he thinks the phone ringing inside might be her. She's almost never here any more—off at her classes, or over in Mt. Judge babysitting, or at the lot consulting with Nelson, or in Brewer with her lawyer and those accountants Charlie told her to hire. He works the key in the lock—maddening, the scratchy way the key doesn't fit in the lock instantly, it reminds him of something from way back, something unpleasant that hollows his stomach, but what?—and shoves the door open with his shoulder and reaches the hall phone just as it's giving what he knows will be its dying ring. "Hello." He can hardly get the word out.

"Dad? What's the matter?''

"Nothing. Why?''

"You sound so winded.''

"I just came in. I thought you were your mother.''

"Mom's *been* here. I'm still at the lot, she suggested I call you. I've got this great idea.''

"I've heard it. You want to open a drug treatment center.''

"Maybe some day down the road. But for now I think we should work on the lot as what it is. It looks great, by the way, with all those little Toyotas in those funny colors of theirs gone. People are still coming in to buy used, they think we must be having a bargain sale, and a couple of companies are interested in the location—Hyundai for instance has this big new place over past Hayesville but the location is up behind a cloverleaf and nobody can figure out how to get to it, there's too much landscaping, they'd love to have a spot right on 111—but what I'm calling about was this idea I got last night, I ran it past Mom, she said to talk to you.''

"O.K., O.K., you're good to include me,'' Harry says.

"Last night I was out on the river, you know over west of the city where they have all these little river cottages with colored lights and porches and steps going down into the water?''

"I don't know, actually, I've never been there, but go on.''

"Well, Pru and I were over there last night with Jason and Pam, you may have heard me mention them.''

"Vaguely.'' All these pauses for confirmation, they are wearing Harry down. Why can't the kid just spit it out? Is his father such an ogre?

"Anyway this guy they know has one of these cottages, it was neat, the colored lights and music on the radios and up and down the river all these boats, people water skiing and all—"

"Sounds terrific. I hope Jason and Pam don't belong to that old Lyle-Slim crowd."

"They knew 'em, but they're *straight*, Dad. They're even thinking of having a baby."

"If you're going to keep coke licked, you got to stay away from the old coke crowd."

"Like I said, they're real straight arrow. One of their best friends is Ron Harrison, Jr., the carpenter."

What is that supposed to mean? Does Nelson know about him and Thelma? "O.K., O.K.," Harry says.

"So we were sitting there on the porch and this fantastic thing goes by—a motorcycle on the water. They have different names for them—wet bikes, surf jets, jet skis—"

"Yeah, I've seen 'em in Florida, out on the ocean. They look unsafe."

"Dad, this was the best I ever saw—it went like a rocket. Just *buzzed* along. Jason said it's called a Yamaha Waverunner and it operates on a new principle, I don't know, it compresses water somehow and then shoots it out the back, and he said the only guy who sells 'em, a dinky little back-yard shop up toward Shoe-makersville, can't keep 'em in stock, and anyway he's not that interested, he's a retired farmer who just does it as a hobby. So I called Yamaha's sales office in New York this morning and talked to a guy. It wouldn't be just Waverunners we'd sell, of course, we'd carry the motorcycles, and their snowmobiles and trailers, and they make generators a lot of small companies use and these three- and four-wheelers, ATVs, that farmers have now to get around their places, a lot more efficient than electric golf carts—"

"Nelson. Wait. Don't talk so fast. What about Manny and the boys over in Service?"

"It isn't Manny any more, Dad. It's Arnold."

"I meant to say Arnold. The guy who looks like a pig in pajamas mincing around. I know who Arnold is. I don't care who he is, he or she for that matter, who heads the fucking service division, they're used to *cars*, big things with four wheels that run on gasoline instead of compressed water."

"They can adjust. People can adjust, if you're under a certain age. Anyway, Mom and I have already trimmed Service. We let go three mechanics, and are running some ads for inspection packages. We want to pep up the used end, for a while it'll be only used just like Grandpa Springer started out, he used to tell me how he kept the Toyotas out in back out of sight, people had this distrust of Japanese products. In a way it's better already, the people without much to spend aren't scared off by the new car showroom and the yen exchange rate and all. So—?''

"So?"

"What do you think of the Yamaha idea?"

"O.K., now remember. You asked. And I appreciate your asking. I'm touched by that, I realize you don't have to ask me anything, you and your mother have the lot locked up. But in answer to your question, I think it's the dumbest thing I've ever heard. Jet skis are a fad. Next year it'll be jet roller skates. The profit on a toy like a motorcycle or a snowmobile is maybe a tenth that on a solid family car—can you sell ten times as many? Don't forget, there's a Depression coming.''

"Who says?"

"*I* say; *eve*rybody says! Everybody says Bush is just like Hoover. You're too young to remember Hoover."

"That was an inflated stock market. The market if anything is undersold now. Why would we have a Depression?"

"Because we don't have any *dis*cipline! We're drowning in debt! We don't even own our own country any more! My image of this is you were sitting there on the porch of that shack with all these colored lights stoned on something or other and this thing buzzes by and you think, 'Wow! Salvation!' You're almost thirty-three and you're still into toys and fads. You came back from that detox place stuffed full of good intentions and now you're getting rocks in the brain again."

There is a pause. The old Nelson would have combatted him with some childish defensive whining. But the voice on the other end of the line at last says, with a touch of the ministerial gravity and automated calm Rabbit had noticed at dinner the other week, "What you don't realize about a consumer society, Dad, is it's all fads in a way. People don't buy things because they *need* 'em. You actually need very little. You buy something because it's be*yond* what you need, it's something that will en*hance* your life, not just keep it plugging along."

"It sounds to me like you did too much mystic meditation at that detox place."

"You say detox just to bug me. It was a treatment center, and then a halfway house for rehab. The detox part of it just takes a couple days. It's getting the relational poison out of your system that takes longer.''

"Is that what I am to you? Relational poison?'' Being snubbed by Ronnie Harrison won't stop rankling, underneath this conversation.

Again, Nelson is silent. Then: "Maybe, but not only. I keep trying to love you, but you don't really want it. You're afraid of it, it would tie you down. You've been scared all your life of being tied down.''

Rabbit cannot speak; he is letting a Nitrostat dissolve under his tongue. It burns like a little pellet of red candy, and induces a floating dilated feeling that adds inches to his sensation of height. The kid will make him cry if he thinks about it. He says, "Let's cut the psychology and get down to earth. What the hell do you and your mother intend to do about that hundred fifty thousand dollars Toyota has to have by the end of the month or else it will prosecute?''

"Oh,'' the boy says airily, "didn't Mom tell you? That's been settled. They've been paid. We took out a loan.''

"A loan? Who would trust you?''

"Brewer Trust. A second mortgage on the lot property, it's worth at least half a million. A hundred forty-five, and they consolidated it with the seventy-five for Slim's five cars, which will be coming back to us pretty much as a credit on the rolling inventory we were maintaining with Mid-Atlantic Motors. As soon as they took our inventory over to Rudy's lot, don't forget, they started owing *us*.''

"And you're somehow going to pay back Brewer Trust selling water scooters?''

"You don't have to pay a loan back, they don't *want* you to pay it back; they just want you to keep up the installments. Meanwhile, the value of the dollar goes down and you get to tax-deduct all the interest. We were underfinanced, in fact, before.''

"Thank God you're back in the saddle. How does your mother like the Yamaha connection?''

"She likes it. She's not like you; she's open, and willing to be creative. Dad, there's something I think we should try to process sometime. Why do you resent it so, me and Mom getting out into the world and trying to learn new things?''

"I don't resent it. I respect it.''

"You hate it. You act jealous and envious. I say this in love,

Dad. You feel stuck, and you want everybody to be stuck with you.''

He tries giving back the kid a little of his own medicine, some therapeutic silence. His Nitrostat rings that little bell in the seat of his pants, and his dilated blood vessels lift weight from the world around him, making it seem delicate and distant, like Neptune's rings. "It wasn't me," he says at last, "who ran Springer Motors into the ground. But do what you want. You're the Springer, not me.''

He can hear a voice in the background, a female voice, and then that seashell sound of a telephone mouthpiece with a hand placed over it. When Nelson's voice returns, it has changed tint, as if dipped in something, by what has passed between him and Elvira. Love juices have flowed. Maybe the kid is normal after all. "Elvira has something she wants to ask you. What do you think of the Pete Rose settlement?''

"Tell her I think it was the best both sides could do. And I think he should get into the Hall of Fame anyway, on the strength of his numbers. But tell her Schmidt is my idea of a classy ballplayer. Tell her I miss her.''

Hanging up, Harry pictures the showroom, the late-afternoon light on the dust on the display windows, tall to the sky now with all the banners down, and the fun going on, amazingly, without him.

The thready lawn behind their little limestone house at 14½ Franklin Drive has the dry kiss of autumn on it: brown patches and the first few fallen leaves, cast off by the weeping cherry, his neighbor's black walnut, the sweet cherry that leans close to the house so he can watch the squirrels scrabble along its branches, and the willow above the empty cement fish pond with the blue-painted bottom and rim of real seashells. These trees still seem green and growing but their brown leaves are accumulating in the grass. Even the hemlock toward the neighboring house of thin yellow bricks, and the rhododendrons along the palisade fence separating the Angstroms' yard from the property of the big mock-Tudor house of clinker bricks, and the shaggy Austrian pines whose cast-off needles clutter the cement pond, though all evergreen, are tinged by summer's end, dusty and sweetly dried-out like the smell that used to come from the old cedar hope chest where Mom kept spare blankets and their good embroidered linen tablecloth for Thanksgiving and Christmas and the two old crazy quilts she had inherited from the

Renningers. It was family legend that these quilts were fabulously valuable but when, in some family crunch when Harry was in his early teens, they tried to sell them, the best offer they could get was sixty dollars apiece. After much talk around the porcelain kitchen table, they took the offer, and now authentic old quilts like that bring thousands if in good condition. When he thinks about those old days and the amounts of money they considered important it's as if they were being cheated, living on slave wages, eating bread eleven cents a loaf. They were living in a financial dungeon, back there on Jackson Road, and the fact that everybody else was in it too only makes it sadder. Just thinking about those old days lately depresses him; it makes him face life's constant depreciation. Lying awake at night, afraid he will never fall asleep or will fall asleep forever, he feels a stifling uselessness in things, a kind of atomic decay whereby the precious glowing present turns, with each tick of the clock, into the leaden slag of history.

The forsythia and beauty bush both have been getting out of hand during this wet summer and Harry, on this cloudy cool Thursday before the Labor Day weekend, has been trying to prune them back into shape for the winter. With the forsythia, you take out the oldest stem from the base, making the bush younger and thinner and more girlish suddenly, and then cut back the most flagrant skyward shoots and the down-drooping branches on their way to reroot in among the day lilies. It doesn't do to be tenderhearted; the harder you cut back now, the more crammed with glad yellow blossoms the stubby branches become in the spring. The beauty bush poses a tougher challenge, an even tighter tangle. Any attempt to follow the tallest stems down to their origin gets lost in the net of interwoven branchlets, and the bottom thicket of small trunks is so dense as to repel a clipper or pruning saw; there is not a knife's-width of space. The bush in this season of neglect has grown so tall he really should go to the garage for the aluminum stepladder. But Rabbit is reluctant to face the garage's grimy tumble of cast-aside tires and stiff hoses and broken flowerpots and rusted tools inherited from the previous owners, who failed to clean out the garage the same way they left a stack of *Playboys* in an upstairs closet. In ten years he and Janice have added their own stuff to the garage, so that gradually there wasn't space for one car let alone two in it; it has become a cave of deferred decisions and sentimentally cherished junk so packed that if he tries to extract the ladder several old paint cans and a lawn sprinkler bereft of its washers will come clattering down. So he stretches and reaches into the beauty bush until his chest begins to ache, with the sensation of an inflexible patch stitched to the inner side of his skin. His nitroglycerin pills got left in the sweat-rimmed pocket of his plaid golf slacks last night when he went to bed early, alone, having fed himself a beer and some Corn Chips after that match with Ronnie ended so sourly.

To placate the pain, he switches to weeding the day lilies and the violet hosta. Wherever a gap permits light to activate the sandy soil, chickweed and crabgrass grow, and purslane with its hollow red stems covers the earth in busy round-leaved zigzags. Weeds too have their styles, their own personalities that talk back to the gardener in the daze of the task. Chickweed is a good weed, soft on the hands unlike thistles and burdock, and pulls easily; it knows when the jig is up and comes willingly, where wild cucumber keeps breaking off at one of its many joints, and grass and red sorrel and poison ivy spread underground, like creeping diseases that cannot be cured. Weeds don't know they're weeds. Safe next to the trunk of the weeping cherry a stalk of blue lettuce has grown eight feet tall, taller than he.

A block and a half away, the traffic on Penn Boulevard murmurs and hisses, its purr marred by the occasional sudden heave and grind of a great truck shifting gears, or by an angry horn, or the wop-wop-wopping bleat of an ambulance rushing some poor devil to the hospital. You see them now and then, driving down a side street, these scenes: some withered old lady being carried in a stretcher down her porch stairs in a slow-motion sled ride, her hair unpinned, her mouth without its dentures, her eyes staring skyward as if to disown her body; or some red-faced goner being loaded into the double metal doors while his abandoned mate in her bathrobe snivels on the curb and the paramedics close around his body like white vultures feeding. Rabbit has noticed a certain frozen peacefulness in such terminal street tableaux. A certain dignity in the doomed one, his or her moment come round at last; a finality that isolates the ensemble like a spotlit crèche. You would think people would take it worse than they do. They don't scream, they don't accuse God. We curl into ourselves, he supposes. We become numb animals. Earthworms on the hook.

From far across the river, a siren wails in the heart of Brewer. Above, in a sky gathering its fishscales for a rainy tomorrow, a small airplane rasps as it coasts into the airport beyond the old fairgrounds. What Harry instantly loved about this house was its hiddenness: not so far from all this traffic, it is yet not easy to find, on its macadamized dead end, tucked with its fractional number among the more pretentious homes of the Penn Park rich. He always resented these snobs and now is safe among them. Pulling into his dead-end driveway, working out back in his garden, watching TV in his den with its wavery lozenge-paned windows, Rabbit feels safe as in a burrow, where the hungry forces at loose in the world would never think to find him.

Janice pulls in in the pearl-gray Camry wagon. She is fresh from the afternoon class at the Penn State extension on Pine Street: "Real Estate Mathematics—Fundamentals and Applications." In a student outfit of sandals and wheat-colored sundress, with a looseknit white cardigan thrown over her shoulders, her forehead free of those Mamie Eisenhower bangs, she looks snappy, and brushed glossy, and younger than her age. Everything she wears these days has shoulders; even her cardigan has shoulders. She walks to him over what seems a great distance in the little quarter-acre yard, their property expanded by what has become a mutual strangeness. Unusually, she presents her face to be kissed. Her nose feels cold, like a healthy puppy's. "How was class?" he dutifully asks.

"Poor Mr. Lister seems so sad and preoccupied lately," she says. "His beard has come in all full of gray. We think his wife is leaving him. She came to class once and acted very snooty, we all thought."

"You all are getting to be a tough crowd. Aren't these classes about over? Labor Day's coming."

"Poor Harry, do you feel I've deserted you this summer? What are you going to do with all this mess you've pruned away? The beauty bush looks absolutely ravaged."

He admits, "I was getting tired and making bad decisions. That's why I stopped."

"Good thing," she says. "There wouldn't have been anything left but stumps. We'd have to call it the ugliness bush."

"Listen, you, I don't see you out here helping. Ever."

"The outdoors is your responsibility, the indoors is mine—isn't that how we do it?"

"I don't know how *we* do anything any more, you're never here. In answer to your question, I'd planned to stack what I cut over behind the fish pond to dry out and then burn it next spring when we're back from Florida."

"You're planning ahead right into 1990; I'm impressed. That

year is still very unreal to me. Won't the yard look ugly all winter then, though?''

"It won't look ugly, it'll look natural, and we won't be here to see it anyway.''

Her tongue touches the upper lip of her mouth, which has opened in thought. But she says nothing, just "I guess we won't, if we do things as normal.''

"If?''

She doesn't seem to hear, gazing at the fence-high heap of pruned branches.

He says, "If you're so in charge of the indoors, what are we having for dinner?''

"Damn,'' she says. "I meant to stop by at the farm stand there at the end of the bridge and pick up some sweet corn, but then I had so much else on my mind I sailed right by. I thought we'd have the corn with what's left of Tuesday's meatloaf and those dinner rolls in the breadbox before they get moldy. There was a wonderful tip in the *Standard* about how to freshen stale bread in the microwave, I forget what exactly, something to do with water. There must be a frozen veg in the freezer part we can have instead of sweet corn.''

"Or else we could sprinkle salt and sugar on ice cubes,'' he says. "One thing I know's in the fridge is ice cubes.''

"Harry, it's been on my *mind* to go shopping, but the IGA is so far out of the way and the prices at the Turkey Hill are ridiculous, and the convenience store over on Penn Boulevard has those surly kids behind the counter who I think punch extra figures into the cash register.''

"You're a shrewd shopper, all right,'' Harry tells her. The mackerel sky is forming a solid gray shelf in the southwest; they move together toward the house, away from the shadow of coming dark.

Janice says, "So.'' Saying "so'' is something she's picked up recently, from her fellow-students or her teachers, as the word for beginning to strike a deal. "You haven't asked me how I did on my last exam. We got them back.''

"How did you do?''

"Beautifully, really. Mr. Lister gave me a B minus but said it would have been a B plus if I could organize my thoughts better and clean up my spelling. I know it's 'i' before 'e' sometimes and the other way around some other times, but *when*?''

He loves her when she talks to him like this, as if he has all the answers. He leans the long-handled clippers in the garage against the wall behind a dented metal trash can and hangs the pruning saw on its nail. Shadowy in her sundress, she moves ahead of him up the back stairs and the kitchen light comes on. Inside the kitchen, she rummages, with that baffled frowning expression of hers, biting her tongue tip, in the refrigerator for edible fragments. He goes and touches her waist in the wheat-colored dress, lightly cups her buttocks as she bends over looking. Tenderly, he complains, "You didn't come home until late last night."

"You were asleep, poor thing. I didn't want to risk waking you so I slept in the guest room."

"Yeah, I get so groggy, suddenly. I keep wanting to finish that book on the American Revolution but it knocks me out every time."

"I shouldn't have given it to you for Christmas. I thought you'd enjoy it."

"I did. I do. Yesterday was a hard day. First Ronnie tied me on the last hole when I had the bastard all but beaten, and then he snubbed my invitation to play again, and then Nelson called all jazzed up with some crazy scheme about water scooters and Yamaha."

"I'm sure Ronnie has his reasons," Janice says. "I'm surprised he played with you at all. How do you feel about brussels sprouts?"

"I don't mind them."

"To me, they always taste spoiled; but they're all we have. I *promise* to get to the IGA tomorrow and stock up for the long weekend."

"We going to have Nelson and his tribe over?"

"I thought we might all meet at the club. We've hardly used it this summer."

"He sounded hyper on the phone—do you think he's back on the stuff already?"

"Harry, Nelson is *very* straight now. That place really has given him religion. But I agree, Yamaha isn't the answer. We must raise some capital and put ourselves on a solvent basis before we start courting another franchise. I've been talking to some of the other women getting their licenses—"

"You discuss our personal financial problems?"

"Not ours as such, just as a case study. It's all purely hypothetical. In real-estate class we always have a lot of case studies. And they all thought it was gro*tesque* to be carrying a mortgage amounting to over twenty-five hundred a month on the lot when we have so much other property.''

Rabbit doesn't like the trend here. He points out, ''But this place is already mortgaged, to the tune of seven hundred a month.''

''I *know* that, silly. Don't forget, this is my business now.'' She has stripped the brussels sprouts of their waxpaper box and put them in the plastic safe dish and put it in the microwave and punched out the time—three blips, a peep, and then a rising hum. ''We bought this place ten years ago,'' she tells him, ''for seventy-eight thousand and put fifteen down and have about ten or fifteen more in equity by now, it doesn't accumulate very fast in the first half of payback, there's a geometric curve they tell you about, so let's say there's still fifty outstanding; in any case, housing prices have gone way up in this area since 1980, it's been flattening out but hasn't started to go *down* yet, though it might this winter, you'd begin by asking two twenty, two thirty let's say, with the Penn Park location, and the seclusion, the fact that it has real limestone walls and not just facing, it has what they call historic value; we certainly wouldn't settle for less than two hundred, which minus the fifty would give us one fifty, which would wipe out two-thirds of what we owe Brewer Trust!''

Rabbit has rarely heard this long an utterance from Janice, and it takes him a few seconds to understand what she has been saying. ''You'd sell this place?''

''Well, Harry, it *is* very extravagant to keep it just for the summer essentially, especially when there's all that extra room over at Mother's.''

''I love this place,'' he tells her. ''It's the only place I've ever lived where I felt at home, at least since Jackson Road. This place has class. It's us.''

''Honey, I've loved it too, but we must be practical, that's what you've always been telling me. We don't need to own four places.''

''Why not sell the condo, then?''

''I thought of that, but we'd be lucky to get out of it what we paid for it. In Florida, places are like cars—people like them brand new. The new malls and everything are to the east.''

''What about the Poconos place?''

''There's not enough money there either. It's an unheated shack. We need two hundred thousand, honey.''

''*We* didn't roll up that debt to Toyota—Nelson did it, Nelson and his faggy boyfriends.''

"Well, you can say that, but *he* can't pay it back, and he was acting as part of the company."

"What about the lot? Why can't you sell the lot? That much frontage on Route 111 is worth a fortune; it's the real downtown, now that people are scared to go into the old downtown because of the spics."

A look of pain crosses Janice's face, rippling her exposed forehead; for once, he realizes, he is thinking slower than she is. "Never," she says curtly. "The lot is our number-one asset. We need it as a base for Nelson's future, Nelson's and your grandchildren's. That's what Daddy would want. I remember when he bought it after the war, it had been a country gas station, with a cornfield next to it, that had closed during the war when there were no cars, and he took Mother and me down to look at it, and I found this dump out back, out in that brambly part you call Paraguay, all these old auto parts and green and brown soda bottles that I thought were so valuable, it was like I had discovered buried treasure I thought, and I got my school dress all dirty so that Mother would have been mad if Daddy hadn't laughed and told her it looked like I had a taste for the car business. Springer Motors won't sell out as long as I'm alive and well, Harry. Anyway," she goes on, trying to strike a lighter note, "I don't know anything about industrial real estate. The beauty of selling this place is I can do it myself and get the salesperson's half of the broker's commission. I can't believe we can't get two for it; half of six per cent of two hundred thousand is six thousand dollars—all mine!"

He is still playing catch-up. "You'd sell it—I mean, you personally?"

"Of course, you big lunk, for a real-estate broker. It would be my entrée, as they call it. How could Pearson and Schrack, for instance, or Sunflower Realty, not take me on as a rep if I could bring in a listing like that right off the bat?"

"Wait a minute. We'd live in Florida most of the time—"

"*Some* of the time, honey. I don't know how much I could get away at first, I need to establish myself. Isn't Florida, honestly, a little boring? So flat, and everybody we know so old."

"And the rest of the time we'd live in Ma's old house? Where would Nelson and Pru go?"

"They'd be *there*, obviously. Harry, you seem a little slow. Have you been taking too many pills? Just the way we and Nelson used to live with Mother and Daddy. That wasn't so bad, was it? In fact, it was nice. Nelson and Pru would have built-in babysitters, and I wouldn't have to do all this housekeeping by myself.''

"What housekeeping?"

"You don't notice it, men never do, but there's an awful lot of simple drudgery to keeping two separate establishments going. You know how you always worry about one place being robbed while we're in the other. This way, we'd have one room at Mother's, I mean Nelson's, I'm sure they'd give us our old room back, and we'd never have to worry!"

Those bands of constriction, with their edges pricked out in pain, have materialized across Harry's chest. His words come out with difficulty. "How do Nelson and Pru feel about us moving in?"

"I haven't asked yet. I thought I might this evening, after I ran it by you. I really don't see how they can say no; it's my house, legally. So: what do you think?" Her eyes, which he is used to as murky and careful, often blurred by sherry or Campari, shine at the thought of her first sale.

He isn't sure. There was a time, when he was younger, when the thought of any change, even a disaster, gladdened his heart with the possibility of a shake-up, of his world made new. But at present he is aware mostly of a fluttering, binding physical resistance within him to the idea of being uprooted. "I hate it, offhand," he tells her. "I don't want to go back to living as somebody's tenant. We did that for fifteen years and finally got out of it. People don't live all bunched up, all the generations, any more."

"But they *do*, honey—that's one of the trends in living, now that homes have become so expensive and the world so crowded."

"Suppose they have more children."

"They won't."

"How do you know?"

"I just do. Pru and I have discussed it."

"Does Pru ever feel crowded, I wonder, by her mother-in-law?"

"I wouldn't know why. We both want the same thing—a happy and healthy Nelson."

Rabbit shrugs. Let her stew in her own juice, the cocky little mutt. Going off to school and thinking she's learned everybody's business. "You go over after supper and see how they like your crazy plan. I'm dead set against it, if my vote counts. Sell off the lot and tell the kid to get an honest job, is my advice."

Janice stops watching the microwave tick down its numbers and comes close to him, unexpectedly, touching his face again with that ghostly searching gesture, tucking her body against his to remind him sexually of her smallness, her smallness against his bigness, when they first met and still now. He smells her brushed-back salt-and-pepper hair and sees the blood-tinged whites of her dark eyes. "Of course your vote counts, it counts more than anybody's, honey." When did Janice start calling him honey? When they moved to Florida and got in with those Southerners and Jews. The Jewish couples down there had this at-rest quality, matched like pairs of old shoes, the men accepting their life as the only one they were going to get, and pleased enough. It must be a great religion, Rabbit thinks, once you get past the circumcision.

He and Janice let the house issue rest as a silent sore spot between them while they eat. He helps her clear and they add their plates to those already stacked in the dishwasher, waiting to be run through. With just the two of them, and Janice out of the house so much, it takes days for a sufficient load to build up on the racks. She telephones Nelson to see if they're going to be in and puts her white cardigan back on and gets back into the Camry and drives off to Mt. Judge. Wonder Woman. Rabbit catches the tail end of Jennings, a bunch of twitchy old black-and-white clips about World War II beginning with the invasion of Poland fifty years ago tomorrow, tanks versus cavalry, Hitler shrieking, Chamberlain looking worried; then he goes out into the dusk and the mosquitoes to stack the already wilting brush more neatly in the corner behind the cement pond with its fading blue bottom and widening crack. He gets back into the house in time for the last ten minutes of *Wheel of Fortune*. That Vanna! Can she strut! Can she clap her hands when the wheel turns! Can she turn those big letters around! She makes you proud to be a two-legged mammal.

By the end of the *Cosby* summer rerun, one of those with too much Theo in it, Harry is feeling sleepy, depressed by the idea of Janice selling the house but soothed by the thought that she'll never do it. She's too scatterbrained, she and the kid will just drift along deeper and deeper into debt like the rest of the world; the bank will play ball as long as the lot has value. The Phillies are out in San Diego and in sixth place anyway. He turns the TV sound way down and by the comforting shudder of the silenced imagery stretches out his feet on the Turkish hassock they brought from Ma Springer's house when they moved and

slumps down deeper into the silvery-pink wing chair he and
Janice bought at Schaechner's ten years ago. His shoulders ache
from all that pruning. He thinks of his history book but it's
upstairs by the bed. There is a soft ticking at the lozenge-pane
windows: rain, as on that evening at the beginning of summer,
when he'd just come out of the hospital, the narrow room with
the headless sewing dummy, another world, a dream world. The
phone wakes him when it rings. He looks at the thermostat clock
as he goes to the hall phone. 9:20. Janice has been over there a
long time. He hopes it isn't one of those coke dealers that still
now and then call, about money they are owed or a new ship-
ment of fresh "material" that has come in. You wonder how
these dealers get so rich, they seem so disorganized and hit-or-
miss. He was having a dream in the wing chair, some intense
struggle already fading and unintelligible, with an unseen an-
tagonist, but in a vivid domed space, like an old-time railroad
terminal only the ceiling was lower and paler, a chapel of some
kind, a tight space that clings to his mind, making his hand look
ancient and strange—the back swollen and bumpy, the fingers
withered—as it reaches for the receiver on the wall.

"Harry." He has never heard Janice's voice sound like this,
so stony, so dead.

"Hi. Where are you? I was getting afraid you'd had an accident."

"Harry, I—" Something grabs her throat and will not let her
speak.

"Yeah?"

Now she is speaking through tears, staggering over gulps,
suppressed sobs, lumps in her throat. "I described my idea to
Nelson and Pru, and we all agreed we shouldn't rush into it, we
should discuss it thoroughly, he seemed more receptive than
she, maybe because he understands the financial problems—"

"Yeah, yeah. Hey, it doesn't sound so bad so far. She's used
to considering the house as hers, no woman likes to share a
kitchen."

"After she'd put the children to bed, she came down with this
look on her face and said there was something then that Nelson
and I should know, if we were all going to live together."

"Yeah?" His own voice is still casual but he is no longer
sleepy; he can see what is coming like a tiny dot in the distance
that becomes a rocket ship in a space movie.

Janice's voice firms up, goes dead and level and lower, as if
others might be listening outside the door. She would be in their

old bedroom, sitting on the edge of the bed, Judy asleep beyond one wall and Roy behind the wall opposite. "She said you and she slept together that night you stayed here your first night out of the hospital."

The spaceship is upon him, with all its rivets and blinking lights. "She said that?"

"Yes she did. She said she doesn't know how it happened, except there'd always been this little attraction between you two and that night everything seemed so desperate."

A little attraction. He supposes that was fair, though tough. It had felt like more than that from his side. It had felt like he was seeing himself reflected, mirrored in a rangy young long-haired left-handed woman.

"Well? Is she telling the truth?"

"Well, honey, what can I say, I guess in a way—"

A big sob: he can picture Janice's face exactly, twisted and helpless and ugly, old age collapsing in upon her.

"—but at the time," Rabbit goes on, "it seemed sort of natural, and we haven't done anything since, not even said a word. We've been pretending it didn't happen."

"Oh, Harry. How *could* you? Your own daughter-in-law. Nelson's *wife*."

He feels she is beginning to work from a script, saying standard things, and into the vault of his shocked and shamed consciousness a small flaw admits a whiff of boredom.

"This is the worst thing you've ever done, ever, ever," Janice tells him. "The absolute worst. That time you ran away, and then Peggy, my *best* friend, and that poor hippie girl, and Thelma—don't think for one moment I didn't know about Thelma—but now you've done something truly unforgivable."

"Really?" The word comes out with an unintended hopeful lilt.

"I will never forgive you. Never," Janice says, returning to a dead-level tone.

"Don't *say* that," he begs. "It was just a crazy moment that didn't hurt anybody. Whajou put me and her in the same house at night for? Whajou think I was, dead already?"

"I *had* to go to class, there was a *quiz*, I wouldn't have gone ordinarily, I felt so *guilty*. That's a laugh. *I* felt guilty. I see now why they have gun laws. If I had a gun, I'd shoot you. I'd shoot you both."

"What else did Pru say?" Answering, he figures, will bring her down a bit from this height of murderous rage.

Janice answers, "She didn't say much of anything. Just the flat facts and then folded her hands in her lap and kept giving me and Nelson that defiant stare of hers. She didn't seem repentant, just tough, and obviously not wanting me to come live in the house. That's why she told."

He feels himself being drawn into alignment with Janice, against the others, with a couple's shared vision, squinting this way at Pru. He feels relieved, beginning already to be forgiven, and faintly disappointed.

"She is tough," he agrees, soothing. "Pru. Whaddeya expect, from an Akron steamfitter's daughter?" He decides against telling Janice, now at least, how in making their love Pru had come twice, and he had felt used, expertly.

His reprieve is only just beginning. It will take weeks and months and years of whittling at it. With her new business sense Janice won't give anything away cheap. "We want you over here, Harry," she says.

"Me? Why? It's late," he says. "I'm bushed from all those bushes."

"Don't think you're out of this and can be cute. This is a hideous thing. None of us will ever be the same."

"We never are," he dares say.

"Think of how Nelson feels."

This hurts. He hadn't wanted to think about it.

She tells him, "Nelson is being very calm and using all that good psychological work they did at the treatment center. He says this will need a lot of processing and we must begin right now. If we don't start right in we'll all harden in our positions."

Rabbit tries to conspire again, to elicit another wifely description. "Yeah—how *did* the kid take it?"

But she only says, "I think he's in shock. He himself said he hasn't begun to get in touch with his real feelings."

Harry says, "He can't be on too high a horse after all the stunts he's been pulling all these years. Coke whores all over Brewer, and if you ask me that Elvira over at the lot is more than just a token skirt. When she's around he sounds like he's been given a shot of joy juice."

But Janice doesn't relent. "You have hurt Nelson incredibly much," she says. "Anything he does from now on you can't blame him. I mean, Harry, what you've done is the kind of perverted thing that makes the newspapers. It was *mon*strous."

"Honey—"

"Quit it with the 'honey.' "

"What's this 'perverted'? We weren't at all blood-related. It was just like a normal one-night stand. She was hard-up and I was at death's door. It was her way of playing nurse."

More sobbing, he never knows what will trigger it. "Harry, you can't make jokes."

"Those weren't jokes." But he feels chastised, dry-mouthed, spanked.

"You get right over here and help undo some of the damage you've done for once in your life." And she hangs up, having sounded comically like her mother in the juicy way she pronounced "for once."

A life knows few revelations; these must be followed when they come. Rabbits sees clearly what to do. His acts take on a decisive haste. He goes upstairs and packs. The brown canvas suit bag. The big yellow rigid Tourister with the dent in one corner where an airline handler slung it. Jockey shorts, T-shirts, socks, polo shirts in their pastel tints, dress shirts in their plastic envelopes, golf slacks, Bermuda shorts. A few ties though he has never liked ties. All his clothes are summer clothes these days; the wool suits and sweaters wait in mothproof bags for fall days, October into November, that will not come this year, for him. He takes four lightweight sports coats and two suits, one the putty-colored and the other the shiny gray like armor. In case there's a wedding or a funeral. A raincoat, a couple of sweaters. A pair of black laced shoes tucks into two pockets of his folding suit bag and blue-and-white Nikes into the sides of the suitcase. He should start jogging again. His toothbrush and shaving stuff. His pills, buckets of them. What else? Oh yes. He grabs *The First Salute* from his bedside table and tucks it in, he'll finish it if it kills him. He leaves a light burning in the upstairs hall to discourage burglars, and the carriage lamp beside the front door numbered 14½. He loads the car in two trips, feeling the weight of the suitcases in his chest. He looks around the bare hall. He goes into the den, his feet silent on the Antron wall-to-wall carpeting, and looks out the lozenge panes at the glowing night-time silhouette of the weeping cherry. He plumps the pillow and straightens the arm guards on the wing chair he fell asleep in, not long but on the far side of a decisive gulf. The he who fell asleep was somebody else, a pathetic somebody. At the front door again, he feels a night breeze on his face, hears the muffled rush of traffic over on Penn Boulevard. He sets the latch and softly slams the door. Janice has her key. He thinks of her over there in the Springers' big stucco house that always reminded him of an abandoned enormous ice-cream stand. Forgive me.

Rabbit gets into the Celica. *Take a Ride in the Great Indoors:* one of the new slogans they'd been trying to push. You can have too many slogans, they begin to cancel out. The engine starts up; reverse gear carries him smoothly backwards. *I Love You When You Set Me Free, Toyota.* The digital clock says 10:07. Traffic on Penn Boulevard is starting to thin, the diners and gas stations are beginning to darken. He turns right at the blinking red light and then right again at the Brewer bypass along the Running Horse River. The road lifts above the trees at a point near the elephant-gray gas tanks and the bypassed old city shows a certain grandeur. Its twenty-story courthouse built in the beginning of the Depression is still the tallest building, the concrete eagles with flared wings at each corner lit by spotlights, and the sweeping shadow of Mt. Judge, crowned by the star-spatter of the Pinnacle Hotel, hangs behind everything like an unmoving tidal wave. The street-lamps show Brewer's brick tint like matches cupped in ruddy hands. Then, quite quickly, the city and all it holds is snatched from view. Groves of weed trees half-hide the empty factories along the river, and one might be anywhere in the Eastern United States on a four-lane divided highway.

He and Janice have done this southward drive so often he knows the options: he can get off at 222 and proceed directly but pokily toward Lancaster through a string of stoplight-ridden Brewer suburbs, or he can stay on 422 a few miles to 176 and head directly south and then cut west to Lancaster and York. This first time he tried this trip, thirty years ago last spring come to think of it, he made the mistake of heading south too soon, toward Wilmington and a vision of barefoot Du Pont women. But the East slants west, and the trick is to bear west until 83, which didn't exist in those days, and then drive south right into the maw of that two-headed monster, Baltimore-Washington. *Monstrous*, she said. Well, in a way, you could say, being alive is monstrous. Those crazy molecules. All by themselves? Never.

He turns on the radio, searching among the jabber of rock music and talk shows for the sweet old tunes, the tunes he grew up by. It used to be easier to search with the old dial you twisted, instead of these jumpy digitized scan buttons: you could feel your way. The scan comes suddenly upon the silky voices of Dinah Shore and Buddy Clark entwined in the duet of "Baby, It's Cold Outside." Thrilling, it turns his spine to ice water, when, after all that melodious banter it's hard to understand every word of, they halt, and harmonize on the chorus line. *Coooold, out, side.* Then this same station of oldies, fading under the underpasses, crackling when the road curves too close to power lines, offers up a hit he's totally forgotten, how could he have?—the high-school dances, the dolled-up couples shuffling to the languid waltz beat, the paper streamers drooping from the basketball nets, the rusty heater warmth of the dash-lit interior of Pop's Dodge, the living warm furtive scent, like the flavor of a food so strong you must choke it down at first, rising from between Mary Ann's thighs. *Vaya con Dios, my darling.* The damp triangle of underpants, the garter belts girls wore then. The dewy smooth freshness of their bodies, all of them, sweatily wheeling beneath the crepe paper, the colored lights. *Vaya con Dios, my love.* Oh my. It hurts. The emotion packed into these phrases buried in some d.j.'s dusty racks of 78s like the cotton wadding in bullets, like those seeds that come to life after a thousand years in some pyramid. Though the stars recycle themselves and remake all the heavy atoms creation needs, Harry will never be that person again, that boy with that girl, his fingertips grazing the soft insides of her thighs, a few atoms rubbing off, a few molecules.

Then, "Mule Train," by Frankie Laine, not one of the great Laines but great enough, and "It's Magic," by Doris Day. Those pauses back then: *It's ma   gic.* They knew how to hurt you, back then when there were two eight-team baseball leagues and you could remember all the players. People then were not exactly softer, they were harder in fact, but they were easier to hurt, though in fewer places.

He has to leave 176 for 23 through Amish country, it's the one really local stretch of road, but there shouldn't be any buggies out this late to slow him down. Rabbit wants to see once more a place in Morgantown, a hardware store with two pumps outside, where a thickset farmer in two shirts and hairy nostrils had advised him to know where he was going before he went there. Well, now he did. He had learned the road and figured out the destination. But what had been a country hardware store was now a slick little real-estate office. Where the gas pumps had been, fresh black asphalt showed under the moonlight the stark yellow stripes of diagonal parking spaces.

No, it isn't moonlight, he sees; it is the sulfurous illumination that afflicts busy paved places all night. Though the hour is near eleven, a traffic of giant trucks heaves and snorts and groans through the sleepy stone town; the realtor's office is full of Polaroid snapshots of property for sale, and Route 23, once a narrow road on the ridge between two farm valleys as dark at night as manure, now blazes with the signs that are everywhere. PIZZA HUT. BURGER KING. Rent a Movie. Turkey Hill MINIT MARKET. Quilt World. Shady Maple SMORGASBORD. Village Herb Shop. Country Knives. Real estate makes him think of Janice and his heart dips at the picture of her waiting with Nelson and Pru for him to show up over at the Springers' and panicking by now, probably imagining he's had a car accident, and coming back with her key to the deserted house, all fluttery and hot-breathed the way she gets. Maybe he should have left a note like she did him that time. *Harry dear—I must go off a few days to think.* But she said never forgive him, *shoot you both*, she upped the stakes, let her stew in her own juice, thinks she's so smart suddenly, going back to school. Nelson the same way. Damned if they're going to get him sitting in on some family-therapy session run by his own son whose big redheaded wife he's boffed. Only good thing he's done all year, as he looks back on it. Damned if he'll face him, give him the satisfaction, all white in the gills from this new grievance. Rabbit doesn't want to get counselled.

The eleven o'clock news comes on the radio. Jim Bakker, on trial in Charlotte, North Carolina, on twenty-four counts of fraud in connection with his scandal-ridden PTL television ministry, collapsed today in court and is being held for up to sixty days for psychiatric evaluation at the Federal Correctional Institute. Dr. Basil Jackson, a psychiatrist who has been treating Bakker for nine months, said that the once-charismatic evangelist has been hallucinating: leaving the courtroom Wednesday after former PTL executive Steve Nelson collapsed on the witness stand, Bakker saw the people outside as animals intent upon attacking and injuring him. Bakker's wife, Tammy, said from her luxurious home in Orlando, Florida, that Bakker over the phone had seemed to be experiencing a terrible emotional trauma and that she prayed with him and they agreed that they would trust in the Lord. In Los Angeles, Jessica Hahn, the former PTL secretary whose sexual encounter with Bakker in 1980 led to his downfall, told reporters, quote, I'm not a doctor but I do know about Jim Bakker. I believe Jim Bakker is a master manipulator. I think this is a sympathy stunt just like it is every time Tammy gets on TV and starts crying and saying how abused they are, end quote. In Washington, the Energy Department is searching for mysteriously missing amounts of tritium, the heavy-hydrogen isotope necessary to the making of hydrogen bombs. Also in Washington, *Science* magazine reports that the new bomb detector, called a TNA for thermal neutron analysis, installed today at JFK Airport in New York City, is set to detect two point five pounds of plastic explosives and would not have detected the bomb, thought to contain only one pound of Semtex explosive, which brought down Pan Am Flight 103 over Lockerbie, Scotland. In Toronto, movie superstar Marlon Brando told reporters that he has made his last movie. "It's horrible," he said of the motion picture, entitled *The Freshman*. "It's going to be a flop, but after this, I'm retiring. You can't imagine how happy I am." In Bonn, West Germany, Chancellor Helmut Kohl telephoned the new Polish Prime Minister, Tadeusz Mazowiecki, in a plea for better relations between their two countries. It was fifty years ago tomorrow, indeed almost right to this minute when allowances are made for time zones, that Germany under Adolf Hitler invaded Poland, precipitating World War II, in which an estimated fifty million persons were to perish. Like, wow! In sports, the Phillies are losing in San Diego and Pittsburgh is idle. As to the weather, it could be better, and it could be worse. *Mezzo, mezzo*. I didn't say messy, but look out for thundershowers, you Lancaster County night owls. Oh yes, Brando also called his new and terminal movie a "stinker." No sweat, for a fellow who began his career in a torn undershirt.

Rabbit smiles in the whispering, onrushing cave of the car; this guy must think nobody is listening, gagging it up like this. Lonely in those radio studios, surrounded by paper coffee cups and perforated acoustic tiles. Hard to know the effect you're making. Hard to believe God is always listening, never gets bored. The dashboard lights of the Celica glow beneath his line of vision like the lights of a city about to be bombed.

The superhighway crosses the Susquehanna and at York catches 83. As Harry drives south, the station fades behind him, toward the end of Louis Prima's "Just a Gigolo," that fantastic chorus where the chorus keeps chanting "Just a gigolo" in a kind of affectionate mockery of that wheezy wonderful voice: it makes your scalp prickle with joy. Rabbit fumbles with the scan button but can't find another oldies station, just talk shows, drunks calling in, the host sounding punchy himself, his mouth running on automatic pilot, abortion, nuclear waste, unemployment among young black males, CIA complicity in the AIDS epidemic, Boesky, Milken, Bush and North, Noriega, you can't tell me that—Rabbit switches the radio off, hating the sound of the human voice. Vermin. We are noisy vermin, crowding even the air. Better the murmur of the tires, the green road signs looming in the lights and parabolically enlarging and then whisked out of sight like magicians' handkerchiefs. It's getting close to midnight, but before he stops he wants to be out of the state. Even that botched time ages ago he got as far as West Virginia. To get out of Pennsylvania you have to climb a nameless mountain, beyond Hungerford. Signs and lights diminish. The lonely highway climbs. High lakes gleam under what is, now, in a gap between clouds, true moonlight. He descends into Maryland. There is a different feeling: groomed center strips, advertisements for Park and Ride for commuters. Civilization. Out of the sticks. His eyelids feel sandy, his heart fluttery and sated. He pulls off 83 into a Best Western well north of Baltimore, pleased to think that nobody in the world, nobody but the stocky indifferent Asiatic desk clerk, knows his location. Where is the missing tritium?

He likes motel rooms—the long clammy slot of hired space, the two double beds, the television set with its invitation to buy an R-rated movie, the shag carpet, the framed prints of big birds, the sanitized towels, the hush of anonymity, the closeted echo of old sex. He sleeps well, as if he has slipped off his body with its troubles and left it lying on the other double bed. In his dream he is back at the lot, with a young woman who seems to be in charge. She wears a white cap and dangly earrings but when he leans close and tries to explain himself to her, to convey his indispensable usefulness to the enterprise, contrary to what she may have heard from Janice, she makes a wry mouth and her face melts under his eyes in a kind of visual scream.

For breakfast, he succumbs to the temptation and has two fried eggs, though the yolks are terrible for your arteries, with bacon on the side. Rabbit likes the very American moment of packing up his car in sleepy unspeaking companionship with the other motel guests, elderly couples, cranky families, as they drift from the breakfast room across the parking lot with its long milky morning shadows. On the road again, with the radio again. The same news as the night before, amplified by the final baseball scores (Phils lost, five to one) and the news from Asia, where it is already afternoon for the busy Japanese currency speculators, the restive Chinese students, the doll-like Filipino hookers, the unhappily victorious Vietnamese, the up-and-coming although riotous Koreans, the tottering Burmese socialists, the warring Cambodian factions including the mindless Khmer Rouge minions of the most atrocious national leader since Hitler and Stalin, the infamous Pol Pot. Like, wow! Wake up, songbirds! The d.j., not last night's but just as crazy and alone with himself, plays some rockabilly song Rabbit likes, about getting down, "make a little love, get down tonight." It occurs to Harry he didn't even jerk off last night, though motel rooms usually excite him. Boy, is he showing his age.

As Baltimore nears, the condominiums multiply, thicken, entire hills and valleys loaded with them, pastel gingerbread staircases containing invisible people. 83 ends seamlessly at 695 and with all the commuters in their neckties he drones around the Beltway, jostling for his space in the world as if he still deserves it. Then he takes up 95, which will be his home all the way to Florida. There are two ways around Washington, he and Janice have tried them both, the boringly expert travellers down in the condo like the Silbersteins say 495 passing to the north and west is actually quicker, but he likes the little glimpse of the monuments you get by staying east on 95 and crossing the Potomac on a broad bridge into Alexandria. The frozen far heart, icecream white, of the grand old republic.

After all that megalopolis, Virginia feels bucolically vacant. The fields seem bigger than those in Pennsylvania, the hills gentler and more open, with meadows and horses, a gracious mist in the air, once in a while a pillared manse on a pale-green rise like something embroidered on a sampler by a slaveowner's spinster daughter. A military tinge: Fort Belvoir Engineer Proving Ground, Quantico Marine Corps Base. Harry thinks of his Army time and it comes back as a lyric tan, a translucent shimmer of aligned faceless men, the curious peace of having no decisions to make, of being told entirely what to do. War is a relief in many ways. Without the cold war, what's the point of being an American? Still, we held out. We held off the oafs for forty years. History will remember that. It becomes hard now to find stations on the radio that are not country music or religion. "Pray for difficult marriages," one preacher says, his grainy molasses-brown voice digging so deep into himself you can picture his shut eyes, the sweat on his temples, "pray for Christian husbands under stress, for Christian wives worried about their men; pray for all hostages, for prisoners in prison, for victims of the ghetto, for all those with AIDS." Rabbit switches the station and resolves to call Brewer when he stops for lunch.

How many rivers there are! After the Potomac, the Accotink, the Pohick, the Occoquan, the Rappahannock, the Pamunkey, the Ni, the Po, the Matta, the South Anna. The bridges thus marked are mere moments of the highway. Unseen towns are named: Massaponax, Ladysmith, Cedar Forks. North of Richmond, shacks in a thickening scatter mark the beginning of the true South, of rural blacks. Harry pulls into a Howard Johnson's on the Richmond outskirts. His ears ring, the ankle of his accelerator foot aches, his neck is stiff, the heat has gone up several notches since the motel parking lot this morning. Inside the air-conditioned restaurant, salesmen with briefcases are at all the pay phones. He eats too much lunch, consuming the last French fry that came with his tasteless hamburger, mopping up salt with it in his fingers like his grandson Roy does, and then ordering apple pie to see if it's any different in Virginia. It's sweeter and gluier; it lacks that cinnamon they sprinkle on in Pennsylvania. A phone is available after he pays the check and with three dollars' worth of quarters ready he dials not the gray limestone house on Franklin Drive but the house where he used to live, the Springer house in Mt. Judge.

A little girl answers. The operator breaks in and Rabbit inserts three minutes' worth of quarters. He says, "Hi, Judy. It's Grandpa."

"Hi, Grandpa," she says, very calmly. Perhaps nothing of last night's revelation has filtered down to her yet. Or perhaps children this young are so innocent of what adulthood involves that nothing surprises them.

"How's it going?" he asks.

"O.K."

"You looking forward to school starting next week?"

"Kind of. Summer gets kind of boring."

"How's Roy? Is he bored by summer too?"

"He's so stupid he doesn't know what boring is. He's been put down for his nap now but is still bawling. Mommy's flipping out." Since Harry seems stuck for a response, she volunteers, "Daddy's not here, he's over at the lot."

"That's O.K., I'd just as soon talk to your mommy actually. Could you get her for me? Judy," he impulsively adds, before the child can leave the phone.

"Yeah?"

"You study hard, now. Don't you worry about those kids who think they're so much. You're a very lovely girl and everything will come to you if you wait. Don't force it. Don't force growing up. Everything will be fine.''

This is too much to try to cram into her. She is only nine. Ten more years before she can go west like Mim and break out. "I know," Judy says, in the safe bored tone, and perhaps she does. After a rattle of the receiver on wood and voices in the background and footsteps hastily enlarging, Pru arrives at the telephone, breathless.

"Harry!"

"Hi there, Teresa. How's it going?" This seductive nonchalant tone, all wrong, but it just came out.

"Not so good," she says. "Where on earth are you?"

"Far away, where everybody wants me. Hey. Wajou tell for?"

"Oh Harry, I *had* to." She starts to cry. "I *could*n't let Nelson not know, he's trying to be so straight. It's pathetic. He's been confessing all this dreadful stuff to me, I can't tell you or anybody the half of it, and at night we pray together, pray aloud kneeling by the bed, he's just so desperate to lick the drugs and to be a decent father and husband, just be *nor*mal.''

"He is, huh? Well, great. Still, you didn't need to turn us in, it only happened once, and there wasn't any follow-up, in fact I thought you'd totally forgotten about it.''

"How could you think I'd forgotten? You must think I'm a real slut.''

"Well, no, but, you know, you've been having a lot on your mind. For me, it was almost like I'd dreamed it.'' He means this as a compliment.

But Pru's voice hardens. "Well, it meant a little more to me than that.'' Women, there's no telling which side they want to dance on. "It was a terrible betrayal of my husband,'' she pronounces solemnly.

"Well,'' Rabbit says, "he hasn't been all that great a husband, as far as I can see. Hey, is Judy listening to all this?''

"I'm on the upstairs phone. I asked her to hang up downstairs.''

"And did she? *Judy!*'' Harry shouts. "I *see* you there!''

There is a fumbling soft rattle and a new clarity in the connection. Pru says, "Shit.''

Rabbit reassures her. "I forget exactly what we said but I doubt if she understood much.''

"She understands more than she lets on. Girls do.''

"Well, anyway,'' he says. "Did he confess to affairs with men as well as women? Nelson.''

"I can't possibly answer that question," she says, in a flat dry voice forever closed to him. Another woman's voice, warmer, courteous, faintly lazy, probably black, breaks in, saying, "Sir, yore three minutes are u-up. Please deposit a dollar ten saints if you wish continuation."

"Maybe I'm done," he says, to both women.

Pru shouts, over their imperilled connection, "Harry, where are you?"

"On the road!" he shouts back. He still has a little stack of change in front of him and inserts four quarters and a dime. As they gong away, he sings a snatch of a song he just heard on the radio, Willie Nelson's signature: "On the road again . . ."

This makes Pru sob; it's as bad as talking to Janice. "Oh *don't*," she cries. "Don't *tease* us all, we can't help it we're tied down back here."

Pity touches him, with the memory of her beauty naked like blossoms that night in the narrow musty room as the rain intensified. She is stuck back there, she is saying, with the living. "I'm tied down too," he tells her. "I'm tied to my carcass."

"What shall I tell Janice?"

"Tell her I'm on the way to the condo. Tell her she can come join me whenever she wants. I just didn't like the squeeze you all put on me last night. I get claustrophobic in my old age."

"I *never* should have slept with you, it's just at the time . . ."

"It was," he says. "It was a great idea at the time. Tell me— how'd you think I did, looking back on it? For an old guy."

She hesitates, then says, "That's it, that's the trouble. I don't see you as an old guy, Harry. I never did."

O.K., he has won this from her. This woman-to-man voice. Who could ask for anything more? Let her go. He says, "Don't you fret, Pru. You're a great dish. Tell Nelson to loosen up. Just because he got over crack he doesn't have to turn into Billy Graham." Or Jim Bakker. Harry hangs up, and the telephone startles him by returning, with a pang and clatter, the dime and four quarters. That operator with the Southern voice must have been listening and taken a shine to him.

As the afternoon wears on toward Fayetteville, North Carolina, where there is a Comfort Inn he and Janice have stayed at in years past, he hears an amazing thing on the car radio. They interrupt a string of Forties swing classics to announce that Bartlett Giamatti, Commissioner of Baseball and former president of Yale University, died of a heart attack on the island of Martha's Vineyard, Massachusetts, late this afternoon. *Pete Rose strikes back,* Rabbit thinks. Professor Giamatti, who was only fifty-one years of age, retired after lunch in his summer home in Edgartown, and at three o'clock was found by his wife and son in full cardiac arrest. *Only fifty-one,* Rabbit thinks. Police took Giamatti to the Martha's Vineyard Hospital where he was worked upon for an hour and a half; the emergency team several times succeeded in restoring the electric mechanism of the heartbeat, but Giamatti was at last pronounced dead. That little electric twitch: without it we're so much rotting meat. One of the first things he ought to do in Florida is make an appointment with Dr. Morris, to keep himself out of the hands of that hawk-faced Australian, Dr. Olman. *Dying to sink his knife into me.* Giamatti had been an English instructor at Yale, the news says, and became the youngest president in the history of the university, and in eleven years reversed that institution's trend into red ink and academic mediocrity. As president of the National League, he had aroused some players' ire by tampering with the strike zone and the balk rule. As commissioner, his brief tenure was dominated by the painful Rose affair, whose settlement a week ago left Giamatti in an apparently strong position. He was a heavy man and a heavy smoker. *At least I'm no smoker.* And now, a tune our listeners never get tired of requesting, "In the Mood."

Fayetteville used to be a hot town, with all the soldiers from Fort Bragg, Rabbit remembers from a segment of *60 Minutes* he once watched. The downtown had some blocks of triple-X movies and sleazy hotels the city fathers finally in despair tore down entirely and made into a park. After a dinner of deep-fried shrimp, with onion rings and white bread fried on one side, a Southern delicacy he guesses, at the Comfort Inn—one of those restaurants with a salad bar big as a little cafeteria, so you wonder as you sit there waiting for the waitress if you're missing the boat—Harry cruises in the slate-gray Celica, his private Batmobile, toward the center of wicked Fayetteville. He can find for a hot spot only a shadowy broad street of blacks loitering in doorways here and there, waiting for some message, some event from beyond. No hookers in hotpants or spandex exercise tights, just a big red-bearded white man in studded black leather who keeps revving his motorcycle, twisting the throttle handle and producing a tremendous noise. The blacks don't blink. They keep waiting. Even at evening the shadowy air is hot, they move through it languidly like sick fish, their hands flapping at the wrists in that angled black way.

Back in his long room with its watery scent of cement from underneath the rug, with walls painted altogether yellow, moldings and pipes and air-conditioning vents and light-switch plates rollered and sprayed yellow, Rabbit thinks of adding $5.50 to his bill to watch something called *Horny Housewives* but instead watches, free, bits of *Perfect Strangers* (it makes him uneasy, two guys living together, even if one of them is a comical Russian) and pre-season football between the Seahawks and 49ers. The trouble with these softcore porn movies on hotel circuits, in case some four-year-old with lawyers for parents happens to hit the right buttons they show tits and ass and even some pubic hair but no real cunt and no pricks, no pricks hard or soft at all. It's very frustrating. It turns out pricks are what we care about, you have to see them. Maybe we're all queer, and all his life he's been in love with Ronnie Harrison. Nice, today, the way Pru burst out with that *Shit* again and then *Don't tease.* That level woman-to-man voice, as if he had his arms about her, her voice relaxing into their basic relation, cock to cunt, doing Nelson in. In bed at last in the dark he jerks off, picturing himself with a pair of coffee-colored hookers from old Fayetteville, to show himself he's still alive.

The morning radio news is dull. Giamatti's death, warmed over. Baseball mourns. Economy shows moderate growth. Bombardments in Beirut between Christians and Muslims worse than ever. Ex-HUD aide says files were shredded. Supreme Court ruling against organized prayer before football games is rousing indignation all over the Southland. In Montgomery, Mayor Emory Folmar marched to the fifty-yard line and led a prayer there. His remarks over the public-address system linked football and prayer as American tradition. In Sylacauga, Alabama, local ministers rose in the bleachers and led the crowd of three thousand in the Lord's Prayer. In Pensacola, Florida, preachers equipped with bullhorns led spectators in prayer. *Fanatics*, Rabbit tells himself. Southerners are as scary as the Amish.

From here on down to the Florida line Route 95 is like a long green tunnel between tall pines. Little shacks peek through. A sign offers *Pecan Rolls 3 for $1.00.* Bigger signs in Hispanic colors, orange and yellow on black, lime green, splashy and loud, miles and miles of them, begin to advertise something called South of the Border. *Bear Up a Leetle Longer. You Never Sausage a Place!* With a big basketball curving right off the billboard, *Have a Ball.* When you finally get there, after all these miles of pine tunnel, it's a junky amusement park just across the South Carolina border: a village of souvenir shops, a kind of a space needle wearing a sombrero. Tacos, tacky. South Carolina is a wild state. The first to secede. The pines get taller, with a tragic feeling. FIREWORKS are offered everywhere for sale. The land gets hillier. Trucks loaded with great tree trunks rumble unstoppably by on the downslope and labor to nearly a standstill on the up. Rabbit is nervously aware now of his Pennsylvania plates being Northern. Swerve out of line a bit and they'll throw him in the Pee Dee River. The Lynches River. The Pocatoligo River. Animals on this highway are hit so hard they don't squash, they explode, impossible to know what they were. Possums. Porcupines. Some dear old Southern lady's darling pet pussycat. Reduced to fur stains amid the crescent fragments of exploded truck tires. Just think, he lay down for lunch and that was it.

Janice must have got the message from Pru, she may be already at the condo waiting, flying down from Philly and renting a car at the airport, better enjoy his freedom while he has it. He has come upon a black gospel station, an elastic fat voice shouting, "He'll be there, but you got to call him names." Endlessly repeated, with unexpected rhythmic variations. "Roll that stone away, do you know the story?" A commercial interrupts at last, and, would you believe, it's for Toyotas. Those Japs don't miss a trick, you have to hand it to them. Selling right in the slave quarters. *Your pruraristic society.* Harry's neck hurts from holding his head in one position so long. He's beginning to feel bloated on radio, on travel. God's country. He could have made it smaller and still made the same point.

He'll be there. Funny, about Harry and religion. When God hadn't a friend in the world, back there in the Sixties, he couldn't let go of Him, and now when the preachers are all praying through bullhorns he can't get it up for Him. He is like a friend you've had so long you've forgotten what you liked about Him. You'd think after that heart scare, but in a way the closer you get the less you think about it, like you're in His hand already. Like you're out on the court instead of on the bench swallowing down butterflies and trying to remember the plays.

Perry Como comes on and sings "Because." Rabbit's scalp prickles at the end, the skin of his eyes stings. *Because—you—are—miiiine!* Como's the best, probably: Crosby had something sly-Irish about him, clowning around with Lamour and Hope, and Sinatra—if there's one way in which Rabbit Angstrom has been out of step with mankind, it's Sinatra. He doesn't like his singing. He didn't like it when bobbysoxers were jumping out of their underpants for this skinny hollow-cheeked guy up on the stage at the Paramount, and he didn't like it when he mellowed into this Las Vegas fat cat making all these moony albums you're supposed to screw to all across the nation: oceans of jism. White with foam. His singing has always sounded flat to Rabbit, like he's grinding it out. Now, to Mim, Sinatra is a god, but that's more a matter of lifestyle, turning night into day and pally with gangsters and Presidents and that square gangster way of carrying your shoulders (Charlie Stavros has it) and Chairman of the Board and Sammy Davis, Jr., and Dean Martin before they dried out finally, if in fact they did, both men have terrible health problems he read somewhere, in one of those ridiculous scandal sheets Janice brings home from the Minit Market. Sometimes Harry envies Mim the glamorous dangerous life he guesses she's lived, he's glad for her, she always had that edge, wanting speed even if it killed her, even if it flipped her off the handlebars, but the fast lane too gets to be a rut, he doesn't regret the life he led, though Brewer is a dull enough town, not New York New York or Chicago my kind of town the way Sinatra grinds it out. What he enjoyed most, it turns out in retrospect, and he didn't know it at the time, was standing around in the showroom, behind the dusty big window with the banners, bouncing on the balls of his feet to keep up his leg muscles, waiting for a customer, shooting the bull with Charlie or whoever, earning his paycheck, filling his slot in the big picture, doing his bit, getting a little recognition. That's all we want from each other, recognition. Your assigned place in the rat race. In the Army, too, you had it: your number, your bunk, your assigned duties, your place in line, your pass for Saturday night, four beers and fuck a whore in a ranch house. *Honey, you didn't pay to be no two-timer.* There's more to being a human being than having your own way. Fact is, it has come to Rabbit this late in life, you don't have a way, except what other people tell you. Your mother first, and poor Pop, then the Lutheran minister, that tough old heinie Fritz Kruppenbach, you had to respect him though, he said what he believed, and then all those schoolteachers, Marty Tothero and the rest, trying to give you an angle to work from, and now all these talk-show hosts. Your life derives, and has to give. Maybe if your mother was in the fast lane like Annabelle's you are naturally leery of the opposite sex.

The pine trees have gaps now. Marshy stretches open the sky up, there are cabins on stilts, trees with shaggy balls on them, colored wash hanging on lines. Homely hand-lettered signs. *Dad's Real Southern Cookin'*. BI-Lo. A long bridge over Lake Marion, this enormous body of water in the middle of nowhere. Highways branch off to the capital, Columbia, where he's never been, though he and Janice did once detour over to Charleston and back on Route 17. Another time, they diverted to Savannah and spent the night in a made-over plantation house with high domed ceilings and louvers on the windows. They did do some fun things, he and Jan. The thing about a wife, though, and he supposes a husband for that matter, is that almost anybody would do, inside broad limits. Yet you're supposed to adore them till death do you part. Till the end of time. Ashepoo River. Wasn't that a comic strip, years ago?

He gets off the highway at a vast rest stop, an oasis in this wilderness—gas pumps, a restaurant, a little department store selling groceries, beer, fireworks, suntan lotion. At the counter a couple of young black men, glittery black in the heat, arms bare up to the shoulder, a mean little Malcolm X goatee on one of them. They have a menace down here, their color shouts, they are a *race*, they are everywhere. But the elderly white waitress has no trouble with these two black boys. The three chat and smile in the same dragged accent, making a little breeze with their mouths. Nice to see it. For this, the Civil War.

To test if he can still use his own voice, Rabbit asks the fat white man one empty stool away from him at the counter, a man who has made for himself at the salad bar a mountain of lettuce and red beets and cole slaw and cottage cheese and kidney beans and chickpeas, "About how many more hours is it to the Florida line?" He lets his Pennsylvania accent drag a little extra, hoping to pass.

"Four," the man answers with a smile. "I just came from there. Where you headin' for in Florida?"

"Way the other end. Deleon. My wife and I have a condo there, I'm driving down alone, she'll be following later."

The man keeps smiling, smiling and chewing. "I know Deleon. Nice old town."

Rabbit has never noticed much that is old about it. "From our balcony we used to have a look at the sea but they built it up."

"Lot of building on the Gulf side now, the Atlantic side pretty well full. Began my day in Sarasota."

"Really? That's a long way to come."

"That's why I'm makin' such a pig of myself. Hadn't eaten

more than a candy bar since five o'clock this morning. After a while you got to stop, you begin to see things.''

"What sort of things?''

"This stretch I just came over, lot of patchy ground fog, it gets to you. Just coffee gets to your stomach.'' This man has a truly nice way of smiling and chewing and talking all at once. His mouth is wide but lipless, like a Muppet's. He has set his truck driver's cap, with a bill and a mesh panel in the back, beside his plate; his good head of gray hair, slightly wavy like a rich man's, is permanently dented by the edge of the cap.

"You driving one of those big trucks? I don't know how you guys do it. How far you goin'?''

All the salad on the plate has vanished and the smile has broadened. ''Boston.''

"Boston! All that way?'' Rabbit has never been to Boston, to him it is the end of the world, tucked up in under Maine. People living that far north are as fantastic to him as Eskimos.

"Today, tomorrow, whatever you call it, I expect to have this rig in Boston Sunday afternoon, twenty-four hours from now.''

"But when do you sleep?''

"Oh, you pull over and get an hour here, an hour there.''

"That's amazing.''

"Been doin' it for fifteen years. I had retired, but came back to it. Couldn't stand it around the house. Nothin' on TV that was any good. How about you?''

"Me?'' On the lam. A bad LAD. He realizes what the question means, and answers, ''Retired, I guess.''

"More power to ya, fella. I couldn't take it,'' the truck driver says. "Retirement taxed my brain.'' The elderly waitress so friendly with the two young blacks brings the hungry man an oval platter heavy with fried steak soaking in a pink mix of oil and blood, and three vegetables in little round side dishes, and a separate plate of golden-brown corn pone.

Harry somewhat reluctantly—he has made a friend—pushes away from the counter. "Well, more power to *you*,'' he says.

And now this fat pale miracle man, who will be in Boston faster than a speeding bullet, who like Thomas Alva Edison only needs a catnap now and then, has his wide Muppet mouth too full to speak, and merely smiles and nods, and loses a snaky droplet of steak juice down the far side of his egg-shaped little chin. Nobody's perfect. We're only human. Look at Jim Bakker. Look at Bart Giamatti.

In his Celica Harry crosses the Tuglifinny River. The Salkehatchie. The Little Combahee. The Coosawatchie. The Turtle. Kickapoo, he thinks—not Ashepoo. Kickapoo Joy Juice in *Li'l Abner*. Between spates of black music that has that peculiar exciting new sound of boards being slapped on the floor, he hears commercials for the Upchurch Music Company ("an instrument that brings musical pleasure to generations to come") and a deodorizer called Tiny Cat. Why would a deodorizer be called Tiny Cat? He crosses the Savannah and leaves South Carolina and its fireworks at last. Because he is punchy from miles of miles, he turns off at the city exit and drives into the downtown and parks by a grand old courthouse and buys a hot pastrami sandwich at a little sandwich joint on the main street there. He sits eating it, trying not to have any of the juice spill out of the waxpaper and spot his pants, like that sickening driblet from the mouth of the guy back at the lunch place hours ago. This piece of Savannah, a block from the river, seems a set of outdoor rooms, walled in by row houses with high steps and curtains of dusty trees; a huge heat still rests on the day though the shadows are deepening, thickening on the soft old façades, sadder and rosier than those in Brewer. A group of pigeons gathers around his bench, curious to see if he will spare any of the bun or Bar-B-Q potato chips. A young bum with long yellow hair like George Custer and that brown face you get from being homeless gives him a glittering wild eye from a bench behind a tree, in the next room as it were. A tall obelisk rises in commemoration of something, no doubt the glorious dead. Little chattering brown birds heave in and out of the trees as they try to decide whether the day is over. He better push on. He neatly packages his wastepaper and milk carton in the bag the sandwich came in and leaves it in a public trash basket, his gift to Savannah, the trace he will leave, like the cloud of finger-moisture on the edge of the bureau back home. The pigeons chuff and chortle off in indignant disappointment. The bum has silently come up behind him and asks him in no particular accent, the limp snarl of the drugged, if he has a cigarette. "Nope," Rabbit tells him. "Haven't smoked in thirty years." He remembers the moment when on a sudden resolve he canned a half-pack of Philip Morris, the nice old tobacco-brown pack, in somebody's open barrel in an alley in Mt. Judge. Left that trace too.

Rabbit moves toward his car with a racing heart, as the bum follows and mumbles behind him about spare change. He fiddles with the key and gets in and slams the door. The Celica, thank God, isn't too overheated after all its miles to start promptly;

George Custer, locked outside, blinks and turns, pretending not
to notice. Harry drives cautiously through the outdoor rooms,
around the tall monument, and gets lost on the way out of Savannah. He is caught in endless black neighborhoods, gently
collapsing houses built of wood clapboard that last saw fresh
paint in the days of Martin Luther King. They talk about assas-
sination conspiracies but that was one that Harry could believe
in. He can believe in it but he can't remember the name of the
man they put in jail for it. A three-name name. Escaped once,
but they caught him. James Earl something. So much for history. Panicking, he stops at a grocery store, the kind with a
troughed wooden floor with shiny-headed nails that used to be
in Mt. Judge when he was a boy, except that everybody in here
is black; a lanky man the color of a dried bean pod, much
amused, tells him how to get back to the superhighway, gesturing with long hands that flap loosely on his wrists.

Back on 95, Rabbit pushes through Georgia. As darkness
comes on, it begins to rain, and with his old eyes, that can't sort
out the lights too well at night any more, the rain is oppressive.
He even turns off the radio, he feels so battered by pellets of
experience. His body from being in one position so long feels
as if somebody's been pounding it with sandbags. He better pull
in. He finds a Ramada Inn beyond Brunswick. He eats a fried-
catfish special that doesn't sit too well on top of the pastrami,
especially the candied yams and the pecan pie; but why be in
Georgia if you can't have pecan pie? The walk back to his room
past the other motel doors, on cement sheltered by the continuous balcony overhead, is secretly blissful. In out of the rain.
Sense enough. They can't catch me. But his snug moment of
happiness reminds him of all those exposed unhappy loved ones
back in Diamond County. Guilt gouges at his heart like a thumb
in a semi-sensitive eye.

Halfway through *The Golden Girls*, it seems suddenly tedi-
ous, all that elderly sexiness, and the tough-mouthed old grandmother, people ought to know when to give up. He watches
instead on the educational channel a *Living Planet* segment about
life at the polar extremes. He's seen it before, but it's still surprising, how David Attenborough turns over those rocks in this
most desolate place in Antarctica and there are lichens underneath, and all through the sunless abysmal winter these male
penguins shuffling around in continuous blizzards with eggs on
the tops of their webbed feet. Life, it's incredible, it's wearing
the world out. A ten o'clock news on the same channel tells the

same old stuff he's been hearing on the radio all day. Poor Giamatti. A female baby panda born in the National Zoo in Washington. Reagan thought AIDS was as mild as measles until Rock Hudson died, reveals his former physician Brigadier General John Hutton. Another tattletale: Navy Commander David R. Wilson claims in this month's *U.S. Naval Institute Proceedings* magazine that the U.S.S. *Vincennes* was known among other ships in the Persian Gulf for her aggressive and imprudent actions for at least a month before the *Vincennes* gunned down an Iranian civil airliner containing over two hundred seventy men, women, and children. Poor devils, Iranians or not. Little children, women in shawls, end over end, hitting the dark hard water. New head of Japan in Washington, provisional government in Panama, mobs of East Germans in Hungary waiting to cross the border into the free world. Poor devils, they don't know the free world is wearing out.

Rabbit makes himself ready for bed, sleeping in the day's underwear, and tries to think about where he is, and who. This is the last night when he is nowhere. Tomorrow, life will find him again. Janice on the phone, the Golds next door. He feels less light than he thought he would, escaping Brewer. You are still you. The U.S. is still the U.S., held together by credit cards and Indian names. Harry becomes dead weight on the twin bed. Lost in the net of thread-lines on the map, he sleeps as in his mother's womb, another temporary haven.

Morning. The rain is just a memory of puddles on the sun-struck asphalt. Sunday. He goes for the French toast and link sausages, figuring tomorrow morning he'll be back to stale oat bran. Janice never cleans out the cupboards when they leave. Efficient, in a way, if you don't mind feeding ants and roaches. He keeps tasting maple syrup and eggs he didn't quite like. French toast is never as good as what Mom would cook up before sending him off to Sunday school: the flat baked golden triangles of bread, the syrup from the can shaped and painted like a log cabin, its spout the chimney. Putting his suitcase in the trunk, he is struck, not for the first time, by how the Celica's taillights are tipped, giving it, from the back, a slant-eyed look.

Within an hour he crosses the St. Marys River and a highway sign says WELCOME TO FLORIDA and the radio commercials are for Blue Cross, denture fixatives, pulmonary clinics. The roadside becomes sandy and the traffic thickens, takes on glitter. Jacksonville suddenly looms, an Oz of blue-green skyscrapers, a city of dreams at the end of the pine-tree tunnel, gleaming glass boxes heaped around the tallest, the Baptist Hospital. You rise up onto bridges over the St. Johns River far below, and Jacksonville shines from a number of angles like a jewel being turned in your hand, and you pay a toll, and must stay alert not to wind up heading toward Green Cove Springs or Tallahassee. Route 95 is now just one among many superhighways. The cars get wide and fat, the trucks carry rolls of fresh sod instead of skinned pine trunks. All around him, floating like misplaced boats, are big white campers and vans, Winnebagos and Starcrafts, Pathfinders and Dolphins, homes on wheels, the husband at the helm, his elbow out the window, the wife at home behind him, making the bed. From all forty-eight of the states these caravans come to Florida, wearing even Colorado's green mountain profile and Maine's gesturing red lobster. He notices a new kind of Florida license plate, a kind of misty tricolor memorial to the Challenger, among the many still with the green Florida-shaped stain in the middle like something spilled on a necktie. And wasn't that the disgrace of the decade, sending that poor New Hampshire schoolteacher and that frizzy-haired Jewish girl, not to mention the men, one of them black and another Oriental, all like some Hollywood cross-section of America, up to be blown into bits on television a minute later? Now the probers think they were probably conscious, falling toward the water, conscious for two or three minutes. Harry descends deeper into Florida, glad to be back among the palms and white roofs and tropical thinness, the clouds blue on gray on white on blue, as if the great skymaker is working here with lighter materials.

You take 95 parallel to the East Coast to 4, and then skim diagonally over through all that Disney World that poor little Judy wanted to go to, next time they come they must schedule it in. Where some of the self-appointed travel experts at the condo (he always did think Ed Silberstein a know-it-all, even before his son tried to put the make on Pru) advise staying on 4 all the way to 75 and saving in minutes what you lose in miles, or at least taking 17 to Port Charlotte, he likes to move south on 27, right through the hot flat belly of the state, through Haines City and Lake Wales, into the emptiness west of the Seminole reservation and Lake Okeechobee, and then over to Deleon on Route 80.

In Florida, there is no trouble finding Golden Oldies stations on the car radio. We're all oldies down here. The music of your life, some of the announcers like to call it, and it keeps tumbling in, Patti Page begging "Never let me gooooo, I love you soooooo,'' and then doing so perkily that Latin-American bit with "Aye yi yi" and the caballeros, and finishing "I've waited all my life, to give you all my love, my heart belongs to you," and then Tony Bennett or one of those other mooing Italians with "Be My Love," speaking of all my love, and then Gogi Grant and "The Wayward Wind," he hasn't thought of Gogi Grant for ages, it's a rare song that doesn't light up some of his memory cells, while the landscape outside the car windows beyond the whoosh of the air-conditioner gets more and more honkytonk—*Flea World, Active Adult Living* and car after car goes by with an orange Garfield stuck to the back window with paws that are suction cups. "Why you ramble, no one knows," Nat "King" Cole singing "Rambling Rose," ending featherily, "Why I want you, no one knows," you can just about see that wise slow smile, and then "Tzena, Tzena," he hasn't heard that for years either, the music doesn't come ethnic any more, and "Oh, My Papa," speaking of ethnic, and Kay Starr really getting her back into "Wheel of Fortune," all those hiccups, hard driving, "Pu*leazzze* let it be now," and "A-Tisket, A-Tasket," that really goes back, he was walking to grade school then with Lottie Bingaman, in love with Margaret Schoelkopf, and Presley's "Love Me Tender," knock him all you want, before he got fat and druggy and spooked in the end he had a real voice, a beautiful voice, not like foghorn Sinatra, and then Ray Charles, now there's another real voice, "I Can't Stop Loving You," "dreaming of yesterdayssss," the way it trails off like that, that funny blind man's waggle of the head, and Connie Francis, "Where the Boys Are," a voice to freeze your scalp all right, but whose life *are* these songs? That was beach-party era, he was all married and separated and reconciled and working at Verity Press by then, no more parties for him. Ronnie Harrison and Ruth fucking all weekend at the Jersey Shore: that still rankles.

The station fades out and in trying to find another he passes through a broadcast church service, evangelical, a man shouting "Jesus knows! Jesus looks into your heart! Jesus sees the death in your heart!" and Harry passes on, coming upon, too late for all of the sobbing, Johnny Ray's "Cry," "If your *sweet*heart sends a *let*ter of good-*bye*," that was around the time he had to go into the Army and part from Mary Ann, he didn't know it would be for good, they argued about Johnny Ray, Rabbit insisting the guy had to be a fruit to sing that way, and then down in Texas he realized the song was for him, his sweetheart sent a letter. Next number, Dean Martin comes on loafing through "That's Amore": by now Harry had come back and taken up with Janice, the quiet girl behind the nuts counter at Kroll's, her little tight body, the challenge of her puzzled dark eyes, he remembers because he would joke, "That's *amore*," after they would fuck in the room a girlfriend of hers would let them use, with its view of the gray gas tanks by the river. "Only the Lonely," the late Roy Orbison warbles. "There goes my baby, there goes my heart," in that amazing voice that goes higher and higher till you think it must break like crystal, as in a way it did; Rabbit supposed his being dead is what makes this one a Golden Oldie.

The songs roll on, broken every half-hour by summaries of the news. A bombing in Colombia has injured eighty-four, the Colombian woes are increased by a drop in coffee prices, President Bush's upcoming speech on the nation's drug problems rouses Washington speculation, can he do a Reagan? Also in Washington, officials are still hopeful that the newborn baby panda, fighting for its life in an incubator, will survive. Locally, manatees continue active in the Caloosahatchee Basin, and the Dolphins were beaten yesterday in Miami by the Philadelphia Eagles, twenty to ten. Rabbit likes hearing this score, but the old songs, all that syrup above love, love, the sweetness, the cuteness, the doggies in the window and Mommy kissing Santa Claus and the naughty lady of Shady Lane, the background strings and pizzicato bridges and rising brass crescendos meant to thrill the pants off you, wear him down: he resents being made to realize, this late, that the songs of his life were as moronic as the rock the brainless kids now feed on, or the Sixties and Seventies stuff that Nelson gobbled up—all of it designed for empty heads and overheated hormones, an ocean white with foam, and listening to it now is like trying to eat a double banana split the way he used to. It's all *disposable*, cooked up to turn a quick profit. They lead us down the garden path, the music manufacturers, then turn around and lead the next generation down with a slightly different flavor of glop.

Rabbit feels betrayed. He was reared in a world where war was not strange but change was: the world stood still so you could grow up in it. He knows when the bottom fell out. When they closed down Kroll's, Kroll's that had stood in the center of Brewer all those years, bigger than a church, older than the courthouse, right at the head of Weiser Square there, with every Christmas those otherworldly displays of circling trains and nodding dolls and twinkling stars in the corner windows as if God Himself put them there to light up this darkest time of the year. As a little kid he couldn't tell what God did from what people did; it all came from above somehow. He can remember standing as a child in the cold with his mother gazing into this world of tinselled toys as real as any other, the air biting at his cheeks, the sound of the Salvation Army bells begging, the smell of the hot soft pretzels sold on Weiser Square those years, the feeling around him of adult hurrying—bundled-up bodies pushing into Kroll's where you could buy the best of everything from drapes to beds, toys to pots, china to silver. When he worked there back in Shipping you saw the turnover, the hiring and firing, the discontinued lines, the abrupt changes of fashion, the panicky gamble of all this merchandising, but still he believed in the place as a whole, its power, its good faith. So when the system just upped one summer and decided to close Kroll's down, just because shoppers had stopped coming in because the downtown had become frightening to white people, Rabbit realized the world was not solid and benign, it was a shabby set of temporary arrangements rigged up for the time being, all for the sake of the money. You just passed through, and they milked you for what you were worth, mostly when you were young and gullible. If Kroll's could go, the courthouse could go, the banks could go. When the money stopped, they could close down God Himself.

For miles in the vicinity of Disney World and beyond, lesser amusement and theme parks hold out their cups for the tourist overflow. Waxworks. Wet 'n' Wild, a water slide. Sea World. Circus World, not the one that's redux down in Sarasota. What a dumb word, as dumb as faux, you see it everywhere suddenly, faux fur, faux jewelry. *False* is what they mean. A museum of old dolls and toys. Old, old, they sell things as antiques now that aren't even as old as he is, another racket. On Route 27, going due south, you enter slightly rolling dry pale farm country, bleached by heat, with pale cattle in wide parched fields and orange groves with their dark dense irrigated green, and giant tanks holding water, shaped like giant mushrooms, like spaceships come from beyond. At the side of the road little wobbly hand-painted signs offer BOILED PEANUTS, tiny Mexican girls manning the stands, and there is, in faint echo of the giant theme parks to the north, a touching dusty amusement park, spindly structures put together for a minute's giddy sensation, idle, waiting for the evening's little customers.

The sun is high now and the morning's tattered gray clouds have melted away and the heat is serious, crushing, frightening when he steps out of the Celica at a Texaco to use the facilities because there is no escape from it, like snow at the South Pole, it even drifts into the men's room, as humid a heat as in the Pennsylvania summer but more searing, as if it hates you. The road is wide but has lights and roads coming from the bleached farmland; the small cities drift by, Lake Wales, Frostproof, Avon Park, Sebring, and he wonders about the lives led there, away from the coasts, away from the condos and the fishing charters, by people who wake up and go to work just like those in Brewer, only everything flattened by the sun: how did they get here, so near the edge of the world, on this sand spit that a little rise in sea level because of Antarctica melting because of carbon dioxide in the atmosphere would wash away? A column of thick smoke appears on his left, toward the Seminole reservation, thick and poisonous, a disaster, an atomic bomb, war has been declared while he's been drowning in musical memories; he expects to run into a forest fire, but nothing happens, the column of smoke slowly recedes on his left, he'll never know what it was. A dump most likely. Harry's whole body feels cramped because of long sitting and he takes a Nitrostat because of the cute little rush it gives you, the inner loosening, the tickle.

The land gets less and less settled and more scraggy. The towns take on funny names like Lake Placid and Venus and Old Venus and Palmdale; just beyond Palmdale, after you cross the Fisheating Creek, at Harrisburg no less, the state capital up there but a nothing down here, you bear right on 29, a narrow road so straight and flat you can see for miles, trucks coming at you through a shimmer that cuts off their wheels, rednecks in pickups pushing in the rearview mirror to pass, hardly any signs, a feeling all around of swamp, so remote from civilization the radio station fades, its last song of your life before it finally fades is somebody called Connie Boswell, way before Rabbit's time, singing "Say It Isn't So" with a rueful little lisp, quietly as if she's just talking it to you, "You've found somebody newww," the band behind her soft and tinny like those that used to play in hotel lobbies with lots of potted palms, a Twenties feeling, they lived hard, no worry about smoking and drinking and cholesterol, just do it, "*Ssay* it isn't sso," he could almost cry, she sounds so sincere, so truly wounded. What *is* Janice's game, anyway? He'll find out soon enough.

You think 29 will never end, between its ditches of swamp

water, its stiff gray vegetation, but it finally comes into 80, at La Belle, streaming west just south of the Caloosahatchee, and then you're almost home, there are signs to the Southwest Florida Regional Airport and planes roaring low overhead, he could shoot them down through his windshield if he were the *Vincennes*. For nostalgia's sake, to get back into it, the Florida thing, he pushes on past Interstate 75 to Route 41. Starvin' Marvin. Universal Prosthetics. Superteller. STARLITE MOTEL. That time he and Janice wound up in a motel like they were an illicit couple when in fact they'd been married for thirteen years. Unlucky number but they survived it. Thirty-three years married this year. Thirty-four since they first fucked. Back in Kroll's he never realized she'd come into money eventually. She just seemed a pathetic little mutt behind the nuts counter, "Jan" stitched to her brown smock, something insecure and sexy about her, a secure independent woman like Elvira probably isn't so much into sex, Jan was, she was amazed when he went down on her like he used to for Mary Ann in the car, only now on a bed. Mom didn't take to Jan; standing in the kitchen with soapy hands she would say Fred Springer was a con artist with his used cars. Now Springer Motors is *kaput, finito*. Down the tubes just like Kroll's. Nothing is sacred.

Harry comes to his turning off 41. The plumes of pampas grass, the flowering shrubs along the curving streets look different this time of year, more florid. He has never been down here at this time of year before. It seems emptier, fewer cars in the driveways, more curtains drawn, the sidewalks looking less walked-on than ever, the traffic thinner even though this is rush hour, with that late-afternoon pall in the air, like tarnish on silver. He doesn't see a single squashed armadillo on Pindo Palm Boulevard. The guard at the security gate of Valhalla Village, a lean bespectacled black Harry hasn't seen before, doesn't know him, but finds his name on the list of tenants and waves him through without a smile, all efficiency, probably college-educated, over-qualified.

The code on the inner entrance door of Building B doesn't work. So many numbers in his life, he may be getting it wrong. But after the third time it fails to click him in, he figures it's not him, the code has been changed. And so, limping from a stiffness in his right leg from pushing on the accelerator for over three days, Harry has to hobble over across the carpeted traffic island and the asphalt, in the dazing heat, through the rush of half-forgotten tropical aromas, hibiscus, bougainvillea, dry palm thatch, crunchy broad Bermuda grass, to the management office in Building C to get it, the new code.

They say they sent the notice to his summer address up north; he tells them, "My wife must have torn it up or lost it or something." His voice talking to people again sounds odd and croaky, coming from several feet outside himself, like the to-one-side echo or chorus that sometimes startles you on the car stereo system. He feels awkward and vulnerable out of the car: a sea snail without its shell. On his way by, he looks into Club Nineteen and is surprised to see nobody at the tables, inside or out, though a couple of foursomes are waiting on the first tee, in the lengthening shadows. You don't play, he guesses, in the middle of the day this time of year.

The elevator has a different color inspection card in the slip-in frame, the peach-colored corridor smells of a different air freshener, with a faint nostalgic tang of lemonade. The door of 413 opens easily, his two keys scratch into their wiggly slots and turn, there are no cobwebs to brush against his face, no big brown hairy spiders scuttling away on the carpet. He imagines all sorts of spooky things lately. The condo is like it always was, as absolutely still as a reconstruction of itself—the see-through shelves, the birds and flowers Janice made of small white shells, the big green glass egg that used to sit in Ma Springer's living room, the blond square sofa, the fake-bamboo desk, the green-gray dead television screen. Nobody bothered to disturb or rob the place: kind of a snub. He carries his two bags into the bedroom and opens the sliding door onto the balcony. The sound of his footsteps makes deep dents in the silence of the place. An electric charge of reproach hangs in the stagnant air. The condo hadn't expected him, he is early. Having arrived at it after such a distance makes everything appear magnified, like the pitted head of a pin under a microscope. The whole apartment—its furniture, its aqua cabinets and Formica countertop, its angles of fitted door frame and baseboard—seems to Rabbit a tight structure carefully hammered together to hold a brimming amount of fear.

A white telephone sits waiting to ring. He picks it up. There is no buzz. God on the line. Disconnected for the season. Today is Sunday, tomorrow is Labor Day. The old familiar riddle: how do you telephone the phone company without a telephone?

But the phone, once it is connected, still doesn't ring. The days go by empty. The Golds next door are back in Framingham.

Bernie and Fern Drechsel are up north bouncing between their two daughters' houses, one in Westchester County and the other still in Queens, and their son's lovely home in Princeton and a cottage he has in Manahawkin. The Silbersteins have a place in North Carolina they go to from April to November. Once when Harry asked Ed why they didn't go back to Toledo, Ed looked at him with that smart-ass squint and asked, "You ever been to Toledo?" The Valhalla dining room is spooky—empty tables and echoing click of silver on china and Bingo only once a week. The golf course has noisy foursomes on it early in the morning, waking Harry up with the moon still bright in the sky—younger men, local Deleon business types who buy cut-rate off-season memberships—and then the fairways from ten to about four bake in the mid-nineties heat, deserted but for the stray dog cutting diagonally across or the cats scratching in the sand traps. When Harry one morning gets up his nerve for a round by himself, planning to take a cart, he discovers the pro shop has lost his golf shoes. The kid at the counter—the pro and assistant pro are both still up north at country clubs that don't close down until late October—says he's sure they're somewhere, it's just that this time of year there's a different system.

The only other person in the fourth-floor corridor who seems to be here is the crazy woman in 402, Mrs. Zabritski, a widow with wild white hair, pinned up by two old tortoise-shell combs that just add to the confusion. The Golds have told him she survived one of the concentration camps when a girl. She looks at Harry as if he's crazy too, to be here.

He explains to her one day, since they meet at the elevator and she looks at him funny, "I had this sudden impulse to come down early this year. My wife's just starting up in the real-estate business and I got bored hanging around the house."

Mrs. Zabritski's little neckless head is screwed around at an angle on her shoulder, as if she's bracing an invisible telephone against her ear. She stares up at him furiously, her lips baring her long false teeth in a taut oval that reminds him of that Batman logo you saw everywhere this summer. Her eyes have veiny reds to them, stuck hot and round in their skeletal sockets, that wasting-away look Lyle had. "It's hell," the tiny old lady seems to pronounce, her lips moving stiffly, trying to keep her teeth in.

"It's what? What is?"

"This weather," she says. "Your wife—" She halts, her lips working.

"My wife what?" Rabbit tries to curb his tendency to shout, since hearing doesn't seem to be one of her problems, regardless of that pained way her head is cocked.

"Is a cute little thing," she finishes, but looks angry saying it. Her hair sticks up in wisps as if it was moussed and abandoned.

"She'll be down soon," he almost shouts, embarrassed as much by his secrets, his hopeful lies, as by her dwarfish warped craziness. This is the kind of woman he's ended up with, after Mary Ann and then Janice and Ruth's silky-sack heaviness and Peggy Fosnacht's splayed eyes and Jill's adolescent breasts and numb compliance and Thelma with her black casket and Pru glowing dimly in the dark like a tough street in blossom, not to mention that tired whore in Texas with the gritty sugar in her voice and that other paid lay in his life, a girl he once in a great while remembers, at a Verity Press outing in the Brewer Polish-American Club, she was skinny and had a cold and kept her bra and sweater on, there in this room off to the side, where she was waiting on a cot like a kind of prisoner, young, her belly and thighs sweaty from the cold she had but pure and pale, a few baby-blue veins where the skin molded around the pelvic bones, her pussy an old-fashioned natural dark ferny triangle, not shaved at the sides to suit a bathing suit the way you see in the skin magazines; he always assumed the girl was Polish because of the name of the club, she might have been eighteen, Mrs. Zabritski would have been that age after getting out of the concentration camp, smooth-skinned, lithe, a young survivor. What time does to people; her face is broken into furrows that crisscross each other like a checkerboard of skin.

"She should wait," Mrs. Zabritski says.

"I'll tell her you said so," he says loudly, fighting the magnetism sucking at him out of the unspoken fact that she is a woman and he is a man and both are alone and crazy, a few doors apart in this corridor like a long peach-colored chute glinting with silver lines in the embossed wallpaper. All his life seems to have been a journey into the bodies of women, why should his journey end now? Say she was eighteen when the war ended, he was twelve, she is only six years older. Sixty-two. Not so bad, can still work up some juice. Bev Gold is older, and sexy.

He tries to watch TV but it makes him restless. The last of the summer reruns are mixed in with previews of new shows that don't look that much different: families, laugh tracks, zany drop-ins, those three-sided living-room sets with the stairs coming down in the background like in *Cosby*, and front doors on the right through which the comical good-natured grandparents come, bearing presents and presenting problems. The door is on the right in *Cosby* and on the left in *Roseanne*. That fat husband's going to have his cardiovascular problems too. TV families and your own are hard to tell apart, except yours isn't interrupted every six minutes by commercials and theirs don't get bogged down into nothingness, a state where nothing happens, no skit, no zany visitors, no outburst on the laugh track, nothing at all but boredom and a lost feeling, especially when you get up in the morning and the moon is still shining and men are making noisy bets on the first tee.

At first he thinks Janice has tried so hard to reach him those four days before the phone got connected on Thursday that she's lost faith in their old number. Then he begins to accept her silence as a definite statement. *I'll never forgive you.* O.K., he'll be damned if he'll call her. Dumb mutt. Rich bitch. Working girl yet. Think's she so fucking hot running everybody's lives with those accountants and lawyers Charlie put her on to, he's known her so drunk she couldn't get herself to the bathroom to pee. The few times Harry has weakened, impulsively, usually around four or five when he can't stand the sound of the golf games beginning up again and it's still hours to dinner, the telephone in the little limestone house in Penn Park rings and rings without an answer. He hangs up in a way relieved. Nothingness has a purity. Like running. He showed her he still had some kick in his legs and now she's showing him she can still be stubborn. Her silence frightens him. He fights off images of some accident she might have, slipping in the bathtub or driving the Camry off the road, having had too much to drink over at Nelson's or at some Vietnamese restaurant with Charlie, without him knowing. Police frogmen finding her drowned in the back seat like that girl from Wilkes-Barre twenty years ago. But no, he'd be notified, if anything were to happen, somebody would call him, Nelson or Charlie or Benny at the lot, if there still is a lot. Each day down here, events in Pennsylvania seem more remote. His whole life seems, as he rotates through the empty condo rooms, each with its view across the parallel fairways to a wilderness of Spanish-tile roofs, to have been unreal, or no realer than the lives on TV shows, and now it's too late to make it real, to be serious, to reach down into the earth's iron core and fetch up a real life for himself.

The local air down here this time of year is full of violence, as
if the natives are on good behavior during the winter season.
Hurricane alarms (*Gabrielle packs punch*), head-on car crashes,
masked holdups at Publix. The day after Labor Day, lightning
kills a young football player leaving the field after practice; the
story says Florida has more deaths by lightning than any other
state. In Cape Coral, a Hispanic police officer is charged with
beating his cocker spaniel to death with a crowbar. Sea turtles
are dying by the thousands in shrimp nets. A killer called Pettit
whose own mother says he looks like Charles Manson is pronounced mentally fit to stand trial. That Deion Sanders is still
making the front page of the Fort Myers *News-Press*: one day
he knocks in four runs and a homer playing baseball for the
Yankees, the next he signs for millions to play football for the
Atlanta Falcons, and the very next he's being sued by the aux-
iliary cop he hit last Christmas at that shopping mall, and on
Sunday he bobbles a punt return for the Falcons but runs it back
for a touchdown anyway, the only man in human history to hit
a home run and score a touchdown in pro ball the same week.

Deion has
right stuff

Enjoy it while he can. He calls himself Prime Time and is always
on the TV news wearing sunglasses and gold chains. Rabbit
watches that big kid Becker beat Lendl in the U.S. Tennis Open
final and gets depressed, Lendl seemed old and tired and stringy,
though he's only twenty-eight.

He talks to nobody, except for Mrs. Zabritski when she catches
him in the hall, and the teenage Florida-cracker salesclerks
when he buys his food and razor blades and toilet paper, and
the people who feel obliged to make chitchat, the other retirees,
in the Valhalla dining room; they always ask about Janice so it
gets to be embarrassing and he more and more just heats up
something frozen and stays in the condo, ransacking the cable
channels for something worthy to kill time with. In his solitude,
his heart becomes his companion. He listens to it, tries to de-
cipher its messages. It has different rhythms at different times
of the day, a *thorrumph thorrumph* sluggish slightly underwater
beat in the morning, and toward evening, when the organism
gets tired and excited at once, a more skittish thudding, with
the accent on the first beat and grace notes added, little trips and
pauses now and then. It twinges when he gets up out of bed and

then again when he lies down and whenever he thinks too hard about his situation, having set himself adrift like this. He could have gone over that night and faced the music but how much music is a man supposed to face? So he and Pru did fuck, once. What are we put here in the first place for? These women complain about men seeing nothing but tits and ass when they look at them but what are we supposed to see? We've been programmed to tits and ass. Except guys like Slim and Lyle, the tits got left out of their program. One thing he knows is if he had to give parts of his life back the last thing he'd give back is the fucking, even that sniffly girl in the Polish-American Club, she hardly said two words, just took his twenty, a lot of money in those days, and wiped her nose with a handkerchief while he was on top of her, but nevertheless she showed him something, she took him in, where it mattered. A lot of this other stuff you're supposed to be grateful for isn't where it matters. When he gets up from the deep wicker chair indignantly—he can't stand *Cheers* now that Shelley Long is gone, that guy with the Cro-Magnon brow he never did like—and goes into the kitchen to refill his bowl of Keystone Corn Chips, which not all of the stores down here carry but you can get over at the Winn Dixie on Pindo Palm Boulevard, Harry's heart confides to him a dainty little gallop, the kind of lacy riff the old swing drummers used to do, hitting the rims as well as the skins and ending with a tingling pop off the high hat, the music of his life. When this happens he gets an excited, hurried, full feeling in his chest. It doesn't hurt, it's just there, muffled inside that mess inside himself he doesn't like to think about, just like he never cared for rare roast beef, as it used to come on the take-out subs from the Chuck Wagon across Route 111 before it became the Pizza Hut. Any sudden motion now, he feels a surge of circulation, a tilt of surprise in the head that makes one leg feel shorter than the other for a second. And the pains, maybe he imagines it, but the contractions of the bands across his ribs, the feeling of something having been sewn there from the inside, seems to cut deeper, more burningly, as though the thread the patch was sewn with is growing thicker, and red hot. When he turns off the light at night, he doesn't like feeling his head sink back onto a single pillow, his head seems sunk in a hole then, it's not that he can't breathe exactly, he just feels more comfortable, less *full*, if he has his head up on the two pillows and lies facing the ceiling. He can turn on his side but his old way of sleeping, flat on his stomach with his feet pointing down over the edge, has become

impossible; there is a nest of purple slithering half-dead thoughts
he cannot bear to put his face in. There is a whole host of
goblins, it turns out, that Janice's warm little tightly knit body,
even snoring and farting as it sometimes did, protected him
from. In her absence he sleeps with his heart, listening to it race
and skip when his rest is disturbed, when kids who have climbed
the fence yell on the empty moonlit golf course, when a siren
bleats somewhere in downtown Deleon, when a big jet from the
north heads in especially low to the Southwest Florida Regional
Airport, churning the air. He awakes in lavender light and then
lets his heart's slowing beat drag him back under.

His dreams are delicious, like forbidden candy—intensely
colored overpopulated rearrangements of old situations stored
in his brain cells, rooms like the little living room at 26 Vista
Crescent, with the fireplace they never used and the lamp with
the driftwood base, or the old kitchen at 303 Jackson, with the
wooden ice box and the gas stove with its nipples of blue flame
and the porcelain table with the worn spots, skewed and new
and crowded with people at the wrong ages, Mim with lots of
green eye makeup at the age Mom was when they were kids, or
Nelson as a tiny child sliding out from under a car in the greasy
service section of Springer Motors, looking woebegone and
sickly with his smudged face, or Marty Tothero and Ruth and
even that nitwit Margaret Kosko, he hasn't thought of her name
for thirty years, but there she was in his brain cells, just as clear
with her underfed city pallor as she was that night in the booth
of the Chinese restaurant, Ruth next to him and Margaret next
to Mr. Tothero whose head looks lopsided and gray like that of
a dying rhinoceros, the four of them eating now in the Valhalla
dining room with its garbled bas-relief of Vikings and sumptu-
ous salad bar where the dishes underneath the plastic sneeze
guard are bright and various as jewels, arranged in rainbow
order like the crayons in the Crayola boxes that were always
among his birthday presents in February, a little stadium of
waxy-smelling pointed heads there in the bright February
windowlight, with icicles and the stunned sense of being a year
older. Harry wakes from these delicious dreams reluctantly, as
if their miniaturized visions are a substance essential to his nutrition, a polychrome finely fitted machine he needs to reinsert
himself into, like poor Thelma and her dialysis machine. He
awakes always on his stomach, and only as his head clears and
re-creates present time, establishing the felt-gray parallel lines
he sees as the dawn behind the curved slats of Venetian blinds

and the insistent pressure on his face as the cool Gulf breeze coming in where he left the sliding door ajar, does his solitude begin to gnaw again, and his heart to talk to him. At times it seems a tiny creature, a baby, pleading inside him for attention, for rescue, and at others a sinister intruder, a traitor muttering in code, an alien parasite nothing will expel. The pains, when they come, seem hostile and deliberate, the knives of a strengthening enemy.

He makes an appointment with Dr. Morris. He is able to get one surprisingly soon, the day after next. These doctors are scrambling down here, a glut of them, too many miners at the gold rush, the geriatric immigrants still hanging up north this time of year. The office is in one of those low stucco clinics along Route 41. Soothing music plays constantly in the waiting room, entwining with the surf-sound of traffic outside. The doctor has aged since the last appointment. He is bent-over and shuffly, with arthritic knuckles. His shrivelled jaw looks not quite clean-shaven; his nostrils are packed with black hair. His son, young Tom, pink and sleek in his mid-forties, gives Harry a freckled fat hand in the hall, and is wearing his white clinical smock over kelly-green golf slacks. He is established in an adjacent office, primed to take over the full practice. But for now the old doctor clings to his own patients. Harry tries to describe his complex sensations. Dr. Morris, with an impatient jerk of his arthritic hand, waves him toward the examination room. He has him strip to his Jockey undershorts, weighs him, tut-tuts. He seats him on the examination table and listens to his chest through his stethoscope, and taps his naked back with a soothing, knobby touch, and solemnly, silently takes Harry's hands in his. He studies the fingernails, turns them over, studies the palms, grunts. Close up, he gives off an old man's sad leathery, moldy smell.

"Well," Harry asks, "what do you think?"

"How much do you exercise?"

"Not much. Not since I got down here. I do a little gardening up north. Golf—but I've kind of run out of partners."

Dr. Morris ponders him through rimless glasses. His eyes, once a sharp blue, have that colorless sucked look to the irises. His eyebrows are messy tangled tufts of white and reddish-brown, his forehead and cheeks are flecked with small blotches and bumps. His projecting eyebrows lift, like turrets taking aim. "You should walk."

"Walk?"

"Briskly. Several miles a day. What sorts of food are you eating?"

"Oh—stuff you can heat up. TV-dinner kind of thing. My wife is still up north but she doesn't cook that much even when she's here. Now, my daughter-in-law—"

"You ever eat any of this salty junk that comes in bags?"

"Well—once in a great while."

"You should watch your sodium intake. Snack on fresh vegetables if you want to snack. Read the labels. Stay away from salt and animal fats. I think we've been through all this, when you were in the hospital"—he lifts his forearm and checks his record—"nine months ago."

"Yeah, I did for a while, I still do, it's just that day to day, it's easier—"

"To poison yourself. Don't. Don't be lazy about it. And you should lose forty pounds. Without the salt in your diet you'd lose ten in retained water in two weeks. I'll give you a diet list, if you've lost the one I gave you before. You may get dressed."

The doctor has grown smaller, or his desk has grown bigger, since Harry's last visit here. He sits down, dressed, at the desk and begins, "The pains—"

"The pains will moderate with better conditioning. Your heart doesn't like what you're feeding it. Have you been under any special stress lately?"

"Not really. Just the normal flack. A couple family problems, but they seem to be clearing up."

The doctor is writing on his prescription pad. "I want you to have blood tests and an EKG at the Community General. Then I want to consult with Dr. Olman. Depending on how the results look, it may be time for another catheterization."

"Oh Jesus. Not that again."

The messy eyebrows go up again, the prim dry lips pinch in. Not a clever generous Jewish mouth. A crabby Scots economy in the way he thinks and talks, on the verge of impatience, having seen so many hopelessly deteriorating patients in his life. "What didn't you like? Were the hot flashes painful?"

"It just felt funny," Harry tells him, "having that damn thing inside me. It's the *idea* of it."

"Well, do you prefer the idea of a life-threatening restenosis of your coronary artery? It's been, let's see, nearly six months since you had the angioplasty at"—he reads his records, with difficulty—"St. Joseph's Hospital in Brewer, Pennsylvania."

"They made me *watch*," Harry tells him. "I could see my own damn heart on TV, full of like Rice Krispies."

A tiny Scots smile, dry as a thistle. "Was that so bad?"

"It was"—he searches for the word—"insulting." In fact when you think about it his whole life from here on in is apt to be insulting. Pacemakers, crutches, wheelchairs. Impotence.

Dr. Morris is making, in a deliberate, tremulous hand, notes to add to his folder. Without looking up, he says, "There are a number of investigative instruments now that don't involve a catheter. Scans using IV technetium 99 can identify acutely damaged heart muscle. Then there is echocardiography. We won't rush into anything. Let's see what you can do on your own, with a healthier regimen."

"Great."

"I want to see you in four weeks. Here are slips for the blood tests and EKG, and prescriptions for a diuretic and a relaxant for you at night. Don't forget the diet lists. Walk. Not violently, but vigorously, two or three miles a day."

"O.K.," Rabbit says, beginning to rise from his chair, feeling as light as a boy called into the principal's office and dismissed with a light reprimand.

But Dr. Morris fixes him with those sucked-out old blue eyes and says, "Do you have any sort of a job? According to my last information here, you were in charge of a car agency."

"That's gone. My son's taken over and my wife wants me to stay out of the kid's way. The agency was founded by her father. They'll probably wind up having to sell it off."

"Any hobbies?"

"Well, I read a lot of history. I'm a kind of a buff, you could say."

"You need more than that. A man needs an occupation. He needs something to do. The best thing for a body is a healthy interest in life. Get interested in something outside yourself, and your heart will stop talking to you."

The smell of good advice always makes Rabbit want to run the other way. He resumes rising from the chair and takes Dr. Morris' many slips of paper out into the towering heat. The few other people out on the parking lot seem tinted smoke rising from their shadows, barely existing. The radio in the Celica is full of voices yammering about Deion Sanders, about Koch losing the New York Democratic primary to a black, about the SAT scores dropping in Lee County, about President Bush's televised appeal to America's schoolchildren yesterday. "The man's not *do*ing anything!" one caller howls.

Well, Rabbit thinks, doing nothing works for Bush, why not for him? On the car seat next to him Dr. Morris' prescriptions and medical slips and Xeroxed diet sheets lift and scatter in the breeze from the car air-conditioning. On another station he hears that the Phillies beat the Mets last night, two to one. Dickie Thon homered with one out in the ninth, dropping the preseason pennant favorites five and a half games behind the oncelowly Chicago Cubs. Harry tries to care but has trouble. Ever since Schmidt retired. Get interested is the advice, but in truth you are interested in less and less. It's nature's way.

But he does begin to walk. He even drives to the Palmetto Palm Mall and buys a pair of walking Nikes, with a bubble of special high-tech air to cushion each heel. He sets out between nine and ten in the morning, after eating breakfast and digesting the *News-Press*, and then again between four and five, returning to a nap and then dinner and then television and a page or two of his book and a sound sleep, thanks to the walking. He explores Deleon. First, he walks the curving streets of low stucco houses within a mile of Valhalla Village, with unfenced front yards of tallish tough grass half-hiding bits of dried palm frond, a Florida texture in that, a cozy sere Florida scent, a feeling of mass vacation in which encountering a UPS man delivering or a barking small dog—a flat-faced Pekinese with its silky long hair done up in ribbons—is like finding life on Mars. Then, growing ever fonder of his Nikes (that bubble in the heel, he thought at first it was just a gimmick but maybe it does add bounce), he makes his way to the downtown and the river, where the town first began, as a fort in the Seminole wars and a shipping point for cattle and cotton.

He discovers, some blocks back from the beachfront and the green glass hotels, old neighborhoods where shadowy big spicy gentle trees, live oaks and gums and an occasional banyan widening out on its crutches, overhang wooden houses once painted white but flaking down to gray bareness, with louvered windows and roofs of corrugated tin. Music rises from within these houses, scratchy radio music, and voices raised in argument or jabbery jubilation, bright fragments of overheard life. The sidewalks are unpaved, small paths such as cats make have been worn diagonally between the trees, in and out of private property, the parched grass growing in patches, packed dirt littered with pods and nuts. It reminds Harry of those neighborhoods he blundered into trying to get out of Savannah, but also of the town of his childhood, Mt. Judge in the days of Depression and distant war, when people still sat on their front porches, and there were vacant lots and odd-shaped cornfields, and men back from work in the factories would water their lawns in the evenings, and people not long off the farm kept chickens in backyard pens, and peddled the eggs for odd pennies. Chickens clucking and pecking and suddenly squawking: he hasn't heard that sound for forty years, and hasn't until now realized what he's been missing. For chicken coops tucked here and there dot this sleepy neighborhood he has discovered.

In the daytime here, under the heavy late-summer sun, there are few people moving, just women getting in and out of cars with pre-school children. The slams of their car doors carry a long way down the dusty straight streets, under the live oaks. At some corners there are grocery stores that also sell beer and wine in the permissive Southern way, and pastel-painted bars with the door open on a dark interior, and video rental places with horror and kung-fu tapes displayed in the window, the boxes' colors being bleached by the sun. One day he passes an old-fashioned variety store, in a clapboarded one-story building, displaying all sorts of innocent things—erector sets, model airplane kits, Chinese-checker boards and marbles—that he hadn't known were still being sold. He almost goes in but doesn't dare. He is too white.

Toward late afternoon, when he takes his second walk of the day, the neighborhood begins to breathe, a quickness takes hold, men and boys return to it, and Rabbit walks more briskly, proclaiming with his stride that he is out for the exercise, just passing through, not spying. These blocks are black, and there are miles of them, a vast stagnant economic marsh left over from Deleon's Southern past, supplying the hotels and condos with labor, with waiters and security guards and chambermaids. To Harry, whose Deleon has been a glitzy community of elderly refugees, these blocks feel like a vast secret, and as the shadows lengthen under the trees, and the chickens cease their daylong clucking, his senses widen to grasp the secret better, as when in whispering knickers he would move through Mt. Judge unseen, no taller than a privet hedge, trying to grasp the unspeakable adult meaning of the lit windows, of the kitchen noises filtering across the yards mysterious and damp as jungles. An unseen child would cry, a dog would bark, and he would tingle with the excitement of being, at this point of time and space, with worlds to know and forever to live, himself, Harold C. Angstrom, called Hassy in those lost days never to be relived. He prolongs his walks, feeling stronger, more comfortable in this strange city where he is at last beginning to live as more than a visitor; but as darkness approaches, and the music from the glowing slatted windows intensifies, he begins to feel conspicuous, his whiteness begins to glimmer, and he heads back to the car, which he has taken to parking in a lot or at a meter downtown, as base for his widening explorations.

Coming back one day around six-thirty, just in time for a shower and a look at the news while his TV dinner heats in the oven, he is startled by the telephone's ringing. He has ceased to listen for it as intensely as in that first lonely week. When it does ring, it has been one of those recordings ("Hello there, this is Sandra") selling health insurance or a no-frills burial plan or reduced-fee investment services, going through all the numbers by computer, you wonder how it pays, Harry always hangs up and can't imagine who would listen and sign up for this stuff. But this time the caller is Nelson, his son.

"Dad?"

"Yes," he says, gathering up his disused voice, trying to imagine what you can say to a son whose wife you've boffed. "Nellie," he says, "how the hell is everybody?"

The distant voice is gingerly, shy, almost not sure what is appropriate. "We're fine, pretty much."

"You're staying clean?" He didn't mean to take the aggressive so sharply; the other voice, fragile in its distance, is stunned into silence for a moment.

"You mean the drugs. Sure. I don't even think about coke, except at NA meetings. Like they say, you give your life over to a higher power. You ought to try it, Dad."

"I'm working on it. Listen, no kidding, I am. I'm proud of you, Nelson. Keep taking it a day at a time, that's all anybody can do."

Again, the boy seems momentarily stuck. Maybe this came over as too preachy. Who is he to preach? Shit, he was just trying to share, like you're supposed to. Harry holds his tongue.

"There's been so much going on around here," Nelson tells him, "I really haven't thought about myself that much. A lot of my problem, I think, was idleness. Hanging around the lot all day waiting for some action, for the customers to show up, really preys on your self-confidence. I mean, you have no control. It was degrading."

"I did it, for fifteen years I did it, every day."

"Yeah, but you have a different sort of temperament. You're more happy-go-lucky."

"Stupid, you mean."

"Hey Dad, I didn't call up to quarrel. This isn't exactly fun for me, I've been putting it off. But I got some things to say."

"O.K., say 'em." *This isn't working out.* He doesn't want to be this way, he is putting his anger at Janice onto the kid. Her silence has hurt him. He can't stop, adding, "You've sure taken your time saying anything, I've been down here all by myself for two weeks. I saw Old Dr. Morris and he thinks I'm so far gone I should stop eating."

"Well," Nelson says back, "if you were so crazy to talk you could have come over that night instead of getting in the car and disappearing. We weren't going to kill you, we just wanted to talk it through, to understand what had happened, really, in terms of family dynamics. Pru's as good as admitted it was a way of getting in touch with her own father."

"With Blubberlips Lubell? Tell her thanks a lot." But he is not displeased to hear Nelson taking a firmer tone with him. You're not a man in this world until you've got on top of your father. In his own case, it was easier, the system had beaten Pop so far down already. "Coming over there that night felt like a set-up," he explains to Nelson.

"Well, Mom didn't think any of us should try to get in touch if that's the kind of cowardly trick you were going to pull. She wasn't too happy you telephoned Pru instead of her, either."

"I kept trying our number but she's never home."

"Well, whatever. She wanted me to let you know a couple things. One, she has an offer on the house, not as much as she'd hoped for, one eighty-five, but the market's pretty flat right now and she thinks we should take it. It would reduce the debt to Brewer Trust to the point where we could manage it."

"Let me get this straight. This is the Penn Park house you're talking about? The little gray stone house I've always loved?"

"What other house could you think? We can't sell the Mt. Judge house—where would we all live?"

"Tell me, Nelson, I'm just curious. How does it feel to have smoked up your parents' house in crack?"

The boy begins to sound more like himself. He whines, "I keep *tell*ing you, I was never that much into crack. The crack just came into it toward the end, it was so much more convenient than freebasing. I'm *sor*ry, Jesus. I went to rehab, I took the

vows, I'm trying to make amends like they say. Who are you to
still be on my case?''

Who indeed? "O.K.," Rabbit says. "Sorry to mention it.
What else did your mother tell you to tell me?''

"Hyundai *is* interested in the lot, the location is just what
they want and don't have. They'd enlarge the building out toward
the back like I always wanted to do.'' *Goodbye, Paraguay,* Rabbit thinks. "They'd keep the service people on, with a little
retraining, and some of the sales force, Elvira might go over to
Rudy's on 422. Hyundai's made her a counteroffer. But they
don't want *me*. No way. Word gets around, I guess, among these
Oriental companies.''

"I guess," Harry says. Too much *ninjō*, not enough *giri*.
"I'm sorry."

"Don't be sorry, Dad. It frees me up. I'm thinking of becoming a social worker.''

"A *so*cial worker!''

"Sure, why not? Help other people instead of myself for a
change. It's a two-year course at the Penn State extension, I
could still get in for this October.''

"Sure, why not, come to think of it," Rabbit agrees. He is
beginning to dislike himself, for being so agreeable, for wanting
to worm back into everybody's good graces.

"Me and the lawyers all think if it goes through we should
lease to Hyundai rather than sell; if we sell the house in Penn
Park we wouldn't need any more capital and should keep the lot
as an investment, Mom says it's going to be worth *millions* by
the year 2000.''

"Wow," Harry says unenthusiastically. "You and your mom
are quite a team. Anything else to hit me with?''

"Well, this maybe isn't any of your business, but Pru thought
it was. We're trying to get pregnant.''

"We?''

"We want to have a third child. All this has made us realize
how much we've been neglecting our marriage and how much
really we have invested in making it *work*. Not only for Judy
and Roy, but for our*selves*. We love each other, Dad.''

Maybe this is supposed to make him feel jealous, and this is
a pang, just under the right ventricle. But Rabbit's basic emotion
is relief, at being excused from having to keep any kind of candle
burning at Pru's shrine. Good luck to her, her and her slum
hunger. "Great," he tells the boy. He can't resist adding,
"Though I'm not so sure social workers make enough to support

three kids.'' And, getting mad, feeling squeezed, he goes on, ''And tell your mother I'm not so sure I want to sign our house away. It's not like the lot, we're co-owners, and she needs my signature on the sales agreement. If we split up, my signature ought to be worth quite a bit, tell her.''

''Split up?'' The boy sounds frightened. ''Who's saying anything about splitting up?''

''Well,'' Harry says, ''we seem split up now. At least I don't see her down here, unless she's under the bed. But don't you worry about it, Nelson. You've been through this before and I felt lousy about it. You get on with your own life. It sounds like you're doing fine. I'm proud of you. Or did I say that?''

''But everything kind of depends on selling the Penn Park house.''

''Tell her I'll think about it. Tell Judy and Roy I'll give 'em a call one of these days.''

''But, Dad—''

''Nelson, I got this low-cal frozen dinner in the oven and the buzzer went off five minutes ago. Tell your mother to call me sometime if she wants to talk about it. Must run. Terrific to talk to you. Really.'' He hangs up.

He has been buying low-cal frozen meals, raw vegetables like cabbage and carrots, and no more sodium-laden munchies. He has lost three pounds on the bathroom scale, if he weighs himself naked and right in the morning after taking a crap. At night, to keep himself away from the TV and the breadbox in the kitchen drawer and the beer in the refrigerator, he gets into bed and reads the book Janice gave him for last Christmas. Its author has joined Roy Orbison and Bart Giamatti in that beyond where some celebrities like Elvis and Marilyn expand like balloons and become gods and but where most shrivel and shrink into yellowing obituaries not much bigger than Harry's will be in the Brewer *Standard*. In the *News-Press* he doesn't expect to get an inch. He read in her obituary that the author had been a niece of Roosevelt's Secretary of the Treasury Henry Morgenthau, Jr. Harry remembers Morgenthau: the pointy-nosed guy who kept urging him and his schoolmates to buy war stamps with their pennies. It's a small world, and a long life in a way.

He has reached the exciting part of the book, where, after years of frustration and starvation and lousy support from his fellow would-be Americans, Washington has hopes of joining up with a French fleet sailing from the Caribbean to trap Cornwallis and his army at York in the Chesapeake Bay. It seems impossible that it will work. The logistics of it need perfect timing, and the communications take weeks, ships to land and back. Anyway, what's in it for France? *Instead of an aggressive ally, they were tied to a dependent client, unable to establish a strong government and requiring transfusions of men-at-arms and money to keep its war effort alive. The war, like all wars, was proving more expensive for the Bourbons than planned.* What was in it for the soldiers? *The American troops, for too long orphans of the battle, unkempt, underfed and unpaid while Congress rode in carriages and dined at well-laid tables, would not march without pay.* What was in it for Washington? He couldn't even have known he'd get his face on the dollar bill. But he hangs in there, patching, begging, scrambling, his only assets the fatheadedness of the British commanders, all gouty noblemen wishing they were home in their castles, and the fact that, just like in Vietnam, the natives weren't basically friendly. Washington gets his troops across the Hudson while Clinton cowers defensively in New York. De Grasse gets his fleet heading north because Admiral Rodney cautiously chooses the defense of Barbados over pursuit. But, still, the odds of the troops and the ships arriving at the Chesapeake at the same time and Cornwallis remaining a sitting duck in Yorktown are preposterous. All that transport, all those men trudging and horses galloping along the New World's sandy woodsy roads, winding through forests, past lonely clearings, among bears and wolves and chipmunks and Indians and passenger pigeons, it makes Harry sleepy to think about. The tangle of it all, the trouble. He reads ten pages a night; his is a slow march.

He does not always gravitate in his health walks to the black section of Deleon; he discovers and explores posh streets he never dreamed were there, long roads parallel to the beach, giving the passerby glimpses of backs of houses that front on the ocean, wooden back stairs and sundecks, three-car garages at the end of driveways surfaced in crushed seashells, plantings of hibiscus and jacaranda, splashing sounds coming from a fenced-in swimming pool, the purr of air-conditioners lost amid the retreating and advancing shush of the surf. *Posh, swoosh.* Some people have it made; not for them a condo where they steal your view of the Gulf from the balcony. No matter how hard you climb, there are always the rich above you, who got there without effort. Lucky stiffs, holding you down, making you discontent so you buy more of the crap advertised on television.

Occasional breaks in the developed oceanfront property permit a look at the Gulf, its striped sails and scooting jet skis, its parachutes being pulled by powerboats, its far gray stationary freighters. Bicyclers in bathing suits pass him with a whirr; a beefy young mailman in blue-gray shorts and socks to match pushes along one of these pouches on rubber wheels they have now, like baby strollers. We're getting soft. A nation of couch potatoes. The man who brought the mail to Jackson Road, he forgets his name, an iron-haired man with a handsome unhappy face, Mom said his wife had left him, used to carry this scuffed leather pouch, leaning to one side against its pull especially on Fridays when the magazines came to the houses, *Life* and the *Post*. Left by his wife: Harry as a boy used to try to imagine what could have been so terribly wrong with him, to earn such a disgrace in life.

His Nikes with the bubbles of air in the heels take him along crushed-shell sidewalks, so white they hurt his eyes when the sun is high. And he walks through an area of marinas cut into coral shell, neat straight streets of water sliced out, full of powerboats tied up obedient and empty, their rub rails tapping the sliced coral, their curved sides seeming to tremble and twitch in the sunlight reflected in bobbling stripes off the calm water as it lightly kicks and laps. *Tap. Lap.* No Trespassing signs abound, but not so much for him, a respectable-looking white man past middle age. Each boat ties up as much money as a house used to cost and a number of them no doubt are involved in cocaine smuggling, put-putting out in the dead of the night when the moon is down, crime and the sea have always mixed, pirates ever since there have been ships, law ends with the land, man is nothing out there, a few bubbles as he goes down under the towering waves, that must be why Harry has always been afraid of it, the water. He loves freedom but a grassy field is his idea of enough. People down here are crazy about boats but not him. Give him terra firma. Away from the water he walks miles of plain neighborhoods, glorified cabins put up after the war for people without much capital who yet wanted a piece of the sun Washington won for them or else were born here, this strange thin vacationland their natural home, their houses shedding paint like a sunbather's clothes, surrounded not by barberry and yew bushes but spiky cactuses fattening in the baking heat, America too hot and dry really for European civilization to take deep root.

But it is the widespread black section that draws him back, he

doesn't quite know why, whether because he is exerting his national right to go where he pleases or because this ignored part
of Deleon is in some way familiar, he's been there before, before
his life got too soft. On the Monday after a pretty good weekend
for blacks—a black Miss America got elected, and Randall Cunningham brought the Eagles back from being down to the Red-
skins twenty to nothing—Rabbit ventures several blocks farther
than he has dared walk before and comes upon, beyond an abandoned high school built about when Brewer High was, an ochre-
brick edifice with tall gridded windows and a piece of Latin in
cement over the main entrance, a recreation field—a wide tan
emptiness under the sun, with a baseball diamond and backstop
at the far end, a pair of soccer goals set up in the outfield, and,
nearer the street, two pitted clay tennis courts with wire nets
slack and bent from repeated assaults and, also of pale tamped
earth, a basketball court. A backboard and netless hoop lifted
up on pipe legs preside at either end. A small pack of black boys
are scrimmaging around one basket. Legs, shouts. Puffs of dust
rise from their striving, stop-and-starting feet. Some benches
have been placed in an unmowed strip of seedy blanched weeds
next to the cement sidewalk. The benches are backless so you
can sit facing the street or facing the field. Rabbit seats himself
on the end of one, facing neither way, so he can watch the
basketball while seeming to be doing something else, just resting a second on his way through, not looking at anything, minding his own business.
    The kids, six of them, in shorts and tank tops, vary in heights
and degrees of looseness, but all have that unhurried look he
likes to see, missing shots or making them, passing back out
and then crossing over in a screen, dribbling as if to drive in and
then stopping dead to pass off in a droll behind-the-back toss,
imitating the fancy stuff they see on television, all together making a weave, nobody trying too hard, it's a long life, a long
afternoon. Their busy legs are up to their knees in a steady haze
of pink dust lifting from the clay, their calves dulled but for
where sweat makes dark rivulets, their sneakers solidly coated
a rosy earth color. There is a breeze here, stirred up by the
empty space stretching to the baseball backstop. Rabbit's watch
says four o'clock, school is over, but the brick high school has
been abandoned, the real action is elsewhere, at some modern
low glassy high school you take a bus to, out on the bulldozed
edges of the city. Rabbit is happy to think that the world isn't
yet too crowded to have a few of these underused pockets left.

Grass, he observes, has crept onto the dirt court, in the middle, where the pounding, pivoting feet rarely come. Shallow semicircular troughs have been worn around the baskets at either end.

Though he is sitting some distance away—a good firm chip shot, or a feathered wedge—the players eye him. They're doing this for themselves, not as a show for some fat old honky walking around where he shouldn't be. Where's his car? Feeling heat from their sidelong glances, not wanting so delicate a tangency to turn awkward, Harry sighs ostentatiously and heaves himself up from the bench and walks away the way he came, taking note of the street signs so he can find this peaceful place again. If he comes every day he'll blend in. Blacks don't have this racist thing whites do, about keeping their neighborhoods pure. They can't be too angry these days, with their third Miss America just elected. The funny thing about the final judges' panel, it held two celebrities he feels he knows, has taken into himself, *loves*, actually: Phylicia Rashad, who for his money is the real star of *The Cosby Show*, with those legs and that nice loose smile, and Mike Schmidt, who had the grace to pack it in when he could no longer produce. So there is life after death of a sort. Schmidt judges. Skeeter lives. And the weekend before last, a young black girl beat Chrissie Evert in the last U.S. Open match she'll ever play. She packed it in too. There comes a time.

Now the *News-Press* wears daily banner headlines tracking Hurricane Hugo—*Deadly Hugo roars into islands, Hugo rips into Puerto Rico*. Tuesday, he walks in the expensive beachfront areas and scans the sky for hurricane signs, for clouds God's finger might write, and reads none. In the hall that evening, happening to be standing with him at the elevators, Mrs. Zabritski turns those veiny protuberant eyes up at him out of her skeletal face and pronounces, "Terrible thing."

"What is?"

"The thing coming," she says, her white hair looking already wind-tossed, lifted out from her skull in all directions.

"Oh, it'll never get here," Harry reassures her. "It's all this media hype. You know, hype, phony hullabaloo. They have to make news out of something, every night."

"Yeah?" Mrs. Zabritski says, coyly. The way her neck twists into her hunched shoulders gives her head a flirtatious tilt she may not mean. But then again she may. Didn't he read somewhere that even in the Nazi death camps there were romances? This windowless corridor, with its peach-and-silver wallpaper, is an eerie cryptlike space he is always anxious to get out of.

That big vase on the marble half-moon table, with green glaze running into golden, could be holding someone's ashes. Still the elevator refuses to arrive. His female companion clears her throat and volunteers, "Wednesday buffet tomorrow. I like extra much the buffet."

"Me too," he tells her. "Except I can't choose and then I wind up taking too much and then eating it all." What is she suggesting, that they go together? That they have a date? He's stopped telling her that Janice is coming down.

"Do you do the kosher?"

"I don't know. Those scallops wrapped in bacon, are they kosher?"

She stares at him as if he were the crazy one, stares so hard her eyeballs seem in danger of snapping the bloody threads that hold them fast in their sockets. Then she must have decided he was joking, for a careful stiff smile slowly spreads across the lower half of her face, crisscrossed by wrinkles like a quilt sewn of tiny squares of skin. He thinks of that little sniffly slut in the Polish-American Club, her silken skin below the waist, below the sweater, and feels bitter toward Janice, for leaving him at his age at the mercy of women. He eats at his table alone but is so disturbed by Mrs. Zabritski's attempt at invading him he takes two Nitrostats to quell his heart.

After dinner, in bed, on September 1, 1781, the French troops make a dazzling impression upon the citizens of Philadelphia. *Ecstatic applause greeted the dazzling spectacle of the French as they passed in review in their bright white uniforms and white plumes. Wearing colored lapels and collars of pink, green, violet or blue identifying their regiments, they were the most brilliantly appointed soldiers in Europe.* Joseph Reed, the President of the State of Pennsylvania, entertained the French officers at a ceremonial dinner *of which the main feature was an immense ninety-pound turtle with soup served in its shell.* Talk about cholesterol. Didn't seem to bother them, but, then, how old did those poor devils get to be? Not fifty-six, most of them. The troops are scared to march south for fear of malaria. Rochambeau has talked Washington out of attacking New York, and at this point seems to be the brains of the Revolution. He wants to rendezvous with De Grasse at the head of the Chesapeake. De Grasse has evaded Hood by sailing the back-alley route between the Bahamas and Cuba. It will never work.

Hugo heading for U.S., the *News-Press* headline says next morning. For breakfast now, Harry has switched from Frosted

Flakes to Nabisco Shredded Wheat 'n Bran, though he forgets exactly why, something about fiber and the bowels. We're all plumbing, the doctors say. He does hope he never reaches the point where he has to think all the time about shitting. Ma Springer, toward the end, got to talking about her bowel movements like they were family heirlooms, each one precious. On the evening news half the commercials are for laxatives and the other half for hemorrhoid medicine, as if only assholes watch the news. After breakfast he walks along Pindo Palm Boulevard in the morning and brings back a bag of groceries from Winn Dixie, passing up the Keystone Corn Chips and going heavy on the low-cal frozen dinners. The day's predicted showers come at noon but seem over by three and in a kind of trance Rabbit drives into downtown Deleon, parks at a two-hour meter, and walks the mile to the playing field he discovered Monday. Today two sets of boys are on the dirt court, each using one basket. One set is energetically playing a two-on-two, but the other consists of three boys at a desultory game of what he used to call Horse. You take a shot, and if it goes in the next guy has to make the same shot, and if he misses he's an H, or an H-O, and when he's a HORSE he's out. Rabbit takes the bench within a chip shot of this group and frankly watches—after all, is it a free country or not?

The three are in their early teens at best, and don't know what to make of this sudden uninvited audience. One of these old ofays after some crack or a black boy's dick? Their languid motions stiffen, they jostle shoulders and pass each other sliding silent messages that make one another giggle. One of them perhaps deliberately lets a pass flip off his hands and bounce Harry's way. He leans off his bench end and stops it left-handed, not his best hand but it remembers. It remembers exactly. That taut pebbled roundness, the smooth seams between, the little circlet for taking the air valve. A big pebbled ball that wants to fly. He flips it back, a bit awkwardly, sitting, but still with a little zing to show he's handled one before. Somewhat satisfied, the trio resume Horse, trying sky-hooks, under-the-basket lay-ups, fall-back jumpers, crazy improvised underhanded or side-arm shots that now and then go in, by accident or miracle. One such wild toss rockets off the rim and comes Rabbit's way. This time he stands up with the ball and advances with it toward the boys. He feels himself big, a big shape with the sun behind him. His shadow falls across the face of the nearest boy, who wears an unravelling wool cap of many colors. Another boy has the

number 8 on his tank top. "What's the game?" Harry asks
them. "You call it Horse?"

"We call it Three," the wool cap answers reluctantly. "Three
misses, you out." He reaches for the ball but Rabbit lifts it out
of his reach.

"Lemme take a shot, could I?"

The boys' eyes consult, they figure this is the way to get the
ball back. "Go 'head," Wool Cap says.

Harry is out on an angle to the left maybe twenty feet and as
his knees dip and his right arm goes up he feels the heaviness
of the years, all those blankets of time, since he did this last. A
bank shot. He has the spot on the backboard in his sights, but
the ball doesn't quite have the length and, instead of glancing
off and in, jams between the wood and hoop and kicks back into
the hands of Number 8.

"Hey man," the third one, the one who looks most Hispanic
and most sullen, taunts him, "you're history!"

"I'm rusty," Rabbit admits. "The air down here is different
than I'm used to."

"You want to see somebody sink that shot?" Number 8, the
tallest, asks him. He stands where Harry stood, and opens his
mouth and lets his pink tongue dangle the way Michael Jordan
does. He gently paws the air above his forehead so the ball flies
from his long loose brown hand. But he misses also, hitting the
rim on the right. This breaks some of the ice. Rabbit holds still,
waiting to see what they will do with him.

The boy in the hat of concentric circles, a Black Muslim hat,
Harry imagines, takes the rebound and now says, "Let me sink
that mother," and indeed it does go in, though the boy kind of
flings it and, unlike Number 8, will never be a Michael Jordan.

Now or never. Harry asks, "Hey, how about letting me play
one game of, whadddeya call it, Three? One quick game and
I'll go. I'm just out walking for exercise."

The sullen Hispanic-looking boy says to the others, "Why
you lettin' this man butt in? This ain't for my blood," and goes
off and sits on the bench. But the other two, figuring perhaps
that one white man is the tip of the iceberg and the quickest way
through trouble is around it, oblige the interloper and let him
play. He goes a quick two misses down—a floating double-pump
Number 8 pulls off over the stretched hands of an imaginary
crowd of defenders, and a left-handed pop the wool hat estab-
lishes and Number 8 matches—but then Rabbit finds a ghost of
his old touch and begins to dominate. Take a breath of oxygen,

keep your eye on the front of the rim, and it gets easy. The distance between your hands and the hoop gets smaller and smaller. You and it, ten feet off the ground, above it all. He even shows them a stunt he perfected in the gravel alleys of Mt. Judge, the two-handed backwards set, the basket sighted upside, the head bent way back.

Seen upside down, how blue and stony-gray the cloudy sky appears—an abyss, a swallowing, upheaving kind of earth! He sinks the backwards set shot and all three of them laugh. These kids never take two-handed set shots, it's not black style, and by doing nothing else from five steps out Rabbit might have cleaned up. But, since they were good sports to let him in, he lets himself get sloppy-silly on a few one-handers, and Number 8 gains back control.

"Here you see a Kareem sky-hook," the boy says, and does sink a hook from about six feet out, on the right.

"When *I* was a kid," Rabbit tells them, "a guy called Bob Pettit, played for St. Louis, used to specialize in those." Almost on purpose, he misses. "That gives me three. I'm out. Thanks for the game, gentlemen."

They murmur wordlessly, like bees, at this farewell. To the boy sitting on the bench out of protest, he says, "All yours, amigo." Bending down to pick up the furled golf umbrella he brought along in case it rained again, Harry smiles to see that his walking Nikes are coated with a pink-tan dust just like these black boys' sneakers.

He walks back to his car at the meter feeling lightened, purged like those people on the Milk of Magnesia commercials who drift around in fuzzy focus in their bathrobes ecstatic at having become "regular." His bit of basketball has left him feeling cocky. He stops at a Joy Food Store on the way back to Valhalla Village and buys a big bag of onion-flavored potato chips and a frozen lasagna to heat up in the oven instead of going down to the buffet and risking running into Mrs. Zabritski. He's beginning to think he owes her something, for keeping him company on the floor, for being another lonely refugee.

In the condo, the phone is silent. The evening news is all Hugo and looting in St. Croix and St. Thomas in the wake of the devastation and a catastrophic health-plan repeal in Washington that gets big play down here because of all the elderly and a report on that French airliner that disappeared on the way from Chad to Paris. The wreckage has been found, scattered over a large area of the Sahara Desert. From the wide distribution of the debris it would appear to have been a bomb. *Just like that plane over Lockerbie,* Rabbit thinks. His cockiness ebbs. Every plane had a bomb ticking away in its belly. We can explode any second.

The rooms and furniture of the condo in these days he's been living here alone have taken on the tension and menace of a living person who is choosing to remain motionless. At night he can feel the rooms breathe and think. They are thinking about him. The blank TV, the blond sofa, the birds made of small white shells, the taut bedspread in the room where Nelson and Pru stayed last New Year's, the aqua kitchen cabinets that seemed too intense once they were painted and still do, the phone that refuses to ring all have a certain power, the ability to outlast him. He is flesh, they are inanimate things. The well-sealed hollow space that greeted his arrival seventeen days ago now does brim with fear, with a nervous expectancy that the babble of the TV, the headlines in the paper, the ticking warmth of the oven and the minutes ticking down on the timer panel, even the soft scuffle and rustle of his body's own movements hold at bay for their duration; but when these small commotions are over the silence comes back, the presence of absence, the unanswerable question that surrounds his rustling upright stalk of warm blood. The lasagna is gluey and like napalm on the tongue but he eats it all, a portion for two, while flipping channels between Jennings and Brokaw looking for the best clips of hurricane damage and wind, wild wet wind screaming through rooms just like this one, knocking out entire glass sliding doors and skimming them around like pie plates. Everything flies loose, the world is crashing, nothing in life can be nailed down. Terrific.

He suddenly needs, as suddenly as the need to urinate comes upon a man taking diuretics, to talk to his grandchildren. He is a grandfather, they can't deny him that. He has to look up Nelson's number in the address book on the fake-bamboo desk, it was changed last winter, he's forgotten it already, your mind at Harry's age lets all sorts of things slip. He finds the book, kept in Janice's half-formed schoolgirl hand, in a variety of slants. He dials, having to hang up once when he thinks he might have dialled an 8 for a 9. Pru answers. Her voice is casual, light, tough. He almost hangs up again.

"Hi," he says. "It's me."

"Harry, you really shouldn't be—"

"I'm not. I don't want to talk to you. I want to talk to my grandchildren. Isn't it about time for Roy's birthday?"

"Next month."

"Just think. He'll be four."

"He *is* four. He'll be five."

"Time for kindergarten," Harry says. "Incredible. I understand you and little Nellie are working on a third. Terrific."

"Well, we're just seeing what happens."

"No more condoms, huh? What about him and AIDS?"

"Harry, please. This is none of your business. But he was tested, if you must know, and is HIV-negative."

"Terrific. One more thing off my mind. The kid's straight, and the kid's clean. Pru, I think I'm going crazy down here. My dreams—they're like cut-up comic strips."

He can picture her smiling wryly at this, her mouth tugging down on one side, her free hand pushing back from her forehead with two fingers stray strands of carrot-colored hair. Sexy; but what has it got her? A would-be social worker for a husband, living space in another woman's house, and a future of drudging and watching her looks fade away in the mirror. Her voice in his ear is like a periscope glimpse, blurred by salt spray, of the upper world. She is up there, he is down here.

Her tone is changing, sinking toward friendliness. Once you've fucked them, their voices ever hold these grainy traces. "Harry, what are you doing down there for amusement?"

"Oh, I walk around a lot, getting to know the town. Nice old town, Deleon. Tell Janice if you ever see her that there's a rich Jewish widow giving me the eye."

"She's right here for dinner, actually. We're celebrating because she sold a house. Not *your* house, she can't sell that until you agree, but a house for the real-estate company, for Pearson and Schrack. She's showing houses for them weekends, till she gets her license."

"That's fantastic! Put her on and I'll congratulate her."

Pru hesitates. "I'll have to ask her if she wants to talk to you."

His stomach feels hollow suddenly, scared. "You don't have to do that. I called to talk to the kids, honest."

"I'll put Judy on, she's right at my elbow, all excited about the hurricane. You take care of yourself, Harry."

"Sure. You know me. Careful."

"I know you," she says. "A crazy man." She sounded Dutch, the cozy settled way she said that. She's assimilating. One more middle-aged Brewer broad.

There is a clatter and whispering and now Judy has the phone and cries, "Oh Grandpa, we're all so worried about you and the *hur*ricane!"

He says, "Who's all so worried? Not my Judy. Not after she brought me in on that crippled Sunfish. The TV says Hugo is going to hit the Carolinas. That's six hundred miles away. It was sunny here today, mostly. I played a little basketball with some kids not much older than you."

"It rained here. All day."

"And you're having Grandma to dinner tonight," he tells her.

Judy says, "She says she doesn't want to talk to you. What did you do to make her so mad?"

"Oh, I don't know. Maybe I channel-surfed too much. Hey, Judy, know what? On the way down I drove right by Disney World, and I promised myself that the next time you're here we'll all go."

"You don't have to. A lot of the kids at school have been, and they say it gets boring."

"How's school going?"

"I like the teachers and all but I can't stand the other kids. They're all assholes."

"Don't say that. Such language. What's the matter, do they ignore you?"

"I wish they would. They tease me about my freckles. They call me Carrottop." Her little voice breaks.

"Well, then. They like you. They think you're terrific. Just don't wear too much lipstick until you're fifteen. Remember what I told you last time we talked?"

"You said don't force it."

"Right. Don't force it. Let nature do its work. Do what your mommy and daddy tell you. They love you very much."

She wearily sighs, "I know."

"You're the light of their lives. You ever hear that expression before, 'the light of their lives'?"

"No."

"Well then, you've learned something. Now go do your thing, honey. Could you put Roy on?"

"He's too dumb to talk."

"No he's not. Put him on. Tell him his grandpa wants to give him some words of wisdom."

The phone clatters down and in the background there is a kind of shredded wheat of family noises—he thinks he even hears Janice's voice, sounding decisive the way Ma Springer's used to. Footsteps approach through the living room he knows so well—the Barcalounger, the picture windows with the drawn curtains, the piecrust-edged knickknack table, though the green glass egg, with the teardrop of emptiness inside, that used to sit on it is now on the shelves here, a few feet from his eyes. Pru's voice says, "Janice says she doesn't want to talk to you, Harry, but here's Roy."

"Hi, Roy," Harry says.

Silence. God on the line again.

"How's it going up there? I hear it rained all day."

More silence.

"Are you being a good boy?"

Silence, but with a touch of breathing in it.

"You know," Harry says, "it may not feel like much to you right now, but these are important years."

"Hi, Grandpa," the child's voice at last pronounces.

"Hi," Harry has to respond, though it puts him back to the beginning. "I miss you down here," he says.

Silence.

"A little birdie comes to the balcony every morning and asks, 'Where's Roy? Where's Roy?' "

Silence, which is what this lie deserves. But then the child comes out with the other thing he's perhaps been coached to say: "I love you, Grandpa."

"Well, I love you, Roy. Happy Birthday, by the way, for next month. Five years old! Think of it."

"Happy Birthday," the child's voice repeats, in that oddly deep, manlike way it sometimes has.

Harry finds himself waiting for more but then realizes there is no more. "O.K.," he says, "I guess that does it, Roy. I've loved talking with you. Give everybody my love. Hang up now. You can hang up."

Silence, and then a clumsy soft clatter, and the buzz of a dead line. Strange, Rabbit thinks, hanging up his own receiver, that he had to make the child do it first. Chicken in a suicide pact.

Alone, he is terrified by the prospect of an entire evening in these rooms. It is seven-thirty, plenty of time to still make the buffet, though his mouth feels tender from all that hot lasagna and the bagful of onion potato chips, full of sharp edges and salt. He will just go down and pick a few low-cal items off the buffet table. Talking to his family has exhilarated him; he feels them all safely behind him. Without showering, he puts on a shirt, coat, and tie. Mrs. Zabritski isn't at the elevator. In the half-empty Mead Hall, under the berserk gaze of the Viking warriors in the big ceramic mural, he helps himself generously to, among other items, the scallops wrapped in bacon. The mix of textures, of crisp curved bacon and rubbery yielding scallops, in his sensitive mouth feels so delicious his appetite becomes bottomless. He goes back for more, and more creamed asparagus and potato pancakes, then suddenly is so full his heart feels squeezed. He takes a Nitrostat and skips dessert and coffee, even decaf. Carefully he treads back across the alien texture of Bermuda grass and the carpeted traffic island beneath the warm dome of stars, really a deep basin we are looking down into, he saw that this afternoon when he did the upside-down set shot, we are stuck fast to the Earth like flies on a ceiling. He feels stuffed and dizzy. The air is thick, the Milky Way just barely shows, like the faint line of fair hair up the middle of some women's bellies.

He gets back into the condo in time for the last fifteen minutes of *Growing Pains*, the only show on TV where every member of the family is repulsive, if you count Roseanne's good-old-boy husband as not repulsive. Then he flips back and forth between *Unsolved Mysteries* on Channel 20 and an old Abbott and Costello on 36 that must have been funnier when it came out, the same year he graduated from high school. Costello's yips seem mechanical and aggravating, and Abbott looks old, and cruel when he slaps his fat buddy. People yelled and snapped at one another like animals then. Maybe the Sixties did some good after all. Among the commercials that keep interrupting is that Nissan Infiniti one of crickets and lily ponds, no car at all, just pure snob nature. The Lexus commercials he's seen are almost as vague—an idyllic road shiny with rain. They're both skirting the issue: can the Japanese establish a luxury image? Or will people with thirty-five thousand to burn prefer to buy European? Thank God, Harry no longer has to care. Jake down toward Pottstown has to care, but not Harry.

He brushes his teeth, taking care to floss and rinse with Peridex. Without Janice here he is becoming staid in his habits, another old-fogey bachelor fussing with his plumbing and nostril hairs. Nostril hairs: he never wants to look like Dr. Morris. His double dinner burns in his stomach but when he sits on the toilet nothing comes out. Phillips' Milk of Magnesia, he should get some. Another of their commercials has a black man talking about MOM and that was unfortunate, his color made the shit too real. In bed, on the march to Yorktown, the allied armies come upon British atrocities around Williamsburg. De Grasse's

Swedish aide Karl Gustaf Tornquist, a latter-day Viking, noted in his journal, *On a beautiful estate a pregnant woman was found murdered in her bed through several bayonet stabs; the barbarians had opened both of her breasts and written above the bed canopy: "Thou shalt never give birth to a rebel." In another room, was just as horrible a sight—five cut-off heads arranged on a cupboard in place of plaster-cast-figures which lay broken to pieces on the floor. Dumb animals were no less spared. The pastures were in many places covered with dead horses, oxen, and cows.* Harry tries to fall asleep through a screen of agitation bred by these images. He has always thought of the Revolution as a kind of gentlemen's war, without any of that grim stuff. He begins to have those slippery half-visions, waking dreams that only upon reflection make no sense. He sees a woman's round stomach, with smooth seams and a shining central fuzz, split open and yield yards and yards of red string, like the inside of a baseball. Then he is lying beside a body, a small man dressed all in black, a body limp and without muscle, a ventriloquist's dummy, wearing sunglasses. He awakes in the dark, too early for the sound of lawnmowers, for the cheep of the dull brown bird in the Norfolk pine, for the chatter of the young businessmen's dawn foursomes. He makes his way to the bathroom amid motionless glossy shapes and slants of dim light—the blue oven-timer numerals, the yellowish guard lights on the golf-course fence. He urinates sitting down, like a woman, and returns to bed. Always he sleeps on his old side of the bed, as if Janice is still on her side. He dreams now of the portal with the round top, but this time it pushes open easily, on noiseless unresistant hinges, upon a bustling brightness within. It is somehow Ma Springer's downstairs, only you step down into it, a kind of basement, brighter than her house ever was, with a many-colored carnival gaudiness, like something in Latin America, like the cruise-ship commercial they keep playing in the middle of the news, and full of welcoming people he hardly knows, or can barely remember: Mrs. Zabritski as a slender young girl, though still with that inviting inquisitive crick in her neck, and wearing a racily short fringed skirt like they wore in the Sixties, and Marty Tothero carrying a mailman's pouch that matches his lopsided face, and Mom and Pop in their prime, looking tall and rangy in their Sunday best, bringing a baby girl home from the hospital wrapped in a pink blanket, just its tiny tipped-up nose and a single tiny closed-eyelid eye showing, and a tall soberly staring dark-eyed man with lacquered black hair like an

old ad for Kreml, who gives him a manly handshake, while
Janice at his side whispers to him that this of course is Roy, Roy
all grown up, and as tall as he. Awaking, Rabbit can still feel
the pressure on his hand, and a smile of greeting dying on his
face.

*Hugo aims at SE coast. USAir jet crashes in N.Y. river. Bomb
probably caused crash of French DC-10. Lee slows boaters in
manatee territory.* Harry feeds himself oat bran and digests the
*News-Press. Chaos reigned on St. Croix, as police and National
Guardsmen joined machete-armed mobs on a post-Hugo looting
spree. Tourists pleaded with reporters landing on the island to
get them off.* What fucking crybabies. It occurs to him that his
dream might relate to all this Caribbean news, the pre-weekend
party they have at resort hotels, to welcome the new arrivals.
He steps out onto his narrow balcony to seize the day. The paper
said today would be sunny despite Hugo and so it is. The distant
blue-green skyscrapers hurl back blobs of light from the east-
ward morning sun. The Gulf cannot be seen but he can smell it
out there. He tries to remember who all was at the party but
can't; dream people don't stick to the ribs. The plane in New
York skidded off the end of the runway and two people were
killed. Just two. One hundred seventy-one died in the Sahara.
A caller in London gave all the credit to Allah. Harry doesn't
mind that one as much as the Lockerbie Pan Am bomb. Like
everything else on the news, you get bored, it gets to seem a
gimmick, like all those TV time-outs in football.

While other, younger men shout and kid on the golf course
behind the curtained sliding doors, Harry makes the bed and
sweeps the kitchen floor, and adds his orange-juice glass and
cereal bowl to the orderly array in the dishwasher waiting to add
up to a load's worth. Not quite there yet. When Janice shows up
at last he wants the state of the place to give her an object lesson
in housekeeping.

At ten, he goes out for his morning walk. He looks at the
northeast sky, toward the hurricane that is snubbing Florida,
and is struck by the clouds, how intricate they are, tattered, gray
on white on blue, with tilted sheets of fishscales and rows of
long clouds shaggy underneath but rounded on top as if by action of swiftly running water, like the rhythmic ribs of sand the
tide leaves. A glassy wind blows through the sunlight. There is
something in the air that makes it slightly difficult to breathe.
Lack of ozone? Or too much ozone? It may be his imagination,
but the sky seems clean of airplanes. Usually you can see them

layered in their slow circling slants, coming in to land at the Southwest Florida Regional Airport. The planes have been chased from the sky. Under the sun a kind of highway of haze in bars recedes to the northeast horizon like the reflections the moon stacks up in a calm ocean.

On an impulse he decides to take the Celica and drive downtown and park at a meter near the First Federal bank and walk toward the black section. This afternoon, he thinks, he might feel like trying to get in some holes of golf. The pro shop called up a few days ago and said they found his shoes.

At the recreation field beyond the empty ochre high school, a lone tall boy in denim cutoffs is shooting baskets by himself. His tank top is an electric turquoise stencilled with a snarling tiger head—orange-and-white-striped fur, yellow eyes, the tongue and end of the nose an unreal violet. On this boy, though, the outfit has a certain propriety, the dignity of a chosen uniform. Older than the kids yesterday, eighteen at least, he is a deliberate performer, making good serious economical moves, dribbling in, studying the ground, staring at the hoop, sizing up the shot with two hands on the ball, letting go with the left hand underneath only at the last while shooting. He wears ankle-high black sneakers and no socks; his haircut is one of those muffin-shapes on the top of the skull, with a series of X's along the sides and back where the shaved part begins. Sitting on the bench, at the opposite end of a small red knapsack the boy has evidently left there, Rabbit watches him a good while, while the sun shines and the glassy wind blows and passing clouds dip the dirt field and the surrounding frame houses in shadow. The houses have the colors of sun-faded wash and seem remote and silent. You don't see people going in and out.

To vary his attitude Harry sometimes tips his white face back as if to sunbathe, coating his vision in red, letting photons burn through his translucent eyelids. One time when he opens his eyes the boy is standing close, darker than a cloud. There is something matte about his blackness, and his high cheekbones and the thinness of his lips hint at Indian blood.

"You want sumpin'?" His voice is light, level, unsmiling. It seems to come out of the tiger's snarling violet mouth.

"No, nothing," Rabbit says. "My sitting here bother you?"

"You after no Scotty?" With the hand not holding the basketball against his hip he makes the smallest, most delicate little motion of cracking a whip. Rabbit darts his eyes at the knapsack and brings them back to the tiger's mouth.

"No, thanks," he says. "Never touch it. How about a little one-on-one, though? Since you seem to be out here alone."

"I *heard* some cheesecake come here yesterday was foolin' around."

"Just foolin', that's what I do. I'm retired."

"How come you come out here to do your foolin'? Lot of foolin'-around places over there in your end of Deleon." He pronounces it the local way, *Dealya-in*.

"It's pretty boring over there," Harry tells him. "I like it here, where there isn't so much glitz. D'ya mind?"

The boy, taken a bit off balance, thinks for an answer, and Rabbit's hands dart out and rest on the basketball, a more worn one than the boys yesterday had, and not leather-colored but scuffed red, white, and blue. It's rough-smooth surface feels warm. "Come on," he begs, growling the "on." "Gimme the ball."

Tiger's expression doesn't change, but the ball comes loose. With it, Harry strides onto the packed dirt. He feels precariously tall, as when this summer he stepped out alone onto the mac-adam street. He put on Bermuda shorts this morning, in case he got to play. Dust and reflected sun caress his bare calves, his chalky old man's calves that never had much hair and now have almost none—actually none, where socks have rubbed for over fifty years.

He goes for a jumper from pretty far out and it lucks in. He and Tiger take shots alternately, careful not to touch and bounc-ing their passes to each other. "You played once," the tall boy says.

"Long time ago. High school. Never got to college. Different style then than you guys have now. But if you feel like practicing your moves one-on-one, I'm game. Play to twenty-one. Honor system—call fouls on yourself."

There seems a leaden sadness in Tiger's stare, but he nods, and takes the ball bounced to him. He walks with a cocky slump—shoulders down, butt out—out to the half-court line scratched in the dirt with the heels of sneakers. From the back, the kid is all bones and tendons, polished by sweat but not too much, the sloped shoulders matte beneath the turquoise straps.

"Wait," Harry says. "I better take a pill first. Don't mind me."

The Nitrostat burns under his tongue, and by the time Tiger has come in and has his layup blocked, and Rabbit has dribbled out and missed a twenty-footer, the pill's little kick has reached his other end. He feels loose and deeply free at first. Tiger has some good herky-jerky moves, and can get a step on the heavier older man whenever he wants, but he wastes a lot of shots. The stop-and-pop style doesn't give you quite the time to get in harmony with the target, and there isn't enough height to Tiger's arc. The ball comes off his hands flat and turns the hoop's circle into a slot. And he is giving Harry an inch or two in height; Rabbit lifts a few close-in jumpers over the boy's fingertips— soft, high, in, just like that, air balls only right through the netless hoop, a scabby orange circle bent awry by too many showoffs practicing slam-dunks and hanging on imitating Darryl Dawkins—and Tiger begins to press tighter, inviting a turn around the corner and a break for the basket if Harry can find the surge. Tiger's elbows and sharp knees rattle off his body and he has to laugh at the old sensation, the jostle and press. He is aware of his belly being slung up and down by the action and of a watery weariness entering into his knees, but adrenaline and nostalgia overrule. Tiger begins to exploit his opponent's slowness more cruelly, more knifingly, slipping and slashing by, and Rabbit kicks himself up a notch, feeling his breath come harder, through a narrower passage. Still, the sun feels good, springing sweat from his pores like calling so many seeds into life. The nature of this exertion is to mix him with earth and sky: earth, the packed pink-tan glaring dust printed over and over with the fanned bars of his Nikes and the cagelike grid of Tiger's black sneakers, stamped earth in the rim of his vision as he dribbles; and sky, wide white sky when he looks up to follow his shot or the other's. The clouds have gathered in an agitated silvery arena around the blinding sun, a blue bullring. Rabbit accidentally in one twist of upward effort stares straight into the sun and can't for a minute brush away its blinking red moon of an afterimage. His chest feels full, his head dizzy; his pulse rustles in his ears, the soaked space between his shoulder blades holds a knifelike pain. Tiger retrieves his own rebound and holds the ball against his hip in his graceful way and gives Harry a deliberate stare. His skin is like a grinding stone of fine black grits. His ears are small and flat to his head and his hair above the row of X's is kinked as tight as nature can make it; sun glints from every circular particle.

"Hey man, you all right?"

"I'm. Fine."

"You puffin' pretty bad."

"You wait. Till you're my age."

"How about coolin' it? No big deal."

This is gracious, Rabbit sees, through the sweat in his eyebrows and the pounding of his blood. He feels as if his tree of veins and arteries is covered with big pink blossoms. No big deal. No big deal you're too out of shape for this. No big deal you aren't good even for a little one-on-one. His sweat is starting to cake on his legs, with the dust. He's afraid he's going to lose the rhythm, the dance, the whatever it is, the momentum, the grace. He asks, "Aren't you. Having fun?" He is enjoying scaring Tiger with his big red face, his heaving cheesecake bulk, his berserk icy blue eyes.

Tiger says, "Sure, man. Medium fun." At last he smiles. Wonderful even teeth, in lavender gums. Even the ghetto kids get orthodontia now.

"Let's keep our bargain. Play to twenty-one. Like we said. Eighteen up, right?"

"Right." Neither player has called a foul.

"Go. Your ball, Tiger." The pain in Harry's back is spreading, like clumsy wings. The young black man whips around him for a quick under-the-basket layup. Harry takes the ball out and stops short a step inside the half-court line and, unguarded, lets fly an old-fashioned two-handed set shot. He knows as it leaves his hands it will drop; a groove in the shape of the day guides it down.

"Man," Tiger says admiringly, "that is pure horseshit," and he tries to imitate it with a long one-hander that rockets straight back off the rim, its arc is too low. Rabbit grabs the rebound but then can't move with it, his body weighs a ton, his feet have lost their connection to his head. Tiger knifes in between him and the basket, leans right in his face with a violet snarl, then eases back a little, so Rabbit feels a gap, a moment's slackness in the other in which to turn the corner; he takes one slam of a dribble, carrying his foe on his side like a bumping sack of coal, and leaps up for the peeper. The hoop fills his circle of vision, it descends to kiss his lips, he can't miss.

Up he goes, way up toward the torn clouds. His torso is ripped by a terrific pain, elbow to elbow. He bursts from within; he feels something immense persistently fumble at him, and falls unconscious to the dirt. Tiger catches the ball on its fall through the basket and feels a body bump against him as if in purposeful foul. Then he sees the big old white man, looking choked and kind of sleepy in the face, collapse soundlessly, like a rag doll being dropped. Tiger stands amazed above the fallen body—the plaid Bermuda shorts, the brand-new walking Nikes, the blue golf shirt with a logo of intertwined V's. Adhesive dust of fine clay clings to one cheek of the unconscious flushed face like a shadow, like half of a clown's mask of paint. Shocked numb, the boy repeats, "Pure horseshit."

The impulse to run ripples through him, draining his head of practical thoughts. He doesn't want to get mixed up with nobody. From the end of the bench he retrieves the knapsack, the kind very small Boy Scouts might use on a one-night camping trip, and, holding it and the basketball close to his chest, walks deliberately away. In the middle of the block, he begins to run, under the high excited sky. An airplane goes over, lowering on a slow diagonal.

Seen from above, his limbs splayed and bent, Harry is as alone on the court as the sun in the sky, in its arena of clouds. Time passes. Then the social net twitches: someone who in the houses bordering the lonely recreation field has been watching through a curtained window calls 911. Minutes later, several of the elderly poor battened down against danger in their partitioned little rooms, with only television for a friend, mistake the approaching sirens for a hurricane alert, and believe that the storm has veered back from South Carolina toward them.

"The infarction looks to be transmural," Dr. Olman tells Janice, and clarifies: "Right through the gosh-darn wall." He tries to show her with the skin and flesh of his fist the difference between this and a sub-endocardial infarction that you can live with. "Ma'am, the whole left ventricle is *shot*," he says. "My guess is there was a complete restenosis since this April's procedure up north." His big face, with its sunburnt hook nose and jutting Australian jaw, looks confusingly to Janice in her sleeplessness and grief like a heart itself. All this activity of the doctor's hands, as if he's trying to turn Harry inside out for her, now that it's too late. "Too late for a bypass now," Dr. Olman almost snorts, and with an effort tames his voice into its acquired Southern softness. "Even if by a miracle, ma'am, he were to pull through this present trauma, where you and I have healthy flexible muscle he'd just have a wad of scar tissue. You can replace arteries and valves but there's no substitute yet for live heart muscle." He exudes controlled anger, like a golfer who has missed three short putts in a row. He is so young, Janice groggily thinks, he blames people for dying. He thinks they do it to make his job more difficult.

After last evening's visit from the Penn Park police (how young they seemed, too, how scared to be bringing their ugly news; the Deleon hospital had called them finally because neither the number of the condo phone nor the number they got for his driver's-license address from Information would answer, she had been out showing a young couple from out of state some properties, one a split-level in Brewer Heights where the Murketts used to live and the other an old sandstone farmhouse over toward Oriole; the police came into her driveway the minute she got home, their twirling blue light licking the limestone walls) and then telephoning to reach Mim, who wasn't answering her phone either, and to get seats for herself and Nelson on some kind of night flight to Florida, with Eastern still mostly out on strike and everything going in or out of Atlanta cancelled or delayed because of the hurricane, and then the drive to South Philly and the airport, the miles of Schuylkill Expressway under repair, and among all the confusing barrels with reflective tape Nelson's taking a turn that wound them up in the dead middle of the city right there by Independence Hall—it seemed to happen in a minute—and then the hours of waiting with nothing to do but soothe Nelson and read newspapers people had abandoned on the plastic chairs and remember Harry all the ways he was from the day she first saw him in the high-school corridors and at the basketball games, out there on the court so glorious and blond, like a boy made of marble, and then the empty condo, so tidy except for the stacks of old newspapers he would never throw out, and the junk-food crumbs in the wicker easy chair, but no traces of another woman in the bedroom, just that book she got him for last Christmas with the sailing ship on the jacket, and Nelson right beside her overreacting to everything so she almost wished he had let her come alone—after a while the mother in you dies just like heart muscle she supposes—and a few hours of ragged sleep that ended too early when the boys began to mow the greens and the men began to play, with Nelson actually complaining at breakfast that there weren't any Frosted Flakes, just these bran cereals that taste like horse chow, after all this Janice felt much like her husband did emerging from his long drive on Labor Day weekend, as if her body had been pounded all over with sandbags. In the hall, the newspaper was delivered to the door on this as on every other day:

Hugo clobbers
South Carolina

Dr. Morris, the old one, Harry's doctor, must have heard she is in the hospital; he comes into the waiting room of the intensive cardiac care unit looking himself not so well, spotty and whiskery, in an unpressed brown suit. He takes her hand and looks her right in the eye through his rimless glasses and tells her, "Sometimes it's time," which is fine for him, being near eighty, or at least over seventy-five. "He came in to me some days ago and I didn't like what I heard in his chest. But with an impairment like his a person can live two weeks or twenty years, there's no telling. It can be a matter of attitude. He seemed to have become a wee bit morbid. We agreed he needed something to do, he was too young for retirement."

Tears are in Janice's eyes constantly ever since the blue police lights appeared but this remark and the old man's wise and kind manner freshen them. Dr. Morris paid closer attention to Harry toward the end than she did. In a way since those glimpses of him shining on the basketball court she had slowly ceased to see him, he had become invisible. "Did he mention me?" she asks, wondering if Harry had revealed that they were estranged.

The old doctor's sharp Scots gaze pierces her for a second. "Very fondly," he tells her.

At this hour in the morning, a little after nine o'clock, with dirty breakfast trays still being wheeled along the halls, there is no one else in the ICCU waiting room, and Nelson in his own agitation keeps wandering off, to telephone Pru, to go to the bathroom, to get a cup of coffee and some Frosted Flakes at a cafeteria he's discovered in another wing. The waiting room is tiny, with one window looking toward the parking lot, damp at the edges from the lawn sprinklers last night, and a low table of mostly religious magazines, and a hard black settee and chairs and floor lamps of bent pipes and plastic shades, they don't want you to get too comfortable, they really want the patient all to themselves. While she's in this limbo alone Janice thinks she should pray for Harry's recovery, a miracle, but when she closes her eyes to do it she encounters a blank dead wall. From what Dr. Olman said he would never be alive the way he was and as Dr. Morris said, sometimes it's time. He had come to bloom early and by the time she got to know him at Kroll's he was already drifting downhill, though things did look up when the money from the lot began to be theirs. With him gone, she can sell the Penn Park house. *Dear God, dear God*, she prays. *Do what You think best.*

A young black nurse appears at the open door and says so

softly, yet with a beautiful white smile, "He's conscious now,"
and leads her into the intensive-care unit, which she remembers
from last December—the central circular desk like an airport
control tower, full of TV sets showing in jumping orange lines
each patient's heartbeat, and on three sides the rows of individual narrow bedrooms with glass front walls. When she sees her
Harry lying in one of them as white as his sheets with all these
tubes and wires going in and out of him, lying behind the wall
of glass, an emotion so big she fears for a second she might
vomit hits her from behind, a crashing wave of sorrow and terrified awareness of utter loss like nothing ever in her life except
the time she accidentally drowned her own dear baby. She had
never meant never to forgive him, she had been intending one
of these days to call, but the days slipped by; holding her silence
had become a kind of addiction. How could she have hardened
her heart so against this man who for better or worse had placed
his life beside hers at the altar? It hadn't been Harry really, it
had been Pru, what man could resist, she and Pru and Nelson
had analyzed it to the point of exhaustion. She was satisfied it
wouldn't happen again and she had a life to get on with. Now
this. Just when. He called her stupid, it was true she was slower
than he was, and slower to come into her own, but he was
beginning to respect her, it was hard for him to respect any
woman, his mother had done that to him, the hateful woman.
Though all four of their parents were alive when they courted at
Kroll's she and Harry were orphans really, he more than she
even. He saw something in her that would hold him fast for a
while. She wants him back, back from this element he is sinking
in, she wants it so much she might vomit, his desertions and
Pru and Thelma and all whatever else are washed away by the
grandeur of his lying there so helpless, so irretrievable.

The nurse slides the door open. Above his baby-blue nose
tubes for oxygen his blue eyes are open but he doesn't seem to
hear. He sees her, sees his wife here, little and dark-complected
and stubborn in her forehead and mouth, blubbering like a wa-
terfall and talking about forgiveness. "I forgive you," she keeps
saying while he can't remember for what. He lies there floating
in a wonderful element, a bed of happy unfeeling that points of
pain now and then poke through. He listens to Janice blubber
and marvels at how small she grows, sitting in that padded
wheelchair they give you, small like something in a crystal
snowball, but finer, fine like a spiderweb, every crease in her
face and rumpled gray saleswoman's suit. She forgives him, and

he thanks her, or thinks that he thanks her. He believes she takes his hand. His consciousness comes and goes, and he marvels that in its gaps the world is being tended to, just as it was in the centuries before he was born. There is a terrible deep dryness in his throat, but he knows the sensation will pass, the doctors will do something about it. Janice seems one of those bright figures in his dream, the party they were having. He thinks of telling her about Tiger and *I won* but the impulse passes. He is nicely tired. He closes his eyes. The red cave he thought had only a front entrance and exit turns out to have a back door as well.

His wife's familiar and beloved figure has been replaced by that of Nelson, who is also unhappy. "You didn't *talk* to her, Dad," the kid complains. "She said you stared at her but didn't talk."

O.K., he thinks, *what else am I doing wrong?* He feels sorry about what he did to the kid but he's doing him a favor now, though Nelson doesn't seem to know it.

"Can't you say anything? Talk to me, Dad!" the kid is yelling, or trying not to yell, his face white in the gills with the strain of it, and some unaskable question tweaking the hairs of one eyebrow, so they grow up against the grain. He wants to put the kid out of his misery. *Nelson,* he wants to say, *you have a sister.*

But does he say it? His son's anxious straining expression hasn't changed. What he next says, though, shows he may have understood the word "sister." "We phoned Aunt Mim, Dad, and she'll get here as soon as she can. She has to change planes in Kansas City!"

From his expression and the pitch of his voice, the boy is shouting into a fierce wind blowing from his father's direction. "Don't *die*, Dad, *don't*!" he cries, then sits back with that question still on his face, and his dark wet eyes shining like stars of a sort. Harry shouldn't leave the question hanging like that, the boy depends on him.

"Well, Nelson," he says, "all I can tell you is, it isn't so bad." Rabbit thinks he should maybe say more, the kid looks wildly expectant, but enough. Maybe. Enough.

Acknowledgments

Grateful acknowledgment is made to the following for permission to reprint previously published material:

Beachaven Music Corp. and *Jarest Music Co*: Excerpt from "Vaya con Dios" by Larry Russell, Buddy Pepper, and Inez James. Copyright © Beachaven Music Corp. and Jarest Music Co. Reprinted by permission.

CPP/Belwin, Inc. and *International Music Publications*: Excerpt from "We're Off to See the Wizard" by H. Arlen and E. Y. Harburg. Copyright 1938 (Renewed 1966) by Metro-Goldwyn-Mayer, Inc., Culver City, California. Copyright 1939 (Renewed 1967) by Metro-Goldwyn-Mayer, Inc. Rights assigned to EMI Catalogue Partnership. All rights throughout the world controlled and administered by EMI Feist Catalog, Inc. International copyright secured. All rights reserved. Made in USA. Excerpt from "All My Love" by P. Durand, M. Parish, and H. Contet. Copyright 1948, 1950 by Mills Music, Inc. (Copyright renewed), c/o Filmtrax Copyright Holdings, Inc. Used by permission. All rights reserved. Excerpt from "Splish, Splash" by Murray Kaufman and Bobby Darin. Copyright © 1958 (Renewed 1986) by Unart Music Corp. Rights assigned to EMI Catalogue Partnership. All rights controlled and administered by EMI Unart Catalog Inc. All rights reserved. International copyright secured. Used by permission. Rights outside the U.S. and Canada administered by International Music Publications.

EMI Music Publishing: Excerpt from "Ramblin' Rose" by Joe Sherman and Noel Sherman. Copyright © 1962 (Renewed 1990) by SWECO Music Corporation. All rights controlled and administered by EMI Blackwood Music Inc. Under license from ATV Music (SWECO). All rights reserved. International copyright secured. Used by permission.

Irving Berling Music Corporation: Excerpt from "Say It Isn't

JOHN UPDIKE

THE COUP

Kush, the imaginary African nation, a large, land-locked, drought-ridden territory, is ruled by Colonel Hakim Felix Ellellou. The good colonel has four wives, a silver Mercedes, and a fanatic aversion to the United States. But the Ugly American keeps creeping into Kush—with all sorts of strange repercussions.

COUPLES

An artful, seductive, savagely graphic portrait of love, marriage, and adultery in a small Massachusetts town in the 1960s.

> "Stylistically brilliant."
> WILLIAM KENNEDY

JOHN UPDIKE

MARRY ME

Updike's classic portrait of intimacy and infidelity in the suburbs.

> "So smooth and miraculously intact that
> it is irresistible."
> *The Boston Globe*

A MONTH OF SUNDAYS

The Reverend Tom Marshfield is literate, charming, sexual, and his outrageous behavior with the ladies of his flock scandalizes his parish.

> "A tour de force...Readable, clever."
> *Chicago Tribune*

JOHN UPDIKE

OF THE FARM

When Joey Robinson, thirty-five-year-old advertising consultant in Manhattan, returns with his new second wife and stepson to the farm where he grew up, it is an adventure. For three days, a quartet of voices explores the air, relating stories, making confessions, seeking solace, finding their way.

PICKED-UP PIECES

A selection of critical essays and humorous pieces by the novelist.

"Brilliant, gentle, self-deprecating yet sure of his view, John Updike is a graceful, inventive, joyous and affectionate writer."
The Washington Post

JOHN UPDIKE

PIGEON FEATHERS

Nineteen short stories in a bestselling collection.

"So full of fire and ice that it almost breaks through to some 'fourth dimension' in writing."
San Francisco Chronicle

THE POORHOUSE FAIR

In Updike's first novel, the setting is a poorhouse—repository of the old, the infirm, and the impoverished—on the day of the annual summer fair. The time is the future, in our century. Crotchety John Hook, with his ninety years of memories ...the administrator, Stephen Conner, caught between his own sense of mission and the old people's human perversity... his young assistant, Buddy, a trifle too eager to please. The people are Updike's own, vividly realized, entirely unforgettable.

JOHN UPDIKE

PROBLEMS

Updike's masterful collection of stories that illuminate and reflect the lives we lead.

"Radiant, dazzling."
The Boston Globe

ROGER'S VERSION

A born-again computer whiz kid bent on proving the existence of God on his computer meets a middle-aged divinity professor who'd just as soon leave faith a mystery. Then that computer hacker, Dale Kohler, begins an adulterous affair with the professor Roger Lambert's wife. Roger himself experiences longings for a somewhat trashy teenage girl. In Updike's acclaimed novel, love and sex and God and faith and modern life are explored with style, passion, and incomparable skill.

JOHN UPDIKE

S.

S. is Sarah Worth—doctor's wife, North Shore matron, loving mother, and now (suddenly!) ardent follower of a Hindu religious leader known as the Arhat. As this brilliant and very funny novel opens, Sarah is fleeing the confinement of her suburban life to become a sannyasin (pilgrim) at her guru's Arizona ashram.

"Entirely satisfying and entertaining."
Chicago Sun-Times

TOO FAR TO GO:

Maples Stories

Seventeen short stories, spanning twenty years, that trace the decline and fall of a marriage, but also a story in many ways happy, of growing children and a million mundane moments shared.

TRUST ME

Twenty-two stories of husbands and wives and lovers.

"As always with Mr. Updike's writing, there is the dazzling variety of perception to which his restless and inquisitive imagination transports him. We certainly can trust him—we are in very good hands."
The New York Times

JOHN UPDIKE

THE WITCHES OF EASTWICK
In a small New England town in the late 1960s, there lived three witches. Alexandra Spofford, a sculptress, could create thunderstorms. Jane Smart, a cellist, could fly. The local gossip columnist, Sukie Rougemont, could turn milk into cream. Divorced but hardly chaste, content but always ripe for adventure, our three wonderful witches one day found themselves quite under the spell of the new man in town, one Darryl Van Horne, whose hot tub was the scene of some rather bewitching delights. Basis for the major motion picture starring Jack Nicholson and Cher.

Nonfiction:
SELF-CONSCIOUSNESS:
Memoirs
"Fascinating...These memoirs, often unabashedly philosophical, take us inside Updike's mind in the way that biography almost never can. Fresh assurance that Updike continues to work his magic on the page."
Chicago Tribune

JOHN UPDIKE

To order by phone, call toll free 1-800-733-3000 and order with your major credit card. To expedite your order, mention interest LM-691. To order by mail, use coupon below.

	SBN	Price
___ RABBIT, RUN	20506	$5.95
___ RABBIT REDUX	20934	$5.95
___ RABBIT IS RICH	24548	$5.95
___ BECH IS BACK	20277	$4.95
___ THE CENTAUR	21522	$5.95
___ THE COUP	24259	$4.50
___ COUPLES	20797	$5.95
___ MARRY ME	20361	$4.95
___ A MONTH OF SUNDAYS	20795	$4.95
___ OF THE FARM	21451	$3.95
___ PICKED-UP PIECES	21203	$4.50
___ PIGEON FEATHERS	21132	$4.95
___ THE POORHOUSE FAIR	21213	$4.95
___ PROBLEMS	21103	$4.95
___ ROGER'S VERSION	21288	$4.95
___ S.	21652	$4.95
___ TOO FAR TO GO	20016	$4.95
___ TRUST ME	21498	$5.95
___ THE WITCHES OF EASTWICK	20647	$5.95
___ SELF-CONSCIOUSNESS	21821	$5.95

Name _____

Address _____

City _____ State _____ Zip Code _____

For postage, please include $2 for the first book and 50¢ for each additional book. Send check or money order (no cash or CODs) to Fawcett Mail Sales, 8-4, 201 E. 50th St., New York, NY 10022.

Prices and numbers subject to change without notice. Valid in U.S. only.

LM-691